Books by Kallypso Masters

Rescue Me Saga

The first seven *Rescue Me Saga* titles are available in the following six books in e-book and print formats:

Masters at Arms & Nobody's Angel (Combined Volume)

Nobody's Hero

Nobody's Perfect

Somebody's Angel

Nobody's Lost

Nobody's Dream

Western Dreams (Rescue Me Saga Extras #1)

Standalone Title

(With Secondary Characters from the *Rescue Me Saga*)

Roar

kallypsomasters.com/books

Lanna,

No guilt, no regrets. It's time to ROAR! Great to meet you at MBLU 2016. You did great!

ROAR

Kallypso Masters

Kallypso Masters

ROAR
Kallypso Masters

Copyright © 2016
Kallypso Masters, LLC
Print Edition
E-book ISBN: 978-1941060230
Paperback ISBN: 978-1941060261

Original e-book version: June 2016
Original print version: August 10, 2016
Last e-book and print revision August 10, 2016

ALL RIGHTS RESERVED
Edited by Meredith Bowery, Rebecca Cartee, and Jacy Mackin
Line edited for print by Christine Sullivan Mulcair
Editing Consulting by Ekatarina Sayanova
Cover design by Michelle Preast
Exclusive rights to cover photo of the couple granted by CJ Gwin Photography
Licensed rights to the digitally altered photo of the bed on the cover was granted by digitalmuseum.no via Creative Commons
Formatted by BB eBooks

To discover more about this book and others, see the *Other Books By Kallypso Masters* section at the end of this book. For more about Kallypso Masters, please go to the About the Author section.

Dedication

To Dave, who shared with me insights into his
more than twenty-two year experience to help me
understand Kristoffer's mindset and pain.

To Toymaker and Corie, whose frightening ordeal
with a different type of brain injury that
might very well have turned out so badly if not for
one very insistent and stubborn subbie who
wouldn't let her Dom go there. You inspired us all!

Acknowledgements

Bringing my eighth novel, **Roar**, to you has been a labor of love—and sometimes great frustration—but I'm so happy to place it in your hands. I couldn't have done so without the help of many on my team or with whom I consulted, so I want to acknowledge them now.

A huge thanks to author Red Phoenix who came up with the idea for our characters to crossover into each other's worlds. In this case, my characters visited Brie's world in **Brie Masters Love In Submission**. You'll see where my characters (Pamela, Kristoffer, and even Adam) make appearances or are mentioned at The Denver Academy, run by Master Brad Anderson in the Brie series. Our intention was to release simultaneously last September, but I knew **Roar** wasn't right yet and it took me this much longer to make it so. Better late than never! We didn't co-write, but merely collaborated on a scene idea and then made sure each other's mentions were true to our worlds. It was fun—although I'm not sure anyone would want to do this with me again given my quirky writing style and inability to meet a deadline! You have great patience, Red!

As you know, I love to research and learn about new things, but the learning curve on this book was monumental and sometimes heart-breaking. But I can't get it right without having a number of subject experts, too. So I'd like to thank Dave (see dedication) for sharing his story, which hit so close to Kristoffer's in ROAR. I also want to thank those who helped me with various detail facts, including Trish and Bill Bowers on some of the early BDSM scenes in the book, Cassandra Caress who corrected my bar maid's German, Tymber Dalton for BDSM insights and references to others I might use, Christine Mulcair for her last-minute medical expertise during proofing, Ruth Reid and Lisa Simo-Kinzer for their help with the psychological aspects, and Ekatarina Sayanova and her Sir (Mr. Sayanova) who helped me finally understand why Pamela was not cut out to be a slave, which led me to finally nailing the story on my third attempt. It flowed so well, thanks to my brainstorming partners—among them Meredith Bowery and Lisa Simo-Kinzer—that in early April I knew I was on the right track.

My editorial team for ROAR includes content and line editors Meredith Bowery, Rebecca Cartee, and Jacy Mackin—and for the print version, Christine Sullivan Mulcair who swooped in at my most frustrated hour. I also had in-person and over-the-phone consultation edits and a BDSM scene edit from Ekatarina Sayanova and Mr. Sayanova (her Sir). Writing a story so unique to the Romance genre required a lot of discussion and soul-searching!

My awesome beta readers came through again for me (and you)! Some worked with me since last summer on earlier versions of ROAR that just didn't work right through to the beautiful version you're holding now. First, those who worked with me on the final version, my thanks to Margie Dees, Iliana Gkioni, Ruth Reid, and Lisa Simo-Kinzer—each of whom read through the entire book *many* times over. I also had early beta help on earlier versions from Khriste Close, Treini Joris-Johnson, and Kelly Mueller. Ladies, you aren't even going to recognize the book!

I also had five amazing proofreaders who found typos and errors galore (usually not the same ones): Barb Jack, Alison K., Eva Meyers, Christine Sullivan Mulcair, Lisa Simo-Kinzer. An after-the-fact reader also found more, so I'm adding Annette Elens to my list of fabulous proofreaders of this book, too!

Of course, I'm always changing something *after* my editorial team and subject experts sign off on a book and that invariably leads to new errors. As always, all new and remaining typos and errors are solely *my* responsibility.

This is one reason why I delay the print version a couple of months in order to find them. (I'll be having a virtual signing where you can order signed and personalized copies of ROAR in September, so please stay tuned. If you see something you think needs correcting, never hesitate to let my assistant, Charlotte Oliver, know by e-mailing her at charlotte@kallypsomasters.com or messaging her on Facebook.)

To the members of the Rescue Me Saga Discussion Group on Facebook who kept me writing by answering questions about past books that might have sent me researching for an hour or more. Usually, they had my answers within half an hour. I'd like to specifically thank Markella Costi who suggested the Forseti name for Gunnar's operation; Sophie Gibbs for suggesting the name Kristoffer; and Jennifer Zenga for being the first to suggest Sprite as Pamela's nickname.

To Christina Gwin of CJ Gwin Photography, thanks for bringing Pamela and Kristoffer to life on the cover. And to Michelle Preast who recreated that awesome antique bed found in an online Norwegian museum.

To Paul Salvette, my unsung hero, who takes my manuscripts and makes it beautiful for e-readers and print books alike. He adds touches I would never bother with (or know about) and I have never had any fear of formatting issues when I've placed a book in his hands.

Last, but never least, to Charlotte Oliver, my amazing personal and executive assistant, who keeps growing into this position she began in August 2013. Her help in bringing the book together, as well as in dealing with all the other matters we have going on from marketing, accounting, purchasing, running the Kally Swag store out of her office, and much more, are invaluable to me. She takes away much of the stress of being a self-published author and lets me focus on the fun parts like writing and engaging with readers and my fellow authors.

Author's Note

To say that **Roar** was a total and complete surprise for me is an understatement. It certainly wasn't the BDSM and sexual romp I intended to write in my first spinoff book from the **Rescue Me Saga**. I'd never met him before and only knew Pamela Jeffrey on the surface level from her brief scene with Marc D'Alessio in **Somebody's Angel**. (Marc didn't even scratch the surface with this woman including knowing her profession!)

There were so many other characters I'd promised stories about or you were screaming for, including Angelina's firefighter brothers, and a trilogy with an overarching romantic suspense theme featuring Patrick Gallagher, Mistress V. Grant, and Gunnar Larson. But those characters didn't come to me with their stories—although the last three are all in **Roar** as is Patrick's lady (Maribeth!).

Instead, when asked by Red Phoenix in fall 2014 about doing a fun crossover with characters from our two worlds, out of the blue came Gunnar's cousin, Kristoffer Roar Larson. I don't plot, plan, or mold my characters in any way, so in April 2015, when I wrote a collaborative scene for Red's series involving Kristoffer unexpectedly seeing a colleague naked in a classroom in Master Brad Anderson's The Denver Academy in Red's Brie world, my thinking was that this would be a lighthearted, fun story. And as I tend to do, there are as lots of such moments throughout the book. Away I went to write the shared scenes from my characters' perspectives to mesh with Red's story from Brie's point of view. Only those of you who follow us on social media or in our newsletters probably even knew Kristoffer and Pamela were from my world when it came out in one of her serial installments last spring or when it was later published in her third full-length Brie novel, **Brie Masters Love In Submission**, in September 2015. If things had gone as planned, I was supposed to release **Roar** that same month. Here I am nine months later finally birthing *Roar*. (For this reason alone, I've learned that any type of collaboration in another author's world is strictly off limits for me if they're on a deadline and used to sticking to them! My apologies, Red, for screwing up what could have been a wonderful simultaneous crossover! I hope some of my readers will now go grab Brie's stories and get to dive in for another great read.)

A month later, I was struggling and worrying about how my readers would accept this different type of Romance. I fought with Kristoffer for a full month starting when he threw me an enormous curve that had no place in a Romance genre. Of course, Kristoffer won; he is a Dominant, after all. But trying to write a happy ending that has never been done before presented me with a lot of challenges. It was during a two-hour editorial intervention just before KallypsoCon 2015 kicked off in New Hampshire last October, where Ekatarina Sayanova and Rebecca Cartee reminded me that I have to tell the story I'm given and listen to the characters rather than worry about how some readers might take my one-of-a-kind happy ending. That discussion and brainstorming session led to me rewriting the book (that would be the second version for those keeping score). But by March 2016 when I was supposed to be finishing up, the story had stalled out again. This is usually a sign that I've taken a wrong turn. Saya once again came to the rescue, along with her Sir, and they helped me see that Marc and I had Pamela incorrectly pegged as a slave. Far from it—she's an alpha submissive (with some dominant traits of her own that won't be surrendered) and a physician to boot as my other brainstorming buddies (Meredith Bowery, Lisa Simo-Kinzer, and Ruth Reid) showed me. Away I went and third time was the charm. With preconceived notions already in published books, I had to tread carefully and try not to contradict what was already out about their story. I think I've managed to do that. Once I hit my groove, the words poured out of me in less than three months—to become my second-longest novel to date (surpassing Marc and Angelina's *Somebody's Angel*). Surprisingly, a lot of the scenes I'd written in the first two *Roar* attempts still worked with major or minor revisions, which helped.

This book deals with a subject matter none of us want to talk about much less read about in our escapist fiction. However, that's never stopped me before! So I hope as you read about Kristoffer's great loss and the consequences we all potentially face in this twenty-first century world that it will spark conversations between you and your loved ones before it's too late and you or they are faced with the unthinkable.

Normally in this space, I warn those who might have triggers and share information about where they can go to find information or someone to speak with if unexpectedly triggered in one of my books. I'm not going to do that in this one because I don't want to spoil the read for you. Kristoffer's decisions may be controversial for some, but ultimately how can we judge what *we* might do in similar circumstance unless we've experienced it?

Roar is one man's journey from darkness to light as he struggles to maintain his dignity and integrity while opening his heart to love again. I hope you will boldly go where no Romance has gone before. (Yes, these two are Trekkies and there will be lots of fun along the way, too!) Hang on as this book takes you on the roller-coaster read of a lifetime.

Playlist for *Roar*

Here are some of the songs that inspired Kally as she wrote *Roar*,
Kristoffer Roar Larson and Pamela Jeffery's story.
Warning: Possible spoilers!

Kristoffer and Pamela

Lady Antebellum – *One Day You Will*

Miles Davis – *Time After Time* and unspecified titles

Chuck Mangione – *Give It All You Got*

Billy Joel – *She's Got a Way*

Bill Withers – *Lean on Me*

The Eagles – *I Can't Tell You Why*

Richard Beymer and Natalie Wood – *Somewhere* (West Side Story)

Carrie Underwood – *There's a Place for Us*

(from *The Chronicles of Narnia: The Voyage of the Dawn Treader*)

John Coltrane – *Blue Train*

John R. Burr – *For the Asking*

Dave Barnes – *Until You*

Dave Barnes – *On a Night Like This*

Paul Brandt – *On the Inside*

Philip Wesley – *Dark Night of the Soul*

Wynton Marsalis – *What is This Thing Called Love?*

Bryan Adams – *Everything I Do (I Do It For You)*

Faith Hill – *Breathe*

Billy Eckstine – *Because You're Mine*

Westlife – *Beautiful in White*

Westlife – *It's You*

Kristoffer and Tori

Sting – *Fields of Gold*

Hollywood Undead – *Coming Back Down*

Bread – *I Would Give Everything*

The Righteous Brothers – *Unchained Melody*

Keith Anderson – *I Still Miss You*

The Williams Brothers – *I Can't Cry Hard Enough*

Darryl Worley – *I Miss My Friend*

Eva Cassidy – *Autumn Leaves*

Thad Fiscella – *Angel Kisses*

New Order – *Elegía*

Miles Davis – *Blue in Green*

Israel "Iz" Kamakawiwo'ole – *Somewhere Over the Rainbow*

CHAPTER ONE

Kristoffer Larson gripped the steering wheel to control the shaking in his hands. As he inched around the curve, flashing blue and red lights on half a dozen emergency vehicles came into view and set his jagged nerves on edge. The emergency flares a quarter mile back failed to prepare him for the enormity of the accident.

Don't let the memories take over.

Fighting for control of his heart, he counted the seconds it took to breathe in deeply and release the air slowly, all the while inching forward in the right-hand lane at a jaw-tightening pace.

First responders blocked access to the passing lane. If only he could teleport himself to Denver and bypass the accident altogether.

Highly illogical.

He didn't even want to think about the nightmares he'd have when he closed his eyes tonight.

The temptation to move onto the shoulder and take the exit up ahead nearly won, but he wouldn't obstruct emergency vehicles needing to reach the victims. Yet having to drive by the carnage and possibly witness the retrieval of bodies—living, dead, or lost somewhere in between—made him wish he were back at Forseti Group headquarters in Breckenridge with Gunnar Larson, his cousin and employer with whom he'd been meeting most of the afternoon.

His mind was plagued with what-ifs from years ago, too.

If only he and Tori had headed home earlier.

If only he and Tori had stayed at Gunnar's thirty minutes more. How many times had he tortured himself with those thoughts about that horrific moment...

Too late to change anything now.

Images of Tori's bloodied and battered face flashed before his eyes as bile burned the back of his throat. Forcing deep breaths, he blew the air out through his mouth—well, when he remembered to breathe, that is. Despite efforts to keep his gaze averted, as he crept closer, he saw what appeared to be four vehicles involved in the pileup. No, *five.* Damn it. One was rammed under a tractor-trailer, practically invisible except for the trunk. Had any of its occupants survived?

Of course, there were fates worse than death. He hoped whoever was in that vehicle hadn't seen it coming. No skid marks. Probably had no clue what had happened to them.

Unfortunately, his beloved Tori *had* seen what was coming—not only the stopped eighteen-wheeler in front of them, but also the pickup truck that slammed into the Mercedes's passenger door as Kristoffer attempted to avoid a similar fate to the poor souls in that car over there. Unknowingly, his knee-jerk response had put Tori in the direct path of the pickup that night.

Almost past the wreck. Eyes straight ahead.

He managed not to see anything more of the wreckage, until a police officer held up a gloved hand for him to halt right beside one of the mangled cars. His heart hammered, robbing him of breath.

Don't look. Don't look, damn it!

Seconds later, an ambulance pulled up on the right-hand shoulder and crossed in front of him to park beside the tractor-trailer. As if in slow motion, he watched the crew exit the emergency vehicle and remove a stretcher from the back.

Kristoffer's chest ached, but he couldn't turn his head away. In strobe-light effect, his mind flashed between this scene and one on that dark night four years ago.

Stay in the moment. Don't let it consume you again.

He forced himself to remember his training with Gunnar, not only a well-respected Dominant and whip master in the Colorado BDSM alternative lifestyle community, but the man who had spent a lot of time mentoring Kristoffer on regaining control of his mind and body. With supreme effort, Kristoffer took several more deep breaths and shifted his focus to the guardrail. Not a mark on the silvery steel, unlike the one his car had rammed into on I-70 that night.

Don't go back there.

The sound of crumpling metal assailed his ears.

Tori's scream for him to stop was cut short, followed by the deadly crunch of metal until all that remained was an eerie silence inside the car.

He shook off the memory with great effort seconds before the low rumble of the Jaws of Life cutting off the roof of a vehicle bombarded him—another sound that sometimes woke him from a deep sleep to this day. As victims were extricated from one of the cars beside him, he turned his head toward the valley beyond the guardrail.

Until a sudden thought occurred to him. What if he made himself view today's wreckage? He didn't know these people. Tragic though their suffering might be, perhaps these images would replace his own memories from that heartbreaking night. Would that help him bury the past once and for all?

Kristoffer turned toward the sound, mercifully finding two police officers holding up a white sheet to shield him and others from witnessing the gruesome sight. Had one of the victims screamed the same way Tori had that night? He didn't remember much about the aftermath, but her horrified shriek revisited him during flashbacks that continued to haunt his days—and most especially his nights.

No one seemed to be paying any attention to the occupants trapped under the tractor-trailer. He wished they'd hidden *that* vehicle instead. Awareness slammed into him as to why they weren't concerning themselves with that car, and he swallowed down more bile. With any luck, new nightmares would now blot out those of the accident involving the love of his life.

Focus on something else. Like tonight's meeting you're now late for. Gunnar is counting on you.

Work had kept him from losing his mind these past two years especially. Safe, unemotional, logical finances. He went over the directives Gunnar had given him this afternoon. His objective was clear—determine if the purchase of the successful BDSM training academy would be a sound investment for Gunnar's portfolio. Far from his cousin's typical venture, this one seemed highly illogical and

3

more sentimental.

His cousin had mentored a number of well-respected Dominants over the years. Mistress Grant, who'd been running Denver's Masters at Arms Club for the past several years, came to mind as one of his most proficient students. Nearly a decade ago, she'd introduced Gunnar to Damián Orlando, a fellow veteran who had been wounded in Iraq. Gunnar had taken the Marine amputee under his wing as well. Of course, his cousin trusted both Damián and Grant with his life and allowed them inside his home and dungeon.

Kristoffer constantly reminded his cousin that he needed to be extremely careful about inviting new people inside his inner circle. But Gunnar hadn't had it easy when he returned from the war and had a soft spot for struggling veterans.

Gunnar didn't reinvest every penny into Forseti Group paramilitary operations. Government contracts aside, he diverted a substantial amount of assets to humanitarian projects. For instance, he had a soft spot for a school for girls in Afghanistan run by a former soldier and romantic interest.

My job is to make sure Gunnar earns enough to continue whatever operations or activities he chooses.

Without a doubt, he owed Gunnar for saving his life and sanity several times over. If Gunnar wanted to open a tent selling arctic moss in the middle of the Sahara Desert, then Kristoffer's job was to negotiate the best deal possible. What else did he have to do with his time since the accident? Focusing on Gunnar's financial interests provided him with great personal satisfaction.

An officer whistled, bringing him back to the present. He waved Kristoffer onto the shoulder of the highway, and a sense of relief overcame him as he left the grisly scene behind and made his way toward Denver once more. He fought hard to focus on the road to keep himself from being involved in a similar accident—again.

✧　✧　✧

Only ten minutes late for the scheduled tour, he pulled into the parking lot and cut the Jag's engine. Staring at the warehouse-like building, home to the prestigious academy, he mentally prepared himself to go in like the tiger of finance Gunnar expected him to be—confident, authoritative, and ruthless when it came to closing the deal.

Without a doubt, this place would require more hands-on involvement than Gunnar had time for at the moment. His covert operations in Afghanistan were heating up after the massive withdrawal of American troops. Too many lives were at stake.

Normally, Gunnar gravitated toward safe, conservative investments as close to blue chip as possible in this day and age. Financial planning that required no personal involvement. What on earth did he see in this BDSM training academy? To Kristoffer, a BDSM relationship was best cultivated in a deeply personal setting between two like-minded adults. Ideally, a Dominant trained his own submissive or bottom. Of course, Gunnar's interest in the lifestyle differed significantly from his own.

Kristoffer and Tori were among a small number of people Gunnar had instructed in his home dungeon, but were far less involved in the lifestyle than the others. Not into a Dominant/submissive dynamic, the two did enjoy some lighter aspects of kink. But whips, knives, suspension, and inflicting pain or harsh punishment didn't fit into their relationship at all. Those were Gunnar's forte. He admired his sadist cousin's talent and expertise with the whip and suspension. Witnessing him in action was a thing of beauty, and sometimes Kristoffer had taken Tori to watch demos, but that's as far as it went with them. Besides, any skills Kristoffer *had* learned were rendered useless when he lost Tori.

In the past couple of years, however, Kristoffer had ventured back into Gunnar's dungeon again to practice and learn new Dom skills and to find a way to release some of his frustration. Gunnar usually hooked him up with a Dom willing to let Kristoffer practice on his submissive. No strings, no sex, and no guilt.

Realizing he was stalling, Kristoffer steeled himself and opened the car door. Quickly traversing the parking lot, the heels of his polished, black leather wingtips clicking a staccato beat on the pavement, he continued his assessment of the property. No visible cracks or potholes in the asphalt lot's surface. The exterior of the building appeared to be sound as well.

The moment Kristoffer walked inside, he recognized Brad Anderson. The headmaster at the academy had a commanding presence with his height and muscular body, but it was Anderson's gregarious smile that threw Kristoffer off-center for a moment.

Anderson greeted him with a firm handshake as Kristoffer explained about the pile-up near Georgetown. He regretted having held up the group even longer while he indulged his case of rattled nerves.

The headmaster waved away his concerns and addressed the group, promptly reminding them all why they were here. "Let me explain the concept behind The Denver Academy. While we run both submissive and Dominant training programs, tonight I will focus solely on the submissive aspect. Our training consists of an intensive six-week course that tests and refines the men and women chosen to attend our classes. Each night, they begin with a formal lesson, then move on to a practice session critiqued by a panel of Dominants, and finish with a personalized practicum centered on each individual's interests and talents."

He went on to explain that an auction was held at the end of each of the first five weeks where fully vetted Dominants were permitted to bid on the submissive trainees and take them on a consensual excursion outside the walls of the academy for one afternoon and evening. Gunnar had mentioned having participated in one of the auctions for the initial training class, but Kristoffer had neither asked for nor expected any details.

Kristoffer learned that the sixth auction was reserved for trainers at the school to work on whatever they deemed important, but the students weren't told in advance about the last one being any different than the other five.

Anderson continued. "In every way, we strive to prepare our students to become skilled submissives who are not only confident in their talents, but also highly sought after by the BDSM community worldwide."

As he listened to Anderson field a question about the origins of the school, Kristoffer surveyed the other potential investors, sizing up his competition. The one who had asked the question about the first academy in southern California wouldn't be a pushover. His gaze then fell on a brown-haired woman with librarian glasses who cast sidelong glances at Anderson. Did the two of them have some kind of personal connection that might complicate a bidding war? She seemed oddly familiar, but he was certain they'd never met. He noticed her respectful and attentive demeanor—laying odds she was a submissive.

Anderson's response to another question forced Kristoffer to stop allowing his thoughts to stray. *Focus, man.* He must still be rattled by the accident. He never let his personal life intrude on business matters. Hell, he had no personal life anymore.

What had Anderson just said?

The headmaster continued as he motioned them to follow him down a long hallway. "We take the privacy of our students very seriously, but I've informed the class of tonight's agenda, and they've graciously agreed to allow an observation of the lesson."

This should be interesting.

Just before entering the classroom, they were given instructions to remain silent and line up against the wall to the left. Anderson stood like a sentinel in the doorway, apparently keeping an eye on things both inside the room and in the hallway. One of the last to enter, Kristoffer was impressed by how everything had been set up, as if he'd walked into a graduate school class. Gunnar had given Kristoffer purchase-bid guidelines based on his earlier observations of the academy, but wanted more detailed information before deciding whether to invest in owning the school in part or outright.

The students seated in the classroom all seemed intent on the front of the room, and Kristoffer's gaze roamed to where the instructor conducted what appeared to be an anatomy class with two nude models. The female model reminded him of…

What the…

Doctor Pamela Jeffrey?

It *was* her. His eyes opened wider. Seriously? A few weeks ago, she'd passionately shared information with the Forseti Group's team about the state of things in the international humanitarian aid hospital where she'd been working until recently. The hospital had become yet another of Gunnar's charities in his efforts to help win the hearts and minds in Afghanistan.

Doctor Jeffrey had also brought Gunnar a package from Heidi Rutherford, his cousin's old flame, who now ran a school for Muslim girls Gunnar provided security for in the same province.

Gone were Doctor Jeffrey's baggy sweater and corduroys that had hidden her body type completely. Hell, gone was every bloody stitch of her clothing. What was she doing standing naked next to an equally nude man in front of a class of submissives in training?

Ogling her was unprofessional and rude, but her flawless skin under the bright lights transfixed him—or had he placed a mental spotlight of his own on her? A natural redhead, judging by the neatly trimmed curls covering the mound at the apex of her thighs.

Turn the fuck away, man!

Heat bore into him as he did so, shifting his feet. He raised his gaze again to her face—thinking that should be safe territory—but found her staring back at him, wide-eyed. Not quite as shocked as he perhaps, but definitely surprised.

The notion of sitting across Gunnar's boardroom table at Forseti Group ever again without seeing her as she appeared before him tonight would be difficult, if not impossible, but he doubted they'd be seeing much of each other. Gunnar had finished deposing her about her recent experiences in Afghanistan and granted her request for humanitarian aid. She would likely never be seen again. Or so he'd thought.

Christ. This image will be branded on my retinas forever.

To her credit, she composed herself quickly, standing straighter as she turned away to stare toward the class. Still, he watched a flush creep from her chest, up her neck, and into her freckled cheeks. While he couldn't see the freckles from here, he'd noticed them the other day.

Only then he'd thought them cute. Not sexy.

Until now.

Wait a minute. Why did he find them sexy now? Tori had ruined him for any other woman since he'd met her in college twenty years ago.

It was so wrong to be thinking these thoughts about another woman.

Doctor Jeffrey locked her jaw and kept her mouth in a straight line. The no-nonsense instructor handed a long wooden stick to a young male classmate who then pointed to the sexual and erogenous zones on both the man's muscular body and the physician's softer body. She'd hidden her assets well—until tonight.

Why the hell wouldn't she? She was a professional woman—a medical doctor, for Christ's sake. No doubt she'd had to fight long and hard in her career to keep her colleagues' and patients' minds from straying the way Kristoffer's was now.

What on earth was she doing here? Was she a submissive trainee at the academy or merely moonlighting as a body model tonight? She'd said during the meeting at Gunnar's that she planned to return to Afghanistan as soon as she could obtain a new assignment. She couldn't possibly need money this badly, not that aid workers were known to bring in huge salaries.

When the pointer touched her pink areola, his entire being zeroed in on the lesson, and his cock stirred to life.

Bloody hell!

Guilt washed over him. He had no more luck in averting his gaze now than he'd had on the highway at the accident scene earlier this evening.

Her nipple peaked, as if reaching out to the pointer. The room grew unbearably hot as sweat dampened the back of his starched collar. Kristoffer reached up unobtrusively to undo the top button of his shirt trying not to call attention to this lapse in professional decorum. At least now he could breathe a little easier.

Realizing he ogled her still, he forced himself to shift his focus to what the student was saying as he pointed out her more than ample attributes. Yes, this was definitely an anatomy class. The student had been instructed to point out the erogenous zones in the female body. No, not just *any* female's body—Doctor Jeffrey's. The pointer moved to the rapidly pounding pulse in her neck.

Seeing such an attractive woman standing naked before him gave him any number of inappropriate, unprofessional musings, but horniness was no reason for him to stray down this dangerous road. What he was experiencing was pure, unadulterated lust borne of long-term neglect of a certain part of his anatomy.

An appendage that would remain neglected.

Would she be asked to advise them on her perspective as a student here before Gunnar made a decision as to whether he would purchase this institution?

He hoped not.

The sooner he regained control of his aberrant thoughts, the better.

Hell, what *hadn't* he seen? *Well, thankfully her backside was hidden from view.*

As if the unknowingly sadistic instructor read his mind, she asked the two models to turn around. Glued to the beautiful display before him, any attempt to turn away failed miserably. He couldn't if his life depended on it.

The unexpected sight of her ginger tresses cascading down her back jolted him from his stupor. She'd worn it up and carefully styled for the Forseti Group meeting. He had no idea her hair was so long, tapering off just above the curve of her ass.

Why am I fantasizing about her ass? Or hair, for that matter? I hardly know her.

He squinted. Was that a tattoo on the top of her ass cheek? She was too far away for him to see what the small design depicted, but Doctor Jeffrey didn't strike him as someone who'd be inked.

Stop staring at her ass.

Good luck with that.

His eyes had ceased obeying the commands of his sex-starved mind soon after he'd entered this room.

Anderson quietly motioned the members of the tour group to leave at the end of the male submissive's anatomy quiz, but once again, Kristoffer found himself glued in place. Just one more glimpse, and then he'd banish all images of a naked Doctor Jeffrey from his mind. Without removing his gaze from the pale skin on her back, he stepped away from the wall to allow the others in the group to precede him out.

When she and her male counterpart were instructed once more to turn toward the class, she immediately faced in his direction, perhaps checking to see if he was still there. She surprised him with what appeared to be a silent plea. Was she begging him to stop staring at her? Or to keep his mouth shut about what he'd seen?

He was fully aware that anything witnessed in a BDSM club or school must remain strictly confidential given the witch-hunt mentality in some communities and professions. He had no intention of outing her. However, she didn't know him well enough to trust him.

He nodded ever so slightly, and she relaxed a bit.

Anderson cleared his throat, bringing Kristoffer's attention back to the headmaster standing in the doorway waiting for him to leave the classroom. Relieved to be taken out of the situation at last, Kristoffer turned and made a delayed retreat; Anderson closed the door behind them.

Now, Kristoffer needed to regain focus on *his* reason for being here. Gunnar had sent him on a mission. As a professional, he would fully investigate whether to recommend this acquisition to Gunnar and, if so, make the deal happen to the greatest financial advantage for his cousin.

Mortified, Pamela watched from the corner of her eye as Kristoffer Larson exited the classroom. The uptight man had been a team member at the Forseti Group meeting last month, exuding an aura of negativity that had put a damper on her energy levels for hours afterward. All business. No nonsense. She couldn't help but sense a deep sadness about him she didn't understand.

Undoubtedly, he was excellent at managing Gunnar's corporate and personal fortune, because Gunnar didn't strike her as someone who tolerated ineptitude among the people on his team. Kristoffer's financial astuteness had made his cousin enough money to finance overt and covert operations in both humanitarian and military realms. For helping with her cause, Pamela was grateful to them both.

Heidi had been right about two things. Gunnar hadn't blinked an eye when Pamela asked him to bring one of her young patients to the States for further reconstructive treatment. In mere weeks, he'd moved heaven and earth, and plans were progressing rapidly to have the fourteen-year-old girl on the return flight from his next mission. She'd be taken to a world-renowned pediatric reconstructive unit in Cincinnati where the next phase of surgeries would commence. Gunnar had assured the hospital that they and their staff surgeons would be rewarded financially, she was certain. The man seemed to have an endless supply of money—which brought her back to Kristoffer, his chief financial officer.

Their efforts would truly change this girl's life. The victim of a vicious acid attack on her way to Heidi's school late last year, Fakhira had never given up on her desire to live and to continue her education, despite being painfully disfigured.

Heidi also had been right about a more frivolous matter concerning Gunnar. He exuded the dominant vibe from every pore. Judging by her own submissive response to the man, he was just the Top to train an alpha sub like Pamela wanting to learn more about the lifestyle. Funny how at one time she'd fancied herself interested in being a slave. How wrong she'd been.

When Heidi had told her she identified as an alpha submissive—a term Pamela hadn't heard before—she'd opened her eyes to the reason why she'd been such a dismal failure to date as a submissive. The more she compared her personality and needs as a strong-willed submissive with what Heidi described, the more she began to think she might be one, too. Among the most revealing traits were that she was not one to kneel before just any Dom, instead seeking a Dom as her equal in many things, and a submissive possessing a need to be in charge in some areas without being mislabeled as a switch.

She still had a lot of questions about this particular orientation. The only sure way to find out if she was truly an alpha submissive would be to find a strong Dom equal to the task. Heidi had encouraged Pamela to talk with Gunnar about training her and exploring the dynamic. When Pamela met him, she'd hoped he would take her on, but he'd sworn off anything in the near future due to his workload.

She only had a small window of opportunity before she'd be heading back overseas so, instead, he'd encouraged her to apply to The Denver Academy, which was about to begin new classes.

And here she was, in her second week of classes, thanks to the strings he'd pulled for her. Gunnar must be highly respected in Colorado's kink community, because everything she'd heard about the school told her it was selective and demanding.

Until tonight's visit by Kristoffer and the group of mostly unknown entities had left her so rattled, she'd enjoyed being here. But the risk of being outed in the community for participating in the much-maligned BDSM lifestyle could destroy everything she'd worked for. When alerted that the headmaster planned to bring a group of carefully vetted strangers into the classroom tonight, she hadn't expected to recognize anyone among them. She hadn't been involved in a Denver surgical practice for years and rarely participated in the social or kink scene when home from assignments these past few years.

After her breakup with Marc D'Alessio nearly four years ago, she'd walked away from the lifestyle. Until this forced rest period from her overseas work, she hadn't had time or inclination to sort out what she wanted in her private life. During her initial interview, Master Anderson assured her this would be the perfect opportunity for her to explore and determine her needs rather than focus so much on what she thought she liked or wanted.

Were the two so far out of sync?

Soon after her arrival here, The Denver Academy trainers and instructors had broadened the list of what she'd be willing to try with the right person. But she wondered if a long-term relationship was in the cards for her.

Her thoughts returned to the tour group. A man in a well-tailored suit was one of her favorite fantasies, and Kristoffer wore his like no other. With his rakishly wavy blond hair falling nearly to his shoulders—loose and disheveled as if windblown or finger-combed—his light-gray, tailored, three-piece business suit made him stand out among the group, and not only because she recognized him.

Her cheeks flushed again as she recalled Kristoffer's gaze homing in on her body and lingering much longer than it should have, in her opinion. His piercing blue eyes bore into her with an intensity not unlike his cousin's. Was he a Dom as well? During those first few moments, Kristoffer had shattered every ounce of courage and poise she'd mustered in order to stand naked in front of the class, while the calm, cool Kristoffer Larson maintained a tight rein on his emotions, much as he had the first time they'd met. What had he been thinking?

The heat in Pamela's cheeks was slow to disperse until Mrs. Fieri tapped her shoulder to regain her attention before sending Pamela back to her seat. *Great*. Now she was losing her focus on her classwork. She slipped into the short, silky robe she'd worn to class and took her seat.

Why had she acquiesced when the instructor encouraged her to do this? Because after her first disappointing auction last weekend, she'd indicated an interest in becoming more comfortable being naked around strangers.

That first week at the academy had gone far beyond her comfort level. In this, her eighth day of classes, she'd gathered the courage to stand naked in front of the class—and look how that had turned out.

The school had respected her hard limits, including not wanting to engage in intercourse with people she barely knew. Sex was so…personal. Jumping in too quickly had resulted in disastrous ramifications for her in the past. With Marc, she'd invested of herself fully in their three short months together, convinced they were well-matched until it became clear that he was unable to commit to anything more than being her Top in the bedroom. She'd needed more from him—she just had no clue what had been missing.

Such a dark, mixed-up time in her life. Just before she met Marc she'd been dismissed from her practice because some jealous wife thought she had designs on her husband. As if she had time to be involved with a married man while trying to establish her career. Christ, she'd barely dated since her undergrad days. What surgeon had time for extracurricular activities? It was one of the reasons she'd decided to take some time for herself during this forced recuperation period following her unexpected illness during her most recent contracted assignment.

In retrospect, perhaps she'd come up with the notion that she wanted to have a Master/slave dynamic with Marc because of the insecurity she'd been experiencing at the time. She'd been so ashamed of being fired from a successful practice that she hadn't even told Marc about her career going down the tubes. She'd hung on to the mistaken belief that she wanted to be a slave long after he'd left although, by the time he showed up on her doorstep a year later, she'd begun the application process for a position with the humanitarian medical team.

The only thing that had become clear in all that misery was that she needed to find a way to serve others. Performing cosmetic surgery on affluent patients wasn't why she'd gone to medical school. However, being sent to war-ravaged, impoverished areas in a global effort to ease suffering had been the best decision in her life.

Meeting Heidi had been a turning point as well. Having been shut off from any BDSM activities for nearly four years, her desire to explore again had become acute. Now she wanted to meet someone interested in at least being her Top for play scenes between overseas assignments to help release some of her stress. Nothing short of submission could keep her from becoming too overwhelmed.

The image of her bent over Kristoffer Larson's desk flashed across her mind, bringing her back to the classroom. Why fantasize about him and not Gunnar? She had no clue if Kristoffer was Dominant. Alpha? Most definitely. But not just any Dom would be able to maintain control of a strong-willed alpha sub like her.

Kristoffer hadn't expressed any interest other than tonight's brief appreciation of her nude body. She needed more than a physical attraction this time around. Before starting another relationship, she intended to take her time and make sure she was compatible for the long haul. At thirty-eight, she had no expectations of marriage or children, but did want someone who, at the very least, shared interests with her, had the ability to hold intelligent conversations, and most definitely possessed a deep, mutual respect for her.

Pamela sighed. She didn't want to shut men out the way her mom did, but she also didn't want to hook up with the wrong one again, either. She enjoyed the company of men as friends and colleagues, but didn't see conventional love and marriage as being in the cards given her pitiful track record.

One thing was certain—gone were the days of trying to live up to someone else's expectations. This six-week course would be her first big step toward living the life *she* wanted.

Speaking of which, focus, woman!

One of the rules at the academy was to remain consciously in the moment, and here she was with her head in the clouds, as Dad would say. She needed to let go of the past, concentrate, and learn everything she could during her brief time here.

"Your attention, please." Mrs. Fieri stared pointedly at Pamela. If she didn't pay better attention, she'd be disciplined.

Pamela tried hard to pay close attention to the remainder of the class, but the image of Kristoffer Larson's dumbfounded face continued to shatter any concentration she could muster. She grinned. In retrospect, his expression had been rather humorous.

After the class was dismissed, her instructor called her to the front of the room. With dread, she moved between the desks to stand before the lectern. "How are you feeling about your role in the anatomy lesson, Doctor Jeffrey?" Pamela kept her eyes respectfully downcast, thankful she didn't have to meet the demanding woman's gaze.

"Look at me."

Drat.

She raised her head. "I wasn't nervous…at first."

"What changed? Was having classmates pointing to and naming the parts of your body problematic, or was it the group coming into the room to observe the class that threw off your focus this time?"

Apparently, her lack of concentration was obvious. "I...I guess I lost my focus when the group arrived. It...was easier being naked in front of my classmates, because we've all had to bare ourselves in so many ways to each other at some point."

Mrs. Fieri tilted her head in a questioning manner, making Pamela even more uncomfortable. Did she suspect Pamela was being less than honest?

The desire to come clean compelled her to explain. "Actually, I recognized someone in the tour group, which was...awkward, to say the least. Probably as uncomfortable for him as it was for me. I can't run the risk of being outed in the vanilla community."

Her instructor held her head higher. "The Denver Academy attracts a number of socially important people in the area. I assure you no one steps inside those front doors without being fully reviewed and cleared after signing confidentiality agreements. Nothing they see inside these walls will be discussed in any identifying way outside without the consent of all parties involved. I hope this lack of trust in our ability to protect you won't continue be a problem for you in the future."

"No, Mrs. Fieri." *Not anymore.*

And yet the image of the uptight and controlled Kristoffer remained steadfast in her mind's eye. Why him? She knew nothing about him. They hadn't even engaged in idle chitchat during or after their one meeting. He'd appeared to be serious and formal to the extreme, even when talking with his cousin during the meeting.

Maybe she hadn't been able to forget about him because he was sexier than sin in the suits he'd worn both times she'd seen him. Well-defined shoulders, but not muscle-bound like his cousin's. Okay, truth be told, she'd felt an attraction to the man.

But only a physical one. Not enough.

"Why don't you get dressed?" The instructor's voice pulled her wandering mind back again. "Tonight's practicum should be much more relaxing, especially for you."

When she didn't elaborate on what to expect, Pamela nodded and returned to her desk to collect her things.

At least she'd accomplished one of her goals—to stand naked in front of strangers. While her body was past its prime, she still had curves in all the right places.

And Kristoffer Larson wasn't able to keep his eyes off of you.

Her heart rate increased. She couldn't escape the image of Kristoffer in that suit—only now the mental picture of him removing it took hold of her.

Pamela smiled. At least her fantasy life had remained active all of these years.

Before leaving the classroom, she turned back to the front of the room. "Have a good evening, Mrs. Fieri. Thank you for the lesson."

✧   ✧   ✧

Kristoffer managed to regain control of his wayward thoughts as the tour continued, viewing the academy's practice rooms. Each was equipped for a wide variety of lifestyle scening, including one set up like a kitchen. His thoughts strayed again, remembering playful moments with Tori in the kitchen of their former home. She enjoyed keeping house, and that room was one of her favorite places to be no matter what activity she was indulging in—be it domestic or sexual.

But the headmaster soon reined in Kristoffer's stray thoughts. "We want every graduating student to please their Master's full range of appetites. I have seen firsthand that some of the submissives we train are in dire need of culinary instruction."

Ah. He was referring to actual *cooking* lessons!

Kristoffer smiled before tuning in to the people around him. Anderson glanced pointedly at the brunette with heavy eyeglasses and chuckled before leading the group down the hall. The two definitely had some kind of history. Would that give her an inside advantage if there was a bidding war?

They stepped inside a large auditorium, which Anderson described as his crowning achievement. He clearly loved this place. This room alone would be worth placing a bid on the facility. Kristoffer imagined a submissive spread eagle and restrained on the stage as his cousin wielded his whip with precision and skill, while a group of Dominants looked on and learned. Would there be enough room for whip play here?

As he conjured up a mock scene, the illusory submissive had ginger hair and a small tattoo on her ass.

Bloody hell.

He shook his head to clear it of errant thoughts and remember his purpose for being here. "This is quite a remarkable set-up you have."

Anderson thanked him. "It's my belief that to create superior graduates, you must utilize superior equipment and hire only the best trainers."

The tour group left and moved down another hall to enter a large dungeon area. "Unlike the Submissive Training Center in California, this warehouse is large enough to include a dungeon area specially designed for use of the bullwhip."

Yes, this space would be even better than the auditorium, but once again, the image of a ginger-haired sprite popped into his mind. *Don't go there.* Still, the fantasy of Doctor Pamela Jeffrey suspended or restrained in any number of ways in this dungeon wouldn't let go. Noticing a tightness in his chest, he reminded himself to breathe.

Tuning in yet again, he learned that all of the high-quality BDSM equipment on the premises would be included in the purchase of the Academy, along with the retention of any staff members wishing to remain. So Anderson apparently intended to separate from the school completely, which would allow the new owner to reopen its doors without missing a beat, thus making ownership even more profitable. He knew the tuition here didn't come cheaply by what Gunnar had told him this afternoon.

A question nagged at him as he tucked a loose strand of hair behind his ear. "Will training continue for the current class of students if the academy changes hands within the next six weeks?"

Anderson spoke to the entire group when he responded. "Rest assured, Mr. Larson, as headmaster of the school, I will not be abandoning my students. Only after this class has graduated will the transfer of ownership take place."

Nodding curtly, he tried not to think about what this might mean as far as one petite, ginger-haired student was concerned. He hoped future business negotiations would be conducted during daytime hours when students were absent from the premises. Still, Kristoffer wanted to pore over some financials with Anderson or his accountant before leaving here tonight.

Would the opportunity to interview Doctor Jeffrey arise in order to gain insights on the institution from a student's perspective? No, he'd try to avoid further contact with her at all costs.

Regaining his focus, he knew Gunnar would appreciate that the school also had tracks geared toward training serious Dominants wanting to learn new skills and improve their technique. With wannabe Doms coming out of the woodwork and so much bad information in the media about the lifestyle in recent years, Kristoffer could see that such an academy would be beneficial in helping submissives learn the difference between posers and authentic Dominants, too.

Fortunately, he and Tori had been mentored by Gunnar even at their elemental level of play, and safety had always been his and Gunnar's first priority. Safe, sane, and consensual was the motto for those in the lifestyle, unless they agreed to take it to the next level with risk-aware kink, but even that was always consensual among those playing at Gunnar's and many other dungeons and clubs, not to mention in the privacy of their homes.

One of the greatest advantages for Gunnar would be to use the school as a place to train those he mentored, thus limiting the number of people permitted inside his private dungeon in Breck. With terrorists infiltrating so many organizations and government systems, Gunnar left himself open to an attack from within by holding play parties in his own home. While he carefully checked the background of everyone who drove inside the gates of his compound, one could never be too careful in his line of work. He'd amassed a number of enemies over the years.

This academy would give Gunnar an additional avenue to explore the lifestyle outside his small circle of trusted friends without risking his personal safety or the security of his missions. Most likely, he'd hire someone to run the place and stay on the periphery. He had little time for much else.

Inside the dungeon, Anderson introduced a respected Domme from the training center in Los Angeles. He learned she would be staying on to help with the transition.

A door opened at the far end of the dungeon, and a heavy-set man carrying a cardboard box entered followed by dozens of cats. Anderson growled in frustration before muttering to himself, "Not again!"

He excused himself from the group, all of whom seemed nonplussed when another staff member pulled a bullwhip from the dungeon wall and began swinging it above the heads of the defenseless creatures until Anderson put a quick end to it.

When a plump tabby rubbed the leg of the brunette with the nerdy glasses, she screamed as she sought refuge with the investor standing next to her. "I hate cats," she whimpered piteously. "They're too much like giant rats!"

More staff members descended upon the dungeon. Several tried, without success, to herd the cats by waving riding crops or paddles in the air, but the desperate plea of the besieged woman in the tour group led Kristoffer to reach down and pluck the tabby up and away from her. He stroked its neck while watching with humor as the chaos unfolded.

The frightened feline purred, much like Tori's pet, Noma. Calming the animal gave him a sense of peace as well. "There, now," he whispered in its ear, which flicked against his lips as if ticklish. "Everything's going to be all right." He wasn't sure if he was speaking to the tabby or himself. Tonight had been unsettling on so many fronts.

Watching the continued failing efforts of the staff at herding cats, Kristoffer shook his head with the strong suspicion that the pandemonium around them had to have been planned. How else would this many cats manage entry into a dungeon deep within the walls of a secure warehouse?

No doubt Anderson had carefully crafted this incident. The man's eyes glinted with merriment rather than irritation as he directed his staff to wrangle up the poor creatures. Was it simply for his own amusement, or did this ruse serve a higher purpose?

Whatever the case, Kristoffer needed this comical ending to a most disconcerting evening. He turned to find the headmaster holding two kittens and decided to call him out. "Herding cats? You can't be serious, Mr. Anderson."

"What?" He feigned innocence, but Kristoffer raised his eyebrow. Anderson dropped the pretense, aware Kristoffer was on to him. The headmaster shook his head, chuckled, and handed the two kittens over to a staff member. He pointed his finger at Kristoffer, laughing warmly. "I *knew* I liked you for a reason."

The headmaster then grew serious. He whistled, a door opened, and the cats headed toward it without protest. Kristoffer assumed someone had opened a can of tuna or some other feline enticement behind the door. Anderson took the cat from Kristoffer's hands and set it down to follow the others. Before it did so, the tabby rubbed against his pants leg, leaving tufts of orange and white fur in its wake. He bent to rub behind its ears one more time before it, too, followed its nose.

Anderson crossed his muscular arms over his broad chest and stared intently at each potential investor, one after the other. "This was simply my way of illustrating how investing can be a lot like herding cats, unless you know what you're doing."

Kristoffer had to give him props for orchestrating this elaborate object lesson.

After reiterating the importance of finding the right person to head up the academy, Anderson continued, "You may think that you came here tonight to decide whether this is the right investment for you, but you'd be only partially correct. I will not hand over this business unless

I feel confident that you or your client is worthy to own this training center."

Kristoffer clapped his hands slowly and with admiration. "Well played, Mr. Anderson." At least he'd made a good impression, which might give Gunnar's proposal a leg up over the others. As they moved toward the boardroom to discuss the details further, he heard a number of the members of the group express interest as well. Kristoffer would have to come up with a solid, tempting proposal that would be advantageous to both parties in order to win the day.

While there wasn't much he could control anymore, Kristoffer intended to make sure he acquired this property for Gunnar, if his cousin's heart was set on it. There were so few checkmarks in his "win" column in any other aspect of his life nowadays, but when it came to business affairs, Kristoffer excelled.

The brunette seemed quite pleased by the subterfuge and met Anderson's gaze. Had she been in on it as well? When she glanced his way, Kristoffer couldn't shake the feeling he knew her until the young woman burst into youthful giggles that echoed down the hallway, making it difficult for him not to smile himself. Such innocence and passion. He hoped she'd never have to face any serious heartache in her life.

With a sudden burst of clarity, he realized what had been bugging him since he'd first seen her. This was none other than Brianna Bennett! While researching the Submissive Training Center in LA in preparation for this tour, he'd watched the documentary she'd made describing her experiences there. Her exuberant praise of the program was one of the reasons he'd agreed with Gunnar to give the place a closer inspection. That also explained her obvious familiarity with Anderson.

Kristoffer shook his head, grinning as he wondered what the two were planning next.

Before entering the meeting room, he glanced down the hallway to the classroom where he'd seen Doctor Jeffrey's naked body in great detail. The chances of another encounter with her—clothed or otherwise—would be slim.

Thank you, God of Thunder.

CHAPTER TWO

Kristoffer let the sounds of Miles Davis's mellow trumpet fill his high-rise condo as the clock's hands crept toward midnight. He stared out the wall of windows at the city lights in the distance as he tossed back the remainder of the glass of scotch. Most nights, he drank wine to relax, but needed something stronger tonight. A single glass of twenty-year-old scotch neat normally was the perfect dose of self-medication to take the edge off a bad day. For some reason, this evening he'd poured a second.

As he sat on the sofa, idly stroking Noma behind her ears, he relaxed a little more. This temperamental feline had been his only companion since the accident. Well, they'd had a rocky start dating back a full decade because Noma had preferred Tori to him from the time she was adopted. Somehow, though, when he'd moved into this new place and the cat's mistress still was nowhere to be found, she'd finally warmed up to him. That had been nearly a year after the accident, coinciding with Kristoffer beginning to escape from his grief-stricken stupor. Coming to the realization his beloved wife would never be returning to the life they'd once shared had taken a major adjustment to put it mildly. On the first night here, with Kristoffer feeling lost and alone, Noma had rubbed against his leg out of the blue, perhaps to let him know she needed someone to comfort her in her loss, too.

Apparently, Kristoffer would do in a pinch.

Had Tori reached out to lay down the law and insist that her pet bond with him? Doubtful. He'd never felt Tori's presence around him, not since the accident, although he hoped she was still with him in some way.

You always took such good care of my needs, Tori.

All throughout that first difficult year, Kristoffer had only been permitted to meet the tabby's physical needs—food, water, and litter.

Until that night. Being allowed to stroke her and sit with her like this helped him feel a connection with Tori he hadn't felt in a long while. Noma fiercely held on to her independence most of the time.

"Is that the way of things, Noma? We're here to hold each other up?"

The cat purred more loudly, but didn't deem the question worthy of a meow. The two of them had reached an understanding. They could communicate silently, each drawing comfort from their mutual love for Tori.

Now, he really needed to get up from this sofa and spend a few hours on that report. Gunnar would expect his preliminary analysis, recommendation, and bidding advice before deciding whether he should make a competitive offer tomorrow to buy The Denver Academy.

Why hadn't Kristoffer been able to string two thoughts together since he'd left the school a couple of hours ago? Knowing sleep would elude him anyway, he put the cat on the couch where she curled into a ball. Standing, he picked up his empty glass and placed it on the bar before strolling out of the room toward his office.

The vision of Pamela's nude body wouldn't release him. *Wait a minute.* Since when had he started referring to her as Pamela? She'd asked everyone at the meeting two weeks ago to call her that, but in light of what he'd seen tonight, using her first name seemed more intimate than he wished to be. Doctor Jeffrey was safer.

He couldn't be attracted to her. No, not at all. No other woman had pierced his armor except Tori, and none ever would.

The only reason he was even thinking such thoughts about another woman was that the last few years of lonely exile had finally taken their toll. His body wasn't dead yet, although the heart and soul he'd pledged to the only woman he'd ever love had become as lifeless as his beloved Tori. Why indulge in thoughts of fleeting, empty sexual pleasure? Nothing could come of any attraction to the woman, so these thoughts were a colossal—illogical—waste of time. He wouldn't jeopardize his work or Gunnar's mission for a brief, meaningless encounter with any woman.

As if the doctor was even interested in him. The pleading look in her eyes hadn't been begging him to make a move, but to pretend he hadn't seen her at all.

Mind over matter won out, and he managed to spend the next ninety minutes outlining the pros and cons of the deal, until his eyelids felt as if they were sliding over sandpaper every time he blinked. He powered down his computer and leaned back as the leather scrunched in his chair. Exhausted, he closed his eyes. He'd have to leave for Breck by seven and ought to stretch out in bed for a few hours, but he didn't have the energy to leave the office. He'd rest his eyes a moment...

✧   ✧   ✧

"Kris! Watch out!"

Kristoffer jerked awake as Tori's scream echoed around the room. A crick in his neck told him he'd been lying in the same position a while. He glanced at the hands on the illuminated clock face on his desk. Four-forty.

Would the nightmares of that night never leave him? Damn it, if he didn't catch some sleep, he'd be a menace on the road later this morning. No, he'd delay his meeting before jeopardizing anyone else's life. Gunnar, of all people, would understand.

Kristoffer unbuttoned his dress shirt as he made his way across the office and back through the living room, heading toward the master bedroom. Jazz strains spilled from the stereo speakers, reminding him he hadn't turned it off earlier. Chuck Mangione's "Give It All You Got," one of Tori's favorite arrangements, played. He'd be sure to remove the CD from the stereo stacker and take it with him tomorrow when he left the house.

But first, some sleep.

The bedroom was free of the frills or embellishments Tori had loved so much. In place of the brass bed he'd shared with his wife, he now slept in this imposing four-poster, canopy bed that had once belonged to his grandfather. It had been in storage for more than ten years, because it didn't go with the décor of his home with Tori.

He left the canopy cloth off, not needing to cocoon himself the way FarFar, his father's father, had done on those frigid, incessant winter nights in Norway. Kristoffer preferred to display the inlaid wood of the canopy frame in all its glory, not that many had ever seen it. The carved headboard and footboard were worn after centuries of use by the Larson family, but the craftsmanship would never fade. Family tradition told of his third or fourth great-grandfather making the bedroom suite by hand.

The matching dresser was the only other large piece of furniture in here. FarFar had also sent the cradle Kristoffer's and Gunnar's fathers had slept in when babies. If he and Tori had wanted children, the babies would have slept there as well. He'd left the cradle in storage, because visions of what might have been were too painful for Kristoffer these days. However, they'd been careless with birth control many times without a pregnancy, so perhaps being a parent had never been in the cards for them. In retrospect, being childless had been for the best. How would he have raised kids without Tori?

Gunnar had chosen to inherit FarFar's weapons and war memorabilia. The two cousins were so different and yet closer than many brothers. Thank God he had Gunnar in his life.

Surprisingly, no sooner did he stretch out on the lonely bed than his eyelids drooped again. Well and good. He didn't want to cancel his meeting with Gunnar. The proposal he'd drafted was a solid one, and he wanted his cousin's thoughts on it before submitting it to Brad Anderson.

The alarm blared in what seemed like mere minutes. He noted with relief that he hadn't had any more dreams about that horrific night. After a quick shower, he downed a cup of black coffee then filled his thermal cup with the amount left in the Technivorm carafe. No surprise. He measured out the same amount of coffee every day, whether working at home or going to a meeting at Forseti headquarters. Kristoffer found comfort in routine. Perhaps because life had thrown him a number of curves. He gave a mental shrug. No matter. Everyone had one idiosyncrasy or another.

His hair still wet, he grabbed a white shirt from the closet and quickly dressed. Gunnar didn't demand formality at their meetings; however, Kristoffer thrived on professionalism and decorum. They provided stability in an otherwise unstable world.

Except for his unconventional shoulder-length hair. But Gunnar's was half a foot longer, and as CEO of his corporation, Gunnar didn't raise an eyebrow or care about Kristoffer's. As if physical appearance would be an issue between them anyway.

He carried his travel mug in his right hand and briefcase in the other with his suit coat draped over that same arm. Minutes later, situated behind the wheel of the Jag, he eased from the condo's parking garage and into the flow of traffic. Most commuters were headed toward the city, but his destination was two hours west. Plenty of time for a leisurely drive to Breck. He felt surprisingly refreshed. That last bit of dreamless sleep must have done the trick.

More likely, he was becoming energized about winning the upcoming deal. Nothing revved him up more than the possibility of going after something to increase Gunnar's portfolio or merely to acquire something his cousin wanted. Kristoffer's visit to The Denver Academy had excited him more than anything had in a long time.

I won't think about why that's so.

Traffic moved steadily as Pamela drove through the Eisenhower Tunnel toward Breckenridge. Gunnar's text last night asking her to join him for a last-minute meeting today at the Forseti Group offices had surprised her. He'd been good about keeping her updated on the progress for Fakhira's transfer to the States via e-mails. Why else would he need to see her in person?

She had a lot of respect for this military man turned humanitarian and couldn't turn him down. Without his help, Fakhira's prospects for obtaining the reconstructive surgeries she needed would be next to impossible. Perhaps he wanted to ask her to be on the jet that flew her young patient and her mother to the children's hospital. She'd give anything to be there to ease the concerns of the girl's family, although her general practitioner had given her orders to rest and not risk a relapse.

Sitting still wasn't in her DNA, however. Neither was idly waiting around for the organization she worked for to send her back to complete her contract abroad. She needed to keep busy.

But poor Fakhira must be terrified of what awaited her in the States. Pamela could at least be at the Cincinnati hospital to greet her. So much tragedy in such a young life. Just when opportunities had opened up for her, she'd been brutally attacked.

Heidi and the teachers had kept their English-immersion institute open despite the danger from extremists, in large part because of the protection Forseti Group guards provided. The attack on Fakhira had been the first one on a student there, albeit occurring outside the school compound, and had left everyone shaken to the core.

Education was the best way for these girls to break away from the rigid standards some might impose upon them. Learning the ways of the world could also bring about changes in the lives of other Muslim women in the region. Malala Yousafzai had been a great inspiration to young and old after fighting back following being shot by the Taliban on her way home from school. One day, these girls at Heidi's school also might become great leaders in their local communities, if not the world. With their help, Afghanistan could become a more egalitarian country where women had more freedom and opportunity.

From what she'd seen, Gunnar's team was fully committed to its mission of shielding the school and its inhabitants from retribution from the Taliban, Islamic State, and Al Qaeda factions over the past five years. Not an easy feat with the recent pullout of coalition forces.

Oh, she had no delusions that he wasn't involved in paramilitary operations as well. Perhaps his humanitarian efforts assuaged his guilt. No, she was projecting her pacifist soul onto his. No doubt his missions were honorable and attempted to right wrongs. She had to tell herself that, anyway.

When she'd tried to look up Forseti Group on the web, she'd discovered the word Forseti also was the name of the Norse god of justice and reconciliation. Clearly, the name of his contracting firm had been chosen to describe its mission and not merely the Nordic heritage of the owner.

The miles ticked by—long stretches of time where she zoned out on the road. In Afghanistan, she'd traveled in caravans with drivers ever watchful of IEDs and other hazards along the route. Americans had no concept of how easy it was to travel from place to place without the fear of dying along the way, except for the occasional motor-vehicle accident.

As she drove on, Pamela replayed last night's encounter at the academy. Heat flooded her cheeks. Would Kristoffer Larson be present today? She hoped not. The man affected her in ways she didn't want to acknowledge.

Pamela pulled into the entrance to Forseti headquarters and waited for the guard to inspect her Renegade Trailhawk thoroughly, much like on her first visit. When the gate swung open, she drove inside and up the winding drive to the secluded building. Even though she couldn't see them, sentries must be posted around the perimeter of the property. It felt as if she'd entered a military base.

Of course, with the threat of terrorism more likely every day, his operation would attract a number of powerful enemies. One couldn't be too careful, not even in the States.

She parked in one of the dozen or so spots at the semicircular parking area. The imposing concrete and glass building, surrounded on three sides by towering evergreens, dominated the landscape, blocking some of the panoramic view of the still snow-covered ski slopes and majestic Rockies. While the solid walls on the first floor didn't allow for much of a view, she'd discovered on her prior visit that the upstairs vantage points were spectacular. Denver's foothills had nothing on the vistas here in Breckenridge. She'd missed the greenery while serving in Afghanistan where everything was so brown and drab.

Grabbing her briefcase, she walked to the front door and entered the lobby. The receptionist showed her to the winding staircase and guided her to the boardroom on the second floor where she'd met a couple of weeks ago with Gunnar and several members of his team, including a man from Albuquerque by the name of Patrick Gallagher, and Mistress Grant, a well-respected Domme she'd met at the Masters at Arms Club.

The receptionist asked how she liked her coffee then went off to prepare her a cup. Inside the room, only Gunnar sat at the table. He stood when he saw her and stretched out his hand in greeting. "Good morning, Pamela." They shook hands as she returned the pleasantry, and he pointed to a padded executive chair on his left side. "Have a seat."

Pamela smiled. Gunnar's military background was unmistakable. Today, he wore a camo T-shirt emblazoned with one word—Army. His muscular arms stretched the sleeves to within an inch of ripping the fabric. As he had the last time, he had pulled his long hair into a simple ponytail. Standing well over six feet to her piddling five foot one frame, one would expect him to be intimidating, but he put her at ease this morning just as he'd done the first time they'd met.

"How have things been going at the academy, Pamela?"

"Really well, thanks." Had he asked her here to talk about that then?

Gunnar's hair was much longer than his cousin's. Both men had sun-streaked blond hair framing faces with icy blue eyes and chiseled chins. Gunnar's nose was more hawk-like than she remembered Kristoffer's being, and the CEO sported a well-groomed beard and mustache. The vision of the two of them standing proudly at the helm of a Viking ship flitted across her mind's eye, and she grinned at her flight of fancy.

Focus.

"What would you say if I told you I'm considering buying the academy?"

Ah, so that explained Kristoffer's presence last night. As his chief financial officer, he'd want to scope out the place, no doubt. Were the others in the group also potential investors? Once again, she had a bout of nerves over who they were and whether anyone other than Kristoffer had recognized her.

"It would be a good investment, especially if most of the current instructors and trainers remain on board."

Gunnar nodded. "Kris assured me in a preliminary report this morning that most do intend to stay." He paused a moment. "You're probably wondering why I've asked you back."

Apparently, this meeting was about to get down to business. At least the younger Larson was missing. *Thank God.*

She smiled. "I assumed you'd tell me when you were ready and am certain you wouldn't waste my time by calling me back here without good reason."

He grinned. "I'd like to ask you to help me with a short-term project." He glanced past her shoulder to the door. "Ah, here you are. We were just getting started."

She turned to find Kristoffer standing there in yet another three-piece suit, this one dark blue. She met his gaze, and last night crashed in on her like a rogue wave. To his credit, he didn't undress her with his eyes, but why would he bother? He'd already seen her in the buff.

Pamela smiled at him, offering her hand for him to shake. Uptight to the extreme compared to his laid-back and casual cousin, he almost seemed reluctant to touch her, but no way would she pull away. At last, he accepted her hand. Firm grip, but not bone-crushing the way some men tried to overpower women.

Well, why on earth would he want to intimidate me anyway?

Yet nothing had been more intimidating than having him see her naked last night in the classroom, even if that was through no fault of his.

Suddenly feeling vulnerable, she retrieved the laptop from her case, took her seat, and busied herself with opening a Word document for her notes. Kristoffer took the seat directly across the table from her and pulled a white legal pad from his briefcase and a silver pen from his shirt pocket. She tried not to stare at how his shirt hugged his chest, but couldn't miss the gold wedding band on his finger.

For the first time since last night, she relaxed. *Off limits. Good.*

Still unable to make eye contact with Kristoffer again, she turned her gaze toward Gunnar. "What is it you need, Gunnar?" The sooner this began, the sooner it could end.

Without preamble, Gunnar brought the meeting to order, his attention first on Kristoffer. "I was just about to tell Pamela why I've asked her to be here, but now I can enlighten you both."

So she wasn't the only one out of the loop here. She waited, studiously avoiding looking at the man across the table.

Gunnar's focus was on her now. "I'd like to commit a substantial amount of money to a project and need the two of you to spearhead it."

Pamela's heart raced at the prospect of seeing Kristoffer on a regular basis. He might be off limits, but that didn't mean he didn't have some strange hold over her.

How to extricate herself from this without appearing rude? "I'm flattered but not sure how much time I'd be able to devote to anything right now. I intend to return to Afghanistan by mid-summer to finish my last three-month assignment."

"That won't interfere with what I have in mind. In fact, it's perfect timing." He leaned forward, resting his forearms on the edge of the table. "This will be short-term in nature, because I know you're a busy woman. Six to eight weeks should be plenty of time."

She hazarded a glance across the table and noticed her counterpart seemed about as enthusiastic as she, although he expressed no reservations aloud. Instead, he asked Gunnar, "What did you have in mind?"

"After hearing Pamela talk about young Fakhira's needs and prognosis, I had some preliminary conversations with the administrators at the hospital where you worked, Pamela, and would like to explore providing for their most pressing needs. As a physician who has been there and seen the hardships firsthand, you can help me determine the institution's greatest priorities as far as medical equipment and whatever else can help doctors provide better treatment for children like Fakhira and other noncombatants."

Pamela sat up straighter in her chair and stared him down. "I am grateful for the opportunity to point out some of the areas where your generosity will be appreciated, but can't accept your offer if there are any strings attached. Yes, we treat children and noncombatants, but no one is asked at the door which side they're on, so there's every possibility we would be treating those fighting against you. You must understand that the staff at the hospital has taken an oath to provide medical care in the areas we serve to *all* in distress. Therefore, we must remain neutral, impartial, and ethical. Will that be an issue for you?"

A muscle clenched in Gunnar's jaw before he nodded. "Point taken. I appreciate your honesty and expect you to continue to speak your mind on this subject. I'll admit that I'm not surprised you would say that, but you can't blame me for trying to increase the odds of my team surviving operations in the area."

Of course, she couldn't fault him for not wanting to help the hospital treat and heal the very people who might cause the death of him or someone on his team.

Perhaps she could appease him somewhat. "What if we focus on the equipment and supply needs in the pediatric, obstetrics, and gynecological wards?"

He grinned. "Anything to lessen the chances of your staff inadvertently healing someone who can later go out and blow up students or teachers at Heidi's school or attack the members of my team would be greatly appreciated."

"*Lessen* is the best I can offer, but there are no guarantees and no way to quantify how successful our efforts are. Naturally, we also can't prevent the patients we treat from growing up and joining enemy forces."

He sobered. "Believe me, I know women and children can hide explosives and weapons just as easily, probably even better with women and girls wearing *chadris* or burqas. Those layers of clothing can conceal an arsenal." He paused a moment. "But, in addition to easing some of the suffering, this is about winning over hearts and minds. Perhaps if someone at the facility is saved due to the staff or equipment provided by American and other coalition forces, we'll be able to stem the rising hatred of Americans there."

"You can't imagine the relief in the faces of parents when their children are saved with modern surgeries and medicines," Pamela continued. "Hopefully, they will tell them the story of how the doctors came and treated them without question of political loyalties."

He nodded. "Let's hope so." He turned to his cousin. "Kris, you need to track down whatever she says is needed and make sure we can get it at competitive prices from the sources. Whatever you have to do to stretch the budget, I want as much bang for my buck as possible."

"Not a problem," Kristoffer responded.

"Good." They spent the next two hours discussing the parameters of the project, both financial and logistical.

Gunnar began to wrap up their meeting. "I see no reason for you to meet on this here, since you both live in the Denver area. But for the next few weeks, perhaps you could drive out here once a week and update me with your progress." He sat back in his chair. "I'm going to leave it to you two to explore every possibility."

Kristoffer cleared his throat. "Gunnar, before we break, you and I should go over my recommendations on the academy I toured last night."

Pamela's face grew warmer, but she refused to make eye contact with either man. Did Gunnar know what Kristoffer had seen last night? Well, if not, he certainly wouldn't hear any details from her. What the two cousins chose to talk about now she didn't care to hear.

She closed her laptop and stood. "I guess I'll head back to the city if there's nothing else." As an afterthought, she asked to borrow Kristoffer's pad of paper. "Let me jot down my cell phone so that you can reach me to arrange for future meetings." She might not want to see him again anytime soon, but she wasn't going to do anything to jeopardize what might be the best thing that had ever happened to the facility she'd spent so many months serving in. The patients there deserved a chance.

✧ ✧ ✧

Kristoffer glanced up from his legal pad before sliding it across the table. No doubt, their first meeting would be an awkward one, but both of them had shown they could be professional and not let what had transpired last night get in the way of business.

"If you two aren't in any hurry, why don't you both stay for lunch? Kris, you can fill me in on the academy while we eat."

So much for postponing the inevitable. Was the doctor blushing? Again? Her freckles faded into the redness of her cheeks. He didn't know if it was from embarrassment or a byproduct of that strawberry-blonde hair. He remembered the strawberry-blonde standing proudly naked in front of the class—and his tour group—and wondered how she'd respond to Gunnar's invitation.

"No, I really should be going. I'd like to do a little research before Kristoffer and I meet."

Thankfully, she wasn't any more interested in hanging out with them than he was, although it sounded as though he'd be spending more time with her in the weeks to come.

But Gunnar dashed his hopes for a brief reprieve. "Nonsense. I insist. We have a fully stocked kitchen down the hall. It won't take us but a minute to whip something up—faster than the drive-through in town." His cousin didn't sound as though he'd take no for an answer, but the equally willful Pamela probably wouldn't kowtow to him.

She busied herself with writing down her phone number. "If you insist."

Submissive. He should have known after last night, although he'd hoped she was merely modeling for the school and not a student.

"Great. Kris, show her to the kitchen. I'll be right there."

After they'd packed away their things, he motioned her to precede him out the door. "Take a right." Walking down the hall, he decided he needed to clear the air before any talk of the academy came up. "Is Gunnar aware that you're a student at the school?"

She laughed from deep in her throat. "He got me into the academy."

So his cousin had known she would be there last night. Did he also know she'd be standing naked in front of her class? Had this been some kind of set-up? A test? Gunnar had been vocal over the past year that Kristoffer needed to move on with his life and at least find someone to engage in BDSM with. Over lunch, he'd feel him out to see if he ever intended to purchase the damned school in the first place.

"If it would help in making the decision, I'd be happy to share some of my thoughts about the academy from a student's perspective."

"Yes, that might be useful. Thanks." He opened the door to the kitchen. "Here we are."

He showed her the fridge and cupboards and helped her prepare a tray of assorted cold cuts, cheese, fruit, and glasses of ice-cold sparkling water. He pulled a loaf of whole-grain bread from the counter just as Gunnar entered the room.

Kristoffer forced himself to engage in social pleasantries, something he'd become quite rusty at, when all he really wanted to do was drive back to Denver and distance himself from everyone. But he'd better become accustomed to spending time with Pamela in the next couple of months. Besides, he owed Gunnar too much, and they hadn't finished their business yet.

Gunnar was the closest relative and friend he had left in the world, including his own mother. Kristoffer would take a bullet for him, but more likely than not, Gunnar would be the one sacrificing himself in that way. Kristoffer spent his days in safe, nonviolent activities, although he did practice aikido, a form of martial arts. However, that discipline was intended more to seek harmony than to take down an attacker.

Being seated so close to Pamela after having inappropriate thoughts about her half the night wreaked havoc with his self-control. Her scent wasn't flowery like Tori's. It was subtle, something more…spicy. Exotic. Passionate.

Hold on a minute.

She was now a colleague, at least temporarily. However, after they'd collided at that inopportune moment last night, he found it difficult to banish thoughts of her naked body from his mind.

Why was he so obsessed with Pamela Jeffrey, clothed or otherwise? Curiosity, perhaps. What had led the seemingly reserved physician to stand naked in front of a class at a BDSM academy?

Was she as nervous around him as he was of her? How could he put her mind at ease? One sure way was to get people to talk about themselves. "Where are you from, Pamela?" He took a sip of his water while awaiting her response.

"Born in Japan, but raised in Colorado Springs." He raised an eyebrow, and she grinned as though expecting his surprise. "I'm an Air Force brat."

"Interesting," Gunnar said.

"My dad was stationed at the Yokota Air Base in western Japan back then, but not long before that he met Mom while he was stationed on the base at Beale near San Francisco. She was finishing high school. They married during her senior year. When he was transferred to Japan, she had to finish high school by correspondence course. Anyway, I was born there a few months later, and by the time I was three, they'd moved stateside again and settled in Colorado Springs."

She certainly was forthcoming.

Flushing, she looked down at her plate, pausing to take a bite and swallow before she continued. "Dad had a teaching job at the Air Force Academy, and Mom attended the University of Colorado there. But my folks split up when I was twelve. They weren't well-suited, but had tried to stay together for me until I guess they just couldn't stand it any longer."

Despite her flippant explanation, he detected a bit of sadness in her eyes. His parents had split up, too, as had Gunnar's.

"That's too bad," Kristoffer said. Few marriages lasted anymore.

But mine has.

She shrugged, but he could see it mattered more than she let on. "Mom went overseas after she left us. I think in something like the

Peace Corps. She never really talked about it much, but her humanitarian work made an impact on me."

He wanted to know more about her and prompted her with, "So you take after her in some ways."

Her smile seemed genuine. "Both my parents taught me a lot about service and giving back. Anyway, Mom eventually settled in California. Dad remarried and retired in Colorado Springs near the Academy. But I prefer living in Denver. More opportunities for jobs and extracurricular activ…"

She cut off the word, and as he watched the telltale blush creep up her neck into her cheeks, he fought back a grin. Before he could bring up the subject of the tour, Gunnar interjected. "Speaking of extracurriculars, Kris, what do you have for me about The Denver Academy acquisition? Worth it?"

He'd much rather learn more about Pamela, but duty called. He turned his focus to Gunnar. "Depends on what your plans and goals are for the place, but yes, it would be a sound financial investment from what I've seen."

Kristoffer laid out the high points of the proposal he'd left in his briefcase. His mind might no longer have a place for cherished memories, but when it came to facts and figures relating to his work, he didn't forget a thing. He rattled off the financials first.

During a brief lull, Pamela chimed in. "Gunnar, Kristoffer is aware that I'm a student there. If you have any questions for me about the student aspects, feel free."

"Great! I was hoping you'd allow me to pry, but didn't want to ask in front of Kris."

This might be his opportunity to put that awkward moment behind them. "About last night, Pamela… Finding me staring at you must have been disconcerting at best."

She smiled and relaxed her shoulders for the first time since he'd arrived in the boardroom earlier. "It certainly was a shock to see someone I knew."

"I was impressed by your poise under the circumstances."

"Thank you. I wasn't feeling poised on the inside. As you can imagine, if anyone in that group chose to talk to the board of the organization I work for, I could be dismissed."

"Rest assured everyone in the group was vetted by Brad Anderson. He'd hold our feet to the fire if anyone spoke out of turn. The man is purported to be very protective of his students and the school."

"Which makes me wonder why he's selling," Gunnar said.

Kristoffer had forgotten about his cousin for a moment. "From what I gathered, he's moving out of the area."

"Ah. Understandable then." Gunnar nodded. "Now I suppose I have to decide if it makes sense for me to buy the place."

Kristoffer wasn't sure it was a sound decision for him. "My biggest concern is the time element. You're a busy man with a lot of irons in the fire already. When would you find time to run the school—or do you know of someone you could put into the role of director or headmaster to take care of the day-to-day operations?"

"I haven't given any thought to who would run it, but point taken. I'm going to have to think long and hard about it. Perhaps I'd prefer being on the board of directors under whomever else decides to purchase it." Gunnar turned toward Pamela. "Your thoughts about the school?"

"Well, I haven't been there a full two weeks yet, but from what I've experienced so far, they do a very good job at helping submissives explore the lifestyle to the fullest extent in a safe environment."

Kristoffer leaned toward her. "One of the hallmarks of their program is the auction nights. What did you think of that aspect? As I understand it, you've been through one now, right?"

She smiled and picked up her water glass to take a sip before answering. "It was...interesting." The blush made the freckles on her cheeks fade. "The Dom who bid on me was excellent at anticipating my needs, but...I just didn't feel any chemistry with him."

Gunnar pushed his plate away. "There are just as many ways to be dominant as there are to be submissive."

Pamela smiled. "Undoubtedly. But figuring out where you fall on the spectrum can help rule out the incompatible ones, although it's hard to connect with anyone for long given my travel schedule. I've had about a dozen assignments overseas in the past three years."

Kristoffer couldn't stop himself. "Meeting the perfect person to spend your life with isn't easy whether you're looking for kink or vanilla. Sometimes they show up when you least expect them."

"How'd you meet your wife?"

A sharp pain pierced his chest as he remembered the first time he laid eyes on Tori. "In college at Penn. We were both nineteen and wound up working late one night on a team project in our introductory finance course." He reached for his glass of water and drained it, hoping to put an end to the subject of his own personal life.

Pamela refilled his glass from the pitcher on the table. "So you're both interested in finance."

No such luck. Obviously, she couldn't know what had happened to Tori. Still, better for her to think him happily married if they would be working together. He trusted her to remain professional, but given his penchant for remembering how she appeared last night, he no longer trusted himself. He hoped Gunnar would keep his mouth shut.

"Not really. It was an elective for her, and she soon found she wasn't all that interested in the flow of money. But she did have an interest in me." He smiled. "We later decided that fate had used that class to bring us together. We had a lot of other things in common, fortunately." And that was all he intended to say about that.

Time to steer this conversation back to business. "Don't say more than you're comfortable sharing, but you didn't have a problem with being auctioned off to a stranger?"

She shook her head but looked away. "Not really. No Doms are allowed into the school unless their backgrounds have been fully checked and cross-checked. They're all made aware of each student's list of limits, likes, and dislikes before they ever place a bid. It's much safer than hooking up with someone at a munch, for instance." She met his gaze, as though making sure she wasn't speaking over his head.

Clearly, she didn't think he was well-versed in the lifestyle. "By munch, you mean where Dominants and submissives meet in public, usually over a meal, to get to know each other better?"

She nodded her eyebrows going up. "I think we learn faster through these interactions with those who win us than we might if we had to attend several munches, play parties, or club visits. Observing how the Dominant relates with other subs beforehand helps determine if they'd be a good match. But, again, if the chemistry isn't there, it can make for a long evening."

"I imagine." He banished the thought of her playing with someone else from his mind for the moment. Not material to what they were discussing. "Well, it sounds as though you still have several more opportunities coming up before your training will be complete."

"Yes. There are six in all." She fiddled with her napkin. "I can't say that it's my favorite part. Trust is a bit of a problem for me. Playing with strangers is another."

Although Gunner reiterated that the academy was a secure facility, Kristoffer understood the trust issues Pamela suffered from and admired her all the more for her tenacious spirit. It seemed, however—with this new project Gunnar wanted to pursue to help the hospital in Afghanistan—that taking on The Denver Academy could prove too time-consuming for his cousin's schedule.

Kristoffer turned his focus back to the pros and cons of this acquisition. "Gunnar, I hope you will give this a great deal of consideration before making a decision. It's the time commitment that worries me most. These students will depend on you and your staff to provide training, but also to keep them safe from backlash and naysayers if attacked by people ignorant of what BDSM means. There were a number of investors there last night, so I can't guarantee that the property will remain on the market long, but don't jump into this without giving it serious thought."

"No worries. I'm not as passionate about that as I am about the project you two are going to be working on, but leave the report with me, and I'll give you instructions tomorrow on how to proceed." He stood. "Now, if you'll excuse me, I have a conference call in fifteen minutes that I need to prepare for. Pamela, Kris, we'll get together in a week to see how you're progressing on the project."

After exchanging goodbyes, Gunnar left the two of them alone. No time like the present to begin making plans, but he wanted to learn more about Pamela first. "Tell me more about your work at the hospital."

Her emerald-green eyes sparkled with excitement. "It's been rewarding beyond anything I'd ever imagined." She shrugged, almost as if she should apologize.

"No doubt a lot of people are indebted to you."

"I hope I'm helping. So many are doing incredible work there, but so much more could be done to save lives." A shadow passed over her eyes, and Pamela glanced down at her half-eaten sandwich.

"I'm sure it's challenging to work in a Third World nation. You've probably seen horrific things."

"I'm one of the lucky ones—healthy and relatively safe. But being able to ease the suffering of the patients, especially the young ones, has been enormously gratifying."

Her selflessness was admirable. Still, she had been working in a war zone, whether she let that concern her or not.

"When would you like to meet to begin our work on the project?"

"No time like tomorrow, unless you're busy."

"Tomorrow's perfect. How about eleven? Where shall we meet?"

"I know a quiet restaurant in Aurora that wouldn't kick us out if we lingered a while. Why not make it eleven-thirty and call it lunch?"

"Sounds good." It truly did. He hadn't enjoyed a conversation this much in a long time. Listening to someone so full of hope and ideals pursuing her passion made him realize that the world had only stopped spinning for him. Everyone else continued to move forward with their lives.

As it should be.

Not that it would be possible for him at this point. He'd chosen his path and had no intention of changing anything.

CHAPTER THREE

Kristoffer entered the darkened room. The scent of flowers assailed his senses. *Tori.* She loved stargazer lilies, so he made sure fresh ones were kept in her room at all times.

"How's my sweetheart doing tonight?"

While facing in his direction, the woman who lay curled up on the bed bore little resemblance to his wife. She didn't smile or acknowledge his presence.

No surprise.

Her arm spasmed. Back when he was more optimistic, he might have interpreted that jerk of her arm as a wave.

Dream on.

Involuntary movement, the doctors told him over and over before it finally sank in after a couple of years. Despite a stream of experts in the first year she was hospitalized and intensive brain scans over the next three, no evidence had been found that she was aware of him or anything around her.

She'd been brought back to life four times in the first two hours after the accident. That night, he'd wanted paramedics and emergency department staff to do everything possible to keep her alive. In retrospect, he wished she'd died instantly. Her brain damage due to the head trauma and lack of oxygen had been massive and irreparable. Tori had always been such a fighter, but even she couldn't overcome those odds.

As he did every evening after work, he prepared to spend the next couple of hours talking to her as if she understood him. As if she knew he existed. As if she still loved him.

Even if she received nothing out of these visits, *he* needed to keep coming every single day. He'd never stop loving and protecting her as best he could. The horror stories he'd read when trying to find a place for her still burned his gut. Stories about how some unscrupulous staff members took advantage of patients like Tori who were unaware of their surroundings.

Good care for persistent vegetative state patients didn't come cheaply; he'd never have been able to afford a place like this on a financial adviser's salary. When she'd first been released to a long-term-care facility, he'd found one he could afford, but fear of abuse convinced him he needed to devote himself to her every waking minute. To that end, he'd shut off every other part of his life, including work, and stayed by her side almost day and night—six months in the hospital and the next year and a half at the first nursing home.

He'd changed more diapers than most parents did with their new-borns. Flushed and replaced the feeding tube to her stomach. Put her through his own intense physical therapy regimen in an attempt to delay the inevitable atrophy of muscle and organ tissue.

Those first two years, his entire focus had been on her daily needs, because he'd promised to protect and provide for her on the day they married. But his determination to live up to his vows came at a hefty price to his sanity.

Kristoffer hadn't seen that he had a problem dealing with every-thing until he woke up one morning at his new condo crying and unable to get out of bed to go see her. The feelings of hopelessness and helplessness overwhelmed him. When Gunnar called to check on him three days later, Kristoffer begged him to take away the pain. His cousin had him in the office of a psychiatrist the next day.

"You need to let others manage her daily needs now, Kris," Gun-nar had advised him. "You won't do her any good if you have to be confined in a padded room somewhere."

Kristoffer had no choice, but his breakdown had been a blessing in disguise. His depression didn't lift for months, even after finding the right meds and a psychologist who understood somewhat. During that time, Gunnar had Tori moved to this place in the Denver suburbs. He'd picked up all the costs, saying that family looked out for each other. This facility was considered the best in the region, and she'd received better care during these past two years than even he could give her, easing some of Kristoffer's guilt. In hindsight, he truly understood he couldn't do it alone, although he'd been stubborn and depressed enough back then to think he was Superman.

Only with tunnel vision, not X-ray vision.

Gunnar loved Tori, sure, but loved and worried about Kristoffer even more. It was at that point two years after the accident that Kristoffer came to the realization he owed Gunnar not only for saving his life, but also for all he'd done for Tori. So Kristoffer had spent every day since working as hard as he could to make money for Gunnar, knowing that a sizeable chunk of it went every month to paying for Tori's astronomically expensive care. His investment efforts had more than quadrupled Gunnar's assets, leaving Kristoffer feeling less of a burden to his cousin.

In this facility, Kristoffer didn't have to provide for her physical needs, so he could simply spend time holding her, talking to her. He'd gone back to daily visits, but now they were more for him than her. This was how his visits would be as long as they both lived.

He tried to envision the once vivacious woman he'd known before, but despite filling her room with framed photos of blissful times together, too often now he couldn't bring himself to look at them. Those memories had faded over the years.

At first, in the hospital, he couldn't see the reality of what she'd become. Nowadays, all he *could* see was the shriveled, distorted woman suffering from years of atrophy. Hands drawn inward at the wrists, almost in a fetal position as her body's muscles contracted from lack of use. Face contorted, mouth open as if in a silent scream.

He'd stopped putting her through agonizing physical therapy after a while, too, hating to hear her groaning as if in pain. Again, the doctors said her brain couldn't register feelings, but the sound nearly killed him.

Her lack of awareness made it futile for him to share what he'd been doing today, but he did so anyway. This was the last connection they had, even if only one of them was aware that they had once been a loving couple. This had been his ritual every night she'd been here.

What would he share about this evening? He couldn't tell her about last night, even though that had been in the forefront of his mind since the tour.

Pamela.

Guilt washed over him for thinking the name of another woman while here with his wife, although nothing had happened between the two of them. Why did a few inappropriate thoughts and a brief conversation with her make him feel as though he had cheated on Tori? His wife hadn't known he existed for the past four years.

He'd done nothing to dishonor his vows since he'd spoken them so many years ago, although last night his mind had wandered into unsafe territory.

If not for his inattentive driving, Tori wouldn't have been left in this state. Tamping down the familiar anger, Kristoffer pulled a chair closer to the bed and placed his hand on Tori's cool arm. Her mouth drew up as if in pain, and her breathing became louder. At times like this, he still wished she recognized him.

How the doctors could be certain all hope was gone, he didn't know, but Kristoffer had to admit there'd never been the slightest spark of awareness from her since the night of the wreck.

"It's okay, Tori. I'm here now." The NG feeding tube from her nose to her stomach that she'd depended on during those early months in the hospital had long since been replaced by the percutaneous endoscopic gastrostomy tube inserted directly into her stomach and well-hidden under her gown. Seeing her once-unblemished skin marred by the PEG tube or any other medical apparatus pained him, but she'd have died without it. The question became whether this, too, had been extraordinary means. Putting her on dialysis or a ventilator clearly crossed the line of what measures he would impose upon her. However, the thought of withdrawing nourishment from her body had been out of the question early on. Feeding her and providing water hadn't seemed like an extraordinary act to him.

Although if he knew then what he knew now, he might have reconsidered.

As her legal guardian, he worried every day whether he'd correctly determined what her wishes would be. They'd never really discussed end-of-life preferences. Who wanted to talk about such ghastly eventualities when they were happily married and going about their lives with no inkling of what horrors the future held?

All right, in retrospect, that sounded irresponsible. If he could do it over again, he'd have made sure they talked about it. Fortunately, her parents agreed with everything he'd done and supported his decision to insert the feeding tube when she'd come out of the coma. While she'd been raised Catholic, neither he nor Tori had been particularly religious, so the situation hadn't encouraged him to seek out religious answers, either. Since the night Tori had been taken from him in that crash, he'd seen no evidence of a benevolent God. What kind of deity would leave her in this state, lost somewhere between the here and hereafter for four goddamned years?

In hindsight, he should have pulled the plug within the first six months when she was deep in a coma and still on the ventilator. But when he finally removed her from the ventilator, she started breathing on her own. Removing the feeding tube had been out of the question. People woke up from comas every day. Look at the police officer in Tennessee who woke up after eleven years. Reports said he even spoke.

Never give up hope. Believe in miracles.

But the media failed to tell people that the man died a few months later with zero quality of life after his "miraculous" awakening.

Kristoffer continued to hold out hope and kept reading about miracles happening to others who had suffered severe traumatic brain injuries. Why not expect one for Tori? She'd been a kind person who was loved by many. Why had her life been destroyed and his spared when both had been involved in the same accident? If he'd been paying attention to the traffic in front of him, he wouldn't have swerved and caused the accident.

Of course, hope didn't always spring eternal. Eventually, one had to face reality.

And here they were. He could take comfort in the fact she appeared to have moments of wakefulness and sleeping, as close to normal as she'd ever be again. But when her body jerked and twitched as if in response to his voice as it had done a few moments ago, he no longer pretended she knew who he was or had heard his words.

He brushed a strand of hair away from her face. Realizing he hadn't kissed her yet—something he normally did the moment he entered the room. He stood and bent over her, placing his lips against her cool cheek.

"How's my sweetheart doing tonight?" he repeated.

No response.

No change.

No surprise.

He settled back into the chair with a sigh. What could he talk about? *Ah, yes.* "You won't believe what Gunnar's up to." No need to wait for any acknowledging murmur like she once had given when he recounted news from his workday. "He's looking into buying a school to train Dominants and submissives in the lifestyle." For the next ten minutes, he told her about his tour—well, most of it. Again, no mention of Pamela. He reminded her how Gunnar had mentored the two of them when they became interested in light kink. Thoughts of those times caused his throat to close off, and the silence closed in on him.

Was a monologue still considered a conversation? At least in a play or stand-up comedy routine, an audience was aware and able to listen and provide feedback.

Tori never would again.

Why so maudlin tonight? What else should he tell her about? "Oh, I almost forgot!" He reached inside his suit coat. "I brought some of your favorite music." He stood, went to the stereo in the corner of the room, and inserted the CD. Soon, the smooth Mangione piece streamed through the speaker system he'd installed in her room. A memory of one of the many times he'd danced with Tori to that very CD flashed across his mind's eye, hitting him like a battering ram to the solar plexus.

Drawing a ragged breath, he returned to the bed and lowered the rail behind her before climbing in. The feeding tube was on the side she lay on, so he didn't have to worry about pulling anything out.

He'd ordered a wider bed than most patients had when she'd left the hospital, and Gunnar made sure it came here with her. The bed was large enough for the two of them to curl up against one another and snuggle. Might not mean anything to her anymore, but it meant the world to him.

Tonight, for some reason, the need to pretend she was aware of him became paramount. In his mind, he pictured her waking up and gracing him with her gentle smile. He could hear her laugh robustly at something he whispered in her ear. God, he missed her laugh. Curling his body against her rigid, curved back, he wrapped his arm around her waist, careful to avoid the tube. Spooned together like this, he could pretend she was merely sleeping as she often was when he quit work and came to bed.

"Come back to me, Tori," he pleaded before he realized he'd spoken aloud.

Stillness. No hint of movement, not even involuntary ones. She wasn't like some of the victims in the countless videos he'd watched showing patients in a vegetative state grunting when spoken to or blinking their eyes to give "yes" or "no" responses to simple questions. While she sometimes made sounds, everyone agreed she had no awareness of what was going on around her. But her moans during physical therapy sessions had always made him worry he was hurting her.

She had no idea tonight that the man she once said was her whole world lay here beside her.

You've been the center of my universe for two decades.

Till death do us part.

"Look at us, Tori." Neither of them had envisioned this outcome when their life together had been so happy.

But she'd have done the same for him if he'd been the one unable to escape the wreck unscathed.

Both had taken their vows seriously, although his definitions of life and of death had been altered by what had happened. No one could describe her state of being as *living* by any stretch of the imagination. Her body continued to exist thanks to modern medicine and tube feedings. Nothing more. Breathing, blinking, and reflexive swallowing, interspersed with moments when she appeared to wake and sleep.

He'd promised to stay by her side in sickness and in health, but had that included being kept alive by artificial means? Did it mean closing himself off from everything and everyone else?

He buried his face against her back and let the hot tears soak her gown. Why was the loss harder to deal with tonight than it had been every other night over the past four years? The future stretched out bleak and lonely with no hope of having the light in Tori's eyes setting him ablaze again.

Hell, you gave up on that fantasy years ago. About two years, to be exact, when Gunnar pulled you back from the brink.

The first two years after the accident, he'd waited for a miracle. The next two, he'd been forced to be pragmatic and realistic or risk losing his mind.

So why start wishing for the impossible again now? Was it wrong of him to hope for more out of life? Tori wasn't coming back.

What in bloody hell had changed since yesterday? he asked himself again. Sure, he'd held on to hope longer than most might. But these days, he had to admit he came here more out of habit and obligation than any other reason. The essence that had been his beloved Tori had been snuffed out in the accident. His visits here usually helped fill some gaping hole inside him, if for only a brief moment or two before the emptiness consumed him once more. While he could touch her and talk to her, he'd been content.

Why couldn't he feel that solace tonight? Why did it hurt so much more now?

The image of Pamela speaking passionately about her work at the hospital flashed across his mind's eye.

Pamela.

She'd breathed life into him today for the first time in...too long. At least he still had his career to immerse himself in, but thoughts of being with Pamela tomorrow to begin work on this project left him more excited than he'd been in ages.

He hugged Tori closer as more tears stung his eyes. The music wrapped around him, infusing a sense of peace into him.

"I love you, sweetheart." His eyelids drooped as he gave in to much-needed sleep.

Shortly after midnight, Pamela entered her upstairs apartment, dropping her canvas bag into the nearest chair and wishing she could plop herself there, too. Night class at the academy on top of a long meeting in Breckenridge today had taken a toll. Despite her doctor's assurances that she was on the road to recovery from the hard-to-diagnose fever that had sent her home from Afghanistan a month earlier than planned, she remained exhausted. Her physician had provided assurances to the academy and her that she was no longer contagious. However, she needed to take better care of herself. Perhaps she'd been pushing herself too hard, but this was the first time she'd had time away from work in years. She wanted to accomplish so much before returning to the hospital this summer.

Adding this project for Gunnar Larson hadn't been among her plans, but this equipment would mean so much to the staff and patients there that she hadn't been able to say no. Why should she put her submissive training on hold because she was feeling a little tired? Things would settle down soon.

The only thing she knew for certain: mastering submission would continue to be pitifully unattainable if she didn't complete the academy's coursework or find a mentor. Her first objective was to learn to turn off the voices in her head that kept her from fully experiencing the moment.

Perhaps this weekend she'd be won by a Dom who could make it happen the way she'd imagined and heard it could be. Whatever *it* was.

Her wish list seemed to be ever-changing. At the moment, she hoped to find a Dom with a sense of humor who was firm yet gentle. Someone who needed her to nurture him, which in turn would help fulfill her need to serve others. A man who would take charge in the bedroom, pushing her limits while guiding her to be the best person she could be.

Her thoughts strayed to lunch this afternoon as she made her way to the bedroom, shedding clothes before tossing them in the laundry basket. Her head ached from all that had happened today.

The conversation with Kristoffer and Gunnar had been eye-opening, especially with Kristoffer. Such an intelligent, thoughtful man. Not at all what her first impression of him had been. He'd surprised her with his candid and solicitous nature. He'd been, well, caring, for lack of a better word. Not cold and distant.

Yet she couldn't help but feel a deep and profound sadness surrounding him. Perhaps his marriage wasn't a happy one. He hadn't said much about his wife, not that he'd revealed all that much about himself, either. She'd certainly dominated the conversation.

Pamela sat at the vanity, removed her makeup, and released her hair from the pins and scrunchie that held it in place. At the academy, she'd been instructed to wear it down, but she preferred to pull it up at other times to keep it out of the way. These days, she typically used a military doughnut technique Heidi had taught her to hold it in place. She picked up her brush and ran it through the loosened strands and let her mind wander.

Thoughts of what she wanted as far as love and marriage invaded next. She did not intend to jump into marriage quickly, if at all. Somehow, the thought of a marriage certificate made her more nervous than blissful. Why have a legal document that most didn't even choose to honor faithfully?

When she met the Dominant she couldn't live without, why couldn't they exchange solemn, heartfelt vows that were meaningful to them without putting their trust in a piece of paper or an institution to hold them to their promises?

Maybe someday I'll find a man I can make that kind of commitment to.

She sighed. If such a man existed.

Deciding to shower in the morning, she stretched out under the sheet and comforter and stared up at the ceiling for a long time, unable to quiet her busy thoughts. She'd gone to the academy to explore and develop her newly discovered alpha submissive side. Until she decided her lifestyle calling was something else, she'd stay on that track.

The bed seemed large and lonely tonight, even more so than usual. The whole apartment was for that matter. On nights like this, she wished she had someone here to share the highlights of her day with or simply to curl up against and feel his strong, protective arms around her.

Her needs were simple. Safety, guidance, and, eventually, maybe even love.

Okay, deep down she wanted it all. Career, commitment, possibly even family. She just didn't like to admit it as much these days as she was closing in on forty with no prospects in sight.

Maybe someday.

Her next cognitive thought was the smell of coffee permeating her senses. She opened gritty eyes and stared dumbly at the clock for a few seconds until the fog of sleep dissipated. Six-thirty. She always refilled the automatic coffee maker for the next day's use, but wished she'd set the timer for later. Sleep deprivation was taking its toll.

Pamela tossed back the covers. No sense lying idly around all day. She wanted to check her e-mails to see if the foundation director or hospital administrator had responded to her with a list of priorities for the facility. She'd like to have specifics to share with Kristoffer when they met in a few hours.

After powering up her laptop, she found an e-mail from the chief of staff in Afghanistan listing two major pieces of medical equipment they could use right away. She did some research on costs and prepared a sheet to share with Kristoffer.

Her stomach growled, and she noticed the time. Nearly eleven! Where had the morning gone? Since lunch was a short time away, she didn't bother to eat anything now. She texted Kristoffer to let him know she was running a few minutes behind. Good thing she'd suggested a place nearby. She closed the lid on her laptop and darted to the bathroom to shower and dress before heading toward the door. She hated being tardy. So unprofessional. She didn't want to jeopardize this equipment purchase.

When she pulled into the restaurant's parking lot, there was only a silver Jaguar and a Ford station wagon. No doubt Kristoffer drove the Jag. She grabbed her briefcase and hurried toward the front door only to have it opened before she could reach for the handle. Kristoffer Larson, in a light gray suit, smiled in greeting.

"Perfect timing."

She knew she was a tad late, but appreciated him for not calling her on it. "Good morning, Kristoffer. Or do you prefer Kris?" She remembered his cousin calling him by the shortened moniker.

"Kristoffer. Gunnar's the only one who calls me Kris. We go way back to my less formal days."

She wondered what Kristoffer was like as a boy. Something told her he'd broken a lot of hearts.

The hostess seated them near a window at the far end of the room where they could enjoy privacy when the place filled up with the lunch crowd. She ordered a glass of lemon water and a Caesar salad; he chose a soup and sandwich combo. Kristoffer instructed the server to put both meals on one bill.

"Thanks for lunch, Kristoffer—and for meeting with me so soon. I'm anxious to get moving on this." Pamela pulled the printouts from her briefcase and passed them across the table. "These are some of the most crucial needs the administrator identified."

He barely glanced at the paper. "Yes, I've talked with him already."

Her eyes opened wider. "You have?"

He nodded. "I wanted to establish a rapport with him, because I'll need him to sign off on a lot of this. Hope you don't mind."

"No, not at all. The sooner we can make this happen, the better."

He finally started poring over her printouts. "You're very much in sync with what he told me."

"We've had a number of conversations about what we'd like to have available to us—mostly wishful thinking sessions. That Gunnar has made this generous offer still has me pinching myself."

He set the papers aside when their meals were served. As she was about to take a bite, he said, "There's just one thing you left out."

She lowered her fork. "What's that?"

"Why didn't you tell me you'd been sick?"

She waved away his concern but wondered why Pierre had spoken out of turn. "I'm nearly one hundred percent again. Just some fluke fever I must have caught from a tick or mosquito bite. Not knowing the source, my physician prescribed a couple of the most effective antibiotics used for fevers contracted in that region, and it went away."

"They weren't able to diagnose what it was?"

"The lab work is too expensive, and some causes won't show up as a positive anyway until much later. Best to treat first and ask questions later."

"Are you under medical care here?" He didn't let up.

"I'm a doctor, remember?"

He narrowed his eyes. "And from what I understand, a doctor often makes a lousy patient."

She laughed, hoping to get him to lighten up. "Probably, but I assure you that when I'm tired, I sleep; when I'm hungry, I eat." *Well, most of the time.*

"Should you be undergoing the rigorous courses at the academy right now? That has to be draining on your energy level so late at night."

"Did I look as though I was suffering ill effects when you toured the school the other night?"

"No. You looked quite healthy to me." Her face grew warm, and she decided to ignore the innuendo, whether he'd intended to be suggestive or not. "But this is only the beginning of the academy's training schedule."

She picked up her fork and speared a leaf of romaine. "I assure you,

I'm taking care of myself. I also saw my primary care physician when I returned stateside, and he's monitoring my situation."

✧ ✧ ✧

Kristoffer couldn't help but grin at the flush in her cheeks that no doubt stemmed from embarrassment now rather than any lingering fever. Still, when he'd learned how seriously ill she'd been a month ago, he wondered why she was putting herself through so much when she should be taking it easy.

Driven. The woman didn't strike him as the type to sit back and take anything in stride. Of course, someone in her chosen profession would have to be driven to make it through medical school and to establish her career.

"Why did you choose plastic surgery?"

She swallowed before responding. "A girlfriend in high school was involved in a serious car accident that crushed most of the bones in her face."

Kristoffer found it difficult to breathe for a moment as the accident that had taken Tori from him flashed across his mind. Only Tori's face hadn't received more than a few bruises. It was her brain that had been crushed. "Did she survive?"

"Yes, she did. And the surgeons did a wonderful job of reconstructing her face. No, not exactly the way she looked before, but when I saw what a difference each of those surgeries meant for her self-esteem, I decided that's what I wanted to do."

"I'm sure you've made a difference in a lot of lives, too."

"Not so much at first, but being one of the few plastic surgeons to join this humanitarian aid group and serving in places where there has been so much trauma has been extremely rewarding. Take Fakhira, for instance. While I know she needs much more reconstructive work, I was able to perform skin grafts to replace some of the facial skin that had been burned off by the acid." She closed her eyes. "I was only able to restore very basic functionality in that primitive facility, though; she still has so far to go."

"She sounds like a survivor."

Pamela nodded before staring pointedly at his untouched soup. "Sorry. This isn't the most pleasant dining conversation."

He brushed off her concern. "Honestly, there isn't a lot that can horrify me anymore. Besides, I'm waiting for my soup to cool." To prove his words, he scooped up a spoonful of the chicken tortilla soup and lifted it to his mouth to test. "Just about right, now." He swallowed, and the two of them ate for a while in silence.

When he'd finished the bowl, he brought the conversation back to where he wanted it. He was worried about the good doctor. "Does Brad Anderson know you've been sick?"

"Key word is 'been.' I'm fine now."

He stared pointedly at her, waiting for her to answer his question. When she glanced away, he wasn't sure if she would continue to evade it or respond.

"Yes. I wouldn't have made it into the academy without full medical disclosure." She met his gaze again, sparks flying. "You worry too much. Now, could we talk about something else?"

Submissive, with a streak of defiance. Intriguing.

"Like what?"

"Have you spent much time in Norway?"

Why the change of subject? Had he struck a nerve—or confronted her with a truth she didn't want to face? He'd humor her, for now. "Only summers. Mother didn't want me to miss school, and traveling to my grandfather's remote village was brutal and unpredictable in winter. Gunnar and I were both sent there every summer during our early to mid-teens. Until FarFar died."

"FarFar?"

"Sorry. The Norwegian word for the father of one's father, although these days it can be used to refer to either grandfather." He shrugged. "He was always FarFar to us. My grandfather's place was along a remote fjord. Man, the adventures Gunnar and I had there." His voice trailed off as he reminisced about some of their adventures. Life had been so simple then. Suddenly, he remembered he wasn't alone. "Beg your pardon. I miss those simpler days a lot. He was a great role model for me. Gunnar has been, too. I owe a lot to them both."

"It's important to have people like that in your life." He wondered whom she would credit as helping to shape who she'd become, but didn't want to pry. "I'll bet that was an amazing experience for two young boys cavorting in the land of Vikings."

Kristoffer laughed. "What happens in Norway stays in Norway."

"I can only imagine all the broken hearts left behind by you two," she said. "Did you see much of Gunnar at other times of the year?"

"No. Not until I turned sixteen. My parents divorced, and I wasn't very happy living with my mother. FarFar had passed away the winter before. So early one June morning, I announced I was moving in with Gunnar, caught a bus, and headed west. He'd just graduated from college and was taking the summer off before heading to boot camp. I didn't think he'd mind hanging out with me, although when I showed up unannounced on his doorstep, he busted my chops more than Mother did."

"Where did Gunnar live?"

"Just north of Denver. He went to Colorado State in Fort Collins and let me stick around a couple of months then sent me packing back east to finish high school."

He took a bite of his sandwich, wondering what else they might talk about. He really had become rusty at making small talk. Ah, yes. Her recent illness.

Before he could bring it up again, Pamela picked up the conversation where they'd left off. "I thought you'd always lived in Colorado."

"I guess I've been here long enough to shed most of my Connecticut accent."

"I didn't think Connecticut folks had accents, at least not the ones I've met."

"I think those of us closer to the Rhode Island or New York City borders tend to have more pronounced accents than those in the middle of the state."

"Which border were you closer to?"

"Southeastern, in New London. Near Rhode Island and just north of the easternmost tip of Long Island."

She nodded, although most people had no clue how far the island extended east. "I haven't been to New England. Actually, with all of my traveling, you'd think I'd have seen more of my own country than I have. But I haven't been to any state east of Colorado except during airport layovers."

He found himself wanting to share with her his love of some of the places he'd been in the States, before realizing that wasn't relevant. Now, where were they? "How do you handle languages when traveling overseas?"

"I studied French in high school and college, and it's one of the official languages of Chad, where I had my first assignment," she explained. Kristoffer had no idea. Must have been colonized by France. "French also is the language preferred by the organization I work for. And I picked up some basic Pashto while preparing to go to Afghanistan the first time. Have you studied any languages?"

"I'm passable at Norwegian, mostly from immersion during my childhood summers, but took German in school. I haven't had a lot of use for it in real life, so I've probably forgotten it all."

"It doesn't take much for a language to fade. I also took a semester of German as an elective in college, but can't remember much. I retained French much better."

She nibbled at her salad, but had barely touched it. How did she expect to get better if she didn't eat? Rather than having a salad, she ought to be eating steak.

"You need to take better care of yourself." He picked up his unused salad fork and speared another anchovy before holding it up to her mouth. He wasn't sure if she opened up willingly or if her jaw dropped in surprise. He realized how presumptuous he was being, but found himself worrying about her. "Good." He'd almost said *good girl*, but caught himself in time. "You need to eat more."

"I can feed myself." She took the fork from his hand and proved it by stabbing another anchovy and popping it into her mouth.

He realized the innate dominant gesture of feeding her might also be misconstrued. Thankfully, she'd called him on it.

She swallowed another bite. "I was just lost in the conversation. If you're in a hurry, feel free to—"

"I'm not trying to rush you. I don't have to be anywhere until this evening. I'm just concerned after hearing you'd been sick."

"Please, ignore Pierre. He's a worrywart. It wasn't nearly as dire as he must have made it out to you."

He'd said she'd been in the hospital nearly two weeks battling the fever. Lord only knew what diseases were endemic to the region. Apparently, the vaccines she'd received to prevent them hadn't covered everything.

After eating several more bites, she asked, "I suppose if you met your wife at Penn, she was from the East Coast, too." She had a knack for deflecting the conversation away from herself.

"Midwest, actually. St. Louis."

"Does she like it here?"

Stalling for the right way to respond didn't occur to him, so he took another bite of his sandwich. "It's been our home for a long time. Neither of us would want to live anywhere else." Not that they hadn't enjoyed trips to wine country in California once a year after honeymooning there. Tori had embraced life to the fullest—until her light and life had been snuffed out.

He needed a new topic of conversation—one that wouldn't lead to thoughts of Tori. "What got you into humanitarian work?"

She swallowed before answering. At least she was eating again. "I was at loose ends mainly. Between jobs and trying to figure out what to do next. Then I saw a news report about the need for surgeons and other physicians. When I checked out the qualifications, I met all of them. Best move I ever made. I think fulfilling my need to serve was a big part of it."

"Don't you worry about your safety?"

She shrugged. "I take precautions, and we're surrounded by security forces. Because we're not taking sides in the conflict, we usually aren't targets. We also make sure all warring factions are aware of our coordinates."

"There's such a thing as friendly fire. No one's safe in a war zone."

"True. But this is what I'm compelled to do. Just as Gunnar makes regular missions in the same region. It's hard to turn your back on those in need."

"There are those in need here, too."

"I know. And when I'm tired of working with this organization, I'll search for a way to help closer to home. I just didn't choose the right practice to work with before and wanted to place some distance between us."

He wondered what had happened. "I'm in awe of those with your courage and conviction."

"I look at it as my job."

"Yeah, that's how Gunnar describes what he's been doing since he joined the Army." Didn't make Kristoffer any more reassured about his cousin's safety. "I'm going to worry about you now when you go back."

"That's sweet, but don't lose any sleep over me."

Too late.

"I've been taking care of myself for a long time." She smiled, but her green eyes shot sparks at him. Clearly, he'd struck a nerve.

If she only knew how much sleep he'd lost in the last few days thinking about her, although not exactly because he was worried about her. Until he'd spoken to the hospital administrator, at least. Still, he wasn't her keeper. He held up his hand in truce. "No offense. I worry about my cousin going over there, too, even though I know he can take care of himself."

Pamela glanced down at her too-full plate. "Sorry. Didn't mean to jump down your throat. That was a knee-jerk reaction. I think you reminded me of my dad for a minute."

Man, I must be getting old. "I can only imagine how worried he is when you're overseas."

This time when she smiled, her eyes actually twinkled. "Yeah, typical overprotective father. Not that he, too, hasn't been in some insanely dangerous situations before. But he never worries about himself. I'm glad he retired before anything bad happened."

"Retiring to teach is a lot safer than what Gunnar did post-retirement."

"I think danger is in Gunnar's blood," she ventured.

"Probably so." Kristoffer tended to gravitate toward much less excitement in his life. Hell, there *was* no excitement in his life. Not anymore.

As it appeared they were finished with lunch, and he had no other business to discuss, perhaps it was time to wrap things up. Unfortunately, there wasn't any reason for them to meet face to face on a project like this, although he tried to think of one.

Before he came up with anything, she spoke. "If you need any help tracking down sources for the equipment, let me know."

"Actually, that might help a lot. Your medical knowledge will be invaluable in choosing the right equipment and supply companies."

"Great!" She seemed as happy as he was they'd be able to continue to work together in person. "When should we meet again?"

"Well, Gunnar wants a detailed preliminary report next week, so why not tomorrow? Lunch or dinner?" He wanted to make sure she ate and more than a salad next time. "I know a great Greek place, if you're into Mediterranean cuisine."

"Love it. Lunch sounds perfect."

He settled the bill and found himself looking forward to meeting again tomorrow. He told her the name of the restaurant. "Oh, one of my favorites!"

"Would you like me to pick you up?"

"No need. I have to run some errands, so I'll kill two birds with one stone."

"Bring your laptop, and we can do some research after we eat."

✧   ✧   ✧

Pamela was first to arrive at the restaurant the next day, having finished her shopping early. Once again, she'd rushed through her morning and was fueled only by two cups of coffee. But shopping had been a breeze. Finding everything was so much easier here than in Afghanistan. She'd never take American conveniences for granted again.

While waiting in her car, she leaned against the headrest. Even making those few stops had worn her out. She hadn't returned home from the academy until nearly one and was so wound up it had taken more than an hour to drift off. After a fitful night's sleep, she'd awakened early enough to make sure she could squeeze everything in before lunch. She might try to take an afternoon nap before class, but right now, she'd just close her eyes for a minute.

Knock, knock.

The sound of someone rapping on the glass of her window startled her, and she jumped. Turning, she saw Kristoffer with a worried expression on his face that quickly became one of relief.

How long had she slept?

Blinking the grittiness from her eyes, she reached for the door handle and exited the car, only to find herself lightheaded. She swayed.

"Whoa!" Kristoffer wrapped his arm around to steady her, holding on to her back and forearm.

Her stomach somersaulted. If she'd had anything to eat, she might have lost it. "I'm sorry! I didn't know I nodded off!" *How embarrassing!*

"You had me worried when I found you like that. And now you almost passed out."

"No. I just stood up too quickly." She glanced at her watch, extricating herself from his arms. As nice as it felt to be held, she didn't like showing any sign of weakness. She'd napped for almost forty-five minutes. Why didn't she feel the least bit refreshed?

He made a noncommittal grunt. "Why don't we skip work and just eat?"

"No, I'm fine. Really!" The thought of postponing this project made her feel even sicker. She reached inside the back seat for her briefcase, bracing herself on the seat when another dizzy spell overcame her. She took several deep breaths, trying to clear her head, and grabbed the case.

He didn't seem pleased with her decision to focus immediately on business, but Pamela wouldn't let anything delay the delivery of the items they were ordering. She noticed his hands were empty. "Did you bring the papers from yesterday?"

He stared at her a moment before returning to his car for his legal pad and a folder. Cupping her by the elbow, he led her toward the entrance as though he thought she might collapse. Once seated inside, she leaned toward him. "I really am fine."

"You're overdoing it. Stress is a killer. Why don't you listen to your body?"

She didn't need a medical lesson, for goodness' sake. "I did listen! When it told me I needed a nap, I took one." She grinned at him, but he didn't even crack a smile. Her stomach dropped as her pulse accelerated. He had the Dom stare down pat.

"Why don't you skip the academy tonight?"

She lifted her eyebrows. "It's only a six-week course. If I miss a night, who knows how far behind I'd fall?"

"Your health is more important."

Clearly, he wasn't going to let this go, so she picked up her menu to peruse the wide variety of Mediterranean dishes. Definitely nothing with starch. She should choose a protein to give her more energy. When the server returned with a pitcher of ice water, Pamela ordered rainbow trout with sides of tzatziki and grilled vegetables along with a spinach salad to provide more iron. That should do the trick. She really was starving.

After he placed his order of moussaka with a Greek salad, he met her gaze. "I'm happy to see you're eating more today than yesterday." That her eating habits were any of his concern surprised her, but she didn't think many things got past his scrutiny.

Why not appease him? She smiled. "I promise to take another nap this afternoon if that will make you happy."

"This isn't about making me happy. It's about having you make choices that will aid in your speedy recovery."

Pamela shook out her cloth napkin and placed it on her lap. "If you only saw what I looked like a month ago…" Okay, that wasn't what the man needed to hear. Time for a subject other than her physical well-being. "Why don't we do a little research while we wait on our food?" She reached for her briefcase in the chair between them, but he placed his hand on hers. A warm tingling sensation raced up her arm and set her heart to pounding, and she pulled away. She must be hard up if her body had such a response to a married man.

"Let's relax first, Pamela. There will be plenty of time to work after lunch."

Easier said than done. One minute she was exhausted and the next needing to expend pent-up energy. "I won't disappoint the staff at the hospital by sitting on my heels."

"No one said you'd be shirking your duties by stopping long enough to have a meal. Are you always this driven?"

He didn't ask as though he thought her inner drive was a good thing. "I have to be." People counted on her. She had responsibilities. Was this some kind of double standard? "Aren't you?"

"Touché, but I'm not recovering from a major illness."

"It was a fever, and it's gone! Would you care to take my temperature? I don't know how else to assure you that I'm over it. And I'm not contagious anymore, either."

He stared at her long and hard. "I'm not worried about catching anything. I just want you to start taking better care of yourself. Perhaps you ought to take some time to reconsider your priorities based on energy levels. Decide whether you continue trying to do it all or if, perhaps, you need to let one of the balls you're juggling hit the ground."

Before she could say more, their salads were served. Wishing to waste no more time on the topic of her well-being, she dove in immediately, partly to show him her robust appetite. Fortunately, she really was hungry and found the combination of veggies in her salad enticing.

But persistence was Kristoffer's middle name. He picked up the conversation without missing a beat. "It sometimes helps me to make lists—pros and cons, 5-year and 10-year goals. What would you list as your number one goal for the next six months?"

She needed no time to consider her response. "Regain my pre-fever health status so that I can return to Afghanistan and complete my obligation to the organization."

"Excellent. What comes after that?"

"Finalize our purchases and see the equipment delivered before I return to Kabul."

"Glad to hear that, because this isn't an activity that might lead to great loss of sleep—or skipped meals," he said, as he raised his fork, almost like a toast, before eating another bite. "Where does the academy fall in your objectives?"

She hadn't thought about it until now, but her training at the academy was the most selfish among her goals. Achieving the status of being a well-trained submissive wasn't critical to her when compared with what was most important. She had time to focus on that later. Did it really matter if she completed the training by next month rather than six months or even a year from now? It wasn't as if she'd be able to do anything with the new skills until after she'd finished her overseas assignment.

"You've given me a lot to think about. Sometimes I have tunnel vision and lose my ability to see the big picture. But ranking them in order of importance will help me come to the right decision to achieve what matters most to *me*."

Pamela would give it more thought over the afternoon before making a decision. She'd go to the academy tonight—either to attend the classes or to let Master Anderson know she'd be dropping out and why.

Having someone—especially a man—make choices for her didn't sit well with her. However, Kristoffer had not tried to force, coerce her, or impose his will on her. Instead, through a few well-placed questions and directives, he'd opened her eyes to see what she'd been temporarily blinded to and did so in such a way she could retain her independence and autonomy.

Clever man.

Not just man. Another question now had been answered—Kristoffer Larson no doubt shared his cousin's predilection as a Dominant. Those two were like Mendel's peas in a pod.

The sudden desire to have a Dom take her under his wing—guiding and nurturing her while she focused on serving others—made her wistful. Would she ever find someone strong enough to earn her submission in that way?

Not if she couldn't put herself out there at the academy and elsewhere. And it didn't look as though her time there would last much longer.

CHAPTER FOUR

Pamela tamped down the sense of dread looming over her as she made her way toward Master Anderson's office before classes began. She'd called his receptionist earlier to schedule an appointment, knowing he was a busy man.

When her lethargy had lingered after lunch with Kristoffer, she knew what she had to do. No sense wasting the time of the instructors and trainers at the school another night.

Her conversation with Kristoffer had helped her see her priorities better. If she didn't rebuild her strength and endurance, she wouldn't be able to complete her contract with the humanitarian aid group. Professional goals had always taken precedence for her since medical school.

Unfortunately, Kristoffer had witnessed her body trying to give her a wake-up call. She needed to pay closer attention and do a better job of self-care.

Of course, she'd also made a commitment to The Denver Academy. The thought of walking into Master Anderson's office almost made her sick. She hated disappointing anyone or falling short of a goal. The headmaster, trainers, and instructors had given her so much in such a short time. But to stay on—especially through tomorrow's auction, which might be physically taxing—wouldn't be fair to anyone.

If only her opportunity to attend this amazing training academy hadn't been so ill-timed. But she was literally exhausted.

She knocked on the door of the headmaster. If ever there was a moment when she was expected to be honest and up front, it would be with him. She owed him her loyalty and respect—and to act responsibly.

Master Anderson asked her to come in. Standing from the leather executive chair behind his desk as she entered, he said, "Please, have a seat, Doctor Jeffrey." He indicated the chair directly across from his gargantuan desk. After she sat, he did so as well.

He hadn't instructed her to make eye contact, so she focused on her hands in her lap.

"How are you this evening?"

She couldn't lie to him. "I'll admit that I've had better days."

"Look at me."

Her stomach dropped as she slowly raised her head to meet his gaze. The concern in his intense green eyes resulted in another wave of guilt.

"Please explain."

She swallowed. "I seem to be suffering from a bit of fatigue." *Be honest with him!* "No, actually a *lot* of fatigue. Earlier today, I had a slight dizzy spell."

"You do appear abnormally pale and tired. This concerns me because you were quite ill a couple of months ago." Master Anderson's voice tugged at her emotions. "Tell me what's going on."

She averted her gaze to her lap again, wishing she could evade his question as easily.

"Eyes." Remembering he'd asked her to look directly at him, she corrected her lapse in protocol, albeit with reluctance.

"I asked you to explain what's going on," he reminded her. The power he exuded compelled her to respond without further hesitation.

She swallowed hard and tried to find the right words. "I've spent the hours following the dizzy spell weighing the consequences of continuing here at the academy versus leaving immediately..." Kristoffer's suggestion of making lists had been a good one. Hers was clearly out of balance, much like her body's circadian rhythm, it would seem.

"And your conclusion?" His voice brought her back to the present. *Stop thinking about Kristoffer. Focus!*

First, she wanted him to know she'd truly thought she'd be able to keep up. "As you know, I was over the fever long before I applied here."

He nodded. "Your application wouldn't have been accepted if you posed any threat to others here."

True. Of course, they'd talked about this during her initial interview. *Move on!* "Since returning to the States, I've been working on rebuilding my body. After a couple of weeks, I felt great and thought I could take on the world. When I applied, I had no doubt I'd be able to complete what I started."

"What has changed?"

"I recently took on an urgent project for Gunnar Larson to purchase much-needed equipment for the hospital where I worked in Afghanistan."

He shook his head. "So you not only took on the demanding curriculum here six evenings a week, but also a project for Mister Larson as well."

She nodded. "Normally, I can do three or four times as much!" *Not now.* Sheepishly, she continued, "I truly thought I could keep up with everything, Headmaster."

"In your professional opinion, what led to the dizziness?"

"No doubt, it's the direct result of skipping breakfast today. Plus, I over-taxed my body last night by missing the nap I always take before attending classes." She'd been so anxious to work on the equipment project yesterday that the afternoon had flown by. When she looked at the clock, she barely was able to change clothes and make it to the academy on time last night.

"Why have you been depriving yourself of sleep and important meals?"

She glanced down, but corrected herself right away, looking at him again. Admitting failure or defeat—especially to a man—did not come easy for her. And Master Anderson was not only a man, but a Dom *and* her headmaster, each role making this moment exponentially harder on her.

But she owed him the truth. "I might have overestimated my ability to keep up with everything given my compromised health situation." Her voice had diminished to barely more than a whisper.

"*Might* have?" He didn't seem pleased at all. "Has Mister Larson been made aware of today's dizzy spell?"

"Gunnar hasn't…" At least, *she* hadn't told him. "But his cousin Kristoffer knows. He was with me when it happened." *Much to my embarrassment.*

He raised his eyebrow slightly, prompting her to add, "He's been working on Gunnar's project with me."

"I see…" Had he almost smiled just now? He and Kristoffer had stood side by side during the anatomy class demonstration. Had the headmaster been aware that Kristoffer had been unable to look away from her nude body or noticed the silent exchange between the two of them? No, surely not. Why would he possibly notice that?

"I'm pleased to hear *someone* is looking after you, Doctor Jeffrey," he said, pointedly reminding her of her professional status. "How can you care for other people so well and do such a poor job in caring for yourself?"

She wanted to reiterate that she'd only skipped one meal and a nap, but remembered her training. "I have no excuse, Headmaster."

He remained silent, making her uncomfortable under his intense stare, and she sat back in the chair to put some space between them. "Understand, Doctor Jeffrey, while you have a bright future as a submissive, pushing yourself beyond your physical or emotional limits is not wise. This is something we teach our students to avoid."

She bit the inside of her lower lip, remembering that instruction on day one of classes. "Yes, I recall it well and take full responsibility for my lapse in good judgment."

"I asked you earlier what conclusion you had come to about your continued presence at The Denver Academy."

Oh, yeah. She'd gotten a little off track.

This prestigious school could open doors for her in the community and give her credentials highly sought after by some of the best Doms in the world.

But she was so damned tired.

"I think I've clearly taken on more than I can handle right now."

Clenching her fists briefly, she began, "I think…" She sat up straighter. "No, I *know* I need to resign from the academy. Effective immediately."

She leaned closer to point out her greatest concern at the moment. "But, Headmaster, I hate letting you down by missing tomorrow's auction on such short notice, knowing the Doms already have our journal entries and have been preparing to try and win one of us to make the fantasy we shared come true."

He waved away her words. "I would be more concerned having you won by a Dom, but unable to fulfill your role as his submissive—or worse, that you might faint or become ill and cause him and my staff a great deal of distress."

"I understand. I saw it as a failure to concede that I wasn't able to complete something, but I wasn't taking into consideration the consequences my decisions might have on others."

He scrutinized her a moment. "Doctor Jeffrey, your passion for your work and desire to grow as a submissive are evident and admirable." His demeanor lightened somewhat, although he didn't smile. "As much as I'll hate seeing you leave, I'm pleased with how you arrived at what I feel is the right decision—with only a little prodding." She definitely caught a glimpse of a grin before he became serious again. "Remember, however, spreading yourself too thin can hinder success in *all* areas."

Is that why she seemed to be racking up one failure after another? Had she taken on too much at once when not at her best? "Yes, Master Anderson."

"Give yourself enough time to recover. You might then consider arranging for a direct mentoring dynamic with someone. After assessing and prioritizing your goals, the Dom you choose could use any number of techniques that are much less rigorous than the academy's full curriculum to help you meet some of your objectives as a submissive."

His mention of prioritizing goals reminded her of Kristoffer. Of course, he hadn't done so as her Dom or trainer, but as a meticulous financial planner who was used to finding ways to identify the pros and cons of a decision.

As for direct mentoring, she'd tried to find that, but Gunnar hadn't been available. "I'll take that under consideration. Thank you."

He nodded his agreement. "It is best to give yourself time. If and when you are ready, I'm happy to provide you with recommendations for a couple of Dominants in the area who might be a good fit for you."

Pamela had always tended to be an all-or-nothing person. Paired with a Dom right now, she'd throw herself into training much as she did everything. "Thank you, Master Anderson. Maybe after I return from Afghanistan. That's very kind of you."

He smiled slightly. "It is not a matter of kindness. As a student of the academy, your success is important to us, whether you remain here or not."

"The attention and concern you and each faculty member and trainer has shown me is deeply felt and much appreciated."

He nodded. "Before you leave my office and the school this evening, I want you to share your short-term plans for how you intend to take better care of yourself."

She drew a deep breath. "First, I'm going home to sleep tonight— and probably through the weekend." She was *that* tired. "Immediately, I plan to eat better and won't be skipping any more meals." What else? "And to increase stamina and endurance, I'm either going to begin an exercise routine at home using DVDs or YouTube, or I'm joining a gym. In addition, I promise not to take on any new projects or activities."

He raised his brows briefly. "A little more detail than I was looking for, but an excellent plan nonetheless. Be sure you follow it. Listen to your body. It will tell you what it needs."

She'd always been a detail person. "Agreed, Headmaster. I will work hard until I am one hundred percent again."

"As with everything you do, Doctor Jeffrey, it sounds as though you plan to tackle your health regimen head-on." A charming smile played across his lips.

She nodded. "My highest priority is to complete my contract. I need to be ready when they call me to head back overseas."

It wasn't lost on her that leaving was reneging on another commitment she'd made. His graciousness in accepting her resignation helped assuage some of the guilt.

"Thank you, Master Anderson, for the opportunity to spend the past two weeks here. I've learned so much and hate having to quit so suddenly."

"We all need to reassess our goals from time to time. Life happens. Situations change." He added in an even more encouraging tone, "It's important that you don't give up on finding your place in this lifestyle if that continues to be important to you. But make sure you screen any potential Dom carefully and that he is meeting *your* needs. I've seen too many submissives hurt by falling for the myth that their needs aren't as important as those of their Dominants. I don't want any of my students to walk away from this school with that misconception."

That he still considered her one of his students warmed her heart, even though she wasn't able to complete the curriculum.

"Thank you, Headmaster. I'll do my best." Someday, she'd find someone to whom she could surrender without losing herself. In the meantime, she'd look for different ways to achieve fulfillment. Yes, she could do that.

Provided it didn't involve any new projects.

He stood, and she did the same. "Thank you for everything, Master Anderson. I'll use this time to reassess my expectations and goals."

"Never one to let that mind rest, are you?"

She laughed. "Point taken. I'll hold off on that for at least a week or two."

He looked at her with kindness. "You're a discerning woman who no doubt will figure out what she wants and go about attaining it."

"I hope you're right, because I'm not getting any younger."

Master Anderson chuckled. "None of us are, my dear." But men like Master Anderson, Gunnar, and Kristoffer grew sexier with age. She wasn't sure she had all that many years left to attract anyone.

As if he could tell where her thoughts had strayed, Master Anderson said, "It appears you've been going nonstop since medical school. Taking this time for yourself will do you good while you reflect on what you've learned and where you wish to go from here."

He walked around the desk to tower over her. "Of course, you're welcome to contact us if and when you'd like to complete your studies at the academy later, or even if you feel a need to start the course of study over with a new mindset and new goals after you return from Afghanistan."

"Thank you for keeping the door open for me, Headmaster. I can't tell you how much I appreciate your invitation."

He nodded. "If you go into future relationships with an open mind and a desire to explore, allowing your Dom to provide you guidance, I'm positive you'll discover what you're looking for in the lifestyle."

She flushed, appreciating his encouragement and confidence in her abilities.

Master Anderson graced her with a melt-worthy smile. "Doctor Jeffrey, tenacity is another desirable trait in a submissive and one quite evident in your character. I'm confident you *will* find a suitable partner when the time is right."

He placed his hand at the small of her back and gently directed her toward the door.

"Thank you for taking the time to talk with me, Master Anderson. I dreaded coming here tonight, but your understanding, patience, and support have alleviated a great deal of my stress."

"My pleasure."

After being dismissed and cleaning out her locker, she left the building and headed to her car under the watchful eye of a staff member who could have been hired as a bouncer at any downtown bar. The school always made sure its students remained safe on the premises, which was comforting given that most of the school's activities occurred after dark.

What the future held for her as far as participating in the lifestyle, she wouldn't begin to guess. But foremost in her mind now was to restore her health and pour her energy into the equipment project. She wondered when she'd see Kristoffer again.

And what would he say when he learned she'd quit the academy?

❖   ❖   ❖

Nearly a week had gone by since his last lunch meeting with Pamela. Kristoffer's world became monotonous again. Most of their work on the equipment project was conducted by e-mail. Despite her absence from his daily activities, he hadn't been able to stop thinking about her. Was she taking care of herself? Overdoing it with her classes?

He missed the excitement of talking with her, too. Just when life had begun to be more interesting again. More times than he should, he checked to see if she'd sent an e-mail. While he busied himself daily on Gunnar's lucrative portfolio making necessary adjustments, he found himself obsessed with finding medical equipment and supplies for Pamela's hospital. He couldn't help but think of it as hers in light of the passion she exhibited for the place.

While he had to admit he was more productive working without her by his side, he couldn't keep from dropping hints about discussing matters over lunch again. She never took the bait.

This past Monday, Gunnar had informed him out of the blue that he was no longer interested in pursuing the acquisition of The Denver Academy. A wise decision given the man's already impossible workload, but he'd never figured out why he'd wanted to pursue ownership in the first place.

That freed even more of Kristoffer's week to work on the hospital project. Armed with Pamela's recommendations and insights, he spent several hours a day in search of medical equipment or in negotiations with firms trying to arrive at a price that would stretch those dollars even further. He hadn't finalized anything yet, but if the deals went through at the rates quoted, he'd be far under budget. He might discuss additional purchases with Pamela before informing Gunnar of the changes.

An alarm went off on his phone, and he pulled up his calendar. Thursday. Forseti. 10 a.m. They were heading back to Breck to update

Gunnar on their progress today. Kristoffer wasn't sure why Gunnar wasn't content with e-mailed reports, but perhaps he wanted a higher level of security than his firewall guaranteed for some reason.

Already, the thought of being with Pamela again was messing with his head—and his libido. The sooner he completed this project, the better, although he had to admit he'd miss her.

Kristoffer continued to visit Tori each evening as usual—sometimes spending the night, other times driving back to his condo to sleep alone. Seeing her became more difficult and painful by the day.

The only explanation he had was that thoughts of Pamela invaded his mind when least expected—or wanted. Throughout his evenings, whether alone or with Tori at the facility, he'd find himself wondering how Pamela's training was going. Had she found a more compatible match at last Saturday's auction?

He wished she would put her training on hold until she'd fully recovered and had been tempted to text her this coming weekend to see if she'd like to have dinner with him before realizing that wasn't proper. They were merely working on a project together and shouldn't mix business with pleasure.

Still, he was dying to see how she looked and whether she'd been completely honest about how well she was taking care of herself. With the purchase of the academy off the table, they wouldn't have a reason to discuss her experiences as a submissive trainee any longer. He'd miss that, too.

Kristoffer noticed a long-absent spring in his steps as he walked across the living room to retrieve his suit coat. Whistling a few bars of John Coltrane's "Blue Train," he pulled out his cell phone on an uncharacteristic whim.

KRISTOFFER: Would you like to share a ride to the meeting today?

Why hadn't he offered before? Because he'd always been so singularly focused on getting through his days and trying to follow a routine that he barely thought of anything or anyone else anymore. She'd probably left already, but he waited for a response, just in case.

Seconds stretched into minutes, and he realized how utterly ridiculous he must look sitting behind the wheel in a parked car wait—
Ping.

PAMELA: **Sounds nice. What time?**

KRISTOFFER: **8?**

PAMELA: **I'll be ready.**

His heart beat erratically for a moment. Why did the prospect of spending a couple of extra hours alone with her during their commute excite him? *Because I'm pathetically lonely.* Having someone to converse with—whether about business or other topics—would make the drive more enjoyable.

Besides, Pamela was nonthreatening. She respected his married status, alleviating any awkwardness. The fascinating life she lived interested him, too, although he still didn't relish the thought of her returning to such dangerous parts of the world.

Seated behind the wheel of the Jag, he set the GPS, exited the garage, and roared off to pick up Pamela. She stood waiting outside the front entrance of her three-story building when he drove up, and he wondered why she hadn't waited for him inside. Her neighborhood in Aurora was an older one. Was it safe? Did she have a keyed entrance?

Her smile as she walked toward the car was infectious, and he barely had time to step around the car to open her door. Her hair was pulled into a bun at her nape. She wore a dark charcoal suit and black heels and juggled a Thermos and briefcase. He took the drink while opening her door.

"Why, thank you. Such a gentleman."

"Thank Gunnar and my grandfather for that. They drilled good manners into me from a young age." With her safely tucked inside, he handed her the Thermos and closed the door, looking forward to this trip for the first time in years. He returned to the driver's side and climbed in. "I see you already have coffee. Need anything else before we head out of town?"

"No. Already ate. But feel free to stop if you need to. Even with traffic delays, I think we have plenty of time." She glanced down at the cup holder between them before placing her travel mug there. "I see you bring your own, too."

"I'm particular about my coffee."

A stimulating exchange about their preferences in coffee blends ensued until they merged onto I-70 and headed west. The conversation flowed naturally with them discussing their preferences in other things, too, especially music.

"Davis and Coltrane are my favorites. Love classical and jazz." Hearing that she shared his taste in music, the conversation moved on to favorite compositions long before they reached their exit. Halfway through the two-hour drive to Forseti headquarters, they still had a lot to talk about.

"How are classes going?"

"They aren't. I quit Friday."

Seriously? Six days ago? Why hadn't she said anything? While he'd hoped she'd consider doing so for her own good, he hadn't really expected her to do it. "How do you feel about that?"

"I miss it a lot, but it was the right decision. I found myself so tired all the time, and I would rather focus on building up my body with food and exercise. But I did learn a lot. Someday, I'll find someone to explore the lifestyle with, but this just wasn't the right time."

He hoped Pamela would find someone to give her the kind of love she sought. She was young enough—only in her mid-thirties, he'd guess. If the universe was kind to the two of them, neither would be struck down in his or her prime. Kristoffer had been lucky to find the love of his life early on and had enjoyed many years with Tori before she'd been ripped away, leaving him with only fading memories.

He found himself curious about what it was she was looking for in the lifestyle. "Describe your perfect dynamic."

"Good thing we have plenty of time. There's so much to say, I don't know where to start." She paused a moment as he drove on. "I used to think I was meant to be a slave, but that wasn't right for me.

I'm afraid I drove away one of the Doms I thought I could be serious with before I came to that realization. He was lost and exploring, too, uncertain of what he wanted. I'm ashamed to say that made him easy to manipulate. I probably topped him from the bottom, but don't think he saw it as such, because I was more subtle than those he'd played with before me."

"The Dom who is right for you would correct that behavior."

She sighed. "I hope so. I've heard how wonderful it can be when you find the one who makes you whole, but also makes you melt. Sadly, I haven't experienced that yet."

"Tell me more about your ideal dynamic."

"For me, it's the psychology that I find fascinating. I'm beginning to identify as an alpha submissive, although I wasn't able to fully explore that before leaving the academy. I'm in search of a Dominant partner worthy of my submission who is intelligent, protective, secure enough in his own identity not to lord himself over me."

"I see." He fought back a grin. Pity the man who ever attempted to do that with this fiery sprite.

Something about Pamela differed from any other submissive he'd met. Perhaps her independent streak, or how she hadn't backed down in the meeting when Gunnar had tried to intimidate her. Not many people went head-to-head with his cousin and won. But Pamela had.

Curious to know more, he asked, "What other qualities would an alpha sub have? I'm not sure if I've met one before."

Until you, perhaps.

Pamela shrugged. "Everyone's going to answer that differently. Some say such a creature can only be found in a polyamorous relationship to establish a pecking order among multiple submissives, but that's too narrow a definition for me."

"One True Way types?"

She nodded. "The know-it-alls who decree their rigid beliefs and protocols are the only way annoy me."

"We're in agreement there."

"I'm not sure what else to say about how I perceive alpha submission other than I'm looking for a Dom who will consider my opinion, consult with me on major decisions, and admit when he's wrong."

"A rare breed of male, indeed—at least among our species." One would think they were zoologists.

She grinned. "Yet I remain optimistic he's out there somewhere."

Hearing the hope in her voice about her future filled a void in his own heart.

"I just have no time for the hunt, so it's a good thing another trait is the ability to thrive on my own without a Dom." She sighed, as though that wasn't her status of choice. "However, when I do find him, as with any good Dom no matter what my orientation, I would expect him to meet and nurture my need for submission and service. More compelling for me, however, is taking away his burdens and worries. It could be as simple as preparing his meal or massaging his shoulders after a stressful day."

The scenes she described opened an aching hole in his chest. He shook off the distant memories threatening to invade. "Doms primarily want to please their submissives. I don't know that you'd get one to ask you to do anything but receive what they wish to give you. Otherwise, if you aren't careful, you'll be disciplined for topping from the bottom."

"True. Definitely something I've been known to do."

"Without providing too much personal information, in what ways would your Dom fill your submissive heart?" He didn't know why he wanted to discuss this with her, but it illustrated how much he'd lost.

"Beyond playing in the dungeon or bedroom, ultimately, I could be fulfilled with simple, non-dominant gestures. Like lying with my head in his lap while he stroked my hair as he read or watched television."

Those quiet evenings with Tori were some of the times he missed most. The sessions in Gunnar's dungeon had been fun and exciting early in their relationship, but they hadn't visited for months by the time of the wreck.

Another regret.

"Trying to anticipate his needs would be my ultimate challenge." Pamela pulled him back to the present.

"Is it the sub's place to anticipate or worry about anything other than what the Dom asks?"

"No. You're right. But I would have this intense need to serve him in some way. Not every Dom is open about his needs, so I'd be compelled to try to determine them on my own."

Lucky man. He, for one, wouldn't have minded being on the receiving end of her caring. "Tell me more about the alpha submissive you feel resides inside you."

She paused a moment. "Trust is harder for me to surrender and could only be given to someone I feel worthy of the gift." She sighed and remained silent a moment before continuing. "Alpha or not, I wouldn't come to him empty. I'm already filled, but merely searching for a relationship where I don't have to be in control of everything. One where I can submit—surrender—to someone who doesn't want me to be 'lesser than' in order for him to feel more powerful or in control himself. Where the directions given to me would not only use my strengths but also push my limits. Does that make sense?"

He nodded. "But I daresay most Doms don't look at their submissives as lesser than. Far from it. They cherish them and know who holds the true power in the relationship."

"True. I'm still sorting it out and didn't get far enough at the academy to determine if my instinct is correct and I am an alpha sub."

"What else makes you think you might be alpha?"

"You sure are digging deep. Certainly making me think."

He laughed. "Sorry. Feel free to tell me to buzz off, but most submissives I've met are strong and have held power positions in their careers and communities. I once met a slave who is an executive for a major airline. Putting labels on people based on their public life and career can lead to some serious miscalculations. From what I'm hearing you say, sounds as though alpha subs like you take strong-willed to a whole new level—in both the bedroom and the boardroom or wherever they hold power."

"I mean no disrespect to other subs. It's dangerous to attempt to peg someone else as this or that kind of sub. It's intensely personal to each person. As I told you, I'm still working this out for myself. I think my professional standing is a large part of how I identify. Some aspects of my life are off limits. For instance, no Dom will tell me how to care for my patients or even who or where those patients can be. So my career is off the table as far as negotiations. And no doubt I have a Dominant streak as well, although I try to use it in not quite obvious ways."

"Topping from the bottom or a switch?"

She shrugged, but grinned. "I've been accused of the former before. But I'm definitely not a switch. I have no desire to be Dominant on the surface."

"Not all Doms allow being topped by a sub."

"No, most don't. Between you and me, I'm excited about finding the Dom who not only recognizes it but also corrects it." She sighed. "However, I won't surrender to just any man."

They drove in silence as he thought about the gauntlet she'd just dropped, although she certainly hadn't intended for him to pick it up.

Soon after, he pulled off the exit ramp at Frisco. Another forty-five minutes to go—and then they'd have the drive back to Denver to dive into other discussions.

Apparently, she hadn't exhausted this one yet. "But can anyone say definitively who they are without a lot of experimentation?" Before he could reveal more than he wanted to about his own relationship with Tori, he was thankful the question apparently had been rhetorical. "I like being in control of everything in my life and will bow down before very few."

The image of her bowing before him flew into his mind out of nowhere. That she was naked in the delusional fantasy didn't help any.

"I'm looking for someone who can earn my respect before I give up control, but who also will take me in hand privately when necessary and provide that piece I long for—be it guidance, dominance, or discipline." She became quiet.

"Only in private?" he asked.

"Unless it's subtle. I'm not "out" to many. Too many closed-minded people with the power to ruin others."

At a traffic light in Frisco, he glanced her way and watched her chewing at the inside of her lower lip. "What kinds of issues do you want to work on?"

She met his gaze briefly. Her voice became softer when she continued. "I have a problem with self-discipline. I'll need a very patient man to help me learn to focus better and rein in my stampeding thoughts. I can't stay in the moment, even during a scene. It's kept me from reaching subspace or anything close. I also have a habit of talking too much. Part of the same issue, I suppose, because it certainly keeps me from focusing."

"An observant Dom would pick up on those things right away and find creative approaches to help you improve." He smiled to himself thinking of any number of ways he'd work with her on such issues.

"I hope you're right, but I also have no tolerance for physical pain. It can go quickly from excited pain to *get me the hell out of this scene!*" Her laugh sounded forced this time. Was she afraid of accepting discipline? He hadn't thought of her as being afraid of anything or anyone before. Perhaps it boiled down to her alpha identification and having not found anyone strong enough to challenge her yet.

The image of Pamela's surrendering to *him* temporarily blotted out those of Tori from a few moments ago. "I hope you're able to find what you're looking for."

"Me, too." She paused to stare out the side window a moment. "Being equal in intellect is important as well. Before he can access my heart, he'll have to go through my head."

"Well, they say the brain is the most powerful sex organ."

"Absolute truth!" Silence ensued a moment. "For the right Dom, I would relinquish control and let him guide me, first in a scene and later perhaps in making decisions and other matters in my life."

"Other than your career."

"Yes. That's a hard limit, although it might be nice to have someone to discuss career decisions with. I just wouldn't surrender control to anyone else."

"Don't settle for anything less. You're right to take it one step at a time." No doubt she'd make some lucky man grateful to have found her someday. "Stay true to your ideals. Never apologize for asserting what your needs are—or your weaknesses, either, for that matter. We all have both."

And you're fast becoming my greatest weakness, lady, whether you know it or not.

"Primal, alpha, or beta, Doms welcome a challenge and admire a submissive who knows what she wants."

"You sound as if you have more than a passing knowledge of the lifestyle."

Not wanting to reveal too much about his relationship with Tori, an almost sacred thing to him now, he said, "Remember, I've been around Gunnar a long time. I've even been to his dungeon on more than a few occasions."

"Are you and your wife active in the lifestyle?" When he didn't answer, she added. "I'm sorry. That's none of my business."

He waved away her concern and chose to respond without revealing too much. Guilt assailed him after she'd been so open with him about her life. But Tori was off limits. "We were at Gunnar's together, of course." Enough said.

He wished he could confide in her about his wife, but there would be no going back once he revealed his marital situation to her. It could change the way she looked at him and most likely talked with him. He'd hate to see pity in her eyes or hear it in her voice. Life had dealt him and Tori a cruel hand, but he tried not to feel sorry for himself and wouldn't accept it from anyone else. Best not to complicate things by bringing up Tori's condition.

Besides, thoughts of Tori kept him from doing or saying anything that might lead him down the wrong path. Yeah, not many would fault him for choosing to move on with his life. Maybe he was hiding behind his wedding band. That might be why Pamela found him easy to open up to; she didn't feel he was on the make.

She was comfortable for him to be with, too—nonjudgmental,

undemanding, and supportive without even knowing he needed propping up.

He could easily let this go further than he was prepared to go. Maybe it was time to distance himself a bit.

Why had she spoken before her brain engaged? Kristoffer's relationship with his wife was none of her business. They were not social friends, although she enjoyed talking with him on just about any topic, even ones she wouldn't dare reveal to any of her colleagues. Thinking back over the depth of their conversation, she felt the telltale heat rise in her cheeks. At least he was driving and wouldn't notice.

Kristoffer seemed to be safe and trustworthy. Most important, he was someone who wouldn't use the knowledge he'd gained about her interest in the BDSM lifestyle against her later. She'd never been this forthcoming with the last Dom she'd dated, perhaps because she was clueless about what she was looking for then.

Kristoffer had also seen her at a vulnerable moment in the anatomy class, which may have broken down some of her barriers posthaste.

Wanting to reconnect, she said, "I'm glad you asked me to ride along, Kristoffer. I hope I haven't talked your head off."

"Not at all. I've enjoyed this immensely."

Until she spoke again, her words about his relationship would continue to hang in the air between them. "A BDSM relationship is based on trust. Until I find someone who has earned my trust and respect, I won't really know what will work for me."

His grip on the steering wheel slackened. "Keep your eyes and options open. Otherwise, you might miss an opportunity right in front of you."

"True!" Perhaps she'd already missed a number of opportunities.

As he continued to drive, they found safer topics of discussion, including her experiences working in Afghanistan.

A short time later, they stopped in front of the gate of the Forseti Group compound and waited to be admitted.

He turned toward her. "You have a lot to offer. Keep the lines of communication open, and for God's sake, make sure you know the guy inside and out before you commit to anything. I'm sick of hearing about abusive men taking advantage of women who are too trusting and jump into a relationship too soon."

"No worries. I don't trust easily and plan to spend a lot of time getting to know him before anything advances too far." She'd made that mistake before with Marc. "With my work schedule abroad, we won't be able to move too quickly."

"Gunnar can help you find potential Doms. He knows many in the area and can clear them using his surveillance and security contacts."

That Kristoffer was worried about her warmed her heart. "Thanks. That's good to know."

Inside the compound, the meeting went by in a blur. Gunnar approved the purchase of anything Pamela deemed necessary. With the green light, they could accept quotes and determine what else to add to the original list up to the full sum of his generous budget. Gunnar mentioned his mission would leave in a matter of weeks. Even more reason to expedite things and get as much equipment on his jet as possible.

Behind the wheel on the drive back, Kristoffer turned toward her. "Why don't you take a nap while I drive?"

"You won't mind?"

"Absolutely not. I usually make the drive alone. Perhaps we can stop for dinner before I take you home."

"Sounds great. Thanks." He probably just wanted to be sure she would take care of herself, but she laid her head back, planning to feign sleep and happy to rest her eyes—and her tongue. She really could take a nap, but her thoughts were in a jumble. Situation normal.

She jerked awake when the engine slowed. When had she drifted off? She didn't even remember driving through Frisco. "Where are we?" Before he answered, she scanned the view from her window and realized they'd traversed most of Denver and were stopped at a traffic light in Aurora already. "How'd we get back here so soon?"

"You slept most of the way, remember?"

How had she dozed that long? "I'm sorry! I must have been more worn out than I thought." She made a mental note to call her family physician to make an appointment for some lab work and checkup. Maybe there was something more going on than the residual effects of the fever she'd beaten two months ago.

When she stared across the seat, Kristoffer gave her a stare worthy of any Dom. "From now on, consider me your chauffeur for any mutual meetings with Gunnar. I don't want you making that long trip alone until you're fully recovered." A shiver went down her spine at the determined look in his eyes.

He's a married man!

She needed to exert better control over her libido.

"Thanks." Her instincts told her not to argue with him on this. Besides, she'd enjoyed most of today's drive to Breckenridge immensely.

He pulled into a Mexican restaurant. They'd eaten a light lunch during a break in the meeting earlier, but it was three o'clock, and she was surprised to find she was hungry.

"Doesn't your wife expect you to be home for dinner? This might spoil your appetite."

He shook his head without another word and exited the car, soon opening her door, helping her out, and escorting her inside. After they were seated and had placed their orders, she began to wonder more about his relationship with his wife. "How long have you been married?"

A cloud passed over his eyes, further puzzling her. "Almost eighteen years. But we've been together twenty, including the years at..." His words drifted off making her wonder what he'd almost said. At college, perhaps?

"Do you want to call her? Maybe she'd like some takeout?"

He shook his head, closed his eyes, and picked up his water glass to drain it. "I didn't expect to get back so early. Hope you're hungry."

She leaned toward him. "Kristoffer, why do I get the feeling you're taking me out because you don't trust me to feed myself?"

He stared pointedly at her. "Might there be any truth to that accusation?"

"Perhaps. But you don't have to worry about me. I'm not your responsibility. To be honest, I wasn't hungry until I saw the menu."

"Promise me you'll do better tomorrow." It wasn't a question. Why was he so obsessed with whether she took care of herself?

"I'll do my best. I also plan to make an appointment for a checkup and labs, if that makes you feel any better." It wasn't as if she needed to be accountable to him, but having someone care about her suddenly mattered.

The rest of their meal was less contentious. She devoured her *carne asada*, hoping the protein in the steak would also boost her iron levels in her upcoming blood work.

All too soon, he drove her home. They agreed to communicate by e-mail and text tomorrow as each worked on the additions to the equipment list and then take the weekend off. They'd come together again on Monday to assess where they were and reevaluate who'd do what next week.

The driveway leading to her parking spot in back was wide enough that he could let her out without obstructing other vehicles. He reached for his door handle, but she stopped him. "No need to get out. I've got it."

Again, the stare he gave her told her she'd better not even *think* about opening the car door. Still, she found the chivalrous gestures nice sometimes. As long as the man didn't think her incapable of doing it for herself, having her door opened left her feeling cherished. He exited, and she picked up her empty mug to wait for him.

Standing beside him, she smiled up—and up. He was so tall compared to her; he had to have at least a foot on her. "Thanks again for driving. I'll be in touch tomorrow and will see you Monday." She turned and reached behind the front seat for her briefcase and met his gaze once more. "Drive carefully, Kristoffer."

"Let me walk you to your door," he said.

As he fell into step beside her, she engaged in small talk. "I'm really excited to see how much we can acquire before the money runs out or Gunnar leaves on his mission."

"I'm confident we can check more big-ticket items off the list by then, but having them delivered in the next couple weeks will be the challenge. He might need to add another mission to his schedule this summer."

She reached out with her key, but he took it and placed it in the lock. Gunnar and his grandfather had been very thorough in his deportment training.

With the door open, she turned to accept the key ring he held out to her. "Have a great evening. Talk to you soon!"

Before he followed her into the building—as if he needed to ensure she reached her apartment—she closed the door behind her and jogged up the steps without a backward glance.

Inside, she undressed and showered before heading to bed. Exhausted didn't begin to describe how her body felt, despite the nap. She'd made the right decision to leave the academy, although she missed her classes and the other students. After her full recovery and return from Afghanistan, she'd consider whether to reapply.

She'd waited this long. What were a few more months? First, she needed to get healthy and stay that way.

After changing from his suit, Kristoffer felt the need to burn off some energy before heading over to visit Tori. Dressed in shorts and a T-shirt, he did some warm-up stretches against a bike rack in the parking garage then jogged into the cool, crisp evening. He spent the next hour trying to get into the zone where he could forget about everything, most especially Pamela, but continuing to avoid telling the two about each other dogged his every step. Sweaty and tired, he gave up after forty-five minutes and walked the rest of the way home.

A cold shower revived him a bit, and he donned black jeans and a polo shirt, combed his hair back but left it loose, and took the elevator down to his Jag. Pamela's spicy scent permeated the interior.

Guilt washed over him. He needed to come clean with Tori today.

With heavy steps, he walked into her room twenty minutes later. The nurses were turning her onto her side, facing toward him. They smiled at him as he came in. "We'll be finished in just a moment, Mr. Larson. She's been having some trouble breathing, so we're moving her more often today to try and make her more comfortable. She's been sitting up for a while now so we're letting her rest a bit."

"Take your time."

The staff here did everything they could to help Tori. Pneumonia was a constant concern, so he appreciated their efforts to avoid it. Gunnar had made sure this facility offered the best of care, and they'd been assured someone would check on her at least every hour. If their treatment of Tori was all for show, he figured his daily presence helped keep them on their toes. But he sensed they took their responsibility seriously, whether being observed or not. Sometimes he arrived at odd hours to convince himself they truly were doing an excellent job. He pitied the patients who rarely, if ever, had visitors and had no one making sure they were cared for. At least this facility, from what he could tell, employed staff members who provided for the welfare and well-being of all their patients.

When he was alone with Tori a few minutes later, he went to the window to open the drapes.

"It's been a beautiful summer day, sweetheart. I took a jog this evening in the foothills. The temps are mild and the sun warm."

He returned to her bedside and bent down to give her a kiss on the cheek. Her mouth and eyes were open. Did he detect a smile? *In your dreams.* "How's my princess doing today? Did you have a good night's sleep?" Or whatever you'd call the state she was in when she closed her eyes for hours on end.

Stretching out on the bed behind her, he stroked her arm as he tried to form the words he wanted to say, but they came with great difficulty.

"I love you, Tori, with my whole heart. I always will."

But I'm so lonely without you.

"I still open my eyes some mornings and expect to find you lying beside me." He still remembered mornings spent in the bed they'd shared, before they'd gone about their busy days.

Only now he sometimes saw another woman in his mind when he woke up in the morning. At least fantasy Pamela wasn't in the bed Tori had slept in. Somewhat less guilt plagued him on that score at least.

His throat nearly closed off. "Tori, I want you to know that I've remained faithful to you all these years, both before and after the accident." *But I'm not sure how much longer I can live like this.* "I know neither of us chose for this horrific thing to happen..." *...and that I'm the one who put you here. If only I hadn't been driving that night.*

"I miss you so much, sweetheart." He pulled her hair away from her face. *Just tell her.* She deserved to know, if by some remote chance she could still understand anything going on. Perhaps her soul hovered nearby, stuck here until her body passed.

"But I've met someone I want to spend more time with. Her name is Pamela Jeffrey. Gunnar asked us to work together on a project." Was that all Pamela was to him? A temporary colleague? "We won't be having sex." He needed to make that clear to her, in case she could hear this confession. "You know I'd never hurt you that way."

Could anything he did now really hurt her anymore?

"But...she needs someone to help her take better care of herself. Not a Dom, really, although I think she'd be more receptive to having a Dom work with her than just anyone. I feel a need to..." *What? Guide and protect her?* Something he was no longer able to do for his wife.

He wished she could give him permission, but that wasn't feasible. He also wouldn't add a lie to his confession by saying his time with Pamela didn't mean anything to him.

If only he could communicate with Tori psychically or know whether she'd moved on to whatever came after this life. Surely, if there were a God, her soul had long ago abandoned this empty shell that had once contained her spirit. But charlatans preyed on desperate, lonely people like him pretending to connect them with their loved ones on the other side. He wouldn't waste his time or money grasping at straws. Hell, he didn't even know if Tori's essence had left this world. Perhaps it was trapped inside her body.

Kristoffer stroked her arm, hearing a rattle in her chest as she breathed. He'd check in with the nurses before he left to make sure they stayed on top of things.

Maybe he'd ask the manicurist to come by tomorrow and do her nails or give her a facial. She'd like that. Tori had always loved being pampered when she was ali—*awake.* He preferred the term awake over alive. Tori had zero quality of life.

No life at all.

Kristoffer didn't have anything else on his mind to talk about tonight. He'd said what he'd come here to confess about his weakness for Pamela. The silence enveloped them, but he no longer needed to fill the awkward silence with words. He stroked her arm and let his hand come to rest around her waist, pulling her closer.

"Let's take a nap together." He'd missed their lazy weekend naps. Okay, so maybe he still wasn't ready to let go of her, even after all these years.

He'd spend the night with her, trying not to think about seeing Pamela on Monday. If only he could be certain Tori would forgive him for moving on. He liked to think he'd want her to do that if their situations were reversed.

If Tori exhibited any expression of emotion, any hint of recognition, he'd put Pamela out of his mind forever.

But there had been no communication from his wife since right after the accident. He'd been given a tiny glimmer of hope when she'd opened her eyes once and seemed to smile at him. Had he only imagined it? Had it been nothing more than a muscle spasm? An errant twitch? Whatever, he'd been certain then that she would bounce back, despite the doctors and their dire predictions.

For months, he'd disagreed with them vehemently. But they'd been right all along. The years that followed had taken their toll.

Pamela had brought light into his world again. His time spent with her showed him how lonely he'd become. He woke up in the morning anticipating getting to see her again.

Was he finally coming to terms with the way things were?

He drew a deep breath. "Sweetheart, I hope you're at peace wherever you've gone. I wish you could assure me that you've truly moved on. That you want me to do the same."

No response. No surprise.

He closed his eyes, alone with his thoughts. Despite how sure he was now that he needed to move on, he could never abandon the woman he'd married.

And no woman should have to settle for half a man. While he wasn't the Dom Pamela was looking for, he could provide some guidance when it came to making her take better care of herself. He didn't have to let on what it meant to him to share a meal or engage in stimulating conversation.

He wanted to spend more time with Pamela, either as friends or as he transitioned back to the living. But he needed to come clean with her first.

CHAPTER FIVE

The weekend dragged into Sunday afternoon. Pamela hadn't been this idle in years. After catching up on the latest journals in her field, she'd taken a nap, probably out of sheer boredom. Now that she was awake again, she wondered what she'd do with the rest of the day. She couldn't wait until tomorrow's working lunch with Kristoffer.

Yes, her thoughts had drifted to Kristoffer quite often this weekend—sometimes to the project they were working on—but mostly to him. Such a mysterious man. She knew very little about him, but realized she'd shared an awful lot about herself with him. Why was he so easy to talk to?

Her phone pinged, and she checked the screen. Speak of the devil.

KRISTOFFER: **Busy tonight?**

What on earth could they do on a Sunday night? They'd agreed to start spending Gunnar's money tomorrow when the medical equipment businesses were open to make deals. But she'd never welcomed anyone's text quite as much as this one.

PAMELA: **No plans. Where shall we meet and when?**

Almost a minute passed before he responded.

KRISTOFFER: **Good. I'll pick you up at 7. Chinese sound good?**
PAMELA: **Sounds great. I'm starving.**

She realized too late she shouldn't say that to Kristoffer. Sure enough:

KRISTOFFER: **When's the last time you ate?**
PAMELA: **Lunch, but Chinese sounds awesome.**

KRISTOFFER: Make it 6.

They'd held all of their meetings over a meal. If he hadn't scheduled their first lunch before finding out about her illness, she'd think he was trying to make sure she ate regularly.

His expedited time frame didn't leave her a lot of time, so she chose to wear black dress slacks and a light blue cotton sweater. She started to pull her hair into the usual donut bun, but suddenly decided to leave it in a ponytail instead.

Kristoffer rang the buzzer a few minutes before six, and she ran down the stairs to meet him. He'd also worn a sweater along with khaki pants. She carried her briefcase with the laptop inside, wanting to be prepared for anything, but he stared at it as if it were a monster.

"You won't be needing that." He wiggled his fingers until she handed it over to him. "But I don't want you going back up the stairs, so I'll just stow it in the trunk."

If they weren't getting together to talk about the project, what were they doing tonight? He tucked her inside the Jag and roared off to their unknown destination. He took the interstate toward downtown.

"How've you been, Kristoffer?"

"Fine. And you?"

She felt awkward for the first time with him. "Well, to be honest, a little at loose ends. I'm not used to having so little to do."

"That's good. Means you're following doctor's orders."

"Oh, most assuredly. I had a CBC yesterday at the clinic and my doctor said my iron's a little low, but otherwise, I'm much improved from the first time he saw me in April."

They must have passed a dozen Chinese restaurants to get to the one downtown, but the meal was scrumptious. He ordered pineapple duck and she the Kung Pao chicken. They even shared a bite off each other's plates.

As the meal came to an end, she realized they hadn't really talked much about anything. She wondered why he'd wanted to come out. He seemed preoccupied, leaving her wondering if something was wrong.

He took a sip of his water, and then he spoke.

"There's something I wanted you to know. It's not something I share with many people, but given your profession, I think you might understand better than most."

This sounded heavy. What on earth was he about to reveal? "I'm listening." Perhaps he intended to dispel some of the mystery surrounding him. Her curiosity was piqued.

"My wife suffered a traumatic brain injury four years ago in an automobile accident." The words came out in a rush, the furthest from what she'd expected to hear.

She found it difficult to wrap her mind around what he was saying at first. He stared straight at her, waiting for a response. She reached out to touch his arm, hoping to find the right words. "Kristoffer, I'm so sorry. I had no idea!" He'd been so reluctant to share information about his wife. Now she understood why.

He blinked and visibly relaxed his shoulders a little. "You couldn't have known."

But he had shared it with her. How badly had the woman been injured? Short-term memory loss? Spinal cord injury? Coma? Christ, while she hoped his wife had made a full recovery, his words didn't portend anything of that nature. Four years ago. Somehow, she managed to keep unspoken the torrent of questions racing through her mind.

He chose to share more of his own volition. "She resides in a long-term skilled nursing facility just outside the city. Persistent vegetative state."

Tears pricked her eyes. "No awareness whatsoever?"

He shook his head. She must be on the worst end of the spectrum for traumatic brain injuries then, although she knew that any brain injury had devastating, long-term effects. "I can't imagine how terribly difficult this must have been for you."

He shrugged. "I won't deny there've been some dark days dealing with denial and depression, but over the years, I've come to accept and have tried to come to terms with it as well as anyone can."

Her heart broke for Kristoffer. She turned toward the wall to regain her composure, blinking away the tears. He was a proud man and wouldn't want her sympathy or pity.

"I'm telling you this so I don't have to keep skirting the truth."

She met his gaze again. "You don't owe me any explanation, but thanks for letting me know. I wish there was something I could do to help."

"Believe me, we've consulted every kind of expert there is. No hope is the unanimous consensus."

"Feeding tube and ventilator?"

"Just the feeding tube. I had her removed from the ventilator when she came out of the coma, but she's hung on. She's a fighter, but I don't know where the fight comes from these days."

She squeezed his arm. "I can only imagine what kind of hell you've been through."

"You'd be surprised what a person can adjust to when given no choice."

"Yes, I've seen that resilience many times over. Just never been on the receiving end of having to deal with such a loss."

She pulled her hand away, suddenly feeling as though she was intruding in an unforgiveable way. Yet her mind couldn't release the image of his wife being separated from him, not by choice but most likely by a tragic and violent accident. What had happened?

Had she been injured alone? Kristoffer exhibited no visible signs of physical trauma.

A million questions bombarded her, but if he wanted her to know, he'd tell her.

She couldn't help but think how extremely exhausting this must be for him. He'd been forced to face this harsh reality day in and day out for years. No wonder he worked hard for Gunnar—work probably provided him the escape he needed from his personal life.

Did he visit his wife still, or was seeing her in that state much too painful?

"Look, there's a reason why I'm telling you this." He ran his hand through his thick mane, raking the loose strands off his forehead before his piercing blue eyes met her gaze. "I've never done anything to dishonor myself or the vows I took the day Tori and I married. I don't plan to start now, either. But…" He drew a deep breath. "I want to ask you to join me from time to time—for dinner, a concert, a play, whatever. I figured eventually you'd begin to wonder why a married man was asking you out, if you haven't already, so I wanted to come clean and make you aware of the circumstances."

"Of course, I wouldn't mind, Kristoffer. I enjoy our time together, too. You're easy to be with." She smiled. "Besides, I was going stir-crazy before you invited me out tonight. I'm not used to sitting still for long."

"So I've noticed." The creases in his forehead smoothed out when he smiled back. "How'd you like to go to the jazz club down the street tonight?" When he mentioned who was performing, she jumped at the chance.

"They're one of my local favorites. I'd love to!" When the server brought the check, she reached for it, only to have it snatched away. "But you've been paying for all our business meals. It's my turn."

"No. That's not how I operate."

"Then at least let me pick up the next tab."

"I don't imagine humanitarian aid workers make what private-practice cosmetic surgeons do."

She laughed. "Far from it. Or any other type of medical professional, for that matter. But we're rewarded in nonmaterial ways."

"I'll be picking up the tabs." He stood and pulled out her chair. His tone told her there'd be no further discussion about who paid.

They chose to walk because the evening was so mild. Inside the darkened nightclub, the mellow strains of the saxophone wound their way into her body as the hostess showed her and Kristoffer to their booth. Sitting side by side so they could both see the stage, she ordered a white-wine spritzer and he a Perrier with a twist. The bar was dark with rich wood paneling on the walls and hardwood floors.

"Have you been here before, Kristoffer?"

He surveyed the room before his gaze came to rest on her. "Yeah. A long time ago."

Had he come here with his wife? If so, why would he take her to a place that conjured up such poignant memories, unless he was attempting to exorcise them? She decided to give him an out if he needed to leave. "If you don't want to stay, we can go somewhere quieter."

"No way. It's nice to be in this place again. Been too long since I've been out for a night of good food and great music." He did seem more relaxed than usual.

Pamela plopped the lime slice into her glass and took a sip. "I can't remember the last time I was here. Thanks for suggesting it." She leaned her head against the back of the booth and listened to the ensemble play. "Aren't they fabulous?" she asked, after the song ended. Fairly new to the local scene, they probably hadn't been performing when he'd last been here. She'd only heard them once herself when she'd ventured out in April.

"I haven't heard them before, but they're very good."

Feeling no need to carry on a conversation while they played, she closed her eyes and let the melodious sound form an intimate cocoon around them.

When the music stopped, he asked, "Enjoying the set?"

"Very much so."

He tossed back the rest of his water.

Compelled to express something she hadn't had the presence of mind to think of back at the restaurant, she said, "Anytime you want someone to talk to, I'm here."

He met her gaze and stared in silence, leaving her wondering what was going through his head. "Thanks. I appreciate that."

When a new set started, they turned their attention back to the stage as the server brought him another bottle. She ordered some salty snacks to munch on, not because she was hungry, but she didn't want to embarrass herself. She'd switch to Perrier herself after this drink, too. Good thing he was driving. She never had been able to drink much.

Pamela closed her eyes again and let the music wash over her. Her feet moved to the beat of the music. Christ, she wanted to dance, but had better leave well enough alone. She lifted her glass to her lips and took another sip.

She didn't want the evening to end, but all too soon, the ensemble announced the final song of their last set. Another group would take its place in fifteen minutes or so, but they weren't as talented as this one.

When the applause faded, he leaned toward her. "How about some dessert? I know of a nice, quiet place around the corner that serves until midnight."

"Sounds great!" She'd have a little more time with him.

They gathered their things, and with his hand at the small of her back, he set off electrical shocks up her back and down her legs.

Stop thinking about him touching you more intimately.

He was Kristoffer, a new friend. He'd established his boundaries, and she'd respect them.

She pulled her wrap more tightly around her shoulders when the cool night breeze hit them, and Kristoffer wrapped his arm around her. "Thanks for the body heat. I forgot how cold it gets at night, even in May."

"No problem. We'll be there in a flash."

And they were. All too soon. She liked having his arm around her even if the gesture had been practical, not romantic. After ordering their desserts, seeming to be at a temporary loss for words, he sipped at his glass of water before Pamela broke the ice. "So what did you think about the musicians?"

"Great talent."

"Yeah. They really are good. Glad I got to catch them again before they move on to bigger and better things. I doubt they'll be hanging around Denver forever."

After more idle chat, they somehow found themselves talking about the time he'd run away to live with Gunnar. "He introduced me to his love of jazz, although I was too young to frequent the clubs." The server brought his bowl of Italian ice and her tiramisu.

Before he took a bite, he continued with his story. "When that summer ended, I moved back home. Gunnar had about given up on me ever amounting to anything, I think. I was a little wild in those days."

She couldn't picture him being anything but the serious, responsible financial expert he was today and wondered what kinds of trouble he'd gotten into, but didn't ask.

"My mom still lives in New London, but I can never return to that rat race in the Northeast, even though I did choose a career in which Hartford or New York City would have afforded me many more opportunities for clientele than Denver did. But Colorado is where Tori loved to be. I can't take her aw—" He stopped and stared at his spoon as though he didn't know what to do with it.

When he met her gaze, he seemed to have come to some decision. "No, Tori wouldn't know one way or another where she was. I guess the real reason I stay here now is because *I* like it. The pristine mountains, the cosmopolitan city. It's the best of both worlds. And I feel closer to Gunnar than anyone else in my family."

"Do you ever go back to visit your parents?" He hadn't mentioned his father at all tonight or in prior conversations.

"I try to visit Mother once a year around the holidays, usually New Year's. Not long after they divorced, Dad married a woman with a son." His mouth flattened into a straight line before he relaxed it again. "He moved that family to Florida."

She'd uncovered another commonality between them, both being children of divorce. Abandoned by his father like that, no wonder he'd been so close to his grandfather and Gunnar. "How old were you when your parents split up?"

"Just turned fifteen. Gunnar's parents had split up when he was a lot younger, so he helped me understand how to survive it all when I moved in with him eight months later."

Interesting that both cousins had come from broken homes. Yet Kristoffer had remained faithful and true to his wife, even though his father had abandoned his mother. Had she been devastated? Perhaps their breakup was what had made him so much more adamant about honoring his own vows.

Gunnar also seemed to be a mate-for-life kind of guy. If Heidi never returned from Afghanistan, Pamela expected he would continue to be involved in her life and support her in anything she chose to do. These cousins shared a lot more than genes.

Pamela wondered if she'd been drawn to them subliminally because of her history. But she hadn't known their story and still, she had felt a pull toward them—probably because they were strong, alpha men and her equals in many ways.

"Your wife is very fortunate to have married you. You haven't abandoned her. I can't imagine what it's like when patients in extended-care facilities don't have a loved one looking out for their best interests."

He spooned a bite of Italian ice into his mouth and swallowed. "I'm no saint. I've let her down sometimes, but FarFar and Gunnar taught me early on to keep picking myself up and trying again. To always strive to be an honorable man. I promised to stay beside her come what may when we married, and I'm a man of my word."

"When those words 'for better or worse, in sickness and in health' and 'till death do us part' are spoken, I don't think anyone really knows what they'd do if the worst should happen, as it did with you two."

"True. But vows are vows. We need to remain true to them."

She wondered if she would be as steadfast and true if faced with the same situation. She'd like to think so, but the thought of those lonely days and nights stretching out before her with no hope of intimacy or having her love returned hurt to even think about. His devotion to his wife was admirable, but had to have taken a toll on him. "Has she ever..."—*How to put this?*—"recognized you since the accident or known that you're there?"

"I have no clue. I don't think so, but I talk to her as if she hears me. She can't speak or even make gestures to respond to direct and simple questions, not like the other patients in a vegetative state that I've seen in YouTube videos."

"So she hasn't been declared brain dead?"

"Correct. She breathes on her own. Opens her eyes when awake—or whatever they call it." He shrugged. "At other times, they're closed as if sleeping. Her gaze used to follow me across the room, but not in a long while. I'm not sure if she was aware of me then or if it was some residual eye reflex where she follows the movement of light and shadow."

Her heart broke for him. "How do you handle continuing to go see her knowing she isn't aware you're there?"

He cocked his head as if she'd grown a second head, and she realized too late how callous her words sounded. Before she could apologize, he answered her question. "*I* know I'm there. *I* know I'm looking out for her needs, connecting with her in whatever way I still can, even if it's only one-sided."

She had no clue how old he was, but the worry lines around his eyes told her he probably was on the other side of forty. He had a lot of years ahead of him most likely. Would he feel the same thing at fifty? Sixty?

"I'm convinced somewhere out there her soul exists and is aware of my visits. I'm sure you've heard the stories about patients coming out of a coma after months and reporting knowing what went on around them while in the coma."

"A coma and a persistent vegetative state aren't the same."

"But who knows if it's the same or not?"

She'd read studies in journals that showed varying degrees of awareness for those in a PVS. Perhaps he'd been given more hope than she felt. "Do the doctors think she could come out of it eventually?"

He avoided her gaze again as he focused on eating before answering. "Not really. They haven't for years."

They must be basing their opinion on science. "Have they conducted an fMRI—functional MRI?"

"Yeah. Several. Years ago, after she came out of the coma. She only has brain function for the most rudimentary of processes—blinking her eyes, breathing. There's been nothing to indicate cognition or awareness since she came out of the coma. Hell, not since the accident really. No reflexes. She doesn't respond to physical stimuli either, although sometimes she grimaces, making me worry that she's in pain."

He gripped the spoon as if a bolt of pain had shot through him then met her gaze again, the intensity of his blue eyes stealing her breath away.

"But they say there are no signs of any awareness or anything re-motely akin to living."

She squeezed his hand. "That doesn't improve with time, Kristof-fer. I worry about how this will affect you over the years."

He pulled his hand away from her. "I'm handling it. It's part of my daily routine now."

She supposed as long as he knew miracles most likely weren't going to happen, he wasn't doing long-term damage to his own mental health. At least, she hoped not. Situations like these took a toll on a person.

"Some believe the soul of patients like Tori transition over to an afterlife somewhere, leaving behind the shell of the body that continues to function on a very primitive level due to the use of tubes and modern medicine. I simply can't take the chance that her soul's still here and have her think I've abandoned her."

She nodded. "Do *you* think her soul has moved on?"

He remained silent for a while and then spoke in a hushed whisper, as though afraid the universe—or Tori—might hear him. "Yeah." He glanced away and blinked his eyes a couple of times. Again, she reached across the table to squeeze his hand, finding no other appropriate way to comfort him.

He stared at their hands. "At least, I'm beginning to think that. It's easier for me to imagine she's somewhere better enjoying some form of existence again."

"But isn't that the definition of death—when the soul leaves the body?"

"That's the belief of some. Others say there's life as long as the brain is functioning, however basic that function is as long as it's keeping the body alive. Legally, I think, death is defined by most courts as when the brain ceases all ability to function cognitively." Defiance entered into his eyes and his voice. "But I have no intention of having her declared dead until she stops breathing on her own, so I don't care what their definition is. Until I know for certain she's gone, I won't play God."

It wasn't her place to tell him what to believe about an afterlife or the definition of death. For obvious reasons, he'd given this a lot more thought and study than she had. Right now, he sounded as though he wanted to accept that she'd moved on, but he hadn't yet arrived at that point where he could let her go.

"Had the two of you talked about end-of-life issues before the accident?"

He shook his head. "Have you talked with your parents about what you want to happen with your body in case something catastrophic happens?"

"Yes. But I've seen what harm modern medicine can do at the end of one's life. I also put myself into situations with my job where the likelihood of death or injury is greater than for the general populace. Anyway, my parents know I don't want to be kept on artificial means beyond any hope of returning to the living. If I can't have quality of life, I wouldn't want to be kept *alive* on tubes and machines." That wasn't living. She wouldn't want to merely exist with no awareness of anything or anyone around her, not to mention be such a financial burden on her family who weren't exactly wealthy, although they were better off than many.

He pulled her back from her thoughts. "Neither do I, now that I've seen what can happen. I had my advanced directive, durable power of attorney, and living will drawn up two years ago. Late, I know, but I wasn't functioning very well before that." He met her gaze in earnest. "Gunnar knows my intentions and preferences, but I'd venture to guess most people haven't had that conversation with loved ones. Far fewer have actually drawn up legal documents outlining their end-of-life preferences. Even with those documents and family support, you still have to hope your doctors and the staff at the healthcare facility you're in will honor your wishes. Some places refuse based on the institution's religious beliefs. But while there are no absolutes or guarantees, I think having the legal papers can help family members by providing some guidance as to what their loved ones would want."

Kristoffer looked down at his bowl as if only now realizing where they were and took a bite. As they were served fresh coffee, she turned her attention to her tiramisu for a moment, trying to digest all she'd learned about him today. They both probably needed a little silence to reflect.

After finishing his dessert, he set down his spoon. "I could have divorced her and moved on years ago if I'd wanted to, and most wouldn't have blamed me. But I won't do that as long as her body is functioning in some way."

"I understand." Well, she didn't really, but admired him for his faithfulness. Many men abandoned their wives—even when their partners were fully functioning—through divorce, emotional or physical absence, work, or other reasons. He was one of a kind. Tori had been—and still was—well-loved.

"Pamela, you asked earlier if I believed her soul had moved on. If it has, it probably would have happened back when she went from being in a coma and on the ventilator to her current persistent vegetative state. I see that now. But at the time, I couldn't give up hope that she'd come back to me eventually. It had only been six months since the accident. That's when I asked the doctors to insert a PEG tube to feed her. I see now that was selfish on my part." He glanced away as the server took their empty dishes away. She barely heard his next whispered words. "I hope she isn't aware of the hell I've put her through since."

The man's anguish was palpable. She wished she could hug and comfort him, but wasn't sure he'd welcome such personal contact. Oh, who cared? He could push her away if he didn't. She stood and walked around the table to his side, wrapping her arms around him. He said nothing and remained rigid. She thought he'd stopped breathing, but eventually, he returned the hug, holding on to her so tightly she found it difficult to breathe herself.

Then the moment was gone, and he pushed her away. "Sorry. Thanks."

"I hate that you've had to go through this, Kristoffer." She returned to her seat. "I hope you don't mind all the personal questions. I'm just trying to understand better." And to learn more about him for a change.

"I don't mind, Pamela. I'm not used to talking about Tori with anyone but Gunnar, and even we haven't really talked the last couple of years because nothing ever changes. The few others who knew about the accident quickly stopped asking about her as the months and years dragged on." He smiled at her, albeit with sadness in his eyes. "I appreciate that you care."

"In college psychology classes and even to some extent in medical school, we're taught about the stages of grief—primarily how to relate to those engulfed in grief or on the journey through the five stages. One of the things that hit me hardest and raised my own awareness was that those grieving often felt, after a while, that no one talked about their loved one anymore."

"But I'm not grieving."

Wasn't he? Based on what she'd studied about the process people went through after a loss like this—and for all intents and purposes, he'd lost his wife during that accident—she'd say he had moments where he was in the acceptance phase but then sometimes backtracked to denial. Even within this one conversation that had been evident. But it probably was easier for someone to grieve when there was a body in a casket or ashes in an urn. Instead, Kristoffer had been left in a state of limbo.

Perhaps someday he'd be emotionally ready to let Tori go, but Pamela had read about cases where someone remained in a state like his wife's for decades. The loneliness and finality of saying goodbye in his heart had to be terrifying, too. Accepting that you must leave behind someone you loved whose body was so accessible in the physical world was different from having nothing but memories and the person's essence to hold on to.

As long as her heart continued beating, he'd continue to watch over and protect Tori physically. While he'd admitted that he didn't expect her to come back and believed that her soul had moved on, he hadn't accepted her being gone yet. Each person had to come to terms with such loss in his or her own way.

But her concern was more with the living. Clearly, she and Kristoffer could become friends socially. They could talk about literally everything from life to death. He'd been isolated a long time, but seemed to be reaching out to her to pull him back among the living.

"What about you, Pamela? Ever married?"

His question brought an instantaneous, "No!" She grinned at the vehemence she heard in the word. With the tables turned, she sat back in her chair, hoping to put an end to the conversation.

He waited for her with a raised eyebrow, and she shook her head reluctantly. "I'm not the marrying kind. It's a monumental commitment, as you've shown tonight. I might be interested in companionship, kink, even cohabitation," she said with a smile. "But I don't know if I could ever trust anyone enough to take that walk down the aisle. Most marriages fail." Look at her parents'—not to mention the marriages of both Kristoffer's and Gunnar's parents.

"Will that be enough in the long run?"

Pamela played with the stem of her water glass and didn't make eye contact as she thought about her response. She sighed. "I'm not sure. I seem to have a habit of painting myself into a corner with absolutes."

"How so?"

She tried to formulate the words to explain something she was only just beginning to understand about herself. "All or nothing doesn't work, especially in relationships, so I need to try to be less rigid in my expectations." She smiled at him. "I hope when I find the Dom I want to be with, we'll be able to talk as freely as you and I do, Kristoffer." When he looked a little uncomfortable, she quickly put them back on safer footing. "I have a tendency to set safe boundaries to protect myself from getting hurt, but then I have regrets when my situation changes and I realize I've hemmed myself in."

"That's what renegotiation is for."

"Sometimes it's not possible to do that, especially in the heat of the moment."

"Ah. No, that's not a good time for any type of negotiation." He smiled. At least this conversation wasn't as deep as their earlier one. "Minds do tend to be slightly illogical then. Often, we find that achieving what we think we want doesn't please us after all. Hence even more regrets."

She smiled back, wondering if he was also a Trekkie. His advice reminded her of something Mr. Spock might say. "I tend to wind up with regrets either way."

"I think if you work on your ability to stay in the moment and focus on the now rather than what has been or might be, you may find yourself experiencing those feelings less frequently. And I don't mean merely during a power-exchange scene."

"I'm not sure I can focus every minute of every day. Or sometimes even one minute of any day." She grinned, but surely, he saw the truth in her admission.

"You just need someone to help train your mind."

Kristoffer was no slacker when it came to discipline and focus. They'd be working together on this project a while. Okay, here she was already trying to fill in some of her free time with something else to be added to her plate. No, she wouldn't ask him to help her work on this problem.

Then he surprised her. "If you'd like, I can devise some exercises for you that will help train your mind to stay in the present."

His offering without her asking surprised her. Her mind flashed to them together in a dungeon. *Whoa, girl!* He wasn't proposing *those* kinds of activities. Actually, she wasn't sure what he was proposing. This represented a major shift for the two of them. If she chose unwisely, would it affect their budding friendship?

"For instance, where did your mind go just now?"

Busted. Man, he was good! She glanced up when the server refilled their water glasses and set down the bill, happy for the brief reprieve.

She reached for the check, but not quickly enough. The man seated across from her wasn't so easily distracted on another matter, either, because as soon as they were alone again, he demanded, "Answer my question." He didn't have to repeat said question. His Dom-like tone made her stomach flip-flop.

She met his gaze. "I was simply wondering what kinds of exercises you had in mind. I'm intrigued, if you think you can help." Her face flamed, probably telling him she'd been thinking more than that.

To be honest, she didn't know what she wanted anymore and had no clue what had changed to make her so uncertain. Was it something she'd discovered at The Denver Academy? Or her talks with Kristoffer? Maybe even her illness, which had shaken her up more than she'd like to admit. All three had made her see things in a different light. Normally, she had tunnel vision, certain of what she wanted with a drive and determination to make it happen. Now she seemed so…confused.

The more she got to know Kristoffer, the more she wanted to know. She'd never had a friend she could be so honest and straightforward with. "Tonight's been really nice, Kristoffer. I hope we can—"

He reached into his pocket, and she heard the staccato buzzing of his phone as he lifted it out. "Excuse me. I need to take this. It's the nurses' station at Tori's facility."

"Go ahead!" She motioned him to answer it.

"Hello." A somber expression came over his face.

"I'm on my way." When he returned the phone to his pocket and glanced across the table at her, it was almost as if he'd forgotten she was there. "Tori's in the hospital. Pneumonia."

"Oh, no!"

He waved the server over to settle the check, pulling his credit card from his wallet. "Her breathing was really labored earlier today. I was afraid this might happen again."

Pamela reached for her shawl and purse. "Let me catch a cab home. You go be with her."

"No, I'll take you home, but I'd like to check in at the hospital first. It isn't on the way to your place; so if you don't mind a delay of a couple of hours, I can take you home soon after. But if I can't break away, then we can revert to calling a cab as a back-up plan."

"I don't want to intrude. Really, a cab is fine."

He stared at her a moment, a pained expression and something akin to a plea for help piercing her heart. "I'd rather not go alone, Pamela. One of these days, it's going to be…" He stopped and glanced down. "Never mind. I can't ask that of you."

She squeezed the fisted hand at his side. "Let's go. She needs you."

Clearly, Kristoffer needed Pamela, too. Her spirits actually lifted knowing that she could be of some comfort to him. She stood and waited for him to sign the receipt before they exited the restaurant, his hand guiding her by the elbow.

At the hospital, he was informed she'd been taken into ICU. He picked up the pace a little more as they headed to the elevator, and she nearly ran to keep up with him. Outside ICU, he announced his presence through the speaker, and a buzzer unlocked the door so he could go back to see her. He turned toward Pamela and grabbed the door before it closed between them. "I'll be back shortly."

She nodded. "I'll go find us some coffee. Won't be what you're used to, but will probably help keep you awake."

"Thanks, Pamela. For being here and…well…for everything." The gratitude in his voice warmed her heart.

CHAPTER SIX

"Go!" Pamela gently nudged him through the door to ICU. His anxiety to find out about Tori's condition sent him in a beeline to the nurses' station. A woman in dark blue scrubs peeked over the top of her computer screen. "May I help you?"

"My wife, Victoria Larson, was brought in tonight. I was wondering what her condition is."

"I can't provide that information without—"

"I have the Health Care Power of Attorney and my driver's license here." The long-term care facility probably had given them a copy of the form already, but he carried it with him at all times, too, just in case. He pulled the worn document from his wallet and unfolded it. "I'm her court-appointed healthcare agent. She's unable to make any decisions for herself, as you know."

She glanced at the ID and nodded, not giving the paper more than a passing glance, so she must have seen a copy in Tori's file already. He was happy to know the system worked, for whenever the decision had to be made as to whether to resuscitate or use extreme measures when he wasn't able to get here in time.

"Mrs. Larson was admitted about an hour ago in respiratory distress. The early X-rays show fluid in both lobes of her left lung. We have her on strong IV antibiotics hoping to control the infection and keep it from spreading to the other lung."

"I heard a rattle today in her breathing when I visited her." Thank God the staff had stayed on top of the situation.

"Let me show you to her room." He waited for her to round the desk and followed her past several curtained doors and windows. "Here you go. Call if you need anything."

"Thank you." He entered and found her receiving oxygen via a nasal cannula. He'd held firm that she wasn't to be ventilated or intubated, but if the antibiotics didn't work, she could be in for some uncomfortable days ahead. If she could feel anything at all.

He'd had her on a ventilator for her first encounter with pneumonia, but the suctioning of the tube was more painful for him than her. Those were some of the most difficult times to stay and hold her hand. The contortions of her body as she fought the invasion were sheer torture for him. How could they be so sure she wasn't feeling it?

At the moment, her eyes closed, she seemed peaceful so he tried to remain silent to let her rest. She might become agitated if she awoke and didn't know where she was.

Wait. She never knows where she is anymore.

Still, her body needed rest, whether she was aware of what was happening or not. Resisting the urge to hold her hand, he sat in the chair beside her.

Her eyes opened. Had she heard him? Could she hear the squeak of the vinyl chair? He stood again and leaned over her. No recognition. No alarm. Just a blank stare.

Nothing new.

"Everything's going to be okay, sweetheart." He stroked her hair away from her face and tried to maintain eye contact. While her eyelids opened and shut, her gaze remained unfocused. "You're in the hospital. Just a little precaution to make sure you don't get worse. You'll be back home in no time."

Home? Well, home for her.

She began coughing, and he held his own breath until she calmed again. He wished there was something he could do to help her, but knew how long it could take her body to fight off the infection. This wasn't the first time she'd suffered from pneumonia; it most likely wouldn't be the last. Eventually, according to the medical experts, pneumonia or some other bacterial or viral infection would take her from him forever.

Was he ready to say his final goodbye if this was the one?

No.

Selfish bastard.

Guessing she wasn't going to rest while he was here, he decided to leave her alone for a while. Nothing more he could do, and he needed to take Pamela home now that he knew Tori was in good hands. He'd seen her much worse than this. No doubt she'd pull through again. Tori was a fighter. Well, her body was, anyway. Did she possess some latent memories of what she'd been like before her brain injury?

Doubtful she had any memories whatsoever.

"Get some rest, sweetheart. I'll be back soon." He kissed her forehead, and by the time he stood and looked down at her again, her eyes were closed once more.

That's it, sweetheart. Rest now.

Making his way back to the nurses' station, he left his cell phone number with a different nurse and asked to be notified if there was any change for the worse in her condition. "I need to run a friend home, but should be back in a couple of hours." He'd stop by his condo, pack a bag, and make sure Noma was set to fend for herself for a few days if need be. Looked like the hospital would be his home for a while.

He returned to the waiting room to find Pamela thumbing through a magazine. Her face showed her concern for him when she met his gaze. So many times, he was alone during spells like this, except for occasional visits from Gunnar.

Bloody hell, he hadn't notified Gunnar yet. Not that he needed to pull him away from preparing for his upcoming mission. Besides, he had Pamela to talk with at the moment.

She stood and picked up a pressed-paper coffee cup to extend to him. "I was right. The coffee is swill, but it's pretty potent swill."

Accepting the offering, he appreciated that she didn't ask questions right off, but having someone taking care of him felt so good.

"I'm glad you're here, Pamela. She's sleeping now. This might be a good time for me to run you home."

"Is she stable?"

"More or less. It will take days, even weeks, before she's out of the woods. They may have to try different antibiotic regimens to knock it out."

Pamela nodded. "Yeah, our bodies develop a resistance over time."

"She's been allergic to penicillin since childhood, which limits them even more. But she looks better than I expected."

"Are you sure you want to leave? Why don't we stay until you see her in the next hour just to be sure? I'd hate for you to be too far away and..." She broke eye contact.

A sense of relief flooded him. "You don't mind? It'll be pretty late then—or early, to be accurate." He'd feel better staying, too, checking her condition over the next couple of hours before leaving, but wouldn't have asked her to do that.

"I lazed in bed all morning. I'm good." Pamela sat and picked up her coffee cup. "Sit and regale me with stories of the Larson boys' escapades in the land of Vikings."

He smiled and joined her in the next chair in the row, absently sipping his coffee. *Gah!* He grimaced. If spitting it out were an option, he would have. With a shudder, he set the cup on the coffee table, content to do without. "I'll call for delivery in the morning. I know all the best coffee shops around here."

Her cup joined his on the table. "You're on."

"I didn't mean to presume you wanted to stay until then. I'll take you home just as soon as I have one more visit."

"Stop worrying about me. Stay focused on Tori."

He grinned that the submissive who insisted she was in need of focus training was instructing him to do the same. Settling back in the chair, he stretched out his legs trying to get more comfortable. They were out of the main traffic areas, although there weren't too many others here.

At her prompting, he chose to talk about his childhood stories. "Have you ever been to Norway, Pamela?"

"No. I haven't seen much of Europe outside a few airports."

"Well, then, I'll start with the basics to set the scene a bit. FarFar lived in a remote fishing village on a fjord off the western coast..."

The next time he glanced at his watch, more than an hour had passed. He stood. "Excuse me. I'll be back after I check on Tori."

"I'll be here."

He stared down at her a moment. "Thanks. I really have appreciated your company tonight."

"That's what friends are for." She smiled, and he turned toward the locked door to announce his name to visit Tori again.

A quick peek inside the room found her sleeping peacefully. Not wanting to risk waking her again, he kept his distance from the bed and merely watched her sleep during his brief visit. Except for the equipment attached to her neck and arms, she might have been asleep in her bed. If only she'd open her eyes and see him—really *see* him—for the first time since the accident.

After a time, he went to the nurses' station to ask if there had been any change.

"Sorry, but it's really too soon. We're checking her vitals regularly, and all I can tell you is that she doesn't seem to be any worse. It'll take time. The residents should be making the rounds in few hours to check on her."

"Thanks. Could you call me back then so I can talk with them? My cell phone number is in the chart."

"I'll try to, but it can be hectic."

He nodded and returned to the waiting room where he found Pamela curled up on a short bench, sound asleep with her flimsy shawl over her arms and chest. He hated keeping her out so late when she needed her rest but decided to let her sleep, too. When the door to one of the elevators pinged and opened nearby, she blinked awake and bolted upright. "Sorry! I was just resting my eyes," she announced like a student caught sleeping in class. She rubbed the sleep from them, and he grinned.

"How's Tori?"

"Sleeping, too."

Pamela began gathering her things, but he stayed her hand. "Pamela, would you mind if we didn't leave right away? I'd like to be here when the doctors make rounds, but I'm afraid I can't make two stops and still get back in time."

"Of course not! These benches aren't as uncomfortable as they look."

She smiled and patted the seat beside her. The least he could do for keeping her here was to give her a cozier place to rest before taking her home. Sitting down beside her, he indicated his lap. "It's late, and you need your rest still. If you don't mind the awkwardness of it all, may I hold you while you take a nap? I don't need to have two women in the hospital."

He'd meant for his remark to put her at ease, but the words took him aback. It wasn't as though Pamela were his woman or his responsibility, although he'd certainly taken on that role with her lately, especially after learning of her recent health issues.

She paused a moment, making him wonder if he should withdraw the offer. Then a half smile lit her face before she stood and settled herself on his lap. He wrapped his arms around her and adjusted her shawl around her as she rested her head on his shoulder.

A sense of comfort and well-being washed over him. He couldn't hold Tori right now with all the tubes, but he could hold Pamela.

He'd make the most of this...for what little time he had.

Having Kristoffer holding her like this calmed Pamela's soul for some odd reason. All the restless energy of the past few months disappeared. She should be comforting him, but perhaps he found some measure of solace, too, by not being alone. Thinking how lonely he must have been on countless nights here waiting for news pained her heart. If they hadn't been together when he received the call, no way would he have asked her to be here for him, either. The man was used to shouldering all responsibility for his wife without help from anyone. Well, if she had anything to say about it, he wouldn't have to go it alone any longer.

They were forming a bond of friendship that might stand the test of time.

Her eyelids became heavy again. *Christ, please don't let me drool on his shirt while I sleep.* Despite having slept in this morning, she couldn't fight the need to catch a few more winks.

A page over the loudspeaker for one of the physicians made her jump.

"Easy. I have you."

She sat up and stared into Kristoffer's crystal-blue eyes. Her stomach did a somersault before she remembered where they were. "How long have I slept?"

His hand left her back to check his watch, sending a chill up her spine at the loss of heat. "About two hours."

She scrambled off his lap. "Seriously? I made you miss your time to visit Tori."

"No. I'm not sure how, but I must have dozed a little myself." His eyes did look a little puffy. He stood beside her. "I'll go back for a little while now." She watched him cross the room and forgot until too late to check for a drool spot, but being a gentleman, he wouldn't have said a word anyway.

There were still several more hours before dawn, which would probably be when the physicians began making rounds. Good thing they'd had plenty to eat before the call came in, because the vending machine food would be unfit for human consumption.

Pamela glanced across the room and saw an older man sitting alone. Not far away was a woman in her late twenties or early thirties. Both appeared alone and distraught. Tragedy and suffering appeared to have struck many people this night. She hoped their loved ones survived—and Kristoffer's wife, too. There had been a time when Pamela would have thought the woman would be better off dead—and maybe she still did—but Kristoffer would be devastated. He loved her with such devotion and didn't seem ready to let her go even after all these years.

It must be difficult to grieve the loss of someone for whom there was no real closure. Would he ever be able to move on?

His brief visit ended, and she looked up as he crossed the room to rejoin her. Probably best she not sit in his lap this time, so she remained seated. "How is she?"

"Sleeping, which is a good thing. I'm sure the antibiotics are doing a number on her right now. Plus, well, it's the time people normally sleep, too." His gaze bore into her. "I slept through the residents' rounds, but the nurse shared their notes."

"Wow, they must have early rounds."

He nodded. "Now I need to take you home and get you into bed."

A flash of him tucking her into bed caused heat to rise in her cheeks, but she quickly waved away his concern. "I just slept two hours. I can sleep standing on my feet when I need to."

"But you don't need to. Tori's my responsibility."

His words took her aback for a moment, but she saw through the bluntness that he was only concerned about her given that near fainting spell at the restaurant the other day.

"I don't want you to have to wait here alone."

He seemed torn, which only meant he wanted her to stay. "You're sure?"

She nodded. "Positive."

They sat in companionable silence, both too tired to carry on a conversation. Or perhaps he just didn't want to disturb the others in the room, who seemed to be trying to catch some sleep between their visits, too.

When Kristoffer went back again at about six o'clock, Pamela walked over to the windows and watched the eastern sky pinken. The horizon was relatively flat in that direction.

"She was awake this time," Kristoffer said. She turned to face him. "Her physician was still making his rounds, so a nurse made sure I had a chance to talk with him."

Pamela turned toward Kristoffer. "Great! What's the prognosis and treatment plan?"

"Too soon to tell if she's responding to the antibiotics. No sign of the pneumonia spreading to the right lung at least."

"That's wonderful!" Pamela was grateful to the doctor who brought a smile to Kristoffer's face.

He motioned toward the elevators. "Let's get some decent coffee and breakfast. We need a change of scenery."

He cupped her elbow and guided her out of the waiting room. They walked to a café two blocks away. "This place has the best crêpes and Belgian waffles, if either of those appeal to you."

"Are you kidding? Now I'll have to choose."

"No worries. We'll order one of each and share."

"Deal." The thought of sharing food with him excited her, but she'd just slept in his lap, so the boundaries of ordinary friendship had long been trampled.

The first cup of dark roast coffee hit the spot, and the cobwebs began to leave her brain. He poked a piece of his waffle and extended the first bite to her. "Open."

She closed her eyes, opened her mouth, and savored the delicious taste. "That's amazing. You were right."

"Here, have a strawberry, too."

She opened again and smiled as she chewed. Remembering her plate, she cut off a bite of the lemon-raspberry crepe and reciprocated. His mouth closed around the fork, and the sudden image of his mouth on her nipple nearly made her drop the fork.

Get a grip, girl.

Where had that errant thought come from?

They finished eating, and she enjoyed every bite, but the ones from his plate were especially satisfying. When the check came, she asked the server, "Would you mind boxing up about a dozen assorted muffins on a separate check?"

"If you're still hungry, we can order something else while we're here."

She grinned at him. "Are you insane? I'm going to waddle back to the hospital as it is. No, this is for some of the others in the waiting room. I thought it would be a nice change of pace for them from the hospital cafeteria and vending machines. Trust me, those get old fast."

He stared at her long enough to make her uncomfortable. "That's really thoughtful of you." He turned to the server and handed him back the check. "Put it on my tab. Hey, you don't happen to sell carafes of coffee, do you?"

"Sure. I'll prepare one and will have everything ready for you in a few shakes."

"I'm afraid I was so wrapped up in my own problems, Pamela, I didn't notice anyone else."

"Your focus belongs on Tori. Let me worry about taking care of you and the others in the ICU waiting room."

"You have a kind and giving heart, Pamela Jeffrey."

She winked. "I'm practicing my service skills for when my perfect Dom comes along, remember?"

"Nonsense. You're just being the beautiful, caring soul you are."

His words warmed her cheeks and her heart, and she had to turn away. Before heading back to the hospital, she excused herself to go to the restroom. When she came back, Kristoffer carried a huge, flat pastry box and two plastic bags that appeared to hold a couple of large thermal containers of coffee along with small plates, cups, condiments, and utensils.

"Here, let me carry something."

"I've got it. You grab the door."

She did, and they made it back to the hospital in no time. When they entered the waiting area, they saw it had filled with a few others, and she hoped they had enough coffee for everyone. She took one of the bags from him and saw that the second container was orange juice for those who might prefer that instead.

Kristoffer excused himself to go back to visit with his wife while Pamela took a muffin over to the elderly gentleman who had been here all night, too, and served him a cup of black coffee after hearing his preference. Everyone in the room seemed a little more animated with the prospect of fresh food and coffee, and Pamela smiled when Kristoffer came back into the room again, but soon sobered at the serious expression on his face.

She excused herself to go check on him. "Is everything okay?"

"They're doing a bronchoscopy with biopsies to check things out.

They seem worried about something."

How had things taken a turn so quickly? She brushed his sleeve with her hand. "I'm sure she'll be okay. Whatever it is, they caught it early." The lame words sounded hollow even to her ears. She wasn't sure of anything of the kind. Pneumonia could be a death sentence for someone with an already weakened immune system, and Tori's system had been decimated.

Kristoffer seemed shell-shocked. "Her life has been out of my control for the past four years. It freaks me out to have her undergo invasive procedures like this."

She wrapped her arms around him, giving him a hug of support. "I know you like being in control, but they're going to take good care of her. Don't worry." Keeping her arm around his back, she steered him toward two empty seats. "Here, let's sit down while we wait for word. These procedures don't take long."

"Yeah, they're doing it right in her ICU room." They sat apart from most of the others now watching them enjoy their unexpected treats. "The muffins were a hit," he said. "Glad you thought to order some."

She nodded. "As was your idea for decent coffee. Luckily, not everyone is as addicted as we are. We had just enough to give a jolt to the four who wanted a cup, and half the OJ is gone, too."

Kristoffer pulled out his phone and pushed a speed dial number. She heard him order two more carafes of coffee, probably from the same restaurant, which spoke volumes as to the number of times he'd been here. He stood and took her hand. "They're too busy to deliver, and I'll go stark-raving mad if I just sit here. Let's go pick them up. We've got time."

They stood, and he took her hand, squeezing it as if needing to hold on. He continued to hold it all the way to the cafe. Half an hour later, each carrying a pot of coffee, they took turns making the rounds to refill cups and pour new ones for a few people who hadn't been here earlier.

A nurse came to the door and called Kristoffer's name. He set down the pot abruptly on the nearest table and hurried through the door without a backward glance.

Please let her be okay. For Kristoffer's sake.

Kristoffer shook hands with Tori's doctor in the conference room. "How is she?"

"Mr. Larson, we found some areas of concern on the admitting x-rays, so we wanted to take some biopsies." The no-nonsense woman didn't pull any punches.

"What are you talking about? Pneumonia, right?"

The Asian woman in the white coat set her lips in a straight line, and Kristoffer prepared himself for more bad news. "I'm concerned about the possibility of a tumor."

Cancer? Was she fucking kidding him? Kristoffer ran his hand through his hair and raked the loosened strands behind his ears. "How much more is she going to have to take?"

"I know you have a DNR order in place and that you've asked that she be treated for infections. As her spouse and legal guardian, it will be up to you to decide what course of action to take if the biopsies are positive—whether you prefer to take action at all or to simply let nature take its course will be up to you."

He stared at her as if she'd grown two heads. "If she has cancer, you sure as hell are going to treat her. I don't want it eating away at her. What if she still feels pain?"

Not resuscitating her if in cardiac arrest was one thing, but letting cancer eat away at her cell by cell? No bloody way!

"Let's wait to find out if the lesions are benign or malignant, Mr. Larson, and go from there. I assure you, we'll do everything possible to make her comfortable if there's any indication she's in distress."

The doctor left, and Kristoffer went to Tori's room. Her mouth, legs, and arms were more relaxed—probably due to the aftereffects of the sedation. She looked so peaceful. He stroked her hair. "Don't you worry, sweetheart. I'm going to make sure you get the best care."

As if she could worry about anything anymore. He'd long since had to carry that burden for both of them.

He stayed longer than before but needed to be with her, even if he couldn't crawl onto the bed and cuddle with her.

Bone weary, he returned to the waiting room and homed in on Pamela's smiling face. Vibrant. Caring. She might be only a few years younger than his forty-one years, but on days like today, he felt older than the octogenarian sitting on the other side of the room.

Her smile faded, and she stood to meet him. "Kristoffer? What did they say?"

He needed to get away—no, to take her away from this before she, too, started to feel as old and helpless as he did. "Come on. Time to take you home. Tori will be sleeping off the sedatives for a while, and I have a cat who might just be destroying my sofa because she's been neglected so long."

"I had no idea you had a cat."

"Well, in her mind, she's still Tori's pet. I'm just the man she allows to take care of her in Tori's absence. Noma tolerates me at best."

She laughed. "Typical cat."

Once behind the wheel, he stared ahead blankly, unable to comprehend what he was supposed to do next. Pamela reached for the keys in his hand. "Trade places. You're in no condition to drive."

"You haven't had much more sleep than I have."

"I had a couple of naps. But I've had a lot more coffee, too—and haven't had to deal with one crisis after another the way you have."

Without waiting for him to move, she exited the Jag. When he relinquished his seat, he waited beside the driver's door to help her in before taking his place on the passenger side.

"Tori asked me to let her drive that night, too, but I wouldn't let her."

Pamela reached across the seat and squeezed his hand. He'd never shared that with anyone before. "Do you want to talk about it?"

"No." She nodded without a word and turned the ignition. Kristoffer closed his eyes as he leaned against the headrest. "Well, maybe. But I don't want you looking at me as I do. Just drive, please."

"No problem."

The squealing tires and Tori's scream exploded in his head. He opened his eyes again. No, he wasn't ready to talk with Pamela about that night. But at the same time, he needed to. First, he'd share this morning's news. "They found some lesions. She might have lung cancer."

"Christ, no! I'm so sorry, Kristoffer!"

He nodded. "Why not me? At least I'm stronger. I can fight back better than she can."

"I'd hate for either of you to have it, but cancer is indiscriminate."

A silence ensued as they traversed several miles. "It was raining that night. I was tired, but being the cocky, macho man I was, wouldn't concede that I might be too tired to drive. We were in my Mercedes. Headed home from a party at Gunnar's place."

Pamela merged onto I-70 East as he continued. "I hadn't been drinking, but was still impaired due to a lack of sleep. I never should have gotten behind the wheel."

"We all drive at least once knowing we shouldn't, whether after a few too many drinks, distracted over something that happened that day, or just from being tired. You're human. Cut yourself some slack."

"I was her husband." He realized he'd said it in the past tense, even though he was still her husband. "It was my responsibility to take care of her."

She sighed. "What happened?"

He closed his eyes again, and the scene unfolded before him. *Face what you've done.* "The rain was torrential and the mountains foggy in spots, so I wasn't speeding. I was in the passing lane because that side had fewer potholes. By the time she screamed at me to watch out, I was only yards from the brake lights of an eighteen-wheeler. I don't know if I zoned out a moment, blinked too long, or what to not see it sooner. I slammed on the brakes and tried to take evasive action into the slow lane, but skidded in front of a pickup truck that hit the passenger door dead center." *And Tori.* "That sent us hurtling into a guardrail. Our front and side airbags deployed, but she was thrown around pretty badly despite them and her seatbelt. Her head hit the passenger window when the truck plowed into us, which is probably what resulted in the brain injury."

Everything remained deathly silent for a moment—both in the scene playing out in his mind and the one in the car right now. "I must have blacked out. When I came to, I was being pulled from the Mercedes. I yelled at them to take care of her, but no one listened. Maybe they thought she was gone already. Maybe she was."

Sirens wailed, coming closer.

"They cut her out of the car. She wasn't moving. Wasn't breathing. Someone did CPR. Firemen. Paramedics. EMTs. I'm not sure who. Apparently, traffic had been stalled because of another accident ahead when I clipped the tractor-trailer." His telling of the story was disjointed, and he hoped she could follow because he had no intention of retelling it. "People came from everywhere to work on her." While he sat on a gurney and watched. Numb. Helpless. "I had nothing but a tiny cut on the head."

"Thank God." He stared at her, uncomprehending her comment until she continued. "I would have hated for you to have been gravely injured, too."

"But it should have been me, not her."

She pulled onto the shoulder, far from the moving traffic speeding by in the slow lane, activated the emergency blinkers, and turned toward him. "Who died and appointed you God?" she demanded, jabbing his chest when she said "you."

Her anger surprised him, leaving him momentarily without a thought as to how to respond. "What? You didn't even know me then."

"But I know you now—and I wouldn't have if you'd died that night. Or worse, you might have been left hanging somewhere between life and death, too, like your wife. What if the outcomes had been reversed, and she was sitting here having to go on without you? Would she be blaming herself?"

His throat closed up, and he cleared it. "Probably not. She tended to accept things as they came, without trying to analyze a dozen actions she might have taken to change the end result." Would Tori have

129

moved on by now? Remarried? Maybe not in four years, but what about six or ten? He'd want her to be happy—wouldn't he?

Why entertain that scenario? "There are fates worse than death, Pamela." Still, he'd change places with Tori in a heartbeat if it meant she could go on living. "I just hope she doesn't feel pain. The tests indicate no cognitive brain activity whatsoever. But what if she can feel it?"

"Oh, Kristoffer." Her fingers wrapped around his wrist and gave him a squeeze to comfort him, but nothing could do that. "I'm sure she doesn't. Don't make yourself crazy worrying about things that probably aren't the case. You said she's usually either awake or asleep. She doesn't cry or scream out, does she?"

He shook his head. "Sometimes she flinched when they'd give her shots or insert IVs when she had to go to the hospital. She always hated needles. Most of the time, she seems serene as long as her breathing isn't distressed. But that's a physiological response to feeling suffocated. If she were brain dead, she wouldn't even respond to that."

"Try to stop worrying about things no one can know for a certainty. She's in one of the best facilities in the area and is now at the best hospital in the Rockies. You've been a devoted husband to her for eighteen years. A lot of other men would have bailed out in a situation like this and moved on, but you've been beside her from the beginning."

He shook his head. "I could never abandon her. I owe her that respect, and I know she'd take care of me if the tables were turned."

"Of course she would. Cut yourself some slack."

He stared at her as her words sank in. Her smile brought a little sunshine back into his day. He needed to stop beating himself up. What's done was done. Pamela was right about that.

"You're a good friend, Pamela. You've made today easier for me in so many ways. Gunnar keeps telling me I need to at least find someone to socialize with rather than remain so solitary. A friend who can take my mind off things now and again." Gunnar had been right, as usual.

All he could offer was friendship. Nothing romantic. He'd never put Pamela in limbo like that. She needed someone who would make a lifelong commitment to her. Nothing like the commitment he'd made the day he married Tori.

Lucky for him, Pamela seemed content with friendship.

Her hand remained on his forearm, and he became aware of it when she gripped him harder. "I'm here for you—whatever you need, Kristoffer. Helping others find joy, peace, and comfort is what makes me happy."

"I saw the way you took care of others in the waiting room this morning."

She swallowed hard. "Kristoffer, your life has been on hold so long that you've forgotten how to take care of yourself or how to accept help from a friend. All I'm saying is that, when Tori's out of the hospital and things go back to normal, whenever that is, I'd like to continue to see you in whatever way you want. I think we're good for each other at this point in our lives. You're a great sounding board for me and have given me a lot of clarity about what I want in future relationships. I understand things about myself that I might never have sorted out without making a lot more mistakes with the wrong guys again."

She glanced at the cars and SUVs speeding by before turning toward him again. "I want to give you a chance to unwind a little, Kristoffer. To do things like go to the jazz club or maybe on a picnic. Constant stress is a killer. You need time to relax most of all."

Platonic. While she sometimes left him wanting something he couldn't have, spending time with someone like her pushed all the right buttons for the latent Dom inside him.

"I'd like that."

Without another word, Pamela put the car in gear and merged back into traffic, continuing toward Aurora. "You going to be okay to drive home after stopping at my place, Kristoffer?"

"Sure. I'm fine now." He had so many thoughts ricocheting around in his head now that he was wide-awake.

Alive. Pamela had the effect of making him feel more conscious of his surroundings than he'd been in years.

This amazing woman seated beside him had awakened parts of him he'd thought long dead. She wanted friendship from him, but would he be content to stop there?

Back in Tori's hospital room the next evening, his phone vibrated, and he checked the caller ID. Liz. He'd called Tori's mother last night to inform her and Ron about their daughter's hospitalization. He'd held off calling right away, hoping for the biopsy results, but then decided to call anyway. They should be aware of the situation in case things took a sudden turn for the worse. Someday, he'd have to make the call to let them know their daughter had passed on.

"Hello, Liz. How are you?" Kristoffer moved to the window and stared out blindly. He'd been feeling alone without Pamela here. This call helped connect him to the outside world.

"How's Victoria? They won't tell us anything over the phone." Well into Tori's second year at the nursing home, her parents had stopped visiting more than once or twice a year. Seeing her that way had become too painful. Because there was no hint that his wife knew her parents were there, it made no sense putting them through that anguish any more often. As they were getting up in age, the drive from St. Louis was hard on them, too.

"She's doing a little better as far as the pneumonia goes. Seems to be responding to the antibiotics." He was glad he'd chosen to have them treat the infection aggressively. After watching her struggle to breathe, along with intermittent coughing fits, Kristoffer needed her to be comfortable above all else. As long as they found drugs that worked, he wanted her treated.

He hadn't shared the news about the biopsy yet, but now was as good a time as any. "Liz, there's a new development you two should know about, though."

"What's that?" The wariness in her voice told him she knew it wouldn't be good.

"They're running some pathology tests because they found some suspicious spots on her lung x-rays. It could just be the infection. Or benign tumors. But it could also mean cancer."

"Ron! Come quick!" Liz's cry tore his guts out. When Ron came to the phone asking what had happened, Kristoffer repeated the news.

"What kind of God would put her through anything more?" Ron demanded.

Kristoffer couldn't answer that. He'd given up on believing in the merciful God of his childhood long ago. If anything, he'd shifted to believing in the Norse god Thor, the sometimes-ruthless deity FarFar had told him and Gunnar about in countless stories.

The physicians all said that she'd be bombarded with infections over time and one would eventually be too much for her to fight off. He'd accepted that, but to give her cancer, too, would be inordinately cruel. "I'll know more after the pathology report comes back. Maybe in a couple more days. Do you want me to call and consult with you before deciding how to proceed?"

Silence on the other end of the call. Then Liz was on the phone again. "You don't plan to put her through chemo or radiation, do you?"

Tori's parents had voiced their opinion long ago that heroic measures should be off the table if they would only result in prolonging their daughter's existence.

Yesterday, he'd given the doctor a knee-jerk response to the question of further treatments, if cancer was detected. But maybe he needed to rethink that. She'd suffered enough. As long as they could assure him that she wouldn't be in pain—was there enough morphine in the world to do that?—he'd forego chemo or radiation treatments. While the thought of watching her starve to death gave him nightmares and was the reason he hadn't pulled the PEG tube years ago, he couldn't put her through anything more. He needed to be fair to Tori.

"Liz, if it comes down to a positive diagnosis, I'll pull the PEG tube, and the doctors will do everything possible to keep her pain-free."

He was aware he'd have to go through Tori's last moments alone. Her parents lived two states away and wouldn't be able to watch their daughter die, not that it would be any easier for him.

Liz spoke next. "We agreed long ago that any medical procedures done would be up to you, son." He wished they'd tell him he was doing the right thing. A long pause ensued. "We'll support you in whatever you choose to do."

Kristoffer drew a slow, deep breath. Being burdened with having to make such decisions on his own left him feeling extremely alone at times like these. He wished he had someone to consult with to help him know what was the right thing to do. Or what was best for Tori. Gunnar had helped some in the past, but he had a lot on his plate right now.

Kristoffer had never known if he'd made any of the right choices, not from day one. What would Pamela suggest? She was a doctor. Maybe he'd talk with her if he needed to make the decision to begin or suspend treatment.

As her guardian, he'd go on trying to do the best he could to keep her comfortable.

Ron broke the silence. "Liz and I will come out for a visit soon. Keep us informed about her condition and the test results in the meantime."

"Of course, Ron. You know I will."

They disconnected the call, leaving Kristoffer alone again. He leaned his forehead against the chilled window pane, staring down at the parking lot. A man carrying a giant teddy bear walked beside a little girl holding a pink helium balloon on a string.

A celebration of new life.

Suddenly, the girl's balloon broke free and began drifting away from her. He couldn't hear her distressed screams through the window, but his attention flew to the balloon as it floated up and mesmerized him for some reason. Above the enormous air conditioning vents on the hospital wing just in front of him, the balloon seemed to stop to dance, undulating just a few yards away from the window.

Tori's rattling cough broke into the silence and made him return to her bedside only to watch helplessly as she gasped for breath. The rattle in her chest was more pronounced. He pushed the button, calling for a nurse.

How much more would she have to bear before she could be set free of her dying body?

As much as you force her to endure.

His anger at a God who would do this surged within him, and he fisted his hand before punching something. But his anger would only serve to agitate Tori more, so he willed himself to calm down.

He imagined the God of Thunder swooping in to destroy the illness, but even the mighty Thor couldn't eradicate the shell of the body that was all he had left of Tori.

Only Kristoffer could do that—by removing the feeding tube. He banished the thought from his mind, hoping he'd never have to make that decision.

When the nurse and tech came in together, he explained again that her breathing was labored, and they said they would see what the doctors had ordered. Perhaps they could give her enough morphine to…

Disgusted with where his mind was going, he left the room. As he passed the nurses' station, someone called out.

"Mr. Larson, the cookies were amazing!"

He turned to find a young brunette in flowery scrubs. "Cookies?"

She pointed to a huge catering tray on the high counter surrounding the desk where he saw a few remaining cookies and lots of crumbs under a plastic covering.

"Please tell your friend we appreciate her thinking of us, too, and going to the trouble to bake them."

Friend? No one had been here except Pamela. Had she made cookies for them? When? He'd been spending more time in Tori's room since she seemed calmer when he was there, so he hadn't been out in the waiting room most of the day.

Why hadn't she texted him to let him know she was here?

"Would you care for one?" she asked.

He reached for one of the macadamia nut cookies, having skipped a couple of meals today. "Thanks." She'd probably be long gone, but he held out hope she'd be in the waiting room so he went directly there and scanned the crowded seating area. No Pamela.

Of course, he wouldn't have expected or wanted her to be sitting here for hours on end if she didn't have to. That she'd taken the time to bring the cookies to the ICU staff was nothing less than he'd expect of the generous servant soul she possessed. He noted a similar tray on one of the coffee tables. Always taking care of the needs of others.

I miss you, Pamela.

Shaken by thoughts of Pamela at a time his mind should be focused on Tori, he was drawn to the chapel for the first time in years, where he sat and stared at the abstract mural on the wall. Lit from behind, it depicted what he interpreted as a sun with flames, or perhaps the sun's rays, radiating out from the center.

He sent up a prayer of sorts that Tori would be made comfortable again and healed from whatever infection was attacking her body. Conversely, his next prayer was for his wife to be taken to heaven while sleeping, without having to suffer a minute longer. He blinked away the sting in his eyes at making such an unholy request.

His eyelids grew heavy. So tired. He probably shouldn't attempt to drive home tonight. He'd nap here a few minutes where it was quiet and set an alarm on his phone to wake him to go back upstairs to check on Tori.

The beeping of his watch jolted him awake, and it took him a moment to remember where he was. As if weighted down by chain mail, he stood and left the chapel feeling not one ounce of solace. Inside her room again, he was relieved to see she rested peacefully, as far as anyone could tell. Not wanting to disturb her, he tiptoed back out, unsure what to do next. The smell of coffee reached him as he entered the waiting room again, and Pamela stood a few feet away, holding a takeout cup toward him.

"You look like you could use this."

He'd never needed her more than tonight. "You're my angel of mercy." He smiled and accepted the steaming brew. "What are you doing here?" he asked, unable to muster up the energy to be upset with her.

She shrugged. "I've been worried about you."

He scowled. "I appreciate that, but there's nothing you can do here."

She squared her shoulders. "Nonsense. I can help take care of you so you can be there for Tori. You look exhausted. When's the last time you've slept?"

"I had a nap earlier."

"How about food? Have you eaten today?"

"Yeah. One of your cookies. That was incredibly thoughtful of you. The nurses asked me to extend their thanks as well."

"You know me. Need to stay busy. But surely that's not all you've had to eat all day!"

Hoping to change the subject, he took a sip of the coffee. "God, that's good." He motioned her to have a seat, but she crossed her arms instead.

"You haven't answered my question."

Bossy little thing. "I'm not hungry."

"Well, I am, so I'll buy. I saw a nice place just around the corner."

He stared at her a long moment, ready to say he needed to stay near Tori, but something kept him from voicing the words. Instead, he said, "You aren't paying, or I'm not going."

The corners of her mouth started to curl into a smile before she caught herself, trying to remain stern, he supposed. "If you insist." She buttoned her jacket and turned to lead the way to the elevators without another word.

Kristoffer grinned, silently thanking her for this reprieve. It had been a long, depressing day.

When they sat across from each other, enjoying two cold beers and a plate of mozzarella sticks, she leaned toward him resting on her forearms. "Has there been any improvement today?"

He shook his head. "Not a lot. She wasn't coughing the last time I went in to see her. I know it's early in her treatment, but it kills me hearing her struggle to breathe. Last time she had pneumonia, she was in the hospital almost a month."

"Not unusual, really. How many times has she had it?"

"This is the third time."

Pamela rested her hand on his sleeve. "How do you deal with everything alone?"

He took a sudden interest in their shared appetizer. When she continued to wait for a response, he asked, "What choice do I have?"

"You don't have to shoulder it all alone." Apparently, she didn't take the hint that he wanted to drop this subject. "We're friends now, Kristoffer."

"If I thought you'd take no for an answer, I'd go on the way I always have."

"Well, I won't. It's time for you to think of yourself in this equation, too." Her sweet smile belied the determination in her eyes.

"Are you this insistent with your patients?"

"Much worse." She grinned.

While he ought to be ticked that she wanted to barge into his personal life, he remembered how she'd made coping easier for him the past few days. Maybe coping wasn't the right word.

No. She made life itself more pleasant. He'd actually found some enjoyment in their times together over meals and the other night at the jazz club.

"I'll concede that I'm enjoying my time with you, Pamela Jeffrey." *Whether I should or not.* "I'd like to continue spending time with you."

✧　✧　✧

The next day Tori spiked a fever and time flew by in a blur of running errands for hot cups of coffee and cold sandwiches. Convincing Kristoffer to leave her bedside had been impossible, but Pamela did what she could to make sure he didn't come down sick himself. She kept Gunnar updated via texts, but sometime midafternoon, she turned toward the elevator alcove to see him approaching.

"How's he holding up?" he asked without preliminaries.

Kristoffer was back with Tori as he had been most of the day, so she could speak freely. "Not very well. He's barely left her side today." She'd kept Gunnar informed about everything she was aware of.

"Maybe the ICU staff can restrict access by telling him they're overcrowded or something." Kristoffer did need to take a break every now and then. "Is he eating? Sleeping enough?"

"No, but even before Tori's fever, I hadn't been able to talk him into leaving the hospital more than once a day, usually for a quick bite, and then back he'd go. He might catch naps here and there, but not enough to matter." He sighed, apparently as frustrated as she was. "Any suggestions would be welcomed, Gunnar. You know him better."

"I've been down this road with him before. I'm sure you're doing as much as I'd be able to. He can be stubborn when it comes to Tori."

Do tell.

"How comfortable are you playing the Domme?"

"Excuse me?"

"You may have to drag him home at least for one night's sleep."

Ohhh! That *kind of Domme.* She smiled. "I'll see what I can manage."

He smiled for the first time since he'd arrived. "I can't tell you what a relief it's been for me that you've been with him the past few days. I've only been able to stop by once before this, so I owe you."

She smiled. "No, you don't. He's my friend, and he needs me. I'm not doing this for any other reason." Yet hearing his words made her feel a sense of accomplishment.

The subject of concern walked into the waiting room and zeroed in on the two of them. Kristoffer stood looking lost a few seconds before she waved him over.

The look of relief that washed over him at seeing Gunnar warmed her heart. The two were like brothers. She saw how strong their bond was by the way Kristoffer's body relaxed as they spoke to one another.

After announcing that Tori's fever had dropped, talk turned to the upcoming mission, and Kristoffer brought up the hospital equipment project. "Sorry we haven't been able to get going on this."

Gunnar looked toward her then back at Kristoffer. "No worries,

Kris. Pamela's been working on it and keeping me posted."

Kristoffer's eyes opened wide. "Why didn't you tell me?"

She indicated their surroundings with a wave of her hand. "You've been preoccupied, remember? Gunnar provided me with information on how to request purchase order numbers, so I placed a few orders."

Kristoffer's initial silence took her by surprise. She thought he'd be happy to hear the project wasn't suffering. "You aren't supposed to be overdoing it," he said. Clearly, he wasn't pleased.

The man was going to drive her nuts if he kept trying to pamper her. "It didn't take any time at all. I placed orders between naps."

Gunnar's gaze shifted from one to the other. "Is there something you two aren't telling me?"

She expressed an emphatic, "No!" at the same time Kristoffer told him about her fever while in Afghanistan. Like his cousin, Gunnar's Dom stare was equally forceful and did strange things to her stomach.

"The project's on hold until you're well," he said, pointing to Pamela first and then to Kristoffer, "and you are back home after Tori's release."

She held up a hand. "But you can't! They need that equipment desperately."

His raised eyebrow told her he seemed surprised that she'd challenge his authority, but then he relaxed somewhat. "Look, I have the detailed reports of what's been purchased and what is still on the list. I'll put someone else to work on the purchasing end." She became the focus of his stare again. "You need to take care of *you*, Pamela—but if you have any energy left, keep this big lug in line."

"Don't worry about me, man. Pamela's been taking great care of me, but I'm more worried about her under the circumstances." Gunnar's enigmatic smile puzzled her as he glanced between the two of them. Then he grinned. "Look after each other, and keep me posted."

She smiled back, happy to have his blessing such as it was. "I'll do my best."

After saying goodbye to Gunnar, she noticed that Kristoffer's shirt was wrinkled and loosened from his slacks. His hair was disheveled, too, probably from running his fingers through it too many times to count. The circles under his eyes attested to the fact that he hadn't slept more than a couple of hours a night since this ordeal began.

"So Tori's fever is down?"

"Yes. The new regimen of antibiotics seems to be working. She's more restful, too."

Time to follow Gunnar's directive before he collapsed. "Good. Time to get you to home to bed."

He cocked his head and scrunched his eyebrows. "I beg your pardon."

She reached for her jacket and slipped it on. "Tori's out of the woods for now. You can't do anything for her if you run yourself into the ground. Gunnar's charged me with taking care of you, so I say it's time you went home and had a full night's rest."

She started for the elevators assuming he'd follow. When she didn't hear the click of his wingtips on the linoleum, she turned around. "Get the lead out, Larson." She couldn't believe she'd just spoken to him that way, but she would not take no for an answer.

"I'm not leaving."

Squaring her shoulders, she pulled herself to her full five foot one frame. "Yes, you are. Either in my car or in a body bag. Your choice. But if you don't take care of yourself, where will Tori be?"

Not waiting for him to say no again, she pivoted and started for the elevators once more.

Follow me, you stubborn fool.

She pressed the button and willed herself not to turn to see if he had, partly because she didn't expect to find him standing there.

"Just a few hours, then I'm coming back."

She smiled, hearing his voice close by, but didn't let him see her face. Her plan was to drive him home in her car and not return until she picked him up tomorrow to take him back to the hospital.

Maybe a few ground rules needed to be laid. "You aren't sleeping with a watch, alarm, or phone."

"What if something happens to Tori?"

"I'll monitor your phone. You'll give me your passcode to unlock it."

Kristoffer shook his head. "You're in no better shape to be up all night than I am. If I sleep, so do you. You'll take the bed, and I'll sleep on the sofa."

CHAPTER SEVEN

Kristoffer jolted awake when the car stopped. A quick scan of his surroundings revealed they were at the gate to his parking garage. He gave Pamela the code to punch in and directed her to his parking spot.

How had he fallen asleep like that? His body didn't feel the least bit rested so he must have only dozed a minute, although he couldn't remember a thing after he'd gotten into her Renegade Trailhawk back at the hospital.

He opened his door and found her standing there as if she had been about to open it for him. Yeah, right. Only he was too exhausted to argue that she should have waited for him to open her door.

"I'll concede I'm more tired than I realized."

He inserted his key, and they took the elevator to the penthouse. He intended to ensure she had enough sleep, too. "I can sleep anywhere, Pamela. Believe me."

She shook her head and, with her hands on his back, propelled him toward the bedroom. "You're sleeping in a bed. Your feet would be dangling off the end of the couch; I'm short, so it'll be perfect for me."

He didn't like the idea of a guest sleeping on the sofa, but the lethargy that had overtaken him on the ride home wouldn't give him any energy to argue. She began to remove his shirt, but he brushed her hands away.

"I'm capable of undressing myself." He'd only go so far with her in here.

Her gaze drifted to the imposing bed that dominated the room. While not a king-sized one, it made up for the lack of width with its impressive height. Crudely chiseled designs worn to a soft patina that spoke of decades—possibly even centuries—of wood polish and age seemed to capture her attention. The canopy frame displayed more of the unique geometric carvings to match the curve in the head and footboards.

As if to give him some space, she approached the bed and ran her hand over the wood, satiny to the touch. "I've never seen a bed with a footboard shaped like this before." The center of the footboard sloped downward in the middle in a concave fashion.

"It was my grandfather's."

"Gorgeous!" She ran her finger over the smooth wood.

"In Norway, where winters are obviously brutal, the bed would have been wedged into a small alcove. Sometimes the crawl-ins were on the sides, but this one had been built so that you crawled in from the foot of the bed, enclosing the occupants of the bed on three sides for greater warmth."

She glanced up at the canopy frame, which would have been covered in heavy fabrics to block any remaining drafts back in those days.

"Ingenious."

He continued. "Gunnar and I often shared that bed, because Far-Far said it was too warm for him in summers. We welcomed it because where he lived was still colder than hell even in the summer."

He removed his wristwatch. "Of course, here I don't use curtains on the canopy, and it's not tucked into an alcove, which makes it much more comfortable."

She extended her hand and waited until he gave her the watch, followed more reluctantly by his phone. Before she left, he needed to lay down a few rules of his own. "My phone's passcode is 0310. You'll wake me if there's any change for the worse in Tori's condition."

She sobered. "I will." Before she left the room, she pulled the room-darkening drapes and unplugged his alarm clock, tucking it under her arm. "Sweet dreams."

If he did dream tonight, they'd be anything but sweet.

After she closed the door behind her, he finished undressing. Too tired to take a much-needed shower, he fell into the bed.

✧　✧　✧

Bacon. Why was he dreaming about bacon? Kristoffer opened his eyes and looked around. Slits of light came in through the drapes. He looked at his wrist only to realize his watch was gone.

Pamela had confiscated it.

He tossed back the covers and walked to the window. Judging by the height of the sun, it had to be close to eleven. He'd never slept this late. He started to reach for his clothes, but they were so disgustingly filthy, he decided it wouldn't kill him to take a shower before heading back downtown.

The warm water sluiced over him and washed away any residual weariness. Grabbing a towel as he left the shower, he dried himself before heading back into the bedroom for some clothes.

A knock sounded on the door as the aroma of strong coffee invaded his senses.

"Are you decent?"

"Just a minute." He grabbed a polo shirt and jeans from the closet and briefs from the dresser and was dressed in record time. "I am now."

A smiling Pamela entered the room, extending a steaming mug toward him. He accepted it, but judged the brew too hot to drink. "Thank you."

"No, thank *you*."

"For what?" *Showering?* Had he smelled that bad?

Her gaze gave him the once over. Good thing he'd dressed before she came in. His cock grew hard, and he returned to the bathroom where he set the mug down and picked up his brush, running it through his hair.

Noma sauntered into the bathroom and wrapped herself around his ankles. He reached down to rub the cat between the ears. Surprisingly, when Pamela followed, the fickle feline left him and went to her.

"I see you've met," he said.

"I won her over by cleaning out her litter box and feeding her last night."

"Damn. I forgot all about her." When was the last time he'd been home?

"No problem. We hit it off immediately."

Figured. Maybe Noma only warmed up to females.

"Breakfast is ready when you are," she announced as she set Noma down. "Oh, the pulmonologist wants to meet with you in about ninety minutes."

Tori.

How could he have forgotten about her? He picked up the mug and lifted it to his face. "I'll be there in a few."

She nodded and started to leave, but turned her head to toss a parting shot over her shoulder. "It's nice to see you back among the living." If he'd slept more than twelve hours straight, he must have been dog-tired.

In the kitchen a few minutes later, dressed and ready to go, she plated scrambled eggs and bacon and a piece of buttered, thick sourdough toast and set it on the table.

"Smells delicious." He sat down and waited for her.

"Tastes even better," she said, filling her plate.

She smiled, and his damned cock stirred. *Bloody hell.* What kind of man was he to have a sexual response to another woman while his wife could be dying?

"I'll admit I had a nibble while I cooked."

They ate in silence a moment. "Man, this hits the spot."

"Glad you liked it. My options were limited in your kitchen."

"Sorry. I don't eat here much."

"Your freezer came through with the bread and bacon, though."

"Yeah, I have a tendency to stock my freezer for times when I might not want to venture out."

"I saw your leftovers from one of my favorite restaurants in the fridge, but I figured they'd been there a while, so I tossed them."

"Thanks." This little scene of domestic harmony felt wrong. His place was at Tori's side. Instead he was across town in his home talking about mundane matters like garbage. Time to refocus before heading downtown again. "What did the doctor say?"

"Just that they had the results of the biopsy and want to meet with you to discuss them."

His heart hammered. "Do they meet with you to tell you everything's okay?"

"They could want the meeting for any number of reasons. Don't jump to conclusions. I personally think her staff member was reluctant to give me any of the information, since I'm not listed on the HIPAA release of information forms."

Damn. He shouldn't have fallen asleep. Kristoffer hurriedly finished the rest of his breakfast and coffee and then stood. "Maybe if we head downtown earlier, we can meet sooner."

"Doubtful. She's probably on a tight schedule," Pamela said as she stood and began clearing the table, seemingly without a worry in the world. He took his own plate to the sink to speed things along.

She tossed him a bone. "But if we get down there early, it'll give you time to visit Tori. I'm sure you're anxious to see her."

He smiled. "Yeah, I am."

But honestly, he hadn't given a visit with Tori a thought. He'd been with her throughout the day yesterday, before and after the physicians came through. He always was when she was hospitalized. The only change in routine was that he'd left her alone last night.

"I'll clean up in here, Kristoffer. Gather whatever you need for an overnight at the hospital, and we'll leave as soon as you're ready."

He appreciated her instructions, because Pamela made simple functions fly out of his head. If she used her power for nefarious purposes, she could be dangerous.

To hell with *could*. She'd passed dangerous somewhere last night when she'd invaded his bedroom.

✧　✧　✧

Kristoffer held on to Pamela's hand tightly as they sat side by side in the conference room across the table from Tori's pulmonologist. He dreaded what they had to tell him, but was relieved he wouldn't have to face the news alone.

"Mr. Larson, as far as we can tell, the lesions are calcified." Kristoffer stared at her, clueless for a moment as to what that meant. He expected to hear "malignant" this or "benign" that. What the hell did calcified mean?

Pamela squeezed his hand and said, "That's great news." Her response helped him relax a bit.

"We'll do more chest scans in a month to be sure there aren't any changes, but my educated guess is that the lesions are remnants of a prior infection."

Needing confirmation, he asked, "So you're saying it's not cancer, right? Not malignant?"

"Yes, that's right. No malignancies showed up in the biopsies we took of the most suspicious-looking lesions."

Kristoffer expelled the breath he didn't realize he'd been holding as he sank back against the vinyl-covered chair feeling as though a ton of bricks had been lifted off his chest. Pamela rubbed his back in support, and he glanced over at her and smiled. What would he have done without her these past few days?

He returned his focus to the doctor across the table. "Is she responding to the treatment for the pneumonia? Is her fever still down?"

"I've noticed an improvement in her labs today, and we don't hear quite as much fluid in her lungs. Too soon to tell, but I'm cautiously optimistic that we're on the right regimen of drugs."

He'd accept that as a positive, too. At this point, it didn't take much for him to be encouraged. He hoped she'd be able to breathe more easily soon. Every time he went in there and heard her struggling for a lungful of air, his gut knotted.

When the doctor left the room, Kristoffer's body began to shake. He buried his face in his crossed arms on the table, unable to fight back the tears.

Strong hands rubbed his back in sure strokes. "Let it out. I know how frightened and worried you've been about her these past few days. Shhh. It's going to be all right."

Suddenly needing this living, breathing woman's comfort, he sat up and swiveled in his seat toward Pamela, wrapping his arms around her. The two of them held on to each other, providing him with a lifeline for who knew how long.

"I don't know what I'd have done without you, Pamela. Thanks for being here."

"This is what friends are for and why it means so much to me to be here with you."

"I didn't think I needed anyone until this week."

"Oh, Kristoffer, we all need someone sometimes. It's not a sign of weakness, but one of strength, to admit you can't go it alone."

As the moments stretched out, his need to retreat again surfaced. How did he extricate himself after crying in her arms? What could he possibly have left to hide? But he experienced no shame for his meltdown. If a man couldn't cry tears of joy after hearing his wife didn't have cancer, then what the hell *could* he cry about?

Still, he didn't like being so exposed emotionally. He pulled away and quickly wiped his eyes with the heels of his hands before smiling at her.

"After I check on her one more time, why don't you go home and take a nap? You can't possibly have slept well on my sofa."

"I got more sleep last night than I have in months. I don't mind sticking around until you're ready for lunch."

While he was far from being hungry anytime soon after the breakfast she'd prepared, he didn't want her skipping meals, either.

He'd compromise a bit, knowing he probably wasn't going to get her to go home while he was here with Tori. "Lunch in a few hours sounds good. And I feel so much better after last night's sleep that I'm going to sleep in my own bed tonight again rather than here. Tori's improving. I won't be far away if they need me."

And I'm more worried about you running yourself ragged right now when you should be taking better care of yourself.

She smiled. "I think that sounds like a good plan. I'll even let you keep your alarm clock and phone this time, as long as you promise you'll not set them for less than eight hours from when you go to bed."

Despite his unexpected tears a few minutes ago, he did feel better after catching some sleep. It wasn't as though he needed to be at Tori's side when she woke so she could see he was there.

Midafternoon, they left the hospital and walked to the now-quiet café where they'd bought muffins the first morning of Tori's hospitalization. Both enjoyed a lunch of field greens topped with grilled chicken, mandarin oranges, dried cranberries, and slivered almonds. He didn't think he could handle anything more after she'd fed him that hearty breakfast. At least she was getting some protein with her lunch.

Pamela set down her fork after finishing hers first. "This hit the spot after all those dry subs I've eaten the last several days."

"You bet. I love a good grinder as much as the next person, but without being able to run those calories off, I've been going easy on the vending machines, or I'll have a middle-aged paunch in no time."

Her gaze flicked to his chest before meeting his gaze again, and a flush blossomed in her cheeks.

Not prepared to process her response, he picked up the check. "I'll pay this and then head back to the hospital. You don't need to hang around. Whether you think you're rested or not, that place is draining on the mind and body."

Pamela smiled. "I *work* in hospitals. I can handle it. Besides I'm smack dab in the middle of a riveting article in *People* magazine and could finish it while you're with Tori."

He shook his head and grinned, doubtful the down-to-earth woman would find anything remotely fascinating about the lives of the rich and famous. Seeing she wasn't going to take no for an answer, after paying the bill, he took her by the elbow and guided her out of the restaurant and back toward the hospital. Despite the emotional roller coaster he'd been on today, he felt incredible. Must be because of the good news from the doctor.

He called and talked to Liz and then Gunnar, sharing positive news about Tori for a change. The afternoon passed in quick visits with Tori—the staff was sticking to the ten-minute rule again for some reason—and forty-five minute conversations with Pamela in the waiting room or while taking a walk around the hospital. Rinse and repeat until he saw it had grown dark outside.

"I'll just go back to see her once more, then let's get some dinner and head home."

"Sounds good. Are you going to be able to sleep tonight, Kristoffer?"

"Like a baby."

"From what I've seen and heard, babies don't sleep all that well."

"All I know is that I'll probably be asleep before my head hits that pillow." He reached up and rubbed his thumb over the circles under her eyes. "I'm glad you're going to go home and sleep, too. Then I want you to take the day off from hospital duty tomorrow."

"You're sure? I really don't mind. I'm enjoying our talks."

He shook his head. "You've been great company, but I plan to take my laptop down tomorrow and do some work between visits."

"Oh, I see." Her disappointment was evident on her expressive face.

No, you probably don't. I need to distance myself from you before I do something stupid and inappropriate.

Too bad Gunnar had taken away their project.

She smiled. "I guess I'll go to the gym a while."

"Good girl."

Her smile faded, and he realized his words sounded like something a Dom would say to his sub. Had she picked up on it? Time to put some space between them.

"I'll go visit with Tori now." He turned and left her.

After his visit, he returned to the waiting room to see Pamela staring into the dark night at the window.

"Ready to go eat?"

She turned around, and concern was quickly replaced by her radiant smile. So beautiful. So alive.

Once again, they walked to a local restaurant to eat, but this time didn't engage in any memorable discussions. Maybe they were talked out.

Or maybe you freaked her out earlier by sounding like a Dom.

After settling the bill, they made their way to her vehicle in the hospital parking garage.

"Text me when you get home."

She nodded. "You're going back to your condo tonight, right?"

He grinned. "I'll just check on Tori once more and then head home if she's all right."

"Night, Kristoffer."

"Night, Pamela. Sleep well."

Try not to think about Pamela lying in bed.

"You, too."

As if he could. He'd gotten way too much sleep last night to be able to repeat the same tonight. Most likely, he'd lie awake thinking about her all night.

On the drive back home, he thought about whether he and Pamela could remain friends if his libido continued stirring back to life at inopportune moments. What was the matter with him? Hell, he was a Dom. He had better control of his body than he'd exhibited in the past day or so. He needed to fight this inappropriate attraction.

No, you need to wake up, man.

He'd ignored his body's sexual needs for years. What he needed was sexual release. And, since sex was out, that meant taking himself in hand, as usual.

He entered the condo, and Noma greeted him halfway down the hallway. After a cursory rub against his pant leg, she turned toward the door as if waiting for it to open again. Was the cat hoping Pamela would join them again? The two certainly must have bonded quickly last night.

Kristoffer stooped to pick her up and rub her behind the ears. "Sorry, baby. It's just you and me again tonight."

The place did seem lonely with just the two of them, however. They'd managed fine for years. How had Pamela invaded both their psyches so thoroughly in such a short time?

And what was Kristoffer going to do about it? Was the answer to spend more time with her or less?

Good luck with the latter. She'd made a difference in his life this week, one he wasn't ready to forsake even if he should.

No better time than tonight to think about what he planned to do about everything.

No, not everything.

About *her*.

Pamela.

✧   ✧   ✧

Pamela hadn't seen or heard from Kristoffer since his wife had been released from the hospital two days ago. He'd actually started to become more distant after they'd had dinner Thursday night before heading to their separate places to sleep.

She'd popped in at the hospital a couple of times in the days before Tori's discharge, but he'd usually sent her home to nap right after taking her out to eat. The man was obsessed with her health habits.

She plumped the pillow and rolled over, hoping sleep would come. Where was Kristoffer now? Home, no doubt. No more late nights at the hospital for him. She could understand he might disappear while arranging Tori's transfer back to the facility, but wished he wouldn't isolate himself again. This hospitalization could signal the coming demise of Tori's ravaged body. Now more than ever, he needed people close by to help him deal with the day he no longer had that body to hold on to. If not this time, it was bound to happen eventually.

He'd asked Pamela to be with him for the meeting where he'd expected to hear devastating news from the doctor. Perhaps the top layer of his formidable wall had crumbled ever so slightly.

She sighed and flipped her pillow to the cooler side. Maybe he was distancing himself because he wasn't comfortable with what the two of them had begun to feel toward one another. She couldn't deny romantic feelings for him, crass as it might seem to some in this situation. But to her mind, his wife had died years ago in a tragic accident. He had nothing to be ashamed of. He'd been by her side all those years, even after he'd finally allowed himself to return to the land of the living in some matters.

In rare moments together, he looked at her not as a friend, but as a woman he felt an attraction to. Some might say they should both feel guilty for such emotions, but most likely, those people had never endured seeing a loved one trapped in this state between life and death thanks to the *miracle* of modern medicine. More like a *curse* in Tori's situation.

Not that she had any intention of pursuing him romantically. But he needed someone, whether a friend or whatever, to ease him back to life himself. Damned if she'd feel guilty or call this cheating with a married man. Emotionally, he'd been a widower for years. His heart just hadn't come to terms with her loss enough to be able to move on yet.

Stretching out before her was another night alone with no one to care for but herself. She ought to get a dog or cat or something. Spending time with Noma the other night had been enjoyable. The cat had curled up on her chest, purring away. She'd never thought about how companionable a pet might be, but maybe one would assuage her need to feel needed.

No, with her job, that would be incredibly unfair to the pet.

Was her feeling of emptiness really about companionship, or did she crave the sense of accomplishment that came from helping someone? She'd had a lot of time to think about what she wanted while sitting in the waiting room at the hospital. Mulling over her life had been sobering.

And made her head hurt.

Ping.

She reached for her phone on the nightstand.

KRISTOFFER: Want to go on a picnic tomorrow?

Her heart began beating faster, and a smile spread across her face. This could give her an opportunity to practice her neglected service skills on someone who could benefit from a little pampering. As long as he came away feeling he was the one being taken care of and he didn't start smothering her again. He appeared to work nonstop from what she could tell. She'd rarely seen the man smile.

PAMELA: **I'd love to!**

KRISTOFFER: **Great! I'll pick you up at 11.**

PAMELA: **What can I bring?**

KRISTOFFER: **A jacket and hiking shoes.**

PAMELA: **No, silly. I mean food.**

KRISTOFFER: **I'm having it catered.**

PAMELA: **No one makes better potato salad than I do. Don't order that.**

KRISTOFFER: **Sounds good. But don't overdo.**

PAMELA: **Yes, Sir.**

She nearly cringed at her submissive response, but he sounded awfully bossy.

KRISTOFFER: **See you in the morning.**

PAMELA: **Night.**

She hadn't been on a picnic in forever. Now how was she expected to sleep? She tossed the covers off and went to the kitchen to boil the potatoes and eggs. She wouldn't mix everything until morning, but this way they'd already be cooled when she worked with them.

Pamela had the salad finished by ten and was dressed and sitting down on the front steps to her apartment building early. She carried her jacket, because the sun was quite warm. Were they going to the mountains?

The purr of his Jaguar coming around the corner set her heart to racing. She'd missed him so much.

She'd been too sedentary since returning from Afghanistan and hoped she wouldn't be too out of shape. Although, knowing Kristoffer, he wouldn't be putting her through her paces. Most likely, he'd want to carry her so she wouldn't exhaust herself.

She grinned at the image and rolled the small cooler down the sidewalk to meet him in the driveway, smiling at him as he exited the car.

He didn't seem as happy at the sight of the cooler. "What's that?"

"A cooler. I need to keep the potato salad on ice."

He narrowed his gaze. "Which floor do you live on?"

Curious why he wanted to know, she blinked and answered, "Third."

"You carried it downstairs by yourself? Why didn't you wait for me?"

Why was he so upset? "I'm stronger than I look."

"You're also recovering from a serious illness. No more heavy lifting."

One bowl of potato salad was hardly heavy lifting, but she'd already learned Kristoffer liked to fuss over her health. Not something she wanted to focus on today.

"Next time, you will wait for me to carry heavy stuff downstairs. Understood?"

"Yes, Sir." He nodded curtly without raising his brows in surprise and opened the door for her, so she decided not to bring attention to her slip of the tongue. He probably just thought it a throwback to her days as an Air Force brat. Unlike her text last night, he couldn't tell from her words whether she used an upper- or lowercased "sir."

"Great day for a picnic," she said, hoping to shift his focus. "I'm in such a good mood today."

He grinned back at her. "Surprisingly, I'm getting there, too. I haven't been on a picnic in years." Today, he wore a jogging outfit with some serious running shoes, but she liked him in suits best.

Kristoffer popped the trunk and stowed the cooler inside next to several bags from a local barbecue restaurant.

"Smells delicious!"

"We'll eat first then hike." Minutes later, they were seated side by side, talking about Tori's condition and all that had happened since they'd seen each other late last week.

She and Kristoffer had all afternoon to enjoy their meal and hike before he'd need to visit Tori. Pamela couldn't imagine that kind of lifelong devotion and love, but hoped she'd find it someday.

Soon they were leaving Denver and heading west. She wondered where they were going until he took the Idaho Springs exit.

"Mount Evans?"

"Yep. Echo Lake to be exact, although if you'd like, we could drive up to the top of the mountain."

"Whatever you want is fine with me. The drive is gorgeous, but there are some good hiking trails at Echo, too."

He pulled into a popular hiking area several miles up Mount Evans Road. After parking and hauling their picnic supplies to one of the lakeside tables—Kristoffer letting Pamela carry the lightest two bags—they spread a blanket over the table next to the lake and started emptying the bags and coolers. Despite her jacket, with the stiff breeze coming off the lake, she might want to huddle *under* the blanket before long. Maybe they were rushing the season, but she loved being outdoors. They'd both dressed in layers knowing how unpredictable the Front Range could be in springtime.

"Are we expecting anyone else?" she asked him.

He quirked an eyebrow. "No, why?"

"Because there's enough food here to feed a small army."

He laughed. "We'll need to build up our strength for the hike."

There were boneless chicken wings, a platter of sliced cheeses and deli meats, fresh fruit salad, and, of course, her potato salad.

A red-tailed hawk screeched overhead, and she jumped at the noise, nearly dropping her plate, then laughed at herself. She was on edge for some reason she couldn't fathom and needed to relax.

Kristoffer opened the bottle of Perrier and poured them each a glass. "Here. Sorry it's not wine, but I didn't want either of us to get dehydrated when we start our hike."

She took a sip and set the glass on the table as Kristoffer stared out over the blue mountain lake in silence. She wondered if he was remembering special times here with his wife? Pamela worried about him not being able to break from the past and enjoy the present.

In an attempt to bring his attention back to the moment, she announced, "Let's dig in! Everything looks delicious."

They took their places on the same side of the bench so both could face the lake, and he refilled her glass before raising his. She did the same. "To blue lakes, brilliant sunshine, and a phenomenal day." They clinked glasses and sipped their water to complete the toast.

Enjoying the beginning of their meal in near silence, both ate heartily and took in the splendid view before them. Being out here with a friend rather than a date, she didn't have to worry about looking like a glutton and helped herself to another chicken wing. Good thing the restaurant packed wipes for their messy fingers.

"I didn't realize how hungry I was," he said. She enjoyed watching him eat with equal gusto. A look of surprise crossed his face when he took a bite of her potato salad. Her recipe used tarragon, dill, and celery seed to give it a special flavor. He swallowed and smiled at her. "This has to be the most fantastic potato salad I've ever eaten. You're a good cook."

His smile and praise warmed her heart. "One of my hobbies, but I don't have a lot of ambition to cook just for me. So flattery might get you invited over for dinner sometime."

She'd never invited him to her place before. When he became serious, she prepared to laugh away the statement until he said, "I'd like that."

His words surprised her, as did his next ones. "Pamela, I can't tell you how much you helped me get through Tori's hospitalization. Thanks for being there."

She felt a familiar heat come into her cheeks. A Steller's jay came begging for food at the end of the table, and she used the distraction to toss it a piece of bread. After it swallowed that piece, it strutted closer to them.

"Brave little thing," she remarked.

"I guess he trusts us."

Pamela tossed another piece of bread to the bird and spoke to it. "You, little bird, will live much longer if you don't place your trust in the hands of strangers."

"You sound as though you speak on experience."

"Oh, do I ever!"

"Could that be one of the things keeping you from staying in the moment when you scene?"

She chewed while she thought. "I suppose. I haven't really analyzed it."

"Well, thinking won't wear you out. While you're on this little hiatus, it might be a good time for you to figure some things out before you dive back into the lifestyle."

"I suppose it couldn't hurt. Hey, the night Tori went into the hospital, you offered to help me on my concentration and focus issues with some exercises."

"Nothing wrong with your memory."

She laughed. "No. I'm like an elephant."

"Well, I did, but haven't had a lot of time to think about it."

"No rush. I'm here for another six to eight weeks, maybe longer depending on the staffing needs at the hospital."

"You sure you'll be ready to return to Afghanistan?" She could imagine the worry on his face, but didn't look his way. The man worried way too much.

"With you barely letting me lift a feather and curtailing my work to a couple hours at a computer each day, I don't see there being any problem."

"I didn't help matters any by having you hanging out at the hospital so much."

"That was my choice." Before he decided to skip the hike and take her home to send her to bed, she stood and picked up her empty plate. "Why don't we pack up all this stuff so we can take that hike and work off this food?"

His grin warmed her. "Good idea." Watching his hands with those long, tapered fingers as he helped clear the table, she wondered what it would feel like to have him massage her entire body.

Sheesh! Get a grip, woman.

They soon had everything packed up and stowed inside his trunk.

He surveyed the area. "Which trail? Besides this one, there's also Goliath and Mount Evans trails."

"The Chicago Lakes Trail is nice, as long as we don't hike to the end."

After they did some warm-up stretches using the bench of the table, she stood again. "Follow me." She started toward the lake and heard the crunch of pulverized gravel behind her. A smile broke out on her face. Normally, she wouldn't be comfortable having a guy checking out her backside while hiking and would insist he go first. But this was Kristoffer. He wasn't the least bit interested in her butt.

Kristoffer tried to take in the breathtaking scenery of blue sky, willowy reeds growing along the banks of the equally blue lake, and bristlecone pines and towering evergreens surrounding them, but hard as he tried, he could *not* take his eyes off the mesmerizing sway of Pamela's hips as she strolled along the trail in front of him. Her slacks encased her sweet cheeks with no visible panty line. Did that mean she wasn't wearing panties? Or did she wear a thong?

What the fuck was he thinking about her rounded assets for?

Because you're not dead yet.

Says who? He'd been dead in that department for years. And as long as Tori remained alive, he intended to remain shut down sexually.

Besides, Pamela was anything but a love interest. Determined not to ruin a nice afternoon with a newfound and much-needed friend, he forced himself to gaze out over the lake toward the mountains. Unfortunately, with little success at banishing the image of her ass from his mind.

His awareness of her would only get worse now. Why had he suggested helping her work on her focus?

As the image of a naked Pamela kneeling before him awaiting his guidance flashed across his mind, he banished it.

I'm not ready to train her.

Could he propose exercises that wouldn't require him to be in the same place with her? Perhaps. But not at first. They were together now. Why not start today?

"We're only going to hike for an hour or so because I don't want you attempting the steep parts yet, but this would be a good time for you to start working on your concentration skills."

She turned and cocked her head. "How so?"

"As you walk along, I want you to look for specific vegetation and animals until you have a list of ten items. Then you'll recite them to me when you reach that number."

Pamela's smile took his breath away. "Sounds good!" She pivoted on the ball of her foot and proceeded on the trail, scanning left and right. He watched her hands as she seemed to count off the items.

Willing himself to simply enjoy this hike and his brief respite from real life, he followed. Something drew him back into the past. Perhaps a bird's call or the sound of the water lapping against the bank. Growing up, the times he'd spent with Gunnar at their grandfather's house in Norway had almost always been spent outside in various Viking-inspired adventures. A far cry from his sedate city life in Connecticut with his mother, although his proximity to the coastal waters off New London had led him on some adventures of his own as a teen. His friend, Jeremy, owned a sailboat, and the two of them had sailed out to Fishers Island once a week in good weather.

Tori never cared for spending time outdoors. Thoughts of his wife dumped a bucket of ice-cold water on him, as usual.

When Pamela stopped in her tracks, he nearly plowed into her. She turned and raised a finger to her lips to keep him quiet before pointing several dozen feet ahead of them. A mule deer drank at the bank of the lake near the trail. They shared the peaceful sight for several moments until something spooked the animal, and it sniffed the air before darting back into the safety of the woods.

"Beautiful," Pamela said.

He found himself staring at the fiery streaks in her strawberry blonde hair, forgetting all about the deer. "Definitely."

She turned to him and smiled, oblivious to where his mind had strayed. "Don't you love it up here?" She didn't wait for him to respond. "If I could move out of the city, I'd do so in a heartbeat."

He hated to end her revealing ramblings, but clearly, she'd lost her focus. "What number did you get to with the deer?"

Her eyes opened wide. "Oh! I lost count—but I can remember. Let me see." Holding her hands in front of her, she ticked off on her fingers what she'd noticed. "Ducks; bristlecone pine; mushroom—or maybe it was a toadstool; a gum wrapper—burns me up that someone would toss litter away on a nature trail; a squawking Steller's jay—I wonder if it was the same one who joined us for our picnic," she said, glancing up at him.

Kristoffer couldn't hold back his laugh.

"What's so funny?"

"Did you keep up the running commentary while making your observations, too?"

Her eyes opened wider, and she scowled. "See what I mean? I just can't stay focused!"

"Well, tell me the rest of the list now—without the sidebars."

She switched hands. "Number six was…oh, yeah, a broken branch across the trail; and seven, the mule deer!"

The smile on her face made him smile, too, which made it hard for him to chastise her, but she'd asked him to help her focus. He forced himself to grow stern. "You fell short by three. I want you to start over at one as we continue our hike back to the car—no repeated items." He motioned her to precede him.

"Yes, Sir." She didn't sound particularly happy, but he knew she didn't like to fail at anything she attempted, especially when following the instructions of a Dom. Apparently, any Dom could elicit such feelings, even one who'd been in mothballs for years.

They hiked along in silence, passing another hiker and his dog about ten minutes in, but she didn't stop or become distracted beyond giving the man a cursory wave.

Suddenly, she spun around and graced him with her beautiful smile. Without preamble or counting on her fingers, she recited, "Daisy, lake, fence, man fishing, aspens, rocks, hiker, dog, clouds, and junipers."

"Good job! You nailed it."

She beamed at him. "I did! Mainly because I didn't want to disappoint you again, but I also needed to prove to myself I could do it." She closed the gap between them and threw her arms around him. He couldn't help but return the hug. "Thanks, Kristoffer. I'm going to enjoy working on these exercises with you."

Her arms around his waist left him speechless with a huge knot in his throat. She was tiny, half a foot shorter than Tori, but soft in all the right places. With reluctance, he nudged her away while he still could.

"Let's head back to the car and drive up to the peak."

She nodded. "I'd love to!"

She'd bombarded his senses during the picnic and hike. Were there acceptable degrees of companionship that didn't cross that line for a married man and another woman? If he lusted in his heart and mind, some believed that as wrong as having an affair. When Tori had been aware of her surroundings, he'd never strayed.

But Tori's gone, and I'm still here.

Not that he was ready to rejoin the dating scene. He hadn't been there in twenty years, not since meeting Tori.

He hoped Pamela would eventually find someone who could give her everything she needed. Someone who would treat her the way she deserved. If he ever caught wind that anyone had done anything to hurt her, he'd step in and set things right. He felt protective of Pamela, much like a brother might be for a younger sister perhaps.

Don't kid yourself. A brother doesn't ogle his sister's ass the way you have hers the past hour.

He'd better tamp down his sexualized thoughts so he wouldn't have to give up spending times like this with her. He just needed to get himself under control and stop—

"Are you okay, Kristoffer?"

He blinked back to the present and realized she'd stopped near the lake to look over the split-rail fence. "Sorry. Had my mind on something else." *Some*one *else. Two someones, actually. You and my wife.* He should be heading over to the nursing home soon. Not that Tori would be missing him, but he suddenly missed her. *Needed* her.

No, he'd promised Pamela a drive to the summit, and he was a man of his word. It didn't matter when he got to the facility. Nothing would have changed.

Pamela made no move to continue their hike. "We can go back now if—"

He reached out and pressed his index finger against her lips to silence her. Warm. Soft. He pulled his hand away as if he'd touched a blazing wood-burning stove. Dangerous territory. "And disappoint all those goats and sheep waiting for us up there?"

The light rekindled in Pamela's eyes making him feel elated and despicable at the same time. Guilt won out. Here he was enjoying life and the world around him while the woman he'd sworn his love, protection, and loyalty to forever had been denied everything. His inability to protect Tori tore at his conscience, leaving an ache in his chest where his heart had been once upon a time.

Why did it seem to hurt more now than it had in years past?

Clearly, he wasn't as morally strong a man as he once thought. His greatest fear was that it wouldn't take much for him to behave unforgivably and hurt his wife. He shouldn't give in to the temptation of being around this vibrant woman who rekindled something inside him that was better left dormant.

But you can't hurt Tori. She's long past knowing or caring what you do.

He motioned Pamela to precede him on the trail, and they returned to the parking lot. Could he slam the door on something that might bring some light back into his life?

Yes. I have to.

How about if he kept his emotions under a tight leash while indulging his dormant Dominant self again? It had been too long since he'd been able to feel the satisfaction that only came from guiding and nurturing a submissive. Pamela probably would be willing.

But was he able?

They drove to the summit in near silence, stopping a few times to see the sheep and goats along the roadside. Before they exited the car in the parking lot at the top, he said, "New assignment. I want you to focus on one sense now—hearing. Tell me the first five sounds you hear as soon as you reach number five."

They hadn't walked a minute and were still yards from the lookout before she reached out to halt his steps. "Wind, voices, footsteps, the bleating of that goat standing on the rocks by the restrooms, and tires crunching the loose stones on the pavement."

"Excellent! I'm proud of you!"

She beamed at his praise. God, he'd missed giving a submissive joy merely by telling her she'd done a good job.

Could he turn his back on Pamela after she'd accepted his offer?

Hell, no.

"You've got short-term focus. Next time, we're going to work on your focus over a longer period of time."

"I'm ready!"

He couldn't wait to continue working with her on these exercises. He'd need to give future ones more thought and preparation.

"How about tomorrow evening? We'll work at my place, where you'll be bombarded by things you aren't familiar with, which will challenge you even more."

CHAPTER EIGHT

D espite some butterflies in her stomach about having Kristoffer training her, even in this nonsexual and non-kinky way, Pamela couldn't help but think they'd turned a corner today at Echo Lake. He seemed more relaxed driving back to the city than he had been when he'd picked her up.

Before dropping her off, he'd arranged to take her out to dinner tomorrow and then back to his place for another round of focusing exercises. She couldn't wait, but hoped she'd do better this time than she had on the hiking trail.

After a night of restless sleep, she spent the morning exchanging e-mails with vendors and updating Kristoffer on her progress. He said Gunnar planned to leave for Afghanistan next week. She hoped some of the equipment would be onboard that first flight.

At Kristoffer's suggestion—okay, it sounded more like a command—she took a nap in the afternoon. She must have been sleepier than she thought, because she slept for more than two hours. Still plenty of time before he'd be here, so she checked the status on the things they'd ordered and let Gunnar know what to expect and the weight of each item so he could plan accordingly.

Finally, the time arrived to dress. He'd told her business casual was fine, so she wore a long-sleeved cotton sweater and black slacks. The intercom buzzed a few minutes early.

"Be right down."

After turning on the living room light so the apartment wouldn't appear deserted, she locked the door and skipped down the stairs. She hadn't looked forward to anything so much since…well, yesterday and their picnic. She opened the door to find him standing there dressed in khakis and a tweed sport coat covering a polo shirt. The man wore clothes better than anyone she knew.

"Hi. You look great," he said.

"I'm well-rested and ready to go! You don't look so bad yourself."

He cupped his hand around her elbow and led her to the car. In no time, they were at the restaurant, a steakhouse about halfway to his condo. He wasted no time once they'd placed their orders.

"Tell me, what do you hope to gain from our work tonight?"

Perhaps he should know what he was getting into first. "I can't focus on a scene or the Dom I'm with more than a few minutes, I can get a little bratty, and I have a need to know what's coming, not just what's expected of me."

"That takes all the fun out of a scene for the Dom, you know."

She nodded. "Believe me, I do. I know on an intellectual level that I'm supposed to let my Dom or Top set the course. But I spend so much time worrying about whether I'm pleasing him that I'm unable to immerse myself into the scene."

"I can't speak for other Doms, but with me, I expect you to follow instructions. Of course, if it's not something you're comfortable with, use a safeword, and we'll talk more. Can you surrender your strong will at that level?"

She certainly hadn't been able to so far. "I'll try."

"That's all I can ask." His smile made her anxious for this evening's activities to begin.

She didn't remember much more about the meal, other than they talked about things unrelated to what he planned to do tonight, even though that was all she could think about.

"Tell me what you just heard."

Heard? He'd been talking about the ultrasound machine, hadn't he? "That you were e-mailed by the company sending the ultrasound equipment, and they thought it would arrive in time."

He shook his head. "That was five minutes ago. Where did your mind go in the meantime?"

Where, indeed? "I was thinking about tonight."

"Why are you worrying about what's to come later when you should be focusing on the present?"

Why, indeed? She'd failed already, and they hadn't even started. Or had they? Apparently so!

"I'm sorry, Kr…what should I call you tonight?"

"You just flitted from one thought to another again."

"See? I told you this is a problem."

"To get your mindset on submission—rather than simple mind exercises—you will refer to me as Roar, my scene name, or as Sir for the rest of the evening and when we are working on these issues in the future."

"Yes, Sir, Roar." The name sent a shiver down her spine. She wondered what was behind it. Sounded so primal. Like a tiger on the prowl.

He pulled her back to the conversation. "Until you can turn off your overactive mind, you're going to struggle to find fulfillment with anyone in the lifestyle."

"I agree. That's why I accepted your offer of help." How well would she be able to perform for Roar? What would be in it for him?

"If you intend to do this, I need you to pay attention only to my instructions and your responding actions. Focus." How had he known her mind had strayed just then? She'd never worked with such an astute Dom and would need to stay on her toes.

Kristoffer settled the check, and they drove to his condo where he parked in his spot near the elevator. Inside his penthouse, he took care of Noma's needs before directing Pamela to the living room. "Have a seat on the sofa. We're going to watch TV. Hope you like *Star Trek*."

"Love it! Any and all versions. You're a Trekkie, too?" She'd been right before then.

"Yes. I didn't realize you were as well."

"I've even seen reruns of all the original series."

This exercise should be a piece of cake. She might even catch something she'd missed while watching the show in the past due to her attention difficulties. She got into her headspace as submissive for the scene.

Roar hadn't taken his seat yet and asked, "Can I get you something to drink before we start?"

"No, thanks. I'm good."

He joined her, sitting a few feet away on the couch. "I want you to focus on the screen until I turn it off. Then I'm going to quiz you at the end."

Sitting side by side, they watched the "Genesis" episode from *The Next Generation* series. This was one of her favorites, where Picard and Data return to the ship to find the crew devolving into primitive creatures.

She paid close attention to which creature each crew member changed into, counted the number of containers in the scene where Picard asked Data what he could do to counteract the virus before it took over his body, and stayed riveted to similar trivial details throughout. When Roar turned off the set with the remote, she prepared to begin her quiz. He stood, but she kept her gaze downward out of respect to his dominance.

Maybe they weren't in a full-blown Dom/sub relationship, but during these exercises, she'd try to behave like someone who had offered her submission.

"What did Data say Captain Picard would devolve into?"

"Possibly some early primate similar to a lemur or a pygmy marmoset." She grinned remembering the show and the response the captain had given to that prediction.

"Very good. What was the second commercial played during the first break?"

"Commercial?" She hadn't paid any attention to the commercials, although she'd wondered why he hadn't fast-forwarded through them since the show had been DVR'd. She'd thought perhaps he'd lost his own focus. And wasn't that about when Noma had decided to curl up beside her on the couch? Later on, he did use the remote to skip the commercials, but she hadn't paid attention to that first set at all. She'd shifted her focus to the cat while trying to remember some of the details of the first segment.

"I'm sorry, Sir. I wasn't paying attention to the commercials. I thought you wanted me to focus on the show."

"I asked you to focus on the *screen*, not merely the TV program."

She thought back over his instructions. "Yes, Sir, you did. I'm sorry I put my focus in the wrong place."

"Did you *put* it somewhere else—or merely let it be drawn away from you?"

"I drifted, Sir." An old Mae West joke popped into her mind, and she grinned.

"Where did you let your mind wander just now?"

Drat. "Sorry, Sir. I was remembering the punch line of Mae West's Snow White joke. I'm an old movie buff, too."

"Remain seated." He didn't sound as though he was interested in what kind of movies she liked. He walked in the direction of the kitchen, leaving her to wonder what he was going to do. When he returned to the room, he stayed out of sight. She heard the sound of something like tiny grains or kernels being shaken in a box.

"Stand and turn toward me. Eyes are to remain on me."

Keeping her gaze on him, she crossed the room until she stood a yard or so in front of him near the entrance to the kitchen. He didn't appear angry, at least. She noticed he held a box of instant rice in his hand.

"By trying to anticipate what I might ask you instead of paying attention, you failed to remain in the moment for the duration of this exercise."

"Correct, Sir. I didn't follow instructions and lost my focus." Did he intend to punish her? With rice? They hadn't really spoken about the consequences of her inability to obey. She thought he'd just challenge her to something harder as he escalated his training regimen the way he had at the lake yesterday. What did he have in mind?

"Pamela, look at me." She brought his face back into focus. "I see you've let your mind drift again trying to figure out how I plan to discipline you."

"Yes, Sir." How could he tell? Besides, wouldn't any sub have been curious about the same thing in this moment?

"I want you to tell me your safewords—one to slow down and one to stop altogether."

Safewords? This sounded serious. Her mind blanked. "Yellow and red, Sir." Those were the most commonly used ones, but she wasn't feeling particularly creative at the moment.

He extended his hand, and she took a few steps to place hers in his. Warm. He squeezed her hand as if to reassure her. Did she look that frightened? Actually, not exactly frightened, but definitely concerned.

"I want you to kneel on this towel and focus solely on your body's responses until I tell you to stop."

Kneel? That shouldn't be too difficult. He guided her into position on the floor, and she suddenly realized what the rice had been for. Dozens of little pellets were digging into her kneecaps.

"I'm going to describe for you my position number three now. Remember it because you may need it again." They were advancing quickly if he was giving her submissive positions already. "Hands on your elbows in a box hold behind you. Back straight. Eyes open and forward. Ass in a straight line with your back."

She maneuvered into the position and stared at the wall in front of her, which was thankfully blank. The lack of distractions would help.

Very little time passed before her knees began to protest their punishment, but she remained in position and placed her entire focus on her throbbing kneecaps. After a while, the pain there dulled a bit, but then she noticed the strain in her shoulders from the way she was clutching her hands and arms.

A bead of sweat rolled down the side of her face. How long would she be required to maintain this position?

Don't think about that. Just focus on the now!

She had no concept of how much time had passed when a swat to her left thigh from what felt like a ruler or yardstick brought her mind into focus again. "Back straight. Ass tucked in."

When had she slouched? She resumed the proper position. The sound of a clock ticking nearby distracted her, so she shifted her knees to bring the pain back into sharper focus. She didn't want to have him catch her out of compliance again. After what felt like hours, but was probably less than half an hour, she wiggled some life back into her fingers.

"Are your fingers numb?" he asked immediately. She'd forgotten he was watching her.

"A little."

"Lower your hands to your sides. Is anything else tingling or numb?"

When he spoke to her like that, she felt a jolt to her clit, but knew that wasn't what he meant. "No, Sir." The last thing she needed to do was get turned on by Kristoffer Larson, a married and emotionally unavailable man. If he suspected she had those kinds of feelings, he'd put an end to their working together—not just on these focusing activities, but also on acquiring equipment for the hospital. She couldn't risk that.

Another swat to her other thigh brought her mind back from its meanderings. How did he know when her mind drifted? Must be reading something in her body language. How had he learned to read her so quickly?

She wished her knees would grow numb, or that he'd let her stand up and escape the rice.

More time passed. Roar moved away, and she heard the television go on.

Focus on your knees!

She shut out the sound from the set and kept her focus on her aching patellas. Not all that difficult, actually. The cocoon of pain now let her focus on nothing else. After an unknown period of time, the pain receded.

A warm hand cupped her chin and tilted her head backward until she saw Roar smiling down at her. "Well done, Sprite." She wondered where he'd picked up that odd nickname, but assumed it was because she was so tiny compared to him. "Especially those last ten minutes."

His face conveying his pleasure with her set off a euphoria inside her, and she smiled back. "Thank you, Sir."

He extended his hand and helped her to her feet, but when her knees buckled, he scooped her up into his arms. "Whoa, there."

The change of position made her lightheaded for a moment, and she rested her head on his shoulder, waiting for the spell to pass. The pain in her knees came rushing back as he carried her over to the couch.

"I'm dropping rice all over your floor," she remarked, wondering why something like that would seem important even as she said it.

"I'll vacuum it up later."

He plopped into the cushions and continued to cradle her back while using his other hand to rub the ache and remaining rice pellets from her knees. She wondered how much worse they might have hurt if she hadn't been wearing her slacks, but decided it best not to think thoughts of being naked in front of him again while sitting on Roar's lap.

"How are your knees now?"

"Better, thanks. Lesson learned."

"Habits can't be broken in a matter of a few exercises, but it appeared to me that, once you forced your mind to focus, you didn't let anything break your concentration—not the television or Noma or me making noise."

"I did! I'm amazed I could stand the pain so long."

"When you truly let yourself go, you'll release endorphins that will produce a morphine-like high. I didn't want you to go that far, because you haven't built that level of trust in me yet. A submissive can be taken advantage of in that state with someone who isn't safe, so be careful who you play with."

"Master Anderson was warning me off certain types, too. I suppose it's no different from the creeps in the dating scene, but wouldn't it be nice if everyone in the lifestyle wanted what was best for his or her partner?"

Too bad Roar couldn't be her Dom for more than these concentration exercises. She'd love to explore more with him, but would settle for what he could give.

"It's going to take more work, but as long as you're willing to try,

I'm happy to help. Would you like to continue?"

"Oh, definitely!"

"Good. This is enough for tonight, but your next assignment will be to sign up for a web site I'm going to e-mail you in the morning where you can do some brain-training exercises in your spare time."

"I've heard about a site like that in commercials. Obviously not the commercials that ran tonight."

He laughed. "True."

They sat in silence a moment as she wondered if they'd have any more face-to-face exercises.

"Pamela, we haven't talked much about doing concentration exercises within the context of a BDSM scene. Since that's your ultimate goal, how would you feel about that?"

It was as if he'd read her mind. "I'd have no problem with it, if you don't." He didn't say anything. Taking this step would be a lot harder for him than for her. "If you'd rather we not go down that road—"

He pressed his finger against her lips to cut off her words. "You, little Sprite, need to stop worrying about your Dom and trust that he can take care of himself."

She reached up to stroke the scruff on his cheek. When she began to feel a familiar tingle between her legs, she pulled her hand away. "You've taken a lot of giant leaps beyond your comfort zone in recent days—maybe even weeks. I know it can't be easy for you, so I can't help but be concerned."

"I have no intention of straying from my marriage vows. Again, you let me worry about that. However, there are any number of activities we can do that would put you in a BDSM frame of mind without crossing my lines of honor."

She nodded, wondering what his limits might be.

"Now, before we go any further, I need to learn more about you, Sprite, so I can know how best to tackle some of the hurdles that have kept you from achieving your goals." He took a deep breath, as though crossing some threshold into new territory. "If you had to name one man from your past who shattered your trust, who would that be?"

A clock ticked away at a deafening clip somewhere in the kitchen as she tried to think of an answer. *Nada.* "I really don't know how to answer that."

"Is it that you don't want to say or that you don't have an answer?"

"The latter. Like any woman my age, I've had my disappointments with men, but none ever hurt me." *Not intentionally, at least.*

"Who were you thinking about just then?"

Busted yet again. *How* did he do that? He wasn't a mind reader, so her body must be sending out signals to him.

"The Dom from my last relationship a few years ago. We weren't looking for the same dynamic and moved way too fast. Now I'm just relieved we broke it off before things went too far." She'd licked her wounds for at least two years before being able to move on. "He was probably as confused about what he wanted in the lifestyle then as I am now, although he seems to have found what he wanted." She was quick to add, "And I'm happy for him!"

"So you've kept in touch?"

"Not really. We had some mutual friends from the Masters at Arms Club, but I did see him a couple of years ago. He wanted closure, I guess."

"Did you get closure?"

"Yeah. He's a really nice guy and I'm sure perfect for his new submissive, but just not the right one for me. I think over time, we'd have had regrets, so we both dodged a bullet by calling an end to it before we went too far. Next time, I'm not rushing into anything."

"Good girl." His praise sped up her pulse rate. "I think if we're going to work on your focus in BDSM scenes, then we ought to put you into a real scene and see how you do. Would you have a problem playing at that club? It's one of the best around."

She lifted her gaze to meet his before she realized she hadn't been given permission and that they were still in their scene. She stared at her lap. "You'd go with me?"

"Of course. How else will I be able to work with you?"

What on earth happened to him out on that hike? Clearly, he'd had some kind of epiphany, but it had all happened unbeknownst to her as she'd blithely walked along the trail trying to focus.

He pinched her thigh. "Still with me?"

She rolled her eyes. She'd lost focus again. "Sorry, Roar." Was she ready to go back to Marc's club? Only one way to find out. "Whatever you think best, Sir. I would have no problem going to the club." *With you.*

"Good." He continued. "Gunnar's dungeon would work, too, but I don't like messing with the security system there when he's away. Besides, that's a long drive, and we could spend our time more efficiently closer to home."

"I'm not a member of the club any longer."

"No worries. We'll get tested tomorrow so we can show them our results. We ought to have our probationary memberships approved by Wednesday. Since we aren't planning to play with others or exchange bodily fluids, I'm sure they won't have any issues."

She nodded to show she heard him, but didn't say anything.

"What else do you do that you think might have annoyed your Doms?" He sounded as though he was biting back a grin. Did he think her a brat who did these things intentionally?

How to explain it to put herself in a better light than that? "When I go into scenes with a Dom I don't know well, it's like walking in a minefield. I do and say what I think will please him, but I always manage to screw up. I seem to have this need to know what's coming at all times."

Now he did laugh. "Sorry, but we Doms want our subs to be off guard—and to push their limits."

"I know." She really must have been a disappointment.

Soon, they were discussing her limits. He didn't pull out a checklist, but no doubt memorized each as they went over a number of kinks. In the yes column, she had flogging, spanking, paddling, bondage and other restraints, blindfolds and other sensory deprivation, wax play, sensation play, and more. Her no-way-in-hell list included knife play, asphyxiation, bestiality, golden showers, other unsanitary practices, and she was certain she left out any number of activities she couldn't think of at the moment—or just never heard of.

By mutual agreement, sexual intercourse was off the table, but she wondered if everything sexual was off limits. "How do you feel about oral, Sir?"

"I wouldn't be comfortable with it. How do you feel about manual stimulation as a means of reward?"

Her clitoris liked that idea. "I'd be very good in order to receive such a reward. But I don't want to be selfish, so I'd want to…"

He pinched her thigh again to quiet her. "I'm able to take care of my own needs in that department. Don't try to top or manipulate me. I'm not like the Doms you've played with in the past."

No, indeed, Sir, you are not. He'd downplayed how involved he'd been with Tori. Where had he picked up his knowledge—Gunnar? If so, no doubt Roar would prove to be a high-caliber Dom with amazing skills. She shivered.

"Cold?"

"No, Sir. I just wanted to say I'm sorry for topping. Giving up control isn't easy for me."

"I've actually been giving that a lot of thought. I've been puzzled about your inability to concentrate during a BDSM scene while you clearly can stay focused at a high level in the operating room or while working with me on the hospital equipment project. What do you suppose is the difference when it comes to doing so during a power-exchange scene?"

She'd never really analyzed it before. "I'm not sure. Maybe it's because I don't like surprises."

"And you don't like surprises because…" He let the statement hang in the air for her to finish.

What was different between performing surgery and being involved in a kink scene? "Well, during surgery or while working with my patients, I'm the one in charge. Even when the unexpected happens, I'm able to deal with it by making choices and taking actions that can affect the outcome."

"How does that compare to being a submissive in a BDSM scene?"

"I'm no longer in control."

"Oh, the submissive maintains all of the control in a scene. You have the safeword, remember."

"True. But I have to surrender to someone else's authority."

"Exactly as it should be if you're submissive and with a Dom worthy of your surrender. The two of you will already have held negotiations, and you will have agreed to receive whatever he wishes to give, whether it's some sort of play or discipline to help you improve in some area. Given your submissive desire to please, I predict you won't use a safeword unless you hit a trigger or he's ignored your limits."

"Probably not. I suppose where I'm hung up is in not knowing what's coming but being expected to respond in the appropriate way even if I don't know the Dom's preferences. That puts me in a vulnerable position."

"The only thing your Dom expects you to do is show respect, obedience, and attentiveness. That vulnerability coupled with a deep trust you have for the Dom—well, after you've been together long enough to establish that—is where the magic happens, Sprite." He tweaked her nose, but had her mind spinning. He made everything so clear. "There aren't any absolutes in the lifestyle unless you're in a dynamic with lots of set protocols. Even in those relationships, the Dom's will spell out his expectations ahead of time so you know how to respond—*if* you need to respond at all. Most of the time, your only responsibility to your Dom is to stay in the moment. If that doesn't give you a sense of excitement and fulfillment, then perhaps you're a closet Domme."

Was she? *No way.*

He didn't wait for her to react to his words. "I think we'll know more after we conduct a few more exercises and scenes. With a little work, I'm confident we'll find ways for you to improve your focus."

Cuddled here in his arms, she felt as if they could conquer anything they set their minds to.

"Because Gunnar's always mentored me in the lifestyle, would I have permission to seek his advice and use your name, or would you prefer to remain anonymous?"

She'd been right about where Roar had learned his skills as a Dom.

"Before Gunnar suggested that I go to the academy, I'd asked him about mentoring me based on Heidi's recommendation, so he knows I'm in the lifestyle. Feel free to discuss my case." She grinned because she made it sound as though she were his patient. "Sometimes two heads are better than one." Besides, she might present problems requiring ideas from both of the Doms.

"I ask that you remain open to surprises and the unexpected while we work together. Any power-exchange partnership, temporary or long-term, will have an element of the unknown to it. Some find that exhilarating. How about you?"

"It's different for Dominants. You guide the scene and can steer it in any direction you wish. There are no scary surprises for you unless something goes wrong."

He chuckled. "Your opinion on how Doms think is based on how many firsthand experiences?"

She blinked and drew a deep breath. "Two—and one was so long ago I'm not even sure he was a Dom. Neither of us knew what we were doing."

"But you still were only in the headspace of the submissive, so stop presuming to know how a Dom thinks."

"True, Sir."

"There are times when no amount of planning is going to eliminate all problems, but I and other Doms do try to minimize unwelcome surprises."

They sat in silence a few moments before he spoke again. "I'm going to give you a new assignment to start tomorrow. Keep a journal. In your first entries, write about what you hope to achieve as a submissive. We'll stop at the drug store and pick up a notebook for you to use, because I don't want you distracted by the Internet while journaling on your computer. Besides, some think the mind is easier to tap into when we write by hand."

"Yes, Sir." Was that why he always had pen and paper in meetings and took his notes the old-fashioned way?

"You'll share pertinent journal entries with me, but I'll let you choose what information you want to share aloud with me. So be honest with yourself. Pour your soul into those pages."

"I'll try, Roar, Sir."

"I'm confident you will. During your second day of journaling, I want you to look back on all the relationships you've had over the course of your life with male authority figures, including your dad, grandfathers, uncles, teachers, bosses, big brothers, Doms—you name it—and determine how they contributed to your desire to serve and submit."

"I don't have any big brothers, and my grandfathers were both deceased before I knew them."

"I'm merely citing suggestions. It's up to you to figure out who qualifies as significant and then write an analysis of your relationship with each one. What moments stand out in your mind? How did each one make you feel as a girl or later as a woman? In what ways did each let you down? In what ways did they build you up?"

Two journaling assignments, plus the brain-training site. Nothing sounded terribly difficult, but it all sounded solitary. When would she spend time with him again?

Their session tonight must be nearing an end. He motioned her to take her seat beside him on the couch again. They chatted more as Roar tried to determine more of her likes, dislikes, limits, and preferences. Added to the no-way list—severe pain, bloodletting, and being passed over to others for scenes without her consent.

When they'd exhausted their negotiations, he said, "I think I'd better be getting you home. First, repeat back to me what you heard me give you as assignments over the next two days?"

"You said you'd be e-mailing me tomorrow with the link to a web site you want me to go on and do brain-training exercises. Also tomorrow, you want me to start a journal, and in my first entry, I'm to list why I identify as a submissive and what I hope to gain from a relationship with a Dominant. Lastly, you asked me to journal the day after tomorrow on the men in my life from childhood on and analyze what each might have contributed to my desire to serve."

"*Significant* men in your life."

"Oh, yes; a much shorter list." She smiled.

"Good job of listening." He stood. "I think we've accomplished enough tonight."

She hated for their time to come to an end, but stood as well. "Mind if I use the bathroom before we leave?"

"No, of course not. Remember the way?"

She nodded. To both of them, actually. She opted for the one at the opposite end of the condo near his office. In another configuration, his office would have been a guest bedroom, she supposed.

After she joined him again, she followed him to the elevator and then to his car. True to his word, they stopped at an all-night pharmacy, and she bought a spiral-bound notebook. Nothing fancy, given the selection, but with lots of pages for her to fill with her thoughts and assignments. If she enjoyed journaling, she might go to a bookstore and find something she could relate to more for her next journal.

On the drive back to Aurora, she realized he hadn't mentioned anything about seeing her tomorrow as Kristoffer or Roar, but wouldn't ask. He'd inform her when he was ready.

She'd just have to become used to surprises from him.

"You've agreed to do *what?*" Hearing the shock in Gunnar's voice through his cell phone caught him off guard before he grinned. Kristoffer rarely did anything spontaneous anymore. Clearly, his cousin hadn't seen this coming. Who could have?

"You heard me. I'm going to train Pamela in some aspects of the lifestyle, namely focus and concentration. We began working yesterday and had a longer session tonight."

"About time. How'd it go?"

"Like getting back on a bicycle."

"Good for you. Even though you may not have had a play partner in a while, once a Dom, always a Dom. With your skill and patience, you'll be perfect for what Pamela needs."

"But I can already see that I'm going to need your help."

"With what?"

"Put in a good word with Grant about expediting our club applications. I'll submit the preliminary test results and paperwork for us both tomorrow, but I'd like to use the club's facilities rather than do this here at my condo. I'm not equipped for anything beyond the rudimentary scene."

"With FarFar's bed, are you kidding? That's a rigger's dream."

Kristoffer grew serious. "I don't think playing in my bedroom would be wise. This will be a strictly platonic relationship."

Silence ensued on the other end until Gunnar spoke, "Keep your options open, Kris." The words echoed the ones he'd given Pamela earlier tonight. "You've merely been hibernating, but spring has come, Cuz. Time to wake up. Come out of your cave."

Kristoffer sighed. Trouble was, there would never be another spring for Kristoffer. "This training will be rudimentary. I can't become involved on an emotional level. You know that."

"I know nothing of the kind."

Kristoffer didn't intend to go into whether he was available or not. "I'll merely be trying to help her improve her focus. I did serve as a Top to a few people in your dungeon, you may recall, without cheating on my wife. I'm not looking for a submissive." Especially not one like Pamela whom he could really become hooked on.

"Kris, you aren't doing yourself or Tori any favors by locking yourself up in a self-imposed monastery. You both got dealt a load of shit, but have to ruck on."

"Look, I didn't call you for an Army training lecture."

"Sorry, comes with the territory. What you're going through was a lot longer and harder than a ruck march, but you've been bogged down in limbo for four years. You aren't a widower, but aren't really married, either."

"I'm very much married."

"On paper, maybe, but Tori isn't a full participant any longer. It takes two to make a marriage, Kris. But before you jump down my throat, nobody said anything about replacing Tori."

"Don't tell me how to be married. You have no clue." Kristoffer regretted his words immediately.

A tenseness entered Gunnar's voice. "Not for a lack of trying. I know all about waiting around for someone who may never be available to me. But I'm not going to become a monk in the meantime. Heidi knew that when she made her choice to move halfway around the globe."

"Tori didn't have a choice. I took that away from her."

"Goddamn it, man, don't you fucking go there. You were both involved in an accident. A fucking *accident*. No one was at fault."

"I was too tired to drive. I shouldn't have been behind the wheel. Or should have headed home earlier that night."

"Well, pardon me, Saint Kristoffer, for thinking all this time you were a mere mortal like the rest of us."

"I nearly killed my wife! Shit, for all intents and purposes, I *did* kill her. Until you've done that to someone *you* care about, you have no bloody clue."

Gunnar became silent again. *Fuck.* Kristoffer rubbed his eyes, wishing he could take the words back. "Sorry, man. You know I didn't mean that. I'm not thinking clearly these days."

Not since a strawberry-blonde sprite invaded my world.

But Gunnar lived with his own survivor guilt after putting his paramilitary troops in harm's way years ago, just a few months before Tori's accident. Not everyone on his team had made it back alive. One loss had been particularly difficult for him. Kristoffer had expected Gunnar to shut down his contracting business as a result, but thought his cousin had gotten over the tragic loss of one of his top operatives—a man who had served in Special Forces with him. But Gunnar had come back with a vengeance, although as far as Kristoffer knew, he'd yet to avenge the loss of that man.

"Pull your head out of your fourth point of contact, Kris, and you might start thinking a whole lot more clearly." He relaxed, hearing the combativeness in Gunnar's voice as a positive sign he wasn't dwelling on the past. "You need someone else to think about for a change, even if it's temporary and platonic."

He hoped he could keep this platonic. Then why was his mind playing tricks on him again? An image of Pamela naked and restrained to his bed made his cock harden. He slammed the lid down on desire before unleashing any more impossible dreams.

No, it wasn't that he didn't trust *her* to remain platonic. She had never crossed the line. The problem was he didn't trust himself. All these years, he'd been strong and faithful to Tori, but that had come crashing down the night he'd seen Pamela standing naked and proud in front of a class at the academy.

Like a fairy sprite. Or a fiery goddess.

On the other hand, the time he'd spent with Pamela these past few weeks did make him feel good. Too good.

Which was wrong on so many levels. He shouldn't be enjoying life with another woman when his wife was doomed to the hell he'd put her in.

Time to change the subject. "When do you plan to fly out?"

"Wednesday. Oh, a freight delivery was made today at the hangar. One of the items you two ordered."

"Great. E-mail or text me the details, and we'll mark it off the list."

Suddenly, he remembered what else he'd wanted to ask Gunnar about Pamela's training. "What do you know about working with an alpha sub?"

"Some of my fondest moments have been with an alpha. Does Pamela identify as such?"

"She thinks so, but I don't know the first thing about how to work with one."

"Prepare for a power struggle, but keep reminding her who's in charge. Over time, she'll come to respect you and find you worthy of her surrender, but it won't come easy."

"I doubt I'll be working with her that long."

Gunnar sighed. "However long, remember she's used to being in control. Don't let her get away with topping from the bottom."

"Yeah, I've already seen a bit of it, and we've hardly started."

Gunnar laughed. "You may want to add a ball gag to whatever else you think you need when you scene with her."

He understood Gunnar's concern Pamela might top from the bottom, but the thought of gagging her didn't appeal to him. He actually enjoyed talking with her, although most of their conversations had been as peers, not in a Top/bottom dynamic. Of course, he wouldn't do her any favors by permitting her to get away with disrespectful behavior. If she did go on to find a Dom worthy of her, it was doubtful he'd stand for it.

God, delving into the lifestyle again after all this time made him nervous as hell, but he reminded himself he'd been trained by one of the best.

The two ended the call, and Kristoffer spent the next hour lying in bed thinking about the scene he'd like to do with Pamela next Wednesday at the Masters at Arms. A smile spread across his lips.

When his cock grew hard again in anticipation, he took himself in hand as he'd done many times since the night of the tour at the academy.

Bloody hell. I'm screwed. The battle may already be lost.

✧　✧　✧

Pamela chewed on the end of her pen. She'd thought journaling would be a piece of cake, but this second exercise was proving harder than expected. Thinking that her biggest issues stemmed from her disastrous relationship with Marc, she'd been unable to come up with more than a few sentences. Kristoffer had asked her to identify significant authority figures. Had she truly seen Marc as having authority over her? No. She also hadn't surrendered much of herself to him.

She ripped out that page and wadded it up then applied pen to paper again. What other man in her past had influenced her? She'd dated a pitifully small number of guys.

Dad.

That would be a minefield she wasn't sure she wanted to navigate. But Kristoffer's instructions came back loud and clear.

"I want you to look back on all the relationships you've had over the course of your life with male authority figures…and determine how they contributed to your desire to serve and submit."

She couldn't very well say she'd been thorough if she left off the first—and possibly only—man she'd ever loved. Dad was her hero. Brave, handsome, doting—well, when he was home and could be. At least his deployments hadn't taken him away as often as other kids' dads and moms in military service. Her friends on base were in the same boat, and the other dads tried to fill in for them on special occasions.

She decided not to journal about her parents' divorce, choosing not to reopen those wounds. Besides, her unresolved hurt feelings were aimed more toward Mom than Dad. Dad hadn't abandoned her.

Trying to formulate how to write about her dad, she thought back to some of their special moments together.

When I was eight, my dad promised he'd be home for my birthday so we could have a special Teddy Bear tea party. Mom tried to prepare me that he might have to go out on a mission or otherwise not be able to attend, but I set up the party on the deck, wore my best frilly dress, and waited. Mom joined me after what seemed an eternity of waiting and watching for him to come through the door. I'd just poured our first cups of fruit juice when the screen door squeaked and out came my dad in his blue Air Force uniform. So tall and handsome with a huge smile on his face. He apologized for being late, but said nothing would keep him away from our special date. Mom faded into the background, and suddenly, it was the two of us. He made me feel like a princess. I'll never forget that day as long as I live.

Wetness rolling down her cheeks brought her out of the memory. A teardrop had landed on the word princess, smearing it. She dabbed her sleeve on the spot to dry it and smiled.

"My hero."

Too bad everything had to change.

Pamela closed the notebook. She'd delved into the past long enough. She didn't know if this journal entry was going to be what Kristoffer was looking for, but she needed a walk in the fresh air. She'd been cooped up too much today.

Grabbing a heavy sweater, she nearly bounced down the stairs and set off for a walk in the neighborhood. Thoughts of childhood drifted away to be replaced by images of Kristoffer.

What could he learn from her ramblings in her journal that would help?

She shrugged and returned to her apartment and opened the journal again. But instead of delving deeper into her feelings about her dad, her thoughts turned again to Kristoffer. He'd said she would only have to reveal to him what she wanted to from her journal, so she decided to be honest.

Kristoffer, as Roar, has broken through to me like no other Dom. If only our relationship could go somewhere, but that isn't possible. Am I going to be able to let go when the time comes? Or is it already too late for me to move on to someone else when he's finished with my training? Given my crazy life and travel schedule, I suppose I could ask if he'd be interested in a Top/bottom ongoing relationship. Would that be possible, given his vows to Tori?

Would that be fulfilling enough for me? I'm not sure. I don't need marriage and the picket fence, but I do need someone who will be a rock for me. Someone who will be by my side through thick and thin.

Was she wasting her time hoping for something that Kristoffer could never offer?

CHAPTER NINE

K ristoffer called her just before she sat down to lunch on Wednesday.

"I'll pick you up at seven. Dress comfortably. No alcohol today. Eat dinner by six, but nothing that would upset your stomach. We're going to the Masters at Arms Club tonight."

Her heart jumped into her throat. He'd said earlier it might be tonight, but they'd only had the lab work done a few days ago. Sounded as though someone had pulled some strings.

Kristoffer hadn't given her any specific instructions on what to wear—or not wear—only that she be comfortable. After selecting and rejecting half of what resided in her closet, she settled on well-worn jeans and a turtleneck. The less skin she showed the more comfortable she'd be.

When she heard a knock at the door after dinner, she took a deep breath as she checked through the peephole. She'd given Kristoffer his own key to her building to avoid having to buzz him through every visit, but she hadn't taken the giant step of giving him a key to her apartment.

Kristoffer—no, *Roar* now—punctual, as always.

She opened the door and smiled, waving him inside. Before he took a step, his gaze swept over her body from head to toes. He smiled, but didn't say anything. Had he figured out her reason for covering so much of her body from view? Of course, he could demand that she remove anything he wanted. She'd made sure to wear a bra and tank under the turtleneck and panties under the jeans. At least she could delay her exposure a little longer.

"I'll just grab my coat."

"Wait. We aren't leaving yet."

Unsure of herself, she met his gaze and waited for instructions.

"Before we make our first foray into the public eye, I want you to know the protocols I expect you to follow."

She glanced at him and tilted her head before remembering herself. "Yes, Sir."

"First, you will look directly at me only when told to. At all other times, you'll keep your gaze somewhere in the vicinity of my shoes—or feet, if I'm not wearing any.

"Yes, Sir." She assumed a submissive pose with her gaze on the floor between them and her hands clasped behind her back.

"That will give you fewer distractions. I hope."

He didn't sound confident in her ability to focus, but that made her more determined to perform well for him tonight. She'd maintain her full attention on him if it killed her, just as she'd done when kneeling on the rice, well, after a while.

Certain she'd nailed the pose he wanted, she couldn't help but ask, "How's this, Sir?"

"You'll not speak unless asked a question or for your opinion. If I need to convey information to you about any corrections I want to see or anything else, I will. Don't seek approval or praise. When earned, you'll receive it from me. You won't have your hearing cut off, so listen carefully to me and only me tonight. I don't care who else is in the club or what's happening around us. You're with me tonight and will give me your undivided attention. Nothing or no one else matters."

She opened her mouth to say she understood, but clamped it shut again before disobeying him.

"Very good."

He walked into her bedroom and returned to place her only pair of four-inch mules on the floor in front of her. "For now and until we're inside the club, you'll wear these. They'll be easier to remove than your socks and sneakers." He bent down to untie and remove her walking shoes and socks then guided each foot into one of the mules.

She waited to see what other apparel he'd demand she change, but when he held up her leather coat, she slipped her arms inside the sleeves, pleased she could keep herself clothed. For now.

"What are your safewords?"

She'd had a little more time to think about them since their first scene. "I'll be using Jeannie for stop, and Cocoa Beach for my slow-down one."

Roar chuckled. "A fan of *I Dream of Jeannie*, I see. How appropriate."

Appropriate? She smiled a little uncertainly, but didn't say anything because he hadn't asked her a question. She'd envied the sexy genie who won over the handsome Air Force officer with wit and charm, not to mention a few blinks of the eyes, in the syndicated show she'd watched incessantly as a teen.

The drive downtown in his Jag raced by, and soon he cruised up and down the streets of Five Points, searching for a place to park. He slipped into a tight space, parallel parking with ease, and helped her out of the car. Before she could take a step forward, he halted her with his hand on her shoulder, setting off a tingling throughout her body.

He opened the trunk and retrieved what she assumed would be his toy bag, wondering what he'd brought to play with.

As she moved along the broken sidewalk beside him, she found her thoughts consumed with not stumbling while keeping up with Roar's longer strides. When he stopped abruptly, she continued for a couple of steps before realizing it.

"Where did you let your mind roam this time, Sprite?"

"Actually, I was concentrating—only paying more attention to my feet than yours. I didn't want to fall."

His laugh told her she wasn't in trouble. He opened an iron gate and led her inside a small yard in front of a familiar and imposing brick structure. At the top of the steps, he stopped and knocked.

It's been a long time.

More than four years. The door opened, and they were ushered inside the entryway, familiar even with her limited view. The scent of leather assailed her.

A soft-spoken woman asked, "May I have your names, Sir?" She didn't recognize the voice.

He answered for them both. "Yes. Scene names Roar and Sprite."

So Sprite had become her scene name, too. It had certainly grown on her.

"Yes, Mistress Grant has arranged for you to play here tonight." So the intimating Domme was one of those in charge now?

Roar stroked Pamela's cheek, bringing her focus back where it belonged.

I can do this. I will make him proud of me.

He helped remove her coat and handed it to the hostess. Without another word, he guided her toward the entrance to the sunken great room. Remaining mindful of his every step, she followed him down the few stairs. She could see table and chair legs set up much as they had been years ago, but didn't look up to see what changes might have occurred under Grant's directorship.

He led them over to a corner and pulled out a chair. She started to sit, but he took the seat and pulled her onto his thigh. Trying not to show any hesitation, she straightened her back as he ordered a glass of ice water with a slice of orange for her and an IPA from a local brewery for himself.

"You're doing very well, Sprite. I am proud to be your Top to-night." He reached up and stroked her cheek. She smiled.

Someone in sleek black leather pants delivered their beverages. When she spoke, Pamela recognized her as none other than Mistress Grant. She'd served as the bartender many times when Pamela had played here before and must still enjoy that duty even with her current status. The woman had the ability to do anything and everything at once, apparently.

"What a pretty lap decoration," Mistress Grant said.

Don't respond. Don't react. She wasn't even supposed to thank her for the drinks, but she wasn't sure she could speak without revealing how insulting she found the label.

"May I touch?" she asked Roar. He must have nodded because Mistress Grant began to stroke Pamela's hair as if she were a dog. While the two women had been equals in Gunnar's boardroom last month, the Domme clearly wanted to put Pamela in her place.

She chuckled as if aware of the effect she had on Pamela. "Roar, I've prepared the room you requested for you and Sprite to play in tonight. No hurry. You have the room for the entire evening."

Roar stroked her back. "Excellent. Thank you. She just began training with me a couple of days ago, but we were in need of something special for tonight's lesson."

The two of them spoke a bit about plans for Gunnar's upcoming mission, and despite Pamela's best efforts to stay focused, other conversations around her filtered into her mind. She tried to see if she heard any voices she recognized, but none sounded familiar. People came and went all the time in clubs like these.

A pinch to her thigh brought her back to the moment. "Mind telling me what you're thinking about, Sprite?"

She worried her lower lip, but knew she would have to respond. Maybe she could also find out some information. "I was wondering if anyone I know is here tonight."

"What difference would it make? You're supposed to be focused on me."

"Oh, and I am, Sir." *Liar.* "It's just that you haven't given me anything to do yet."

He chuckled. "Why do I get the feeling I'm going to be working with a brat?" She batted her eyes innocently, and he chuckled. "Finish your water. I want you to stay hydrated tonight."

She picked up the glass and chugged it, anxious to start. Well, continue. They'd started back in her apartment tonight.

"Thank you again, Mistress Grant." Roar indicated for Pamela to stand, and she did.

He took her forearm and directed her toward the hallway that led to the eight private play rooms.

Don't anticipate.

Don't analyze.

Stay in the moment.

She kept up the mantra all the way down the hallway until he stopped at the second door on the right. She'd never been inside this room before.

He knocked, which seemed odd. Hadn't Mistress Grant just told him the room was available and reserved for them for the night?

She didn't hear any sound from inside before Roar reached for the knob and opened the door. The scent of candles or incense—an exotic mixture of scents that included patchouli and possibly jasmine— greeted them, but the room was empty of other people's feet as best she could tell.

Trying to peek at the room without lifting her head enough to be noticed by him, she was able to make out a round tent of heavy maroon and gold curtains at the opposite end of the room. The flaps to the entrance were open enough to see piles of enormous pillows inside. The room was decorated with faux gold-leaf ornamentation against sky-blue walls and ceiling. The floor looked like marble, but had to be fake.

Lifting his hand to point toward the corner, Roar commanded, "Go behind the privacy panels and choose whatever costume you'd like to wear for me tonight. No need to remove your panties, but lose the bra and tank."

How'd he know she also wore a tank? Observant man. Before heading off to the dressing area, she wanted to ask if he had a favorite color but hadn't been given permission to speak and wasn't supposed to concern herself with his pleasure tonight, so she'd have to do her best in choosing. Behind the panel, she found an array of harem pants and bra tops with beading and sequins. Lots of scarves in every hue lined what looked like a tie rack.

Shucking off her mules, she felt the cold floor beneath her. Wow! Maybe it was real marble. Regaining her focus, she removed her turtleneck, tank tee, bra, and jeans, before trying on several pairs of harem pants until finding the best-fitting pair. The decision on what color he might prefer was answered for her—the ones that fit. Green. A peaceful color that complemented her eyes. She hoped he liked it. The matching bra was a little tight in the cup area, but that probably was intentional because most Doms would want cleavage. She'd never dressed in such a revealing manner before with Kri—*Roar*.

Good thing her panties were skin-toned. Otherwise, they might have shown through the sheer material of the pantaloons. She saw a vanity at the far end of the dressing area and started toward it to apply some color to her eyelids, but he hadn't asked her to do anything but put on a costume. Unsure if harem makeup was part of her costume, she stood indecisively for a moment.

Don't anticipate what he wants. Just follow his exact instructions.

He clapped three times, summoning her to his side. Giving the bra one more tug upward to cover as much of her breasts as possible, she grabbed several green scarves to tuck into the bra and hide her bare middle. She'd been doing sit-ups and walking more, but had gone a little flabby since she'd returned to the States.

For good measure, she grabbed one more scarf and used the hair-pins available to secure it over her nose and lower face leaving only her eyes showing. No time to check the mirror to see if she'd achieved her goal of being alluring. She scurried barefoot out from the dressing area to see the flaps drawn back and resting on hooks near the entrance. Inside, Roar lounged against the pillows.

He'd dressed as a sultan in gold lamé robes, but without a sultan's turban. His hair had been loosened from its usual leather thong. He motioned her to join him on the bed.

"Crawl to me like a proper harem girl."

She'd only gone a short way on the marble floor before realizing the veil was in the way so she quickly tucked the end into her cleavage at the top of the bra. Thankfully, he hadn't given her the instruction to crawl until she was only six feet away from the cushions, because her knees ached in a very short time from crawling across the cold, marble floor. The pillows in front of her appeared to be plush and comforta-ble, and she made her way toward them.

"Eyes on me. Seduce me as you come to me. Pay attention to noth-ing else."

She lifted her head, smiling as she closed the distance between them. The veil now hid her most obvious charms from him, so she wasn't quite sure if she was succeeding in seducing him. She moved like a cat on the prowl, slow yet purposeful.

Before she reached the entrance, he ordered, "Position number three."

She nibbled the inside of her lower lip as she knelt, straightening her back and tucking in her butt as he'd shown her the other night. She hoped there'd be no more kneeling on rice, especially on this hard floor. In his apartment, the hard grains had been scattered on a towel on top of carpeting.

She placed her open hands in a box hold as she raised her head once more to meet his gaze and wait for him to inspect her pose. Rising to a kneeling position, he moved toward her. The first thing he did was to remove the veil from her face. The scarves she'd hoped would hide any sagging parts were yanked from her cleavage and cast aside next.

"Better."

"Thank you, Sir."

"Did I give you permission to speak?"

But she'd only thanked him! *Oh!* She'd better adhere to the letter of the command from now on. "No, Sir. Your harem girl apologizes for her lapse in obedience."

"Your apology is sweet, but another transgression nonetheless. You'll pay for them all later tonight as part of your discipline."

Oh, dear. That didn't sound good! He sounded as though he expected her to fail at a number of things. She'd show him!

"We are going to work more on mindfulness and keeping you in the moment. You are not to think about, say, or do anything unless I tell you to do so. Your only duty tonight is to please me with your obedience and your attention. Is that understood?"

She nodded.

"When I ask a direct question, you're to answer with words."

"Sorry, Sir. Yes, I understand." Had she just added to her punishment with her apology?

Focus. She didn't want to have any more slip-ups tonight.

"Crawl closer to me." She moved onto the round mattress and

progressed forward until a leather-tipped riding crop and a bowl of stemmed grapes and hulled strawberries filled her view. He instructed her to stop mere inches away from him.

"With your mouth, pick up the crop and present it to me." She opened her mouth and caught the leather between her teeth, lifting her head and turning it in his direction as she maneuvered over the bowl, hoping not to spill anything. "Very good," he said as he took the crop from her. He stroked the leather tip down her back, causing goose bumps to rise.

He hadn't told her to change position, so she remained on all fours, face lowered.

Her stomach growled. What the heck? She'd eaten both lunch and dinner today. But Roar didn't offer her any fruit. Instead, he continued to stroke her with the crop. Would he use it on her—and where? Her breasts? Her butt?

He laid the crop sideways at waist level on her back and stretched out on his side with his elbow on the pillows, propping his head in his hand to admire his handiwork, she supposed.

"Turn your head toward me." She'd gotten a bit of a crick in her neck from straining in this unnatural position, so she moved slowly to allow the muscles to cooperate.

"Feed me. No hands. And do *not* let that crop fall off your back."

How was she supposed to achieve any movement without that end result? Pamela glanced at the bowl of fruit and quickly realized that feeding him meant using only her lips and teeth. Bending to retrieve a plump strawberry between her teeth, she crawled toward him. Balancing the crop seemed impossible, and she groaned when she felt it slipping toward the waistband of her harem pants, but it stopped there. She breathed a sigh of relief.

Moving even more cautiously, she lowered her head to his. He smiled before opening his lips and accepting the berry.

"Now, one for you, Sprite. Didn't you eat dinner?"

"I did, Sir, but the fruit looks delicious." She wanted to refuse for fear any more movement would send the crop tumbling, but refusal to obey wasn't an option. She crawled backward the short distance until she could choose another strawberry and chewed slowly, savoring its sweetness. He must have found a source for berries from the valley. Delicious.

"Continue to feed us both alternately until the bowl is empty."

Why had he chosen such an enormous bowl? She dipped her head again and moved forward, wishing she could just move the bowl closer. But he most likely had placed it there for a reason. She safely delivered a grape into his mouth and returned gingerly to the bowl, silently cursing him for placing it so far away.

"What was that thought?"

Drat! "I wondered if this might be easier if we moved the bowl closer to you so that I might feed you more efficiently, Roar." Normally, efficiency was important to the man, at least in business dealings.

His laughter made the mattress shake beneath her, and she worried that movement alone might topple the crop. "Nice try, my sweet girl. Remember—*I'm* the Top in this scene."

One of the things she'd fought against in medical school and beyond was being deemed childish and therefore lesser than, but she knew in the presence of a Dom, it often was just another way of establishing authority over the submissive.

He grinned. "I wouldn't be surprised if you had a few choice words for your sultan as well, given the look on your face."

She needed to school her features better. The man seemed an expert at reading expressions. Maybe he read minds, too. Of course, she'd left off the part about swearing at him, not that he hadn't guessed anyway.

"I'm adding two more minutes to your punishment for taking so long to resume your duties just now."

Pamela wondered how many total there would be by the time they finished. Not to mention how many would be added if she dropped the blasted crop. But she quickly went back to work, alternating between feeding first him and then herself while keeping the crop balanced on her lower back. She fed him the last strawberry and then bent her head to await further instructions. He reached out to stroke the top of her head.

"Thank you, Sprite. You did well."

She smiled. One thing was certain; she'd remained focused almost the entire time on the tasks she'd been given. When he said nothing else but only continued to stroke her head, she wondered what would be next. She dared not move for fear of losing the crop.

She'd never acted out the harem-girl fantasy with anyone before, but enjoyed it, wondering how he'd guessed at her love of *Jeannie*.

Roar thumped her on the head with his finger, bringing her back to the present. She wasn't paying attention, but what was she supposed to be thinking about? He hadn't really given her any new instructions.

"Your only duty tonight is to please me with your obedience and attention."

Why was it so difficult for her to empty her mind of everything but what he'd instructed her to do? She'd have to try harder.

Once again the minutes stretched out without any additional instructions from him. Whenever her mind started to wander, she reined it in—and waited. Voices from the hallway drifted in, momentarily distracting her.

Another thump on her head told her she'd been busted again. How did he catch her so quickly? What tells were giving her away? She felt the crop slipping and straightened her back again, curving her spine until she'd managed to right it to a balanced position again. That was close. She didn't want to think what punishment she'd receive if the crop fell off.

His hand fell to the pillows beside her. He remained silent, and she wondered when he was going to give her another command. Merely being here on all fours with a crop balanced on her back didn't seem like it would provide him with much pleasure.

A soft snore broke the silence. Sleeping? He'd fallen asleep? Seriously? She might be here all night if he didn't awaken soon. No, someone would clear the rooms at some point. She ventured a glance at him and saw his features had softened, almost to that of an innocent boy. The man had to be exhausted from all the responsibilities he shouldered with Tori's care and Gunnar's financial empire. Why he'd taken her on as well was beyond her. She shouldn't have agreed to let him do this.

As another ten or fifteen minutes dragged on, her mind wandered several times to a conversation in the hallway.

Oh, no! The crop slipped off without warning, landing on Roar's thigh. She waited for him to awaken and chastise her for not keeping her mind focused on such a simple task, but he didn't move. Surely he'd felt it. Would he know if she picked up the crop and placed it on her back again? Probably. Even if he wouldn't, she didn't want to disobey him. There would be consequences when he awoke, but she'd prefer to suffer those than to add a punishment for willfully doing something without permission.

"Quite a predicament."

She startled when he spoke. His eyes were still closed, but his lips held a hint of a smile. Had he been sleeping at any point, or had he only wanted her to think he was asleep and no longer attentive? Thankfully, she had used good judgment.

At last, he opened his eyes and caught her staring at him. She quickly remembered her place and lowered her head and gaze to her hands, because his feet were behind her. He picked up the crop and placed the end under her chin, forcing her to meet his gaze.

"Now we need to carry out your discipline for the many times you failed to keep your mind focused on me tonight."

She said nothing, as if anything she said would make a difference. She wondered what type of corrective measures he had in mind. The crop? Probably not. He knew how much she liked spankings of all types. His disciplinary action would be something she didn't care for, no doubt, or it would be funishment, instead.

"Still trying to figure out what happens next, Sprite?"

Damn it. She'd done it again—and so soon!

"I'm sorry, Sir. I can't seem to turn off my brain."

"Pray tell, what were you thinking just now?"

"I was wondering what implement you would use to punish me, Sir."

"Is that any of your concern? Do you expect to affect the outcome by dwelling on such matters? Why worry unnecessarily about something that might not happen at all?"

"No and no, Sir. And, yes, it is a waste of my time to worry and takes me away from paying full attention to you."

"Exactly. I will say you performed better than I expected you to do when you had actions to perform. I'm pleased you've only racked up the six for dropping the crop plus another six for inattentiveness and letting your mind wander several times."

His words of praise were lost momentarily as she continued worrying about what he would use to deliver those dozen strokes, but she pulled her errant thoughts back, cleared her mind, and waited.

Roar rose from his reclining position to his knees and crawled off the pillows to stand outside the harem tent's entrance. She waited some more. After a moment, he said, "Crawl out, Sprite." When she reached the edge, before she placed her hand onto the marble flooring, he reached for her arm. "Stand." He helped her to her feet, making sure she was steady before releasing her.

"Follow me." He turned toward the corner, and she followed until he stopped. "Tell me why you're being disciplined."

"For my inability to maintain my focus on you and for allowing the crop to fall from where you had asked me to hold it for you."

He nodded and reached into his robes to pull something out. Placing a quarter on the wall, she knew her punishment immediately. He commanded that she press her nose against the coin and keep it from slipping away from her.

Why couldn't he just paddle her with a crop or spank her with his hand?

You are not to question his actions.

The coin was placed slightly higher than where her nose would be with her feet flat on the ground, so she stood on tiptoe.

"Twelve minutes. You will remain attentive to the position of the coin. If it falls, you'll begin again until you complete a stint of twelve consecutive minutes."

Nothing was going to distract her from *this* assignment. Only a dozen. *I've got this!* The coin was warm from where it had been against his skin, she supposed. After some unknown amount of time, Pamela began sweating and worried that the coin would slip, so she pressed it even harder.

Focus.

Roar would let her know when the punishment had been completed to his satisfaction. He said nothing, but she was certain he stood directly behind her.

Don't think about him or anything but the quarter!

A hitch in her shoulder made her twitch, and the coin clanged to the floor. Damn it!

"Five and a half."

That's all?

"Straighten up." Pamela corrected her posture, and he worked the kinks out of her shoulders with strong, sure hands. He gave an excellent shoulder rub. She cringed when, all too soon, he placed the coin against the wall again and indicated for her to move forward again and hold her nose there.

"Let's make it to a full count this time."

Focusing her mind on one simple task was more difficult than she thought. Determined not to fail him again, she gave it her best. Nothing existed in the world right now but her nose and this coin.

Before she knew it, Roar spoke. "Time."

A sense of elation soared through her, but she hadn't been instructed to pull away yet. He chuckled. "Very good, Sprite." He stood behind her, his body warm against her chilled backside, and held her face between his hands as he pulled her away from the wall, letting the quarter drop to the floor unheeded.

"You did well that second time. I'm proud of you." When he lowered his hands, she wished he'd touch her again, but knew tonight had been far beyond his comfort zone. "Let's get dressed, and we'll go out

to the great room for a while to discuss tonight's exercises."

With a mixture of satisfaction borne of pleasing him and pride in having maintained her focus better tonight than she had in the past, she returned to the dressing area and tossed the costume into the bin marked laundry. After changing into the clothes and shoes she'd worn here tonight, she followed Roar to the great room where music poured from speakers near the stage. She kept her gaze on the floor once more as he held out a chair for her. She'd hoped to be his *lap decoration* again, because he never made her feel humiliation, but instead, she felt him pull away.

"Would you care for something more than water now?"

"Yes, Sir. A Wallbanger, please."

He laughed and walked over to the bar to retrieve their beverages. She listened to the music and conversations flowing around her. Roar hadn't told her what to do other than wait for him, but she assumed she was not to make eye contact with anyone.

He returned with their drinks. "What are your thoughts about tonight's scene, Sprite? You can look at me when you speak."

She met his gaze and smiled. "My mind did wander some, but not as badly as it usually does. Being in the private room with fewer distractions helped, I think. And you didn't allow me to go too long without bringing me back to the moment. I'm surprised at how quickly you pick up on the fact that my mind is drifting."

He smiled, but didn't reveal his secrets. "Was there anything that made you uncomfortable?"

"When I thought you'd fallen asleep and that I might be there until the club closed." Again, he only smiled enigmatically, keeping her guessing as to whether he actually *had* fallen asleep.

Whatever the next few weeks held, no doubt Roar would have a profound effect on her psyche.

CHAPTER TEN

L ater that evening, Kristoffer tossed back a double scotch and stared out the window. He tried not to reflect back on his time with Pamela tonight in the harem room, but images of his little sprite bombarded him nonetheless.

No, not mine.

But as long as he was committed to training her, he needed to at least consider her his bottom, if not his submissive. She'd improved greatly in her concentration skills. Perhaps he'd be able to finish working with her soon, and his world would return to normal again.

What? Predictable and dull?

Pamela was neither. She made him feel...*alive* again, for lack of a better term.

And with that came feelings of hurt, pain, and loss—all of the emotions he'd tried to tamp down over the past few years. Every minute he spent with Pamela opened up wounds he thought had healed over—or at least no longer festered. She stirred everything up again.

Reawakening feelings displaced the guilt he'd carried so long. Tori would want him to get back in the game, not cut himself off and be numb to life.

But allowing himself to feel again meant making some decisions about Tori he didn't want to face. While he would do nothing to hasten her departure from this world, he also couldn't see anyone ever replacing her in his heart.

Yet Pamela opened up a door to a world he hadn't realized he'd missed so much. Inherently, he was a Dom. He wanted to explore that world again and in more depth than in the past, but felt disloyal to Tori.

This realization hadn't only been born as a result of the momentary thrill he'd experienced tonight watching Pamela as she crawled panther-like toward him, her emerald eyes sparkling with...he didn't want to put a name to it for fear he'd misjudged the look. While he tried to make it clear what his limits were as far as a commitment to her, sometimes he thought perhaps she wanted more than he could offer.

Or was that merely wishful thinking on his part? Most likely, he was reading things into her eyes that weren't there.

And while being an active Dom to someone again charged him up, some of the times that stood out most were dining out or sharing a love of jazz music with her. The key? Doing those things *with* someone. They held no meaning when done alone.

Going through the motions alone had never fed his soul the way spending time with Tori had—before the accident.

Now, with Pamela, he'd begun to find joy again. After learning firsthand how fleeting life could be, he no longer took such moments for granted as he might have done in the past.

Kristoffer set the empty glass on the coffee table and made his way to the bedroom. After removing his clothes and crawling into bed, he tried to read but couldn't focus. Setting the book back on the nightstand, he saw the business card he'd received last night from a grief counselor named Rick something or other who was making the rounds at the nursing home and talking with caregivers. He'd chatted with the man a bit—about nothing in particular—but the two had hit it off.

He picked up the card and stared at the name and number. Would scheduling an appointment to talk about these conflicting emotions help in any way? He wasn't actually grieving.

Okay, maybe I am. Finally.

Tori wasn't coming back to him. Time to accept that and move on.

He didn't so much want to talk with Rick about coping with Tori's situation. He'd done that for years. Nothing he could change there.

Instead, he wanted to discuss these new emotions he was experiencing and explore this developing relationship with Pamela. Her presence in his life this past month had brought about an unsettling shift in his mindset. The more time they spent together, the more he wanted to be with her. A year ago, the thought of spending time with another woman would have scared the shit out of him, because the thought of replacing Tori made him physically ill.

But now I'm…tired.

Tired of being alone, of having no one to carry on a two-way conversation with, no one to hold who could hug him back, no one to care for who knew he existed. Gunnar tried to fill some of the void, but he had a full plate dealing on so many fronts. While he made time for Kristoffer whenever he needed him, Kristoffer didn't want to burden his cousin.

Besides, women are different.

Pamela had only asked for something it was easy for him to give her while maintaining his dignity. All she wanted was to spend time with him socially and for submissive training. No sexual demands, which helped. He couldn't handle that type of relationship yet, if ever.

So why did feelings of guilt continue to bombard him? Could a therapist bring resolution to the conflicted emotions he was experiencing? Help him find answers?

Doubtful.

He put the card down again, but it continued to nag at him for a long time as he tried to find a comfortable position. It wouldn't hurt to schedule a session and see what the therapist had to offer. The walls of this self-imposed prison were closing in on him. Gunnar had been telling him to start living again for years, but Pamela had been the first to show him he truly wasn't dead yet.

Would he take a counselor's advice if he saw him? Is that even how therapy worked? From scenes he'd seen on TV, the counselor was more a sounding board than a dispenser of wisdom, but talking to someone who didn't have a vested interest in whatever he decided to do might help. Rick said he helped caregivers move on if they weren't living to the fullest because they'd become stuck in working through the stages of grief. He'd probably be good at understanding people like Kristoffer with a loved one in a persistent vegetative state.

Maybe it was time to reach out. He'd call for an appointment in the morning. Merely making that commitment helped push back the restlessness, and he turned onto his side and fell asleep.

After a dreamless night, he woke up with no viable reason to change his mind. Dressed in his suit, as he'd done for years to remind himself he was still a financial advisor, even if he had only one client and worked from home, he walked to his office at the other end of the condo and glanced around. Sterile, cold, not a single functional object out of place.

Much like my life has been since Tori was ripped away so suddenly.

Kristoffer wanted to rejoin the living, not simply go through the motions. Picking up the card again, he called the number and scheduled an appointment for tomorrow.

With that chore behind him, maybe he could get some real work done. But first, he texted Pamela a new assignment.

KRISTOFFER: Journal about something you need that might only benefit you directly. Be specific.

He'd be interested in seeing what she identified when he met with her tonight. She tended to put her needs on a back burner in order to serve and meet the needs of others. Would she be able to identify a need of her own? If so, would he able to fulfill that need?

Pamela read her texted assignment on her way home from the gym. She'd joined in an effort to build stamina so she could go back to work and finish her contract. Even though the hospital in Afghanistan had no openings for her in July, they thought she might be able to replace one of the surgeons in August.

After a quick lunch, she went to work on the assignment. Instead of immediately diving into an entry she'd be willing to share with Roar, she journaled for an hour about a fantasy she'd like to fulfill with Kristoffer. As if that would ever happen.

Why hadn't she been able to separate her wants from her needs?

And why was it so blasted hot in here? She set the notebook aside. The central air was barely keeping the temperature inside her top-floor apartment comfortable on this unseasonably warm day.

Oh, let's be real, Pamela. You're not hot because of the mid-eighties tempera-ture outside. You've suffered through temps a lot hotter where air conditioning was nonexistent.

No, she was horny. Since she was still on orders from Roar to take afternoon naps, she went into the bedroom and stretched out on the bed. Not one to let sexual frustration, heat, or boredom get the best of her, she reached for her vibrator in the nightstand drawer, remembering the words she'd written describing her fantasy.

Kristoffer, I have this need at the moment that only you can help me with.

She grinned at her silly words. Good thing he didn't ask to see her notebook entries, but allowed her to share what she wanted to with him. Deciding that fantasies involving Kristoffer might make her time with him a little too weird, she opened her e-reader to continue a reread of the sexiest BDSM club series by her favorite author. Soon she was so wrapped up in the story again—trying her best not to picture the Dom as Kristoffer and failing miserably—that she forgot both about the assignment and her need for release.

She remained immersed until her vibrator started up on its own. *What the heck?* When she reached down to pick it up, she realized it was her phone vibrating and rolled her eyes at her flight of fancy.

Her heart beat a little faster when *Kristoffer* showed on the screen.

"Hello." Her voice sounded winded, so she forced her breathing to a steadier rhythm as she sat up. "Is everything all right?" He usually preferred to text rather than call.

"Yeah, everything's fine. Did I catch you in the middle of something?"

"Oh, no! I was just reading." *And fantasizing about you.* God, she was messed up. "Um, how's Tori?" Had he visited with her yet today? She pulled the phone away from her ear to check the time. Too early.

"She was doing well when I saw her yesterday. Back to normal anyway."

"That's great." Her words sounded ridiculous as soon as she said them, but at least Kristoffer sounded less stressed now that his wife was out of the hospital.

"Do you want to eat out or in tonight?"

"In, if that's okay with you. I have something in the crockpot already. I can bring it to your place or we can eat here."

"Your place sounds easier. I should be there about six-thirty."

They'd already had the time arranged. What had he really called about?

"Would you like me to bring anything?" he asked.

"Maybe stop by the store and pick up your favorite frozen pie for dessert. I was busy…at the gym this morning and forgot all about picking something up after I received your text."

"Cherry crumb sound good?"

"Excellent. Grab some vanilla ice cream, too."

"Will do."

A silence opened up between them. After a few awkward moments, she asked, "Is there something you need, Kristoffer?" She was never quite sure when to address him as Kristoffer and when as Roar, but unless they were involved in an actual scene, she reverted to Kristoffer.

She wished he'd ask her to do something for him once in a while, but he tended to keep the focus on meeting her needs.

"No, I'm fine. Guess I just wanted to hear your voice. I'm looking forward to tonight."

After ending the call, she sat there a while trying to make heads or tails of what that call had been about.

Less than three hours later, her heart skipped a beat at the sharp knock on the door.

When she opened it, Kristoffer greeted her with a smile. "Smells great!"

Nothing pleased her more than to hear his praise, and he appreciated everything so much, even little things. "Thanks. It's a new recipe I found online. I hope it tastes as good as it smells."

"You've yet to prepare a bad meal. Oh, here's dessert." He followed her into the kitchen. "I practically salivated all afternoon thinking about coming over here." He seemed to look forward to their time together as much as she did, which warmed her heart, although her anticipation of his visits had nothing to do with food.

After dinner, Pamela placed the cherry pie in the oven and set the timer. They moved to the living room. Soon Roar emerged and sent her to retrieve her notebook. Suddenly, she remembered that she hadn't finished today's assignment other than the fantasy she'd poured out on the pages this afternoon.

She needed to think quickly, because no way did she intend to share that with him. What other need did she have? She'd interpreted his assignment as choosing something to make herself feel better that probably would have no impact on anyone else. But not something like her getting off on a fantasy of him in his sexy suit.

Picking up the incriminating notebook, she dragged her feet on her way back to join him in the living room. Roar was seated on the couch and patted the cushion next to him. She settled next to him, a bundle of nerves.

"Share with me the entry to today's assignment."

She didn't open the notebook for fear he might catch a glimpse at her actual words. What selfish need did she have? Suddenly, one popped into her mind that seemed perfect. It might not be the stuff fantasies were made of for most, but because he'd been very reluctant to touch her thus far, she could think of nothing that would satisfy her more and yet remain within their set limits.

Or did it?

"Is there a problem?"

"No, Sir. I did come up with one. It might seem a little silly—"

"Share it with me. There's nothing silly about you expressing your needs."

"Well, I have always..." Why was she stalling? Tonight wasn't about fantasy, but need.

She took a deep breath, and he furrowed his brows. "Everything all right, Sprite?"

She nodded before standing to pace a little. "Sir, I love that I can talk about almost anything with you, whether as my Top or as

Kristoffer." She smiled down at him as much to reassure him as herself.

"As do I. You've filled a lot of dark places for me these past few weeks."

She sobered. "I can't tell you how much you've helped me see what it is that I want. No, what I *need*." She glanced away. *How do I put this into words?*

His smile reassured her a bit. "Repeat back what you were asked to journal about."

Pamela drew a deep breath and exhaled. "My assignment was to journal about something I need. This is the hardest homework you've given me so far, Roar. It's much easier for me to determine the needs of others and to find ways to serve them than to take a hard look at myself and voice what would help fulfill a need within me."

"I understand, which is one of the reasons I wanted you to do this assignment. Tell me what it is you need. Ask me, Sprite, before you make yourself sick."

"Sir..." She bit the inside of her lower lip until she winced in pain. As if a dam had been breached, the words burst out in a rush. "I just...I wondered if perhaps you might consider allowing me to..." If he laughed at her, she'd...

"To?"

"I'd like to lie with my head in your lap and have you stroke my hair while you're watching TV." His eyes opened wider. *Darn.* Afraid he'd say no outright, she hurried on. "I know that seems like a bizarre thing to ask for—or need—but, well, having my hair and scalp touched is so comforting to me." *And it also seemed like a safe place for you to touch me without either of us crossing any lines.*

He stared at her a few moments more before speaking. "You honor me with your request. I don't see what harm there could be."

She sighed deeply, and her body relaxed. "Really? You'd do that for me?"

He chuckled as he nodded his head. "I'm a Dom. How could I deny such a heartfelt request when all you're doing is responding to my assignment? You did well, by the way."

She wanted to launch herself into his lap immediately, but showed a bit of restraint. "Thank you! Can we start tonight?"

"Of course."

"Why don't you pick out a movie to watch in case you get too bored?"

"I doubt I could get bored when I'm with you, Sprite." But he went over to the entertainment stand and flipped through the DVDs in the basket by the television, scanning the titles of her collection that was a mixture of romantic comedies, chick flicks, and classics. He held up a special-edition copy of *The Wizard of Oz*. "How about this one?"

"Oh my gosh, I haven't seen that in forever!"

He grinned. "It's always been one of my favorite films, so the *Wizard*, it is." He placed the disc in the player and returned to the couch with the remote.

He rolled up the sleeves of his dress shirt, reminding her of the fantasy she'd written that took place in his office, but thought it best that she put that scenario entirely out of her mind. Perhaps she'd just pretend this was aftercare instead.

"Can I fix you something to drink first?" she asked.

"No, I'm fine." He sat at the end of the couch. While anxious to begin, she was nervous about jumping in until he motioned her to join him. "Stretch out on the sofa and place your head in my lap."

She did as instructed, but before she placed her head on his lap, he put a throw pillow there. Probably a good idea if this was going to remain as G-rated as the movie they were watching.

He fiddled with the remote, and soon the familiar music and opening credits were playing. She lay waiting for him to touch her hair. Instead, his hand came to rest on her arm. He stroked up and down her exposed flesh to relax her, but goose bumps broke out wherever he touched.

"Cold?"

Not on your life.

"No. Are you?"

"No." He chuckled and the vibration came through the pillow.

"Relax your body." The firmness of his voice sent a thrill down her spine.

Her heart raced faster when his hand finally stroked her hair, starting at the nape and weaving his hand up and over the back of her scalp. *Yes!* She closed her eyes, able to picture the movie in her head without watching after having seen it dozens of times.

He tucked a lock of hair behind her ear and continued to run his hand through the strands, this time massaging her scalp as well.

"Mmm." She'd died and gone to heaven.

"Like that?"

"You have no idea how many women can be turned to mush by having someone play with their hair."

"Really?"

Apparently, his wife hadn't been like her in that regard if he wasn't aware of this. She smiled, welcoming differences between what Kristoffer had done in the past with Tori and what he did now with her. Not that she was in any kind of competition.

Ding!

She jumped at the sound, yanked from her not-quite-fantasy musings, and realized the pie needed to be checked. Bounding up from the couch, welcoming the break in contact to regroup from letting those thoughts about Kristoffer become dangerous, she headed toward the kitchen. "Be right back."

"Take your time." His voice sounded husky.

After placing the pie on the cooling rack, she returned to the living room to find Kristoffer standing at the window, staring down at the street or something outside. He didn't turn when she entered the room, so she announced her presence. Still no response.

"Everything okay?"

He turned to face her, a look akin to anguish on his face. "I'm sorry, but I need more time before I can do this."

His words surprised her. As best she could tell, they hadn't done anything to compromise his vows. Would time really help if he continued to shut down?

"Perhaps we can talk about what's going on."

"Pamela, I'm not comfortable with the feelings being stirred up when I touch you, even when it's perfectly innocent."

She felt the heat rise into her cheeks as she remembered the thoughts that had been going through her head when he touched her. If he needed to take it slower, then she'd slow down. She sat in the middle of the couch and patted the cushion beside her. "Come on. Let's just watch the movie, have some pie after it cools, and call it a night."

He stared at her a long time before closing the gap between them and sitting down. "I'm sorry."

"No worries. I kind of hit you out of the blue without giving you a chance to prepare mentally."

While they didn't actually make body contact, heat emanated from his body. She pressed play, and the movie resumed. They watched silently until Dorothy encountered the scarecrow before Pamela paused it again.

"Pie time. Do you want ice cream on yours?"

"Is there any other way to eat cherry pie?"

She shook her head and laughed, happy they'd gotten past the tension from half an hour ago. "Never!"

Pamela led the way to the kitchen and served each a generous portion with a huge scoop of vanilla bean ice cream. As they sat at the dining room table, he praised her baking skills, and she laughed, considering she'd done nothing but heat it up. But he'd come out of his earlier funk, which made her happy, too.

Give him time. She could only imagine how such a domestic scene must have rattled his memories of similar times with his wife.

After finishing her pie, she yawned, hoping he didn't see through her ruse. "Would you mind it if I called it a night a little early?"

Relief showed on his face. Should she let him off the hook for future evenings together? No, she didn't think that would help him learn to move on and start living again. She hoped that, over time, he'd see the benefits of companionship.

They carried their dishes to the sink, and she rinsed them off before turning to him. "Thanks for bringing dessert."

He shuffled his feet and looked down. His sudden shyness—or whatever she wanted to call it—charmed her. When he met her gaze again, he surprised her. "Why don't I pick up dinner tomorrow, and we can finish the movie?"

"I already know how it ends."

He smiled. "As do I. But I dropped the ball tonight and didn't follow through on my promise."

"No one set a time limit for when you had to fulfill this need of mine." He'd opened the door a crack at least. She should at least let him in. "Okay, you're on for dinner. I'm looking forward to it."

He touched the tip of her nose with his index finger, warming her insides more than the pie had. "You're so easy to please, Sprite."

No, I just know when not to push you too hard.

✧ ✧ ✧

Don't get used to this, man.

During their almost nightly visits over the last two-and-a-half weeks, sometimes at her place and others at his, Pamela made sure he ate well and had a sounding board to talk with about Tori, work, or whatever was on his mind. He'd grown more comfortable with their "couch time," as they came to call it, and quickly made it through much of her DVD collection. At his place, they accessed a popular movie streaming subscription service he'd neglected for years. They managed to watch a complete film each night now without him suffering a meltdown.

Some nights they simply had dinner, took a stroll in his or her neighborhood, or lingered at the table after dinner to talk. However, having Pamela lying with her head in his lap still gave him some anxiety and made him wish there could be something more. He stroked her silky hair, trying not to think about touching her in other ways, in other places.

While those desires went against everything he believed in, Pamela fulfilled his yearning to be needed again. Tori didn't know he existed anymore. He'd continue to watch over her and ensure she was well cared for, but the days of her longing for him were gone.

Yet here was Pamela wanting him in more vital ways—a woman who would be aware who was meeting those needs.

His sessions with Rick had helped him come to terms with some of his feelings of guilt. Still, he couldn't be hers or she his in his current situation. Why lead her on? Some might consider his being with her this way to be cheating, but he'd come to see it more as an emotional joining of their minds, not their bodies. He hadn't abandoned his wife.

How much longer could he be kept imprisoned along with Tori? One of them had survived the accident.

Yeah, keep justifying this shit, and you're going to find yourself up to your knees in it.

Pamela turned her face upward and smiled. "This is nice. Thank you for indulging me."

"I'm enjoying it, too." The word "sweetheart" almost came out, but he wouldn't use that endearment with anyone but Tori.

"I probably should head home soon." *Before I get us both into trouble.*

She sat up. "I understand."

That's the problem; you're too understanding.

"I wish I didn't have to go, to be honest, Pamela, but I'm having a hard time reconciling being here like this with you."

"It hurts me that you're feeling that way." She laid her hand on his thigh. "We've done nothing wrong."

Not tonight, maybe. Not yet, anyway.

"Yeah, but if you knew how much I want to do something I shouldn't..." Her eyes grew smoky with desire, and his balls tightened in response.

Damn it. Don't look at me like that.

"Why do you waste your time with me, Pamela? You should be with someone who can love you one hundred percent. I don't know if or when I'll ever be free to be with you."

"My needs are rather simple. This is the perfect evening, if you ask me. Sitting here together watching a movie, having your hand stroke my hair or talking about…well, whatever. These evenings make me happy."

"Don't you get frustrated?" He certainly did.

"That's just physical. I've been taking yoga classes at the gym and learning to channel some of that frustration in other ways." She laughed, somewhat embarrassed. "We're both healthy adults. We know how to take care of our basic urges and rid ourselves of pent-up sexual frustration."

He didn't want to think about her pleasuring herself. Not that he could banish the image without a struggle at the moment.

Luckily, she continued. "We have a strong emotional connection. Look at you and Tori. It's not a physical love you share with her now, but don't you still gain something from your time with her?"

"Yeah. I need those visits every day, even though I'm not sure what either of us gets out of them anymore. But with you, it's different."

"It has to be. No two people can share the same dynamic." She nibbled on her lower lip, making him want to kiss her.

You need to go home, man.

But before he could act on either, she went on. "Tell me about your marriage. What was it like before the accident?"

Did he really want to remember those times? He'd blocked them out in order to be able to function with reality and make it through each day.

Perhaps he could share a less personal account. "I suppose we had a fairly traditional marriage. She wanted to stay home and take care of me and our home. I was driven to make money for my clients and spent long hours working. I didn't work solely for Gunnar at the time." He'd lost most of his other clients through inattention in the first year after the accident. "But Tori always made all my worries vanish when I came home. I could forget about work for a few hours."

"You didn't have children."

"No. It was a mutual decision to delay having kids. Tori didn't think she was cut out to be a mom, and I never thought about fatherhood one way or another. We decided to wait and see if our feelings changed, and then…well, it was too late."

"I'm sorry." She stroked his arm.

"Don't be. I couldn't have been emotionally present these last four years for any children we might have had. Even worse, what if our kids had been in the car at the time of the accident?"

He couldn't even contemplate that possibility.

Enough about him. "How about you? Did you ever think about being a mother?"

She sighed and returned her head to his lap. "Not seriously. Never found anyone I thought would make a good spouse and father."

An interesting choice of words. He should drop it, but was intrigued now. "What was your own father like?"

"Wonderful. I was his princess. Until my mom moved away, at least. We were alone for almost a year while I took care of him and the house."

"At twelve?"

She shrugged. "It is what it is." Both remained silent a moment as he smoothed her hair away from her forehead. Finally, she continued. "He remarried soon after the divorce came through, I guess. Monica and her kids were part of the family by the time I was fourteen. Anyway, he didn't need me anymore then."

Kristoffer stroked her hair, trying to absorb some of the sadness of that little girl who'd been left behind by her daddy. How did that factor into her decisions about later relationships?

"Like you, I'm glad I didn't bring kids into the world. It isn't fair to a child to run off to Timbuktu and leave them behind while you pursue some need to save the world." She expelled a puff of air as if frustrated.

"Like your mother did to you?"

She blinked as though she hadn't connected the dots yet. "I suppose."

The hurt in her eyes made him fight the urge to bend down and kiss her in an attempt to take the pain away. Instead, he feigned fighting back a yawn. "I think I'd better hit the road, Sprite."

She sighed as she sat up again.

Without intention or good sense, he leaned forward and placed a kiss on her cheek. "Thanks for being you."

"Who else can I be?"

"No one. Stay true to yourself."

She stared at him so long, she made him uncomfortable. Then she grinned, confusing him further. "No worries. I'm finally beginning to figure out who I am and what I want."

"Good for you." They discussed tomorrow's assignment, and he headed home. She'd given him a lot to think about tonight.

During his appointment with Rick the next afternoon, before visiting Tori, Kristoffer talked a bit more about Pamela. Still no mention of his role as Roar. He wasn't sure yet if Rick was kink aware.

Out of the blue, Rick asked, "When's the last time you spent time away from Denver?"

"I go to Breckenridge once or twice a week."

"No, I mean really away, where you aren't within a few hours of Tori's bedside?"

Kristoffer thought back and realized he hadn't left Colorado since the accident except for two visits in recent years to see his mother. "Tori and I used to travel all the time, but I haven't had any interest in going anywhere in a while." Not since the accident.

Rick nodded. "Is it that you truly lost interest in travel or that you feel guilty about going places now without Tori at your side?"

"Probably both." *Where's the fun in traveling alone?* "I think what I loved most about our ventures was sharing the experiences with her." *And reminiscing about them for years to come.*

"What do you think Tori would say to you if she were able to participate in this discussion right now?"

"She'd tell me to find someone and go." Her words rang out in his mind as though she were speaking to him. He smiled. She'd always told it like it was.

"Listen to her. A vacation—a change of scenery—could help you gain a new perspective." Rick leaned forward in his chair. "You love Tori. Nobody doubts that. You two share a soul-deep love very few people experience. Nothing can break that."

Kristoffer's eyes stung, and he shifted his gaze to the window behind Rick where the mountains formed not only a backdrop, but a kind of barrier that represented the walls he'd put up between himself and the rest of the world these past four years.

"Kristoffer, Tori wouldn't want you to stop living life to the fullest. What happened to her was an accident. Hang on to the memories of the good times before the accident and keep those in your heart, but consider taking a few steps forward. Create some new memories. If the tables had been turned and you were the one confined to that bed, what would you want her to do?"

When he put it that way, even though Kristoffer had heard the same question put forth from Gunnar over the years, the words finally began to sink in. He wouldn't wish what had become of his life on anyone, much less his beloved Tori, had their roles been reversed. So why was it supposed to be acceptable for him?

Rick continued, "From what you've shared here, Tori loves you too much to have you give up on living."

Unable to speak to the truth being laid out before him, Kristoffer merely nodded.

Perhaps the time had come for him to make some changes in his life. No, more like time for him to *get* a life, period.

✧   ✧   ✧

Pamela let Kristoffer into her apartment, and he placed his suit coat on the coat rack in the hallway. He seemed more subdued than he'd been lately.

"How'd your day go?" she asked.

"Same old."

He didn't seem himself. "Is everything all right with Tori?"

"Yeah."

Whatever was on his mind, he didn't seem to want to talk about it. No doubt he was worried about his wife. Tori could live this way until she reached a ripe old age unless some infection or disease claimed her first. Kristoffer took his wedding vows seriously, and without anyone else to care for his wife, he would always take an active part in her care.

If I were in Tori's place, would I want that kind of undying commitment from my husband? Perhaps. What a testament of his love for her.

Be real. No way would she want anyone to go through that on her behalf. Being trapped in a shell of a body that many years and putting her family through such anguish would be unbearable to her soul, even if she didn't know what was happening.

Of course Tori had no idea of the sacrifices her husband made for her every day, namely giving up his own happiness in order to remain by her side. While honorable, such devotion had taken a toll.

He seemed resigned to his fate, but was nowhere near happy. Kristoffer didn't seek love or even sex elsewhere.

Would she be satisfied in the long run to spend evenings like this without any physical intimacy? Did he crave anything other than friendship and providing her with guidance as her Dom or Top? She admired his faithfulness, but not his stubbornness, if that made any sense.

Actually, nothing made sense anymore.

Better to continue playing it safe with Kristoffer and not test the waters any further. Tonight, she'd give all thoughts about the future a rest and stay in the moment.

Inside the kitchen, she pulled the salad from the fridge. "I hope you're hungry. I'm trying something new tonight"

He smiled. "Sounds good. Can I help with anything?"

"Why don't you take the lamb out of the oven?"

While it rested, she prepared the bread to go in, enjoying working side by side with him like this. Her feelings for him grew deeper every moment—and the thought of his leaving later tonight hurt her heart.

You've got it bad, girlfriend.

She filled him in on her day. With so little going on other than her visits to the gym, that didn't take long. Bored didn't begin to describe how she felt. She'd caught up on medical journals, read some books for fun, and reorganized her pantry. Whatever Kristoffer would be comfortable doing with her, she would welcome.

Even if all they could do was continue to spend quiet nights cuddled on the couch, she'd try to be content. He made her feel cherished. He hadn't promised her anything more than friendship and training.

"Why don't we start with the salads?"

After dishing them out, she carried them to the table. Shaking the homemade vinaigrette into a frenzy, she poured some over her salad and passed the bottle to him.

They ate in tense silence until the smell of bread wafted to her. "Oh! I almost forgot!" She jumped up and ran to the kitchen.

Luckily, she rescued it before the loaf burned, although it might be crispier than she preferred. While in here, she removed the leg of lamb from the pan and transferred it to a platter before checking on the vegetables.

Kristoffer joined her. "What can I do?"

"Why don't you slice the roast?"

As he did, she plated their vegetables followed by the meat. "Mint jelly?"

"How else does one enjoy lamb?"

A man after her own heart.

Seated together again, Pamela picked up the basket of bread slices and butter and offered them to him.

"Now we can sit and enjoy the rest of our meal without interruptions," she said. Perhaps she was a little preoccupied tonight. Normally, she'd have no trouble having everything served at one time.

He seemed quieter tonight as well. Before she could take her first bite of lamb, Kristoffer's gaze drew her to him like a magnet. "I need to ask you something, Pamela."

He sounded deadly serious, causing her to set down her fork. "What is it?"

Was he about to tell her they could no longer continue to meet like this?

He took a deep breath, making her worry even more. What on earth was the matter? She needed her couch time more than ever and hoped it wouldn't be a thing of the past.

"How would you like to take a little vacation with me? For a week or so?"

Excitement stirred in her once more as she released the tension that had been building up all evening. "That sounds awesome. What did you have in mind?"

"I thought maybe we could go out to Sonoma Valley, enjoy fine wine, good food, and reliable sunshine. Are you up for a trip?"

"My next overseas assignment has been postponed until mid-August at the earliest. We can handle anything that comes up with the equipment purchases through the Internet while on vacation. So, yes, I'd love a chance to get away." *Especially with you.*

He visibly relaxed. Is that what he was so nervous about tonight? She'd expended a lot of energy worrying about something that wasn't even the problem.

But there was one issue they couldn't ignore. She'd hate herself for reminding him, but needed to make sure he'd thought this through. "What about Tori?"

"Well…" She expected him to say he'd reconsidered. "I've only been away from her side about five or six days in more than four years, and…" He sighed. "I didn't mention this earlier, but I've been seeing a grief counselor the past few weeks."

"Good for you!" Finally, someone who could help him figure out what he wanted out of the rest of his life, rather than remaining tied to the past.

He rushed to add, "Don't think I'm going off the deep end or anything. He's a relationship counselor as well as a grief expert. Anyway, he's been helping me to see it's not healthy to hold on to Tori this tightly."

No kidding. She'd been worried about how long he'd be able to do so.

"I think it's great that you're talking with someone who's objective and trained to help people sort out situations and deal with warring factions in their cognitions." When his eyes glazed over, she grinned. "Sorry for the lapse into jargon. All I'm saying is he could help you find ways to a new happiness and to let go of some of the internal conflict about letting go of the past."

"Ah, agreed. Today, he helped me see that I need to allow myself a mental-health break every now and then. I know this all sounds sudden, and it's unlike me to be spontaneous, but I decided a short getaway might do me some good. I just don't care much for traveling alone."

"Me, either, except for work. So you want to go to Sonoma?" She'd only been there once, with her mom, but she'd been too young to drink wine at the time.

"Yeah. We'll want to beat the Fourth of July weekend crowd, but I found a rental that's available starting this Friday night. Is that too soon?" He quickly added, "We'll have separate bedrooms, of course."

She smiled and mentally shook her head, knowing he wasn't ready to take *that* kind of leap yet, if ever. Regardless, she wasn't used to Kristoffer being spontaneous at all, and what he was proposing was an enormous step forward. "I can be ready whenever you are."

"Great. Going with you will be a lot more special than going alone or with anyone else."

Pamela's chest grew tight at the last part. He didn't want just any travel companion. He wanted *her*. "I can't wait."

A whole week together without one or the other having to go home at the end of the evening. Not to mention that being away from Tori and the heavy burden of responsibility that he carried daily would be freeing for Kristoffer, too. She felt a little guilty for thinking that, but selfish though she might be, having him all to herself could help her figure out whether he'd be worth waiting for. One day, he'd be free to love again, but putting herself on hold for a man had never been something she'd considered doing. Not in a million years.

Kristoffer was different than any man she'd ever met, and she was fast approaching the point where she wouldn't be able to imagine her life going forward without him in it. Of course, there was no guarantee Kristoffer would want anything permanent when the time came.

Raising her hopes too high might be a monumental risk to her heart.

✧   ✧   ✧

Had he done the right thing to ask Pamela to spend a week with him in Sonoma? Would he be able to control his desires during that time when every moment spent with her only made him want her more?

They settled down on the couch after dinner to watch a movie. He couldn't say which one, but he stroked her bare arm and cradled her head in his lap. Kristoffer couldn't believe he of all people had sought out a therapist but had to admit his anxiety level had decreased about spending times like this with Pamela. He increasingly looked forward to these nights.

Somehow, talking with another man had been easier than trying to explain his carnal conflict with a woman. He and Rick also had the stock market as a common interest. Often their sessions started out discussing markets and other subjects comfortable for Kristoffer before Rick zeroed in on something personal and pushed him into talking about his personal life. While most adjustments Kristoffer had made so far had been subtle, the upcoming trip would be monumental.

Rick had nailed it this afternoon when he said, "It sounds as though you haven't allowed yourself time to grieve." He'd spelled out the stages of grief, as if Kristoffer needed any more stages to wade through.

In fact, Kristoffer hadn't considered a need to grieve at all over the years, because Tori wasn't dead. Not in the sense she'd been buried, anyway. Not in the way that would have allowed him to move on with his life when emotionally ready.

She remained alive in some ways, but dead in so many others. Trapped between two worlds.

This trip with Pamela would open a new door for him. He hoped he was doing the right thing.

Pamela brought him back to the moment when she sat up. "I think I dozed off. Was it good?"

He gave a noncommittal grunt. "I wasn't paying much attention either, but I'd better be heading home."

"Text me when you get there. You look as worn out as I feel."

He nodded and left. As soon as he let himself into his condo, he texted to let her know he'd made it home safely and to say goodnight. He pocketed his phone, walked across the living room, and started to pour himself a stiff drink, but he hadn't even removed the stopper from the decanter of scotch before realizing he really didn't want a drink at all. Another bad habit he'd developed in recent years. Self-medication, Rick called it.

He ought to be preparing for this imminent trip. Glancing back at the sofa, he saw a stack of unread *Wall Street Journal* newspapers. He definitely needed to clean the place up before Liz and Ron arrived to stay with Noma while he was gone.

That his in-laws had agreed to help him get away on such short notice surprised him, but they'd been checking in more frequently since their daughter's bout with pneumonia, so when they'd called while he was visiting Tori tonight, the request was out before he gave it another thought. Perhaps they were more aware than before that it might only be a question of time before their daughter lost her tenuous hold on this world.

His thoughts turned to Sonoma. Would going back to a place steeped in memories of Tori be what his therapist had in mind? He hadn't revealed that to Rick—or to Pamela. But when he thought about traveling, the valley was the first place that called to him.

Sonoma.

He'd rented a house not far from where they'd honeymooned eighteen years ago this August. The thought of returning to that other house churned his stomach, but his need to relive the happy moments he'd spent in the valley with Tori then and over the years was too strong to ignore.

Noma rubbed his pant leg, and he picked her up. Petting her while staring out the window at the skyline miles away, he remembered the day they'd rescued the cat soon after an anniversary trip. They'd named her Sonoma, but Noma fit her better.

He reminded himself that he'd need to be as attentive as possible to Pamela during the upcoming trip. She'd have no fun if all he did was wallow in the past.

Should he tell her about the significance of where they were going?

Maybe—once they were out there. It wasn't as though they were going as lovers. *That* would have been supremely tacky and thoughtless. But he needed to revisit a place where the vivacious Tori had still been a part of his life. Not to relive the past. Instead, the time had come to say goodbye to that chapter in his life. To close the door and move on.

With Pamela?

He hoped he could.

CHAPTER ELEVEN

Kristoffer tried to shed the lethargy that had grown worse the farther away from Denver they flew. He carried the remainder of their suitcases into the vacation rental house as Pamela set the brown-paper grocery bag on the kitchen counter. They planned to eat out, but had bought coffee, creamer, and a few snacks. Without hesitation, she made a beeline for the patio doors where he joined her, looking out over the rolling hills covered in vineyards.

"I can't believe we're here, Kristoffer." She smiled up at him. "I like surprises like these."

"Thanks for being open to the trip." He'd said goodbye to Tori eight hours ago, and here he was about to spend a week without her in their favorite place. His heart felt encased in ice. Numb.

Guilt threatened to weigh him down. Should he have come here alone? Why drag Pamela out here on the pretense of a carefree vacation when his mind intended to wallow in the past?

Consider this yet another roleplay scene.

Refusing to disappoint Pamela, he resolved to make this week enjoyable for her while still honoring his memories of Tori. Maybe her spirit would be here with them if she truly were free of her broken body.

"Which bedroom would you like?" she asked, drawing him back.

"Doesn't matter to me. I doubt either one will be bad." The vacation property listed two master bedrooms, so they'd have plenty of room to spread out without stepping on each other's toes.

"Why don't you take the master bedroom on that side then?"

He picked up her carry-on bag in one hand and the larger suitcase in the other. "Let's settle in before going out to dinner in a couple of hours. I made a reservation at a wonderful place you're going to love. Do you mind dressing up a little?"

She raised herself on tiptoes and placed a quick kiss on his cheek, throwing him off guard. "Sounds wonderful! I rarely get a chance to dress up."

How could she be so upbeat when he'd just abandoned his *wife?* Sharing this vacation with Pamela seemed wrong on so many levels. Whatever had possessed him?

You aren't here to have sex.

Still, he needed to make Pamela the focus. For her, this was a vacation getaway, not a homework assignment from a therapist. His depressing mood would only put a damper on her experience if he didn't shift gears into a Sonoma state of mind.

After carrying her bags to her room, he rolled his own into the room she declared to be his. He'd unpacked and put everything away in drawers or the closet within twenty minutes. Unable to relax or nap, he walked over to the window, but the view barely registered with him. All his mind could see was Tori, not as she was when they'd last come to the valley, but as she'd looked when he kissed her goodbye this morning.

He missed her already.

Shaking off the feeling that he'd made the wrong decision to come here, he turned and chose what to wear tonight. He hung the coat to his Italian cotton suit on the wooden valet stand. He probably could go casual in the valley at most places this week, but felt more comfortable in a suit and tie for where he planned to take Pamela tonight.

Two hours later, after checking on how the market was doing before the closing, he responded to Pamela's knock at the door. "Come in." He looked up from his computer to find she'd dressed in a flowing skirt with a tight-fitting blouse that showed off her breasts to perfection.

Why was he noticing her breasts?

Because you aren't dead yet.

Her telltale blush told him she was aware of his wayward gaze. Her gaze shifted toward the window. "Mind if I see what your view is like on this side of the house?"

His arm swept toward the windows. "Be my guest."

She walked to the balcony window and stared out. "Oh, you can see the villa from here! This is what I imagine Tuscany must be like."

He suddenly didn't care about any view other than the one of the woman standing before him. Right or wrong, they were out here together now.

'Give this thing a chance, Cuz. You need a life again.'

Gunnar's words from last night's phone call from Afghanistan reverberated through his mind. Kristoffer wanted to get to know Pamela better. Not as lovers, of course, but as friends. Gunnar probably had the wrong idea, but that was his problem.

He'd agreed to help Pamela further her training, too. Being in a new setting—well, new for the two of them together, anyway—might be the perfect time for that.

He wouldn't let things go too far, but there were any number of things he could do to continue working on her focus issues.

The sudden urge to flee nearly overwhelmed him, but instead, he retreated to the closet where he pulled out a white dress shirt and a tie. "Be right back." He went into the bathroom to change out of the polo shirt he'd worn on the plane. Damned if he'd let Pamela down by running back home the first day. He owed her more than that. She'd been his rock ever since Tori had been hospitalized.

Not to mention his temporary submissive—no, bottom was more accurate for their level of power exchange.

After dressing, he returned to the bedroom to see she still stood in the window taking everything in. Pamela's excitement was childlike, but the way he was staring at her ass in that flowing skirt was anything but.

He made a fist at his side, determined to keep his hands off her. "Ready for dinner?"

She turned and smiled. "More than! Let me just grab a wrap and my purse."

Her ginger hair was swept up into a doughnut-style bun, but a couple tendrils had come loose and caressed her neck. Why was he tempted to pull her hair loose to cascade around her shoulders? Or to run his fingers through her tresses the way she loved so much?

A few moments later, his hand rested on the curve of her lower back as he guided her from the house and down the stone path to the Ford Mustang. When Pamela had said she'd always wanted to drive the winding California roads in a convertible, he hadn't been able to tell her no and upgraded their rental at the airport.

Traveling with Tori hadn't been spontaneous like that in their later years, perhaps because they'd seen and done everything here so many times before. Usually, they just made a point to hit all their favorite spots.

Stop comparing Pamela to Tori.

Kristoffer held open the passenger door to the red sports car. He'd keep the roof up on the way to dinner so as not to mess up Pamela's hair. For tonight anyway. They had all week to enjoy the wind in their hair as they drove the valley, perhaps even heading over to the coast highway at some point.

Before he'd closed her door, she smiled up at him. "Let's put the top down."

"What about your hair?"

She grinned as she reached up to remove whatever held her hair in place and shook it out to cascade down her back just as he'd imagined a few minutes ago. He fought the urge to wrap his fist in her hair and pull her head back for a deep ki…

He squeezed his eyes shut to banish the image. Denying his rampant sexual desire for her would be difficult this week. He took his seat, turned over the motor, reached up to lower the sun visors, and released both levers. He pressed the button until the roof was tucked into place behind them. Glancing over at Pamela, he saw she'd donned her sunglasses and rested her head against the backrest, a huge smile on her face.

So full of life and easy to please.

Damn it, this week, I want to experience life with that much exuberance again, too. "Buckle up and hold on, Sprite."

His use of her scene nickname had begun to come up more often in their everyday encounters, too. She'd certainly shone her light into his dark world.

Determined not to overanalyze everything, he shifted into reverse, backed out of the drive, and tore off down the road toward his favorite Sonoma restaurant.

Pamela leaned back and closed her eyes, letting the wind toss her hair into a frenzy across her face. She didn't care. She and Kristoffer were going to make the most of every minute this week. She imagined they'd be enjoying many glasses—maybe even bottles—of wine in the days to come, but she couldn't imagine feeling any higher than she did now.

Even the air smelled different out here. Drier, but sweeter, too. No wonder the area produced so many exquisite wines. Realizing she was missing the scenery, she opened her eyes and glanced out the passenger side. Rows and rows of lush vines tied to wires provided a splash of greenery in an otherwise brownish landscape.

Kristoffer pointed to a sign as they passed a winery. "That winery's been in the same family for more than a century."

"Wow. I can't imagine wanting to be in business with my family that long." She laughed. "We'd drive each other crazy."

He chuckled. "Well, it seems to be working for them. They win top international competitions every year."

"Will we get to sample some of them?"

"Of course. One does not come to Sonoma Valley to simply look at grapes on the vine without trying a few...or a few dozen. We can spend at least one day doing some wine tastings, if you'd like."

She grinned over at him. "Sounds wonderful!"

While still dressed more formally than she'd like him to be while on vacation, his shoulders were less rigid, and some of the creases around his eyes had smoothed out. Hopefully, before the week ended, she'd be able to relax him even more. While he'd done most of the planning for the trip, she'd asked him to give her all day Monday to be in charge. He was in for a treat—or a nightmare, if he didn't have the right frame of mind.

He pulled into the gravel parking lot leading up to a restaurant emblazoned with the name she'd seen numerous times on signs as they'd driven past hectares and hectares of grapevines on wires for the last ten minutes. Taking the brush from her purse to detangle her hair, she was surprised when Kristoffer wrested it from her hand. "Allow me."

She closed her eyes and turned her back to him, letting loose a moan of pure delight as he went to work. "I love having my hair brushed by someone else." Or touched. No, *pulled.* As if he ever would.

"Good to know."

She sighed. His gentle persistence managed to tame the mess much more quickly than she wanted. When she started to pull it into a bun, he stayed her hands.

"Leave it down." She met his gaze. If this would make him happy, she'd comply. "Beautiful." His praise warmed her chest. She wished he'd place a kiss on her neck, but knew that wasn't part of the deal this week. Vacationing friends. Perhaps they'd engage in some Top/bottom exercises, but nothing more.

"I don't know about you, Sprite, but I'm famished. You're in for a treat."

"You've been here before?"

"Yes. Tori and I tried to come out here at least once a year."

His words dumped ice water on her spirits. He'd brought her to a place he'd visited before with his wife? Pamela wasn't jealous of his love for Tori, but the whole point of getting away from Denver was for him to *stop* thinking about his wife for a short while.

She knew he adored Tori. To be loved that deeply by anyone made Pamela's heart ache. Maybe there was a little jealousy involved, but only that Tori had been so lucky to find something Pamela wasn't sure she'd ever find for herself.

Maybe she was the one making more out of this than intended. Regardless, she wouldn't let petty anger or perhaps even jealousy spoil their week together. Despite what his therapist had tried to achieve, Pamela shouldn't have expected so much in such a brief time. He might never be available to her, even after Tori breathed her last. When would she stop pursuing emotionally unavailable men?

Pamela hated that their time together in Sonoma would be riddled with constant reminders of Tori at every turn, but Kristoffer would never stop thinking about the love of his life no matter how far removed he was from the woman physically. What made Pamela think she could help this man start living again when he chose to remain entrenched in a past that could never be again?

After putting the top up, he walked around the car and opened her door. He took her hand, helped her out, then cupped her chin, forcing her to meet his gaze. "You okay?"

Determined not to let her sour mood ruin the evening, she forced a smile and decided to do her best to steer his thoughts away from any previous meals he'd enjoyed here. Tonight was about her and Kristoffer creating new memories.

"Couldn't be better."

The raising of his eyebrows told her he was dubious. She'd have to do better than that. They walked toward the entrance, but before he reached for it, the door to the restaurant opened.

"Mr. Larson! So good to see you again! It has been much too long. We have prepared your favorite table."

"Carlo, good to see you." The two men shook hands before the maître d' turned his gaze to her unable to hide his obvious surprise that she wasn't Tori. He quickly recovered as Kristoffer propelled her inside the door with his warm hand at the small of her back. "Madam, would you like to check your wrap?"

Feeling as though a ghost had just walked over her grave, she pulled it tighter around her. "No, thank you. I'll keep it with me for now."

The chill permeated her bones as they followed the man toward their table. Even Kristoffer's hand resting on her lower spine did nothing to warm her spirits. They were shown to a secluded table in a dark corner of the otherwise crowded restaurant when Pamela noticed a terrace bathed in sunshine just beyond the wall of windows. Surprisingly few patrons had opted to be seated out there, which made it even more inviting.

"Oh, Kristoffer! Let's eat outside. The sunlight looks so inviting." She hoped he wouldn't think her too forward, but the thought of sitting in perhaps the same chair his wife had sat in would have made taking a single bite tonight impossible.

The maître d' deferred to Kristoffer for the final decision. She noticed for the first time the stiff lines that had returned to Kristoffer's face when he stared at the table in the corner.

Break from the past, Kristoffer.

When he looked toward the patio seating area, he visibly relaxed. Perhaps he, too, wanted to create new memories.

He smiled at her. "That's a great idea. The day's heat shouldn't be too bad this evening."

"I'm sure it will feel divine to bask in the sunshine." She smiled. Perhaps a small victory, but a win nonetheless.

He turned toward the host. "I'm sorry, but would you mind seating us outside?"

"Of course not! Excellent choice."

As they meandered between the tables to the terrace's entrance, her steps grew lighter as did her heart. This trip was going to turn out beautifully—for both of them—if she could keep him in the present.

After seating her with the most amazing view of the vineyards and gardens, Kristoffer took his seat and leaned across the table to take her hand. A tingling spread from her hand and up her arm at his touch. "Thank you for this. I wasn't expecting them to remember me after all these years, so Carlo took me by surprise in there." His relief at not having to be seated at the table he'd shared with Tori seemed palpable.

He turned, and his gaze swept over the landscape as his once-rigid demeanor relaxed even more. "Lovely. Just what I needed tonight." He turned back to her and smiled.

Pamela's heart soared. Happier than she'd been since finding out about his history with Sonoma, she returned her attention to the menu. No way would she ask him for a recommendation and let him go with an old favorite of his or his wife's.

Instead, she suggested, "Let's be adventurous tonight and order something we've never tried before."

"Sounds good to me. I sometimes get in a rut when it comes to dining."

You're in a rut not only with your choices of foods, my friend.

✧   ✧   ✧

They spent several minutes perusing the menu in silence. Something new? He'd always gone with the beef tenderloin when he dined here with Tori. Deciding to take Pamela's advice, he veered as far from that as he could go.

"The broiled bay scallops in white wine sounds good. I've never tried them here at least."

Her face lit up with approval. "Sounds wonderful. I'm going to try the wine-braised pork myself. And let's order a basket of grilled focaccia."

"I'll admit that's not new for me, but it's the best you'll ever have."

"Sold."

They closed their menus and waited for their server. His mouth suddenly dry, he reached for the lemon-flavored ice water and downed half a glass. When he met Pamela's gaze across the table, he was taken by how alluring she looked tonight, especially with her hair down. He wished she'd wear it loose more often. The early evening sun brought out the fire in her strands and left her kissable lips full and enticing.

Don't think about kissing her.

His hands, at least, remembered how soft her skin was, but instead of reaching out to indulge himself, he reached for his napkin instead, placing it over his lap. Not that she'd have been able to see the erection he now hid.

Time to divert his focus. "Tell me about your college days, Pamela. I don't think we've talked about that before."

"Well, they were pretty typical, really," she began. "I went to State for undergrad with a double major in biology and psychology. After that, I was accepted at the University of Chicago for medical school."

"I imagine that was a challenging program."

She laughed. "All medical schools are challenging. But I thrived on the competitiveness and found my niche."

"Excuse me, Mr. Larson." He turned his attention to the server. "Would you care for something from our cellars this evening?"

He nodded. After consulting the extensive wine list, he chose a rare chardonnay that would complement both meals, and the man went off to chill it.

She leaned forward, worry in her eyes. "May I ask you something personal?"

"Sure." He wasn't at all sure he wanted to answer a personal question, but he'd made no promise that he would answer, only that she could ask.

"First, it means the world to me that you took me under your wing and have worked with me on my focusing issues."

"I've enjoyed working with you, Sprite." He smiled, hoping to convey a lightness he didn't exactly feel at the moment.

"I was wondering if you might be willing to work on something else with me, too."

"What's that?"

"Would you mind helping to keep me on track this week as far as my workouts? I've gained a lot of strength and stamina spending time at the gym, but I don't want to backslide."

He relaxed. This he could handle.

"Sure. We can jog, walk, or even play golf or tennis at the club, if you'd like."

She smiled. "Sounds great. I wouldn't mind having Roar make an appearance or two, too."

"Are you topping from the bottom now?"

Her eyes opened wider before she grinned. "Busted. I just wanted to make it clear that I wasn't only talking about vanilla workouts."

He shook his head, but couldn't keep the grin off his face, either.

Their salads were served along with the bottle of wine he'd ordered, and he proposed a toast. "To a week of sunshine, flexing new muscles, and creating fond memories."

"I couldn't have put it better myself." She clinked his glass, and they each took a sip. Her smile lit up her face. "I adore this wine. Can we stock up before we fly back to Denver? I brought an extra suitcase to fill up with all the things I don't want to live without." She savored another sip.

"I doubt they had more than one or two bottles in the cellar. It's quite rare."

She swallowed, eying the bottle, and then asked, "How much does it cost?"

"That's not for a lady to ask when the gentleman is picking up the tab."

She set the glass down. "No wonder the wine list had no prices. I don't know if I can keep drinking it, knowing how much it's costing you."

"Nonsense. The entire bottle is paid for. We should not let a drop go to waste."

And they didn't, although they drank more slowly, enjoying most of the bottle after their entrees had arrived to lessen the effects of the alcohol. He'd take her for a walk in the gardens before heading back to the house, even though he didn't feel any buzz from the wine.

After declining dessert, Pamela wiped her mouth and set her napkin on the table beside her plate. "That was the most succulent meal I've enjoyed in ages. Thanks for bringing me here."

"I'll have to admit, trying the scallops was a wonderful discovery, but nothing compares to your cooking. However, I'm happy to give you a break from the kitchen this week."

"No way! I rarely cook for myself and never when I'm overseas. But you're welcome to join me in the kitchen anytime. I enjoy anything we do together."

The mention of her being overseas put a damper on his mood. He didn't want to think about her being in harm's way again, whether from militants or some new virus or infection that might not be as easy to cure this time. But he knew she'd be going again sometime this summer.

"Any word on your next assignment?"

She shook her head. "No change from the last estimate."

About six weeks. "I'm going to miss having you around when you're gone."

"And I, you, but it's only for a month."

Seemed like a lifetime.

"There's so much I still want to accomplish." Her eyes opened wider. "Any word on when Gunnar expects to fly back with Fakhira?"

"No. I spoke with him yesterday, but he's knee-deep in something he thinks might take two or three more weeks to sort out."

"Oh." Her disappointment was fleeting because she smiled again, lighting up her face. "Well, without Gunnar agreeing to do this, I'm not sure she'd ever have been given this opportunity—not this soon, at least—so I'll just be patient."

The server left the check, and Kristoffer placed his card inside the folder.

When they stood after settling up with the restaurant, the sun was low on the horizon. "Why don't we walk off some of this dinner before we head back to the house?" he suggested.

"I'd love to."

"There's a path into the gardens for patrons." He pulled out her chair and placed his hand at the small of her back to guide her down the steps.

A breeze kicked up and blew a wisp of her hair against her cheek and mouth. He reached up to capture it and tuck it behind her ear before realizing what he was doing, although she didn't seem bothered by the intimate gesture.

His stomach knotted up.

"What's that I smell?" They were in the red wine garden. She lifted her pert nose into the air.

He drew a deep breath to test his rusty skills. "I smell basil, rosemary, and tobacco."

"Tobacco? Seriously? I thought that was only grown in the southeast."

"The vintner tries to bring together a variety of scents for his wines. Tobacco has an affinity for merlot and cabernet sauvignon."

She closed her eyes and drew a deep breath. "Yes, I can smell all of those scents now. And...sage?"

"Excellent."

She met his gaze and smiled. "How do you know so much about wines?"

He shrugged. "Picked it up here and there over the years." Much of his knowledge had come from the many times he'd visited here with Tori. "It's one of my guilty pleasures—enjoying good wine and learning everything I can about its vintage." A new one was spending time with Pamela, it seemed.

When the stones in the path became uneven, he took her hand. "Don't want you falling." He remembered lifting her into his arms when her knees had given out the night he'd made her kneel on grains of rice. Holding her hand satisfied something inside him, but he didn't want to send her the wrong signal. Keep the focus on the garden's flowers and plants.

They walked side by side in silence until she leaned closer to some of the plants, trying to determine what scent they emitted, he supposed. The pathways were well-lit by torches, but the planting areas were difficult to see in the waning daylight.

"We need to come back during the day," she suggested. "This is such a beautiful place."

"Not a problem, but there are lots of other places I want to take you to as well."

"I can't wait." She turned to him and, before he knew what she planned to do, placed a kiss on his cheek. "Thanks. I'm having a wonderful time. But would you mind if I moved my plans up to tomorrow rather than Monday?"

He grinned. "Be my guest." He wondered again what she wanted them to do but found himself anticipating whatever she had in mind more than the places he'd planned to take her.

This week would be the perfect opportunity for him to try new things and discover his favorite place through Pamela's eyes.

❖   ❖   ❖

Pamela's resolve to help Kristoffer see Sonoma in a new light was never stronger than when she mounted her rented bike late the next morning. Her mission became clearer after realizing he'd most likely intended to show her all of his and Tori's special places. She wanted to flood him with new memories this week. Kristoffer wouldn't think of this valley again without remembering Pamela, too.

"Ready, set, go!" She set off down the road from the bike rental place. Soon the clicking of his spokes told her he was in hot pursuit. After a short sprint, she laughed and surrendered, slowing the pace. "Okay, now let's take it a little slower."

"Whatever you say. You're in charge." He didn't even sound winded. Man, she hoped she was able to keep up.

The route she'd mapped out called for about twelve miles round trip riding along fairly flat lanes until they reached the final climb to a place in the hills where they would have a late lunch or early dinner, depending on how long it took them to reach that point. She'd made sure they ate a hearty breakfast to last them and packed some power snacks in her backpack. His backpack carried their water bottles. The GPS on her handlebar had been programmed, and she looked forward to the hours ahead.

The sun soaked into her skin. What a difference it was to experience the valley without motorized vehicles distorting the natural sounds enveloping them—the rustling of the leaves on the grapevines, songs of western birds she couldn't identify, and their tires on the pavement. She wished they could stop and sample some of the grapes, but they weren't ripe yet. Besides, the pesticides would probably kill them. They'd sample the wines instead.

Out of the blue, her thoughts meandered to her mother, a strong advocate against pesticides—and champion for any number of other environmental and social-justice causes. She ought to have told her she'd be traveling so close by this week.

Kristoffer rode abreast of her along a deserted road and touched her arm. "Where'd you go?" She turned toward him, puzzled. "I asked if you'd like to take a break for a bit."

"Sorry. I was thinking about my mom."

He raised his eyebrows. "Didn't expect that answer." They pulled to the side of the road, and he retrieved a sports bottle from his backpack to hand to her before extracting his own.

She grinned. "One thing led to another in my head as we were riding along, and suddenly, I was thinking about her."

"You do have a tendency to let your mind do that. Perhaps I should have prepared an assignment for you to help you focus on the now." He grinned. "Instead, I'll indulge you while we rest. Tell me more about her."

"She lives in Carmel-by-the-Sea. I guess the lure of free spirits and dog-friendly beaches were too strong." Pamela forced a laugh, but remembered how devastated she and her dad were when Mom left them to find herself, or whatever it was she was searching for. Thankfully, both of her parents seemed much happier now. "Mom is happily free of male oppression, I suppose. Dad did like being in control, which I can see in retrospect. Fortunately for him, his second wife had no problems giving in."

For the first time, she wondered if they had a Dom/sub relationship, but didn't really want to think about that. Besides, he'd asked her about her mother.

"Mom had a difficult time adjusting to the role of Air Force officer's wife when they returned from Japan. She's much happier now fostering rescue dogs."

"Would you like to go down for a visit later this week? It's a beautiful drive along the Pacific Coast Highway, and we do have the convertible. Shouldn't let it go to waste."

While she missed her mom and the thought of driving along the iconic highway with the wind and sea air blowing through her hair and against her face sounded lovely, she wasn't sure what Mom would think of Kristoffer. He wasn't far off the mark from the highly disciplined people on the base or at the Air Force Academy's campus where she'd never fit in. What if she went into a panic thinking Pamela was dating an uptight man who might give her equally uptight little grandchildren?

Whoa, I'm not dating Kristoffer at all. But she didn't want Mom to get that wrong impression, either.

"No pressure, if you'd rather not."

She realized she hadn't responded to his suggestion. Why was she reverting to old bad habits when she'd been doing so much better while working with Roar?

"I'm not sure we'll have time."

"Don't let that hold you back. I'd hate for you to be so close and not get to visit her. If you want to, that is."

Had she just sealed her fate? Kristoffer took family ties seriously, at least with Tori and Gunnar. Perhaps his mother, too.

Suddenly, something occurred to her. Taking him away from all the memories of his wife here in Sonoma might be just the thing to help *him* relax more on this vacation. She could even suggest stops along the way at some of her favorite spots.

She took a swig of water before committing one way or another, but her mind was made up. "I think a drive down the coast would be perfect." Hopefully, he and Tori hadn't done that many times before, too.

"Consider it done. We could leave here Monday or Tuesday to meander along the coast then come back to close up the house and catch our flight home."

Everything had shifted in a matter of minutes. She hoped she wouldn't regret the decision to visit her mom, but looked forward to excursions showing him some of her favorite places, perhaps going as far as Big Sur.

They mounted their bicycles again and rode along the windy road in silence while she drew deep breaths of the ultra-fresh air. Not as crisp as Colorado mountain air, but not unpleasant either. Simply different.

Their GPS alerted them to the approaching highway sooner than expected, and she signaled for the turn. At this point, the road became steep on the approach to the restaurant, and she put the bike into a lower gear. Near the crest, she was never so happy to see the restaurant's roadside sign come into her field of vision.

Dismounting, she stretched her legs. Man, her butt was sore. She gasped for breath and retrieved the unfinished water bottle from the holder on her frame to squeeze the now-warm liquid down her parched throat. The thought of getting back on the bike for the return trip held zero appeal, so she looked forward to a leisurely meal. As long as they made it back to the house by dark, they'd be fine.

"It's beautiful up here," Kristoffer said as he surveyed their surroundings.

"The restaurant's online menu boasted a number of fresh entrees. I thought it would be perfect to break up our ride."

"Must be new to the valley. Wasn't here last time I visited."

That's why I chose it.

She looked forward to this meal and his company without any chance of him getting stuck in the past. Inside, the hostess seated them at a table overlooking the vineyards. They were between major mealtimes and had the place to themselves. She was certain it would be a zoo here over the weekend.

Kristoffer emptied his water glass and refilled it from the carafe before surveying the hillside. "No wonder this place came so highly recommended. The view alone is spectacular."

She ordered a duck confit dish prepared in a red wine reduction and accompanied her meal with the same wine while he selected pan-roasted sea bass and a glass of Chablis. After a toast to good friends and relaxing getaways, both sipped and proclaimed their vintage to be the best.

Kristoffer set down his glass. "I'll order a case of each to be shipped back to my place for us to enjoy again sometime."

"Sounds great—and there's less chance of them being broken that way than in my spare suitcase."

She looked forward to their reliving what she hoped would be idyllic memories of this adventure for many years to come.

Their salads arrived, and they ate until she broke the silence. "I can't believe how hungry I am. Riding bikes is quite a workout."

"And yet it doesn't feel like work when we have such beautiful scenery along the way. We ought to do this back home. Lots of Rails-to-Trails routes and other great places to ride in the back country without scaling any Fourteeners."

"I'd like that a lot." Any time spent with Kristoffer would be something to look forward to, but going home again wasn't what she wanted to talk about now. This respite from real life would help heal both of them. She just hoped he wouldn't be called back for an emergency. He needed this break from Tori. With her parents visiting and having temporary guardianship and responsibility, Pamela hoped they would handle any minor crisis that might arise.

Kristoffer set down his fork after finishing his salad—all except the onions, she noted. "Now, to continue our earlier discussion, tell me more about your mom. When's the last time you saw her?"

She wished they'd find another topic of discussion. "About a year ago."

"That's a long time."

"Oh, we talk on the phone a couple times a month and have certainly gone longer than a year between visits before." Money had been too tight for her to travel much for pleasure, and during medical school, she'd gone five years without seeing her mom. "But Mom wants nothing to do with Colorado, even though I live hours away from Colorado Springs, so the only time we see each other is when I travel to California. Last year, I booked a layover in San Francisco for a few days on one of my trips to Afghanistan just to see her."

"All the more reason for us to make a reunion happen this week." He pulled out his cell phone, as if he intended for her to call Mom at this very moment. "No signal. But you can call her when we get back to the house."

This seemed more important to him than to her. "How do you get along with your mother?"

He chuckled. "We love each other in our own way, but she isn't easy to be close to." He sobered. "She became severely depressed after my father left, and I was just a kid myself and had no clue how to help her."

"It wasn't your place to assume the role of counselor or crutch."

He opened his mouth to say something, but didn't because their entrees were served at that moment.

Alone again, before he took the first bite, he met her gaze and grew serious, but something must have triggered a memory of his wife, because he veered off into a polar-opposite direction.

"Since the accident, nothing's stable anymore. In some ways, it's reminiscent of how I felt as a kid when my father moved out. It took a long time for me to process that."

No doubt the abandonment issues were churned up by Tori's being ripped out of his life so suddenly.

"I still sometimes feel as though Tori's going to walk through the door to my condo any minute, though we didn't even live there before the accident. And somehow we'll be transported back to our former world, as if this was some nightmare and we're holograms on the Holodeck in *The Next Generation*." He shrugged, but he must really wish that could happen sometimes—to have a chance to see Tori one more time and say everything left unsaid.

If only I could make it so for him.

But then he'd have to struggle through the loss all over again when the make-believe world was over.

He cleared his throat. "Then I remember she's not coming back, and the world tilts on its axis yet again."

She reached across the table and squeezed his hand, but had no words to offer in comfort. After a moment, she pulled back and their meal progressed in companionable silence.

By the time they'd finished, she regretted ordering such a heavy dish. The thought of getting back on the bicycle again was daunting.

"Did we save room for dessert?" the too-chipper server asked.

Both responded with an emphatic, "No!" They laughed, and Kristoffer asked for the check.

"Maybe we'll work this off on the ride back to the bike rental office," he said. "We can pick up dessert around there and take it back to the house."

"I shouldn't be thinking about eating again for the rest of the week—but that sounds like a plan to me. I have a feeling the ride back will make me hungry for something."

Like you.

She banished the improper thought from her mind.

After settling the bill, they walked around the property and took some photographs and a couple of selfies with an incredible view of the evergreen-covered mountains behind them. His long arms made her look much better than she did when taking them herself with her phone.

All too soon, the time came to mount their bikes again. Just as she suspected, the bruised area on her butt screamed at being back in the saddle, but unless she wanted to walk the six miles back, she'd just have to suck it up.

Kristoffer groaned, too. "You'd think they could make bicycle seats more user-friendly."

She laughed at the similar direction of his thoughts. "Yeah. I have new respect for those professional cyclists who spend three weeks in the bike saddle during racing tours."

"Well, at least they train for it."

"True. Maybe there are padded biker shorts they can wear, too."

"Well, let's make a pact not to sign up for an international cycling team or anything."

"Done," she said, holding out her fist to bump knuckles in agreement. "But I'll race you to the next stop sign." Without giving him a chance to insert his foot into the pedal, she was off, but he quickly made up ground on the downhill grade, and they reached the sign neck and neck.

The exertion caused Pamela to gasp for breath between each word. "No. More. Racing." She took a deeper breath and glanced at him. He'd barely broken a sweat. "You're in better shape than you led me to believe with your sedentary office job."

"I run sometimes when I need to quiet my head. Guess I built up some strength in my leg muscles in the bargain."

"Anytime you want to whip my ass into shape, take me running with you sometime."

The look on his face was priceless. He glanced at her shorts-encased backside for a fraction of a second before his eyes smoldered to a deeper blue. He grinned. "Nothing wrong with your ass. But you do need to expand your lung capacity..." His gaze rested on her heaving chest a moment before he continued in a now-raspy voice. "Perhaps we can do some training on your quads and hamstrings to give you more strength for the hills." Again, his eyes focused on the part of her anatomy he was discussing—her legs this time—and her body tingled with awareness.

"You're the Dom who wants to train me. Just remember, I'm not a masochist. Go easy."

Anything that would give them more time together sounded perfect to her. With all the plans they had for when they returned to Colorado, she wasn't dreading how fast this week would fly by.

His gaze bore into her, causing her girly bits to tingle a bit, and not from rubbing against the bicycle seat. "I'm demanding. You might want to reconsider what you're asking for."

The benefits of improving her body while spending time with Kristoffer far outweighed any worry about his being too tough in that area.

"If you're game, then I'm willing." Images of him standing over her in the gym caused the slowly dissipating heat to return to her cheeks. "When do we start?"

"I'm not one to rush into something as serious as physical training for someone." His words surprised her, because he had jumped into training her on improving her focus. "Tonight, we'll discuss your long-term and short-term goals and map out a plan to reach key targets over the next few months, including ways to stay in shape while overseas."

"I'm sure it will take me a while to get to where I want to be." The thought of his training her over the course of months pleased her. "You're on. I'm going to enjoy working out the kinks." She flushed at the double entendre. After all, weren't personal trainers dominating and even a bit sadistic? She smiled and gave him a wink before they hopped back onto their bikes and took the next stretch side-by-side, talking as they rode along.

"We'll need to spell out the rewards and consequences in relation to how you are at meeting your goals." His husky Roar voice made her wet. He'd never been quite so suggestive before. Adding this arrangement might be the next best thing to having a full power exchange with him. He'd be guiding her every day, pushing her to improve her body and mind, and then rewarding or punishing her in accordance with the goals and standards they agreed upon.

"I wouldn't expect anything less than being punished if I don't follow instructions."

"I prefer to call it discipline, not punishment. Think of it as suffering the consequences of poor decisions or misbehavior. But you're not a child, Pamela. I expect you to behave responsibly and follow whatever regimen and protocols we establish for your own sense of accomplishment. You'll enjoy a lot of satisfaction in meeting your goals. But be warned that I won't tolerate cheating, topping from the bottom, or slacking off because you want a funishment."

"I wouldn't expect you to. And I never cheat."

She laughed, although she had to admit the thought of being spanked for missing a goal had already crossed her mind. She'd better not play those games with him. No doubt, he already knew her well enough to suspect that a spanking would actually be more of a reward than a fun "punishment."

"Good girl."

Her stomach dropped into her pelvis, and a delicious heaviness spread into her lower abdomen. She hoped to hear those words often.

✧   ✧   ✧

Back at the rental house, they went to their separate bathrooms for showers. As the water poured over him, more than sweat and grime washed away. Years of pain and sorrow followed them down the drain.

If left to his own devices this week, he would have wallowed in memories and might never have experienced the incredible awakening he had today. Actually, it began last night at the restaurant. When the host inadvertently tried to put him back into the past, his mind had been too numb to even see any other option. If he'd been alone, he'd have taken that table in the corner, hoping to feel close to Tori one more time.

He wished he'd been able to wake up and shout, "Bloody hell, no!" Instead, he'd been too…guilt-ridden to take that step, open his mouth, and ask to be seated elsewhere.

Then Pamela spoke up and literally saved him from the abyss. No, he hadn't figured all this out at the restaurant. It wasn't until spending this incredible day with her—seeing old places through reawakened eyes, exploring new things—that he'd finally begun to sort a lot of this out.

As they had biked back to the house an hour ago, along some of the same roads he and Tori had traveled every year, he realized he'd never said goodbye to her. Why? Because he hadn't been honest with himself. He'd never fully accepted that she was never coming back. Sounded delusional when he put it that way. What sane man could look at her body day after day for years and not figure it out?

No, his mind *had* figured it out at least two years ago and maybe earlier.

The holdout all this time had been his heart. Tori occupied every inch of that space for twenty years. When she'd been ripped away from him, the wound gaped open…

He hadn't known who or what could heal his heart and fill it again until last night when Pamela not only helped him to choose the table on the sun-touched terrace over the one in the shadowed corner. She also made him see that he preferred light over darkness. The future over the past.

He'd been stuck there too long, unable to find a way out.

Today, his eyes and heart had both opened wider. Pamela showed him possibilities he hadn't imagined since losing Tori.

Kristoffer blinked, reaching for the shampoo bottle yet unsure if he'd already washed his hair. He'd been going through the motions like that for years. Now, he had a chance to start living fully again, but there was something he still needed to do.

No, two things.

First, he needed to apologize to Pamela for bringing her out here on false pretenses. Second, he needed to let Tori go. Way past time for that, actually.

He set the bottle down and leaned his forehead against the granite wall. "Tori, I know I ought to do this somewhere more dignified, but I'm not going to lose another minute. My heart says it has to be right now, right here."

He drew a ragged breath.

"Sweetheart, I've held you earthbound too long. But starting in this moment, I am going to stop agonizing over and mourning what we've lost. We can never get back what we had. We can't live out the dreams we had for our lives together. But I'll make these new promises to you."

I'll never forget what we shared as long as I live.
I'll never abandon you no matter how long you linger.
I'll be the keeper of our memories, but let our hopes and dreams go.
And, most of all, I'll set you free, Sweetheart.

A new start. In the shower, everything had seemed clear as day, but by the time he'd dressed and prepared to meet Pamela as agreed at seven to discuss her training program, once again, he seemed clueless as to what to do. Then it dawned on him. Today was a day of epiphanies, now that he'd opened his heart a little.

One day at a time. One step at a time.

And first up, he'd agreed to train her physically starting tomorrow. Maybe even tonight. As much as he liked to prepare for everything, sometimes he needed to learn to take things as they come.

Like the idea to train Pamela physically. It hadn't come completely out of the blue. Ever since she told him she'd joined a gym, he'd flirted with the idea of adding some of that work to her concentration exercises. When she gave him the perfect chance to engage with her in such a nonthreatening activity, he'd jumped at it. The physical training would bridge the gap from California to Denver, too, allowing them a little more time to spend together.

Kristoffer put on his watch a few minutes before the time he'd told her he'd meet her in the kitchen to prepare their snack. He found her already busy putting the finishing touches on their filled plates.

Wearing form-fitting biker shorts and an emerald-green tank top, she looked over at him and smiled. "Impeccable timing, as always."

She'd pulled her hair up in a clip, probably while still wet from her shower, and he fought the urge to release the clip and let it fall loose.

Not my place.

The tops of her breasts were exposed by the scooped neck, but he forced his gaze to meet hers, noticing instead that the tank also brought out the color in her eyes.

He surveyed the dessert plates filled with much healthier fare than they'd originally intended. "Looks great. Light, but satisfying." By mutual agreement after returning the bikes to the shop, they'd opted to pass on desserts and purchased a bottle of wine and an assortment of fresh fruits, soft cheeses, and crackers for dinner. "I'll open the wine and pour."

Only their second day in Sonoma, and his original plans had flown out the window, but he found himself enjoying every minute spent with her.

While nibbling on their light dinner, they jotted down a number of short- and long-term goals. The page was filling impressively when she became distracted.

"Look at the sun!" Pamela pulled him out of the task at hand to look out the window at the golden light bathing the valley just as the fiery ball slipped behind the horizon.

He couldn't chide her for her lack of concentration, because if not for her, he'd have worked right through, and it would have been dark by the time he looked up.

"Let's go for a walk before it's too dark," he suggested. "Some stretches and a power walk would be the perfect thing to loosen up our muscles after all those hours on the bikes. Might help us sleep better, too."

"Sold! I'll get my shoes and be back in a flash."

After the two were ready, he motioned her to precede him out the door and followed. They spent a few minutes stretching their leg muscles—and groaning at how tight they'd already become.

When she would have strolled away after their warm-ups, he halted her with a hand on her arm. "As you walk, crook your elbows and fist your hands. Pump them back and forth in rhythm with your stride."

When they took off, he went over a mental list of what he wanted to pick up when they were in town tomorrow. Some light weights for one. Nothing expensive, because they'd probably leave them behind rather than add to the weight of their checked bags.

His longer legs made the pace more difficult for her, but he didn't go easy, either. She managed to keep up. She may lack stature, but had an abundance of determination and motivation.

Watching her breasts bounce to each step caused him to note that a sports bra might be a good addition to their shopping trip tomorrow as well. Or not. He cast sidelong glances her way, constantly pulled back to those mounds.

His inappropriate thoughts made him happy the sun had gone down and his hard-on wasn't evident to her. He hoped not, at least.

"I think we should head back before it's too dark." He had a flashlight app on his phone, but didn't have to use it until they reached the driveway to the house. He was satisfied she'd gotten off to a great start today.

Back at the house, they showered and returned to the common area where they turned on the stereo and flopped onto the couch.

"I had an awesome day, Kristoffer. Thanks for everything."

He sat and motioned her to stretch out and rest her head in his lap. Pamela's hair was still damp from the shower as he ran his fingers through it, but he smiled as she moaned the way she often did during their couch time back home.

Keeping her eyes closed, she said, "That feels heavenly."

"I wasn't sure how I was going to handle this week, but you've made today better than I could have imagined."

She smiled. "Your turn tomorrow. What's on tap?" she asked.

"You'll see."

She quirked an eyebrow, but didn't ask for details. She trusted him, he supposed, even though she had no idea where he intended to take her. He enjoyed surprising her.

Kristoffer grinned like a kid in a candy store. He'd just come up with an idea and couldn't wait to see if he could make it happen.

CHAPTER TWELVE

On Sunday, Kristoffer took her shopping. Her dad always indulged her stepmother Monica on such trips, but he actually seemed to enjoy it. Okay, most of what they shopped for was in athletic stores—three- and five-pound weights, better running shoes, and even a couple of sports bras.

At a clothing store, he asked if she'd packed a swimsuit, which she had, and now she wondered where they planned to swim. They were rather far from the beach, although he might be looking ahead to Carmel. While the water would be cold, the beach made up for it.

But after dropping everything off at the house in the afternoon, he suggested she grab her suit and a towel, and within half an hour, they were swimming laps side by side in an Olympic-sized pool at the local country club. He must have signed them up for short-term memberships.

After only three laps, she could barely move her arms.

"You go on without me," she said as she hoisted herself onto the edge of the pool and sat. Watching him swim freestyle two more lengths of the pool, she marveled at his athletic physique. She'd never thought he'd be flabby, but for a man who worked at a desk all day, he had muscles on his torso and legs in all the right places.

He had nice tight buns, too.

I can look as long as I don't touch, right?

He ended his last lap beside her right knee and rested his elbows on the edge before smiling up at her. "Tomorrow, no excuses. I want you to give me five."

"If that's Roar speaking, then okay. Otherwise…"

"Don't be a brat. You don't have to make world-record time, but we won't leave the pool until you finish. By the way, I'm impressed with your breaststroke."

With any other man, she'd have thought he was flirting, but with Kristoffer, she took his words at face value. "I was on the swim team in high school."

"We'll have to make use of the pool at my condo when we get back from California."

"You're on."

Knowing he still wanted to hang out with her made her happy.

In one fluid motion, he dragged himself out of the water—splashing her, probably intentionally, and sat on the ledge a moment. "Let's go." He stood and reached for her hand, pulling her to her feet. "I have something special planned for tonight."

How had she ever thought she didn't like surprises? She couldn't wait to see what he had in mind.

After they returned to their rental and were about to head to their separate rooms, he said, "In case you're wondering, dress in business casual tonight."

"Skirt okay?" She hadn't attended a lot of business functions; at the hospital, she usually hid behind her white coat.

"Whatever is comfortable to sit and walk in. We'll be making a number of stops tonight."

Intrigued, she went to her room. After showering and applying makeup, she quickly donned a cerulean blue, gauzy skirt decorated with fine beadwork. Probably a little dressier than he'd suggested, but she felt like getting gussied up. Instead of a blouse, she wore a black short-sleeved cotton sweater free of adornments.

Before leaving the room, she retrieved the beaded purse that matched her skirt, both of which she'd purchased at a market in Kabul, handmade by one of the locals.

When she entered the common area between their bedrooms, he whistled his appreciation. "I might need to step up my game." He wore black slacks and a polo shirt.

"Don't be ridiculous. You look great. I just felt like wearing something fancier tonight."

"If you're ready," he said, crooking his arm for her to place her hand there.

When he walked by the car keys without picking them up, she stopped. "Don't forget the keys."

But he nudged her to continue on. "We won't be driving."

"Oh? Do I need to change into walking shoes?"

"No."

He opened the door, and she found a white stretch limo parked in the driveway. "What on earth?"

"Your chariot awaits, Sprite."

She shifted her attention to Kristoffer, who beamed with pride, perhaps because he'd succeeded in surprising her. "I'm floored. But what's the occasion?"

"We have a number of wineries to hit tonight on our quest for the perfect home wine collections. But I don't want either of us driving under the influence, so I hired a driver."

In a luxury limo. "You always think of everything—and then some."

He led her down the steps to where the uniformed chauffeur waited beside the limo's open door to help her inside. She scooted across the white leather bench to just before where it curved around behind the privacy window. In front of her, an incredible feast had been laid out on the bar. Kristoffer took his seat beside her and reached forward to prepare her a plate of assorted small bites and finger sandwiches.

"I didn't want to drink a lot of alcohol in transit and ruin our taste buds for the wine, so I opted for having our meal in stages while we ride from vineyard to vineyard." He filled a water goblet with Perrier. "But because our first stop is the farthest away, we'll have our main course now."

"You sure know how to swell a girl's head. I've never been in a limo before, stretch or otherwise."

"Not even on senior prom night?"

"I didn't go to either of my proms." His arched brow and sidelong glance made her laugh. "Why the skepticism? I was a geeky nerd long before it was cool."

"Well, clearly the boys at your high school were blind fools. Not only are you intelligent, but beautiful as well."

"I may have to show you some of my high-school pics—braces and all."

She waited to begin eating until he filled his own plate. The windows were tinted, but they'd ridden all over Sonoma Valley by either car or bike the last couple of days. She was content to look at Kristoffer and enjoy this meal beside him without needing to peek outside.

"Oh, I almost forgot." He reached over to the bar and buffet area again, and soon the mellow strains of Miles Davis surrounded them. It took her only a few seconds to make out the tune as Davis's unique rendition of "Time After Time."

The song always made her sad, especially this version, but she wouldn't let anything dampen her spirits tonight. "How long have you been planning this?"

He grinned. "Since last night. I went online and arranged it after we got back from our bike ride. I wanted to experience another first here with you."

He hadn't done this with Tori? She could barely contain her pleasure. "And I thought the light under your door meant you were working hard again."

He shrugged. "I'm taking this vacation thing as seriously as I do my work."

"You're doing better than I expected. When's the last time you were on a vacation?"

"Two and a half months before the accident." He still told time in before and after that traumatic night. "Tori and I celebrated our seventeenth anniversary in Sonoma."

Let him talk about her. Even if it kills you.

She placed her hand on his arm. "I know how much Tori means to you. I know her situation isn't going to change for the better, but I admire that you've remained true to her all these years."

"I love her. You do whatever you have to for the ones you love."

How to say this without overstepping? "My heart breaks for you both, Kristoffer, but I worry that no one is seeing to *your* needs."

"I don't need anyone taking care of me."

"It's the human condition that we can't survive without each other. Just remember I'm available anytime you ever want to reach out—for anything."

An awkward silence stretched out between them. Kristoffer took her empty plate and set it and his own down on the seat beside him before turning back toward her. His somber face made her worry.

"I owe you a deep apology, Pamela."

"You don't owe me anything of the sort."

"No, I wrongly invited you as a crutch to help me deal with the memories I knew would bombard me. But I didn't tell you that's why I wanted you to join me. Hell, when my counselor hears that I went on vacation to Sonoma—of all places—I bet he'll lose his cool for the first time ever."

"Please, you don't have to explain—" His warm finger against her lips cut off her words and left her body tingling when he pulled his hand away.

"Yes, I do. Stop arguing with me." He smiled, taking some of the sting out of his admonishment. "I think deep down I expected to feel closer to Tori by coming back to all the places we loved. But nothing's gone as planned. The minute we arrived and walked into the house, I felt that familiar depression settling over me. By the way, this isn't a place I ever stayed with Tori."

A worry was lifted off her mind, because she *had* wondered since dinner that first night.

"Friday night at the restaurant, when we were shown to the table Tori and I… The thought of sitting there…" He glanced away. "I was almost sick to my stomach. Partly because I knew I could never share it with Tori ever again, but also because I saw how unfair I was being to you. Your exuberance for this vacation was snuffed out because I couldn't get my head out of my past."

She grinned, wanting to lighten the mood. "Nothing can curb my excitement. I will have fun regardless. Besides, we all have times when our heads are in the wrong place." She wouldn't dare say his had actually been up his ass, but from his self-deprecating grin, he knew she alluded to it.

"Then you steered us to the patio. Pamela, it was as if I was able to begin to put the past in perspective and open a door to new opportunities and memories to come. I've been training you to live in the moment, and I was doing anything but. Ever since that night, you've shown me Sonoma through your eyes and helped me create new memories—with you."

He glanced at the floor. "Tori and I came here a lot, and I'm always going to hold on to those memories." She reached out to squeeze his hand and bring him back to her, but when he met her gaze again, she saw he hadn't really left. "I never set out to make this vacation intolerable for you. I don't want to ruin tonight for you, either. I just needed to get all that off my chest and move forward." He shrugged with an apologetic grin.

"I'm glad you did. Now, maybe you can fully relax and enjoy the rest of our vacation."

He marveled at her taking his confession in stride without resentment. Such a forgiving and compassionate woman. He brushed a loose strand of hair behind her ear. "I haven't felt this alive since the accident. You've gradually been shining a light into the dark corners of my soul. It's one of the reasons I call you Sprite." He grinned. "That and your pint-size body."

She rolled her eyes, but was charmed that he credited her for making a difference in his life. "I wondered where that came from."

He sobered again. "Bottom line—I was wrong. Can you forgive me?"

"As I said, nothing to forgive. You're a grieving man who has been stranded between the living and the dead for a very long time." She reached up to stroke his cheek. "Kristoffer, we'll have to make this up as we go. Unlike a D/s relationship, there aren't any protocols for building a close friendship between a man and a woman."

"True, but we have a more serious issue to tackle."

What else? When he took her hand and squeezed it reassuringly, she only became more nervous.

"Pamela, I stopped seeing you as a mere friend a while ago, although I've fought against those feelings because I can't offer you everything a woman deserves." She started to interrupt, but he held up his hand. "Hear me out. Rick—my therapist—has been helping me to see that it's not wrong for me to be attracted to you or to want to have something more than friendship with you."

Her throat closed up, and she wouldn't have been able to speak even if she had any words to say. She was so confused at the moment.

"I'm not trying to put you on the spot or anything. Hell, I don't even know what I want. I made a commitment to Tori I need to keep as long as she's living." He ran his free hand through his hair, seemingly at a loss for words himself. "But I'm not dead yet, either. I guess what I want to ask is whether we can renegotiate our limits—not just for the Dom/sub relationship but for our everyday one, too. Could you be open to having something more with me, even if I can't define what *more* means yet?"

She closed the gap between them and gave him a hug. When she pulled away again, she saw the worry in his eyes and realized he needed to hear the words. He'd taken an enormous step, but still didn't seem to know what to do next.

"Kristoffer, neither of us has any illusions that life will be easy or perfect. Why not carve out our own happiness? We're both adults. We don't have to answer to anyone but ourselves."

"We don't live in a vacuum, although being out here is pretty damned close to it. Back in Denver, people will talk. It might even affect your career."

"I don't think either of us cares particularly what others think, especially not the judgmental ones. Besides, I've dealt with wagging tongues before and didn't let them control how I live." She leaned closer. "Kristoffer, we're going to take it one step at a time. One day, we'll look back and realize how far we've come on the path."

A tear surprised her by splashing on her hand, but she needed to say this. "I'm so proud of you for taking this first step. I've been terribly worried about you with all you've shouldered in silence for so long. You put so much pressure on yourself to honor your commitments and take care of Tori's and Gunnar's interests that you seem to forget you're still human. You have needs, too."

His shoulders relaxed, and he smiled. "As I'm discovering again. You're an amazing woman, Pamela." He picked up and handed her the water goblet before lifting his own in a toast. "Here's to wherever our journey takes us."

This was happening more suddenly than she'd expected. This trip had been good for him—but she knew not to celebrate until they were back in their day-to-day lives. That would be the test of whether he was prepared to enter into something more than friendship on a long-term basis.

She drew a ragged breath and smiled. "I've never enjoyed any man's company as much as yours."

"I enjoy being with you. No pressure, and I'm able to talk with you about anything and have been able to right from the start."

She couldn't resist adding her assessment. "Seeing me naked at the academy probably gave us a sense of intimacy most people don't have when they first meet."

He laughed, but almost instantly became serious again. "Honestly, Pamela, I can't promise you anything but today. I may return to Denver and go back into my cave."

That he voiced the same concerns she'd had only a moment ago confirmed they were well-matched and that he was aware of the hurdles ahead. "We'll take this one day at a time. No doubt there will be days when you're in that dark place, but I hope you will allow me to comfort you in those times and let me coax you back to the light."

He stared at her in silence a moment. "You make our having some kind of deeper relationship seem plausible."

"Oh, Kristoffer. It is. It really is. I'm not saying it will be easy, but I do believe we are going to make it work."

"I haven't allowed myself the luxury of thinking about living my life again since the accident. In some ways, it still seems as if it never happened and that I'll wake up from the nightmare. In others, if feels as though I'm forgetting Tori and I ever had a life together, and that scares me just as much."

"You've spent almost half your life with her. She'll never be gone from your heart." Would he be able to let Tori go when the time came? Pamela wanted to be strong enough to help him through that, but what if she was in Afghanistan or somewhere else when he needed her? He had Gunnar, but his cousin traveled even more than she did. It pained her to think of Kristoffer facing that day alone.

"I'll fight off the demons as best I can before they destroy what we're trying to create here."

She smiled. "You won't have to fight them alone. You have me. And I'll also help *you* work on staying in the moment."

"Deal." He leaned forward and kissed her cheek. While she wanted more, shifting gears from friends to a couple wouldn't come easy for him.

She'd been craving—no fantasizing about—kissing him since the night he'd made her kneel on that bed of rice. Maybe earlier.

Turning her head, her lips grazed his cheek, and she heard him draw in a short breath. She leaned away until they were face to face. His pupils dilated. Should she break down the barrier or wait? Hoping this wouldn't be seen as too aggressive, she leaned forward again and lightly pressed her mouth against his. Barely the whisper of a touch. Slowly moving her head back and forth, her lips tingled at the butterfly kiss as she enticed him to continue.

When Kristoffer retreated, she let him go with a sigh, seeing he wasn't ready. But this was only the beginning. They'd have many more opportunities to explore the feelings growing between them, as long as they continued on their path.

However, he surprised her when he wrapped his hand around her nape, keeping her from moving away, as if she had any intention of doing so. He searched her eyes—and growled.

The primal sound set her body on alert for what she hoped would be an exquisite assault on her senses.

Or did the growl signal his frustration and that he was about to flee?

Don't pull away. Kiss me back, Kristoffer!

A chasm opened up before him, one he wasn't sure he was ready to jump. But if not now, when? It was a bloody kiss, not hot, passionate sex in the backseat of a limo.

But once he crossed this line, his world would never be the same. He wanted Pamela, but this kiss would be the first time he'd acted on his selfish, primitive urges.

He waited, giving her a chance to change her mind about whether this was right for her, but the look of longing in her eyes told him she'd reached the same level of frustration at not being able to express their true feelings for one another.

"Close your eyes, Sprite."

Momentary confusion flashed across her eyes before she did as he told her, slipping with apparent ease into her submissive mindset. He leaned closer while holding her head between his hands, even though he didn't get the impression she wished to escape. Her moan of passion when their lips touched again was all the encouragement he needed.

Kristoffer trailed light, tentative kisses from her neck to her ear, stopping there to nibble on the lobe. Her hands grabbed his shoulders as if to hold on—or perhaps to keep him from moving away.

When she tried to tilt her head, he placed his hands on either side of her head to keep her still. Exerting physical control over her thrilled him, reminding him of... She moaned, bringing him back to the moment and empowering him to go further.

Her skin was so soft. He grasped a hank of her hair and tugged her head back as he moved to capture her mouth for the first time. His cock strained against his zipper. His tongue traced her lips, and he gave a silent roar of victory when she opened to invite him inside.

Although the move lacked finesse and he ought to tease her a while longer, his tongue entered her warm mouth, branding her as his in some primal, symbolic way. They could work out the details of what that meant later, but for now, he'd focus on making her feel cherished and important to him and hoped one day she'd yearn for something more, too.

He released her hair and lowered one hand to stroke her back. Longing to touch her breast, he chose instead to lift his hand up to her nape. When he tried to draw away again, her hand reached up to hold him in place.

"More," she whispered.

The blood rushing to his head nearly drowned out her voice.

More.

Happy to oblige and wanting to explore further, he slipped his other hand under her sweater, seeking the warm flesh of her back. Gooseflesh popped up in his hand's wake.

As he lowered his head to capture her lips again, the limo came to a stop. *Bloody hell.* He'd forgotten where they were. How appropriate that they were making out in the backseat, because he felt like a teenager again—testing boundaries he was unsure of while being in a complete state of uncertainty.

Not wanting to embarrass Pamela when the man opened the door, he sat up and pulled away. He handed her a napkin. "Your lipstick," he said with a grin as he pointed to the mirror behind the bar. She scrambled to sit up and lean forward to check out the damage to her makeup.

"How's this?" Her lips looked swollen and well-kissed.

"Beautiful."

She handed him a napkin. "You might want to wipe my lipstick off *yourself*, too." As he did, she glanced toward the door. "Why do I feel like I'm sixteen and my dad's on the other side waiting to catch us at being naughty?"

He laughed until the door opened, and the liveried chauffeur stepped aside. Kristoffer exited then helped Pamela out. With her hand in his, they made their way to the tasting room. He couldn't describe a single wine they sampled, because all he could think about was the amazing woman at his side.

Pamela seemed better able to focus on wine tasting, and they placed an order to ship three bottles to her place. Suddenly, he had zero interest in winery hopping. Before they walked back to the limo, he turned her toward him and stared into her eyes.

After a moment, he asked, "How would you feel if we went back to the house and did a scene together?"

Her pupils dilated, but he waited for a verbal response.

"I'd like that, Sir. What did you have in mind?"

"Not your concern, Sprite. But while we've spent a lot of time talking about what you don't want, you might share with me some of the activities you'd like to try for future reference." For tonight, he'd formulated a rough idea for a scene and mentally checked off what he'd brought with him and what he needed to purchase. His toy bag had most of what he needed, but when he was packing, he'd only planned to continue their mind training exercises, so he'd left restraints at home.

She drew a breath and held it a moment. "I can't wait." The huskiness of her voice told him she was as excited as he.

They returned to find the chauffeur waiting for them. After helping Pamela into the back of the limo, Kristoffer addressed him. "Change of plans, David. Please drive us back to the house. No hurry."

The man smiled and tipped his cap. "Yes, sir."

Kristoffer started to turn away when he had a second thought and stopped. "Are there any hardware stores still open tonight?"

The chauffeur cocked his head. "Is there a problem that needs fixing?"

No, there's a Dom here who just realized he was traveling without all of the necessary equipment.

Time to improvise. "No, I just need to pick up a few things for the house."

Pamela snickered from inside loud enough for him to hear, no doubt well aware of his intentions.

"Santa Rosa has several that stay open late." The driver mentioned a familiar national chain.

"Perfect."

Inside the limo again, he found Pamela grinning. To her credit as a submissive, she didn't ask what he wanted to purchase.

"Now, where were we?" he asked.

✧　✧　✧

Pamela was wound tighter than a steel spring at the promise of a scene with Roar tonight. He'd lowered some of his barriers. Now they could take things a little further. Would they be doing more than mind-training exercises? What had been on her extensive list of things she'd like to do? She had no clue what he had planned on the spur of the moment.

But she couldn't wait to find out.

If he planned to stop at "Dom Depot," as her friends called it, he apparently needed something he hadn't thought to bring with him.

She'd just have to wait until they made it back to the house.

"Water or soda?" he asked. How could he be so calm?

She leaned forward. "I can get it."

He pressed her shoulder back against the seat. "I'm taking care of you tonight."

She smiled. "Water, please."

He refilled her glass and handed it to her. "Would you care for anything else to eat?"

"No, thanks. I couldn't eat another bite." Her stomach was a bundle of nerves already.

They arrived at the hardware store sooner than she expected. "You stay here and eat. Drink, too. I don't want you becoming depleted or dehydrated tonight."

Sounded as though he planned an active session. Her body thrummed with excitement. She munched on a few more finger sandwiches and drank another gobletful before he returned carrying a bag that concealed his purchases.

Setting it near the door, he rejoined her on the seat. "Listen carefully, because I will be watching to see how well you carry out my instructions." She sat up straighter and made eye contact. "When we get back to the house, you're to go to your room, shower, and pull your hair up in a way that it won't distract you or be uncomfortable when you're lying down."

She'd be in a bed for this scene? Sounding better all the time.

"I'll be waiting outside your room for you. When you join me, I expect you to be naked—that includes shoes and underwear. Will that be a problem for you?"

She smiled. "You've already seen everything there is to see."

"Yes, but I wasn't close enough to touch you then."

Her heart pounded, taking her breath away.

She didn't want to keep him waiting while she prepared herself for him. Good thing she'd shaved earlier today before going shopping and swimming, so she wouldn't have to do that tonight. Her pulse raced at the thought of him finally touching her intimately. Unable to speak, she nodded her acquiescence.

"What are your current limits?" he asked. "List all of them again so there are no miscommunications."

"As long as we stick to what's conventionally considered safe, sane, and consensual, I'll probably have no problem trying things. But my hard limits still include most forms of edge play, up to and including knives, bloodletting—including needle play, bestiality, practices involving excrement or urine, asphyxiation or extreme breath play." Some of these she assumed he wouldn't want to do, either, but it was important to spell everything out. "And while I've had mixed results with severe pain in the past, it's subjective and tolerance can increase over time, so I'll just rely on my safeword to let you know if something becomes more than I can take. Oh, and I still am not open to being shared or turned over to anyone else for scenes without my specific consent."

She took a breath and grinned. "Glad all that is out of the way. Now, it's time to get into the gray areas. Well, not gray for me, but possibly for you."

"Such as?"

"When the time is right for you, I'm more than agreeable to oral and manual stimulation, both giving and receiving." Did his grin mean he might be as well? Something had changed in him tonight. Walls were coming down. When more blocks tumbled away, she wanted him to take it to the next step without stopping to negotiate.

She may never learn what all of his own limits were; he'd simply avoid them, unless something triggered him. Perhaps he needed to hear one more thing from her. "You're in control of the scenes, and I have my safeword. We should have no trouble exploring together."

She added, "Oh, intercourse with you is no longer off limits for me, but I respect your decision to wait until *you're* ready to take that step." More like a giant leap.

He glanced away momentarily. When he met her gaze again, she heard his reservations. "I don't want to hurt you for anything in the world. If I run cold on you when we return home, I don't want the added guilt of taking our relationship to that level of intimacy."

She nodded her agreement. She'd never known a man with such restraint, but his honor and integrity were two major factors she'd found desirable in Kristoffer in the first place. "I appreciate you for slowing things down, Kristoffer. I'm not a prude and enjoy healthy sex, but my impulsiveness in past relationships has led me to plunge into the deep end when I should be putting in my big toe and testing the waters first."

She leaned forward. "But when our test days are over, I'm ready to high dive into the deep end with you whenever—*if* ever—you are."

"You'll be the first to know," he said with a disarming grin. Then he sighed. Doubt or guilt must have blasted him again, because he grew serious almost immediately, raking his fingers through his hair. "I've only started to come to grips with this new world order. So until I'm certain I can commit to something more long-term, we won't have intercourse."

Pamela grinned and placed her hand on his sleeve. "I agree." *Yes!* He hadn't taken oral and manual off the table. Trying to maintain her composure, she said, "Thank you for taking care of me so well, both as Kristoffer and as Roar. Look how far we've come tonight alone. I'm excited about the prospect of more advanced play scenes. Whatever you're comfortable with works for me. You're in charge."

Their negotiations seemed very thorough, but then Kristoffer was used to having deals spelled out in minute detail. What could be more important than negotiations between a Dom and a submissive?

Kristoffer closed the space between them and placed a kiss on her lips. Not a peck, but not as deep as before, either. However, he prolonged the kiss long enough to make her lips tingle before he pulled away. "Thank you, Pamela. We'll continue to reassess our relationship and communicate like this periodically to be sure both of us are having our needs met."

With impeccable timing, the limo dropped them off at the house at that point. After tipping the driver, and eager for tonight's scene, Kristoffer sent her off to follow his earlier instructions, not repeating them. She hoped she'd remember everything. First and foremost, she didn't want to disappoint him.

After towel-drying her hair, she brushed and pulled it into a scrunchie high on her head and perfected the Heidi bun. She'd loved when he'd kissed her neck earlier and wanted to leave that part of her anatomy bare and accessible. She started to slip on her mules to give her some height, but remembered he'd said no shoes.

Placing her hand on the doorknob, she inhaled deeply and let the breath out over several seconds. And again. Why was she so nervous? He'd seen her in the nude before. Ah, but they were two strangers then. Tonight would be vastly different.

They had turned a page. If only she knew what would be written on it and the following ones. The not knowing was frustrating.

Therein lies my problem
Stop trying to figure out his every move.
Let him be in charge.
Surrender.

✦   ✦   ✦

Kristoffer had prepared the scene in the bedroom. Now all he had to do was wait. In his mind, the time was right. But his heart and head weren't always on the same bar in the sheet music. When her door opened, he drew a deep breath to brace himself for the monumental shift their relationship would take tonight.

Holy hell, am I in trouble.

Her bare breasts registered with him first: High, rosy areolas, begging to be touched.

Not yet.

He met her gaze, surprised to find a glimpse of insecurity there.

"So beautiful, Sprite." At his words, she smiled and relaxed. Moving into gear, he closed the space between them and placed a kiss on her cheek. "Ready?"

"I think so."

She'd been hurt by someone she'd submitted to before. He would need to reassure and praise her frequently to let her know he was pleased until she came to know him better.

Wrapping his arms around her, he hugged her close. "I'll do nothing to harm you, Sprite, not intentionally anyway. Even though we've only known each other a short time and not in the capacity of an intense, intimate relationship, we've always been able to share with each other. Communication will be key, but there are more ways to communicate than verbally."

He kissed her cheek, released her, and stepped back. "Because I want to strengthen your powers of concentration and improve your discipline over your body, I've decided to put you into sight and voice deprivation tonight. Are you okay with that?"

"Yes, Sir. I welcome the challenge." Her confidence level seemed higher already.

"If you need to safeword, of course, you should feel free to speak up. Tell me again your safeword and slow-down word."

"Jeannie and Cocoa Beach, Sir."

The words never failed to conjure up the sexy genie and the astronaut and leave him smiling.

"I should point out that if you break voice restriction, the consequence will be a ball gag." He hoped she hated it as much as he did, but the gag wasn't on her limits list.

She nodded, apparently afraid to speak even now.

"Time to get you into the proper headspace. Turn around, Sprite." Holding both ends of the necktie he planned to use as a blindfold, he situated it over her eyes and tied it securely at the back, below her bun. While he loved having her hair down, playing with fire and wax could be both dangerous and messy.

Coming around her, he took the liberty of enjoying her body more slowly without worrying about being a gentleman. As in the classroom, when he'd seen her standing proudly naked during his tour, his gaze went immediately to her neatly trimmed bush. He loved that she didn't shave completely bare, not that he would express his preferences to her. Still, she had spent time recently at least working on the bikini area from what he could see.

Taking her by the arm, he led her through the great room to his bedroom. He'd removed the top sheet and duvet already, so he guided her to sit on the edge of the mattress. He lifted her feet and swung her legs onto the bed. She was half sitting up. "Lie back." She followed his command without hesitation, her response flowing over him like a fine Miles Davis trumpet solo.

He re-engaged his brain after his flight of fancy. "I want you to think of your favorite fantasy now." While she was busy with that, he reached into his toy bag on the floor to retrieve the white soy candles, a saucer, and the butane lighter he'd packed in Denver and set them on the nightstand. He'd already stowed the kitchen fire extinguisher near the nightstand as a safety precaution. He'd kept everything out of sight in case he decided not to blindfold her in the other room.

He took a moment to reassess where and how he intended to restrain her. The bed wasn't nearly as full of possibilities as his own back home, but he'd make do with what he had.

The tie-downs he'd bought at the store tonight awaited him at the four corners of the headboard and footboard. He'd tested their strength earlier and found them substantial enough to hold a willing submissive firmly in place. One of the areas he planned to work on with her tonight was her ability to control her movements, too, so he wouldn't expect her to struggle against them.

Before he restrained her, he needed one more item from the kitchen. Gunnar would have strung him up by the balls if he'd left her alone while tied up. "I'll be back in a moment. I want you to focus on your fantasy and on your breathing. Nothing else."

When he returned to the bedroom and set the bowl on the nightstand beside the other items, he found her lying exactly where he'd left her. Back in Denver, she'd told him she enjoyed a variety of sensations.

Glancing away, he reached for the bottle of baby oil. As liberally and as dispassionately as possible, he coated her nipples, areolas, and breasts with the oil to make it easier to remove the wax later. Soft, yet firm. His ability to maintain control would be impossible if he kept touching her breasts. Making a fist, he pulled away.

Deep breath. Slow it down. Make it last.

Moving lower, he applied the oil to her belly and thighs. He ought to do the same on her mound but wasn't ready to touch her there yet.

"Cup your right hand." He squirted some oil into her hand. "Now, spread it on your mound and labia. Try not to miss a spot." She did as instructed. Seeing her touching herself, even in a nonsexual way, turned him on even more.

With his hand at her side, he nudged her toward the center of the mattress and fastened the soft leather cuffs he'd bought for her wrists. He'd never dreamed he'd use them so soon.

After hooking the cuffs together and threading linen rope through the clip, he lifted her arms above her head and secured her to a clip on the bungee cord spread tightly between the two posts. Anxious to see her progress after only a few weeks of mind-focusing exercises, he left her feet unrestrained to test how well she would maintain focus and discipline.

Taking a moment to admire her stretched out on the bed, he smiled when his cock grew stiff. He fought back the urge to bend over and place a kiss on one swollen nipple. As if sensing where his gaze had fallen, both nipples bunched and became even more aroused.

Kristoffer picked up one of the candles and flicked the lighter until the wick ignited.

"Mmmm." She smiled, no doubt aware of what was to come.

He might have to be more specific. "Behave. To me, voice depriva-tion includes making any sounds with your mouth, unless I ask you to make some noise for me or answer a direct question. I want this to be a night of pleasure and rewards, not consequences. But I will take corrective measures, if need be, in order to improve your training as my submissive. Understand?"

My submissive. He liked the sound of those words. *Please don't force me to use the gag, Sprite.*

She nibbled the side of her lower lip, properly chastised, he hoped—or perhaps worried. "Yes, Sir."

Punitive actions held no appeal to him—but he couldn't shirk his responsibilities as her trainer—her Dom tonight. He'd deliver whatever discipline necessary to help her grow in areas they deemed in need of improvement.

With his head back in the scene, he tested a drop of wax on his inner wrist and determined that it would be safe at the height he intended to let it drop. Reaching over her, he let the next drop fall into the valley between her breasts. Her torso surged upward, and she screamed, "Oh!"

"Silence." A second transgression. He blew out the candle and set it down on the saucer. While he had to admit there might be nothing sweeter to his Dom ears than to hear squeals, moans, and groans, those same sounds would also lead to his undoing. If her self-discipline truly was this weak, how would she handle what was to come?

He reached into his bag and removed the breathable ball gag from its packaging. As usual, Gunnar had seen this coming almost from the first. Kristoffer had hoped not to have to even open it, but had chosen one suitable for beginners with a smaller ball.

"Sprite, you've shown me that you aren't yet able to control your mouth during a scene. Before I place the gag in your mouth, there are some changes to how you will safeword because you will no longer be able to speak."

Good thing he'd considered the possibility of having to use a ball gag while shopping earlier, because he hadn't brought a clicker to use as her safe gesture. He picked up the squishy toy he'd found in the office supply store next to the Dom Depot. The stress ball was shaped like a man, and dressed in the odd combination of a business suit and hard hat. Perhaps he represented an executive visiting a construction site.

Wanting to assess her anxiety level by making eye contact, he slid the blindfold up to her forehead. She blinked a couple of times, then smiled at him.

"I want you to become familiar with the item you'll be using as your safe gesture now." He held it above her head for inspection. "You're temporarily out of voice restriction as well, in case you have any questions about either the gag or how to use a safe gesture."

She nodded.

"You'll use this talking stress ball instead of either safeword. All you have to do is squeeze, and I'll know to stop."

"What if you don't see me do it?"

Like him, she'd never used a safe gesture like this before. "Good question, Sprite. Let me demonstrate." He squeezed it, and the cheerful falsetto voice said with a lisp, "Remember, safety is our number one goal. So smile, be safe, and enjoy your day!"

Pamela fought to control her giggle at first, but seemed unable to regain her composure and soon broke into full-out laughter. How could he keep from smiling? Actually, the combination of the silly toy's voice and her laughter relieved some of his tension, too.

After she'd regained her poise, he explained, "Sorry, but there wasn't time to track down a party store to find a Gunnar-approved clicker to use. I'm still putting our toy bag together, but left many things at home. I didn't realize what I would need." He certainly never expected to have a scene this intense.

"We have our own toy bag?" she asked, eyes opening wider. Did she think he would use his and Tori's?

"Of course."

She smiled.

Not only did he prefer new items and implements for hygienic reasons, even the ones that could have been sterilized would hold too many memories.

In her right hand, he placed what would forevermore be deemed Mister Safety to him.

She looked up at the thing. "Sir, what a perfect mascot to promote safe, sane, and consensual play!" He shook his head at how in sync they were.

"Oh, look! He's in a business suit. That's one of my favorite fantasies."

She'd never mentioned *that* before. Was it one of the reasons she'd been attracted to him in the first place? He'd almost left his suits behind before realizing they might want to partake of some fine dining on this trip. Now he wished he hadn't gone so casual tonight if she thought his suits were sexy.

Get this scene back on track, Roar.

"Any other questions before I strap on the ball gag? Have you ever been in one before?"

She sighed. "Oh, yes."

Why did that not surprise him? Would the annoying thing do a better job of deterring her from future disobedience this time? He hoped so.

"No more questions, Sir." She sounded resigned, but not upset.

"Open wide and keep your tongue on the floor of your mouth." She nodded when ready, and he wedged the ball between her teeth. "Wider." It filled the space in her mouth, but should still make it possible for her to breathe and swallow. "Inhale through your nose." She didn't seem to panic and did as he'd asked. "Good girl."

"I think you're going to do fine, but just in case, after this is strapped on, I'm going to lift your shoulders and head with pillows.

Being elevated won't do anything to stop the drooling, I'm afraid, but should make it easier for you to swallow. Don't worry about the drool, and I won't. It can't be helped." Humiliation wasn't his kink, but couldn't be avoided when using the ball gag.

"Lift your head." He wrapped the strap around the back of her head and fastened the hooks at the side of her mouth. She looked ridiculous, but her eyes remained calm. While her head was up, he supported her shoulders and placed a couple more pillows under to help her breathe and swallow with more ease.

"I'm returning your blindfold now." He slipped it over her eyes again. "If you can't breathe or swallow, squeeze Mister Safety before you are in full-blown panic. Because we don't have your Jeannie and Cocoa Beach safewords to differentiate between totally stopping and just slowing down to talk about what's going on, we won't consider your using the squeeze toy to be a scene-stopper. If you use it, I will halt whatever I'm doing and check in with you to see what's wrong."

She nodded.

Other than the ball gag, she looked delectable stretched out before him. Waiting. Wondering when and where the next drop of wax would fall. He relit the candle, let the wax build up again preparing for another...

Splat!

This one hit the areola of her left breast. She inhaled quickly in surprise, easily breathing through her nose. Her body relaxed as soon as the heat dissipated. Not giving her as long to wait this time, another opaque droplet hit her right areola. Her left hand clenched, but she was careful not to squeeze Mister Safety. Her legs remained in place as well.

"Very nice, Sprite."

He picked up a second candle and ignited it from the first before letting two drops land almost simultaneously, one on each nipple.

She moaned from the back of her throat. Not giving her time to rest, he soon had both breasts covered in white wax. He moved the candles closer to her body, hovering just below her belly button and building up a good amount of melted wax. These drops would be hotter than the others due to the candles' proximity to her skin.

As if anticipating where the next drops would fall, she started to lift her legs to protect herself, but apparently thought better of it and stretched them out straight again.

"Good girl."

He tilted the candle sideways, a few inches lower than her naval so that the wax wouldn't flow inside, where it wouldn't be fun for either of them to remove it later. The wax splashed onto her skin and ran a few inches toward her mound before the rivulet solidified. Sprite's knees flew up toward her abdomen in a defensive response.

"Tsk, tsk." *No, that won't do.*

She straightened out her legs immediately and held them rigid on the bed. The creases on her forehead conveyed her worry.

"Too late, Sprite. We'll deal with disciplining you for that later. Remember, legs are to remain stretched out unless otherwise instructed."

He needed to work on helping her find ways to control her body's responses. Training her to be *his* submissive, rather than preparing her to please some other Dom, put a smile on his face.

She could be mine for life.

Hold on. He shouldn't jump too far ahead of the game. *Focus and remain present*, as he often reminded her to do.

To test her concentration again, he gently kicked the toy bag with his foot hard enough to make her think he was searching for restraints for her legs. When he rained an unexpected barrage of wax droplets onto her abs, her muffled squeals and hisses delighted him.

Then what sounded very much like "Oh, Christ!" emitted from around the gag.

"Sprite, you still being able to express yourself in words even with a ball gag truly amazes me. I'd be lax in my duty as your Dom to let these transgressions go uncorrected. Do you understand?"

She nodded.

Kristoffer blew out the candles and returned them to the saucer. "Lift your hips." He placed two pillows underneath her to raise her pubic area to an angle where the wax would hit its intended marks with the greatest impact. Her short curls would keep her from feeling the most intense heat directly on her mound, but if she shaved her lower lips, as he suspected she did given her neatly trimmed bush, she'd be in for some serious discomfort.

"Tent your legs and spread your knees open." Her slight hesitation told him she expected the worst, but to her credit, she followed through with his command.

This should be interesting.

He picked up the two candles again and re-lit them. After letting the melted wax build up, he let the first large drop from each fall from a height of two feet onto her inner thighs. The muscles of her legs contracted, but she held her position perfectly despite the discomfort she must be experiencing on such tender and new areas.

"That's my girl."

Without pause, he let two smaller drops hit the area between her mons and the juncture of each of her thighs. A drawn-out moan escaped her gag, as sweat broke out on her forehead. Her left hand clenched the rope as she struggled for control and to prepare herself for the next, no doubt.

"Excellent control of your legs that time, Sprite."

Making a sudden change in plans, he extinguished the candles once again, laid them on the saucer, and reached up to untie both hands. The frown lines on her forehead spoke volumes. She must be thinking they were finished.

Not by a long shot, Sprite.

"Lower your arms." She did so, moving stiffly. "Hands on your inner thighs." She complied, careful not to release the squeeze toy in her right hand.

Picking up a candle from the saucer again and reigniting it, he crawled onto the bed and knelt between her calves, careful not to touch her. They were moving into dangerous territory. He wasn't ready to give her an orgasm with *his* hands yet, even though he'd told her it might be used as a reward sometime.

One step at a time.

He stared at Pamela's labia. Shaved, as he'd suspected.

My dear Sprite, this is going to hurt like hell.

"Remember Mister Safety, if you need him." He couldn't help but smile at the wrinkling of her brow before she moved her hand, as though remembering the stress toy. "Ready?"

She nodded as her entire body tensed in anticipation and fear. He waited until she relaxed ever so slightly before letting the wax drip over her labia.

Yet again, he made out her muffled curses. Unable to control her response, she tried to clamp her knees shut only to encounter his body blocking the movement.

Fuck. Okay, so he hadn't thought through the possibility of being squeezed between her thighs like this. Who was tormenting whom?

"That's number three. Where should your knees be?" *And why aren't they anywhere but clamped around my sides?*

Pamela flung them open and away from him. She took a deep breath and let it out in a hissing sound around the ball gag. Drool escaped the corner of her mouth. With a foreign object as large as this one in her mouth, drooling was a natural response and nothing he could control or alleviate for her.

As the silence dragged out between them, her brows knit together as if in preparation to accept more pain. So brave. So beautiful. The thought of returning to a world where the two of them were nothing but casual friends had officially flown out the window. Tonight, he'd unleashed a torrent of emotions and feelings that could never be buried again.

He removed himself from between her legs and knelt at her side before letting more wax fall on her shaved labia. Her hips rose slightly from the pillow, but he heard no curses, and she quickly recovered her composure.

Thankfully, her legs remained open for him this time, too. "Better, Sprite. Now, spread your folds for me." She didn't move. "Don't make me wait." She started to reach with both hands. "Use only one hand—

two fingers. You may need Mister Safety for this." His warning made her hand tremble, but she reached down to spread open her lower lips with her other hand.

Her trust and obedience melted his heart.

He should force himself to focus on her face. Her forehead. The gag. Anywhere safe.

Instead, he couldn't take his eyes off her clit as the swollen nub slowly came into view the wider she spread her wax-covered lips. She stopped, fully exposing the tender flesh to him.

So trusting. So willing. So...

How would she handle what was to come? He couldn't wait to find out.

CHAPTER THIRTEEN

P amela's index and middle fingers halted their outward movement. She took a slow, deep breath. Unless he was trying to psych her out, Roar intended to drip hot wax directly on her exposed clitoris. No one had ever taken wax play to this extreme with her before. Not even close. Was she ready? Or should she use her safe gesture?

Don't wimp out during your first scene as his actual submissive.

She had no clue if she could take what he intended to do, but owed it to him and to herself to allow him to try. After the first drop of wax fell, if it was too much to handle another, she'd bail.

"Sprite." His stern voice brought her back.

Had he given her another command? Or had she not performed the last to his satisfaction? *Focus, Pamela—now more than ever!* She spread her lips wider for him.

Before she could prepare mentally, the first drop scorched a new spot on her outer lips where she'd shaved herself bare. Intense heat ripped through her genitalia. She prepared for the next, but it hit her finger instead. Had he intentionally missed? Probably, because he'd been extremely accurate as far as she could tell up to now.

Forcing her mind to slow down her heart rate and breathing, she still wasn't prepared for the next searing drop of wax landing on her exposed and vulnerable clit hood.

Fuck! Oh, Christ! Every nerve ending in her body exploded. Her hips lifted off the pillow an inch or two before she forced them back down as she breathed slowly and tried to regain her composure.

Had she made the sounds, or merely screamed the words in her head? And where were her legs? She returned them to their widest span. How much had she moved a moment ago? Her mind had focused solely on the pain but not how well she was holding her position. She hoped she hadn't clamped them completely shut.

Her focus homed in again on her distressed clit hood. Was it caught in the crosshairs of another drop of wax? When would it fall? Would it hit her even more sensitive clit hidden inside, afraid to come out?

Don't anthropomorphize your genitalia, Doctor Jeffrey.

She tried to steel herself and block out all other sensations.

"Because you can't speak or use your right hand, I want you to give me your pain level in this moment on a scale of one to ten. Use your left hand. If you need to go higher than a five, make a fist before the second set of numbers."

She'd been a six at the point of impact, but was already down to a three now. It had been intense, but quickly dispersed. She flashed three fingers at him.

"Very well. Let's continue." His voice sounded huskier, deeper.

Did watching her in such agony turn him on? Was *that* his kink? The man must be a sadist like his cousin.

"Push the hood aside and expose your clit to me." No time to guess at his preferences. She'd have to learn them firsthand.

"For taking so long, I'm going to have to add to the consequences you receive later. Now, do as I asked."

With no choice, she opened her labia again, this time catching the edges of the hood with each finger, and held her breath. Her clit throbbed, totally unaware her hood wouldn't protect it this time. But *she* was fully aware of what was coming next. This was going to—

Plop!

The wax hit her clit dead center. "Oh, my fucking Lord! Shit, shit, shit!"

She didn't know if the ball gag did anything to distort her curses, but the energy she put into them certainly made her feel better. Pamela no longer cared how long she'd be disciplined later. She needed to vent as vulgarly as possible.

Wait! She had another option before he let a second drop of scorching wax hit her there. While the pain dissipated quickly, the next one might be worse. Her grip tightened on Mister Safety. She could let him do the talking this time. Kristoffer had promised her using the safe gesture would only halt the scene and give him a chance to assess her situation. She wasn't at a point where she'd want to end totally—just affect where any other drops of wax fell.

Do it! Now!

She squeezed. "...So smile, be safe, and enjoy your day!"

Time to regroup—and not a moment too soon. Suddenly, the silliness overtook the pain and she began giggling before breaking out in hysterical laughter.

Roar pushed the blindfold up, but his face swam before her because of the tears welling in her eyes. He must think she'd lost it. He unstrapped the ball gag. "Open wide, Sprite." She followed his instruction, finally bringing her laughter under control. She realized the pain in her clit had gone away, too.

When he pulled the ball out of her mouth, she shifted her jaw back and forth to get it working again. He gently wiped the embarrassing trails of drool from her face and neck, the movements oddly comforting.

Her spirits tumbled next. She didn't even want to hazard a guess as to how long she'd be disciplined for all her outbursts and failures. She'd performed horribly.

"Sprite, thank you for using your safe gesture when you'd reached your tolerance limit. It helps me to know where your limits are, as we're just beginning to explore. Knowing I can trust you to safeword when you need to goes a long way toward building trust between us." He brushed her hair back with his hand, his gaze never leaving hers. "Now, before we move to aftercare or discipline, whichever you decide you'd like first, there's something I need to reveal to you first about this scene. A surprise." He smiled.

She liked Roar's surprises. And the pain *was* gone. Besides, this would postpone moving into the disciplinary phase. "What would you like to show me, Sir?"

He wasted no time. "Touch your clit." The corners of his lips quivering as he seemed to fight back a laugh of his own.

She targeted her wax-covered clitoris. To her surprise, there wasn't any wax on either the clit hood or the sensitive bundle of nerve endings. Instead, it was as cold as ice! What the heck?

"Confusing, isn't it?" he asked.

She glanced at her breasts and saw the splotches of white wax. "But you dripped hot wax on me. I felt it. I smelled it. How did you make it disappear?"

"Those last two drops on your clit and hood weren't wax—they were drops of water off this ice cube." He held up the ice and a drop slipped between his fingers and fell onto her abdomen.

"That was cold, but I felt intense heat earlier—both times!"

"Your mind played a trick on you."

No way. But clearly there *was* a way, because she couldn't deny the evidence.

A mindfuck? Roar was good!

One thing she knew for certain was that she was now hornier than ever. It wouldn't take much for her to get off, but he hadn't said anything about allowing her to orgasm. She'd already incurred a long list of infractions, but this one would make the discipline worth it. Not even bothering to hide what she was doing, she slid her middle finger into the cleft and touched her wet vagina. She hadn't been this turned on in a long time. Gliding back up, she rubbed her clit, hopefully in the guise of dispersing any lingering discomfort. It wouldn't take much. So close. Her breath hitched as her vaginal muscles contracted.

"Enough." His abrupt voice stilled her fingers. "You do not have permission to pleasure yourself."

"I'm sorry, Sir. But you've left me wanting more after that scene. And I know you aren't ready for sex, but I can please you in any number of ways if you need to come—"

"Topping from the bottom, now?"

Well, technically, yes, but I really just wanted to help you.

Oh, he'd asked a question. "Guilty as charged, Sir."

"I can see that no ordinary discipline session will be needed tonight."

The mattress jostled. Now the scene was ending and in a much different way than she'd hoped it would. What kind of consequences would she suffer to learn her lessons?

He began peeling the wax off her breasts and abdomen. The wax on her breasts where he'd applied the oil seemed to be coming off more easily.

"Peel off the rest," he commanded. His voice sounded strained, probably from his disappointment after spending so much time training her.

She sighed. Having no doubt which area he intended her to focus on, because her torso was well under his control, she began to remove the wax from her mound, pulling at her short hairs a few times. The wax broke off in tiny pieces. This could take all night. Good thing he'd used ice water on her most sensitive areas, but she still couldn't believe her mind had registered it as searing heat.

"Haven't you done wax play before, Sprite?"

"Yes, Sir, but never like that. Only on my breasts and abdomen." After she'd removed all of the wax she could from her mons and labia, her hands stilled. She didn't want to be accused of playing with herself again without instructions to do so but wasn't sure what she should be doing. So she waited.

"Is the need to come an urgent one, Sprite?"

"Oh, yes, Sir!" At last! Roar was going to touch her.

"I very much looked forward to watching you pleasure yourself to orgasm, so I regret now having to deal with one naughty submissive's disciplinary needs instead."

She tamped down a groan of frustration, which would only add to her troubles. Not only did he not intend to touch her, he wasn't going to allow her to touch herself, either. But she wouldn't add to her ever-growing sentence by complaining. With no question hanging in the air, she remained silent.

He reached for the wrist cuffs and pulled her up and into a seated position.

"Stand."

She rolled onto her side, planted her feet on the floor, and stood.

When she swayed, his strong hands steadied her. Instead of quickly releasing her, he wrapped his arms around her.

"We can do aftercare now or wait until later," he whispered in her ear. "Which would you prefer, Sprite?"

While she longed to sit in his lap, she might need it more after her punishment.

"I'd like to wait, Sir." *Let's get this over with.*

"Let's put this back on before we continue." The blindfold was secured over her eyes, and the familiar sound of rice in a box came to her ears. She had an inkling she'd be kneeling on those damned pellets again.

Without a word, he took her hand and led her out of the bedroom. She had no clue where she was, but she trusted his hands on her shoulders to guide her onto a chair. Perhaps he needed to put her in a safe place before setting up the scene for her to accept her discipline.

"Sit."

He gave commands as if she were a dog, further making her regret her inability to focus during the scene. What was wrong with her? Why couldn't she control her mind…and her mouth?

Roar shook out the rice, but the tinkling noise sounded like he was pouring it into a bowl. When she heard a bowl being set in front of her, she became even more confused.

"Let's review why we're in this position." It sounded no more pleasant for him than her. "What misbehaviors are we correcting, Pamela?" She hated when he used her real name in a scene, because it meant he was not pleased with his little sprite.

"Most recently, I topped from the bottom and tried to take control of your scene."

"And that is a problem for us, why?"

"Because it undermines your authority, Sir."

"True, but even more problematic for me is that it keeps you from truly surrendering to my authority. What are some of the other actions requiring correction?"

"I didn't control my legs and hips consistently. And cursed a blue streak, although thankfully, you couldn't hear the actual words because of the gag, my Lord."

He grinned and shook his head. Incorrigible to the bitter end. "Believe me, Sprite, I am fluent in ball-gag-ese."

He would be. "And, of course, the cherry on top—pardon me, but I couldn't resist—is that I tried to steal an orgasm you hadn't given me permission for."

Had she covered everything?

"Sprite, one of the reasons you have difficulty focusing, and therefore reaching the euphoria of subspace, is that you don't have control of yourself yet. You need to free your mind of all thoughts and concerns except for receiving whatever your Dom wants you to experience in the moment. Don't let your mind, body, or mouth stray. I assure you, scening will be much more rewarding for us both when you are able to reach your maximum potential as a submissive. You'll have more fun, too. Perhaps even reach subspace. That's why I'm continuing to push you on mind control first, and now body control. As for that mouth, well, not even the ball gag seemed to curb your tongue."

She sighed. She'd not really thought about it that way. She wanted to say something, but he hadn't asked a direct question. So she conveyed the thought telepathically. *Thank you, Sir. I understand better now.*

"Being aware of what you're doing wrong without me having to point out every infraction is a good step in the right direction." He stroked the back of her head, and she couldn't wait for him to take her in his arms and comfort her later. But this wasn't the time.

"Now, to help you learn, I'm going to give you a lot of time to think about not repeating these mistakes again. You're no longer in voice deprivation. If you need me, call out to me. But your mouth and mind will be too busy for idle chitchat, so make sure it's important and that you won't lose your focus again."

Before she had time to contemplate her punishment any further, he took her left hand and placed it inside the bowl. "Because I don't want to strain your back, I'm allowing you to sit at the table to do this. You may be here a while, so I'm going to set a glass of water to the right of the empty bowl."

"Thank you, Sir." She wasn't sure what he wanted her to do yet but soon found out.

"You are going to count—out loud—each grain of rice." Her fingers sifted through the rather deep bowl of rice. There must be hundreds, if not thousands, of pieces!

He placed her right hand in another bowl, this one empty. "As each one is counted, you will place it into this bowl on your right. When you have emptied the bowl on your left, give me the number you have arrived at. If you lose concentration at any point, carefully pour the contents of the bowl on the right into the other and start over."

"Will the blindfold be removed as well so that I can see better and not spill any?"

She heard more grains of rice being poured into what she assumed was the bowl on the left.

"That's for trying to top me yet again. If I wanted the blindfold removed, I'd have done so. Now, I want you to take a moment to gather your bearings and picture in your mind the layout of the two bowls. You may begin whenever you're ready."

Pamela wondered if he wanted her to count out loud then remembered that's what he said. Why was she so nervous? Because she wanted to perform well for him. Hearing the numbers out loud should help her to maintain focus.

"One." She transferred the first pellet to the other bowl. "Two." Dear God, this would take her all night! When she reached number twenty-three, the television came on. He wasn't even watching her. Had he pre-counted each piece? How could he when he'd randomly added more at the last minute?

Drat! What number had she been on?

She sighed and dumped the contents of the bowl on the right into the original container and started over. This would definitely take care of any orgasm she might have hoped for tonight. Honestly, she was feeling anything *but* turned on anymore.

She tried to sync her counting to the ticking of the clock above the stove, but was taking several seconds to count each one.

"Seventy-five. Seventy-six. Seventy-seven."

A tug at her topknot sent her hair spilling over the back of the blindfold and onto her shoulders. He didn't say anything or touch her hair, but she knew he stood nearby from the heat of his body against her shoulders.

"Seventy-eight." Nothing would make her have to start over again. She pushed thoughts of Roar from her mind and kept counting for an undetermined time.

Tick-tock. Tick-tock.

"Three hundred forty-eight. Three hundred forty-nine. Three hundred fifty." She ran her hands through the remaining pellets. She'd barely made it through a third of them yet. Her mouth dry, she reached for the glass of water and took a sip.

Just keep counting, damn it.

"Three hundred fifty-one. Three hundred fifty-two." Time marched on until warm hands massaged her shoulders. She hadn't realized how tight the muscles there were until he began to work out the kinks.

Focus!

Was he deliberately trying to distract her? Well, she wouldn't let him. "Four hundred six. Four hundred seven. Four hundred…"

He placed a kiss on her left shoulder blade, momentarily throwing off her count. She began counting louder. "Four hundred *eight*. Four hundred nine. Four hundred ten."

Take that, Sir! You aren't going to make me start over again!

The program on the television changed. She realized she no longer felt his body heat behind her. The air conditioning kicked on, and one of the blowers must have been pointed directly at her, because she felt the cold draft on her bare breasts. Her nipples bunched, making her uncomfortably aware of her nude body.

Wait! What number was she on? The last she remembered saying was four hundred ten, but she couldn't remember if she'd continued to move pellets beyond that. Probably not, and he was distracted with the television, so he wouldn't know if she missed a few.

"Four hundred eleven. Four hundred—"

"Tsk tsk."

Dammit! His admonition stopped her. He must have been using a remote for the TV. Without being told, she dumped the contents of the right-hand bowl back into the left and started to count again.

✧   ✧   ✧

Kristoffer nearly groaned for her, but what a trouper she was to just start over after coming so far. He went to the fridge to pour his own glass of water before sitting down across the table from her with a magazine. It was going to be a long night, but he wouldn't leave her in the kitchen by herself.

He wouldn't do her any favors by being lax on teaching her to control her actions. Only from that level of surrender would she become the submissive he knew she could become with more work. He looked forward to the day when she'd submit to him at that level.

The building of trust wouldn't happen overnight, but he no longer felt the pressure of fighting against time with her. She'd agreed to take their dynamic to a deeper level, as well as to start dating or being together to see how their relationship might develop. Assuming he could sort out where he wanted his life to go.

He flipped the page and realized his mind wasn't registering anything in the magazine. He set it aside. Bored as he was watching her count, he couldn't relieve her from the onerous task. Knowing she'd be honest in completing the challenge, he didn't have to scrutinize her so closely. He walked into the bedroom and retrieved his legal pad and a pen.

Rick had given him a couple of homework assignments, although he hadn't given them much thought this week. The counselor asked him to make a list showing how he intended to bring structure to his days when he added Pamela to his life. Neither man had expected her to become such a key part so soon, no doubt. How would Pamela affect the way he interacted with Tori and took care of his own needs? Perhaps if he started by listing what each person in this triangle of life needed…

Tori's physical demands were handled by the facility, which took excellent care of her. He visited her, loved her, but if he wasn't there every evening, she'd never miss him. Those times had been more a way to meet his needs, not Tori's. Of course, he'd continue to visit his wife regularly. He'd never abandon her.

Before Pamela entered his life, that had been enough, but if he intended to form a committed relationship with her, she'd require more of him than Tori currently did. The list included companionship, affection, guidance, training, and…what else? It had been so long since he'd been in a two-way relationship.

One thing was certain—he couldn't go back and forth full-time between them, or he'd become emotionally and physically drained.

"Twelve hundred forty-three. Twelve hundred forty-four…" Pamela continued to count. He regretted pouring so much in the bowl now, poor thing.

Realizing he hadn't tried to distract her in a while, he reached for the remote and changed the channel on the television, but Pamela didn't miss a beat. She continued to count one tiny grain at a time. Wondering if she'd truly reached the zone, he turned off the set and fired up the stereo with one of her favorite Coltrane numbers, but the only numbers she seemed focused on were the ones related to the rice she was counting.

"Twelve hundred ninety-three. Twelve hundred ninety-four. Twelve hundred…"

Amazing concentration. She must have counted two-thirds of the rice already. He had confidence she'd make it this time.

Back to *his* counting. He'd need to take care of his needs as well. What were his limitations so he could achieve balance between his time with Pamela, with Tori, and by himself? *Keep up with the financial world.* That was business, though, not quality alone time. It was a given he'd spend a large portion of his weekdays, at least, on the job.

Take time to run and work out. That really was his only leisure activity now. Was there something else he wanted to do?

Spend time with Pamela. He smiled. That would be his greatest need of all. She filled his soul. Their time together should also help meet her needs. What he'd missed more than anything these past few years was not having someone who depended on him, looked forward to seeing him, and appreciated the little things he did to show her how special she was to him.

Glancing across the table, he saw she was nearing the end of her task. How did he plan to reward her diligence? He wouldn't send her to bed focusing on the negative aspects of the night, because there were a number of times she'd done well. Encouragement would go a long way toward her trying harder to please him and obey the next time. And this was, after all, their first major scene.

The two bowls hid her breasts from his sight, but he wondered if a little nipple torture might excite her. He had found a pair of massage cups for nipples he was anxious to try. They didn't use fire, but some kind of suction mechanism. Then again, he needed to consider how much *he* could stand, too.

How far could he lower his walls? He'd save nipple play for another time.

Her alabaster skin was freckled in a few places on her shoulders, captivating his attention. He'd kissed the back of her shoulder earlier after massaging the knots out.

Was he ready to share his bed with her, holding her close to him all night long without succumbing to wanting to make love to her? Hardly.

What did that leave? Numerous floggers and paddles. Based on her list of likes, any of them would do the trick and would also be safe for him.

He stood, knowing Pamela would be fine while he prepared the next part of their scene. When he returned to the dining room, she was past fourteen hundred. Almost finished.

✧   ✧   ✧

Pamela had no idea how much time passed, having tuned out everything but the counting of the rice. Roar must have tired of testing her ability to concentrate. Nothing existed but these goddamned rice pellets in the two bowls, her water glass, and counting and transferring each grain.

"Fourteen hundred twenty-four. Fourteen hundred twenty-five. Fourteen hundred twenty-six…" Her fingers felt around the bottom of the bowl, but she could feel no more rice. "I'm finished! I did it, Sir! There are fourteen hundred twenty-six!"

How anyone could be so excited about a bowl of uncooked rice confounded her, but she felt a ridiculous sense of accomplishment.

"Very good, Sprite." He seemed far from enthusiastic, but she didn't care. She'd done it. That's all that mattered.

"What sounds did you hear during the last…ninety-five minutes in your third attempt that met with success?"

She'd been counting rice that long? No wonder her shoulders were stiff again.

"Sounds? I didn't hear anything except for my counting, Sir."

"Not the refrigerator door opening or the music from the stereo or any of the other sounds I made?"

She beamed. "Not a single thing! I concentrated for more than ninety minutes without being distracted?"

"That you did, Sprite." The pleasure in his voice made her smile. "I'm proud of you for sticking to it. That wasn't an easy task, and despite a couple of false starts, you succeeded."

One would think she'd just completed a brain transplant, but she couldn't be happier. She'd pleased Roar. That's all that mattered.

No, she also had achieved something that had eluded her for so long. She'd kept her focus on the task without letting her mind wander or become distracted.

"Let's return to the bedroom."

Yes!

She grinned from ear to ear. She stood before realizing she had no idea where the bedroom was with the blindfold. His chuckle made her grin. He guided her with his hand, and soon she was seated on the mattress before realizing she hadn't let her mind play twenty guesses about what he planned for her. She awaited his instructions, eager to please him with how quickly she could respond.

"Stretch out on this side of the bed."

She did as he said, waiting.

"You're beautiful."

Pamela smiled, happy that he liked what he saw.

"Tell me what you fantasized about earlier this evening while waiting for our play scene to begin." It must be past midnight. Well, of course. She still couldn't believe how much time had passed while she'd been counting rice.

Her cheeks flamed hot at the thought of sharing her erotic musings, but she did as he commanded. "I'm lying on a sandy beach in a string bikini." Well, this was her fantasy, after all. Might as well look hot and sexy in it. "My sunglasses block the sunlight, and I'm unaware of any sounds or people around me. All alone, I slip my hand inside my bikini bottom's triangle and stroke my clit."

"Touch your clit and continue with your fantasy."

Once again, she wet her finger in her vaginal juices and lubricated her clit.

"Then what happens?"

An image of Kristoffer in his suit and tie emerged before her mind's eye, and she smiled as she suddenly found herself in Gunnar's boardroom dressed in her sweater and slacks.

"What was that thought?"

"At that point, there was some kind of spatial anomaly out of *Star Trek*, and I've been transported into Gunnar's boardroom. I see you sitting there in your starched shirt, silk tie, and pewter-gray suit staring at me from across the table. You seem to be undressing me with your eyes. Not that you need to use much imagination, because—"

"Focus, Sprite, without unnecessary commentary."

Oh, Sir, why the hurry? The devilishly sexy Dom was hiding in the details.

"Yes, Sir. Well, the temperature in the room suddenly shoots up for some unknown reason, and you loosen your tie, never taking your eyes off me. I'm finding it getting uncomfortably warm, too, and pull my sweater over my head."

She heard his sharp intake of breath and smiled. Would he think back on tonight when alone and masturbate to thoughts of her? She hoped so.

"What are you wearing underneath?"

She mentally glanced down. "The string bikini top?" *How bizarre.*

He chuckled at her confusion about the mixed-up worlds of her imagination. "Go on."

She shrugged. "Maybe it's a bra. Anyway, instead of simply loosening your tie and letting it hang around your neck, you take it off, followed by your suit coat, and place them neatly over the back of one of the leather chairs." She licked her lips and stroked her clit faster. "Next you unbutton the dress shirt, and..." She could easily picture his chest after seeing him swimming yesterday.

"Continue," he prompted her.

Did his voice sound huskier? Was he becoming turned on, too?

"You've obviously been working out in the gym or the pool or something. Your pecs are...lickable."

"What do you do about that?"

Do? She hadn't gotten that far earlier but, at his prompting, decided to advance the scene in her head. "I stand and walk seductively around the table toward you."

"What else are you wearing?" he asked.

Men are so visual. "Black slacks."

"Oh." He sounded disappointed.

Time to spice it up a bit. "I unbutton them. Your eyes are riveted on my slow movements as I slide them over my hips and down my legs until I step out of them. Somehow, I manage to keep my stiletto-heeled mules on." He'd seen her in those shoes and would better be able to envision them as the sexy scene played out in his head, too.

"You remove your belt, and I'm wondering what it would feel like to have you use it on my butt." Would that be considered topping? How could it? He'd asked her to describe her fantasy.

When he didn't say anything, she went on. "But you only lay it on the table and begin unbuttoning your slacks. I kneel down in front of you and brush your hands aside so I can do it for you."

She licked her lips. "I lower your zipper, feeling your erection against the back of my fingers. You're hard." *For me.*

Roar cleared his throat, so she continued. "You stop me before I can release your cock. You command me to stand, bend at the waist over the table, and lean on my elbows." *Talk about hot!*

Her clit became more swollen as she stroked, wondering where she should take this fantasy. She slowed down her strokes, not wanting it to end, but she'd already reached the point of no return. If she didn't finish this soon, her orgasm would fizzle out. On fire, she rubbed in small circles wondering what Kristoffer intended to do with her in this position.

Before she could come, Roar spoke. "Sit up." *No!* But she kept her feelings to herself and, with his help, did as instructed. He swung her legs over the side of the bed. "There's a pillow on the floor to your right. Kneel on it facing the bed, and stretch your arms out toward the middle of the bed."

She tried to follow his instructions, growing wetter by the second, but the mattress cut her off at the ribs just below her breasts, making it impossible to stretch out.

He chuckled. "I forgot my sprite is a pixie. Here, let me put another pillow under your knees." He lifted her with one hand while positioning a firmer pillow for her. She maneuvered into position, waiting for further instructions. The muffled rattle of chains told her he was searching for something in his toy bag.

"What happens next, Sprite?" he prompted.

"You paddle, whip, or flog me."

"Choose."

He was going to let her choose? "Flogging, Sir."

The swishing of a flogger instantaneously told her he had been holding the implement already. She smiled and tried to be as prepared as he seemed to be.

Her vagina contracted as he teased her with the tips, warming her butt. She accepted each stroke and reveled in it, not worrying about what might come next. She didn't care what came next. This moment would provide enough fantasies to last her a lifetime. She appreciated that he didn't pull her out of the imaginary scene by asking her to describe it any longer.

In her mind, in this moment, she was bent over the boardroom table as Kristoffer flogged her.

But the blows of the flogger ended without warning, and he slapped her butt with something stiff and hard. A belt? Tawse? She clenched her hands. Another blow wiped away any concern about what he was using. All she cared about was that it had a delicious sting.

He didn't fall into a predictable rhythm or pattern, but rained a variety of hard and soft blows all over her butt and upper thighs.

Oh, Christ! So good. Harder!

Had Roar's breathing grown louder, or was it merely a byproduct of his exertion? "Your ass is red. You mark nicely."

She wished he'd take a photo, but wouldn't ask. Something about imagining his marks on her body nearly sent her over the top without even touching her clit.

"Spread your legs wider for me."

She extended them to the edges of the top pillow, and the next few swats fell against her labia and clit.

Closer. So close to coming.

She'd never gone from zero to sixty this fast before.

"Put a finger inside yourself."

She buried her finger inside herself and rubbed the wetness over her slickened nubbin.

Slap!

"Ow!"

The stiff leather implement came down hard where her thighs met her butt. "I did not give you instruction to touch your clit. Now, two fingers inside you." This time, she did only as instructed. "Pump them in and out."

He stopped whipping her. *But I'm not there yet!* Had she groaned out

297

loud or only to herself?

He definitely breathed harder. Was he merely taking a break? No, he was in much better shape than that. She bit the inside of her lower lip and buried her middle and pointer fingers inside her to her third knuckles.

Was he touching himself now as he watched? She pictured him firmly stroking the length of his hard cock. She moved faster, imagining him ramming it inside her.

Would he let her touch him tonight? Jack him off? Suck him off?

You'll do whatever he tells you to do and nothing more.

CHAPTER FOURTEEN

K ristoffer released his cock from his pants and, using his thumb and index finger, stroked its rigid length. Watching and listening as she pleasured herself stirred up a need inside him. He ached to bury himself inside her, but wouldn't do so until he was sure he wouldn't bail on her when they returned to Denver. He needed to be able to face himself in the mirror—not to mention *her* in the morning—without guilt or regret.

He pulled on his cock's most sensitive nerve endings and let his mind wander to Gunnar's boardroom where her fantasy—and now his—unfolded. The tattoo that he'd noticed high on her ass cheek the night of the Academy tour was now visible in vivid detail. Its simple design of a skeleton key intrigued him. Definitely something to ask her about.

Later. He needed to focus on this scene now.

Kristoffer's breathing grew more rapid as he pictured himself fulfilling her fantasy. When she moaned, nearing her climax, his hand froze.

Fuck. What the *fuck* was he doing? He wasn't ready to be pleasuring himself with someone other than Tori. Remembering to make this about Pamela, he returned his cock to where it belonged and picked up the tawse.

Slap.

He aimed for high on her ass to avoid her hand. Pamela moaned. His gaze rested on the globes of her reddened ass. She panted for air, her mewling sounds torturing him even more. He needed to put an end to this scene.

"Come for me, Sprite."

Her fingers returned to her clit, and her hand moved faster.

Slap. Slap. Slap.

"I'm coming! Oh, Christ! Yes!!!" Her hips bucked, and he imagined what it would feel like having her squeezing his cock at this moment if they ever made love. "Yes! God, yes!"

When she screamed her release, his cock jolted, but he kept it inside his pants. She continued to rub her clit in slower movements as she came down from her orgasmic high.

"That's my girl."

"Did you come, too?"

"Topping again so soon? Didn't you learn anything from your time with those bowls of rice?" He'd thought she'd maintained focus fairly well after that session.

"I did, Sir!" She sighed, sounding a bit frustrated—whether at him or herself, he wasn't certain.

"Your submission alone is what pleases me, nothing else." Would she ever just stay in the moment and stop worrying about meeting his needs? Probably not. Apparently, it was in her makeup, just as the Dom couldn't stop trying to meet his submissive's needs.

But he wasn't in the headspace yet where he could go any further than they had tonight.

"Let me help you up." Placing his hand on her upper arm, he guided her onto her feet. He removed the tie from her eyes. She blinked a few times, and he realized he'd had the blindfold on her for several hours.

"I'm sure my hair is a wreck."

Her strawberry-blonde strands were tousled, looking as if she'd just gotten out of bed.

"No, it's fine." *Sexy. Beautiful.*

When Pamela tried to take a step, she nearly collapsed until he steadied her. "Sorry. I didn't realize how far I'd spread my thighs apart. I might need a minute to get them back into their joints." She laughed, bringing a smile to his lips as well. He held on to her until she nodded that she could proceed on her own. Still, he was reluctant to let her go.

"You probably need some privacy in the bathroom to clean up before we move on to aftercare."

"I'm looking forward to my couch time tonight, Sir."

The image of a naked Pamela sitting on his lap flashed before his mind. Fire and brimstone had been licking at his ass all night. Why not feed the flames a bit more?

His primary duty as a Dom was to see to Pamela's needs.

But he had to admit that the thought of cuddling with her pierced the wall of loneliness surrounding his heart. Tori had been the complete opposite, preferring to be alone after an intense scene. She'd soak in the tub for an hour before joining him in bed. How many times since the wreck had he indulged his own need to hold her by wrapping himself around her unyielding, contorted body? She could no longer push him away, but couldn't show him any affection, either. Not the way a vibrant Pamela could.

Don't compare the two women. Play fair.

"Be thinking about what you've experienced tonight, and meet me in the living room."

She smiled, warming his heart even more. "Thank you, Sir!" She ran off to the bathroom to do as he'd instructed.

Alone in the bedroom, he selected a dress shirt from his closet, thinking it best she not remain nude. When she walked back into the room a few minutes later, sooner than he'd expected, he wasted no time slipping her arms into the shirtsleeves. "There."

The sight of her in his dress shirt nearly made him come undone anyway. *Damn.* He really hadn't thought anything through very well tonight when it came to how he'd respond to her. "Button yourself up."

As it was, he'd be doomed to face some potent fantasies in rather close quarters with her the rest of their days here in California, especially after whipping her to orgasm as she fantasized about him.

Truth be told, the memories from this night would haunt him even longer if he didn't figure out what kind of relationship he wanted with Pamela. At a minimum, they'd agreed to date and to continue her training, but with him as her Dom, not merely a Top or trainer.

When he saw her grappling with the front of his shirt and that she hadn't lined the buttons up into the correct holes, he brushed her hands aside. "Here. Let me."

"Sorry. Men's shirts confound me. Everything's backwards." Her self-deprecating smile charmed him. The warmth of her breasts radiating through the fabric of the shirt as his knuckles brushed over them led him to pull the shirt away from her body and close each one from collar to tails in record speed.

He took her hand and led her into the living room. "Let's listen to some music." He realized the stereo still played from when she'd been counting rice earlier. The mellow trumpet of Wynton Marsalis playing "What is This Thing Called Love?" filled the room.

He reached to skip that selection until Pamela said, "One of my favorites." His hand stilled. *Figured.* They had so much in common.

Kristoffer sat on the sofa and pulled her onto his lap, covering her bare legs with a fleece throw. His mind kept warning him this was a colossal mistake. In the past when he'd held her like this, she'd been fully clothed.

While they both needed a little aftercare tonight, her needs came before his. He wrapped his arms around her. With his right hand, he pressed her head against his shoulder. Something inside him calmed, as if a roiling sea had been reduced to a serene lake.

Pamela sighed. "This is nice, Sir."

Swallowing against the lump in his throat, he closed his eyes. For a brief moment, he imagined holding Tori in his arms like this, but cuddling after sex or a scene had never been her thing.

"I could stay like this forever." Pamela's words jarred him back to the present before he drifted too far into the past. His focus needed to stay on the beautiful submissive who had given herself into his care.

Dom up, and treat her right.

"I'm enjoying our time together, too, Sprite. Having you submit to me like this was incredible." He hadn't expected to become this attached to her in such a short time.

"I tried. Nothing intruded on the scene after the rice counting, and it was—unbelievably intense."

To lighten the mood and steer away from reliving the moment when she'd exploded in that orgasm, he tapped her nose and grinned. "Not to mention you made a noteworthy transformation from earlier this evening."

"Thank you, Sir. I never want to have to count another grain of rice as long as I live. But it really did seem to help me with my focus."

"Glad to hear that the discipline I chose helped."

She grew silent. Then, out of the blue, asked, "How did you come to be called Roar?"

"My full name is Kristoffer *Roar* Larson. Roar is my paternal grandmother's maiden name."

"What an unusual surname."

"In Norway, it's not all that rare."

He might as well continue to do a debriefing on tonight's scenes. "What else have you learned tonight?"

"So much that I'll need time to process most of it. Would it be okay if I sort it out in tonight's journal entry?"

"Good idea, but overall, what are your thoughts?"

"You clearly showed me the benefits of maintaining my focus." She laughed. "Counting the rice was the most tedious thing I've ever done, but it was still so fresh in my mind when we returned to the bedroom that I think it helped me to focus on what you were doing and to not worry about what might be coming. That scene was earth-shattering, for lack of a better word."

He shrugged, but smiled inwardly. "That works. You might swell my ego if you go any further."

She grinned. "I'll definitely be sure to be more attentive in the future, too." The thought of having more scenes with her both thrilled and terrified him, but he'd promised to try. "You've also shown me something else about myself tonight, Sir."

"What's that?"

"I like surprises." She sat up and smiled at him. "Not knowing what to expect all the time made the scene much more exciting."

"Keeping you from trying to anticipate my every move isn't easy."

She nodded. "Bad habit of mine. One I need to break myself of if I want to enjoy what's going on rather than always trying to figure out what might never happen."

"Well stated."

"Besides, your surprises are so much better than anything I could dream up on my own. Even when I thought I knew what was coming, like during the wax play scene, well, you turned the tables on me."

"Doms take great delight in surprising their charges." He met her gaze. "Whenever you find yourself trying to outguess your Dom, take a deep breath and find something to focus on, like your breathing or a spot on the wall if you aren't blindfolded. Anything that will recenter you firmly in the moment."

"Good tip. Your Dom instincts are spot on. You always know what I need, even if it's not what I might want."

"I want to reiterate how proud I am of you for using your safe gesture. Now I know going forward that I can trust you to communicate when you've hit your limit. It's difficult to know limits for someone you haven't played with much before. Don't ever get so wrapped up in pleasing me that you won't take care of yourself and me in that way."

"I was nervous about it, but not as nervous as I was about another drop of wax—or so I thought—on my clit."

He chuckled. "Just know that if I ever find out you've risked your safety by not using your safeword or gesture when you should, you're going to be counting a lot more than fourteen hundred grains of rice.

They sat in silence a while, neither needing to talk. Then, out of the blue, he said, "Tell me about your tattoo. It has intrigued me since the night of The Denver Academy tour."

She'd forgotten all about it and wondered what had made him think about it now. "I had it done when I came to a realization after getting some closure on a past relationship." She sighed. "I had a period of feeling sorry for myself and thinking that I'd never find a Dom who would be anything but a fleeting part of my life."

Kristoffer hoped he wouldn't wind up being another disappointment for her.

"I found a quote that resonated with me—'When one door closes, another one opens.' I thought a key would be an excellent symbol to depict that sentiment. Not only is it the key to my future happiness, but one day that key would be used by one special man to unlock my heart."

Her romantic notions surprised him. She always seemed to be grounded and logical. The pressure to do no harm ramped up even more.

Before he turned her loose to go to her bedroom, he wanted to impart a little advice, in case he wasn't able to fulfill her romantic dreams. "Sprite?"

"Yes, Sir?"

The obligation of being responsible for her happiness tore at his insides. What if he returned to Denver and Tori's bedside and couldn't continue to provide what Pamela needed? The duty to protect and care for her overwhelmed him for a moment. But the list he'd been working on earlier left him wondering if he knew what she wanted out of this relationship.

"What would make Pamela happy?"

She didn't answer for several moments. "Finding a man who's a friend first, Dom second. I think that's what I love about how our dynamic has developed. Slowly, without sex derailing us before we started. In the past, I'll admit I tended to jump into bed too soon."

He found it hard to get the image of her sharing his bed out of his head.

She touched his chest. "That's one of the reasons I placed most sex acts on my hard limits list at the academy and later with you when you first started training me. Now, I'm ready, if it's what we both want."

They were approaching unsafe territory again. *Rein her in.* "When's the last time you were happy?"

"I find something to be happy about every day."

"Not an answer to my question."

"Sorry." She paused so long he wondered if she meant she was sorry, but wouldn't answer the question. Then she spoke again. "I guess I have to be honest. I'm happy right now. I was happy swimming laps at the pool. Happy in the limo. Perhaps living in the moment helps. All we have is one moment at a time."

She was beginning to sound like him—although what he'd been doing these past four years was anything but living.

"Krist...Roar...No, actually I do mean Kristoffer." He grinned as she tried to say whatever it was she had on her mind. "I hope our being together doesn't cause you any...regrets. I know we've come a long way—since we came out here, especially. But I'm open to taking this relationship further when you're ready."

"I'd like that, too, Sprite." He truly did, more than anything he'd dared to hope for in ages.

"If we can't find our way as a couple and the Dom/sub dynamic doesn't work out for us, then I'd still want you to be my Top. You have amazing skills with mind training—and mindfucks—not to mention the flogger and whatever else you used tonight."

"Let's take it one day at a time." In reality, she might not want to continue seeing him as a Top or in any other capacity. It was never easy to backpedal after becoming more intimate with someone. Choosing not to speculate about their future together, he asked, "You couldn't tell what it was?"

"Well, as you may have noticed, my mind can trip me up."

She brought him back to the moment. "In my fantasy, I wanted you to use your belt on me, but I suspect in the real-life scene, you actually used a tawse."

"You would be correct."

She smiled in triumph.

"I need to have a better idea for when we have another scene as to your tolerance level. On a scale of one to ten, how would you rate the highest pain level reached in the various scenes we did tonight?"

"A ten."

He raised his brows. Why hadn't she used her safewords?

Then she broke out in a grin. "That would have been for the rice counting part."

Such a brat.

"But the paddling and flogging was a four. The wax play? Well, the mindfuck came in at an eight, but only briefly."

For someone who had said she wasn't particularly into pain, she had a high tolerance. Over time, no doubt it would become even higher. Paddling and flogging seemed to be areas where she could go much further.

"I don't always want to hit my limit on pain, of course. This was perfect for a short scene, just enough to send me into an orgasm."

"I'll keep that in mind next time." He closed his eyes and pulled her toward him, resting his chin on the top of her head. A comfortable silence stretched out between them.

Despite earlier worries about whether he'd been right to suggest they date and continue in their Dom/sub explorations when they returned to Denver, he forced down the anxiety he felt about Tori. His head told him there wasn't much he could do for her these days except provide a safe environment and visit her.

Pamela had offered to see to his needs, something he'd been missing.

Face it, man, you've enjoyed beyond reason what the two of you have shared these past few days.

Especially tonight.

Pamela's body grew heavier. Was she falling asleep?

Intense didn't begin to cover the range of emotions he felt, but in this moment, he was providing Pamela with what she needed. That gave him an immense level of comfort.

He'd worry tomorrow about what the hell to do about his little sprite once the magic of tonight had ended.

✧   ✧   ✧

"Time to wake up, Sprite."

Pamela blinked her gritty eyes a few times, but only saw darkness. Gradually, they adjusted to the dim lights from the stereo.

Feeling the hard chest her head rested against, she remembered where she was—sitting on Roar's lap.

No, Kristoffer's.

Both, actually.

Awareness made her sit up straight. "Sorry, I didn't mean to pass out on you."

"Stop apologizing. I'm honored you trusted me enough to fall asleep like that. I enjoyed holding you."

His arms surrounding her made her feel cherished. "Kristoffer..." Calling him Roar or Sir now didn't feel right at the moment. "About what happened tonight."

He stopped her flow of words with a finger to her lips. "Let's not discuss it further until you've had a good night's sleep and time to journal your thoughts."

She nodded. Maybe that would help her sort out her feelings better.

"Why don't we head down to visit your mom tomorrow?"

He was going to put up walls again. Clearly, he needed some space. She started to extricate herself from his lap, but his arms impeded her escape. Confused about his mixed signals, she met his gaze.

"Pamela, I want to do more exploring with you, but I'm going to need some time, too."

"I understand."

He sobered. "That makes one of us. You confuse me, Sprite, flitting into my life and shining your brilliant beams of light into the caverns left dark so long ago."

A wistfulness in his eyes made her act on impulse, if only to ease his pain. She leaned forward, brushing her lips on his whiskered cheek in a chaste kiss.

"I'm here for you, Kristoffer. You set the pace."

Before she could continue, he took her head between his hands and guided her lips to his. Hard and unforgiving, his hands held her captive, drawing her in. *Yes!* She wanted this. A tugging at her hair pulled her head back, and her mouth opened wider. His tongue invaded and danced with her own as she held onto the back of his head, afraid

Kristoffer would come to his senses and end the kiss sooner than she wanted.

And then he retreated. Before he added another apology to the mix, she placed her fingers against his lips where seconds ago he'd been plundering her willing mouth. "I think I'd better get off your lap before we venture down a path you may not want to take to its logical conclusion." Not waiting for him to say anything more, she stood and faced Kristoffer. "Thank you for taking such good care of me tonight. And for allowing me to have that incredible orgasm."

His face looked thunderstruck for a moment before he grinned. "The pleasure was all mine." Kristoffer stood and lifted her hand to his lips. "Good night, Sprite. Sleep well." His lips brushed her knuckles, and a thousand butterflies took flight in her abdomen.

Oh, man. She had it bad.

He lowered her hand, turned her around, and patted her on the butt to encourage her to move toward her room. She grinned.

Before she left, she turned back to him. "When did you want to hit the road tomorrow?" She'd hoped they'd get to stay here and explore longer, but if he wanted his space, she'd give it to him.

"No set time. Let's sleep in without alarms and just head down whenever we're ready."

"Sounds good. See you at breakfast."

The door closed behind her with a snick. Inside, she realized she still wore his dress shirt, covering her to below the knees. Deciding to sleep in it, she crawled into bed, reaching for her journal and a pen.

Kristoffer needed space to grow, but not enough to bury him alive again. He might try to push her away again, maybe as early as tomorrow morning, but she was more determined than ever to focus on bringing more joy and light into that man's life. While his loyalty and faithfulness were honorable—and she'd never pull him away from his wife—Kristoffer deserved happiness, too.

She was glad he was talking with a counselor in Denver. He could be dealing with trust issues. Survivor guilt. Perhaps even punishing himself for what had happened to Tori. He might not be able to accept comfort and solace from anyone, choosing instead to cut himself off from the world.

If stuck there, would she ever be able to reach him?

Well, like her and most people, what Kristoffer wanted and what he needed were two different things. She had no doubt that he needed her.

She wasn't going to give up on him.

CHAPTER FIFTEEN

O ut of the corner of his eye, Kristoffer noticed Pamela picking at her nail polish as they drove across the Golden Gate Bridge and exited onto California 1 to continue south. He didn't understand why this visit to her mom's had put a damper on her mood when they'd left early this morning, but life was too precarious. He'd hate for her to have regrets if something should happen to her mother.

For him, leaving Sonoma for a while would help him escape the past, which should have been the whole point of this vacation. He'd botched the job by hitting the automatic button and choosing a place where he'd be bombarded with memories of Tori.

To his credit, he'd corrected that trajectory and allowed himself to create new memories—with Pamela.

The floodgates of loneliness had burst open in Sonoma, and now his heart was filling up with new memories—those involving Pamela. The realizations he'd come to in the shower after their bike ride left him feeling no shame or regrets about any of it, which surprised him. Was he coming to terms with Pamela being a major part of his life? With being her Dom?

He hoped so. He enjoyed being with her.

But the valley had still been filled with too many ghosts, so taking a break from Sonoma would give them a chance to slow things down, explore the Central Coast for a day or two, and regroup. They'd have to head north again by Friday morning at the latest to pack up the rest of their stuff before returning to the real world.

He still didn't have a clue what was bothering Pamela. Did she have regrets about last night, or was she worried about explaining his presence to her mother? Hoping to lessen her anxiety if it was the latter, he suggested, "I don't mind fending for myself while you visit with your mom."

She turned to face him, but he needed to keep his eyes on the late-morning, bumper-to-bumper traffic. "No, I want you to meet her."

He wasn't convinced by her words and reached across the seat to pull her hands apart so she wouldn't continue to decimate her cuticles. She relaxed her fist—slightly—and he smiled. "Want to tell me why you're so stressed today?"

She took a deep breath, but didn't fool him. Was her mom some kind of nutcase? Should he be worried? After all, what well-balanced mom abandoned her family to go in search of who knew what, leaving behind a daughter who blamed herself in some irrational way for driving her mother away.

"Are you worried she'll jump to the wrong conclusions about us?"

"What makes you ask that?"

He took his left hand off the steering wheel and pointed to his wedding band with his thumb.

"Oh, that." She didn't sound as though she'd given any thought to his being married. "Mom's pretty open-minded. Live and let live. I wouldn't worry."

"Then would you mind telling me why you're wound tighter than the Wicked Witch of the West at a pool party?" She laughed, but made a fist in her lap again. "Pamela, take a slow, deep breath. Count to five as you inhale. Then let it out to an equal count of five."

Her response to his Dom voice registered immediately. She opened her hands and placed her palms flat on her thighs as she followed his command. When she'd finished exhaling—albeit to a faster count of five than he'd wanted—he told her to do it again but more slowly this time. After the third time, he smiled, even though she probably didn't see it. "Feel better?"

"A little. Thanks. I'm being honest when I say I have no clue why I'm so nervous."

"Want to make this a quick visit and then find a hotel for the night? We could even head back to Sonoma after visiting your mom, if you'd prefer."

"No. I want to see her. And you're going to love the beach there."

"No beach is worth it if you're too anxious to enjoy it."

The traffic cleared unexpectedly, and soon he took the ramp onto the interstate heading out of the city. They were on the Pacific Coast Highway in no time and would spend the next couple of hours driving along the coast.

"Why don't you look out the window and enjoy the scenery? Or take a nap, if you'd like. We were up pretty late last night." He'd been surprised to find them both up by nine this morning.

Pamela apparently chose to stay awake. "I love this drive."

"This coast is gorgeous." He'd left the top down, and the landscape surrounded them.

"Have you ever been to an elephant seal sanctuary?"

Where had that busy mind of hers gone now? "Can't say that I have."

The sign for a state preserve came into view. "Turn into this park. Año Nuevo is something we can't pass by without stopping in, although it will take us a few hours to get out to where the seals are and back. Do you mind?"

"Is your mom expecting us at a certain time?"

"No. I only told her we'd be there tonight. She'll be immersed in some project or the dogs and won't expect us until we show up. But if there's cell phone service in the park, I'll text her and tell her we'll definitely be late."

"Good idea. I wouldn't want her to plan on having us for dinner or something."

Pamela laughed. "She doesn't cook."

"Where'd you pick up the skill?"

"My stepmother insisted that I help her in the kitchen. I guess I learned most of it from her." Sounded as though she hadn't given it much thought before. "I'll admit to being a little jealous at how much Dad raved over her cooking, so I wanted to learn as much as I could."

As he tried to banish thoughts of a young teenaged Pamela seeking her daddy's love and and approval, he wove his way to the nearly deserted parking lot after paying the admission fee. She was still searching for that, no doubt.

After he opened the trunk, she helped pack water bottles and snacks in a backpack and grabbed her camera bag. Apparently, this would be a substantial hike. As they crossed the lot to the exhibit area, she sounded like a tourism spokesperson telling him about how wonderful the California park system was and that their admission would be good for all parks they visited today. Did she intend for them to park hop all the way to Carmel? How many more diversions would she find before showing up at her mom's doorstep? What was she trying to avoid or postpone?

He tried to get her to talk more about her mom without much success as they walked along the paved path, but as soon as she heard the barking of the seals on the approach to the first vantage spot, he lost her attention altogether.

"Look! There they are! Aren't they incredible?"

He glanced at the far-off beach, but only saw tiny black blobs from this overlook. He wondered if they'd be able to get any closer to them.

"I'll take some photos here, but the best shots will require a much longer hike."

"I'm up for a hike if you are." The longer it took, the better chance he'd have to get her to talk about whatever was bothering her, although she seemed to have relaxed now that they weren't navigating any closer to her mom's.

After taking some telephoto shots of the seals at the first lookout, they continued on a bit before veering off to the right at a fork in the trail. Twenty minutes later, they found themselves trudging through dry, loose sand dunes.

The muscles in his legs were getting a workout. "Man, not as easy as walking on a wet-sand beach."

Pamela laughed. "True. I was afraid to warn you about it, because I really wanted you to see this, but be prepared to feel the effects in your legs tonight and tomorrow. Better than the workouts we've been doing at the country club these past couple of days."

"Never mind my legs. What about yours?" he asked.

She grinned up at him. "It's not my legs that hurt. You swing a mean tawse, Sir."

He laughed, feeling some of the tension disappear. He'd wondered how her ass was doing after that paddling.

After what seemed an eternity, they reached a boardwalk that made the hike much more enjoyable. At a curve, a park ranger had set up an information station with binoculars mounted on a tripod to give visitors a closer glimpse at the enormous elephant seals.

He and Pamela took turns sharing the scope and drinking water while she took more shots. From here, the now-giant blobs of blubber sunning themselves on the beach were much more visible—and comical. Every now and then, one would lumber over another sleeping seal before plopping in exhaustion and falling asleep. Out in the water, a fight of some sort seemed to be under way. The ranger explained that those were some of the young pups involved in play that would help them fight off predators and even competitors when they were older.

"I've never seen anything like it. Thanks for suggesting we stop here, Pamela."

"Glad you liked it."

Watching the seals, otters, and ocean birds, while learning more about them from a wildlife expert, had been an eye-opening experience. Tori would have enjoyed this excursion. Too bad they hadn't ventured far from Sonoma during their visits.

But exploring with Pamela was a treat. They had been out here over an hour, so they decided not to continue on to the farthest vantage spot, given they still had a way to go to reach Carmel. They also wanted to stop for dinner along the way.

While he hated to break the spell, it was time to go. "We'd better head back."

His leg muscles nearly groaned when they arrived back at the sand-dune stretch. They hadn't really had much of a chance to talk, trying to conserve their energy for walking.

She was breathing harder than usual, too.

He reached for her hand. "Hey, we're in no hurry. Let's stop and rest."

"If you need to, I'm all for it."

He grinned. She wasn't going to concede that she could use a break, too. Pamela never wanted to appear weak, sometimes to the detriment of taking care of herself by pushing too hard.

She pointed ahead. "How about that footbridge?" They traversed the remaining yards, and as she went to sit, a lizard of some sort scampered from its sunbathing spot. "Darn! Wish I had my camera ready for the umpteenth time today. I've missed so many shots."

"But you must have captured at least a thousand other images."

She laughed and plunked down on the sandy plank. "Ow!" She wiggled her ass to try to find a comfortable position. Kristoffer smiled as he joined her.

Catching their breaths, they listened to the distant barking of the seals and watched the wind ruffle through the grasses in the dunes.

"Kristoffer?"

When she didn't continue, he prompted, "Yes?"

"About my mom." Was she finally going to open up to him? "She's...well, kind of a free spirit." Nothing surprising there from what she'd told him before. "As I've come to know her a little better as an adult, I have the feeling she's searching for something, but doubt she'll recognize it even if she finds it. For a long time, she seemed to be anxious all the time. I do think Mom attained a sense of peace with her dogs in recent years."

"Any idea what she's looking for?"

"No clue. I love her dearly, even if I can't understand her sometimes. I've always wished she'd been a little more...family-oriented." She shrugged and smiled at him. "You two are polar opposites."

He wasn't sure why contrasting the two of them mattered, but she didn't elaborate. "I'm looking forward to meeting her. Perhaps I'll learn a little more about you from observing and listening to her."

Her eyes opened wider as she turned sideways to face him. "Oh, I doubt that!"

"Why?"

"We're nothing alike. I tend to be more pragmatic and family-oriented, like my dad. Mom wasn't in touch with either of us for a long time after she left. She was completely absent from our lives until I went to college. Her solitary life out here is removed from most of the activities I'm a part of."

"Tell me more about your parents' personalities." He assumed one day she'd introduce him to her dad as well. He wanted to learn what to expect from each of them. "Start with your mom, since we'll be seeing her today."

"Mom's driven by many passions in life that I don't understand, because she doesn't talk much about them. As a preteen, when she first left us, I used to imagine she was a covert spy for some secret government agency." She grinned, shrugging away the notion, but the pain her younger self must have experienced trying to understand why her mother had left made him ache to comfort Pamela. He reached out to squeeze her shoulder.

She placed her hand over his. "I wish I could explain why she'd just leave like that, so abruptly. Fueling the flames of my imagination, a cloak-and-dagger atmosphere surrounded her before she left. A room I was never allowed to enter, phone calls she'd get freaky about if I happened to overhear."

Trying to lighten the mood, he suggested, "Perhaps the room that was off limits was filled with kink toys or sex furniture."

She seemed to consider the possibility before shaking her head. "I don't think so—and really don't want to have that idea planted in my head. Thank you very much, Sir." She smiled, which pleased him.

"Anyway, my visits with her after the divorce were nonexistent for the first five or six years. When I went to college, we'd meet in places far from either of our homes. My mind was eager to fill in the blanks. If she were on a mission to save our country or something, it might make more sense as to why she had to leave us."

She shrugged again. "We've tried to make up for it since my college years, but we may never be able to relate to one another the way normal mothers and daughters do."

"There's no such thing as normal."

"Okay, I'll give you that. But there are *norms*. My family didn't fit *any* of those." She pursed her lips and glanced down at the sand a moment, whether actually seeing something or merely needing some space to regroup after baring her soul. "She's become more accessible in recent years, thank goodness." Pamela didn't appear to have any more answers to her many questions now than she had as a teen.

She smiled. "But I think fostering abandoned and abused dogs fills a void in her heart."

Sounded to him like she discarded dogs the same way she had her daughter. "She doesn't keep any of them?"

"Mom has trouble making emotional attachments. With the exception of the unadoptable ones, she keeps most only until they can find a permanent home." She paused. "I never really thought about it, but maybe taking them through the healing process is why she does this work. Not everyone is strong enough to do that."

"A healer, like her daughter."

Pamela beamed for the first time all day. "Maybe we have something in common after all."

"Anything else you want me to know going in?"

She became quiet, perhaps choosing her words. "Mom can be exuberant at first then kind of cools off and becomes more distant."

"Does she still distance herself from you?"

"I never really thought about it, since we're closer now than we were in the nineties. But you're right. She's somewhat detached." Pamela bit her trembling lower lip, and this time he pulled her into his arms. No wonder she was nervous about today. She and her mom had a lot of unfinished business.

Sitting up and moving away from him after a moment, she forced a smile. "My mom loves me the best way she knows how. It's hard to relegate childhood hurts to the past sometimes." Pamela drew a deep breath. "Mom once told me leaving me was the best thing she could do for me at the time. While I don't pretend to understand those words, I know she believes that. Maybe someday I'll understand."

She stood abruptly. "But I assure you we won't be getting into any of that on this visit. I hope my revelations don't make you uncomfortable around her. Trust me, she's great at keeping conversations superficial, so I'm sure we'll find plenty to talk about."

Not ready to let it go as easily, he stared up at her. "It must have been hard for you going through your teen years without a mom." Her chin quivered before she regained control. He wanted to comfort her before getting behind the wheel again. "Sit back down, stretch out, and put your head in my lap."

She crossed her arms in defiance a moment but acquiesced. He rubbed the furrows from her forehead and stroked her hair, watching her body relax over the next few minutes. Soon her words flowed again, more easily this time.

"I wouldn't be the person I am today if not for both my parents. I got my strength and sense of order from my dad, and my independence and a desire to save the world from my mom. While I was in elementary school, she immersed herself in taking college classes and doing homework and was a role model to me for lifelong learning. But I think because I didn't understand Mom's motivations and actions at all until later, I leaned more toward emulating my dad."

"How does he differ?"

"He's very regimented, of course. There are rules and protocols for everything in the military."

"To win his acceptance and love, you learned to obey?"

"Maybe to a degree. But I think I learned about service from both of them."

He wondered if some of her service orientation might be her search for the unconditional love she didn't receive in her teenaged years.

She went on. "But Dad's also loving and demonstrative. He always gave more hugs and kisses than Mom did. Maybe because Mom was so young when she had me, she just seemed overwhelmed a lot."

He brushed a strand of hair from her cheek and tucked it behind her ear. "I'm looking forward to meeting both your parents. And I don't care if your mom's nothing like me, if that's what you're worrying about. Life would be terribly boring if we were all alike."

She tilted her head back. "I'm not worrying!"

Kristoffer tapped her on the nose. "Yes, you are. You have been ever since we left Sonoma this morning. Perhaps not about me so much as about seeing your mom again. However, now that I understand your mood a little better, I'm looking forward to this visit even more."

"You are?"

"Yes." Maybe he could help Pamela find answers in what he learned from her mother. "But we'd better think about how we're going to explain this." Once again, he held up his hand and indicated his wedding band. "I'm fond of touching you in ways inappropriate for a married man to be touching someone not his wife. I don't want her thinking badly of you for being with me."

She seemed to give it some thought. "Honesty would be best, if you're open to that. I wouldn't tell her we're dating or anything. But trying to pass you off as a friend would come across as false. Are you okay with telling her about Tori?"

He nodded. "That's probably the best thing to do. I'll wait for the right time, assuming she notices the ring at all."

"That's a big if. I don't think she pays any attention to marital status of the men around her. One thing I know for sure is that Mom *isn't* looking for is a man."

The mystery of this woman who birthed Pamela became more intriguing by the moment. He helped Pamela to sit up. "We'd better get going if we're going to turn up in Carmel tonight." They stood and began their hike again.

They'd left Sonoma many hours ago, and she hadn't had much to eat at breakfast. He retrieved two energy bars from the bag and handed one to her. "Where would be a good place to eat?"

"Santa Cruz has a nice pier with a number of restaurants."

"Sounds great." They plodded the rest of the way through the shifting sand back to the paved path that took them to the parking lot. After using the facilities and texting her mom their ETA, they were soon on their way.

The drive to Santa Cruz had Pamela asking him to pull over a couple more times so she could snap photos of the coastline, a kite surfer, and other sights. He wondered if she was stalling still, despite their talk, but he enjoyed seeing the places they stopped at and figured she probably just wanted to share her love of the drive.

Their seafood dinners were deliciously fresh. Seated at the window, they watched a sailboat regatta returning to the marina.

After dinner and a walk on the pier, their drive to Carmel-by-the-Sea passed faster than the GPS estimated. He navigated down Ocean Avenue past late-night shoppers and jay-walking pedestrians before driving past a couple of blocks of residences.

"It comes up pretty fast," Pamela said, learning forward to look. "There it is!" *Damn, didn't these people know what a wonderful invention the street light was?*

He turned onto the narrow, one-way Scenic Road a few blocks down. Lighting was sparse here, too, making it difficult to see house numbers. They still had the top down, and he heard the ocean waves crashing against the shore directly below them. The evening had grown chillier since entering Carmel.

"If we spend the night here, maybe we can take a walk on the beach in the morning," he suggested.

"I'd like that. Mornings and evenings are the best. On certain nights of the week, they allow beach fires. That would be nice, too."

"You're not as worried about staying?"

"I was more concerned about you than me. If you're comfortable after you two meet, we'll spend the night."

"Deal."

"Oh, slow down! Here comes Eleventh Avenue."

"Where?" He scanned the area to his left, but didn't see a street.

"There," she pointed. "Right after that gnarly-looking cypress tree."

She pointed at what could barely be called a footpath between two houses. "It's not even wide enough for a bike, not that anyone would want to take a bike up or down that hill."

She giggled. "I know. It's really just a rocky path for those up the hill to gain access to the beach or to walk their dogs."

He pulled into the tight drive beside a canary-yellow Volkswagen Beetle convertible and pressed the button to put up the top on the Mustang. Before exiting the car, he cupped her chin and turned her face toward him. "What's your safe gesture in case you need to leave early?"

She laughed. "You don't have to worry about me, Sir."

Too late, Sprite. "Your gesture?"

Pamela sighed and rolled her eyes. "I'll tug my ear like Carol Burnett used to do to signal her grandmother at the end of her show. Know the one?"

"Yes. I'm older than you are, but apparently, we both enjoyed vintage TV and movies."

"But you may be ready to go sooner than I, Kristoffer. What will *your* signal be?"

He chuckled. "I'm in this for as long as you want to stay. As I told you, I'm looking forward to learning more about you via your mother."

While he harbored some resentment toward the woman for deserting her daughter, leaving aftereffects that still haunted Pamela, he could see the advantages of the two meeting and talking, too. Maybe Pamela would find healing.

He exited the car, opened her door, and helped her out. Taking her hand in his, he led her up a few steps to a side door. "Let's leave the luggage in the car in case we need to beat a hasty retreat."

She laughed and shook her head. He looked up at the two-story blue-gray house. The paint was weathered from exposure to the salty air and sun, but had a warm, beach cottage feel to it.

Before she lifted the knocker, their presence set off a cacophony of dogs barking inside. "How many dogs did you say she has?"

"It varies, depending on how many have been adopted. Last time I visited, there were five."

From deep timbres to high-pitched yaps, it sounded as though several distinct breeds were represented. Kristoffer had never had a pet until Tori adopted Noma as a kitten. In recent years, the picky feline had become his close companion. He didn't have much familiarity with dogs or their behavior, though.

The door swung inward to reveal a ginger-haired woman the spitting image of Pamela—except her hair had thick curls liberally sprinkled with silver strands. She smiled at them as she tried to restrain a Great Dane by one collar and a Doberman by another. Two smaller dogs of unknown lineage growled from their perches on the sofa behind her, but didn't jump down to come any closer.

"You're here!" She seemed genuinely happy to see her daughter, but cast him a wary glance. "Let me kennel these two. I'll be right back." She started toward the back of the house and soon was out of sight.

"Let me help, Mom." Pamela called out before turning to him, winking, and whispering, "Save yourself!" More loudly, for the benefit of her mother, she said, "Why don't you wait here, Kristoffer?" She grinned before slipping inside the house. A slate-gray pit bull came barreling down the hallway and jumped on her with its paws on her shoulders. Kristoffer moved toward her, in case he needed to rescue her, and the dog growled at him.

"Arlo," Pamela admonished. "Where are your manners? This is my friend, Kristoffer Larson." The dog lost interest in him immediately as it began to rain kisses over her face. Pamela's joy was contagious, and he couldn't help but relax, seeing she was in no danger. "Sorry, Kristoffer," she said as she tried to curb the dog's enthusiasm. "Believe me, this guy is all bark with a heavy dose of false bravado. I met him the last time I visited. Maybe she's decided to hang on to him."

Kristoffer entered the house and closed the door behind him. A rat terrier of some sort jumped in the air as if catching an imaginary Frisbee, but landed against Kristoffer's chest instead. He wrapped it in his arms and soon was being showered with kisses as well. "They certainly are a friendly bunch."

"Most are, except the ones needing kenneling, I suppose. They might be relatively new and not used to strangers." She glanced toward the direction her mother had gone, but must have decided against joining her. Of course, she had the weight of a sixty-pound pit bull on her shoulders.

Her mother called out to Arlo and two other dogs to get their treats, and the terrier sailed from his arms and scrambled on the slick hardwood floor to gain traction before tearing up a couple of stairs and into a room off the dining room. Arlo and a black lab he hadn't noticed before followed close behind. He'd never seen so many dogs in one home.

"Let me take these two back there." She picked up the two dachshunds from the sofa. They appeared to be unable to use their hind legs. They, too, showed their love of Pamela by dispensing more licks. Their squirming made it hard for Pamela to hold them both.

"Here, let me carry one." He reached out and took the long-haired, bluish one from her and followed Pamela.

"I don't want them to miss out on their treats," she explained to him.

"What happened to them?"

"Bad hips. Peril of the breed. Malcolm and Abbie haven't been able to use their back legs for years. Mom has no plans of adopting them out."

Sounded like at least three of the dogs were long-term pets.

He began noticing a trend in the naming of them—all icons of the Sixties radical hippie movement and civil-rights era.

Pamela led him to the right, and they entered what would otherwise have been a bedroom, now filled with kennels of all sizes. Her mom had caged the two biggest ones and they were contentedly chewing on their rawhide treats. Pamela indicated the cushion next to the one where she placed either Abbie or Malcolm, and he set the other down next to it.

"I'll let them out later, once they settle down," her mother said, indicating the two largest dogs. "They're always excited when company comes, but I don't know them well enough to trust them yet."

After the dogs were content, the woman walked over to Pamela and wrapped her in a hug. "I've missed you so much, Sunshine."

Apparently, her mother saw her as a beam of light, too. "Glad you stopped by for a visit while you're out here."

"Missed you, too, Mom." Pamela squeezed her mother tighter. They'd done the right thing by visiting.

Breaking apart, Pamela took her mom's hand to bring her to him for introductions. He extended his hand to her, and she shook it as firmly as any business acquaintance, which surprised him. "I'm Maribeth Jeffrey." A wariness in her eyes told him she wasn't quite sure about him yet.

"Pleased to meet you, Ms. Jeffrey."

"Oh, it's Maribeth. Mrs. Jeffrey is my former mother-in-law."

"Call me Kristoffer."

She released his hand. "I had no idea Pamela was out here with someone."

Pamela shot him an apologetic look. Maybe she'd considered not having him here. "When Kristoffer invited me to join him in Sonoma for the week, I couldn't resist."

Her mother cast a quick glance at his ring finger. "You're married."

That didn't take long.

CHAPTER SIXTEEN

I f the tables were turned, he'd be worried, too, if his daughter showed up with a married man.

"Yes, ma'am. For eighteen years." Probably not what she expected to hear, but he hadn't been prepared to get into this so soon.

Her mom's eyes turned toward Pamela, and he reached for Pamela's hand. "Let me explain, Maribeth." He drew a deep breath. His mind flashed back to when he'd met his future in-laws. He'd offered them the reassurance he'd take care of their daughter, although he'd failed miserably.

He nodded as he decided how much to reveal. "Four years ago, my wife and I were involved in an accident. She suffered a traumatic brain injury."

"Dear God! How awful!"

Most people who said things like that had no clue. Lucky them. He wasn't usually this blunt, but wanted to put this behind them without having Maribeth thinking badly of her daughter for being with him.

Kristoffer let the rest come out. "She's been in a persistent vegetative state since coming out of the coma. Doctors hold no hope for a reversal."

"What a nightmare for you," Maribeth said, and he believed her sincere.

"Your daughter has helped me a lot in the last two months. She's amazingly supportive and understanding." Her hand squeezed his this time.

"Mom, we were just going to be friends at first, but...well, things have changed." Pamela smiled up at him. "We're limited in what kind of relationship we can have, because Kristoffer's first responsibility is to his wife."

He didn't hear regret in her voice, although that was one of the things weighing heaviest on him. Was he being fair to Pamela? Who would be content to be the other woman, even if it wasn't a case of infidelity, but of modern medical breakthroughs allowing someone to linger in a state like Tori's for years beyond their natural life?

Pamela directed her next words to her mom. "I don't have time for relationships and commitments, as you can imagine, but I love spending whatever time I have together with him." Her eyes twinkled at him before returning to meet her mom's gaze. "Kristoffer and I enjoy the same music, hiking, and working out. We met through a special project we're collaborating on." More or less truthful. "I've never cared for a man the way I do for Kristoffer." He hoped there would be no regrets if they began dating each other, given their uncertain circumstances.

He wanted to kiss her right now, but held back. "Ma'am, you know this already, but your daughter's compassion has led to some amazing healings." He wasn't talking about her patients, either. "She's enriched my life in so many ways."

Maribeth looked from one to the other. He hated to see the pity in her eyes for both of them. He didn't want or need her pity, but Pamela might.

He turned his attention back to her mom. "I care deeply about Pamela. I'd never do anything to harm her."

Pamela wrapped her arm around his waist and pulled herself into his embrace. "Kristoffer and I keep the lonelies away for each other." Pamela smiled at him, and he realized how true those words were. "We both needed this getaway." Her tone said this topic had reached an end.

Thank you, Sprite.

He kissed the top of her head.

Maribeth smiled. "I see. I'm glad you found him, Pamela. You seem to be good for one another." All three of them relaxed somewhat. "Where are my manners? Let me fix you something to drink."

Her mom led them into the kitchen around the corner where she poured a flavored tea for each of them—raspberry, he thought from the coloring, not the Long Island tea or other spirits he'd expected.

After making sure no one wanted anything to eat, they carried their glasses into the living room. She motioned them toward the smaller overstuffed sofa. "Have a seat."

As mother and daughter caught up on family news, Kristoffer took the opportunity to survey the room. Decorated in a mix of California mission style and early thrift shop, he found the decor cozy. Two large picture windows must provide incredible views of the ocean during the day. Three skylights would allow in even more sunlight, as well as moonlight on a nearly full-moon night like this. He wondered why she didn't pull the blinds at night. Not knowing who stared in as they drove or walked by left him feeling as if he were in a fishbowl.

Ferns, spider plants, and some kind of flowering plants hung from poles and macramé hangers in three corners of the room. Potted impatiens and gardenias lined a shelf made of water-stained, weathered boards propped on three stacks of red bricks across the length of the windows. Among the bookshelves near the fireplace were a few knickknacks including two beaded purses similar to the one Pamela carried that night in the limo and one Gunnar had brought back from Afghanistan for Tori.

When there was a lull in the conversation, Maribeth offered, "Would anyone care for dessert?"

Kristoffer glanced at his watch and saw they'd been talking more than an hour. Pamela nodded and set down her glass as she stood. "Sounds good to me. Let me help." Pamela followed her mother into the kitchen.

He decided to stay put and placed his glass on a coaster beside Pamela's before picking up a women's political magazine to flip through the pages. Unable to focus, he stood and crossed the room to the fireplace to inspect the framed photos. Most were of Maribeth and Pamela at various ages—up to about twelve, he supposed. Two were of Pamela as a graduate—alone in the high school one, and with Maribeth and a man who must be Pamela's father at a college commencement. Fascinated to see Pamela age from a baby into a young woman, he remained captivated by this rare glimpse into her past. He'd seen no such photos prominently displayed at her place.

In one of her about middle-school age, she posed holding a soccer ball.

"Oh, my. What secrets are you learning over there?"

He turned as she returned to the living room. "That you played soccer."

Pamela stared at the photos as if surprised to find them there before zooming in on the sports one. "Don't be too impressed. I was only junior varsity and for one season. Never made varsity or scored any goals. I was as bad as you might expect."

"I didn't expect anything of the sort."

"You're sweet. Sports weren't my thing, although I did enjoy swimming and wrestling during middle school much more than playing soccer."

She'd been on the wrestling team? "Intriguing. That opens up training possibilities I hadn't considered before." Her pupils dilated, and he grinned, confident they were on the same page.

"I doubt I'll remember anything."

"No worries." Not wanting to take the fantasy any further now, he said, "I wasn't much into sports, either, but I spent a couple seasons on the wrestling team as well."

"Seriously?"

"Why would I lie about something that important?"

"I just find it a coincidence. Any other activities I should know about?"

"In addition to the investment and chess clubs—yeah, I was one of those—I developed my passion for sailing in high school. A friend of mine owned a sailboat."

"When's the last time you sailed?"

"Probably in high school. Gunnar didn't have a boat." He glanced at the photos again. "I'd say you must have had some kind of athletic ability if you made all those teams, whether varsity or not."

She shrugged. "I did it mostly to make Dad happy."

He turned to her. "But not for you?"

She shook her head. *How sad was that?*

"Anyway, I came in to tell you dessert's ready."

He put his arm around her shoulders and walked with her to join her mother in the dining area.

✧   ✧   ✧

"You're going to love these cupcakes, Kristoffer. Thanks again for remembering, Mom!"

The chocolate-raspberry flavored Bundtlets were piped with sour-cream icing and always her must-have treat during a visit with Mom in Carmel.

They sat, she and Kristoffer, side by side across the table from her mom. Out of Mom's eyesight, he squeezed Pamela's knee, and she smiled at him.

"Sunshine's great in the kitchen, unlike me." Pamela cringed to see Kristoffer's smile as he heard her nickname for the second time. Would she be hearing it again—from him?

"She's also methodical, whether working on a recipe or a surgical procedure," Mom added.

Pamela flushed, wishing Mom would find some other topic of conversation than bragging on her daughter. Next thing she knew, Mom would be bringing out the photo albums and showing her life in agonizingly incremental detail. Actually, she'd been surprised to see some of those photos displayed on the bookshelf. They hadn't been there the last time she visited. She'd always been puzzled why Mom kept her childhood photos anyway, but, oddly enough, it made her feel special, too.

"I just like order in my life, Mom." Pamela hadn't been able to maintain control in her childhood so she made up for that in her career and adult life.

"You take after your dad in that regard." While Mom's words weren't said in a bitter way, Pamela didn't want to talk about Dad behind his back.

"What brought you to California, Maribeth?"

Kristoffer's question took Pamela off guard. Had he forgotten what she'd told him about her mom? No, he never forgot anything she said as best she could tell. He must be trying to steer the conversation away from Pamela. She beamed at him to show her appreciation.

Mom's hand had stopped midway to her mouth with a forkful of cupcake. She glanced at Pamela before setting the fork down. Pamela's heart pounded. Would she reveal anything more about herself than what Pamela already knew, which was so limited?

"I was raised just north of San Francisco. I inherited this house from a maiden aunt at a time I needed a place to…live, so it became my…haven." Why was she choosing her words so carefully? Pamela did know Mom met Dad in northern California, but not about her great-aunt's bequest.

Mom continued. "I've come to love this area. I'm working now at a center in Salinas Valley that provides services to migrant families. Keeping middle-school girls in this after-school program motivated and away from drugs and gang violence is a challenge, but rewarding."

"When did you start doing that, Mom?" She hadn't heard her mention it before, but Mom had always had large gaps in her life unknown to Pamela.

Her mother picked at a dog hair or something on her slacks before turning her gaze to Pamela again. "Six months ago." Pamela had noticed her mom seemed more relaxed and content now than she had during her last visit. Was her new job responsible for the change? Whatever the reason, Pamela was happy about it.

"Enough about me. Tell me, Sunshine, how have you been feeling? You scared me to death when you told me you'd caught some kind of rare fever."

"Not rare in that part of the world, only difficult to diagnose under the primitive circumstances. But I'm fine now."

Pamela told her mother about the medical-equipment project she and Kristoffer were working on, which morphed into talk about Heidi's school for Afghani girls and Fakhira's imminent arrival in the States for further surgery. They then launched into a lengthy discussion about the deplorable plight of girls in that region of the world and made comparisons to some of the conditions faced by immigrant girls here.

"Among other things I do at the youth center in Salinas is lead a book club once a week. We recently read and discussed Malala's remarkable story of courage against the Taliban. The Mexican-American girls felt empowered by her story and her choosing to face unthinkable dangers in the quest for an education for her and other Muslim girls. I think they began seeing parallels between their lives and hers and are making some connections as to what might be possible for them if they pursue their educational goals."

She and her mom hadn't talked about anything that mattered this much in a long time. Sharing a common interest made Pamela feel a bond with her mom she'd rarely experienced since her childhood.

Mom grew pensive, and the conversation ended as they finished eating their enormous cupcakes. Kristoffer, who hadn't been talking as much, finished first. "Dessert was delicious, Maribeth. Thank you."

"I can't take the credit."

He laughed. "I have several restaurants on speed dial myself. Knowing which ones are good takes a certain knack, too." They smiled at each other in understanding before he turned toward Pamela. "I have to agree your daughter's cooking is fabulous. I don't rely on takeout as often as I once did."

"Tell me, Kristoffer, what is it you do?" Maribeth asked.

"I'm the chief financial officer for a government contractor. Basically, I find ways to make money so that the CEO and his team can carry out their missions."

"Contractors? Does that include military involvement like Blackwater in Iraq?" Pamela heard the edge in Mom's voice. That her mother kept up with what had happened in Iraq didn't surprise her, but the sudden tension between the two of them did.

Kristoffer laughed off her concern. "Today's contractors are under much more scrutiny, I assure you. You wouldn't believe the amount of regulations and paperwork involved these days."

Mom remained silent a moment before relaxing her shoulders

again. Even though she smiled, Pamela saw strain on her face. "You both sound equally committed to humanitarian work. I like that."

"Kristoffer's cousin runs the firm and is doing some wonderful things in Afghanistan, Mom. He's making a difference. If not for his generosity, Fakhira, the girl I told you about, wouldn't be coming to the States for more advanced surgeries."

Kristoffer nodded in agreement. "Many missions, like his current one, are focused primarily on providing the school Pamela mentioned with adequate supplies, security, and food, but they also work to obtain the release of Allied Command prisoners, rebuild infrastructure destroyed during the war, and such."

"And the project to buy equipment for the hospital where I worked is making a huge difference, too, Mom." Pamela didn't want to digress into whether the war was right or wrong or whether it had done any good.

Mom leaned onto the table. "Sunshine, if you're involved with them, I'm certain they're aboveboard."

This might be a good time to change the subject.

"Mom, we were thinking about going down to the beach. Are beach fires permitted tonight?"

"Sure. Monday through Thursday. There's some seasoned drift-wood in the garage. Help yourself. Perfect night for it." Mom seemed happy to send them off, not used to having anyone around perhaps.

They cleared the table and loaded the dishwasher before taking the dogs for a walk up and down the street with her mom. The sound of the waves called to her. Pamela noticed half a dozen fires lit on the beach already.

Back at the house, Mom shooed them toward the door leading to the garage. Kristoffer went out to gather what they'd need as her mom pulled her aside. "I only have the one bedroom upstairs. Unless you want me to kennel the dogs that usually sleep on the sofa."

Pamela had originally planned to sleep on one of the couches, but saw the Doberman and Great Dane curled up in those two spots now.

"Don't worry about us. I'll talk to Kristoffer, but we'll probably take the upstairs." If Kristoffer didn't want to share a bed, it would be a beautiful night to sleep under the stars on the balcony.

Pamela closed the space between them and hugged her mom. "Night, Mom. Thanks for everything. It's so good to see you again."

Uncharacteristically, her mom didn't push her away first, but seemed to want to hold on a little longer. "Love you, Sunshine." When they separated, her mom pressed the house key into her hand. "Enjoy your time on the beach." She started to turn away, stopped, and faced Pamela. "I like Kristoffer. Hang on to him."

Pamela had never asked her mother to weigh in on anyone in her life before, but having her support meant a lot.

After giving her mom another quick squeeze, Pamela turned toward the garage as Mom picked up the dachshunds to take them to her room at the back of the house. Before Pamela joined Kristoffer, Mom tossed back over her shoulder, "See you at breakfast!"

Inside the garage, Kristoffer picked up a small bundle of firewood and the butane lighter while Pamela grabbed the beach blanket, a bucket to extinguish the fire, and a flashlight. They crossed Scenic Road lured by the sound of the waves crashing against the shore. She could never live at the beach year-round, but did enjoy occasional visits like this one.

The air was chilly, not unusual for Carmel. If the daytime temperature reached seventy degrees this time of year, it was considered a heat wave. Good thing she and Kristoffer had worn jackets while walking the dogs.

"The moon's almost full enough that we don't need the flashlight," he said. The stars twinkled above, and she spotted the Big Dipper, too.

At his suggestion, she turned it off after both had reached the bottom of the steep rock steps. There were only two fires burning in this area, rather close together, so they ventured closer to the crashing waves to find themselves a secluded spot. Kristoffer soon had the fire blazing, and they stretched out on the blanket, curled together for added warmth.

"I can't believe how cold it is here. It's almost July," he remarked.

"Carmel's temperatures vary only slightly in any given season, but tend to be on the cool side year-round. After today's warmer-than-usual temps, the marine layer probably will roll in tomorrow morning and leave everything blanketed in fog until at least afternoon. San Francisco gets that fog, too."

Leaning against him, his arms wrapped around her, she relished being held by him again. Would they share a bed tonight? Before she could bring it up, he spoke.

"This week has been quite an adventure. Who'd have thought we'd wind up here in Carmel when we set out on this adventure last Friday? I've enjoyed traveling with someone spontaneous like you, Sprite, and I'm going to hate to leave."

"I feel the same way. We've had an amazing time. Even though our week is only half over, when can we run away together again?" She grinned, but found herself waiting for his response.

"I haven't managed to get any work done out here. Gunnar might not grant me another vacation for a while." He laughed.

"Don't you hate for a good vacation to come to an end?" She hadn't had many, but this was at the top of her list of favorites. Would they do this again someday?

They sat quietly and listened to the waves. "Want to take a stroll?" he asked.

"Not tonight." His arms around her, strong and protective, with the sound of his beating heart against her head was all she wanted. If only they could stay like this forever.

They wouldn't return to Sonoma for four days. Where should she take him next? "Want to drive down to Big Sur tomorrow, Kristoffer? There's a fabulous restaurant overlooking the ocean. Maybe we can still get reservations since it's not a weekend."

"Sounds good to me. Whatever you want to do."

She sighed. *That* was off limits.

A strand of hair whipped against her face, and Kristoffer's fingers brushed it behind her ear. Her heart beat erratically at his touch.

They lapsed into a comfortable silence.

✧   ✧   ✧

Listening to the sounds of lovers on the beach, Kristoffer ached to make love to Pamela, but was helpless with a fear of failure. Their fledgling relationship needed more time before they made a decision that might leave her hurting. What if this was a vacation anomaly and not something they'd be able to sustain back home? Had he truly broken down walls for good?

Pamela had been clear she wasn't looking for casual sex. Hell, neither was he. They'd wait.

Even if it kills me.

Holding her like this in such a romantic setting, his defenses lowered even more. Perhaps he should shift his thoughts in a safer direction and douse his libido. Talking about her mom ought to do the trick.

"Your mom is quite interesting. I can't help but feel there's a lot more to her than meets the eye."

"Join the club. She's always struck me that way, too. I'd love to know more. She did share things tonight that were new to me, including those photos on the bookshelf."

"Why don't you ask her specific questions?"

"Lots of reasons. Deep down, I don't think I want to hear the answers. I mean, what if she left because she hated having me as her kid?"

"I don't get that impression with her at all. She's proud of you and clearly loves you."

"I know. Logically, I don't believe she left because she didn't want to be my mom. Something must have scared her."

Silence settled around them until he asked what was foremost in his mind. "What are the sleeping arrangements tonight?"

"That's something I'm supposed to talk with you about. Mom's an early riser and has already gone to bed. She gave me the key so we can let ourselves back in tonight." That didn't answer the question. Pamela turned to face him, but reading her expression in the shadow cast by his head was difficult. "We have the upstairs to ourselves. It's really the best part of the house, but…there's only one bed."

One bed. He'd suspected one bedroom judging by how the upstairs looked from the outside, but had hoped for two beds. Interesting that her mother didn't make the upstairs room her master suite, rather than a room at the back of the house that had no view of the ocean, but that had nothing to do with determining where he and Pamela would sleep.

At the moment, they shared a beach blanket and hadn't crossed any line. Could he sleep with her and not let his libido get the better of him?

"If you aren't ready for that, Kristoffer, I'll be happy to sleep on the balcony's chaise lounge and give you the bed."

"Nonsense, Sprite." *Man up, Roar.* "A tiny thing like you would freeze out there without a fire—or me—to keep you warm." Why was he flirting with her? Before volunteering himself to sleep on the floor or the balcony, he needed more information. "How big is the bed?"

"King."

That helped. A lot. He relaxed some. "We'll share the bed."

Passionate moans from down the beach reached his ears, igniting a flame inside him to match the one in their fire pit nearby. He hoped he wasn't making a huge mistake.

"Someone's getting lucky." Apparently, she'd heard them, too. Unless she was referring to the two of them, but he didn't think so.

"Ah, to be young and in love again," he said.

"Sometimes I think love is wasted on the young. Sure, their bodies are firing on all cylinders, but they're clueless about what true love and lifelong commitments are about. One unwanted pregnancy and their lives will be changed forever."

Was she thinking about her parents now? Had her mom's unplanned pregnancy contributed to their inability to stay together? Had she gone in search of whatever she hadn't been able to enjoy while in high school? Seemed doubtful. Something more powerful had sent her away.

Pamela continued, "There's much more to being intimate than the sexual act itself can provide."

Maybe, but his memories of sex were all fond ones. "You're too young to write off finding someone special, Sprite." While he hoped he could be that man for her one day, he needed more time to know for certain.

She shivered, and he pulled her more tightly against him.

After a moment, he asked, "Warmer?"

"Mm-hmm." The dreamy tone in her voice made him wonder if she might fall asleep. The fire would take a while to burn out. He'd content himself to lie here, watch the moon arc over them, listen to the waves, and hold his tiny sprite.

Not for the first time, he wished their situation could be different.

Stay in the moment.

Right now, holding her like this had to be enough. When her head lolled, she jerked it back. He decided it was selfish of him to stay out here. They could snuggle like this in the bed, too. As long as it went no further than that. Time to go back to the house. She needed her sleep.

He separated from her and stood. "Why don't we walk on the beach in the morning instead of tonight?"

"Sounds great. All our hiking today wore me out."

"The sound of the waves isn't helping, either."

"We can leave the doors open tonight and let the waves put us both to sleep."

Sharing a bed with her would *not* be conducive to sleeping. Not for him, at least.

He offered her a hand and pulled her up. They looked out toward the darkened bay. The moon's reflection shimmered across the water's surface much like Pamela had shone a beacon of light into his dark, dark world.

With a sigh, he went to the water's edge and filled the bucket with water to douse the flames—the ones in the campfire at least. Once certain it had been extinguished, they trudged through the loose sand to the nearest stairway, this one putting them a block or so down the street from her mother's house. Snatches of moonlight shining through the branches of the gnarled and windblown cypress trees cast an eerie mood over the street.

Kristoffer reached for her hand when she stumbled on the uneven pavement and held on tightly to steady her.

They continued along, and he noticed some of the houses. Few people opted to close blinds or drapes, and soon, he was engaging in the very behavior he'd decided he didn't like when he'd looked out Maribeth's picture windows earlier this evening.

"I've always heard about this place as where the rich came to shop and play, but never really thought about its incredible beauty."

Yet nothing compared to the woman walking beside him. He couldn't fathom how different she was from the woman he'd first met during that business meeting with Gunnar at the end of April. Or the one he'd seen standing naked in front of the class during his tour of The Denver Academy. Perhaps her poise and physical beauty had opened his eyes to her initially, but they paled compared to her inner beauty. The spark of life this vivacious woman had breathed into his soul these past two months. He didn't want to imagine what life might be like without her.

When would he be ready to admit his true feelings for her? Not until he was completely certain of them—or as certain as anyone could be.

In the driveway, they removed their sandals and brushed any residual sand from their feet, legs, and clothing. "Let's get our bags from the trunk first," he suggested. He opened it, retrieved their carry-on bags, and followed her to the side door. When they heard the large dogs let out a couple of warning barks, she reassured them of her presence through the door and pulled the key from her pocket. Inside, the two biggest dogs bounded up to greet them and accepted their reward in some vigorous behind-the-ear rubs from Pamela before returning to the beds they'd made on the sofas.

The door to the upstairs was off the dining room, beyond the one to the garage. They climbed the stairs to their own little sanctuary. The windows had been opened, and the room aired out. The sound of the waves came to him as soon as he exited the enclosed stairway.

A king-sized bed dominated the room. "Which side would you

prefer?" he asked.

"Doesn't matter to me. I sleep in the middle of my queen one, so no preference."

The thought of her unconsciously making her way to the middle of this bed tonight made him wonder if he ought to take the floor or balcony. Would he make it through tonight without doing something he couldn't undo?

"Do you want the bathroom first, Kristoffer?"

"No. You go ahead." He set down her suitcase on the side of the mattress nearest the bathroom and walked around the bed to what would be his side near the entrance to the balcony. Restless, he walked outside. The view took his breath away. The moon sank lower on the horizon, within only an hour or two of setting. It illuminated a few clouds high above the cypress branches across the street.

At his left was the silhouette of a deck chair. If he were smart, he'd sleep out here tonight.

Chicken.

Guilty as charged. But he was fully in control of his body and faculties. No doubt, she would be equally cautious about running the risk of making a mistake both might regret. What was he worrying about?

Footsteps on the boards behind him alerted him to Pamela's presence. "Wow. It's even more breathtaking from up here." He turned to watch her come closer, her hair wet from the shower as she quickly donned a robe over the knee-length T-shirt she wore.

"You took the words right out of my mouth." And every thought from my mind.

Get a grip, Roar. You've seen her in a lot less.

She came to stand beside him, looking out at the horizon. They stared silently—her at the water, he at her.

"Thanks for bringing me on this trip with you, Kristoffer. I needed this time away from home more than I realized, but today has been especially eye-opening."

"In what way?"

She turned to look up at him, and he faced her. "Talking with mom about you and me has helped me see things more clearly. I really don't care what anyone else thinks or says about us. As long as you and I know what we have is right for us and we are not ashamed of it, what does it matter what anyone else thinks? We're calling the shots. The only people in our relationship are you, me, and Tori."

He hadn't expected her to bring Tori into it, but appreciated Pamela for thinking of her, too. "I'm not ashamed of anything we've done." He took a strand of wet hair plastered to her cheek and curled it around her tiny ear. There still were so many things he wanted to try with her, once he was sure of himself and their future. "Once we're home again, we can reset our boundaries and see where we go with this."

"We'll sort everything out when the time comes," she said confidently.

She didn't seem to have any concerns at all. He wished he could be so self-assured. "We owe it to ourselves to grab whatever happiness we can have or make for ourselves. Life's too short. We both know that better than most."

He needed to stop trying to think in terms of marriage as the be-all in relationships. That was off the table. Their commitment to one another would be centered more around their Dom/sub dynamic. "You'll be my submissive, regardless of whatever else we choose to be to one another. I'm content with that even if there's never anything more, because at this moment, the thought of not having you in my life at all is unthinkable."

She smiled up at him. "No regrets, no guilt."

"That should be our mantra."

"Works for me, but those are powerful words to live by, but not always easy to live up to."

He moved closer to her. "Like any changes one makes, it takes repetition to get it to sink in. All I know is these past few days have changed me, Pamela. My heart has opened up again." Or had it been ripped open with a sudden awakening? He groaned as he turned away, looking out to sea again.

Her arms wrapped around his waist. "Stop torturing yourself, Kristoffer. We want to be together. We're going to figure out a way to make this work for us."

He turned back to her and pulled her into his arms with a fierceness that surprised him—and her, as well, given her wide-eyed expression. Holding the sides of her head, either to anchor himself or to keep her from retreating, he lowered his face to hers. Their lips brushed before he kissed first her upper lip, lightly sucking it between his, then the lower. They breathed into each other's mouths and when he could stand it no longer, he ground his mouth against hers, forcing his tongue between her lips.

God of Thunder, he wanted Pamela so badly. No way could he revert to the passive, barely alive way he had existed the past four years. His heart was big enough to include both Tori and Pamela.

How could it be wrong for him to love these two women who meant the world to him?

CHAPTER SEVENTEEN

Y *es!*

Pamela relished the feel of his hands on her face, his lips on hers, his tongue inside her mouth. She didn't know when his passion might cool again, so she'd bask in it every chance she could. Did the thought of going back to the way things were lack appeal for him as much as it did her? She meant each and every word she'd spoken. Together, they'd figure this out and do what was best for them, but in the meantime, any time spent in Kristoffer's arms would be time she'd cherish forever.

His mouth broke away, and she feared he'd retreat again. Instead, he trailed hot kisses down her neck to the hollow of her throat, igniting her passions even more. Her knees nearly buckled, and she held on to his shoulders to keep from falling into a puddle at his feet.

Once again, he pulled away, this time apparently to control his breathing.

"Kristoffer, please. Don't stop."

Not tonight.

He pulled her lower body against his, and she felt his erection against her abdomen.

Yes, yes, yes! He wants this, too!

Every nerve ending burst to life in her body. Barely half an hour ago, she'd almost fallen asleep in his arms on the beach. While the shower had revived her, this man had lit a fire inside her in a matter of seconds. They had so few days left before this magic bubble they'd surrounded themselves in would burst. She needed to make each precious moment last as long as possible.

When he pulled away once more, she expected him to call an end to this before they reached the boundaries set in place. Instead, he scooped her into his arms and carried her into the bedroom to lay her on the bed.

"I'm going to take a shower. A cold shower."

No! You can't leave me like this!

But he did just that. The moment ended as quickly as it had begun.

Kristoffer, his lips tight with determination, pulled some clothes and a toiletry bag out of his suitcase and walked into the bathroom, closing the door behind him. She heard the shower running and pictured him torturing himself under the cold spray.

She fought the urge to join him and at least give him a blow job to relieve his sexual tension, but she would wait for him to tell her oral was on his list of approved activities. Pushing him too far, too soon, might backfire and send him running.

Just be patient with him.

Tempted to shuck her gown and sleep in the nude, Pamela quashed that thought, too. She removed the bolsters and throw pillows from the bed before turning down the sheets and duvet. He'd come closer than ever tonight to admitting he desired her in a physical way. Not as her friend. Not as her Top. But as her lover.

But his attraction ripped apart everything he believed about faithfulness in marriage. His traditional values were butting up against the realities of the twenty-first century. How many spouses faced this harsh reality of modern medicine?

She didn't want to compete against the love he had for his wife, because she'd only get hurt. But their feelings for one another were growing stronger. If not in love yet, they were certainly on the road to it. Could they find a way to be together that wouldn't leave him riddled with guilt and regret?

She's his wife. I'm his submissive.

Pamela had only begun to submit to him, but that only made her anxious to delve more deeply into the lifestyle with him.

With the turmoil Kristoffer must be experiencing now, she wouldn't want to hazard a guess as to her chances with him once they returned to Denver. But he'd been teaching her to live in the moment. Why worry about what the future held? *Carpe diem.*

Pamela stretched out on the mattress and punched her pillow several times, as if that could help relieve her frustration. The bathroom door opened, and she turned around to see him standing there wearing only his boxers. He dried his muscular torso with the towel, but his gaze never left hers.

"Sorry about that. You okay, Sprite?"

She forced herself to smile. "I think so." Yet she negated her words by shaking her head.

He tossed the towel on the bathroom floor, crossed the room, and crawled onto the mattress from the other side of the bed. She didn't want to face him until she brought her emotions under control, but he closed the space between them and pressed against her back. He wrapped his arms around her, his warm body smelling of deodorant soap.

Warm? So he hadn't taken a cold shower after all.

"Sex is out, of course, but how would you feel about cuddling?"

Baby steps. She rolled over and smiled at him. "I'd love that."

"Good, because I need your body against mine tonight, Pamela." He sighed, and she thought he was going to say something more, but he remained silent. When he sighed again, she knew something was on his mind.

Pamela stroked his cheek. "What's wrong?"

He took a few moments before he answered, making her worry more. "I took care of myself in the bathroom." It took her a moment to realize what he meant. "I wouldn't be able to touch you, lie beside you, without exploding otherwise."

She grinned. "I understand completely. I'm here if you need me to..." She didn't know why she couldn't come out and say the words. As far as she knew, the man hadn't come since they'd been on this trip, although she had no idea what he'd done in the privacy of his room in Sonoma. Pamela had no problem with him seeing to his own needs if he wasn't ready to allow her to do so.

"I know you would. Perhaps I'll be ready to ask for that soon. But not tonight. And especially not with your mother downstairs." He half shrugged, and she laughed. "But I don't want to be a selfish bastard on top of one very confused one. Can I help relieve some of your frustration, too?"

Intuition told her allowing him to go any further tonight would only result in more guilt on his conscience and destroy all they'd achieved the past few days. Rather than let her rampant hormones dictate how fast this relationship moved, she'd give him some breathing room.

"No, thanks." She grinned. "Next time, perhaps we can consider taking care of each other—hands and mouths are both on my okay list, whenever they are added to yours."

He drew a deep breath. "Keep putting images like that in my head, and you'll send me back to the bathroom."

"Not without me this time, I hope."

He chuckled, telling her she hadn't pushed too hard. Never hurt to remind him where the current level of negotiation lay.

"Turn over so we can spoon, Sprite." She did as instructed and pressed her back and butt against him again, feeling the sting left from last night. His hand reached up to cup her breast, but she halted the movement and placed it around her waist instead.

"Don't get me wrong, Kristoffer. I want you to touch me more intimately, but not until we're ready." His breathing sounded labored; the only other noise she heard was the waves lapping against the beach. "Snuggling with you is all I need tonight."

She scooted closer against him, ultimately deciding to bring his hand up to rest between her breasts. A compromise of sorts. Tonight, she would lie nestled in his arms, snug against his warm, hard body in a protective cocoon.

Tomorrow? Well, they'd continue to negotiate this relationship like two rational adults before jumping into anything that might cause regrets for either of them. She'd jumped too fast before and had only wound up hurt. He hadn't permitted himself to be close to anyone since Tori. Both had a lot to overcome before they could move forward together. But neither seemed ready to cut and run.

He lifted her hair and kissed the back of her neck. "Thank you, Sprite."

The rasp of his scruff made her body tingle to the core. "For what?" Her voice sounded husky to her ears.

"For understanding me better than I do myself sometimes."

She smiled and closed her eyes. "I'm trying."

✧   ✧   ✧

Kristoffer's heartbeat slowly returned to normal. He doubted he'd sleep much tonight, but holding her like this left him with a sense of peace he hadn't felt in…a very long time. Pulling away from her would gouge a hole in his chest.

How had this little sprite become so precious to him in such a short time?

Each step closer to intimacy left him torn in two directions: Faithfulness to his marriage vows and the need to seek comfort—and perhaps more—from a woman he'd come to care deeply about.

"Pamela," he whispered.

"Yes?"

"In a perfect world, where do you see our relationship going from here?"

"We don't live in a perfect world."

Such a pragmatist. "Okay, where do you *want* this to go?"

"Go? Some things can't be planned or forecasted, Kristoffer, unlike your investments. I know you're used to controlling everything around you, but romance doesn't work that way."

While he wasn't ready to say this was a romance, they'd certainly become more romantic since coming to California. Clearly, by her words, she saw this as a romance.

He ought to close his eyes and mouth and go to sleep, but the need to figure this out outweighed caution. "It would be selfish of me to string you along when you could be spending your time at clubs or play parties looking for a Dom who can offer his entire heart and mind."

She rolled onto her back and stared at him. "I thought we agreed in the limo we're going to take this one step at a time." She propped herself up on her elbow, a stern expression on her face. "Right now, you're the only Dom I want. I agreed to be your submissive, because I'm comfortable with you and am coming to trust you more each day. You've had an amazing effect on my submissive skills. Bottom line, I choose to be with you rather than search for some unknown Dom who may or may not understand and care for me as well as you do."

"There's no guarantee I'll be able to continue when we go home."

She brushed a strand of hair off his forehead. "Look, at the very worst, we go back to me being in training with you. That worked before, and there's nothing to say it won't work again. But what might have you concerned is that other aspects of this relationship have advanced faster than either of us anticipated while we've been out here."

To say the least.

"Kristoffer, it's only natural to become nervous when exploring new territory in a relationship—and this is definitely new to us both." A steely determination came into her eyes. "But I, for one, have zero regrets about anything we've done. I can't imagine anything that would make me change my opinion. I hope you feel the same way. Guilt and regret are wasted emotions and a total drain on your energy. I suggest that you cut them out like a cancer."

Easier said than done, but her bossy lecture made him smile. "Yes, ma'am."

She smiled back, lightening the mood. He rose up on his own elbow and rested his head in his palm. "You always say what I need to hear." He brushed an imaginary hair from her forehead and let his hand trail down her cheek to her chin. "I don't want to spend the rest of my life beating myself up because I didn't allow myself to experience something I want this badly."

Pamela closed her eyes and shook her head before meeting his gaze again. "You sound as though you have to make a decision immediately. Take all the time you need. I'm not going anywhere. Well, except maybe to Afghanistan in a month or two."

He didn't like the thought of her being in harm's way again. As her Dom, he could voice his opinion, but they hadn't negotiated for him to have any authority over her profession.

"I know we've talked about security measures at the hospital before, Pamela, but I wasn't your Dom then. Now, I expect you to set up regular check-ins. I'm still going to worry every minute you're gone, but at least at those times—once a day, if not more often—I'll be able to breathe."

"It's really not as scary as it sounds, but knowing you care and expect to hear from me will help me feel less isolated. Oh, my parents care, too, but they haven't required daily updates."

"Never confuse me with your parents."

She laughed. "No, Sir. No chance of that happening." She leaned forward and gave him a chaste peck on the lips. "But thanks for not going all he-man Dom on me and demanding that I give up my career."

"I know how much your work means to you. Nothing would end this fledgling relationship faster than me trying to control every aspect of your life. I can just imagine how well that would go over."

Surrendering her independence to him career-wise wasn't going to happen with her. No more than he'd give up working for Gunnar. Even if watching her go was going to kill him, he'd have to suck it up.

"How long do you think you'll be gone?"

"Right now, I'm only planning to finish out my last contract. I've applied to join the plastics and reconstructive surgery department at Children's in Aurora and have an interview with the chief of surgery Monday."

"That's great!" Knowing she wouldn't be planning any more dangerous overseas assignments relieved him somewhat.

"I haven't been offered a position yet."

"You'll bowl them over. I have every confidence in you. Why didn't you say anything before?"

She shrugged. "We seem to have a deplorable lack of interest in discussing one another's careers, as best I can tell."

"True." He chuckled. He'd been too consumed with her submissive training and his attempts at moving on with his life to waste precious time together talking about their work.

"Children's has a wonderful program and even lead a team of surgeons on a trip to Guatemala every year, so I won't completely be giving up my humanitarian activities."

He wasn't sure Guatemala was all that safe, either, but at least she'd be closer.

He shook his head as he continued to stare at her. So beautiful in the moonlight. Her lips beckoned him, and he pulled her head toward his to kiss her. She moaned and opened her mouth to receive him, but he ended the kiss almost as quickly as it had started.

"Let's spend a night or two in Big Sur."

"I'd love to!"

Being alone with her, away from her mother, would be far less inhibiting. Was that a good or bad thing?

"Why don't we leave right after breakfast?" he asked.

She nodded. "Perfect. There are a few stops I'd like to make on the way."

He chuckled. "I know how you are on scenic drives."

She picked up her phone from the nightstand. "I'm setting the silent alarm on my fitness tracker bracelet so I won't wake you up, but I want to have a talk with Mom before we leave." Had the light in her eyes dimmed a bit? "I'll just go down before breakfast, but you sleep in, or take a walk on the beach."

Sounded serious—and something he didn't need to be a part of. "I'm sure I'll manage just fine for a couple of hours on my own." If there was one thing he knew how to do, it was be alone.

"A walk sounds good. I have some thinking to do, and I'm guessing you could use some time alone with your mom."

She studied his face a moment. "Sure. It's a great place to find answers."

He wasn't sure he knew the questions to ask, but nodded. "Now, let's get some sleep," he suggested, lying on his back. He rolled onto his side facing away from her, worried being so close to her might turn him on. But when she snuggled against his back, leaving him wanting so much more, he wondered if he could manage to hold out until they returned to Denver.

All he knew for certain at this point was that the thought of ending all contact with Pamela now would rip his heart in two...again. He still hadn't figured out what kind of relationship he could offer that was worthy of her commitment, but perhaps he'd find answers on the beach in a few hours.

Pamela tried to be as quiet as possible and grabbed her tank top and shorts to carry downstairs and dress so as not to awaken Kristoffer, who was sleeping as though he hadn't a care in the world. She smiled. This trip had been good for him.

After dressing at the base of the stairwell, she walked into the kitchen to find an array of fruits laid out on the counter along with bacon, a bag of potatoes, and a carton of eggs. The door to the patio was open, and she peeked outside to find Mom doing yoga. Rather than disturb her, she began cutting up potatoes for home fries and frying some of the bacon. She was halfway through preparing the one healthy part of the meal—fruit salad—when Mom came into the kitchen.

"Smells wonderful!"

"Thanks for going shopping this morning." The fridge had been nearly empty last night.

"I woke up early and thought you might be hungry when you got up. Hope I didn't forget anything."

"I can't think of anything you've left out." Pamela couldn't help but wonder if Mom was trying to send them on their way as early as possible, although she didn't seem to be stressed out by their being here.

As she hulled and quartered one strawberry after another, her thoughts swarmed around the question foremost in her mind all morning—and for a large portion of her life. She'd never asked, but all of the recent talks with Kristoffer about her childhood had stirred up a lot of feelings. She wanted answers, but didn't want to rock the boat, either. She and her mom had been getting closer for more than a decade. Why jeopardize that?

"You're awfully quiet, Sunshine. Everything all right with you and Kristoffer?"

"We're doing great. Thinking about driving down to Big Sur and spending a couple of nights there." Pamela didn't make eye contact, but picked up the stems and peels from the salad and tossed them into the waste bin after asking if they could be recycled here.

"Should be a lovely day for the drive if the marine layer doesn't roll in to shore." Mom pulled plates and bowls from the cupboard and carried them out to the patio table. When she came in again, she seemed to notice the silence between them. "Is something else the matter?"

Her mother wasn't usually tuned in to Pamela's moods. She'd given her the perfect opening—twice—but asking the question was harder than expected. The closing of the front door told her Kristoffer must be off on his walk. She wished she'd asked to go with him, but last night, he sounded as though he wanted some time alone. Sharing a room—and a bed—offered no privacy for someone used to fending for himself. She hoped he wasn't tired of traveling with her, but he seemed excited about Big Sur.

As her mother counted out silverware, Pamela inhaled deeply before the words tumbled out in a rush, "Mom, why did you leave Dad and me?"

Mom's hands stilled then began to shake slightly. She didn't meet Pamela's gaze right away, but when she did, there were tears in her eyes.

"I'm so sorry I hurt you, Pamela. That wasn't my intention, but I had to protect you both."

"From what?" Or would *from whom* be the better question? Neither made any sense. How could Mom protect her daughter and husband when she was thousands of miles away? Not that she knew where her mom went during those years.

"Let's sit outside." She turned away and walked through the door;

Pamela followed. Mom continued setting the table as the silence drew out between them. Was she trying to formulate an excuse or to find the perfect words to defend the unexplainable?

"Sit down, Sunshine." She was using her nickname again, so she must have regained her equilibrium.

Taking the seat next to her mom, she sat and waited. Mom wrung her hands in her lap a few times before meeting her gaze again. A tear ran off her jaw and splashed onto her arm. "I want you to know that I only left because I loved you. I'm...I was involved in something I still can't talk about, but my decisions put you and Bryce in danger. To protect you both, I had to disappear."

"What kind of something? Mom, that's no answer at all." Her cryptic response left Pamela with a million more questions.

"I know. You'll just have to trust me. If I could explain further, I would. Maybe someday—"

Were her childhood fantasies of Mom as a spy more real than she thought? No, that's preposterous. Who had a mom who was a spy? The Cold War ended long ago. Actually, the Berlin Wall fell in 1989, about the same year Mom left.

"Were you spying on East Germany?" Or worse yet, *for* them—or the KGB in Russia?

Mom's brows furrowed in confusion. "Of course not! How would I have contact with anyone in Eastern Europe? We didn't even have a World Wide Web yet."

Then who? What? None of this made any sense!

Mom had lived in Japan when Pamela was born until a few years after. Did Americans spy for or against Japan? But Mom hadn't even earned her high-school diploma until nearly the time they returned to the States. Weren't spies more highly educated?

Anger boiled up inside her. Not only at her mother but also at herself now for opening up this wound in the first place. "Mom, what the hell did you do?"

She dashed a tear from her cheek. "I destroyed my family. If I had it to do over again, I don't know if I'd make the same..." She let her words trail off.

"I love you, Mom, no matter what, but I've spent more than two decades wondering what I did that made you want to leave us."

Mom reached out and squeezed Pamela's arm. "Oh, God, Sunshine! You must believe me when I say it had nothing to do with you!"

"You deserted me! That had a *lot* to do with me!"

Tears streamed down her mom's cheeks unheeded now, and Pamela felt guilty for causing them, but then remembered admonishing Kristoffer for that wasted emotion. "Mom, my whole childhood felt like a lie. I don't want to continue believing that the rest of my life. How can whatever happened back then still be affecting your life now?"

Neither woman spoke for a while, and her mom picked up a paper napkin to dab at her eyes. She said in a voice so low Pamela had to lean closer to hear, "I thought I was doing the right thing. I know you want answers—*deserve* answers—but I won't risk putting you in danger again."

Again? How could what happened then still be a threat? This was surreal.

Mom closed her eyes. "Please accept my apology, Pamela. I was young and saw no other option. But at least neither of you was punished because of what I chose to do. I intend to keep it that way."

"Mom, with Dad's help, I forgave you years ago."

"Thank you. If I'd known you thought that…" Mom dabbed at her eyes again and blew her nose in the napkin before picking up another.

"For a long time, I explained away your absence picturing you working as a kick-ass, international spy." She laughed with a shrug. "I had an overactive imagination. Or maybe spent too many nights watching spy shows on TV."

Mom smiled. Seeing she wasn't going to obtain any additional answers this morning, she needed to end this on a high note. "Dad eventually convinced me that whatever drove you away wasn't my fault, but you've cleared up any lingering doubt."

"Sunshine, you were the best daughter a mother could have. I was so proud of you. Even after I left, I tried to keep up with your accomplishments and activities."

Now Pamela found herself in tears. "I hadn't noticed the photos in the living room before last night."

"I only put them out last Christmas. I guess I was thinking back over all the things I'd missed and needed reminders that I had been there for some of those milestones at least."

Pamela stood up and closed the gap between them. Wrapping her arms around her mom, she hugged her tight. "I hate that we lost those years and hate even more that you continue to live in fear like this, Mom. Have you thought about going to the police?"

Mom held on to Pamela as though she were a lifeline. This was why guilt was such a useless emotion. They had both harbored a lot of guilt all these years—and for what?

"Are you going to be okay, Mom? I probably shouldn't have stirred all this up just before I'm about to leave."

Mom nodded, took a step back, and searched Pamela's gaze. "How about you?"

"Yeah, I am. But I have Kristoffer to talk with if I'm not."

"Oh, you'd be surprised at what good listeners my dogs are." They both laughed.

"Call me if you want to talk more."

"Will do. I'd like us to keep in touch better, even if by phone or Skype."

"I'd like that, too, Mom. I may never understand what happened back then, but it helps to know it had nothing to do with me."

"It pains me that you thought that all this time. I'm so sorry, Sunshine. If I had it all to do over, I might have made different choices. But I definitely would have assured you more that you weren't to blame for anything I did or didn't do."

"Thanks, Mom. Just cut yourself some slack. What's done is done. You have a lot of living yet to do, and I hope you can let go of the past."

"I'll try. Want me to help with breakfast?"

Pamela grinned. "That would be interesting." The two laughed out loud, agreeing that was a preposterous notion. But the tension washed away.

Before Pamela turned to go into the kitchen again, Mom asked, "Pamela, I wondered if you would share with me Heidi's contact info for the school in Afghanistan."

"Sure, Mom. Why?"

She glanced away. "I'd like to see if she'd be interested in connecting her girls with mine via videoconference or something."

"That sounds like a wonderful idea! I know Heidi would love it. Let me grab a pen and paper, and I'll jot down her online contact info."

❖   ❖   ❖

Kristoffer startled awake upon hearing voices outside. The ocean waves must have lulled him to sleep. Daylight streamed inside the door, but Pamela was up already. Then he recognized her voice drifting inside. She was talking with her mom.

A quick glance at his watch told him it was only seven. Pamela must have risen early. She'd mentioned that her mother was a morning person, so they were probably deep in discussion now. He didn't want to intrude, knowing Pamela wanted to talk over some private matters with Maribeth before they left.

He'd slept better than he had in a long time. Perhaps the sea air agreed with him.

No, be real, man.

Having Pamela share the bed with him had given him this sense of peace and security he'd been missing since he'd lost Tori. He appreciated that Pamela liked to snuggle, too, which no doubt had led to his feelings of contentment this morning. He'd always wanted more of that, but it wasn't Tori's thing.

As he headed down the stairs, he realized for the first time in a long while there was a woman who cared about him and whether he existed. Not just any woman, but one he found fascinating and enjoyed spending time with.

He didn't want to lose her due to indecisiveness or an inability to commit to her in a significant way. The other day in Sonoma, in what one might call a cleansing ceremony given the shower, he'd said goodbye to Tori's spirit and unilaterally revised his vows to her to fit the dilemma modern medicine had left him with that shattered their original ones. But how do you negotiate with someone who doesn't have any awareness? Someone whose mind died but left her body behind?

Same old questions. No new answers.

After dressing in shorts and a polo shirt, he headed down the narrow stairway to the dining room. The door to the patio was open and he could hear the women talking. To signal his leaving, he shut the front door behind him with more force than necessary. Perhaps knowing he wasn't about to interrupt them, they could talk more freely.

Before going outside, he'd booked them a room in one of Big Sur's exclusive resort hotels for tonight and tomorrow. If they hadn't packed the right clothes, he was sure there would be shops eager to sell them whatever they needed.

All that mattered was that he'd soon have Pamela all to himself again. He wanted to give this budding "whatever *it* is" relationship a chance and would need to keep his heart and his options open. He hadn't yet exercised his full potential as her Dom. That might be the safest and best course to chart.

At the base of the stone stairs, he removed his sandals and left them against the wall and out of the way from where a group of caterers—according to the words on the pink and yellow decorations—were setting up for a birthday party. That should make the shoes and stairs easy to spot on his return walk.

He crossed the dry sand, remembering his walk with Pamela yesterday to see the elephant seals. She certainly was one to stop and capture special memories, rather than go from point A to point B.

But he had a purpose for being out here this morning, so he traversed this much shorter sandy expanse quickly, and soon the surf lapped at his feet. Damn, it was cold for nearly July.

He stood staring out at the bay awhile watching surfers in wet suits trying to catch a wave. Something farther out caught his eye as a lone sloop hoisted its sail again in the center of the bay. Kristoffer sighed wistfully. He'd spent some good times on the water with Jeremy, his high-school buddy who owned a sailboat, and learned a lot about sailing and life on the open sea. Not always in the Atlantic. Most of the time, they sailed either the Fisher's Island Sound or the Long Island Sound.

He closed his eyes, and his body swayed as if he could feel the hull and keel beneath him tacking into an upwind. Jeremy described the wind as being at twelve o'clock. If one tried to sail into it, they stalled. But by tacking—shifting the sails a little this way and a little that on either side of the direct wind current—they could move forward again. The closer he hauled between the eleven and one o'clock positions, the faster he could go.

Kristoffer opened his eyes. He'd come out here to walk and think. A power walk might help burn off some pent-up frustrations. He wanted to give Pamela and Maribeth enough time to talk and maybe even sort out the distance between them. Time on earth was too short to develop or sustain resentments between loved ones.

Glancing south then north, he opted to head north toward the Monterey Peninsula and Pebble Beach—not that he'd walk that far, of course.

He prepared himself to sail into the unknown with Pamela, having no clue where they'd wind up or even what their destination might be. One day, Tori's body would pass, but he wouldn't continue to put his life on hold. She might hang on like this for years. Rick had told him about one woman at the facility who'd been in a persistent vegetative state for more than twenty years. Tori would be the first to kick him in the ass and tell him to get on with his life.

Yet divorcing her wasn't something he was able to do either, even though he didn't see himself so much as her husband as her legal guardian and caregiver now. Looking back, he could pinpoint where he'd first known all hope was lost. He was preparing to move into his condo and out of the house they'd shared that had become too painful to live in. He'd asked Liz to take Tori's jewelry, clothing, and knick-knacks and do with them whatever she wanted.

He wouldn't have done that if he'd thought Tori would be coming back to him. He kept her wedding ring, which had been cut off her finger at the hospital due to swelling in her hands after the wreck, as well as the photo albums depicting their life together. But he hadn't opened those since he'd scanned the photos while putting together a slideshow of Tori's life for her eventual memorial service. Going over their life in photos had helped him to look back over their lives, but he'd been stuck in those memories ever since.

If Tori had died outright in the wreck or soon after, she would have expected him to mourn for a period of time, but eventually seek love again. After the accident, he'd wailed, he'd grieved, but, dammit, he hadn't died. Why, then, had he chosen to bury himself alive? He could live another forty or fifty years, but not if stress and misery sent him to an early grave.

The foamy surf washed over his bare feet as he walked. He thought about how much he'd enjoyed his time with Pamela. But how long would she be satisfied to be a traveling companion and friend? Yes, they had the occasional Top/bottom scene, too. Funny how setting out to become her trainer and to teach Pamela how to stay grounded in the moment had actually shown him how little he'd done of that himself for years.

If he truly wanted a future with her, he needed to figure out a way to make her the center of his universe every single day.

He'd already screwed up once by bringing Pamela along on this trip and telling himself he could be content with her companionship, but perhaps his subconscious had already begun steering him in a new direction. Only he hadn't been the one with his hand on the tiller; it had been Pamela, especially in the restaurant that first night. She'd firmly, but gently, guided him down a new path.

What did the future hold for them? He hadn't bothered to think beyond today in a positive way in...forever. He had a choice to make.

He couldn't think about the days ahead anymore without picturing Pamela at his side. But would she be content with living together in a lifelong committed relationship without marriage? What if she wanted children someday? She'd apparently never been in a relationship where the idea had been discussed seriously. Would being with him keep her from living life to the fullest?

When he reached the end of the public beach area, Kristoffer faced the bay again and watched the sloop spin in circles. Must be novice sailors on board.

Kristoffer had been caught *in irons*, too, as Jeremy called it. Spinning and going nowhere.

The time had come for him to re-chart his life.

He turned south and realized how far he'd walked. All he knew in this moment was that there was a beautiful, caring, dynamic woman waiting in that house down the beach who saw something in him worthwhile enough that she'd ventured to California with him. He sure as hell had an interest in pursuing something more with her.

He and Pamela had the next few days to explore where this relationship might go, but only if he could let go of the past and allow her into his heart. Why waste one more minute out here alone? He'd been alone long enough.

He began running down the beach toward the ginger-haired sprite who had shone her light into his dark, lonely world. He searched for the caterers and soon spotted the tables. As he drew closer, he saw two of them tying pink and yellow balloons to the chairs for the kids who would soon arrive for their party.

Life had given him a new reason to celebrate as well. Normally, before making any major changes in his life, he'd spend hours if not days carefully analyzing, assessing risks, and planning. But from now on, he intended to take a new tack. Life had given him a precious second chance at love with Pamela.

As he left the wet sand and made his way to the staircase and his shoes, one of the pink balloons escaped the hands of the caterer. As he walked, he watched it float on the wind toward him. As it drifted over him, he paused and turned to watch it dancing on its merry way out to sea, never even to be missed by the kids at the party.

Time, too, was a precious commodity that could be ripped away in the blink of an eye. For however long he and Pamela chose to be together, he wanted to share every moment with her, both here in California and back home.

Kristoffer wanted to be like that balloon, reveling in being free of its moorings and floating free. He'd wasted too many opportunities with Pamela as it was.

Not anymore.

Chapter Eighteen

No sooner had Pamela retrieved the information for her mom than the front door closed with a bang. The dogs barked enthusiastic greetings. Kristoffer must not be aware that the dogs would more than alert her of his return. But she appreciated he didn't want to walk in on her and her mom unexpectedly, knowing Pamela had planned to have a serious talk this morning.

"Good morning, ladies." Kristoffer stepped onto the patio, Arlo enjoying a prolonged top-of-the-head rub at his side. She'd never envied a dog so much in her life.

Pamela smiled at him, but his initial happy expression was soon replaced by one of concern. Not wanting to explain why she must look as though she'd been crying, she kept the moment light. "Enjoy your walk?"

"Immensely." He seemed more relaxed.

Had he come to terms with something out there? Would he share it with her? "I'd better get back to work in the kitchen if we're going to make a dent in all this food before we leave."

He fell into step behind her, as she'd expected, but when she would have turned toward the counter in the galley kitchen, he took her arm and gently led her to the living room. Arlo took his spot on the couch, yawned, and returned to his morning nap.

Kristoffer turned her to face him, cupped her chin, and tilted her head back to meet his gaze. "You okay, Sprite?"

"I'm fine. I'm glad you had a good walk." She wanted to ask the question on the tip of her tongue—*Did you figure out anything about us out there?*—but wouldn't. He'd tell her when he was ready.

"You've been crying. How'd it go with your mom?" He stroked her cheekbones as though erasing her tear tracks.

She smiled, hoping to reassure him. "I don't have any more answers now than I did before—although apparently Mom wasn't a kick-ass spy as I'd fantasized in my teen years." She grinned with a shrug, hoping to convey she wasn't upset about having no further answers. "But for the first time in my life, I am one hundred percent certain that it wasn't anything *I* did or didn't do that sent her running. Dad almost had me convinced of that, but there was always a niggling doubt."

"That's progress, at least. I know how much you've questioned yourself all this time."

"How about you? Find any peace of mind during your walk?" She hadn't meant to pry, but preferred to have the spotlight off her neuroses.

"Very much so. Beautiful beach. And I did manage to make one decision."

"Oh, yeah? What's that, if I may ask?"

"You'll find out tonight." His answer left her frustrated and in high anticipation of whatever he planned to tell her—or better yet do to her.

She wrapped her arms around him and hugged. Kristoffer and Mom were two hurting people in her life that she couldn't fix with a scalpel. If only she could place a few sutures and make everything better for them. But perhaps all three of them had made some kind of peace with the past today. Pamela had, for sure.

"I'm famished and will settle right now for food for the stomach." He pulled away and framed her face. "I promise not to get maudlin on you again. I intend to enjoy the time I have left with you out here."

She searched his eyes for whether that meant they would only have this time together, but no need to conjure up things he hadn't said or meant. "I've never found you maudlin, so stop beating yourself up. There are going to be setbacks along the way. You've embarked on a new life, and that's not easy for anyone to do."

"Thanks, Sprite. You're too good for me. How can I ever repay you?"

Accept me. Love me as much as I love you.

She smiled, not ready to admit she was falling in love with him, not even to herself. There were still so many obstacles in their path. "Help me in the kitchen."

"You know I have no cooking skills, so don't give me anything too important to screw up," he said, laughing as he followed her.

In the kitchen, she pointed to the stove. "I'll fix the scrambled eggs. You can fry up the rest of the bacon. I'd rather you get splattered than me." She stuck her tongue out at him.

Kristoffer peeked out on the patio, apparently to make sure Mom wasn't close by, then leaned down and whispered, "I didn't hear you complaining when I was splattering you with hot wax."

Her pulse quickened, and she caught her breath as the sensory memory of their wax play returned. "You, Sir, are a sadist to bring that up when there's nothing we can do about it here." Would they play again tonight? Is that what he'd decided out on the beach? She hoped so.

Twenty minutes later, the three sat down to breakfast on the patio. No one seemed to want to talk about anything too deep. *Thank you, baby Jesus!* She and her mom had come further in those fifteen minutes earlier this morning than they had in fifteen years. There was hope. And, if they were lucky, time to reveal all the secrets.

As for Kristoffer, he'd need time, too. She intended to enjoy the rest of their trip and keep things light, unless *he* needed to talk.

After putting the bedroom and bathroom back the way they'd found them, with clean towels and linens and making the bed, they hugged her mother goodbye with a promise to visit more often. This time, she might even follow through.

Moments later, she and Kristoffer drove out of Carmel-by-the-Sea, passed Mission Carmel, and headed south on the Cabrillo Highway. Kristoffer pulled off a couple of times at her request so she could take photos. The wind nearly whipped the phone out of her hands once—good thing she'd left the good camera in the car—but they managed a few selfies to prove they'd been here.

"I booked us into a hotel for tonight and tomorrow," Kristoffer revealed. He went on to say he'd even scored premium seating for dinner overlooking the sea at sunset. While it must have set him back, as always, he refused to let her pay for anything. Perhaps when she was working for Children's or whatever hospital would hire her, he would be more willing to let her pay for something.

Despite having so much up in the air, she experienced a sense of freedom and optimism that everything would turn out fine when they went home.

Arriving at Big Sur too early to check in, they decided to hike Julia Pfeiffer Burns State Park for a couple of hours. When they reached the overlook above McWay Falls, Kristoffer wrapped his arms around her from behind and held her against him as they watched the slim waterfall cascade onto the beach. He'd become much more demonstrative in the past few days. She loved it when he touched her, hugged her, held her out of the blue like this.

"Beautiful," he whispered in her ear.

"Yes, it is."

"The falls, too, but I'm talking about you."

Her heart beat so rapidly she found it impossible to speak. But no words were necessary. They were finding their way. He continued to lower his defenses, as if the stars and planets aligned to clear a path for them now that they'd told the universe their intentions to continue on this journey together—not just to California, but into the future.

She could have stayed here in his arms forever, but all too soon, he pulled away with a kiss to the top of her head. "Why don't we head back to the car? We ought to be able to register now. That'll give us time to shower and maybe even take a swim in the infinity pool before dinner."

Pamela nodded, even though she had no clue what an infinity pool was, and they walked the trail hand-in-hand back to the parking lot. The rich lived a very different lifestyle than she'd been accustomed to. But it sounded divine. As long as he didn't intend to make her swim laps for infinity. With this morning's breakfast, she'd sink like a rock.

They checked into the opulent hotel and located their private cabin overlooking the rock cliffs and ocean. All too soon, she found herself in the most amazing pool where the edge of the water met the sea and sky as if the three were one.

"It's magical," she said. "I feel as though we're at the top of the world overlooking our own piece of paradise."

Kristoffer stood behind her in the water, massaging her shoulders and neck, as she propped her arms on the edge and took in the panoramic view. His hands went underwater to grasp her sides, tugging her away from the edge and against him. The cool air chilled her rapidly, and her feet dangled in the water. She tried to tilt her head to the side to encourage him to kiss her only to have his teeth capture her earlobe instead. *Even better.* The direct hit on her erogenous zone made her clit throb for attention.

"Mmm."

He pulled away. "Like that?"

"You know I do, Sir."

"Would my sprite like to play after dinner?"

"Definitely."

"I'd like you to scream for me when you come."

She would get to come tonight! Her lower body tingled in anticipation. The thought of their neighbors hearing them occurred to her, but she didn't care. She'd never see any of them ever again.

"Do we have to wait until after dinner, Sir?"

He pinched her butt cheek. "Who's in charge, Sprite?"

Not wanting to jeopardize her imminent orgasm, she bowed her head. "You, my Lord."

He placed a finger under her chin and forced her to make eye contact. "I won't neglect my submissive's needs, and you haven't eaten since morning."

His taking care of her made her feel good, but how could he ever neglect or disappoint her?

"Thank you, Sir."

He released her sooner than she'd have liked, leaving her resting her forearms on the edge again. Despite the heated pool exceeding one hundred degrees, he left her body chilled after he'd ignited a fire in her only a moment ago.

"Time for your massage."

The thought of him giving her a massage further excited her, but she soon found out he'd made an appointment for her at the spa. "Afterward, we'll prepare for dinner. I understand we're in for a treat— not only a gorgeous sunset, but a taste of Big Sur with some incredible wine pairings."

"Sounds wonderful. I feel like a princess." She smiled. Being spoiled by Kristoffer would never grow old.

The dress code was casual elegant according to the binder in the room. Thank goodness she'd packed a nice pair of slacks and a silk blouse for their trip down the coast.

In the bathroom, she quickly applied her make up with a light touch and put up her hair in a quick twist. When she came out, Kristoffer whistled as his gaze roamed her body from head to heels.

"Turn around." The familiar fluttering in her womb as he commanded her to obey made her smile. When she presented her back to him, he placed a cold stone pendant around her neck.

She turned toward the mirror to see what it looked like. "It's gorgeous!" The circular jade stone was strung on a thin piece of leather.

He came up behind her, wrapped his arms around her, and presented her with a small jewelry box as well. She opened it. "Matching earrings!" The stones in the studs were about a quarter-inch around. "You shouldn't have gone to such an expense."

"I wanted to give you something to remember our time here by."

She shook her head. As if their time together here wouldn't be etched on her mind forever.

He smiled. "It's called Big Sur jade and comes right out of the ocean waters here. I thought the set might be a nice souvenir."

"When did you have time to go shopping?"

"While you were having your massage this afternoon."

Ah. "Thank you for that, too, by the way. It was incredibly relaxing. I just might have fallen asleep." She switched out her earrings for the new studs and turned to show them off.

His pupils dilated. "Now that's what *I* call gorgeous. They bring out the green in your eyes."

He bent to place a kiss on her cheek and loosened her hair, emitting a low growl that sizzled her nerve endings. Wrapping his arm around her, he tilted her head back by grasping her hair. Any thought of maintaining an elegant look went out the window, but she didn't care. She felt his breath on her face a second before he lowered his lips to hers, demanding more.

Clasping him around the neck, she held on tight and reveled in his kiss. When he pulled away, she groaned in frustration. His inability to catch a deep breath told her he'd been affected as well. He grinned impishly as he reached up to remove the remaining pins that had held her updo in place.

"I prefer it loose." He ran his fingers through it, tousling it. "Yes. Much better. I love the way your hair looks when you first tumble out of bed."

That might be a little too casual for the restaurant, but if that's what he wanted... "As you wish, Sir."

He placed a trail of kisses along the column of her neck, sending shivers coursing down her body. As abruptly as his sensual assault had begun, it ended. "Ready for dinner?"

"I think I'm more ready for us to go to bed." He smacked her butt. "Promises like that aren't helping to change anything," she teased.

"I don't think I'll ever forget how much you love to be spanked."

She grinned, completely reluctant to leave the room now. "Trust me, Sir, my butt is available anytime you have a need." She winked.

He lightly bopped her nose. "Keep that up, brat, and I'll have you waking up the sleepy hamlet of Big Sur begging me to let you come—and not allowing you to do so."

"You wouldn't." As he'd pointed out, she did have a bratty personality. Might as well own it.

"Don't test me, Sprite." His Dom stare unleashed butterflies in her belly.

"I don't think I shall, Sir."

"Good girl. Perhaps if you promise not to bring security to the room with your screams, you might receive what your inner brat deserves—and is begging for."

His words left her cheeks overheated. They hadn't had a scene since Sunday night.

She enjoyed this playful, spontaneous Kristoffer and hoped he wouldn't retreat on her again.

At the moment, however, they had hard-to-obtain dinner reservations to keep.

"Are you sure I shouldn't run a brush through my hair so I won't have everyone speculating as to how we've spent our afternoon?"

He shook his head, an even more primal stare capturing her in a web of desire. "I want every man in that restaurant to know you're with me and that they can't have you."

He'd marked his territory both with his gaze and her sexy hair. She reached for her emerald green devoré shawl, only now realizing how appropriate it was that she'd packed it. The color was perfect for the jade necklace and earrings.

Feeling anything but cold at the moment, she handed him her wrap. Smiling, he placed it around her shoulders, his warm hands giving them a squeeze.

Hardly ten minutes passed before they were in the restaurant and seated near a window overlooking the sea outside the resort's gourmet restaurant. A symphony of new and enticing aromas permeated her senses. She immersed herself in the experience of trying course after course from an apple-watercress salad to an entree of flounder.

An hour and a half later, as they awaited the dessert, she and Kristoffer reminisced about their trip so far. When the chocolate ganache cake was served, all other thoughts left her mind. She smiled as he fed her a bite of the mouthwatering delight. There would be a fourth course as well, but she couldn't imagine stuffing another bite into her mouth. That is, until the server brought them the Charlie Cashio Bixby Bloom. The small dish of brie on acorn bread provided the perfect ending to one of the most memorable meals she'd eaten in her thirty-eight years. She'd have to see if her local baker would try baking this incredible-tasting bread.

"I can almost see the wheels turning and imagine I'm in for a treat from your kitchen when we get home."

She laughed. "I'm sure I won't come close to recreating these dishes, but the chef has given me some wonderful ideas!"

"I can't wait."

But she could. She didn't want the magic of this getaway to wrap up. When they returned to Denver, this all might come crashing down around them and put an end to this fantasy.

"What's wrong?"

She forced a smile. "Nothing."

"Sprite." His stern tone reminded her she wasn't supposed to keep anything from her Dom.

"I'm sorry. I was just thinking how much I wish we could stay here forever."

"What have I tried to teach you about living in the moment?"

"I know. I should. I'll stop worrying about the future if you will."

He brushed his thumb over her cheek, and she closed her eyes as she melted against his hand. "I know it's scary not knowing what awaits us, Pamela, but I've made a promise to you to be your Dom. I don't renege on my promises."

Pamela nodded, smiling. "Yes, Sir."

He leaned toward her and whispered so that only she could hear. "Good, because I do believe I promised my sub a paddling for her bratty behavior."

She grew wet hearing his words, and her breath hitched. "Ready when you are, my Lord."

Kristoffer watched fiery streaks of light dance through her hair in the candlelight. Freckles he'd barely noticed back in Colorado had become more pronounced after this week's exposure to the sun; they fit her personality. While Pamela presented the image of a competent, revered surgeon to the world, with him, she let her playful spirit shine.

Not to mention her laugh, which never failed to make him smile and lift his mood.

He'd have to make sure she spent more time outdoors. The image of her restrained to a tree while he played with her flashed across his mind. Tori hadn't been into playing outdoors. More new territory for them to cover. Finding new memories without ghosts lurking in the corners would be his objective moving forward.

He'd planned a scene for tonight that, with a few adjustments, could let them begin to explore a bit outdoors.

Pamela's eyes radiated happiness. He wanted to keep that spark there always. His time spent on the beach this morning hadn't given him any answers concerning Tori, but he'd come to realize that being away from Pamela even for that short time felt as though a piece of him was missing. She'd taken up residence in his heart, and he was more determined than ever to find a way to make her a permanent part of his life. Commitment. He wouldn't dishonor his vows to Tori, but his heart could love both women. Rather than feeling split in two, he actually felt his heart and soul mending for the first time since he'd lost Tori.

Damned if he would feel guilty, either. He'd been a good husband to Tori. Never cheated on her. Stayed by her side every single day of their marriage, well, until these past few days in California. Bottom line, he still loved Tori, and their marriage would last until she breathed her last.

For all intents and purposes, her life had ended on that highway four years ago. But *he* wasn't close to dead yet and refused to continue to live like he was.

No more incessant worrying about right or wrong. His moral compass wasn't broken, but his world had tilted on its axis four years ago. He was finally finding his bearings based on a new magnetic north— and the needle pointed directly to the woman sitting across the table from him.

"You're thinking awfully hard. Should I be worried about tonight?" she asked.

He smiled. "I like keeping you off guard, but I was simply thinking what an amazing person you are and how grateful I am to have you in my life."

Her eyes opened wider in surprise before she laughed with embarrassment. The blush he loved crept into her cheeks. "And here I thought you were planning all manner of delicious torture for me when we get back to the room."

His cock surged to life. "That, too. But I'm trying to be a little more serious now. Your cooperation would be appreciated, Sprite."

Feigning innocence, she asked, "What's not serious about a well-executed play scene?"

He stared at her until the smile left her face. "Better." Why was she deflecting the seriousness in the conversation? Maybe because he hadn't said anything to her about his revelation on the beach. Of course, she might not be ready for yet another cosmic shift in his thinking.

Hell, man, you might not be, either.

"Pamela, we have only two more full days here before heading back to Denver. I know we've spent a lot of time talking about what we want and need in a Dom/sub relationship. And that we agreed to wait and see how my reentry into real life goes before taking plans for our relationship any further."

She reached across the table for his hand. "We have all the time in the world. No need to rush into anything."

"But I realized something out on that beach today. My life is empty without you in it."

Her eyes opened wide, and she smiled. "I feel the same about you."

"I may be confronted by powerful emotions when we get home—in fact, I'm sure I will be. But I don't want to face them alone. Before we leave here, I want us to at least determine a plan to move toward laying the foundation for something that could last a lifetime—not only an emotional bond, but physical and intimate ones as well." He squeezed her hand.

"That was one productive walk!"

He glared at her, and she reined in her brat and became serious again. "Sorry, but I'm afraid to get my hopes up too high. It makes me nervous."

His whole reason for having this conversation was so that he could reassure her. He wasn't going to lose her because of his indecisiveness. Okay, perhaps his insecurities were getting the best of him now, but someone as beautiful, desirable, and independent as Pamela wouldn't put up with that shit forever. He needed her to know how important she was to him and that he was willing to make a commitment to her, as soon as he figured out what type of one would be worthy of her. "I never want you feeling as though I'm taking your needs for granted."

"I never ha—" He cut off her words with his fingers pressed to her lips.

"I know, but please hear me out. Pamela, I don't know what the future holds, but I do know that I want you to be a part of mine. I'm going to find a way to make this work—whatever *this* is." He stared intently at her. "I'd never do anything to harm you or take advantage of your trust in me."

Her half-smile told him she was cautiously optimistic. "I wouldn't expect you to. You've shown you're a man of your word."

"The *only* thing I'm certain about anymore is that I want something more with you, starting tonight." Had someone turned the heat up in here? He loosened the top button of his shirt under his tie. "Pamela, you've become an indispensable part of my life in the past two months. I can't offer you all that you deserve. And we both know marriage isn't an option, but dating is. Perhaps what we're working toward is a relationship that's *like* a marriage, just without government or church documents binding us together." Once again, he'd relegated a discussion about their future together into negotiating the terms of a business acquisition.

Smooth, man. Bloody smooth.

Before he could rephrase his poorly chosen words, she spoke. "I've told you before that I don't view a marriage certificate as the be-all and end-all of long-term relationships and happy endings. Half end with one or both parties breaking their vows. No guarantees exist in life.

Besides, I'm not any more religious than you are, so I have no ethical or moral need to be wed in a church."

She leaned closer and whispered, "But like you, if I commit myself to someone for life, it *will* mean for life. So if you're wondering if I'm open to an unconventional relationship with you, I think I've already proven that I am."

As if a two-ton anchor had been lifted off his chest, he relaxed and smiled. "Just what I needed to hear before I..." He started to say *propose*, but ended with, "...take this to the next step." He reached for the check. After charging it to their room, he stood and placed her shawl over her shoulders again before taking her hand and leading her from the table.

His hand wrapped around her back then lowered to rest on the swell of her ass—as though marking his territory for every man in the restaurant to see.

Mine.

She didn't envy him the job of finding a way to make it so.

✧   ✧   ✧

Pamela wasn't sure what metamorphosis had occurred over dinner or why, but she sensed Kristoffer coming to some sort of peace and contentment about moving forward with their relationship. For the first time since realizing she was falling for him in a big way, she had hope that they would be able to carve out a life for themselves.

But tonight, he had planned a scene for them so she prepared herself mentally.

Roar closed the door. "Go into the bathroom and remove your clothing. Shower if you wish. I'm going to do a little setup, so please wait there until I come for you."

She grinned as she removed her jewelry and shawl, placing them on the dresser. Slipping out of her shoes, she made her way into the bathroom.

Anticipation ran high. He'd hinted at something different tonight, not to mention that she'd been dying for another scene since leaving

Sonoma. Wanting to be as fresh as possible, and hoping it would relax her a little, she hopped into the shower but used a plastic cap to keep her hair dry. No sense spending a lot of time with a dryer. She wanted to be ready when he opened that door.

Brushing out her slightly tangled hair, she then knelt on the bath mat in front of the vanity. Because he hadn't specified how he wanted her waiting, she decided to present herself in a modified kneeling position, keeping her gaze and head cast downward in submission. Instead of placing her arms and hands in a box hold behind her, she rested them palms down on her bare thighs. She straightened her back, rested her butt on her heels, and bowed her head.

I am yours, Roar.

A number of minutes passed with no sign of him. She could hear no sounds beyond the door, either.

Don't clutter up your mind with worry. Focus on your breathing. In…out. Prepare yourself for…

The door opened without a knock or warning. She kept her gaze on the tiles in front of her.

"Beautiful submission. Thank you, Sprite."

Her heart soared with pleasure at his compliment. Roar came toward her and placed his hand under her chin, tilting her head back until she stared up at him. He wore the same slacks, dress shirt, and tie. *Sexy.*

Mine.

Tall. Silent. Commanding. The power he exuded melted her to the core.

"Give me your left hand." She lifted and placed it in his outstretched one as he helped her to her feet. Standing naked before him, a sense of vulnerability overcame her, but he'd seen her naked before and seemed to like what he saw.

He stroked her cheek, his hand warm and unwavering. She knew where she stood with him, what was expected of her.

"Trust me?"

"Yes, Sir."

"My intention is for us to go further tonight in your mind-centering exercises, among other activities. Any parts of your body I should be aware of as being off limits?"

"No. I am yours completely."

"Any restrictions you have concerning my body?"

Was he going to permit her to touch him, pleasure him this time? "None other than my hard limits, Sir."

He stepped back, released her hand, and took a chunk of her hair, pulling her head back. She didn't fight against him. This was what she'd trained for. She wanted to please him with her entire being.

He bent to claim her lips, teasing her into responding to him with tiny nibbles and sucking on her lips. She didn't open her mouth right away. He seemed content to tease a moment then, suddenly, he invaded her mouth. When his tongue pushed between her lips, claiming her at the same moment his hand reached up to pinch her nipple for the first time, her knees buckled. Thankfully, he held her upright with his left arm around her back, or she'd have collapsed on the floor.

His tongue retreated and advanced repeatedly as his thumb and finger tormented her tender peak. Was he preparing her for...

Don't think about anything but this moment. This kiss.

He tugged her hair harder, opening her mouth to a deeper plundering. She tangoed playfully with his tongue, simulating her licking the sides of his penis. He groaned and gently pushed her away.

His breathing was rapid and shallow, eyes dilated. "Come with me before it gets too dark for this to be fun."

Puzzled by his words, she took his hand, and he led her out to the balcony. The sun had set forty-five minutes ago, and while private and removed from other cabins, she had no idea if anyone was on the beach below or the rocks nearby. The cool evening breeze made her nipples bunch in anticipation.

"I want your hands on the top of the railing, like so." He positioned her hands in front of her, shoulder height. Tapping her shins with his shoe, he guided her feet away from the railing until she stood bent over at the waist at a forty-five degree angle.

"See that group of trees over there?" Tilting her head back, she saw he pointed down the hillside a hundred yards away. She nodded. "Keep your focus on it until I tell you otherwise."

She'd noticed someone hiking there earlier in the day. Her naked body would be visible in the balcony lights if someone was out there, but it was too dark for her to make out any shadows moving. *Wait.* Had she just seen something move in the trees? Her face grew warm at the thought of being seen in this compromising position.

Her breasts dangled underneath her as Roar positioned himself behind her, pressing his erection against her butt as he leaned over her back. He reached around her ribs to cup her breasts. "I can see I'm going to enjoy the hell out of these." *Apparently so.*

She grinned but didn't respond. His lips nuzzled her neck, and she moaned then wondered if she was in sound restriction. He hadn't said anything about it, but she'd try not to be too vocal until certain she was in the clear.

When he released her breasts, she ached for more. "Maintain that position. I'll be right back."

Again, she began to worry whether anyone was watching her, but only found herself getting wet at the thought. Who knew she had an exhibitionist streak in her? Well, she had agreed to stand naked in front of her classmates at The Denver Academy.

Focus on now. Inhale…exhale.

She brought her wandering thoughts under control as she waited and stared at the evergreen trees.

Roar returned and stood on her right side. "I've been fantasizing about placing clamps on your nipples since I saw you standing in that anatomy class."

That he'd fantasized about her during that brief incident surprised her. That he loved nipple clamps didn't. No, it thrilled her.

He pinched her nipple to make it swell before placing the first tweezer clamp on her right nipple and sliding the rubber ring up the metal to tighten it. She sucked in her breath. While tight at first, given how little she'd played in recent years, the pain quickly dissipated to leave only a dull pressure.

"How does that feel?"

"Delicious. Enough pressure to know they're there, but not painful."

"I'll see what I can do to add to your enjoyment." He slid the ring closer to the clamp's tips, and they mashed the base of her nipple until she suddenly rose on tiptoes trying to escape. "Better?"

She nodded, unsure of her voice.

"You will answer direct questions aloud, please."

"Yes, Sir." Her voice came out in a squeaky whisper. "Much tighter now."

He chuckled. "I see we're going to enjoy finding just the right clamps to command adequate respect from you in the future."

She'd heard of a number of clamps that had more bite than tweezer ones did and decided it might be a good idea to work on conditioning her nipples for that eventuality.

With most nipple clamps, the discomfort in the beginning was fleeting as the blood flow was cut off and the nipples became numb. The real pain would come later, when he removed them. After he attached the other clamp and adjusted the tension until she hissed in pain again, she realized there was a chain between them. No sooner did the thought register than he tugged on it, enough to make her breasts bob and nipples start to ache again.

He stood behind her again, wrapping his arms around her and cupping her breasts as though assessing their weight. His thumb and finger pinched her areolas and pulled them away from her body making her push out her chest to try and relieve the pain.

When he released them, he stepped away, taking his body's heat with him. The cool night air raised goose bumps on her back and arms.

"Nice. We'll let those work their magic for a while. The real fun will come later."

The swish of a flogger made her grip the railing harder, anticipating the first falls hitting her backside, but he didn't begin there. Instead, they slapped against her outer thigh. As the skin grew warmer, he switched sides and applied the tips of the flogger to her other thigh.

Hardly missing a beat, the falls of another flogger—probably a leather one—came down hard across her butt cheeks without warming her up whatsoever. "Ow!" The sting surprised her more than anything. The first flogger had been thuddy, but this new one actually hurt. She took a deep breath to center herself again and prepare for...

Slap! Slap! Slap!

She hissed, but didn't utter a sound otherwise. The tails of the leather one landed on her butt and the softer one, her upper thighs. Just when she thought she'd begun to predict a rhythm, he reversed them and the stings now fell on to her thighs. Holding on to the rail, she tried to maintain her focus on the trees, but it was now too dark to see them.

"Let me hear how much you're enjoying this, Sprite."

He wanted her to make noise? Would anyone in a nearby room hear the sound? Would they be aware of what was going on next door?

"Yes, Roar, Sir." The next blows were high on the backs of her thighs, stinging more than the others. "Mmm." She loved the sting of the flogger and once again became used to the rhythm, moaning in pleasure.

Suddenly, the tails became silent and a new implement cracked across her butt. "Christ!" Unrelenting, he paddled her with whatever it was until tears streamed down her face. "Oh, God! My butt's on fire." The paddling stopped.

"What color are you?"

The sting burned even more now that he'd stopped. But she wasn't ready to stop, even though she welcomed this break. "Green."

"What number is your pain level?"

"Five to six."

"Sounds like you are far from your limit, but why don't we cool off that ass of yours a little before we continue? Let go of the railing."

She'd held on for so long, her joints refused to budge. He chuckled and helped pry her fingers free. Standing upright took an effort, too. Surely she wasn't getting past her prime to enjoy a little kink. Wouldn't that be the ultimate torture—she finally found the right Dom only to have arthritis...

"Come with me." He guided her toward the sliding-glass door, but before he walked into the hotel room, he stopped, blocking the way. "Turn around and press against the glass from shoulder blades to ass." She cocked her head, but after she followed his instruction, the cool glass became the perfect balm for her stinging butt.

"Clasp your hands over your head, arms straight."

The movement made her breasts rise as well, defying gravity for a moment. Glancing down at her tortured nipples, she found herself fearing the moment the clamps would be removed had arrived.

"Ready for me to remove these?" he asked, tugging on the chain between them to rekindle the sting in her nipples.

She clenched her fists. "I'm ready whenever you are, Sir." The sooner, the better, but conversely, she wasn't in any rush, either. And yet, with Roar, she was discovering she had a higher threshold for pain than she'd once thought.

He reached for the right one, which had been on the longest. While it had only been a few minutes, she braced herself given how angry red the tip appeared to be.

"Spread your legs wide for me." Confused by his words when her attention was held captive by the clamps, she hesitated. "Don't make me repeat myself, Sprite."

She spread them at the same instant he removed the first clamp. Focusing on moving her feet should have diverted feeling some of the pain, but… "Goddamn, that hurts!" His chuckle registered in some distant part of her brain, so she let loose a few more choice words she'd never uttered before in his presence.

Roar rubbed the offended nipple as it became swollen and much more sensitive, then he lowered his mouth to suck on it.

"Oh, yes!"

When his free hand touched the juncture of her thighs and rubbed her swollen clit, she nearly came. Apparently, he knew how close she was because he stopped touching her there and his finger slid between her folds. She hadn't realized how turned on she was until now. "So wet. I see you're enjoying yourself tonight."

"Immensely, Sir." Most likely, her wetness stemmed from the flogging and paddling a few minutes ago, but having him touching her so intimately for the first time obliterated semantics all to hell. "Please, Sir, may I come?"

"Not yet, Sprite. But soon." At least he wasn't going to make her wait too long for relief.

The weight of the dangling chain on the other clamp reminded her there was some unfinished business to be dealt with first. He removed his hand from her cleft, but instead of going directly to her nipple, he lifted his hand to his face and licked her juices off his finger, his gaze never leaving hers.

"Sweet. A taste of things to come."

She throbbed in need. Did that mean he planned to go down on her? How could he mean anything else?

Don't anticipate. Stay in this incredible moment!

"First, my girl needs some relief of another kind."

He reached for the other clamp and quickly removed it. *Oh, no!* Wait for it… Wait for it… The rush of pain was even worse with this one. "Christ! Oh, fuck, that hurts!" He took her aching nipple into his mouth and sucked—hard—until the pain began to recede.

Before she could fully recover, he scooped her into his arms and carried her inside the bedroom. After placing her on the bed, he closed the glass door then opened his suitcase and sorted through it.

He pulled out rope and wrist cuffs. So he had planned on playing when they left Sonoma. Everything seemed to be happening so fast and spontaneously she'd wondered, although those were the basics of any scene, and he might have merely brought them in case. How could he have known they'd wind up in Big Sur when they set out for her mother's house yesterday?

Having something other than her tender nipples to concentrate on helped, but she was letting her focus stray.

She grounded herself once more as he placed first one cuff then the other on her wrists. "I'm afraid the designers of this luxury hotel room haven't made it easy for me by providing bed posts." He glanced around, and his gaze landed on the high-back chair at the desk. Taking the rope with him, he retrieved it and placed the back against the side of the mattress. "Lie across the bed with your head near the chair."

She scooted sideways and took her place as instructed. "Move about three feet away from the chair." She adjusted herself toward the other end of the mattress. "Perfect. Now stretch your arms above you." He threaded the rope through the D-rings of the cuffs and tugged at them as he fastened her securely to the heavy oak piece of furniture.

Roar walked around the other side of the bed and stared down at her nude body. Her nipples peaked, still smarting from their earlier torture. No doubt in her mind, she was wetter than ever before. His enigmatic smile made her wonder what he was thinking—or planning.

"Bend your knees and open for me, Sprite."

She slid her feet up the mattress until her knees were tented and spread apart. His gaze went to her genitals warming the area the air-conditioned room had cooled. He'd seen the area before, but tonight was different. With her hands restrained, he wouldn't be asking her to pleasure herself—and he'd touched her earlier on the balcony promising more. The opening of her vagina spasmed.

"You're clenching in anticipation."

Was he going to reprimand her for anticipating? How could she *not*?

Instead, he grinned and knelt on the floor, leaning on his elbows on the bed to take a closer look. At the sight of him wearing his dress shirt, tie, and slacks, she almost came after having had this fantasy so many times before.

Don't stop now, Roar. Please don't leave me hanging like this!

He continued to stare at her. "Beautiful. So incredibly perfect."

She flushed at his praise—or perhaps it was because of his up-close-and-personal scrutiny.

His fingers spread open her lower lips, and he continued to stare. *Please, Roar! Make it so!*

She wouldn't beg out loud. For him to be this close was a huge step. Just when she thought he'd release her and instruct her to masturbate, his head leaned closer, closer, until she felt his breath on her clit hood. The tip of his tongue flicked against her clit. When her hips tilted upward to give him better access, he stopped and pulled back.

"I want you to concentrate on keeping your ass on the bed. Can you do that for me?"

She nodded then remembered he wanted her to speak her responses aloud. "Yes, Sir."

"Good girl." He wasted no time placing his tongue on her again, but this time avoided direct contact with her clit. His tongue laved the sides of the hood, teasing her to distraction, and then slid lower to press into her vagina. She performed Kegels on his tongue, causing him to chuckle and withdraw momentarily. But he entered her again, and it took every ounce of discipline to keep her butt on this mattress.

By preventing her from moving around, he was able to target where he wanted his tongue to touch her, making it that much more powerful.

All too soon, he pulled away, resting his head against her inner thigh. His breathing was rapid and shallow. Was he going to stop now? Was he remembering Tori?

While not surprising, given this was the first time he'd gone down on a woman since... Still, she didn't want him to be thinking of anyone else right now.

"Roar, Sir," she began, hoping to bring him back to her. He opened his eyes and looked at her, a crooked smile on his face. "Are you okay?" If she weren't in restraints, she'd have stroked his hair to comfort him. He nodded curtly. "You don't have to do this if—"

He cut off her words. "Don't top me, Pamela." His rebuke and reverting to her real name made her realize she'd been about to do just that. Instead, she needed to wait for him to compose himself and decide what *he* wanted to do.

"Don't move or make a sound—until you come. Understand?"

Oh, yes!

A weight lifted off her chest. "Yes, Sir!"

He smiled before lowering his head again, his thumbs spreading her open as his tongue continued to work her into a frenzy. He played around her clit without touching it directly until she was ready to scream in frustration. Then one long finger slid inside her.

Don't buck!

It was all she could do not to ride his finger, but her reward for staying still was another finger inside. He pumped them in and out, watching the motion a few times before he met her gaze.

"Come for me, Sprite."

His tongue flicked against her clit as his third finger joined the other two and pushed deep into her. Instead of pulling out, they curled around and stroked her G-spot. An involuntary spasm raised her pelvis toward him. He must have assumed she'd begun to come, but she really was close. However, he didn't slow down his tongue or fingers as the crescendo built.

"I'm going to come!"

His fingers alternated between pumping in and out and pressing against that sweet spot deep inside, while his tongue didn't let up on its assault. She began to buck up and down, simulating the sex act, as she rode to the crest.

"Oh, yes! Don't stop, Sir! Oh, my God!"

She soared over the summit and continued to revel in the incredible feeling as he slowed down his movements, but continued to touch her. When her clit became ultrasensitive, she wanted to beg him to stop, but groaned instead, hoping he'd understand how hypersensitive it was.

Her heart pounded as he pulled away, his fingers remaining inside her. Filling her. Making her want more.

Making her want what she couldn't have.

She panted, her chest heaving as she tried to take a deep breath. When she glanced down at him again, he smiled at her in triumph.

"That was absolutely incredible, Sir."

"For me as well." He withdrew his fingers and stood. Was this it? He didn't want something in return for what he'd given her? It wasn't her place to suggest that she knew what he needed or wanted, but clearly, judging by the tent in his pants, he needed relief, too.

He circled the bed again and began removing the restraints. She tried to hide her disappointment.

Give him time.

He'd taken a giant leap tonight. She wouldn't push him. Perhaps they'd snuggle now. Maybe he'd let her stroke him, even if he didn't want to come.

He moved the chair away and helped situate her into a sitting position facing him. He leaned closer and pressed his wet lips against hers, allowing her to taste herself on his lips. He grabbed her head with both hands and plunged his tongue inside her mouth. His kiss signaled anything but an end to this scene.

As she suspected, he took her arms and guided her to her feet.

"Undress me."

Don't think about how far he intends to take this tonight. Just follow one instruction at a time.

She tugged his now-loosened tie through the starched collar and tossed it on the bed. Next, she released the second button, because he'd already undone the first one at dinner. Unbuttoning his shirt from this side wasn't a challenge at all, and she smiled. When she'd undone the last one, she reached for his belt and drew the end through the loop before releasing the prong.

Slowly, she tugged on the buckle, taking one step and then two backwards until the backs of her knees hit the mattress. She met his gaze and released the belt from the pants loops, tossing it on the bed with the discarded tie as she closed the gap between them again. Starting with his left arm, she removed the cuff link and moved to the right one to do the same. Taking more care with these, she walked over to the dresser and laid them beside her jade jewelry.

Pamela smiled as she returned to where he stood and hooked a thumb inside each of the flaps of his shirt, unhurriedly sliding it over his shoulders and down his arms, taking in the view of his bare chest. No undershirt. Perfection. She loved his chest, especially his pectorals.

She longed to lean forward and take one of his nips into her mouth, but hadn't been instructed to do anything but undress him yet. No topping from the bottom. This was his scene to control.

She was his to control, as well.

Removing the shirt, she folded and laid it on the bed before turning her attention to his pants once more. No sooner had she placed her hands on the button than he halted her with, "Shoes and socks first."

Of course.

He crossed to the bed and sat down. "Kneel, eyes on my feet as you remove them," he ordered. She did so, unlacing first one shoe and then the other. Slipping each off in turn, she placed them neatly at the side of the bed. Then came the socks, which she tucked inside the shoes before awaiting his next command.

But it didn't come. He sat silently. She was tempted to look up and meet his gaze, but hadn't been given permission to do so. Something told her he needed his space right now, so she remained patient, sitting back on her heels and staring at his feet. Strong veins crisscrossed the dorsal surface of his feet.

This isn't another anatomy class, Pamela.

He stroked her cheek, his thumb brushing over her lips. When he pressed his thumb between her lips, she accepted it inside her mouth. Should she suck on it? Simulate going down on him? Was this a test to see whether she'd please him at the risk of being accused of topping? Should she wait for him to tell her exactly what he wanted her to do?

She would wait.

His thumb retreated until it almost left her mouth before he pushed it back inside. Slowly, he pressed deeper inside. It had been a long time since she'd gone down on a man. Would she be able to please him if he asked her to do so tonight?

As Roar pulled his thumb completely out of her mouth, she gave him a parting kiss. He stood and faced her, his crotch at eye level. "Now, the pants." When she reached out to steady herself on the mattress in order to stand, he added, "Remain on your knees."

She needed to listen more carefully to his explicit instructions and not anticipate what she thought he wanted her to do.

Extending her hands, she undid the button on his waistband. His erection strained against the zipper, and she longed to stroke him, but would only do what he'd told her to do. She carefully lowered the zipper, in case he went commando, but soon revealed his boxers just as he had worn the other night.

Hooking her thumbs in the waistband this time, she slowly lowered his slacks. His cock sprang free of its confines, but still remained covered by his underwear. When he lifted one foot, she slipped the pant leg off and then did the same with the other. She smoothed and folded them neatly before placing them on the mattress with the rest of his clothes.

Turning toward him again, she waited, her gaze riveted by his erection. She licked her lips, hoping he would allow her to pleasure him tonight, but oral sex might not be something he was ready for, either.

Uncertain what to do, she waited. He hadn't asked her to remove the boxers yet, so she did nothing.

Roar cleared his throat. "Take out my cock."

Smiling, without hesitation she pulled his cock out of the slit in the boxers. The plum-colored head stood erect and enticing.

"Kiss my cock."

Needing no further encouragement, she leaned in.

Chapter Nineteen

K ristoffer's heart pounded as he watched her mouth move closer to his throbbing cock. Something had broken loose inside him when he'd brought her to orgasm. He hadn't planned to ask her to go down on him tonight, but it had been so bloody long. Now, he couldn't wait for her to finish him off. If he couldn't let himself be vulnerable to her in this way, he'd go home to Denver and sink back into the hole he'd been buried in for years. Tonight was one of letting go of the past and embracing the future.

Focus on the present.

To ground himself, he reached out and stroked her hair. But he wanted more.

"Worship my cock, Sprite."

As though straining on a tight leash until this moment, eager to be turned loose, she smiled up at him. "I'll give it all I've got, Roar, Sir."

She kissed his cock open-mouthed.

For the little imp to quote Scotty at a time like this was…so like her. He smiled. As always, she gave him just what he needed. His stress evaporated.

Wrapping her lips around the pulsating head, she first licked the underside. Maybe he hadn't slowed this down at all, because he nearly exploded in her mouth right then. To savor this incredible moment— he didn't want this to come to an end anytime soon—he went over Gunnar's stock portfolio in his mind. But her amazing mouth wasn't to be ignored. She took his cock deeper inside then pulled back repeatedly. A few times he hit the back of her throat, which only made him crave more, but he let her determine how deep she took him.

Needing to ground himself again—he said, "Look at me, Sprite." She stared up at him with those sexy green eyes, his cock held between her lips and the hint of a smile on her face. "You know what to do.

You know what I need. Show me."

Yes, definitely a smile. Her eyes twinkled as she maintained her gaze on him while taking him so deeply into her mouth that his head rammed the back of her throat. She gagged slightly, her shoulders heaving as she eased off him, before taking him even deeper.

"Feels so good, Sprite." He closed his eyes, and she began to piston faster. When he thought he might lose it, he placed his hand on the top of her head to slow her movement and set a new pace.

Breathing hard, after a few moments, he released her head. Her face moved closer to the base of his cock. This time when she gagged, she didn't back away, but closed her eyes and held it until she became accustomed to his length and girth inside her mouth.

"No rush. We have all night."

Empowered by his words, he supposed, she braced her hands on his hips and inched him into the canal. Only letting the first couple of inches of him to enter her throat, her muscles squeezed at his head as her tiny body convulsed with each inch in an instinctive attempt to push him out. Already fighting the urge to come, he knew he wouldn't last much longer, but he hadn't confirmed that swallowing his cum was something she'd want to do. Too late for negotiations, he held her head and pulled out, grabbing his cock in his hand and pumping.

"Play with my balls."

With the perfect amount of pressure—not too bold, not too meek—she cupped him in one hand while the other wrapped around the base of his cock and squeezed, matching the rhythm of his strokes, as though sheathing him in her tight vagina.

"I can't hold back, Sprite."

She smiled her encouragement, flicking her tongue to try and make contact with his throbbing cock. He'd warned her, but she hadn't halted her delicious ministrations. Her consent was what he'd been waiting for. He exploded, and his semen spilled onto her face and breasts. When her tongue ventured out to lap up some of it, even more erupted onto her. He pumped harder and gave her everything he had.

Realizing she still held onto his testicles, a little more tightly than was comfortable in their current state, he tried to brush her hand away, but she continued to stroke him a moment longer.

He reached into the pocket of his folded pants and pulled out his clean handkerchief to wipe her face. "That was better than anything I could have dreamed of." He helped her to her feet. "Now, why don't we go shower before sitting out on the balcony for some aftercare?"

She placed her hands on his shoulders, tugged him toward her, and kissed him. Holding the back of her head, he explored the mouth his cock now knew intimately. Drawing back with reluctance, he led her into the shower where he washed her face, hair, and body with slow, loving care.

Afterward, she took the bar of soap and washed his back, ass, and cock with equal care. He looked forward to playing with her in the shower again sometime, but his mind and body were blown—in more ways than one.

Drying her off, he promptly wrapped her in one of the luxurious resort bathrobes. If not, he'd never make it through aftercare without igniting another fire in one or both of them.

On the balcony, he sat and settled her onto his lap, her head naturally resting on his shoulder. The sun had long since set and stars had begun to twinkle. So far from the city, he couldn't believe how many he could see.

He wondered if Tori were up there somewhere looking down. Was she okay with his moving on in this way? He hoped so, because he needed someone to take care of again. Someone who was aware of him. Someone who could give back.

His eyes burned as the roller coaster of emotions tried to overwhelm him.

"Thank you, Sir."

"No need to thank me." His hoarse whisper made her sit up and search his eyes. Fortunately, it was too dark for her to detect any stray tears. He cleared his throat.

Her hand cupped his face. "I think that was pretty intense for both of us. Making the choice to seek happiness and start living again has to have you feeling a lot of mixed emotions."

He nodded. Tonight was a perfect example of a Dom needing aftercare, too. She must have heard how shaky he was a few minutes ago. Sprite didn't miss much.

"Kristoffer…I hope it's okay to call you Kristoffer now."

"Sure."

"I'm never going to replace—" His fingers against her lips stopped her from saying her name.

"I know you aren't. And I assure you there were no ghosts present while we played tonight. I stayed grounded and in the moment—until after. I'm sorry, but—"

This time she pressed her fingers against his lips. "No regrets, no guilt, remember?" The light from the bedroom illuminated the beaming smile on her face. "I just hope someday you can find a way to make me a part of your life, because I would very much hate the thought of returning to Denver and losing what we've found out here."

"Me, too. Trying to compare the two of you would be like comparing apples to oranges. You're both women, but the similarities end there. You're very special to me, Sprite. I don't have the words to express what… I hope you realize that…"

How could he botch this so badly? He made business presentations all the time. Speaking with others was never a problem. Why couldn't he tell her that…

Just say it.

"I think I'm falling for you in a way I never expected to feel about any other woman, Pamela."

Once the words tumbled out, he felt as if he'd be sick. Tears glistened in her eyes. "That's good, because I've already fallen for you. Hard. Knowing I might stand a chance at finding my own place in your heart has me feeling hopeful. Seeing how far we've come this week has me thinking it's only a matter of time before we figure this out."

He placed his hand behind her head and pulled her toward him for a kiss. And then kissed her again. "I'm working on it. I think the only thing keeping me from an all-out declaration is not wanting to hurt you."

"Nonsense. You would never do that intentionally, and if I get my feelings hurt otherwise, we can talk it out."

"I hope so. Tell me, when did you think you were starting to fall in love?"

"I'm not sure when the exact moment was, because it's been building since—I guess since you agreed to train me, although I certainly was smitten before that. Definitely, something happened in the limo and again later that night at the house in Sonoma. But tonight, you sent me over the moon."

"You aren't mistaking an orgasm for love, now, are you?"

She grinned. "It wasn't *my* coming that clinched the deal for my heart." She kissed him again. "You put yourself in an extremely vulnerable position, and to surrender to me in that special way...well, I'm honored you trusted me that much."

She sighed before continuing. "Honestly, I have been falling for you for a long time. I tried to protect myself with a warning not to make the same mistakes again. I've been attracted to unavailable men before and was afraid it might be some kind of pattern with me. I think I mistrusted myself more than I did you. So I wanted to be cautious. And I knew you were just beginning to take steps toward healing and starting a new life. I didn't want to get my hopes up."

"Your encouragement, support, and the occasional guiding hand—like that first night in Sonoma when the host wanted to seat us at the table Tori and I used—helped me turn the page on my future sooner than I'd imagined possible. Certainly, nothing prepared me to welcome you into my heart this fast."

"You didn't want to let go. I understood that. I wasn't sure if you'd want me steering you in a new direction, but thought it was worth a try. I think Rick has helped you a lot, too. I owe him a box of chocolates for suggesting that you get away from it all and that you take me along."

"He didn't suggest I take you. That was all my idea."

She smiled. "Even better."

"Thanks to you, I can redeem myself when I go for my appointment next week. He wouldn't have been too happy to hear I'd come out here expecting to visit old haunts. Now I can tell him all the places—and things—I discovered here."

"Well, you could leave out *some* of the details." The light wasn't bright enough to see her blush, but he knew she did.

"I don't kiss and tell."

"Good. That's a load off." They sat in companionable silence, listening to the waves crashing on the rocks far below.

"Pamela, I've been fighting what I feel for you for so long; I'm not sure how ready I am for the next step or even what that step will be. I treasure that you understand what a huge leap this has been for me."

She brushed her thumb over his lips. "Kristoffer, I think if we hadn't started as colleagues, then friends, and moved on to the D/s explorations first, neither of us might have let down our guard enough to consider something more."

"Having you by my side during Tori's last hospitalization was a major turning point for me. I'm not saying I fell in love with you that night. But that you would drop everything to stay with me, neither of us knowing what the outcome would be, made a huge impact. I tried to stay away right after that, but I missed you so much. It was as if a light bulb had blown out in my life—again."

"I don't know how you've kept it together these past four years. I know you have Gunnar, but he's a busy man. You also have your pride, and I'm sure there were many times you didn't even let Gunnar know what was going on with Tori."

Kristoffer glanced up at the stars. "He was there when I needed him most. I don't want to burden anyone else with my worries."

She couldn't possibly see his face, but took his chin and guided it back toward her. "Well, from now on, you have me. If you need a shoulder—or someone on your lap like this to talk things over with—please call me. If I'm around, I'll be there. If not, I'll get to you as quickly as humanly possible."

His throat closed. He nodded, knowing her hand on his chin would feel the movement.

When he could speak again, he said, "No one could be more perfect for me. I have to pinch myself trying to figure out how on earth you came into my life."

"I guess the stars aligned in just the right order," she said.

Both glanced up just as a meteor shot across the sky and simultaneously shouted, "Did you see it?"

She grinned. "Yes! I think it's a sign!"

A sign. He'd never been one to pay attention to cosmic signs, but if that falling star signified the universe wanted to steer him toward a future with Pamela, he'd believe.

✧   ✧   ✧

Late Friday night, Kristoffer unlocked the door to his condo and wheeled his suitcases into the foyer, bone-weary from saying goodbye to Pamela, even if for only one night. However, they'd made plans for dinner tomorrow with her dad in Colorado Springs. After visiting Maribeth, Pamela had thought it only fair that she introduce Kristoffer to him and her stepmother as well. Family was important, and this was one more step in moving forward with their relationship.

And once all their family obligations were out of the way, they'd start laying the foundation for their future together.

"You're home!" Tori's mom came up and embraced him before taking a step back and searching his face. "I can see this trip was good for you. You look so relaxed."

The change was that visible? What of the other changes in him? He needed to let his in-laws know about the decisions he'd made, but worried that they might not be ready to hear he'd moved on.

"Have you eaten dinner yet?" Liz asked. "We have some leftovers I can heat up."

"No, thanks. Pamela and I stopped on the way to her place from the airport. I didn't think she'd have anything much to eat in her apartment after being gone a week."

"I wasn't expecting your flight to be on time. Ron's just taking a nap now."

"No, I'm awake!" Ron countered, rubbing the sleep from his eyes as he joined them. "Nice to see you home, son." He patted Kristoffer on the back before scrutinizing his face. "California agreed with you."

Kristoffer smiled at their similar assessments. "I suppose I was overdue for a vacation."

He couldn't let them leave tomorrow without telling them what had happened and what was going to take place next, but reentry was proving difficult. He needed some space.

Noma ambled into the foyer to join the party, took one look at him, and stuck her nose in the air as she pointedly ignored him and walked away again. "I guess not everyone is happy with me being home."

Liz laughed. "You know cats. They don't forgive easily when we desert them, even for a short while."

After such an eventful week, Kristoffer felt he'd been gone a year. When should he talk to his in-laws about his plans for the future? While they'd always given him lip service for their support of his moving on, were they actually prepared for him to do so?

"How's everything with Tori?" Kristoffer asked first.

"Fine," she said. "No problems at all. She's been very peaceful when we've visited. No new issues with her lungs."

Situation normal. "Glad to hear it."

"Why are we all standing here?" Liz asked, indicating the way to the living room. "Come in and sit down. You must be exhausted after the flight. It's such a hassle to fly anymore. I dread going to the airport tomorrow." They'd opted to fly this time rather than drive, neither of them able to take the long drive from St. Louis, especially with all the summer construction projects on I-70.

In the living room, they sat down, Liz and Ron on the sofa and Kristoffer in a wing chair facing them.

"Tell me all about your trip," she asked. "Where did you go?"

After recounting much about the sightseeing aspects of Sonoma, Carmel, and Big Sur, he was at a loss for words. The only ones left unsaid were the ones foremost in his mind and heart.

"Liz, Ron, there's something I need to tell you and I'm not sure how to start."

They glanced worriedly at one another and then back at Kristoffer. "What is it, son?" Ron asked.

Kristoffer swallowed, forcing himself to maintain eye contact when he wanted to look anywhere but at his wife's parents. "There was an unexpected consequence of this week. Not something I'd planned—far from it, actually."

Liz reached out for Ron's hand, and Kristoffer knew he shouldn't prolong it any further.

"I think I'm falling in love. I don't know how you feel about that."

Both of them sank into the sofa and something much like relief bordering on joy shone on their faces. "Kristoffer, you had us worried." His mother-in-law rose and walked around the coffee table with her arms outstretched. Needing her approval more than he'd realized, he stood to accept her embrace. "We're so happy for you, Kristoffer. We worried that you'd never be able to find happiness again, and that broke our hearts all over again."

"Liz, I need you to know I'll never stop loving Tori. I have no intention of abandoning her."

She pulled away and looked up at him. "I had no such concern. But Victoria wouldn't want to hold you to vows that don't take into consideration extenuating circumstances like these. She'd want you to remarry."

"I have no intention of divorcing Tori."

She cocked her head. "Then how are you and Pamela going to be together the way you should be?"

"We haven't figured that out yet. Right now, we're going to date and nurture this budding romance while still allowing me to honor my marriage vows."

Ron blew his nose in a handkerchief and said from his seat on the sofa, "You have our full support, whatever you decide. No one could have been a better husband or provider to our daughter. We know you will never abandon her, but if the legalities of it all require that you divorce Tori to marry Pamela, you have our blessing. Tori left us not by choice, but we need to keep on living. You've more than fulfilled your end of the bargain."

Kristoffer didn't think of his marriage as some kind of *bargain*, but understood what Ron was trying to say. This couldn't be easy for either of them to talk about.

"Listen, I'm going to take a shower before going over to visit Tori. Would you like to come along?" He intended to tell Tori what had happened with Pamela tonight, which he should do alone, but didn't want to be rude to her parents, either.

"We were there this morning," Liz replied. "Why don't you take some time alone with her? You can run us over to see her in the morning before we head to the airport."

He nodded. "Sounds good."

After showering and dressing in khakis and a polo shirt, he pulled his hair into a ponytail and said good-bye to his in-laws. Noma met him at the door with a stare as if accusing him of abandoning her again. He smiled and stooped to pick up the fussy feline.

"I'm not going to stay away long this time. Just going to visit your mommy." Noma meowed as if she had a message for him to deliver. "Don't worry. I'll let her know you miss her, too," he whispered in the cat's ear.

He kissed the top of the cat's head and set her down again to wander off if she'd like.

Half an hour later, he walked into Tori's room. The lights hadn't been turned on, so he flipped on the nightlight to see if she was awake or asleep. Her eyes were open, so he went ahead and turned on the floor lamp. Not too bright to be annoying.

As if Tori could be annoyed about anything anymore.

He stroked her cheek, but got the response he expected. Nothing. "Hey, sweetheart. I'm back." He started to tell her he'd missed her, but didn't want to lie. Sure, he'd thought about her while in California, but mostly in the context of how to get on with his life and the business of living.

'No regrets, no guilt.'

Pamela's words came to him, and he steered clear of those useless emotions. Crawling into the bed behind Tori, he wrapped his arm around her, careful to avoid the feeding tube.

"Tori, thank you for being the best wife a man could ever ask for. Thanks for putting up with my workaholic ways. I know I left you alone many times, and if I had it to do over again, I would have ditched work to spend more time with you."

He blinked away the sting in his eyes.

"We always think we have forever, but that wasn't possible for us."

Kristoffer didn't know how to continue this conversation, so he remained quiet a while. "Sweetheart, I have something to tell you. A while ago, I told you I'd met someone—Pamela. I didn't intend for this to happen, but it did." He drew and expelled a deep breath. "I'm falling in love with her." Might already have fallen. Hard.

"The two of us are talking about making plans for our future together. I want you to know I'll never abandon you, but I need Pamela in my life, too. I've been so lonely since you were taken away from me. I thought I could be content to go on like this until...but...I can't. She takes care of me and I her. We comfort each other. I know this sounds bizarre, but if you had picked out someone for me to be with after you, it would have been Pamela. You'd like her."

Not that he'd have asked Tori to choose someone. He'd thought they'd grow old together. A tear trickled inside his ear, as he closed his eyes before clearing his throat. Exhaustion overtook him, and he kept his eyes closed and listened to her breathing.

Sometime later, he crawled out of bed, kissed her goodnight, and returned to the condo. Ron and Liz were asleep in his bedroom. Liz had made up a place for him on the sofa, and after pouring himself a Scotch, he downed it and went to the bathroom off the office to prepare for bed.

Tomorrow he'd see Pamela again. Tori's parents were closer to him than his own mother in many ways. Having them meet the woman he intended to spend the rest of his life with was suddenly important to him. On the spur of the moment, he texted Pamela to see if she'd like to join them for lunch or brunch.

For two people who weren't planning to marry, they sure spent a lot of time meeting each other's family members. But he, at least, wanted to know more about her family. He could learn a lot about her that way.

He wondered if he should be nervous about Pamela's father, knowing how rule-oriented an Air Force officer could be. How much influence would he have on his daughter's life choices? Only time would tell if the man would be an asset or a liability to their happiness.

However, meeting him was important. While they couldn't enter into any kind of legal commitment at this point, they could share with their loved ones what they did have. It made it more visible, more real, more valid.

He just hoped the man wouldn't have a problem with their living together, because the day was going to come soon when Kristoffer wouldn't be able to send Pamela back to her apartment again at night.

CHAPTER TWENTY

"You're here! Come in!" Monica cried, holding out her arms. Her stepmother seemed genuinely happy to see them, despite the short notice and it being the Fourth of July. Pamela had expected them to be celebrating with friends from the Air Force Academy and hadn't wanted to intrude. To be honest, she thought they'd suggest she and Kristoffer come down the next weekend, instead.

Kristoffer's hand at the small of her back helped tamp down her nerves. How would Dad react to him? She wanted them to hit it off, but he might not be too happy about Pamela's plans given Kristoffer's marital status.

Speaking of which, her smiling dad came up beside Monica. "Here's my girl!" He reached out to give Pamela a bear hug that stole her breath away. "So good to see you, Punkin. It's been too long."

Oh, Dad. Don't use that nickname today!

But Pamela laughed the moniker away to diminish its power. Another childish nickname to live down, although Kristoffer hadn't pounced on the Sunshine one her mom used. "Good to see you, too, Dad."

He braced her upper arms as he backed away and gave her a thorough inspection. "Look at the freckles on you."

"Yep. Still there, Dad." He'd always teased her about her freckles. Most of the time, they were nearly invisible, but she'd spent a lot of time in the sun last week.

"And who have we here?" he asked, turning his attention to Kristoffer. While he wasn't blatant, the intense stare told her he was sizing Kristoffer up. All she'd said to Dad on the phone was that she was bringing a friend, but she hadn't mentioned it would be a *male* friend, one she was very close to, besides.

Chicken.

"Monica, Dad, I'd like you to meet Kristoffer Larson. Last month, we finished consulting on a project for the hospital I worked at in Afghanistan." What else should she reveal in these crucial first moments? "We've also become close friends. We took a recent trip together to California. Kristoffer rented a convertible, which is probably why my freckles are so pronounced, Dad."

Dad raised his eyebrows and gave Kristoffer a closer look. She might need to explain more over dinner, but after introducing them to Marc during their oh-so-brief engagement, Pamela was afraid to call this anything deeper and jinx it. The universe had a way of laughing when she made plans. Besides, she and Kristoffer hadn't figured out how they planned to move forward, other than they knew they wanted to be together in some type of committed relationship.

Kristoffer reached out to shake her dad's hand while Pamela gave Monica a quick hug. "Pleased to meet you, sir." Her embrace ended while Dad continued to grip and shake Kristoffer's hand. To his credit, Kristoffer didn't flinch at all.

"Only the cadets call me sir. It's Bryce." Pamela relaxed some. He didn't ask people to call him by his given name unless he liked them.

"Bryce, it is. I am Kristoffer."

She stood aside as Kristoffer pecked Monica on her upturned cheek before handing her the premium bottle of wine they'd stowed in their luggage on the flight home yesterday. Thankfully, it hadn't been stolen or broken in transit.

"Nice to meet you, too, ma'am. Pamela and I chose a little something for you both to enjoy sometime at one of our wine-tasting stops in Sonoma."

Her stepmother looked at the label, and her eyes opened wider. "Wonderful vintage. A Cabernet blend will be the perfect complement for the steaks, too, and this label tops anything we have on the wine rack. Chilled or room temperature?"

"Chilled—about 60 degrees would be ideal."

Monica nodded with a smile. "I'll see what I can do."

Dad stepped to the side and indicated for them to enter the living room. "Kristoffer, why don't you come out and help me on the deck? How do you take your steak?"

"Medium, please."

"And to drink? Beer? Wine? Cocktail?"

"Water would be perfect, thanks. With the long drive ahead, we'll save the wine to enjoy with your wife's fabulous cooking."

Dad nodded. "Smart and responsible. I like that in my daughter's...friends."

Clearly, Dad already suspected more between them. *How could he not, with Kristoffer's hand at the small of my back when we came in?*

Dad turned and led the way to the deck while Monica headed toward the kitchen. Pamela started to follow the men, but Kristoffer turned to her. "Why don't you see if there's anything Monica needs help with, Sprite?" He didn't say the nickname loud enough for the others to hear, but she took this as a signal he was speaking to her as her Dom. Was he seeking out alone time with her dad already?

Because it wasn't really a suggestion, she nodded obediently and whispered, "Yes, Sir."

Her heart pounded as he walked away, but she turned to follow Monica down the hallway to the kitchen. She knew it was more from worry about what Kristoffer and Dad would talk about than spending time with her stepmom. They got along pretty well, especially in the kitchen.

Monica closed the fridge and went to the oven to place the tray of hors d'oeuvres in to bake.

"What can I do to help?" Pamela asked, watching Monica set the bottle in the wine chiller to a temperature of 60 degrees just as Kristoffer had suggested.

"Well, if you'd like to help, wrap these asparagus spears in prosciutto. They only need five minutes to bake, so we'll put them in when we know the men are closer to being ready to eat."

Monica's words made her worry that Dad was grilling Kristoffer instead of steaks, so her mind went back to the men outside. But

Kristoffer could take care of himself.

Forcing her anxiety down, she washed her hands and went to work, letting the silence drag out until it became uncomfortable after a few minutes.

"How are Whitney and William doing?" She hadn't seen her stepsiblings since the holidays.

Monica's continued silence caused her to look up to find tears in the woman's eyes. Her chin quivered, making Pamela wonder what was wrong. Was someone ill?

"Whitney's pregnant."

Pamela didn't get the impression those were tears of joy on the imminent grandmother's face, but a baby on the way should be cause for celebrating no matter what. "Congratulations. When's she due?"

"Six months. She wants to have a big wedding and invite all of our friends. How does she expect me to pull that off on such short notice? And you know how conservative this community is."

Pamela wondered how well her choice to spend the rest of her life with a legally married man would go over.

But this wasn't about her. She reached out to stop Monica's hands from breaking the ends off the asparagus, compelling Monica to stop and meet her gaze. "I'm sure she'll be happy with any type of ceremony if it means joining her with the one she loves." At least she hoped the two loved one another. Her parents had found themselves in a predicament that might have forced them to marry, but they'd seemed happy in the earlier years at least.

Pamela realized marriage wouldn't be in the cards for her anytime soon—if ever. Would she miss sharing that moment with family and friends? No, not really. She and Kristoffer would figure out a way to honor their commitment when the time came, and if they wanted to celebrate with family and friends, they could host a reception following whatever kind of ceremony they decided upon.

"If there's anything I can do to help, Monica, let me know. I should be stateside when the baby arrives." She wouldn't mention her interview tomorrow at Children's, just in case it didn't pan out.

"Whitney's too young to be having a child. She's still a baby herself."

Pamela smiled. Whitney was twenty-eight years old. Heck, Monica had gotten pregnant at seventeen and again at nineteen by a high-school boyfriend who wasn't able to handle the responsibilities of a wife or two kids at a young age. And Pamela's own mom had gotten pregnant at seventeen, too. Seventeen was what she'd call too young, not twenty-eight. Why was she so worried about her daughter?

Be sympathetic and understanding.

"How do you feel about them as a couple? Is her boyfriend good to her? Will he be able to provide for the physical and emotional needs of his new family if they marry?" Her questions seemed to shift Monica's focus away from feeling sorry for herself and her daughter.

"She's dated him for more than two years. We've met him a few times and liked him. And he has a civilian job on base that provides a steady income." While that didn't address how good a husband and father he would be, at least it seemed he wasn't likely to shirk his financial responsibilities.

"I think it's wonderful they've chosen to have the baby and build a new life together. They seem to have everything in their favor."

"I suppose you're right." Monica looked away, apparently at a loss for what else to do or say.

She didn't sound convinced this was going to work out. "What's worrying you?"

She met Pamela's gaze again. "They hadn't spoken of marrying until she found out she was pregnant. I know from experience that's not a sound reason to marry someone. Whitney and William's father was a disaster to be with."

Pamela closed the gap between them and wrapped her arms around her stepmom. "Keep the lines of communication open, and if anything seems to be wrong, don't sweep it under the rug. It's hard to predict who will or won't be abusive. You and Dad raised Whitney to know she deserves better than an abusive man. She's strong and self-assured. I don't see her standing for that kind of treatment for one minute if it should ever occur."

Monica held on a little longer. When she pulled away, she reached for a linen towel and wiped her tears.

Pamela had no doubt Monica would embrace being a grandmother, once the initial shock wore off. "I hear grandchildren are so much more wonderful than children because you get to love on them and then send them home to their parents."

Monica smiled and looked at the countertop. "We'd better get busy before they wonder what happened to us."

As she wrapped the asparagus spears, Pamela wondered for the first time how Dad felt about becoming a grandfather. He'd raised Monica's children as their father, and he had adopted both as his own. Whitney's baby would very much be his first grandchild.

Truly, Pamela had never given much thought to having children— or providing her parents with grandchildren. Good thing, because rug rats probably wouldn't be in the cards for her and Kristoffer. She had no qualms about having a baby outside of marriage as long as she was certain the relationship would last, but Kristoffer and Tori had chosen not to have kids. There was little reason to believe he'd suddenly want them now with his… girlfriend. What would her status be? Submissive, yes, but that was in private and only open in the lifestyle community. Close friends, as she'd introduced him to Dad and Monica, didn't convey the relationship she hoped they were building together.

Something else to discuss with—

"Smells delicious." She turned to find Kristoffer in the doorway. He entered and crossed the room to stand beside her. If her hands hadn't been greasy with prosciutto, she'd have given him a hug. He seemed relaxed and carefree. She wondered what he and Dad had discussed, but wouldn't ask here. There was plenty of time to talk on the ride home.

"I told you Monica's an excellent cook. She taught me a lot of what I know."

Her stepmother's tears had dried up, and she beamed at Pamela. "Thank you, honey. I wish Whitney had enjoyed spending time in the kitchen as much as you did. Those are moments I'll always treasure between the two of us. Who knows?" she asked as she dried her hands on a towel and arranged the wrapped spears on a cooking tray. "Maybe I'll be able to enjoy doing that again with my granddaughter—or grandson."

Pamela turned to Kristoffer. "Monica and Dad are expecting their first grandchild in six months."

"Congratulations, Monica." Kristoffer's attention quickly returned to Pamela, perhaps trying to gauge whether she had any strong emotions about the news one way or another.

She smiled up at him. "I'll be a favorite aunt. Okay, perhaps the only aunt, but that baby is going to be spoiled rotten with love if the Jeffreys have anything to say about it."

Kristoffer stroked her back, and she leaned into his hand. "What can I do to help you ladies?"

"Not a thing," Monica said, back to her old self and in command of her domain. "Men don't belong in the kitchen. Pamela and I have everything under control here. Let Bryce know we'll be finished here in about five minutes, if you don't mind."

He gave Pamela a look silently asking her to confirm she was okay, and she nodded almost imperceptibly, but apparently he was satisfied enough to smile before leaving the room. She felt cherished when he checked on her that way.

She and Monica spent the next fifteen minutes moving like a well-oiled machine with Monica arranging the appetizers on trays while Pamela placed the warm rolls she'd just pulled from the oven into a basket she covered with a linen napkin. Lifting that and the large salad bowl, she carried them to the dining room where the table had already been set. Kristoffer and Dad joined her, the latter carrying a covered platter and a plate of four foil-covered baked potatoes.

"The steaks smell wonderful, Dad." He smiled as he expertly opened the bottle of Cab Monica brought in along with the appetizers. He poured each of them a glass. Kristoffer would probably have some wine now that it was being consumed with food.

"You seem to be a wine connoisseur, Kristoffer," Dad remarked.

"One of the few hobbies I've been able to indulge in the past few years."

Pamela searched Dad's face to gauge his response, but he didn't indicate whether he knew Kristoffer's story yet or not. What had the two talked about outside?

Soon the four were seated, two each on the long sides of the table, with Kristoffer by her side and directly across from Dad.

After the platters and bowls were passed, Monica apologized for not having the appetizers ready to enjoy out on the deck.

"Nonsense. Everything's delicious, Monica, Pamela." The way Kristoffer acknowledged her small contribution in nearly the same breath made her smile.

"My girls are the best cooks ever." Pamela acknowledged Dad's compliment, too, with a nod.

"I can't take credit for this feast, guys," Pamela said. "Monica did all the prep and hard work."

Conversation continued in a similar vein until Monica cleared the salad and appetizer plates and the steaks were served. Dad had a set of markers indicating doneness, and each was served a porterhouse cooked to a different temperature. Pamela noticed she and Kristoffer both chose medium.

"So, Kristoffer, tell me more about your work," Dad prompted.

As Kristoffer launched into his usual low-key description of his work and even mentioned the equipment purchase project, Pamela watched Dad's and Monica's responses. They seemed genuinely interested, and she relaxed. *What's not to like about Kristoffer?* Dad asked a few questions, especially concerning the type of jet Gunnar used on his missions, and Kristoffer surprisingly knew the answer, but he'd probably been responsible for the jet's purchase.

In under a week, Kristoffer had survived meeting both of her parents and her stepmother. She glanced in Kristoffer's direction and found him gazing at her. He smiled warmly at her, and she sent her own back to him. Was he aware of the direction her thoughts had taken? Skilled Dominants could interpret body language, and he'd shown numerous times he could read her like a book.

"Pamela, what's been keeping you so busy these days?" Dad asked. "Or should I ask who?" Dad's pointed look at Kristoffer made her blush.

"The project we worked on took up quite a bit of time. Of course, I had some restrictions due to my recovery period." Hoping to steer him in a different direction, Pamela changed the subject. "Oh, I'm interviewing Monday at Children's Hospital in Denver for a possible position on the plastics and reconstruction surgical team."

"Does this mean you intend to stay put for a while?"

She shared her plans to spend one more month in Afghanistan to finish out her contract. "I'll be glad when that's behind you. Not to say I'm not proud of you, Punkin. There's a lot of haters in this world, but knowing you're doing something to make life better for some of the casualties..." He broke off and cleared his throat. "You definitely inherited a mix of your mother's idealism and my practicality."

His praise washed over her like a brilliant beam of sunshine. "You two passed down to me the best you each had to offer."

The meal neared an end too quickly, but they had yet to say anything to Dad about what the two of them meant to one another. She'd follow Kristoffer's lead but regretted not introducing him accurately at the front door. Now it seemed awkward to bring up their status again.

Kristoffer reached for his untouched wine glass and lifted it as if to propose a toast. Everyone followed suit and raised their glasses. In his sexy, deep voice, he said, "To Pamela, one of the bravest, kindest, and most proficient people I know—and the woman who has filled an enormous void in my life with her presence."

Pamela's vision blurred as she blindly clinked her glass with his and completed the toast with Monica and Dad. She blinked rapidly, not wanting to turn the end of their meal into a weepy mess. Glancing nervously over at Dad, she was met with his smile and a twinkle in his eye. He wasn't the least bit surprised by Kristoffer's announcement. Clearly, the two men *had* spoken on the deck.

She turned to face Kristoffer, furrowing her brows, but he only shrugged matter-of-factly. "I couldn't very well ask you to be a significant part of my life without first knowing we would have your father's approval, especially given our unique circumstances. Call me old-fashioned, but I spent a lot of my childhood being raised by a grandfather in the old country—and my late teen years under Gunnar's authority."

"Rest assured, Punkin, I warned Kristoffer what would happen if he ever hurt you in the slightest way." While Dad winked at her, an edge to his words left no doubt the two had spoken quite seriously earlier. "You two have a lifetime to figure out what to make of your relationship. Don't let anyone else's standards dictate what's right for you."

She'd never thought of Dad as particularly liberal, but he certainly sounded open-minded about the prospect of his daughter living with a man outside of marriage. That lifted a great weight off her shoulders.

His voice grew husky as he finished. "As long as you're happy, Pamela, you know I'll be happy." Perhaps the twinkle in Dad's eye was unshed tears.

She stood and rounded the table to give him a hug. "I love you, Dad. And I love Kristoffer, too. He's very good for me."

Only Monica seemed as surprised as Pamela by this turn of events. "Well, does this mean we'll be planning *two* weddings this summer?"

Pamela's gaze shifted to Kristoffer, whose smile became stiff, but before he could speak, Dad said, "Monica, all you have to worry about is Whitney's. I'll explain it to you later."

Kristoffer stood. "Monica, Bryce, if you'll excuse us, Pamela and I have some things to discuss—in private. Pardon my manners, but please continue without us. This might take a while."

"Take all the time you need, Kristoffer," Dad said, grinning. No doubt in her mind that those two were going to become good friends—and accomplices.

She wasn't sure if he meant they were leaving or what, but he eased her hand into his and guided her out onto the deck, releasing her to slide the door closed behind them. Once out of sight of the two in the dining room, he turned her toward him.

"This might be the longest speech I've ever made, so please bear with me." His serious expression caused the blood to pound in her ears.

"Two months ago tomorrow, I walked into a classroom at The Denver Academy and found a beautiful ginger-haired sprite standing naked and proud before a group of her fellow students." A flush heated her cheeks. She hadn't remembered the date, but it pleased her that he had.

"I was wearing blinders before that, or I'd have noticed you in the boardroom the day you came to Gunnar asking for help for Fakhira. But suffice it to say, you definitely captured my attention *that* night." He was quick to add, "And not because you were nude, although that didn't hurt any." He shrugged unapologetically, endearing himself to her even more. His humor helped relieve some of her tension, but he grew serious again.

"That night was the wake-up call I needed. At one point, I don't know if you remember, but you looked at me with a silent plea in your eyes, begging me not to expose you outside those walls. At least that's how I interpreted it."

"I knew you had to have been vetted, but it was definitely my initial reaction when I saw someone I knew standing there."

"The thing is, you needed something from me."

The moment had been obscured by time for her, but apparently had made an indelible impact on him.

He took a deep breath and sobered. "That extremely awkward moment changed my life forever. Yeah, I fought it at first, thinking it wrong of me to even be attracted to another woman, much less act on it. I'm a married man, so it was even more wrong of me to fall in love with her."

The pounding in her ears might have blocked out some of his words.

"…mere mortals like me can't dictate the will of our hearts." He cleared his throat and stared deeply into her eyes. "I was doomed the moment my enchanting pixie flitted into my dark, gloomy days, casting a dazzling light into every corner." He shook his head and grinned. "No, truth be told, you came in with a blowtorch and brought me roaring back to life."

They shared a laugh at the image he'd spun of her as Tinkerbell on steroids.

He reached out to cup her cheek. "You, Sprite, are the most amazing, selfless woman I've ever met. Rarely with a thought to your own needs, you go about making sure *my* needs and those of others are met. In my case, it required igniting a stick of dynamite to break loose some of my barrier walls."

She swallowed against the lump in her throat, blinking rapidly. "You, Sir, have always made certain my needs were met, even ones I was unaware of."

He pressed a finger to her lips. She kissed it, leaving him grinning and shaking his head simultaneously.

Soon, he grew serious again. "Pamela, you've never asked me to compromise my principles or abandon my obligations to Tori. From the beginning, you've accepted the fact that I can't divorce her, even though I now know in my heart, as well as my head, that she's gone. While we were in Sonoma, I made my peace with her and said goodbye."

"You and I began as friends, but we've become much closer."

She smiled. "Oh, *much* more."

He continued as if she hadn't spoken, as though he'd practiced this speech at some point and needed to let it out verbatim.

"When you agreed to be my submissive trainee and recently became my submissive—knowing I had a list of intimacy hard limits a mile long—you never complained about what we couldn't have. You simply accepted the moments we *could* share together."

Drawing his hand back, he began fiddling with his wedding ring. "In Big Sur, we both admitted we were falling in love with each other." He sighed heavily. "I know you must wonder whether I'll be able to love you the way you deserve given this." Pausing a second, he then slowly removed his wedding ring.

What was he thinking? "No, Kristoffer! I'd never ask you—"

The white band left on his tanned finger showed that his years with Tori had left their mark in more ways than one. He'd worn her ring for eighteen years.

"This doesn't mean I'm divorcing Tori or shirking my duties to the shell she left behind." He held the gold band up between them. "But continuing to wear this on my left hand is a lie. It tells the world that I'm an actively married man. I've finally admitted that's not true. Rick explained it best—how can it be called a marriage if one partner is unable to participate in the relationship in even the most basic of ways? Someone whose body is alive only because of artificial means?"

Confused at what he was saying and doing, she cocked her head.

"Pamela, I've been trying to figure out how to show you I'm ready to move on with you emotionally, not to mention declare in some public way that we're committed to one another now."

He then slipped the band onto his right ring finger. "While not wearing Tori's ring at all might send a message we're divorced, I think wearing it here serves as a reminder to me of my duty and promise to oversee the care of her body until she passes. That could be tomorrow...or twenty or forty years from now."

Pamela's took his hands in hers and looked into his eyes. "One of the things I love most about you is that you don't shirk your duties or go back on your promises."

"But I also love you, Pamela. Why shouldn't we be allowed to express that love openly? Neither of us is religious, although most religious doctrines would agree with me that Tori died four years ago— or at the very latest three and a half, when she went from the coma to a persistent vegetative state."

He dragged his hand through his hair. Perhaps he still wrestled with the decision he'd made. "Pamela, the moment I moved my ring, I pledged in my heart to cherish and love you for the rest of my life forward." He smiled. "I'd go so far as to say you're going to be the dominant force in my life, but I don't want your alpha to misconstrue my words."

She smiled through her tears. "I am also willing to pledge the same to you for the rest of my life."

He knelt on one knee, and her hand flew to her mouth. What on earth was he doing?

"Pamela, I'd rather die than spend another night alone without you in my arms. Last night was pure hell for me."

She trembled all over as her eyes filled with more tears. She wasn't normally the weepy type, but her emotions were riding a roller coaster ever since California. "I cried myself to sleep last night, Kristoffer. I missed you, too."

He reached into his left pocket and pulled out a jewelry box. The insignia on top seemed familiar, but she had too many tears in her eyes to read it.

"We're eventually going to have to define what type of relationship we have—if for no other reason than to be able to explain it to others. But, while we can't marry, I don't plan to put our love on hold. Tonight, I am ready to show the world how important you are to me." He opened the box and held it toward her. Inside were two identical silver bracelets consisting of a simple silver chain joined by the infinity symbol and a lobster clasp closure.

Forever.

"To symbolize the commitment I'm making to love you, Pamela, I want to ask if you will wear this bracelet as a token of our love."

He'd found the perfect way to profess their love without using a traditional symbol of marriage like a ring. That he would honor their commitment in such a way left her speechless.

"I've been carrying this box with me since Big Sur, waiting for the right moment to share them with you."

That's where she'd seen the insignia on the box—the jewelry store where he'd bought her the matching Big Sur jade earrings and necklace.

"I probably should wait until we drive back to Denver and are alone to do this, but..." A shadow passed over his face. He'd lost one love on a Denver highway and was afraid of losing her before he could do this. Oh, Kristoffer. The fear he'd lived with every time they ventured onto the road, worrying if the unthinkable would happen again, must be unbearable. She reached out to stroke his cheek.

He cleared his throat. "I can think of no better time than tonight, Pamela, to put this bracelet on your wrist and stake my claim. And if someday you to decide to place the larger one on my wrist, I will wear it with pride and love."

"I'm more than ready, Kristoffer." She had been since California, but hadn't been sure how they would manage to pull it off.

Setting the box on the deck beside him, he lifted the smaller of the two bracelets out and opened the clasp. She rarely wore rings or bracelets, because she couldn't wear them in the operating room. Some believed a wedding band should never be removed, and this was very much that type of symbol for them.

"Kristoffer, I feel I should tell you I'll have to take it off to scrub and perform surgery. Will that be a problem?"

He gave her a funny expression then shook his head. "No. If you wore my wedding ring, you'd have to do the same, wouldn't you?"

"Yes. It's considered best practice to remove everything below the elbows to maintain a sterile environment in surgery."

"Of course, you need to follow the rules your job requires. If I were a mechanic, I probably wouldn't wear jewelry, either, for safety reasons."

"Safety first!" *Oh, Christ!* Where had *that* come from? Well, she knew, but it was decidedly inappropriate in such a solemn moment. When he grinned, she knew he remembered her safe gesture squeeze toy Mister Safety from their scene in Sonoma. She wondered if he'd kept it afterward.

Focus, Pamela!

"Now, where was I?" He only sounded teasingly annoyed at her interruption. That he was able to find humor in life again and not be so serious was a good thing.

He held it by the ends and moved toward her left wrist, so she extended her arm and he secured it in place. He then raised her wrist to his lips and placed a kiss on the underside that sent tingles up her arm. The bracelet fit perfectly, slightly loose, but not so much that she would lose it. This simple, yet elegant piece of jewelry symbolized their commitment to each other and the world.

Kristoffer stood and kissed her lips next. "I love you, Pamela."

He'd said it!

"I love you, too, Kristoffer, which is why I need to do this right now."

Pamela knelt and removed the remaining bracelet from the box. Looking up at a very tall Kristoffer, she began, "Present to me your dominant wrist. Please," she added with a smile, so as not to appear too bossy.

"I can see you're going to be a handful. But you're *my* handful!" He held out his right arm. She had guessed it would be that one, given that he wore his wristwatch on the left. While it was the same side he now wore Tori's ring, she had no problem placing her bracelet around that wrist. He'd made commitments to them both.

He tilted his palm upward as if waiting for her to fill it—and his life. She hoped she would never disappoint him.

She met his gaze. "This bracelet signifies my acceptance of you—not only as my lifemate, but also as my love. While I can't promise to control my strong alpha nature at all times, Kristoffer, please know you are the only man I've found to be worthy of my complete surrender in the bedroom—and in my heart." She glanced down to place the bracelet on his wrist and kissed him in the same place he had kissed her, feeling his radial pulse beating fast against her lips.

She looked up at him again. "This bracelet will be the manifestation of my love for you for all the world to see."

"You honor me with your trust and love, Pamela. I will never make you regret entering into this commitment."

"No regrets, no guilt. Remember?"

He nodded then smiled, caressing her cheek. "You know what it does to me to see you on your knees for me, don't you?"

She nodded, unable to suppress a grin as her pulse quickened. "But my father is on the other side of that wall, so behave."

"Wait until I get you home, Sprite."

Home. Another decision they needed to make. "I can't wait, Sir!"

He helped her to her feet. As if on the same wavelength, he said, "Pamela, I want us to be together for the rest of our lives, starting tonight."

He framed her face with his hands. As he lowered his mouth to hers, they affirmed their heartfelt promises in a kiss free of reservations or regrets. Her stomach flipped in somersaults as he playfully tugged at her lower lip until she opened her mouth to him. Deepening the kiss, he held the back of her head. When it ended, they clung to one another, reluctant to pull away.

Until a neighbor's dog barked, breaking the spell. They grinned at each other like teenagers caught necking on the porch. Well, the back deck, in this case.

Still trying to determine what had just happened, she said, "I think you've found the perfect way to honor us both. When did you decide to do this?"

"On our last morning in Big Sur, when I left the room while you slept in, I went shopping again. I'd had so much luck at the hotel jeweler that I went there."

So he had purchased it after their most intimate time together—when she'd first admitted she'd fallen in love with him.

"I said goodbye to Tori the way I should have four years ago when we were in Sonoma that second night. During that walk on the beach two mornings later, I was determined to find a way to profess my love in a visible way, because I knew we were headed toward something permanent even then." Permanent. She liked the sound of that. "So I asked the jeweler what were some traditions other than an exchange of rings where someone might make a commitment, and he mentioned love bracelets."

"Love bracelets are perfect," she said, looking down at his again. "I hadn't heard of them before, but I tend not to keep up with the latest social or fashion news." She reconnected with his gaze, basking in *that* visible sign of love, too. "So when did you decide to ask me here at my dad's?"

He brushed his thumb over her cheekbone. "Pretty much the moment I met him this afternoon."

Her eyes opened wider. "Wow! Kristoffer Roar Larson being spontaneous?"

"I seem to be doing that a lot lately. You're a good influence on me, I guess." He grinned. "After spending a little time with us, it wouldn't have taken long for an observant man like your dad to notice the two of us were more than close friends, as you described us to him earlier. You might have noticed that I can't keep my hands to myself around you."

She grinned back at him. "True, although you showed great restraint before and during dinner. I thought I'd go mad missing you touching me."

His pupils dilated. What would tonight hold for them? She couldn't wait, but needed to remain in this amazing moment.

"Of course, I was waiting for the right moment. I'd planned on it being tonight when we got home, but I've been carrying those bracelets in my pocket since I bought them. When we went through airport security in San Francisco and I was told to empty my pockets, I was afraid they'd ruin the surprise for you. Luckily, you were ahead of me retrieving your own things and putting on your shoes. You didn't seem to notice."

She smiled. "I assure you that I saw nothing."

Kristoffer would always be a planner, which was fine with her, given the instability of her childhood and her career. She'd be able to count on him to be her rock and to always have a contingency—or twelve. That something as serious and significant in his life as this moment hadn't been planned to the nth degree made her smile.

She admired the bracelet from several angles. "Well played, Kristoffer." He definitely had the potential for pulling impromptu moments out of his bag of tricks when he wanted to.

Not to mention his bag of toys. Hadn't he promised some play time tonight? And that he didn't want to spend the night apart?

Kristoffer was a man of his word. His promises were as good as gold—or silver, in the case of her bracelet. No doubt in her mind, they would find a way to make this relationship happen, too, and be together for the rest of their lives.

Kristoffer sobered and took her hands in his to squeeze them and hold on tight. "Last night, when I visited Tori, I told her everything about us."

"I love that you still talk to her like that."

He shrugged. "I know some might think it strange, given that I know her soul doesn't reside in the shell left behind. But I like to think her spirit visits there and that she's aware of me from wherever she exists now."

"I have no doubt she does. You two have a connection that transcends anything here on earth."

She could never replace Tori, even after her body breathed its last, but as long as Pamela, too, had a place in his heart, she'd be happy.

"I know we're both mature adults and that I didn't have to ask your father for permission to be with you, but I wanted him to understand about Tori and why you and I don't want to put our lives on hold until Tori passes. I assured him I'd love and cherish you and that I would never desert or harm you in any way. He said that's all he cared about—and that you were happy."

Standing on tiptoes, she grasped his shirt and tugged, signaling she wanted another kiss, and he obliged.

When their lips parted again, she smiled. "Do you think Dad and Monica are wondering if we're ever going to join them again?"

"I apologized ahead of time, didn't I? All I know is that we have a seventy-mile trip ahead of us so we're going to be even ruder by going in there, saying our goodbyes, and heading home."

Home.

Before she could ask which home that would be, he added, "I'd like it to be to *our* home—my condo for now, at least."

A grin spread across her mouth. "I thought you'd never ask. Oh, wait. You didn't."

He shook his head. "Brat. *Will* you move in with me?"

"I don't want to spend another night without you."

After one more kiss, they went back inside, made up for their manners by staying through a wonderful, quick dessert, and at last were able to say their goodbyes. To Monica, Pamela offered, "Let me know if there's anything I can do to help with Whitney's wedding or preparing for the new baby."

"I may come to Denver to do some shopping," Monica said. "Maybe we can get together then, if you're not busy with your new position."

"I hope I get the job, but thanks for the vote of confidence. Anytime. Just let me know a little ahead of time. Bring Dad, too. There are some great new jazz clubs you two would love. Kristoffer and I have been trying them out one by one."

At the door, Dad pulled her aside for one more hug and spoke quietly so only she could hear. "I like Kristoffer. A lot. You two are good together. I'm glad you finally found the right one."

"Thanks, Dad. I couldn't agree more."

Back in Denver that night, with fireworks lighting up the skyline as if to celebrate his and Pamela's new status, Kristoffer stopped by her apartment so she could pack some essentials. For someone who wasn't particularly spontaneous—hell, far from it—he'd sure been full of surprises lately—because of Pamela.

Today alone had started out with him introducing her to Tori's parents over lunch and being given their blessing just before his in-laws headed through security to catch their flight.

That was nothing compared to tonight. They'd promised to commit themselves to each other for the rest of their lives, and now he waited as she packed her clothes to move in.

He sat on the sofa and used this time to flesh out a rough idea for a scene tonight. But it was what he hoped happened afterward that would bring the next barrier tumbling down.

I'm ready.

He fiddled with the bracelet she'd placed on his wrist, smiling as he remembered her reason for putting it on his dominant side. Something she'd said earlier this evening had gotten him thinking about a way he might be able to make an even more permanent commitment to her. He needed to talk with Gunnar and make some plans first.

"All set. I think I have it all," she said, coming out of the bedroom with two suitcases. "Luckily, I hadn't unpacked yet from California. I was so tired when you dropped me off last night I went straight to bed. Not that I slept much. Hope you don't mind my doing laundry tomorrow."

How something as monotonous and mundane as laundry could sound exciting baffled him. But it signaled a degree of the ordinary he'd missed sharing with someone for a long time.

"My laundry room is yours, Sprite."

She smiled before glancing around the room. "This place came furnished, so most of it stays. Two more trips with both our vehicles should manage the rest. But it can wait a while. The month's paid up, and I have that interview tomorrow."

Maybe they should skip the play scene and go straight to bed, although he thought the scene would be a great segue. Her interview was in the afternoon, so she could sleep in.

"I don't expect you to make irrevocable life changes at the drop of a hat," he said. "Keep the apartment as long as you'd like."

His condo would suffice for now, but eventually, he'd like to find a place just outside the city where they could have more privacy. The thought of playing with Pamela in an outdoor scene appealed to him immensely. He hadn't done one with anyone else before, so this would give him and Pamela one more unique experience not mired in memories of Tori.

"What are you grinning about, Sir?"

"You'll find out soon enough." He met her across the room and placed a quick kiss on her lips before he commandeered her suitcases and headed for the door. She retrieved a carry-on sized bag, and they made their way down the two flights of stairs to his Jag.

Thoughts about what he planned to do tonight bombarded him all the way home. He had no idea where to start or what type of scene…

Do you have to plan every damned thing out, man?

Well, spontaneity was nice for his love life, but a Dom ought to put some thought into a scene to make sure nothing went awry.

After taking time to settle her into his bedroom and make room in his dresser and closet for her things, he turned to her. Holding open his arms, she stepped into them, looking up at him.

"Would you like to take a shower before we play?"

"I'd love to—if you'll join me."

He grinned. "Thought you'd never ask."

He reached for the hem of her shirt and pulled it over her head. Next, his hands moved to the bra clasp, in the front this time. His knuckles brushed her firm breasts, and when they sprang free of the binding cloth, he cupped them, squeezing the nipples between his thumbs and index fingers.

Her hiss of excitement made him rock hard for her. Bending to take one peak into his mouth, he sucked as she held on to his head for balance. He flicked his tongue against her nipple before his teeth clamped down hard enough to hurt.

"Yes!"

While she said she didn't enjoy pain, whenever he'd tested her limits, he'd yet to find them. Perhaps she hadn't been wrong to seek training at the academy to explore her submissive side. He was just glad that now she'd be exploring it with him.

Emboldened, he moved to the other nipple and sucked it hard into his mouth, but his cock demanded to get in on the fun, too. Before he threw her onto the bed like a barbarian, he let her go and helped her shed the rest of her clothes. His quickly followed.

"After you," he said, motioning toward the bathroom.

CHAPTER TWENTY-ONE

Hair still wet from their shared shower, Kristoffer prepared for their scene by setting out on the top of his dresser the implements he wanted at the ready. Pamela was in the living room finishing up her journaling after their eventful evening at her dad's. No doubt her journal would reveal a number of her own anticipatory thoughts about the evening ahead, despite his instruction to focus on her feelings about their exchange of love bracelets earlier.

Tonight, they'd be doing some roleplaying after he'd noticed a number of sexy costumes in the luggage she'd unpacked earlier. He'd told her to surprise him with one and looked forward to improvising a scenario to match whichever she chose. A worthy test of his newfound spontaneity. He planned to try some new toys on her, too, but would also bring out some of her favorites.

Because his wearing a suit turned her on, he donned one, skipping the vest and boxers. Anxious to rejoin Sprite, he picked up the pervertible nipple clamps and attached the rubber bands tightly to either end of two bamboo skewers, then fashioned a second one for her other breast. His pinky finger wedged between them was a bit tight, but should mean they'd be just right for her. He placed them in his inside breast pocket and covered the tray of other toys he might use tonight with a hand towel. He checked the timer he'd be using to ensure he didn't clamp her nipples overly long. Twenty minutes max this time, unless she used a safeword sooner.

Would Sprite's inner brat remain under her control? He doubted it but wouldn't mind if she made an appearance. He and Sprite were serious about so many things that their playtime should be a place to let loose and have fun.

Kristoffer also enjoyed mindfucks and teasing her. His options tonight were endless, although he wanted this to be a fairly quick scene so they could go share his—now, their—bed for the first of many such nights.

Tomorrow afternoon, she would interview for a surgical position at Children's—and no doubt be hired. But that meant they wouldn't have as many opportunities to play. Surgeons kept long hours, and Pamela would spend even more time working, because she took a personal interest in her patients.

But he would enjoy every minute he didn't have to share her with the world; he'd treat the next couple of weeks like their honeymoon.

Thinking perhaps she ought to have finished journaling by now, he crossed the room and entered the living room to find her kneeling beside the sofa with her pen lying on top of the notebook in front of her as if an offering to him. The page was full of her handwriting and probably one of several pages she'd used to express herself. He'd delve into that with her later, interested to find out what she'd chosen to share.

Her hands rested on her thighs, palms upward, while she appeared to be centering herself in the moment.

"Very nice, Sprite. Thank you. Now, stand."

Using the sofa for leverage, she followed his command, her gaze remaining downcast in full submission. He grinned. She'd chosen to wear a German beer maid costume with a flouncy petticoat peeking out below an über-short skirt. A string-tied bodice lifted her plump breasts over the elasticized neckline of a puffy-sleeved peasant blouse. She stood before him as though awaiting inspection. Her hair was tied in loose pigtails draped over each breast.

"Nice." He might even let her keep her hair like that tonight, rather than completely loose.

She smiled. He'd play with this fantasy a bit before he played with her body. Cold, hard implements only went so far for him. He enjoyed conveying his emotions to her as well as touching her.

She kept her focus on the notebook in front of her. Drawing near, he pinched one nipple through her blouse with thumb and finger. Her sexy hiss and the instantaneous swelling of the bud told him she was primed and ready. He'd left her in her head the perfect length of time.

"You please me with your choice of costume."

When she didn't respond, he realized she might think she was under voice restriction. "You are permitted to speak tonight. In fact, it will be quite necessary. Understand?"

"*Ja*, thank you, *mein Herr.*"

He chuckled. *My Lord*, huh? His brat was going to have a very red ass before the night was over.

"Now, let's begin." He walked around her body as if inspecting her and affected his best German accent as he entered into his role tonight. "*Fräulein*, you will do nicely. Come to the back room with me."

She lapsed into character seamlessly. "But, *Herr*, I have thirsty customers to serve." Apparently, her brat would be front and center tonight.

So it's Sir now. Love it.

He kissed the side of her neck, and she moaned. "Not as thirsty as I am for you, wench." He pressed his erection against her and whispered, "You will spread your legs for me tonight so that I may taste your charms."

Her voice hitched. "I look forward to it, but please let me take care of one more table, *Herr*, and then I'll slip away with you. However, I can't be away too long, or I'll lose tips."

She appeared to be begging for a nice, long paddling tonight. *Good.* Kristoffer wrapped his arms around her waist and cupped her breasts. She hissed, preparing for the clamps.

"Pleasing me—and being pleased *by* me—will make up for any loss in wages or tips. I will reward you well, if you're my good girl."

"I will be your *very* good girl, *Herr.*"

In front of her now, he bent and lightly bit one of her ripe buds before standing upright again. "I have every confidence you will."

A frustrated moan told him she was more than ready. He'd indulge his naughty little brat a while longer as she appeared to be enjoying this roleplay as much as he. But she'd receive her *funishment* paddling later on.

Her beer maid costume gave him an idea for a new pervertible to add to his arsenal tonight. Before moving into the bedroom, he let her go and walked over to the bar. Finding what he wanted hanging against the wall as a decoration, he carried the beer flight tray back to where she stood. While her gaze was downcast, he wanted to make sure she could see it.

"Have you ever seen one of these before?"

She lifted her head, and her eyes widened in surprise when she saw the wooden plank with its four evenly spaced holes. She didn't seem to be much of a beer drinker, but he would have expected her to have seen one while in a bar with friends. Perhaps she hadn't gone bar hopping much.

He'd been given this one as a souvenir at his favorite pub in Philadelphia during his college days, but truthfully hadn't thought about its more perverted uses until a few moments ago.

"Hands in front, palms upward." He placed the instrument across her palms. "Bring this with you to the back room, beer maid. Keep in mind that for each minute it takes for you to join me, I'll add another swat from this beer flight paddle to your backside. And know that you've already earned four swats for not agreeing immediately to join me in the back."

Her body remained relaxed. Sprite enjoyed being paddled, so he wouldn't expect her to follow for at least a few minutes, but her uncertainty about how she'd respond to a new implement might hasten her joining him. Tonight was about rewards, testing limits, and having fun. He'd give her what she wanted as long as she didn't become too bratty. But his brat-tolerance limit was fairly high.

"I won't be long, *mein Herr.*" Her voice conveyed her excitement. His own anticipation grew along with the size of his cock as he looked forward to lifting her skirt for any number of delights. Merely imagining the sound of the heavy wood smacking against her ass cheeks and upper thighs made him harder. The paddle's holes would leave some sexy markings, too.

He glanced at his watch and left the room, wondering how long she would linger in here.

About six minutes later, she entered the bedroom with the improvised paddle still perched on her upturned palms. Six more swats making a total of ten—so far.

"One might think you enjoy the thought of this paddle striking your ass, sexy maid." He removed the object from her still outstretched hands as she smiled. To her credit, she maintained her position, awaiting his instruction to lower them.

"I would have put this…paddle to use serving two of my tables their beer, *Herr*, but it's not conducive to serving beer in steins."

He chuckled. "You may lower your arms to your sides. And the beer flight tray isn't for serving at all. Besides, watching a bar wench struggle with multiple steins or glasses is too much fun. No, its intended use is to present a series of up to four brews to pub patrons wanting to try a number of different beers or IPAs at one sitting, similar to a wine tasting. But enough about its more mundane uses." He slapped the soon-to-be-paddle against his hand to make a nice, loud crack. She flinched at the sound, and he laughed heartily. He obviously hadn't tried this on himself, so he'd need to assess her often.

"*Fräulein*, because you chose to serve other men tonight before me, you've earned a paddling, haven't you?"

"*Ja, Herr.*"

Roar set the paddle on top of the hand towel covering his other implements. He returned to where she stood and lowered the neckline of her blouse to expose her breasts, running his hands over the firm peaks, cupping them while occasionally pinching her nipples to prepare them for what was to come. "Beautiful."

She smiled at his praise. He'd see how long she'd be able to continue smiling. At her dad's, he'd commandeered four leftover bamboo skewers from the package Bryce had used for the grilled veggies earlier this evening.

"But we're also going to try something else that's new tonight. He reached inside his breast pocket and pulled out the bamboo skewers and rubber bands he'd fashioned earlier. "Have you had bamboo used as nipple clamps before, Sprite?"

"No, Sir." The breathy response told him she was willing to try. He always loved finding new experiences for her—for them both.

Roar rubbed the sides of the thin sticks over every inch of her breasts, occasionally poking her nipple with the pointy tips or slapping the long ends against her nipples to keep them engorged in anticipation.

He'd begun conditioning her nipples in Big Sur with the tweezer clamps, and eventually would introduce the intimidating clover clamps, but he wanted to explore her tolerance levels slowly. He detected no sign of anxiety or fear.

"Tonight, I ask you to show me how well you've learned to discipline your mind, body, and mouth as we test your pain boundaries. The scene might be uncomfortable at times, but I have yet to reach your pain limit. Remember that I expect you to use your safeword if you even come close, unless you want to forego making love tonight and count about three thousand grains of rice."

She quickly masked her distaste for that prospect and nodded. "I will obey, Roar, *Herr.*"

"It pleases me when you're honest with me and keeps me from doing any harm. I want to know the second you've reached your limit no matter what activity we're enjoying. Now, tonight you will keep your gaze downcast regardless of position unless instructed otherwise."

"*Ja, Herr.*"

"Now, assume position number one." She lifted her hands and interlaced them behind her head, elbows pointed outward at ear level, legs spread to shoulder-width.

"Well done." He pinched her nipple again before separating the two sticks of one pair and tried to determine the best position for them. Secured too close to the base, and they wouldn't be any more intense than the tweezer ones. Too close to the tip might be more intense than she was prepared for. He decided halfway between the tip and the base would be a happy medium.

He remembered his own Dom training and experiencing bamboo clamps for the first time. Gunnar had made sure Kristoffer didn't try anything on a submissive or bottom he hadn't first tried on himself, but always took great joy in making sure Kristoffer knew the outer limits of pain he could inflict. Now *that* man was a genuine sadist.

Focus, Roar!

She watched his every move, but he'd asked her to keep her gaze down, too. He spread the sticks of one set apart and eased them over her erect left nipple. When he released them suddenly, she gasped, *almost* trying to shrink away from him. Her arms bowed forward slightly as she absorbed the pain, but she promptly regained her composure and returned to the proper position.

"Well done." She smiled and relaxed. He stroked the area around her breast to sooth away some of her pain. Then he clamped the other nipple, tightened the bands on them both another twist or two, and set the timer for twenty minutes.

"You seem to be taking the pain well, wench. Is that so?"

"*Ja, Herr.*" The strain in her voice was evident.

He rubbed her areolas and bent to lick the tips of her nipples exposed beyond the sticks. She moaned. "Like that?"

"Oh, *ja, Herr!*"

He grinned. "Remember to take slow, deep breaths throughout the evening to help control the pain and improve your concentration." She took a deep, cleansing one for him. "That's my good girl." He kissed her cheek to ground *himself*, and said, dropping the accent, "Assume position number five over the end of the chaise." She sashayed to the foot of the padded lounging chair in the corner of the room, head held high and showing no anxiety. This may be funishment, but he couldn't let her disobey, either. "Two more whacks for not keeping your gaze down, wench."

Kneeling, she bent at the waist, stretched her torso gingerly over the length of the chair, trying not to twist the bamboo sticks, and placed her hands on the floor, palms downward. While not a spanking bench, it should work well, especially given her short stature.

This position caused her crinoline petticoat to lift just as he'd hoped, baring her ass to him nicely. No panties, of course. Her pale, rounded globes begged to be reddened, and time was running out on the clamps. He slapped the paddle against his palm several times, watching her ass cheeks clench each time.

"Hold that position for me as you think about why you're about to receive a dozen swats and how they are delaying the fun we could be having now, wench."

Both of them were enjoying the hell out of this, though.

Kristoffer wouldn't need to restrain her unless she was unable to maintain her position without too much movement, at least until her ass began to sting and burn too much. Oh, yes, how he planned to make *those* muscles dance. Lifting the crinoline petticoat and skirt up to reveal even more of her backside, he applied a few light warm-up taps to bring the blood to the surface in preparation.

Quickly, without warning, he lifted the paddle and landed it firmly on her left cheek. "Count for me, bar wench."

"One, Sir."

"In German." She'd told him about taking a semester of German in college and ought to at least remember the basics of counting, he would expect.

"*Eins, Herr.*" He grinned.

Slap!

"*Zwei! Danke, Herr.*"

'Thank you, Sir?' Nice touch.

Seeing her left cheek begin to pinken, his next blow fell to the right one followed by another on the same side in quick succession. She continued to count and thank him for each one. The next three fell squarely across both cheeks in the same spots he'd hit before. The four holes were making nice marks, indeed—sometimes whole and other times crescents, depending on how the flat beer flight tray connected with her not-so-flat ass. She'd want to see them later, no doubt, so he pulled out his phone and took a picture. Even though his phone camera wasn't connected to his cloud, he made a mental note to erase it before the image accidentally made it into the wrong hands. This sight was for his eyes only.

The eighth blow fell a little lower, where her thighs met her ass. Her uncharacteristic groan made him pause, and he watched as she lifted her torso off the chaise. Apparently, her movement had twisted the skewers. He grinned. She'd lost her composure and hadn't held position. "Tsk, tsk, *fräulein*. This session is intended to teach you to control your body and mind. You now force me to add two more swats for moving without permission, as I try to drive home this important lesson."

The removal of the clamps would become more painful with time, but he had a paddling to finish first.

"We're more than halfway through, *if* you don't incur any more infractions."

To make sure she wasn't afraid to end the scene for fear of disappointing him, he advised, "Sprite, if you are beyond your pain limit and don't use your safeword, I would be terribly disappointed. Are we clear that would not be acceptable?"

She nodded her head. "*Ja, Herr!*"

"Tell me what pain level you are now."

"*Drei, Herr.*"

Only a three? Not even close. Returning his attention to her now-reddened ass, he delivered without hesitation one more blow to each cheek.

"*Neun und zehn, Herr.*" She paused to take a breath before adding a thank you.

He smiled as he lifted the beer flight paddle for the next swat, which landed squarely across her upper thighs. But he heard no number.

"What are we forgetting, *fräulein?*"

"I know I'm supposed to count out loud, Roar, *Herr*...but I can't remember the number for eleven in German."

"I'm happy to help. It's *elf*." Ironic that his little sprite hadn't remembered that word, given his nickname for her. "What's the highest number you can count to in German?"

"*Zwanzig.*"

Twenty? Now to make this even more interesting. "Very well. I will be lenient and give you permission to lapse into English when necessary until we reach the maximum number of earned swats."

"*Danke, Herr!*" Her relief was evident as she accepted his offer, but it would be short-lived.

He grinned, even though she couldn't see his face. "*However...*" He let the word hang in the air a moment for maximum effect and watched her body stiffen. "*...only* those swats in which you use the correct German word will be counted. But I am not unreasonable, so I will not exceed *zwanzig*, the highest number you remember in the language."

"*Danke, Herr.* Um, you are very kind." She didn't seem upset at all that he'd potentially added more swats, but he didn't know how well she could speak German, either.

Perhaps he needed to switch things up now, in case they were nearing the end of the paddling.

Kristoffer stepped over to the dresser, lifted the towel, and picked up a new implement. He wondered how she felt about this one. Well, he was about to find out.

Pamela waited in anticipation of the remaining swats. What a creative and innovative Dom she had. That beer flight paddle had become an instantaneous favorite. Surely she'd demonstrated to him how well she could handle it, too.

Her backside burned, but she was far from her pain limit. Not even the bamboo nipple clamps hurt, except for the time she'd twisted one. Of course, that was because her nipples were numb. The pain for them would come later.

A minute must have passed, and she wondered what he was waiting for. She used the time to refresh her memory about the remaining German numbers. If she could count in German, she had four swats left, but because she didn't know the number for twelve, either, that would mean five to go. If she missed too many others, she wouldn't be able to sit for a while. Fortunately, for most of the remaining numbers after twelve, she only had to add -*zehn* to the ending of the root number.

But what was the blasted German word for twelve?

A higher-pitched swish of air told her he'd changed implements even before the leather slapped against her burning cheeks. She squealed in pain, and her upper body jerked in a futile attempt to escape. The cursed nipple clamps caught in the velvet fabric of the chaise and pulled at her tender flesh.

Sweat broke out on her forehead. She took a slow, deep breath to regain composure.

"I didn't hear you."

Because I didn't say anything. Dammit! What's the word I need?

She gave up. "I'm sorry, Sir. I can't remember the number for twelve either."

"*Zwölf,* for future reference."

Zwölf! That's it! He'd retained his German better than she had. Not knowing she'd be in a German costume tonight, he couldn't have brushed up on the numbers beforehand, although she now wished she had.

And what implement was he using on her now? Not a cane, but definitely thinner than a tawse. A riding crop maybe? Not her favorite by a long shot, but this session was purely a fun roleplay, not one requiring discipline, which lessened the sting a bit.

The next blow landed across her upper thighs, jarring her again, although she managed to move very little. She eked out her thank you in German, followed by "*Dreizehn, Herr.*" Another swat landed squarely across her butt's curve making her want him inside her so badly. Would this be the night?

Focus!

"*Vierzehn. Danke, Herr.*" Her voice was barely above a whisper as she fought to regain her composure. The sting was slow to subside in any of the places he'd struck her with the crop.

"What pain level are you now, Sprite?"

"*Vier, Herr.*"

"Shall we continue?"

"Oh, *ja, Herr.*" *I want to get this over with.* If she'd paid better attention in her German classes in college, she'd be finished. Instead, she still had at least two more to go—*auf Deutsch!*

Steeling herself to remain absolutely, perfectly still this time, she breathed in through her nose and exhaled slowly though her mouth.

Swat!

Once again, the thin leather landed on her rounded flesh, in almost the exact same spot. The sting was becoming unbearable, but she had this.

"*Fünfzehn!*" She'd always loved the way the word felt on her lips. One more, and she'd be done. But the words barely came out in a squeak this time.

The swishing sound of the riding crop sailing toward her made her hold her breath. He seemed in a hurry to complete the final count.

Swat!

"*Vielen Dank, mein Herr!* That's *sechzehn!*" She thanked him profusely for speeding it up, even though she didn't think tonight's session was intended for anything other than having a good time and celebrating. Still, she was thankful this part of the scene would soon be over.

His hand touched her left butt cheek and squeezed. Hard. Not expecting that, she moaned and then fought to regulate her breathing. The pain heightened as he squeezed her other cheek. They *were* finished, weren't they?

"You've been such a good girl for me, how would you like two more swats as a reward using the beer flight paddle? I could tell how much you enjoyed it."

Confused, but excited at the same time, she prepared to tell him yes when his finger slid between her folds. "So wet. Should I take that as a yes?"

"*Ja, Herr! Bitte!*" He knew what she loved.

Because her butt was even more sensitive now that he'd brought more blood flow to the surface, not to mention the soreness of where the riding crop had struck her a minute ago, these swats would be delicious.

Instead of delivering them, though, he stroked her clit. Feeling his fingers there, she nearly came. Would he make love to her soon? Her butt rose in invitation, and she moaned.

So close.

So wet.

So ready.

A foil wrapper ripped open, and his penis probed against the opening of her vagina. She hadn't expected their first time to be like this, but didn't care. Having him inside her was all she wanted right now.

Fighting the urge to push against him for fear of further aggravating her nipples or getting out of position, she braced her hands on the floor. His cock spread her open more, inching inside—until she heard a plopping noise.

What the—?

When the vibrations began, she clenched her fists. He'd made her think he was sheathing his cock with a condom when he'd only intended to stick a vibrating egg inside her?

The man loved his mindfucks. And her mind had been sufficiently blown this time, as always—although he'd have to work hard to top the wax and ice scene.

She sighed, but the vibrations soon ramped up her excitement again. She hadn't been given permission to come—and to avoid another rice counting consequence or worse, she'd endure the last two blows with the damned egg thrumming inside her.

The next swat came from the beer flight paddle she now loved immensely. It landed over her vagina, pressing the egg against her G-spot ever so briefly. "Oh!" Her entire body felt electrified. She wasn't sure if she was supposed to count still, but once she regained her senses, she did so anyway. What number were they on?

"*Achtzehn, Herr! Danke schön!*"

His chuckle made her smile in the hope that he would deliver the final swat with a little more force and give her that thrill again.

But his words dampened her joy. "Sorry, Sprite. That was actually number seventeen, not eighteen. You'll have to backtrack in your numbering, and I'll keep trying to deliver your two reward swats until I receive the appropriate responses."

The vibration of the egg increased and took her breath away just before he delivered another swat, this time closer to her clitoris, landing in such a way as to have her clit in the center of one of the holes, accentuating the pressure and excitement.

He still hadn't given her permission to come. Would she be able to hold on much longer?

Count! "*Siebenzehn, Herr!*"

Slap!

The final blow landed seconds later directly against the egg again. Rather than lift the paddle off, he pressed it firmly and held it against her G-spot. Her legs shook uncontrollably, the nipple clamps twisting in delicious waves of pain.

"Ah-ah-ah-*achtzehn, Herr! Ohhh!*" She screamed the last word as the pressure built to an unbearable peak. She couldn't hold back any longer. "*Bitte.* Please, Sir! May I come, Roar, *Herr?*" Her mind fractured between the two languages, but she couldn't form a coherent thought any longer if her life depended on it. She prepared to ride the crest of what would be an amazing orgasm.

Until the pressure stopped, along with the egg's vibrations. Not the answer she'd hoped for. "I'll determine when the time is right for your release, Sprite."

Bastard. She knew that word meant the same in both languages but gave it a German accent in her thoughts.

Roar's hand lightly stroked her burning ass, so lightly he caused goose bumps to rise, only bringing the pain to the forefront and intensifying it. Was he trying to dampen her enthusiasm? Or test how far she'd go before using her safeword?

I want my ultimate reward—an orgasm!

The timer dinged.

"Let me help you up, maid." He grasped her around the waist and did most of the work, careful not to drag her nipples against the chaise.

She swayed as dizziness overcame her, whether from the rapid change in position or her near orgasm, she wasn't certain. He didn't let her go until she nodded that she would be able to stand on her own.

The loss of his body heat signaled that he had walked away, but she didn't turn or lift her gaze to see what he had in mind next. His silk tie landed on the bed, followed by his suit coat, shirt, and slacks.

He seemed to be in a hurry. Did that mean... He faced her and pressed his lips to hers. All too soon, he pulled away. "Be brave for me, Sprite."

The moment she'd been dreading had arrived. He reached down to rub his thumb over one tortured nipple. Could she take the pain without screaming like a baby—or a banshee?

"You've handled these bamboo clamps very well for the first time. I'm proud of you, Sprite."

The euphoric rise in emotions at his praise gave her a natural high. She still wasn't sure if pain might be her thing, but she enjoyed it with him.

"Brace yourself."

Before she could even catch her breath, first one pair of skewers then the other was simultaneously released. Oddly enough, there was no pain at first. "Sir, please..." She had no idea if she wanted to beg him to stop or to do something more, but when the blood rushed back into both nipples all at once, she screamed despite her best intentions.

"Oh, fuck! Fuck, fuck, fuck!" *Did I just say fuck in front of Roar? Yeah, four times, I think.* A burning sensation blazed through her chest and into her shoulders before making a beeline into her genitals.

"That's it. Take the pain for me, Sprite," he coaxed, gently rubbing her sore nipples.

Suddenly, something snapped in her head in a moment of total clarity. "I will gladly take the pain from you, Sir." Her words made no sense, yet accurately described her feeling.

He tilted his head and furrowed his brows, but continued to play with her nipples until the pain was replaced by excitement. Before she could analyze anything further, Roar sheathed himself in the condom he must have opened a moment ago.

He pressed her body backward, easing her onto the length of the chaise lounge. The scratchy crinoline grated against her sore butt in a delicious way.

"I promise our next time will be slower, but I need to be inside you, Sprite. Spread yourself open for me."

Yes! Finally!

She smiled up at him. The last thing she wanted right now was a slow hand—or cock, for that matter—after waiting so long for this moment. As she drew up her knees, he pulled out the egg and let it drop to the floor. Propping himself on his elbows, he pressed his cock against her. This time she knew it was Roar and not some inanimate object.

"Eyes on me, Sprite." She opened them and stared directly into his. "Don't ever forget that I love you. This is right and we're exactly where we're supposed to be."

She nodded. "Always."

His delicious weight came down on her. Her nipples stung at the friction his chest hairs created when he drove himself into her in one fluid movement. She gasped. Her well-spanked butt rubbed against the crinolines, adding to her state of frenzy.

So full. Even better than she'd imagined.

"You feel so good wrapped around me. Hang on, Sprite. I am about to send you over the edge. But you are *not* come until I say you can."

"Yes, Sir."

He withdrew almost to the tip and rammed himself inside her again. Soon, they found a pace that left them both breathing hard. Despite being on the edge of exploding, she waited.

"Wrap your legs around my waist." The position tilted her pelvis, and he slipped his finger between their bodies to rub her clit.

"Come for me, Sprite."

He began pumping in and out of her again. In a perfect storm of sensations, the combination of his cock pressed against her G-spot and his finger against her clit made her world explode. "I'm coming!" She actually saw stars! "Oh, God! Don't stop! Come inside me, Sir!"

She realized she was topping him—*literally* from the bottom this time—but perhaps the infraction would be forgiven with him caught up in delivering his powerful thrusts. Suddenly, what could only be described as a roar erupted from his mouth as he came inside her. His orgasm seemed unending as he continued to pound into her causing her hypersensitive clit to protest, but she wouldn't ask him to stop. He needed this release.

When the world ceased spinning, a million emotions bombarded her, and she began to shake—arms, legs, her very core. Tears swam in her eyes.

He withdrew from her. "Satisfied tears, I hope," he said.

She nodded her head. She'd just had an amazing orgasm following the most intense, mind-blowing scene with Roar. "Very satisfied."

He kissed her. "That was incredible for me, too. I need to dispose of the condom. Are you okay? Do you need to go to the bathroom first?" She shook her head and watched him walk away, his tight buttocks a beauty to behold. He ought to be a model in the anatomy class at The Denver Academy.

Then again, no. I don't want to share him.

He returned with a washcloth to clean her off, then helped her to her feet before slowly undressing her, scooping her into his arms, and carrying her to the bed. "We're going to have aftercare in bed tonight." He pulled the sheet and duvet up to her shoulders.

Pamela closed her eyes and smiled, waiting for him to join her. He crawled into bed and pulled her against his rock-hard chest. His arms around her upper body wrapped her in a cocoon of sated bliss.

When he didn't speak, she opened her eyes and turned toward him. The smile on his face warmed her heart.

"'Thank you are probably the two lamest words right now, Kristoffer, but that was amazing."

"Sprite, I'd hoped to make love with you the first time in this bed and a lot slower, but the intensity of your surrender and trust blew me away."

"You won't hear any complaints from me, Sir. I think we were both ready. Waiting another instant wouldn't have shown us living in the moment as we're striving to do."

"Nice try, Sprite, but there will be times when you're very much in the moment and wanting to come and I'll delay your orgasm even longer."

She groaned inside, not sure she could have held out much longer tonight.

"Even before sex, Sprite, you were taking everything to a new level, open to anything I wanted to try. Thank you."

She grinned. "I think what you're describing was a big reason for my eye-opening moment."

"Which moment is that?"

She still had no words to describe it, but wanted to reveal what had happened in that flash of an instant. "After you removed the clamps, when you asked me to take the pain for you, something was branded in my brain. Not that I was simply taking the pain of the bamboo clamps, but that..." She chewed on her lower lip.

"You knew you were safe with me, Sprite, which helped you let go like that."

"I suppose, but..." What had she been on the edge of realizing before her world exploded? "Maybe I..." *Oh! What* was *it?* The self-realization lay just beyond the reach of her mind.

"Maybe what?"

She groaned. "I don't know! My mind is mush. It's right on the tip of my tongue, but I can't find the words."

He leaned forward, kissed her, and then pulled her head into the crook of his shoulder. They lay in silence for an undetermined time, his hand playing with her sore nipples.

"I'm going to become the best submissive I can be under your guidance and sure hand."

"You're already the best you can be, but I know over the years we'll be able to—"

"Tonight started out like other scenes, but ended so…differently." Why was she so spacy?

"Well, we did have sex for the first time."

"Even before that. It happened right after you removed the clamps. I'm having trouble putting it into words," she admitted with frustration.

"Could it have anything to do with this?" He lifted her left hand and indicated the bracelet he'd placed there earlier this evening.

Had his profession of love been the thing to take her trust to a whole new level? *Yes!* In her heart, she knew that had to be the difference.

"I think that could be it!"

"Go back to the scene in your mind. At that point you say your eyes were opened, what were you thinking? Feeling?"

She thought back. "I was elated that the nipple clamps were about to come off."

He chuckled. "Then what?"

"You asked if I could take the pain for you and—" She bolted upright in the bed and faced him. "My God! That's it!"

He looked puzzled. "Explain."

"Everything about tonight was different. I focused better—still not perfectly, but better. I trusted you completely. I surrendered my entire self to you!"

He smiled. "That you did. I could see it in your demeanor and body language."

"Before I met you, I'd only been playacting at BDSM. But the level of trust I've felt for you from the beginning—from that reassuring nod during the anatomy class to the way you took me on for training with the sole purpose of meeting my needs—you've always assured me you would take care of me and my needs." The happiness in his eyes warmed her heart.

"But this time, Sir, the pain was different, too. Even though I didn't really enjoy the crop, you wanted me to experience it and I did so for you. Only I didn't just take the pain *for* you, I took it *from* you as well."

He eased himself onto his elbow and propped his head in the palm of his hand. "I'm not sure I follow. I thought this epiphany happened when the clamps came off."

She groaned. "It's so hard to explain. It was the strangest sensation, but yes, in that instant right after the clamps were removed—when an intense wave of pain coursed through my body as if on an electrical current—I visualized me drawing *your* pain away from you and into me. The years of pain, of loss, of loneliness. *All* your suffering absorbed into me."

She lay down again and scooted closer, cupping his cheek. "Kristoffer, I can never know what you've been through, but if what I felt was even a tenth of what it must have been for you, I—"

Tears welled in his eyes. She wasn't sure she understood it still, but couldn't continue. She'd made him cry, not her intention at all.

"Sprite, saying that you surrendered yourself to me as a receptacle for my misery, draining my body of those emotions, well, that's just about the most incredible thing a submissive can do for her Dom—or a woman for her man."

She stroked his face from temple to jaw. He did understand. This man meant more to her than life itself. "I've hated seeing you aching, Sir, and being unable to comfort you."

"You have no idea how much comfort you've given me, Sprite, especially tonight."

"That pleases me. I wanted to open you up, reach inside, and remove all the pain as a surgeon might excise a tumor. I hated watching you hold yourself back from experiencing life, especially during those first weeks we were together." Pamela took a cleansing breath. "Seeing you experience life, love, and joy again makes me ecstatic."

She pulled his head toward her and kissed him. When they separated, she said, "When I heard those beautiful words 'I love you' tonight I knew we'd make it and eventually move in together. Just not *this* soon." They both grinned. "You've become insatiable for spontaneity, Sir."

"Because you keep me on my toes—and in the moment, Sprite."

She grew serious again. "Back to what happened tonight. I think a part of me still wonders how we'll ever pull this off. Love is grand, but we have so many hurdles to overcome, not the least of which for me is that you might change your mind over time and regret or feel guilty about making a commitment to me. I think that's one reason our mantra resonates so well with me. That niggling doubt kept me from completely surrendering myself to you because I feared you might leave me one day. Until tonight."

He seemed to be the one at a loss for words now. Had she said too much? She was aware she wasn't making total sense and probably should have journaled about it before trying to explain it to him. But she didn't want to wait for fear she might lose the ability to tap into that feeling if she waited until tomorrow.

This was what their aftercare time was for, after all—expressing their feelings and insights about a scene.

Perhaps she should start again. "I saw your pain leaving your body on a wave of raw, dark red color and pouring into me. But instead of making me weaker, I grew stronger." She glanced away. "I know I'm rambling. I don't know how else to describe it." She met his gaze. "Suffice it to say, I'm here for you, Kristoffer. I am yours. Forever." She held up her infinity bracelet for emphasis.

"Pamela," he said in a strained whisper, "I never asked you to take on my pain. I'd never inflict that on anyone."

"Don't you see? We're one now. Your pain is mine and vice versa, Kristoffer."

She didn't want to admit it, but she no longer felt she had to compete for his affections with Tori. Each woman held a special and separate place in his heart. Pamela would love Kristoffer in the present and for every moment the universe gave them together. She wouldn't take a single second for granted.

"Thank you, Pamela. I'm about as blessed as any man has ever been. Together, we're a force to be reckoned with. Nothing can stop us once we set our minds on what we want."

"And our hearts, bodies, and minds know what we need long before we do, sometimes."

CHAPTER TWENTY-TWO

The next month passed in a whirlwind for Pamela. Children's Hospital hired her and she had joined the staff two weeks ago today. She worked long, not always predictable hours—this evening being no exception. She and Kristoffer were supposed to go out for a special dinner tonight, but she was over two hours late, and he'd changed their reservations to a place closer to the hospital in Aurora. Otherwise, they'd have been eating at ten at night by the time she arrived home and went back out.

He'd tried to insist on picking her up at the hospital, but it would just require him to backtrack, so she'd brought her alpha personality to the fore and told him to meet her there. As she parked and made her way to the restaurant, she made some mental notes about things she needed to do before leaving for Afghanistan next Tuesday. As luck would have it, right after she accepted the job at Children's, the humanitarian physicians group she worked for had let her know there was an opening for her to complete her contract starting mid-August. While she'd informed the Children's Plastics Department's Chief of Staff about the possibility during the interview process, the timing could have been better.

To keep them from regretting their decision to hire her, she'd been working longer-than-expected hours, cramming as much training and orientation as possible in at the Aurora hospital campus. Her caseload would remain small, mostly handling emergencies, until she returned to Denver in September.

When she walked into the darkened restaurant, it took her eyes a minute to adjust. She gave the hostess the Larson name and was shown to where Kristoffer waited. He stood and gave her a hug and kiss before they sat across from each other near the window.

After ordering, they caught up on their days.

Before Kristoffer entered her life, she'd have worked, gone home, slept, and then awakened the next day to repeat it all *ad nauseam*. Having someone else to consider helped her find balance in her life. Not to mention that he nurtured her by making sure she ate, exercised, and slept. While all aftereffects from her fever in March had disappeared, her intense work schedule exhausted her some days. Kristoffer seemed to know her moods and when she needed more rest and care.

She tried not to feel guilty that she wasn't doing as much for him at the moment. All couples went through periods where one gave more than the other—and she'd make up for it when her career settled down. He insisted on seeing to her needs right now—needs she'd put on a back burner for a long time.

Coming home and playing out a scene with him helped her shed the stress and sometimes sadness of the day and maintain her focus strictly on the two of them during their time together. The difference in her life from before and after her sexy Dom stole her heart amazed her when she thought back on the last decade.

Most nights, they made love after their kink scene. Afterward, they always fell asleep in each other's arms. Despite the demands of her new job, she felt like they were enjoying their honeymoon.

"Why don't we go hiking Saturday?" he suggested. "The weather's supposed to be hot in the city, so we can cool off up there. Or maybe even drive out to Independence Pass, hike a while, and have dinner in Aspen."

"Either sounds good to me."

They continued eating until halfway through their meal when something caught her eye outside the window. She glanced out to see a balloon with a long string float by. If the windows had been opened, she'd have been able to reach out and grab it and possibly return it to whoever lost it.

She leaned over to look down to the first-floor level, but there was no one standing there.

"What's the matter?" Kristoffer asked.

Pamela pointed to the balloon that was now much higher, floating over the street. "That pink balloon. I don't see anyone it might have escaped from."

Kristoffer stared at the balloon a long while then seemed to shake himself out of his reverie. A few minutes later, he remarked, "The sun's setting."

She looked out again and watched it sink. "Gorgeous."

"Mm-hmm."

She turned to find Kristoffer staring intently at her, rather than the horizon.

"I'm looking forward to the rest of the evening with you, Sprite."

She smiled. "I'm wide awake for a change."

He grinned back. "I'm sure I'd have no trouble reviving you, if need be. You usually catch your second wind after dinner and some couch time. Well, when you don't fall asleep on me." He grinned.

Too soon, his smile faded. Intuition told her he had something on his mind—most likely worrying about her imminent departure. Her flight to Kabul in six days weighed heavily on them both.

"I miss having you all to myself, but..." He shrugged. "I know you're doing important work." He glanced out the window in the direction the balloon had drifted away.

What was he going to do when she was gone for a little more than a month? Tomorrow, she'd call Gunnar and suggest he keep Kristoffer busy with work or whatever while she was away.

She became his focus again when he faced her. "Promise your Dom you won't wear yourself out before you even leave for Afghanistan."

If he knew what kind of pace she'd have at the hospital overseas... This was a picnic compared to that.

She reached across the table to squeeze his right hand, noticing their love bracelets shining in the candlelight. Remembering last night and how he'd restrained her to his antique bed, she grinned.

"What's so amusing?"

"I was thinking what FarFar's reaction might be if he saw how you restrained me to the Larson family heirloom last night."

He shook his head, and his grin widened. "And here I thought I'd broken you of the habit of letting your mind wander, although that you're remembering a time spent with me makes up a little bit for your lack of being present in the moment tonight."

"But I am present! Now we can talk about all the delicious things you did last night. However, it might make me crazy wanting to get you home again to see what you might have planned for later."

"No, Sprite. That's *not* living in the moment, and you know it. Now, you're musing about what *might* happen in the future."

She sighed dramatically. "I suppose you'll just have to continue to work on my focus, Sir."

"My pleasure."

The remainder of their meal was leisurely, sprinkled with small talk about how she was fitting in at Children's with the other staff. But she didn't want to waste their precious time together talking shop.

The topic of her trip to Afghanistan didn't come up, although he must also be thinking about it. While she'd only be working four weeks, she'd have at least three days travel both to and from, adding nearly another week apart.

Kristoffer had made it clear he worried about her going. She had concerns this time, too, because she'd be based at a trauma center in a more remote region. Best not to talk about it, or they'd both have indigestion.

To his credit, he hadn't forbidden her to go. He understood that she was a woman of her word, like him. She'd made a commitment to serve three full months there last winter and spring, and she intended to fulfill that contract.

But she'd promised him not to sign up for any additional assignments with the organization once this one was completed. Their upcoming separation would be difficult for her as well. Children's Hospital would satisfy her need to help children both here in Colorado as well as on the hospital's annual trip to Guatemala. That would meet her humanitarian needs and her desire to serve those in poverty.

"Oh, I spoke today with the doctors in Cincinnati. Fakhira's family wanted me to know she has come through her latest surgery with flying colors."

"Wonderful! I know you've been worried about her."

She nodded. "I feel personally responsible for her in some ways, so not being actively involved in her treatment has been frustrating. However, she's in excellent hands."

"You care a lot about your patients—but don't set yourself up for burnout. Not everyone can be saved. I'm sure you're going to face a lot of heartache in Afghanistan again this time."

"I know. But it's hard to be objective and keep your distance when working with such innocent lives." She squeezed his hand. "You help me leave it all behind when I come home. Thank you."

He waved off her words. "That's what Doms do. Would you like to go visit Fakhira sometime?"

"I'd love to! Maybe we can get away one weekend this fall. She still has a long road ahead and a number of surgeries and procedures to come, but Fakhira's a survivor."

The server brought them the dessert they'd ordered to share— molten chocolate cake. Kristoffer scooped up the first spoonful and held it out for her to eat.

She opened her mouth, maintaining eye contact, and a mixture of cold vanilla ice cream, hot fudge sauce, and a bit of chocolate cake hit her taste buds all at once. "Mmm. Oh, my God, that's sinfully good."

"You're healthy and take care of yourself, so you need to indulge once in a while. That's all that matters." They hadn't been working out together as much as they had before she joined the hospital staff. Taking time to go to the gym for a swim or a workout stole from the limited time the two of them had together at home. But they tried to get there once a week.

Leaning forward on his forearms, his voice grew husky. "Tonight's plans won't involve that kind of workout. But I should warn you that you might not want your stomach to be too full."

Her body tingled with excitement and anticipation.

"I can't wait to see what you have planned."

Kristoffer fiddled with the stem of his water goblet, lost in thought a moment before meeting her gaze. He seemed about to say something monumental, but out of the blue, asked, "How would you like to travel to Norway next summer? I'd love to show you one of my all-time favorite places on earth."

Not at all what she'd expected, but exciting nonetheless. "I'd love to! With enough notice, I ought to be able to take a couple weeks off at the hospital, especially if we delay leaving until after my first full year on staff." Scandinavia had been on her bucket list forever, as were a number of other places. The thought of exploring the sights with Kristoffer made her incredibly pleased she'd put that trip off instead of traveling alone. Sharing it with someone who knew Norway intimately would make the experience wonderful, but having him with her anywhere made it better.

"There's something else I've been wanting to talk with you about." Ah, so there was another matter making him a little nervous. "I'll try not to make this as long as my last speech." He smiled.

Sounded serious. The last time he'd given a speech, he'd proposed they enter into a committed relationship and move in together, exchanging bracelets as a token of their love. He seemed even more nervous tonight. What could he possibly say to top that? Unless, maybe, he was ready for some kind of ceremony to publicly declare their intentions before friends and family.

Stop guessing and wait!

"Pamela, you've become the most important person in my life, especially after agreeing to a permanent relationship with me. But I've given it a lot of thought over the past month."

But? Was he having reservations?

"Something's missing."

The blood rushing through her ears must have distorted his words. She reached for her water glass and took two large gulps.

He reached for her hands and pulled them toward the middle of the table, but continued to hold on. "Nothing would mean as much to me as you surrendering to me so completely…" She squeezed his hands to encourage him to say whatever seemed to be troubling him. "…that you would consider wearing my collar."

She had no words. Kristoffer wanted to collar her—so soon? The honor of having a Dom, or for some a Master, want to take it to that level usually came after being together and building on their relationship for years.

"For me, your collar would be as binding as a marriage. There will be no walking away on my part. I'm talking *forever*."

His declaration wasn't so unlike the one he'd made at her dad's, but in so many ways, it touched her more. Doms didn't take collaring lightly, and neither did submissives. That moment when he placed the symbol of his love, protection, and devotion around her neck would be the ultimate tribute. He had chosen her to be his one and only submissive for all time, because Kristoffer did not go back on his promises.

His.

This decision meant much more to her—and to many in the community—than would a marriage proposal or wedding ring offered by the same person. For him to make such a commitment made her love him even more.

While she tried to process what he'd asked, he grew more serious and continued. "I know this probably seems sudden to you, but I first got the idea when we exchanged these bracelets a month ago. Something you said made me perceive your bracelet as a mini collar. I've been talking with Gunnar about it, and he reiterated that the bond between a Dom and his or her collared submissive is stronger than any other—except perhaps for fellow comrades in combat."

The analogy seemed odd until she remembered Gunnar's military background. She could easily see how the level of trust, love, and protection among their fellow troops must be at their greatest during a combat situation.

"I'm blown away and honored that you'd ask. But do you think we're ready for such a step in our relationship? In some ways, I feel we're barely brushed the surface of what it will ultimately be."

"Thank you. I know we've already made a commitment to be together for the rest of our lives, but through the ritual of collaring and all that entails, we can seal our lives in a bond that would be unlike any I've ever had." He loosened his tie, as if breathing had suddenly become difficult. "You are the only woman I've ever asked to wear my collar. And the only one I ever plan to ask."

He hadn't asked Tori in the fourteen years they spent playing together before the accident?

She smiled. For him to have found a unique way to make her his one and only in this revered and esteemed manner tempted her to agree on the spot, even though she had never before given a thought to being collared by anyone. If entered into solemnly and truthfully by both parties, this could take their relationship to a much deeper level—exponentially so.

Marriage wasn't an option for them, and neither wanted to put their lives on hold, hovering like vultures over Tori, waiting for her body to finally give up the fight. What better way could there be for them to live in the present, move step-by-step together into the future, and cement their relationship more solidly than for her to accept his collar?

Looking into his intense blue eyes flustered her, so she closed hers to focus on hearing his words before trying to formulate her response.

"Pamela, if you agree to taking this step, we'd have a special ceremony with Gunnar officiating in his dungeon. I'd present you with a special necklace I've had created especially for you, a symbol of your surrender to me and my acceptance of that surrender as my collared submissive."

He took a deep breath before continuing. "I don't want you to accept my proposal out of fear that, if you don't, our current relationship will end. Banish such thoughts immediately. If being collared isn't right for you—now or far into the future—simply say no. No matter what you decide, I'll continue to love, cherish, and protect you as long as I live. We have the rest of our lives to find ways to declare our love, trust, and commitment."

"How would our relationship change afterward?"

"That's for us to discuss and negotiate. In our case, we seem to gravitate toward a Dom/sub dynamic, but I don't see this collar stopping at our BDSM relationship. It would encompass the whole of our lives together."

"If I allowed you to collar me, I'd take it as seriously, too." She nibbled her lower lip, unsure how to say this. "I suppose my biggest worry is about how it would affect my continuing to have autonomy over myself in matters of career."

"I'd expect you to include me in discussions before making any major decisions that might affect our lives together, but you would have the ultimate say in matters concerning your career."

Such as her going to Afghanistan, no doubt? She glanced down, knowing she hadn't consulted with him before agreeing to take the assignment, much less asked for permission to go. However, he'd known of her passionate mission from the first time they met, when she'd shared details of her work in Gunnar's boardroom on the day she'd pleaded her case with the Forseti Group to help Fakhira. And he'd become even more aware of her commitment to humanitarian causes since they'd been seeing each other.

Even though he'd just said he wouldn't impose his will on her when it came to matters of her career, without question, she wouldn't make such a decision without consulting with him in the future. They were partners in life now.

"Eyes on me." Her pulse raced as she met his gaze. "I'm only asking for one thing—the complete and unconditional surrender of your heart."

Silly man. "I thought you knew you already have that."

He smiled for the first time since this conversation had begun. Even the server had steered clear of their table, possibly sensing something monumental was being discussed here. And she'd be right.

"Something I am eternally grateful for, but the vows I intend to make as I place my collar around your slim, beautiful neck should give *you* an even deeper assurance of my pledges to you and that we belong to one another." He tapped her bracelet. "This came with many promises from my heart. However, my collar will not only set those promises in stone, because you will wear it for the rest of your life, but will help us take this relationship much further. Deeper."

In her heart and mind, she saw no reason to deny his request. However, he continued before she could speak.

"I don't want your answer until you return from Afghanistan, because this isn't something to rush into or take lightly. I've been doing a lot of research on this commitment, and I'll be e-mailing you some blogs from other submissives sharing their deliberations as they decided whether to accept their Dom's or Master's collar, the rituals they used, and their lives after the ceremony. But you need to see both sides, so I'll also send some articles from those whose experiences weren't as positive as they had hoped. If you have time and energy, I encourage you to do some research on your own, as well. But I'm sure your time will be limited."

She nodded. After her shift, she normally crashed into bed a few hours then went back to work. She planned to fit in time for exercise and healthier meals, so that she wouldn't come home sick and exhausted the way she had the last time. Kristoffer had promised to give her self-care assignments as well.

"About the only good thing I can say about our separation is that it gives you a chance to be apart from me while objectively weighing the advantages and disadvantages of your decision."

She'd never seen such a ceremony before, but had spoken with collared submissives at the Masters at Arms Club. What struck her most was the peace of mind each had expressed feeling after being collared. Having never trusted anyone enough to want to be bound to him in such a permanent way, the thought of being collared simply hadn't crossed her mind.

Until now.

She opened her mouth to speak, but he held up his hand to halt her. "One more thing—a very important piece of information to consider." After taking another sip of his water, he added, "If you agree to wear my collar, I will make it absolutely clear this is for life.

Obtaining a divorce from a husband would be a hundred times easier than erasing your promises to commit to being my collared submissive."

"I'll do whatever I can to assure you of my lifelong commitment."

"Including having my name tattooed on your body?"

She smiled. "I'd permanently wear your name in a heartbeat. You might recall I've been inked before."

"Would you be agreeable to altering the existing tattoo if that's what I wanted you to do?"

"Yes. The key inked on my backside was significant to me at the time, but no longer bears the same importance." The door she wanted unlocked had been opened when Kristoffer came into her life.

"All right, but you *will* take the time I ask for you to think this over before we take this permanent step. Committing yourself to someone forever and in every way isn't something you jump into."

"Fine. I'll do as you say and give it a lot of thought first." She was certain that the pro column would far outweigh the con one. She squeezed his hand. "No matter what, Sir, I want you to know I am honored that you would find a way to join us together that is unmistakably different than the way you committed to Tori. Having that unique bond would be at the top of my long list of pros."

"You two are nothing alike, yet you both chose to love me." He picked up his water goblet and indicated that she do the same. "I am the one who is honored—and humbled—by your devotion and love, my lady."

Tears stung her eyes as they clinked glasses and drank to the toast. "No more of that, or I won't be able to see to drive home."

"If you aren't able to drive, give me your keys." He held out his hand, but she waved it away.

"I'm fine. And I can't wait to get home so I can find out what else you have planned for me tonight."

Kristoffer followed Pamela's car back to the condo, keeping his focus on her and the road, while thoughts of what he'd proposed threatened to distract him. He probably should have waited to ask until just before she left, but his mind would have been too muddled to make any sense.

He clenched his jaw. Worry about her trip had consumed him since he'd heard she was leaving. Being supportive was bloody hard sometimes.

Had he made sense tonight? If not, they still had a few days to talk about it.

Tori's only remaining needs were physical, but Pamela's were emotional, spiritual, moral, physical—everything. She was vibrant, and their relationship could take any shape they chose as long as they worked at it.

Pamela's Jeep took their exit ramp, and he followed. Almost home. He had planned a scene meant to relieve her of any lingering stress from work—and to take his own mind off saying goodbye to her in the days ahead.

He pulled into the spot he'd been assigned in the parking garage for his second vehicle, now that Pamela had his premium one, and joined her at the elevator door. Unable to resist, he bent down and placed his lips on hers, but what was intended as a quick peck soon became an impassioned kiss.

When the elevator dinged, he pulled away. Her eyes sparkled even in the darkness. "You're always going to own my heart, Kristoffer Roar Larson, no matter what."

Her smile melted him even more than tonight's heat. "And you, mine, Sprite."

She cocked her head, fanning herself playfully. "Not to mention that you make me hot, my Lord."

He shook his head. His brat wanted to play tonight, apparently.

"While I'm preparing the scene in the bedroom, I want you to journal your initial thoughts and questions about what we discussed over dinner."

"Our trip to Norway next year? Can't that wait?" She tried to remain serious, but fought back a laugh even under his most intense glare.

He swatted her backside then kept his hand on her ass as he guided her into the elevator car. "I'll make another promise to you tonight—one you won't have a choice in."

"What's that, Sir?"

"Your ass will be much hotter before the night's over."

She grinned, her eyes dilating.

"If you must, Sir. How else will I learn?"

Each time she submitted to him, whether playfully like this or with great seriousness as she had so many times now, she filled more of the chasm that had once been his heart.

After opening the door to the foyer, he tried to ground her before she started her writing assignment. "If you have questions about the collaring proposal you haven't asked, write them down, and I'll answer as best I can over dinner tomorrow."

"Yes, Sir." She picked up her journal and pen from the coffee table and curled up on the sofa.

Inside the bedroom, he decided he wanted to make love to her more than play. He lit scented candles and turned on the lights to set the proper mood.

Unable to wait any longer, he walked into the living room and found her forehead scrunched as she thought about what to write. A Miles Davis track played on the stereo. *Perfect.*

He closed the space between them and reached for her pen. "You can finish tomorrow. There's something you and I started that can't wait."

He pulled her by the hand until she stood next to him. He was still dressed in his suit from dinner, and she in the dress she'd worn to work.

"But first, let's not waste such beautiful music." He pulled her into his embrace, and they swayed to the music, staring into each other's souls. When a Coltrane song came on, she closed her eyes and rested her cheek against his chest, but they continued to dance through several songs before he lowered the zipper of her dress. His hand stroked her back, unhooking her bra to get it out of the way.

"Mmm. I love when you touch me."

Kristoffer had lost all interest in whatever else he'd planned. Tonight, he wanted to make love to her. He pulled away and framed her face.

"Change of plans. Let's shower and go to bed. I need to be inside you."

She smiled up at him. "Sounds divine."

After a quick shower, they dried off, more or less, and tossed back the duvet. The foreplay in the bathroom made him that much more eager to stretch her out on the bed and love every inch of her beautiful body.

"Hands touching the headboard. Honor bondage." While there weren't places to grab onto, he wanted her to surrender to his touch rather than worry about pleasing him. He'd find his pleasure later.

Kristoffer stretched his body over the length of hers, propping his weight on his elbows. He dipped his head to kiss her lips and pulled her lower one with his teeth. She moaned.

Moving to her ear, he nibbled on her earlobe, and her hips bucked up in response.

Better.

He trailed tiny bites down her neck to the crook and across her shoulder before moving to the other shoulder and going up her neck again. This time when he tugged at her lower lip, she opened her mouth to invite him in.

But that wasn't what he wanted now. He maneuvered down the bed until he hovered over her breasts. Her buds were already swollen and probably super sensitive right now. He grinned as he lowered his mouth to one and kissed it before taking it between his teeth and pulling upward. Her back lifted off the bed to follow him when the pressure became too much, but he hadn't told her she couldn't move. Yet.

He let the nipple go with a plop and stared into her eyes. "Keep your back on the mattress, or I'll have to return to Plan A."

Not that he'd told her what that was. He trailed his finger lightly down the underside of her arm and continued downward to her hip. He eased to his side and played with the curls at the top of her mound. She maintained control of her body well this time. Teasing the area around her mound, he then stroked her thighs with his hand.

"Bend your left leg outward."

She granted him easier access, and using only his finger, he grazed her curls once more before leaning over, taking her nipple and areola into his mouth again. He flicked his tongue over the sensitive peak, his mouth continuing to lavish attention there while his hand explored her abdomen, belly button, and mound. When his middle finger slid along her cleft, he dipped his fingertip into her. So wet. But he was having too much fun with this slow exploration of her body. Pushing himself up to a seated position, he reached for a bolster pillow.

"Lift your hips." She did so, and he positioned it underneath. Crawling between her legs, he lowered his face and spread her folds open. Her lips had been shaved this morning, just the way he instructed her to keep them, which made going down on her that much hotter for him.

He dipped his head closer, closer, until just the tip of his tongue licked her up one side, across the top, and down the other. He pulled away and checked her. Hands fisted against the headboard, teeth nibbling on her lower lip, eyes clenched shut.

He grinned. Not ready yet.

Lowering his head to her again, he opened her labia wider again, and his tongue teased the less sensitive area of her clit, delved inside her vagina, and slid up to flick against her clit in earnest.

The mewling sounds she made might have brought Noma in here to investigate if he hadn't shut the bedroom door earlier. His right hand moved to where he could slip first one then two fingers inside her while he continued to torment her clit.

Her breathing grew more shallow and rapid as she came closer to the edge.

Stretching out over her again, he said, "Look at me."

Pamela opened her eyes, pleading with him to bring her relief.

"Soon, baby. Touch me." He'd have to put the condom on in a bit, because he wouldn't send her to Afghanistan with a baby growing inside her. But after she came home, he intended to talk to her about when would be a good time to get pregnant. He wanted a complete life with her, and the thought of having a little girl with strawberry blonde curls or a boy who reminded him of himself or Gunnar at that age, brought him up short.

Would she want kids? He'd never given it a lot of thought before, but then they'd only recently committed to each other in a relationship. Talk of babies could wait until after she accepted his collar.

She lowered her left hand and grasped his hard cock. Feeling her hand squeezing and stroking him brought Kristoffer to the edge, too. They were both so combustible that trying to take things slowly rarely met with success.

Unable to wait another minute to bury himself inside her, he reached onto the nightstand to grab a condom, sheathed his cock, and maneuvered himself over her. "Guide me inside with your hand."

Rising onto both elbows again, he waited. He wanted her juices to lubricate the condom. She pulled his cock toward her until the head was inside. She squeezed her vaginal muscles around him.

He hissed at the sensation, even with a condom on. "So tight."

Smiling, she slid his head in and out, going a couple of inches deeper every time. His hips moved to her rhythm. When his fingers played with her clit again, her breathing hitched, signaling that her orgasm was close.

Wanting to try a new position that would be much more likely to hit her G-spot consistently, he pulled out. "Turn over and get on all fours, Sprite, facing away from me."

She cocked her head then grinned as she quickly got into position. He knelt behind her, but quickly realized his little sprite's legs were much shorter than his. Taking another bolster pillow, he had her lift each knee one at a time to raise her to the right height. He'd have to invest in a wedge cushion if they wanted to try this again, but he was close enough now to make this work.

"Lower your head onto your arms."

Lining himself up at her opening, he held onto her hips as he entered her halfway, pulled out, and then thrust the rest of the way inside.

"Oh, Christ!"

Was that what he thought it was? He pulled out and rammed into her again, eliciting the same response. Definitely stimulating something. He developed a faster pace, and soon her words and sounds merged into incoherent noises that were all pleasure—for both of them.

Lying over her back, he reached between her legs and began stroking her clit, his cock still buried inside.

"Oh, yes! Please, don't stop!"

He grinned. Now to see how close she would get before she begged for release. Alternating positions, sometimes upright, others bent over her back, he pounded against the bundle of nerves inside before changing things up and stroking her clit into a frenzy.

"P-p-please, Sir! I can't wait any longer!"

"It will be even more incredible if you do."

She groaned in frustration.

He slapped her ass, and her muscles squeezed his cock. As he pumped in and out, he delivered more slaps to the side of her ass. When he reached the point of no return, he said, "Come for me. Now."

He climaxed before lowering his body over hers again and reaching for her clit. "Yes!" She clenched his cock, drawing every last drop from him as her own orgasm exploded seconds after his.

When both were spent, he remained inside her, not wanting to break the connection. In five days, she'd be on her way halfway around the world. He'd try to go a little easier on her ass the next few days, because she'd be sitting in uncomfortable airplane seats for several long flights, but he intended to take advantage of every moment they had together.

While he disposed of the condom and cleaned himself, he returned to the bed to see she'd straightened the bed, blown out the candles, and gotten into bed with her sexy back toward him. He turned off the light and got into bed, curling up against her, his arm wrapped around her waist and his hand cupping her breast.

"I'm going to sleep like a baby tonight, Sir. That was incredible. So much deeper—and you hit all the right spots."

"My pleasure." He kissed her shoulder. After a pause, he said, "Not to overwhelm you with anything else after our talk at dinner, but when you return from Afghanistan, we should start looking for a house together. Owning a house jointly in both our names where we can start fresh will be an important step for us to take in our relationship."

One without any ghosts. Tori might not have lived here, but two of the saddest years of his life had been spent within these walls. He wanted them to live in a place filled only with joy—and with Pamela's touches throughout. "We'll select it ourselves to fit us and furnish it the way we want."

"Sounds a bit overwhelming, but if you give me a few days to recover, I'm sure I'll be ready to house hunt. If I left you to your own devices, everything would be white or neutral colors."

"Are you saying the condo is bland?"

She rolled onto her side and propped herself up on her elbow to search his eyes. "I'm saying that white walls and white carpets are just too—dull, for lack of a less polite word."

He grinned. "The condo folks told me I could have it painted, but I didn't really care when I moved in."

She brushed a strand of hair from his forehead, but didn't need to say anything for him to understand her empathy for where he had been in his life back then.

After a brief moment, she smiled. "I'm glad it's not a personal decorating choice then. I'm not into knickknacks and wallpaper, but I do love southwestern colors splashed on the walls."

"Good idea. The decorating ball's solidly in your court." He pulled her on top of him, framed her face, and moved in for a kiss. Which led to another opportunity to worship her body.

More than an hour later, she straddled his spent cock buried deep inside her. A smile on her lips, she collapsed beside him. "I am the luckiest woman on earth."

He grinned over at her. "And I, the luckiest man. Now, if you'll excuse me." He went to the bathroom to dispose of the condom and wash up before rejoining her in bed with a washcloth to clean her. He wouldn't have the chance to care for her this way for almost five weeks.

"I could have done that, you know. I need to pee anyway."

While she was in there, he tried to think if anything had been left unsaid. They had very little time together before she'd have to leave him.

"Sprite, you hold the power as to whether you choose to be collared. Consider all of the pros, cons, and ramifications of each answer until you know in your heart what's right for you." He stroked her hair. "After you've had sufficient time to rest up from this assignment, I'll be waiting for your answer. But I'll wait as long as it takes you to decide."

"I don't think I'll need any more time than you're forcing me to take, Sir."

"I want to be sure you consider everything."

They remained silent a moment, until she propped herself up and revisited their earlier conversation. "Let's look for a house in the hills."

"We can look anywhere you'd like. How about Genesee or Morrison?"

"Oh, I love Red Rocks Park! Let's see if there's anything around there in Morrison."

He grinned. So much enthusiasm. "Will this be your first owned house?"

She nodded. "First property owned, actually. I always rented inexpensive apartments before."

Maybe he'd scout out some listings while she was in Afghanistan so they could hit the ground running when she returned—after she rested up a few days. This would give him something to do while she was gone to maintain his sanity.

She nibbled her lower lip.

"What is it, Sprite?"

"I was wondering…"

"Wondering what?"

"Not wondering exactly, but I want to change my position on something."

The thought of positions had his cock twitching, but he was more than depleted for the night.

"Do I have to pry it out of you?"

She grinned. "No, I'm just trying to choose the right words to tell you I'd be open to having a baby with you."

His throat closed tighter. "I think you just did—tell me, that is. I'd planned to ask how you'd feel about babies when you returned. My biggest concern is how it will mesh with your profession."

"I love what I do, but doctors have babies all the time."

"Doctors' *wives* more often than not."

She shrugged. "I can take a paid maternity leave of six weeks and then there's the Family Medical Leave for another twelve if I want to take longer. If Children's isn't able to accommodate my needs for family time after that, I may need to change jobs."

"But you just landed that one."

"Family comes first. And I've never been a mother before. I don't know how I'm going to change when I become one. But how do you feel about adoption if we aren't…"

"I'd love our adopted baby as much as one you give birth to. But let's try for at least a year before going that route."

"I love you, Kristoffer Roar Larson. I just want to make sure you know that before…"

He pulled her by the back of the neck until his lips on hers broke off any reminders about leaving.

Kristoffer and Pamela had been in each other's arms near the ticket counters for the past thirty minutes. The airport security lines weren't unbearably long, and they wanted to grasp every possible moment together before she had to leave to catch her first flight in the long journey to Afghanistan. She wouldn't arrive in Kabul for nearly thirty-eight hours.

"The next month is going to be one of the most difficult ones of my life," he said. "Hell, I missed you when I took that thirty-minute walk on the beach at your mom's. How am I going to survive thirty days?" More like thirty-four-and-a-half, but who was counting?

"I feel the same way." She pulled away and searched his face. "Promise me you'll keep busy and try not to think about me too much. I won't have it as hard, because this new hospital will be in perpetual motion if it's anything like the last one."

He raised a brow hoping his Dom stare spoke volumes. "Don't run yourself ragged. I don't want you having a relapse."

"I won't. I'll eat, rest, and drink lots of water." She smiled. "But I know you're still going to worry about me too much. It's second nature for you to worry about the ones you love."

"Don't you forget it, either."

She pulled him down by his lapels until she could kiss him on the cheek. "You've calmed me down already. I promise to follow your long list of instructions, and I'll be in touch at least once daily. I can't promise a set time each day, so don't freak out on me if one day it's morning and the next one nighttime. For the most part, I'll be asleep when you're awake and vice versa, but I'll try to get a message or call out to you before or after each shift."

He held up his arm and pulled the sleeves of his suit coat and dress shirt back to reveal his watch. It wasn't a new one, so she quirked a brow at him.

"I've already purchased a dual-zone watch and set it to Afghan/Denver time so I'll always know when it's the best time to text, e-mail, or call you." *So I can feel closer to you.* "You let me know how you're doing every day." *Reassure me you're still alive and well.*

"Kristoffer, I'll be fine. And back in Denver before you know it. I've been making these trips for years and have a dozen under my belt already. Please, try not to worry."

He bent to brush his lips against hers before grabbing and holding her against him, kissing her with something akin to desperation. When their lips parted, he ached to keep her close to him like this forever.

While he admired her for sticking to her commitments, she also had a commitment to him. In the future, he might become a little more selfish and demanding about her time overseas saving the world. Yeah, she'd already saved him, but that didn't mean he couldn't use regular maintenance.

"I'd better go, or they'll be paging me."

The pain in his chest was unbearable. "Don't forget your home-work assignment. It may be some of the hardest work you've ever done, but consider everything so you can give me your answer when you get home."

As a businessman, Kristoffer wasn't one to ask a question without being almost certain of the response. But in affairs of the heart, he was far outside his comfort zone. And after her breakthrough the other night in the condo, he was even more certain of her answer. It wouldn't be the end of the world if she chose not to wear his collar, but after the idea came to him, it seemed the perfect way to make a one-of-a-kind commitment to her. One that didn't put her in competition with Tori.

Not that he saw this as any kind of contest. "Call me when you get to Frankfurt. And Dubai."

She nodded. "You try to get some sleep, too. Don't be waiting by the phone all hours of the day and night."

"I'll do my best."

Grasping her hand in his while wheeling her carry-on beside them with the other, they started toward the TSA line. Before he reached the point of no return for him, he kissed her again. "Stay safe, Sprite. No shopping in the marketplace. Stay inside security."

She smiled. "Yes, Sir. I'll take care of myself and be back with you before you know it."

The only way for that to happen would be if he were placed in a drug-induced sleep for the next month.

He shuddered at those words and pulled them back from the uni-verse. Being comatose wasn't anything to joke about.

He tried to keep the fear out of his voice. "Come home safely."

"I will. I love you."

One more kiss, this one initiated by Pamela, and he watched her walk away. His heart felt as though it had been ripped in two again.

She stood in line five minutes before turning around and racing back to him. "Kristoffer, in my heart, I'm already home. Right here." She touched his chest, left of center—right over his heart.

Before he could respond, she was back in the line. He watched her go through the scanner and lined himself up to see her as far as he could before she turned one last time to wave at him, and then she walked out of sight.

How am I going to get through the next thirty-four days without her?

He returned to his car in the parking garage and drove home. Noma greeted him at the door, looking to see where her new mistress was, no doubt. Pamela had been here long enough that her scent, her memory, her very being was on just about everything in the place.

He'd hang on to those until she returned.

God of Thunder, bring her safely back to me.

CHAPTER TWENTY-THREE

Kristoffer slammed the lid down on his laptop and pushed it away as he sat back in his chair. He hadn't been able to concentrate on a bloody thing since seeing Pamela off at the airport three weeks ago. But it would be nearly two more before she finished her contract and made it back home.

Before he'd know that she was safe.

He tried to take it day by day, but not only did he miss her, he was worried sick about her. How did military spouses handle the deployments of their loved ones who could be gone for a year or more at a time? Gunnar told him not to watch the news, but Afghanistan wasn't a daily item as it once had been. Unable to help himself, Kristoffer had found sources of information via internationally focused news sites, but after a few days of assuming every roadside bomb or mortar attack had taken her, he'd had to quit looking.

He was worried she'd be killed before he could prove to her what she meant to him. He'd lost Tori in the blink of an eye, and while he hoped his wife had known how much he loved her, Kristoffer wanted to make sure there were no doubts about that with Pamela.

Trying not to pour out his loneliness—and neediness—to her in his daily e-mails, he forced himself to focus on work. She'd kept up her agreement to text or e-mail daily, although her correspondence was brief. He knew she must be extremely busy and didn't want to become a distraction to her, but restricting himself to sending just a single daily e-mail was a challenge. If he could, he'd hold an ongoing, nonstop back-and-forth Skype conversation with her. At least then he'd know she was okay for that moment in time.

Could he survive until he held her again? The only pain worse than this had been losing Tori, but he reminded himself this separation with Pamela was finite.

His phone pinged.

GUNNAR: **Meet me in the garage.**

KRISTOFFER: **What garage?**

GUNNAR: **Ur fuckn garage!**

What the hell was he doing in Denver again? He had just been here Thursday—two days ago—and seemed to drop by all the time lately.

KRISTOFFER: **Give me 10. Come up?**

GUNNAR: **I'll wait.**

Kristoffer hurried to the bedroom to dress. He hadn't bothered putting on suits to work in at home since Pamela left. And he wouldn't wear one tonight, either. Gunnar wouldn't be dressed formally. After donning a polo shirt and jeans, he slipped on his loafers. A few minutes later, he exited the elevator to find Gunnar leaning on the rear spoiler of his restored 1968 Ford Mustang Fastback. That car just might have saved Gunnar's sanity after his discharge from the Army. He'd practically slept in it the first six months.

But he rarely drove it unless he was in a particularly nostalgic mood—or had a hot date he wanted to impress with something more than his mansion, kink, or good looks.

Dressed in jeans and a green *Army of One* T-shirt, Gunnar shook his head. "You're a soup sandwich."

Kristoffer cocked his head. "Speak non-Army English."

Gunnar shook his head. "Civilian. You're a *mess*. Have you eaten since the last time I was here?"

"You came all the way back to Denver to ask me that?"

"No, I came to take you out to eat, because every time I've seen you the past few weeks, you've looked like fucking death warmed over."

Kristoffer shook his head, but couldn't fight back the grin. When Gunnar was in one of these moods, Kristoffer felt like a teenager again, back when he'd idol worshipped his cool older cousin. While only six years older, Gunnar was decades ahead of him in wisdom and experience. But Kristoffer had come away with quite an education that summer he'd hung out with Gunnar after running away from home.

Man, had his mother ever been pissed at the language Kristoffer had picked up. Lots of disparaging words had been thrown out about the riffraff around the fishing town in Winter Harbor, Maine, where Gunnar and both their dads grew up. Special Forces had nothing on those fishermen and their salty language.

"Shotgun." Kristoffer opened the passenger door, settled into the bucket seat, and buckled his seatbelt. Gunnar had told him once this was the first model to have shoulder belts, a safety feature Kristoffer appreciated.

Gunnar settled in and started the engine, gunning it a few times for effect. "Steaks?"

"Sure." Kristoffer didn't eat a lot of red meat, but he hadn't had anything since breakfast and had skipped most meals yesterday, too. He wasn't sure he had much of an appetite. He'd lost it when he'd dropped Pamela off at the airport. His body didn't crave anything—well, nothing except Pamela.

But he welcomed Gunnar taking his mind off worrying about her for a few hours. His cousin had been finding ways to get him out of the house a few times a week over the last three weeks by either calling him to Breck for last-minute meetings to discuss nothing that couldn't have been handled by phone or e-mail or, like tonight, coming to Denver to hang out.

"Did Pamela tell you to keep an eye on me?"

"You'll have to ask her." Gunnar put the muscle car in gear and burned rubber out of the garage to punctuate his words.

Kristoffer grinned and shook his head. "Show off."

"Just blowin' off some steam. Fucking wasted on you, Cuz. You never let your hair down. How'd you get so highfalutin?"

They'd tried to analyze this many times before. "I suppose living with my mother. Stiff upper lip and all. How she and Dad hooked up in the first place is beyond me."

"You know how those summer romance things go."

"Yeah, well, there is that. But it wasn't like they had to marry. She didn't have me for a couple more years."

"Maybe she miscarried or something."

Kristoffer shook his head. "Doubt I'll ever know. Their marriage lasted more than fifteen years—longer than your parents, who both came from the same social class."

"True." Gunnar was silent a moment then sighed. He drove in silence a few miles. Out of the blue, he asked, "How'd you get rid of the guilt over the night of the wreck? I know you blamed yourself in the beginning." The question was so far out in left field that Kristoffer wondered where his cousin's mind had gone.

He hadn't told Gunnar about seeing Rick for counseling. Not out of shame, but they hadn't had as much time together since he'd been with Pamela. Okay, not so the past three weeks. Maybe he needed to come clean.

"Before I went to California, I starting talking with a therapist at Tori's facility. He helped me sort out a lot of stuff, including the fact that sometimes random shit happens. After the wreck, I tried to micromanage and plan everything, thinking it gave me more control. Rick—the counselor—helped me see that what happened that night was just a horrible accident. I could make myself crazy with all the what ifs, but that wouldn't bring Tori back."

"No." He paused then added, "He's right. You did get fucking anal about planning, even more so in the past two years."

Kristoffer shrugged. "I wouldn't say *anal*. It's not unusual for a financial manager and planner to be that way, you know."

"Yeah, but you were controlling every fucking aspect of your life down to how to put your shoes on in the morning."

He hadn't been *that* bad. *Okay, maybe at first.* Man, did anything get by Gunnar?

"I think Pamela helped a lot, too. I set out trying to train her to live in the moment and realized I'd better start practicing what I preach."

" 'Bout time." The corners of Gunnar's lips lifted. "Now, how the fuck did we get talking about deep shit like this? We're supposed to be celebrating."

Kristoffer went quickly through the internal database of special occasions in his head and came up blank. September fifth. Labor Day was still two days away. "What's the occasion?"

"We'll talk about it over dinner."

How he was supposed to celebrate something he didn't know about was beyond him, but at least he wasn't pacing around the condo waiting for tomorrow morning's e-mail from Pamela.

When they merged onto I-70 East, Kristoffer had a clue they weren't stopping at the neighborhood steakhouse. They discussed some business until, instead of taking the downtown exit, Gunnar headed north on I-25 instead.

"Have you given any more thought to how you'd like to do the collaring ceremony, Kris?"

"I don't have her answer yet."

"Pfft. She's crazy about you—and it really is the best way to show her how special she is to you. She'd have probably said yes before she left, but you wouldn't let her."

"You're the one who said make sure she thought it through a while."

"Yeah, but I thought you'd give a few days, not almost five weeks."

"What's done is done." Kristoffer shrugged. "But to answer your question, yes, I have. I looked up the ceremonies you mentioned and think the white rose is the one I'll use."

"Bullseye."

"I'd like her tattoo redone as part of the ceremony."

"I know a great ink artist who'd come out to Breckenridge for a chance to see my dungeon. I'll call her as soon as you give me the go-ahead and some dates."

Kristoffer had fantasized for weeks about Pamela—dressed in a simple white gown, surrendering herself to him as he placed his collar around her slim neck. He'd had the choker specially made by the artist in Big Sur after calling and explaining what he was looking for.

Having her key tattoo altered would be highly symbolic and meaningful for them both. He'd looked over a lot of designs and found one with a heart-shaped padlock, a chain connected to the key, and a ribbon banner below, where the artist would ink the name "Roar."

If she didn't say yes right away, he'd keep all the plans at the ready for the day she would trust him enough to make that commitment. They had time.

Don't jinx it.

When they passed Thornton, he knew they were heading to their old stomping grounds in Fort Collins. Did Gunnar have a class reunion at Colorado State or something? Kristoffer hadn't gone to school there, but had hung out with him and his friends that summer and kept up with the couple of guys Gunnar enlisted with immediately after graduating.

He glanced at his cousin's T-shirt and ragged jeans. Doubtful he'd go dressed like that, although with Gunnar you never could tell. He liked to buck the status quo.

Driving into Fort Collins, Gunnar skirted the campus and drove into the Old Town area, parking on the street near Sonny Lubick's Steakhouse. When Gunnar had splurged on dinner the one previous time they'd been here, the restaurant had been called Nico's Catacombs. It was the place Gunnar had taken him the night before sending him back to Connecticut to finish school.

Inside, he noticed that the atmosphere in the renovated version was reminiscent of the original incarnation. While they'd lost the cellar-like feel of the Catacombs with more lighting, the brickwork was the same.

Gunnar gave the hostess the Larson name for their reservation. They were seated soon after, Gunnar oblivious to the young woman's flirting as she showed them to a table at the end of the room.

Kristoffer took the seat with his back to the room and other patrons, knowing Gunnar would need the one with his back to the wall if he was going to enjoy dinner while at the same time remaining aware of his surroundings. Old habits died hard.

"Haven't been here since the last time you brought me, Gunnar."

"Me, neither," Gunnar opened his menu. "More affordable now. The Catacombs was way over my budget at the time. Of course, Aunt Claire paid for our meals that night."

"Mother sent you money?"

He shrugged. "I'd just graduated and only had a part-time job while waiting for boot camp. Those couple months you were out here, she sent me enough to keep you in food—you ate like a horse—and whatever else you needed."

He'd never known she'd done that. Kristoffer looked at the prices for the successor to the Catacombs. Definitely not the fine-dining prices he remembered, even adjusting for inflation, although Gunnar's fortunes had increased significantly in the last twenty years. He was a self-made billionaire a few times over. Kristoffer hoped to continue to build on his net worth for years to come.

After they'd ordered beverages and the signature steakhouse salads, Kristoffer looked across the table. He still had no clue why they were here. But Gunnar would get to it when he was ready.

"I remember being pissed as hell at you that night for making me go back home."

Gunnar laughed heartily. "Good thing I was headed off to the Army, because I don't think you'd have talked to me even if I *could* make any calls home."

"If they'd have let me follow you into the Army, I probably would have. I was a lost little puppy back then."

He shook his head. "Not without a high school diploma, you wouldn't. You'd had your rebellious summer. Time to go home and get back to the work at the business of growing up." Gunnar grew serious for a change. "I'm sure glad you and Pamela hit it off. I wasn't sure I was doing the right thing, but all's well that ends well. You were ready to rejoin the living—just needed a little nudge in the right direction."

Kristoffer cocked his head. "What are you talking about?"

The server filled their glasses with water before presenting for Kristoffer's approval the unopened bottle of Sonoma wine he'd ordered. At Kristoffer's nod, he opened the bottle and poured.

Kristoffer would drink the lion's share, because Gunnar was driving and would barely have one glass before switching back to water.

"Since everything turned out, I might as well 'fess up." He lifted his glass. "But first, a toast."

Kristoffer wondered what the hell was on Gunnar's mind, but lifted his as well.

"Here's to the land we love and the love we land. May you and Pamela have many joyous years together."

Kristoffer shook his head and grinned as they clinked glasses. But Gunnar wasn't smiling. Something told him the mood was about to shift. *Damn.* He'd been ready to maintain this good mood after the last three weeks of hell.

"Thanks, man. I'm lucky to have found a woman like Pamela to share the rest of my life with."

The server returned to prepare their salads tableside, the only difference in ingredients being Gunnar's red chile dressing versus his own sherry shallot one. Then they were left alone again.

When Gunnar's mood remained uncharacteristically somber, Kristoffer leaned forward. "Stop being so bloody cryptic, and tell me what you've been going on about."

"Kris, you've been through hell since you lost Tori. Something no spouse should have to go through."

Why was he stirring up those memories? What the hell kind of celebration was that? Kristoffer took another sip of wine, his salad untouched.

"So when Pamela came to meet with us and ask us to bring that little girl here for additional surgeries, I thought I caught a spark of interest on her part when she first met you, until she noticed your wedding ring. Or maybe your sour mood. You were having one of those black days where you're only half there."

He couldn't argue that there were times when he was physically present but mentally absent, so he let that slide. But *a spark of interest?* "What the hell are you talking about? I barely spoke two words to her."

He grinned. "Yeah, but your eyes spoke volumes the couple of times I saw you looking at her. I hadn't seen you give any other woman the time of day since you'd met Tori. That's when this idea came to me. I knew if anyone would be able to pull your head from your fourth point of contact, it would be this classy, intelligent, tough-as-nails spitfire."

Kristoffer shook his head. He had no clue how he'd looked at Pamela that day, but in his denial that he resided among the living, he supposed he could have sent a signal at least Gunnar noticed. But that wasn't the point of Gunnar's story. "I probably don't want to know, but what exactly did you do?"

Gunnar's shit-eating grin was infectious anyway. "Well, she'd talked to me about training as a submissive, so I encouraged her to apply to The Denver Academy. But, of course, I needed to pull some strings with Brad Anderson because it was so close to them starting a new class."

Before he could continue, their steaks were served—Gunnar's medium-rare porterhouse steak and Kristoffer's medium-temperature ribeye. After checking them for the correct doneness, they nodded to send the server away and returned to their conversation.

"While talking with Brad about having the school take on one more student, I found out he was planning to move and would be putting the academy up for sale."

"What does all this have to do with Pamela and me?"

"Patience, Grasshopper. All in good time." He glanced down at his plate. "But our steaks are going to get cold. Let's dig in."

"Yours is still twitching." Gunnar's baked potato swam in the steak's bloody juices.

Gunnar smiled, took a bite, chewed slowly, and swallowed, savoring the succulent beef—and dragging out the moment to full effect. Then he repeated the ritual for several more bites.

Kristoffer might as well eat, too. He could starve to death waiting for Gunnar to come clean about the rest of the details concerning Pamela.

Halfway through their steaks, Gunnar set down his fork and knife, took a sip of wine, and continued where he'd left off. "So I asked Brad to help me out. The night before I sent you to the academy for that tour, he called to tell me this might be an excellent opportunity to bring the two of you together and show you a different side of the lovely doctor."

Kristoffer stopped mid-chew. "You arranged for me to walk in and find her naked? What the fuck's the matter with you?"

"Stop right there. Brad and I had no idea she'd volunteer to be the nude model that night—although when he called to report your response to the situation, we had a good, long laugh about it."

Kristoffer was dumbfounded for a moment then shook his head. "You placed us both in an extremely awkward situation, intentionally or not. Her eyes had pleaded with me not to out her to anyone. She was placed in a most vulnerable state."

Gunnar took another bite and grinned. "No one in the group would have outed her. And everything worked out, didn't it? But I swear on your Dad's cheating ass, I had no idea about her planning on being naked that night."

His cousin had never forgiven Kristoffer's dad for deserting his family. At least Gunnar's parents had remained amicable. They just couldn't live under the same roof.

"I guess you're right." Kristoffer still didn't know what to think about Gunnar's involvement in that night. A sudden thought had him looking at his matchmaking cousin again. "Then, I suppose, you cooked up the hospital-equipment project for us to work together on."

Gunnar waved his words away with his fork. "I'd have probably done that anyway. Some of the girls from Heidi's school have been treated at that hospital. They do good work." He sobered. "If the day ever came where Heidi herself needed to seek treatment there, I'd want them to have everything they'd need at their disposal."

Now that Kristoffer had found someone to love and protect, he wanted that for Gunnar, too, but he and Heidi might never come to their senses and realize they belonged together. A pity. Life was too short, and they'd missed out on so many years together already.

Trouble was, one of the two stubborn people would have to agree to give up his or her life and move halfway across the world. Seven years ago, Kristoffer's money would have been on Heidi winning that bet, given Gunnar's love for her.

But Gunnar had remained firmly entrenched here in Colorado, and the stalemate had begun. To his credit, Gunnar had found ways to hook up with Heidi four or five times a year. Whether those visits were conjugal or strictly humanitarian, Kristoffer had no clue. He'd never gone there himself and hadn't seen Heidi since she'd retired from the Army the year before she'd gone back to Afghanistan to establish the school for girls.

"So by putting you both on the acquisitions project, I had hoped your spending time together might help you see what you'd been missing. Things were going great until she had to quit the academy. I swear on Thor's hammer I had no idea she wasn't in top form health-wise. I regret that a lot."

"I can't say that I have any regrets, because my becoming her Top to help train her on some issues was one of the things that brought us even closer together."

Gunnar smiled. "See? It all worked out, Kris!"

How could he fault Gunnar? He'd done everything out of love for his lost and grieving cousin. And Anderson had merely been doing a favor for a friend.

"Yes, it did. I'm not sure how given all the twists, turns, and barriers, but it certainly did."

They moved on to talking about the good times they'd had in Norway. He hadn't been sure he had enough of an appetite coming in here, but had nearly finished his twelve-ounce steak. After dinner was over, Kristoffer thought they'd soon be leaving, but Gunnar showed no signs of being in any hurry.

Throwing him for a loop again, Gunnar asked, "Got any plans for the coming week?"

"Other than working for you?"

"You have vacation time coming."

"I'd rather save it for when Pamela and I can travel together. We're planning to go to Norway next August or September."

Gunnar leaned forward. "You didn't take a day off for two years—not even weekends—until that recent trip to Sonoma." So he *had* noticed how Kristoffer spent his weekends, too. No surprise. Not much got past the man. "Before your mental health break two years ago, you didn't take any time off, either. So I figure I owe you five or six weeks of vacation. Pamela's not going to have a lot of time off, just starting a new job, so take advantage of a getaway while you can."

"All right. As long as we're back by the time Pamela comes home. Where to?"

"How quickly can you pack?"

"Pack for where?"

"I'd like to check on some investments."

He hadn't taken Kristoffer along on any business trips before, mainly because Kristoffer wouldn't leave Denver. Was there a problem with one of the companies Kristoffer had invested in? "Which ones?"

"You'll see when we get there. Pack for a week. Leave the suits at home. I'll provide you with some special outer gear, so just wear what's comfortable."

"Road trip?"

Gunnar shook his head. "Oh, fuck no. Flying."

"Where. To?" he asked again, reiterating each word for emphasis.

"Man, you're a Debbie Downer, you know that? You could trust me."

"You know I trust you with my life." Apparently, Gunnar thought he needed a diversion to kill the rest of the time before Pamela came home. "When do we leave?"

"Early Monday morning." Day after tomorrow. "Bring Noma out to my place, and I'll have my house sitter take care of her, too."

"As long as I'm home in time to pick up Pamela at the airport."

"I'll personally see that you two connect without spending a minute more apart from each other than necessary."

Kristoffer set down his glass as a smile erupted on his face. "We're flying to Kabul?"

Gunnar looked exasperated for only a moment. "Well, you just blew my surprise." But he couldn't keep the grin from returning to his face. "You'd better not tell Pamela we're coming. If I'm flying halfway around the world, *somebody* needs to be surprised."

✧   ✧   ✧

Pamela set down her shower caddy, stripped off her scrub top, and tossed it in the laundry bin before making a beeline for the shower. Twelve grueling hours on her feet in surgery, but she wouldn't crawl into bed until she'd removed at least a couple of layers of grime from her body.

The line of patients had been never-ending today. This time, she'd heard the IED and several mortars exploding in the distance—much closer than she'd liked. Within an hour, new casualties arrived at the trauma center. She hadn't lived in such fear in any of her past assignments.

Without a doubt, the hospital near Kabul seemed like a country club in comparison to this remote place in Kunduz. So primitive—like an outpost in the wilderness, despite being surrounded by buildings and a city. She and other staff members rarely left these walls. Not only because the staff here was dedicated to its mission and patients, but because they had no clue whom to trust or where the next explosive device might go off or a mortar round fall.

At the end of tomorrow's shift, her month-long assignment would be over. She'd catch some sleep and then be on her way back to Kristoffer. The thought of the long trip home was too daunting to dwell on, especially the grueling five-hour trek to Kabul on a road that could be lined with IEDs.

Please, don't let anything happen to my convoy. Kristoffer needs me.

He'd already lost one love in his life. She wasn't sure he could survive another being ripped away from him. Her anxiety for him was almost higher than for herself.

She also feared for the staff left behind and for the Afghans who had to live day in and day out in this war zone with no hope of escape—except through death. Man's inhumanity to man never ceased to confound her.

After her shower, she wrapped her hair in a towel, donned her terrycloth robe, and picked up her caddy to make her way down the hall to her sleeping cubicle. Staff members who occupied the house slept in shifts. When they went back to work in the trauma center, another crew would come in to catch some sleep.

She rarely managed more than a few hours any given night. One more night after this and—

"Pamela! Which house are you in?"

Kristoffer?

For a moment, she stopped and prepared to rush to the front door. God, she must be more tired than she thought if she was hearing his voice like he was standing outside the house.

"Sprite, answer me!"

Her heart hammered as she dropped the caddy and ran to the door. Standing in the dirty courtyard in the center of the staff housing units was Kristoffer. He was dressed in camo with backpack straps showing and wearing a military helmet, but she couldn't mistake his height, voice, or chin for anyone else's.

"What the—?"

Hearing her voice, he homed in on her position and ran toward her, lifting her into his arms and holding her against his hard body as her towel slipped free and fell to the concrete porch. They kissed, her tongue plundering every blessed inch of his warm mouth until she had to break away to catch her breath.

She stared into his beautiful blue eyes. "What on earth are you doing here?"

"I've come to take you home—after your shift tomorrow. We weren't sure how long it would take to get here, so my timing is a little off."

Tears of joy and exhaustion spilled down her cheeks before her brain engaged. "Who's *we?*"

Kristoffer set her on her feet and pointed to where she could see the gate to the common yard area where Gunnar stood, also in camo and helmet, but holding a rifle. He nodded a greeting in her direction and smiled. Another man she didn't recognize stood nearby.

"Gunnar and Patrick copiloted around the clock, with only the legally required ground time, until his jet touched down in Kabul late Sunday."

"We've been in the same country an entire day and I didn't know? Your e-mail last night mentioned that you and Gunnar were on a business trip."

By now, Gunnar had joined them, grinning. "I invested a fuck-ton of money on some equipment at a hospital in Kabul and wanted to see if I got my money's worth."

She broke free of Kristoffer and wrapped her arms around Gunnar's waist, hugging him and whispering, "Thank you. Lame words, I know, but I appreciate this from the bottom of my heart. As long as we don't get killed or attacked trying to get out of here."

"I've got your six, Doc."

She shook her head, incredulous she was standing here with these two beautiful men. Kristoffer pressed his body against her back, and his hands spread open over her ribs, his thumbs grazing the undersides of her breasts. He bent to murmur, "And I've got your front, Sprite." She grinned. Of all the nicknames people had given her, she liked Sprite best.

Gunnar gave them a nod. "I know when I'm not welcome anymore. Sleep well. Patrick and I will keep an eye on things." Ah, Patrick, the Marine from New Mexico who had attended the meeting in which she'd pleaded Fakhira's case for being brought to the States. She hadn't recognized him from this distance with his gear on.

She wriggled out of Kristoffer's arms and turned to face him. "Where on earth are you going to sleep? I only have a cot."

He grinned and took her hand to go inside. "I'll be your mattress tonight."

She shook her head. "This isn't my private residence, you know."

He feigned indignation. "I didn't say I was going to let you have your way with me, woman. Show some discipline."

She laughed. "Well, I might be a little rusty because I haven't seen my Dom in a month. I'm probably running on adrenaline now, but I do need to catch some sleep so I don't make any mistakes on my last day here. Come in. I'll give you a tour."

After showing him the shared kitchen and bathroom, she led him back down the hall to her sparse room. "You weren't kidding." He walked the few steps to the cot, dwarfing the room with his size. "Now, let's get you ready for bed, Sprite." He turned and shut the door before removing her robe. "Where's your brush?"

"Probably on the hallway floor where I dropped my caddy after I realized I wasn't hallucinating—or hearing things."

He grinned and shook his head as he opened the door again and went to retrieve her toiletries. Back inside the room, he told her to present her back to him and began brushing out her hair, which was a tangled mess. Such a simple gesture of caring.

"I've missed having you taking care of me like this. The past month has been so stressful, and I haven't had any way of processing it other than sleep—when I could catch a few hours."

"You'll enjoy a full night's sleep in my arms tonight."

She still didn't know how the two of them would fit into such a tiny bed, but they'd somehow make it work.

As he brushed the knots out, she relaxed so deeply she swayed. "Whoa!" He dropped the brush and scooped her up and carried her to the cot. "Bedtime, Sprite."

Exhaustion overtook her, and she started crying again. "I'm sorry for the waterworks."

"Never apologize for showing your emotions. They're real, and shedding tears can be cathartic in many ways."

"Thanks." He always understood and accepted her as she was.

"What do you usually wear to bed?"

She pointed to her carry-on bag sitting on the floor beside two others. "There's a T-shirt in there. The blue one." He unzipped the bag, found the shirt, and returned to her side.

"Arms up." His voice had grown husky, and she felt the heat of his gaze on her breasts. After such a long absence, he had to be horny as hell, but she appreciated that he didn't intend to act on it. She was bone weary and wanted nothing more than to feel his arms around her to make sure she wasn't imagining this.

After he tugged the shirt down to hide her attributes, he lifted her legs and swung them around onto the foot of the cot. Surveying what little bed was left, he smiled. "Plenty of room." He began to remove his boots and clothing, his eyes never looking away from hers. If he said it would work, she'd believe him. He was much more spatial than she was.

As he stripped down to his boxers, she laughed. He'd worn a white pair covered in red hearts.

"Eat your heart out, Sprite. I knew we wouldn't be making love tonight, but I wanted to give you something sexy to dream about."

"I'm sure if I dream tonight, it will be nothing but sexy thoughts of you—and your boxers, Sir." She smiled, holding out her hand in invitation.

"Turn on your side facing the wall, and scoot that way as far as you comfortably can. I'm coming in."

The cot groaned under his weight, but didn't collapse. She held her breath, unsure the flimsy bed would survive the weight of them both. But when he wrapped his arm around her waist, cupped her breast, and pulled her against him snugly, she sighed.

They might not be back in their condo, but they were home.

"Welcome home, Master Roar."

His breathing stopped a moment, telling her he'd noticed her new title for him. She'd let him know her decision later, when she could be lucid, but she had long ago decided she would accept and wear his collar proudly.

He kissed the back of her head. "It's good to *be* home, Sprite."

From now on, home would be wherever they happened to be, as long as they were together.

✧   ✧   ✧

Peace. The world had righted itself again, because he held his sleeping sprite tonight. She'd zonked out in a flash, but the light she exuded through every pore burned brightly for him. He'd slept on the jet and was wide awake.

Seeing her standing in the doorway an hour ago, dark circles under her eyes, her face showing the ravages this month had taken on her, he'd wasted no time taking her into his arms. She'd lost a lot of weight judging by the ribs he felt on her back through her terry robe.

He'd get right to work building up her stamina again once they were out of this hellhole. Until then, he'd pamper and care for her. And kiss her, hold her, sleep with her. Nothing else on his agenda for the foreseeable future.

Gunnar said they couldn't chance the road to Kabul after dark, which meant another night here. Unless she could be released early enough to make the five-hour trip in daylight.

He kissed the back of her head again, careful not to wake her but needing to assure himself he actually held her like this. As if he could wake her.

He took a deep breath.

Man, did he ever owe Gunnar—again. The thought of her flying home on three commercial flights after spending a grueling month in this…

She wouldn't have to. Along with the help of copilot Patrick, they would reach home safely much sooner and in a lot more comfort.

Kristoffer shuddered as he remembered hearing a mortar blast on the drive to Kunduz. Everything he'd imagined about the fear felt by those in the military and in harm's way flew out of his mind. The terror he'd felt—listening for the next one, wondering if it would hit the vehicle he rode in—God of Thunder, what had his woman endured this past month?

And why hadn't she shared what a dangerous area she was in? She'd told him remote, but he'd figured fewer people might lessen the danger. Maybe that only worked in the States.

Gunnar hadn't seemed fazed by any of it. In fact, he might have been exhilarated by it. The two cousins shared no resemblance to one another at the moment.

Truly sitting shotgun—assault rifle locked and loaded with Patrick behind the driver ready to provide cover to that side of the vehicle—the Army Delta and Marine had been vigilant. If anyone could get them out of here safely, it was these two—along with the other members of Gunnar's team in the convoy.

Kristoffer didn't own a single weapon, but wished he'd bothered to learn to use one now. All he could do was shield her with his body if they came under fire.

Pamela jerked in her sleep, and he held her tighter. "Shh, Sprite," he whispered. "I have you."

Mine.

No one would ever hurt her if he could prevent it. But if she ever signed on to do something this dangerous again, he'd...well, she wouldn't be able to sit for a week.

Of course, he'd promised that her career was off limits as far as his authority, but he'd damned well ask more questions next time and do a lot more investigation to determine the risk factors and make sure she was aware of them.

And if they were blessed with kids, well, he'd have no problem playing the guilt card to keep her home, regardless of their "no regrets, no guilt" mantra.

At least, this would be her last assignment in a war-torn country. Central America had drug lords and guerillas. Maybe he'd go along in some capacity. When they returned home, he'd ask Gunnar to teach him to shoot a weapon at the firing range. He'd encourage Pamela to learn, too. Maybe if he presented it as a bonding experience for the two of them...

He almost laughed at the image of himself in his three-piece suit wielding a .357 Magnum or whatever weapon Gunnar suggested he fire. Having spent his life tucked safely behind a desk, this wasn't something he'd given any thought.

But violence and evil existed back home, too. Colorado had seen its share of senseless massacres. He wanted to be able to protect her—and while she couldn't carry a weapon into the hospital, at least she could have it in her glove box for the commute.

You need to get some sleep, man.

Perhaps Gunnar could spare one of his teams to shadow Pamela in Guatemala—and him as well, because never again would he be separated from her this long, especially when she was in harm's way.

He sighed. While having someone to look out for and care for was great, the responsibility weighed heavily on him tonight.

And they still had some unfinished business, although he wouldn't push her for an answer to his proposal to collar her until she'd recovered from this nightmare first.

Had he given her enough time to think about all the problems being collared might present? Or too much? He'd been clear, he hoped, that the collar he'd place around her neck wouldn't make anyone suspicious of its meaning unless they were familiar with the BDSM lifestyle and noticed that she never wore any other necklace.

But had he pushed for collaring her too soon?

No. The bond they'd formed at her dad's house far exceeded what most people achieved after years of being together. Perhaps their ages had something to do with the speed in which things were happening. He'd be forty-two in two months.

All he knew was that, collared or not, he wanted her beside him the rest of his life. But the collar offered a deeper sense of belonging to each other for both of them.

He couldn't wait to see if she was ready to take that step with him in the near future along with many others.

Pamela awoke suddenly, thinking she'd missed her shift, only to realize she'd worked her last one yesterday. After the grueling drive to Kabul, they hadn't wasted any time before hopping on Gunnar's luxury jet and taking off. Tonight, sitting on Kristoffer's lap—soon to be her

Master Roar—on her way home to Colorado, she couldn't stop touching him. He'd traveled all that way, thanks to Gunnar, to bring her home.

She sat up and smiled at him. "I could sleep for a month."

"I'm sure you missed out on a lot of it this past one. I know I ought to let you stretch out and sleep, but I don't want to turn you loose to move even that far away from me."

She smiled, searching his eyes. "I sleep better in your arms than anywhere." She leaned in for a kiss, but her growling stomach killed the mood.

Kristoffer slid her onto one of the curves in the U-shaped leather seat. "I'll get your dinner, Sprite."

He walked over to the kitchen and pulled a plastic-covered dish from the fridge and popped it into the microwave. "I'll be right back. Let me see if Gunnar or Patrick want to eat now, too."

Alone while he went to the cockpit, she looked around. She'd known Gunnar had money, but he didn't flaunt it. This was pure opulence. She still marveled that anyone could have a fireplace in an airplane—well, a simulated-fire one anyway.

Except for takeoffs and landings, they'd remained entwined in each other's arms. They'd left Frankfurt and were on the final leg of the journey. Soon, they would be home. She'd expected to still be on the ground in Dubai, assuming her original flight from Kabul had taken off on time and she'd made all her connections. Instead, she'd have more time to spend with Kristoffer before having to return to work at Children's.

And one very important matter to discuss with him—how soon they'd try to get pregnant.

Kristoffer returned. "They're good for now. That dinner we had in Frankfurt must have stuck with them as it did me. But you, Sprite, hardly ate enough for a bird."

The microwave dinged, and while her meal remained inside another minute per the instructions, he walked over to her and reached for her hand. He started to guide her to an upholstered seat where the dining area was, but stopped to wrap her in his arms and kiss her again, his hands splayed on her butt as he pulled her against his erection.

They separated and he smiled. "I can't wait to get you home."

"Who said we had to wait?"

He chuckled. "I do, at least until you've had your dinner—or lunch. My internal clock is so far off I don't know what time it is, but I'm sure it's time for some meal. Then we'll see what you feel up to." His smile promised something delightful, for sure.

After he had her sit and buckle up in case of turbulence, he retrieved her leftovers from the German restaurant and served them along with a glass of chardonnay.

"Aren't you going to eat anything, Kristoffer?"

"I'll join you for dessert later." While they had ordered apple strudel to go, she somehow didn't think by the tone of his voice that's what he meant.

She finished every bite, not realizing how hungry she'd been. "That was fabulous!" Pamela glanced around. "Have you traveled in this jet before?"

He shook his head. "Gunnar's only had it a few years, and I was rooted in Denver those years."

She nodded her understanding. Wanting to lighten the mood again, she grinned. "Maybe we should talk him into a trip to Norway next summer. He could coax Heidi away, and the four of us could explore together."

He raised his eyebrows. "Not a bad idea. I'll talk with him about it."

"I missed hanging out with Heidi this time. Man, if I'd known where they'd be placing me before I went, I might have declined."

He grew stern. "In the future, we're going to ask more questions, do more research, and make certain you aren't taking on any unnecessary risks."

Her heart warmed at his words. Not only that he intended to look out for her—and perhaps even save her from herself—but that he hadn't laid down the law and commanded her not to take on such assignments anymore.

Roar

But she ought to lay his fears to rest. "I've tendered my resignation from the organization and plan to stay put for a long time to come. The way I feel right now, I'm not even sure about Guatemala, although I have a hunch I'll change my mind again after I put this behind me in a few months." At the look of worry on his face that she might traipse off again sometime soon, she quickly added, "Or years."

"Better."

After he cleared her dish and utensils away, she peeked out the window but saw nothing but ocean below them. Unbuckling herself, she carried her wine glass over to the fireplace and switched it on.

"Cold?"

"Not really. Just wanted to stare at the flames."

He wrapped his arms around her. She loved that he couldn't seem to stop touching her. Cherished. He made her feel so loved.

"Master Roar," she said, signaling a change in tone and topics, "I'm ready to give you my answer."

His body visibly stiffened, and she smiled. "Sir, have you been worrying all this time whether I'd accept? How can you doubt I would say 'yes'?"

"Well, as proposals go, I'm not sure it's what every woman dreams of when she thinks about her happily-ever-after ending."

She set her glass on the shelf behind the fireplace and turned toward him, death rays probably streaming from her eyes. "*I'm* not every woman, and don't you forget it."

"No, indeed, Sprite, you are not."

Appeased, she lightened up some. "For the record, my answer is an unequivocal 'yes, yes, yes.' To wear the collar of such a strong, protective man—someone who changed my life forever in such profound ways—is an honor and a great tribute to what we're trying to forge for our future." He started to lean down to kiss her, but she held up her hand. "It's my turn to speechify, Sir. I'm not finished yet."

He silently held up his hands in surrender, and she smiled sweetly before continuing.

"Your request was the most perfect—albeit perfectly unexpected—

and phenomenal proposal any man has ever uttered to a woman since the beginning of time."

"That good, huh?" She saw the twinkle in his eye.

"I know there will never be another man I could love more than life itself. No other man can make me feel one-billionth as worthy, protected, cherished, and loved as you do me."

She peered into his eyes. "That you would find the perfect solution for us—one that would make me feel like the most important person in your life—makes me the happiest alpha brat around."

He kissed her, but before they wound up making love on the floor of this jet, she pulled away.

"I love your brattiness. Always have."

"Even when I'm supposed to be behaving?"

"Especially then, because it means you have some funishment coming."

Her breath caught in her throat, and she glanced cautiously at the cockpit door. Would they be interrupted if…

"Good, Sir, because I can't be anything other than who I am. At least I know you've seen the real me and aren't expecting someone else, which might lead to regrets."

"No regrets, no guilt."

"*My* only regret at the moment is that we're not alone right now, Sir, so you can take your brat in hand."

"Do you think I'd have a problem hauling you over my knee, if needed, because we might be overheard by Gunnar and Patrick? I assure you, neither would be shocked by anything we do here, but they've promised to alert me before checking on us."

She smiled. "Why do I have the feeling I'm not going to make it to Eagle Vail Airport without a very sore bottom?"

"Because somehow I doubt you're going to be able to curb your tongue even half that long—and I left the ball gag at home."

He dug his fingers into her hair and tilted her head back, leaning down to capture her lips in a searing kiss. But before he proceeded to make love to her, or whatever he had in mind, she needed to discuss one thing.

"How would you feel about us ditching the condoms starting now? I don't want to wait. I'm thirty-eight and you're forty-one."

"Well, I brought condoms along," he said, "but I'm ready whenever you are. How's your chief of staff going to feel if you now take a maternity leave so soon after being hired?"

"I guess we'll have to find out, but legally, he doesn't have a leg to stand on. Though if it would cause too great a hardship on the patients if there was no temporary replacement, I'm not above resigning." She smiled up at him. "All I know is that it could take us months to conceive even if we're both fertile. Why wait?"

He grinned. "Why, indeed?" Kristoffer kissed her again and lowered her to the rug in front of the fireplace.

CHAPTER TWENTY-FOUR

Pamela awakened in their bed the following Monday, the day she would have just been arriving home by commercial flights, to find Kristoffer carrying a tray filled with a continental breakfast of fruit, pastries, and a glass of orange juice. She wouldn't report to Children's until next Monday, and Kristoffer seemed intent on pampering her in new ways every day. She already felt as good as new and excited about what they had planned for this week.

"If you don't quit spoiling me like this, I'm going to get lazy, quit working, and lie here eating bonbons while watching daytime dramas all day."

"Having you in my bed twenty-four/seven can be arranged," he said, wiggling his eyebrows as he placed the tray over her lap. "But I'd have your hands restrained, your eyes would only be on me, and I'd be the one feeding you those bonbons." He bent to place a kiss on her lips. "Good morning, Sunshine."

She'd known the nickname her mother had revealed would pop into his vocabulary at some point, although he might be referring to the sunlight streaming in the window onto her face.

"Now, this morning you are to eat, shower, and dress, in that order. We have an appointment with the Realtor at ten." He straightened up. "I'll leave you to those tasks while I take care of a few things in the office."

Now or never.

"Wait. I need to ask you something." She'd put it off for days, not sure how he'd respond to her request, but the collaring was set for tomorrow evening. She needed to talk with someone first.

He cocked his head when she didn't continue and then prompted, "What is it? You know you can ask me anything."

She set the untouched breakfast tray to her side and swung her legs over the side of the bed to stand beside him. Embracing him, she looked up at the love in his eyes.

For me.

But another woman had been gazed upon that way before Pamela had, and it was time the two of them met. "Would you take me to meet Tori?"

His eyes narrowed as he furrowed his brow in confusion. "If you'd like, but may I ask why?"

She swallowed. "Tomorrow, I'll be joined to you forever, and I want to meet and thank the woman who loved you first."

His eyes welled, and his voice grew husky when he spoke. "I'd like you to meet her and to introduce her to the woman who filled the void in my heart she left behind."

That went better than expected. "Thank you!"

He bent to kiss her. "I love you so much."

"And I, you."

Their lips met briefly before he took her by the shoulders and turned her around, patting her butt as he pushed her toward the bed. "Now, eat. I'm going to reschedule house hunting until this afternoon. We'll see Tori first."

"Perfect." Once she met Tori, she would be able to wrap her head around the search for a place to start their new life together.

An hour later, she walked into the bright room with him to see the atrophied woman curled on her side, vacuous eyes open and mouth gaping.

Kristoffer squeezed Pamela's hand before letting her go and crossing the room to his wife's side. "Good morning, sweetheart." He stroked the side of her head, but there was no visible response. How heartbreaking the past four years must have been for him, to come here alone every day to see her, talk to her, care for her—and for her not to know he existed.

"There's someone I want you to meet. I've already told you a lot about her." He stood up and held out his hand to her. "This is Pamela Jeffrey. Pamela, meet Tori."

She walked over and wrapped her left arm around his back for support—for her. He seemed to be fine, which reassured her he was ready to take the next step in their journey.

Pamela then let him go and bent down beside Tori's face, holding and squeezing her shriveled and distorted hand. "Tori, I've heard so much about you. So happy to finally meet you."

No response. With tears in her eyes, mainly for Kristoffer, she looked up at him. "Would you mind giving us girls a moment alone?"

He cocked his head, glanced at Tori, and then back at her. "Sure. I guess. I'll just be outside."

Pamela watched him leave and waited until he pulled the door closed before turning her attention to his wife again. She'd tried to practice the perfect words for days, but they all deserted her at that moment.

Others took their place, coming more from the heart. "Tori, I've come here today to reassure you that Kristoffer loves you and always will. We'd never have met if not for the accident because he took his vows seriously."

She swallowed, her throat suddenly parched. "I know it's hard to let go of a loved one, but I wanted you to know that I'm going to do my best to take care of him for the rest of my days. Not as his wife. That will be your title and rightly so."

She teared up. "Tori, he loved you so deeply and still does. Don't ever doubt that." What else needed to be said? Had she conveyed everything she wanted to? "What the two of you shared is real and can never be diminished or destroyed." She licked her dry lips and stared at the cool hand she held, unable to look into Tori's empty eyes any longer. "I know you wouldn't want him to be sad or lonely or depressed. He was so devastated by the accident."

She drew a deep breath. "But he's asked to collar me as his submissive, and I've accepted. You don't have to worry about him anymore. I'll take this next watch."

Kristoffer also believed she was gone from him, so she wouldn't pretend otherwise, but even though the body in front of her wasn't filled with Tori's presence, she had no doubt that the soul that once inhabited this body hovered nearby.

"He will never abandon your earthly body, nor will he ever forget or forsake the love you shared. But your perpetual absence from his life left Kristoffer alone and hurting. I am simply refilling the broken half of his heart."

Each woman's place in his heart was secure, side by side. "We've inadvertently formed a triad relationship. Not in life, but if there's something beyond death, we will be together." She liked to think Tori approved of her as the alpha submissive in the relationship and gave Pamela her blessing. Whether that was wishful thinking or truth, she couldn't say, but a sense of peace came over Pamela in that moment. Tori was his wife. Pamela was about to become his collared submissive. Pamela was okay with sharing him—once they got there. Wherever *there* was.

But she and Kristoffer still had a lot of living to do.

"Tori, for the first half of his adult life, you were his primary concern, and now for the last half or however long we have together, I will be. But please know that he loves us both, just as we both love him. It's just a matter of focus."

Having no other words to say, Pamela stood. She saw that Tori's eyes had closed.

"Rest now, Tori. I've got this covered, and I'll take good care of him."

When she opened the door and rejoined Kristoffer, he searched her face for answers. She smiled, but what she'd shared with Tori was between the two women who loved him.

She could tell it was on the tip of his tongue to ask what this visit had been about, but all of a sudden, he smiled and bent to place a kiss on her cheek.

After he went inside to say his goodbye, he joined her, took her hand, and squeezed it. They were ready to embark on the next phase of their journey. So many milestones today and tomorrow alone.

"Shall we grab some lunch before we hunt for our dream house?"

he asked.

"Absolutely."

His mood seemed to lighten exponentially as they left the facility. In no time, they were bantering back and forth and anticipating what life had in store for them.

Perhaps he found peace in knowing Tori had "met" the new woman he'd fallen in love with. She hoped that would reassure him and help him let go of any lingering guilt about rejoining the living himself.

Time to start a new chapter.

Pamela's request to meet Tori had taken him aback, but whatever it was she needed from the visit, she seemed to have attained. Her smile as she walked out of Tori's room was radiant, more relaxed than it had been in days. He wasn't sure why he'd never thought to bring her here before, but was glad she'd asked. Somehow, he knew Tori would approve of having Pamela in his life now that she could no longer be here.

He'd never kept either woman a secret from the other, but this meeting between the two great loves of his life made it possible to close the score on one symphony and start a new one.

He'd spent the past few days making sure Pamela restored her body and soul after the arduous ordeal in Afghanistan. He didn't want her getting sick because her immune system was compromised or she was too run-down and exhausted to fight off whatever germs might be making the rounds at the hospital.

She didn't mention the visit at lunch, either, so he decided whatever happened was going to stay between his girls unless Pamela shared with him one day.

After lunch, they met the Realtor at the first house in the Morrison area, west-southwest of Denver. Despite the commute she'd have, Pamela wanted to live in the foothills, and this area boasted a number of state parks and green areas they could enjoy just outside their door. Pamela's schedule kept her busy, and his job was to make sure, when she was home with him, that she found peace and respite.

Her tastes were simple, but the houses here weren't. Despite her protests that they find something smaller, he insisted they look here first. This one boasted three stories from finished basement to loft, with amazing views of both Red Rocks Park on one side and downtown Denver on another.

The gourmet kitchen and ceiling to floor windows in most rooms seemed to be what Pamela loved most. "I don't think I'd know how to act in a place like this," she said, as she ran her hand over the granite countertops on the island.

"Like the adorable sprite you are, no doubt."

She shook her head and laughed before taking a swig from her water bottle.

"Let's see the yard and property." While he could picture them living in the house, he also wanted a buffer zone from the world in which they could play and explore.

The acreage surrounding the house is what sold him. A small waterfall trickled down among strategically placed rocks in a landscaping feature tucked away in a quiet corner of the yard.

"Oh, Kristoffer! Can you imagine how peaceful it would be sitting here and reading, journaling, or meditating?"

The serene elegance of the property was another selling point. Not unlike the traits the woman beside him exuded from every pore.

As far as he was concerned, it was all over except for the closing on this place. They continued to walk around the six-acre lot. It would provide enough privacy that they would be able to indulge their kink outdoors anytime they chose. That would be one of the first things they'd do when they moved in.

He was particularly interested in one bristlecone pine tree with a missing branch at just the right height for restraints. Man, he wished they could move in today.

Before rejoining the Realtor on the patio, he pulled her into his arms and kissed her long and hard. He smiled. "Can you picture yourself living here?"

"As long as you'll be here with me, yes, I can."

"Good, because with the mortgage this place will come with, we aren't going to be able to afford to get away much for a while."

Her concern was immediate as her eyes opened wide. "What about Norway?"

"Don't worry. That's a done deal. Gunnar's agreed to provide the air transportation, so our expenses will be limited." He grew serious. "How about the commute to the hospital? It would take you a minimum of forty-five minutes each way."

"From the condo to work is already thirty to forty-five minutes." She broke free and took in the view down the hillside from the house. "This will be a much more scenic route."

"I'll drive you on days when you're too tired or the roads are bad." His schedule was fairly flexible, and he'd be working mostly from home. Surely the universe wouldn't take Pamela, too. He tamped down his rising fear, banking that the probability of such a loss happening again was astronomical.

No regrets, no guilt.

He took her hand. "Are we ready to make an offer?"

"After only looking at one place?"

He grinned. "I know what I want when I see it." *Like you.* "I also know from a little research on prices in the area that this place is priced competitively and won't last on the market long. There's no time to lose."

"I love your spontaneous side, Kristoffer Roar Larson. Let's do it, but I'll leave the negotiations to you and our Realtor."

After discussing an offer with the real-estate agent, they signed a bid contract at the full asking price. They'd know in a day or so if their offer had been accepted. On the way back to the condo, he shifted gears to tomorrow night's ceremony.

"The plan for tomorrow is for me to drive out ahead of you to Breck. Gunnar wants to pick you up and bring you to me for some reason. I think he wants to speak with you alone. Just don't believe anything bad he says about me." Kristoffer grinned at her.

"I'll defend you, Sir."

He shook his head. "I wouldn't want to take bets on which of you would come out the victor." He drove a few more miles before continuing. "In the meantime, I'll be setting up the dungeon to make sure everything's just right."

"I'm looking forward to every minute of it. I intend to take each second as it happens and drink it all in. After all, it's not every day a girl gets collared. This will be the most important day of my life and one I'll treasure always."

He glanced her way, and they smiled at each other. At least she wasn't nervous or worried. She exuded confidence in her position with him and the choice she'd made. She wouldn't be intimidated by Gunnar, either. They would be family now. By all appearances, she was ready to take the monumental next step in their journey together—not only the collaring, but becoming a member of the Larson clan.

"Tonight, I'll give you the full list of what you need to do or bring with you. Remember that the tattooing will be part of the ceremony. Stay hydrated. Continue applying lotion to your key tattoo in preparation for the new ink on it."

"I will. You seem quite concerned about this process. I don't think I did anything but show up at the shop for my first one. You've been shaving the area nightly since we came home from Afghanistan. You do know that the ink artist is going to do it, too, just before the tattoo machine comes out."

"Really? I've never had one myself. I was just going by what I learned on the Internet."

She chuckled, shaking her head. "Perhaps one day you'll be wearing your sprite's name on your body."

He'd never really thought about having one done. "You're already branded on my heart and mind, Sprite. Why not on my skin, too? We'll discuss it later."

"Just wish mine wasn't in a place where I can't admire the finished product."

He chuckled. "I'm sure I'll be ogling it enough for the both of us in the decades to come."

Kristoffer took the ramp to their neighborhood and continued sharing some of the plans for tomorrow. "We'll do the first part of the ceremony and then enjoy some refreshments so you don't go too long between meals. I'm told it could be about two hours for the design I want to be inked on you. I'll be with you the entire time," he assured her.

"Thank you for taking such good care of me, Sir."

He pulled into their parking spot in the garage and turned to her. "How could I not?" Reaching out and in no hurry to get out of the car, he stroked her cheek. "It's not only my duty to watch over and protect you, but my great privilege and honor to do so as well." He leaned over and met her in the middle for a kiss. "Thank you, Sprite, for coming into my life and giving me a reason to live again. You've mended my heart and made me whole."

While waiting for Gunnar to pick her up the next evening, Pamela went over Kristoffer's instructions a third time to be sure she hadn't forgotten to pack anything. The ceremony would take place in the dungeon at Gunnar's house, high on a mountain outside Breckenridge, so she'd be two hours from here.

After house hunting yesterday, she'd gone dress shopping—alone. Clothes shopping had never been a pastime she enjoyed, so she made a beeline to the department store that always seemed to have fashions that appealed to her. After trying on only three dresses, she'd found the perfect one. Kristoffer had told her it should be a simple white gown. The chiffon dress had an ankle-length flowing skirt—which probably would have come to mid-calf on an average-sized woman. No time for alterations, but it was perfect in her eyes. The bodice had a soft, overlaid fabric clinging in such a way around her breasts as to place a knot solidly over her heart. Well, the center of her chest, anyway. A love knot, she thought, smiling.

Her neck and shoulders would be completely bare above the bodice, front and back, except for the capped, sheer lace sleeves that covered little more than her shoulder joints. She planned to wear her Big Sur jade studs and her silver love bracelet, but no other jewelry. The collar would be the focal point.

She'd spent nearly ninety minutes this afternoon having her hair styled just the way anthropologist Doctor Carolyn Palamas had worn hers on the original *Star Trek* series' episode "Who Mourns for Adonais?" in which the god Apollo captured her heart, well, along with the Enterprise and crew. Would Kristoffer recognize it? Somehow, she bet he'd focused more on Doctor Carolyn's sexy costume when he'd watched the show.

The elaborate updo piled curls at least six inches high above the crown of her head, with thin white satin ribbons intertwined among the swirls. The light touch of hairspray should keep every strand in place while dressing at Gunnar's. The stylist had tried to talk her into what she called event spray, but Kristoffer preferred her hair loose, so she wanted to make it easy for him to release the locks whenever he chose to do so.

Realizing Gunnar would be here any minute, she brought the dress in its bag to the living room and draped it over the couch. The overnight bag she'd packed for her and Kristoffer waited by the door. She'd checked already to make sure she remembered everything as per Kristoffer's instructions—and that she'd left out the things he'd expressly told her not to bring, like underwear. She wasn't to wear any tomorrow, either.

Very few people would be present for the ceremony, and only those in the lifestyle had been asked. Kristoffer had chosen their attendants—Mistress Grant as hers and Patrick his. The woman intimidated her enough that she'd made sure her dress had a side zipper so she could take care of preparing herself without all that much help.

The sharp rap on the door made her jump. Peeking through the peephole, she saw Gunnar and opened the door to greet him.

His gaze went to her hair, and then met hers. "Kris isn't going to be able to take his eyes off of you tonight, Shortcake." He bent to kiss her on the cheek.

"Shortcake?"

He grinned. "I'm about to welcome you into my family. I'm entitled to give you a nickname if I want." Her heart swelled. "With your size and the reddish strawberry-blonde hair, it was the natural choice."

She gave him a quick hug, momentarily too choked up to say anything without breaking down. But soon she'd composed herself. "You didn't have to come all this way to pick me up. I could have ridden out with Kristoffer."

"Nonsense. Then we wouldn't have a chance to talk about some things before Kris lays claim to you forever."

What did he want to say? Despite his commanding personality and height, she'd never been intimidated by the man—until now.

He grabbed the suitcase and she her dress, and they went down to the garage. Instead of his high-bodied Ford Raptor truck, he'd driven a sleek and sporty black Mustang Fastback. It reminded her of the 1969 Fastback her dad restored after he retired from the Air Force.

Gunnar maneuvered easily through late-afternoon city traffic. They would be about an hour ahead of the hordes leaving work and hitting I-70 West at rush hour, so shouldn't find themselves in a bottleneck on the interstate as long as there weren't any accidents or construction projects.

Once outside the metro limits, Gunnar wasted no time saying what he'd wanted to talk with her about.

"Shortcake, I want to thank you for all you've done for Kris these past four months. My gut told me the day you came to tell us about Fakhira that you two would be good for each other. But I never imagined things would move this fast or this far. You achieved a miracle in an extremely short time."

"Miracle?" She laughed. "We simply fell in love."

"Don't shortchange it. I'd nearly given up on bringing that man back among the living, despite two years of serious trying. Then you walked into the room, and it was all over but the shouting. That part happens today."

"I'm not sure he noticed I existed during that meeting. Even he admits he didn't."

"Oh, he noticed all right. That was one of his demon days, but several times, I saw his gaze stray in your direction. Maybe his logical brain hadn't noticed, but his subconscious had."

She smiled. "And here I thought it was my being naked in the classroom the night he toured the academy."

"Happy bonus, I'm sure, but Kris and I talked about this recently. It wasn't your body that night—okay, not entirely that, anyway. The real clincher was the vulnerability you conveyed to him that evening with your silent plea to which he could not help but respond as any Dominant would." Gunnar grinned.

"Kristoffer told me pretty much the same thing, but I thought he was just being a gentleman."

Gunnar laughed. "I'm glad to hear you see him behaving like a gentleman. FarFar, Aunt Claire, and I all tried our best. In all seriousness, he's not a man controlled by his hormones, but rather by a need to guide, protect, and nurture the woman he loves. He never breaks a vow, and that's what has kept him stuck for so long, because with Tori in that state, deciding when she'd died wasn't cut and dried."

Still wasn't, perhaps, although he seemed to have accepted the fact Tori died the night of the accident.

"But that night at the academy you threw him the lifeline he needed. Watch over him, as he will you."

She reached across the car and squeezed his arm. "I'll take good care of him and do everything in my power to make him happy, Gunnar. You can count on that."

He glanced quickly at her and smiled before turning his attention once more to the straight stretch of road. "You're my sister now, Shortcake. If you or Kris ever lack for *anything*—material or emotional—you call me, because I know he's not one to reach out half the times he should. I wouldn't have half the money I do if not for his savvy investments, and family takes care of family. But it's a good thing you two figured out a way to be together so I don't have to butt in anymore."

"Anymore?" When had he before?

He grinned. "Some night when you two have nothing better to do or talk about, ask Kris to fill you in. Just know, Shortcake, he was as clueless about it as you are."

She grinned, shaking her head. "I'm honored to be welcomed into the Larson family too. If I wasn't strapped into this seatbelt, I'd kiss you right now."

He smiled. "I'll take a rain check after the ceremony tonight." His gaze on the road, he sobered. "I've loved your man like a brother for a long time. But I'm not losing my brother, I'm gaining a sister."

His welcoming her to the family left a warm spot in her heart for him. "I'm happy to call you brother, too. All I can say is you two must have been something growing up. But you know what they say."

"What's that?" he asked.

"God made you cousins because He knew neither set of parents could handle you both as siblings!" Gunnar's laugh was long and hearty.

How had Pamela been lucky enough to cross paths with these two? Well, she owed Heidi a debt of gratitude for starting the ball rolling by pointing her in Gunnar's direction. She would have to find a way to repay her someday.

Dressed in black tails, Kristoffer surveyed the dungeon. The lighting would be provided primarily by candles. Once Gunnar had come in, and he knew Sprite was preparing upstairs, the three of them, including Patrick, had set about lighting the seven white tapers on each black floor stand of the same number. Seven for luck. Three stands lined either side of the white runner she'd walk down and the last one was behind Gunnar.

Grant had gone upstairs to check on her, although Sprite had insisted she could do everything herself. When the candles had been lit, Patrick headed to the kitchen to give Kristoffer's check to the caterers so they could be sent on their way before the ceremony started. Only the five main parties would be here. The tattoo artist wouldn't even arrive to set up until after the collaring and reception were over.

Gunnar had given them a guest suite in his mansion to enjoy on this special night. From what the artist had told him, Sprite would be tender given the position of the tattoo. Avoiding lying on her back tonight would prove interesting, but Sprite's agreeing to alter her ink in a permanent way was important and symbolic.

Patrick turned up the dimmers on the wall sconces, casting a little more light and drama to the setting. Kristoffer walked over to the silver tray that held the single long-stemmed white rose with unsnipped thorns and carried it to the room where Sprite would await the signal to join him.

Gunnar rang a bell signaling Kristoffer and the attendants to take their places, not unlike the positions at a wedding. Grant, also dressed in black with her blonde hair in a ponytail high at the back of her head, took her place at the sound system. At Gunnar's signal, she began the song Kristoffer had chosen.

Westlife's "It's You" spoke what was in his heart better than he ever could. Sprite truly had lit up his life and made it a different place. He'd instructed her to listen to the words as she walked toward him. After he heard the cue—"Baby, it's you"—Patrick handed Kristoffer the bell to ring.

His heart pounded and then seconds later, Sprite entered the room from the back dressed in a long, flowing gown, her chest bare above the top of her dress. Her alabaster skin begged for his hands, his lips, but he reined in his libido. They hadn't made love since last night, but would tonight—gingerly, depending on how comfortable she was after being inked.

Her hair was swept up in an incredibly sexy style that reminded him of someone, but he quickly banished thoughts of anyone but his precious Sprite from his mind.

She carried the single white rose in her hands, the bud resting between her breasts and against her heart, as she walked toward him. The soft skirt of the dress swirled as she appeared to float toward him, barefoot and in complete submission.

The song ended just as she reached his side. Having eyes for no one else, Kristoffer and Sprite faced one another. He took her right hand in his, looking deeply into her eyes for any sign of reluctance or uncertainty. All he saw was love and acceptance. He smiled at her, overwhelmed that someone so beautiful, so precious, had chosen to submit to him and to wear his collar.

Gunnar began the ceremony. "Welcome, friends. We have gathered this evening to unite Kristoffer Roar Larson and Pamela Darlene Jeffrey in a bond no one—not human or superhuman—can shatter. The power they will exchange before us will bind them together as surely as any rope or chain ever could. Roar and Sprite, as they will be referred to in this ceremony, have come together to pledge themselves to love, cherish, and support one another for all eternity as Dominant and collared submissive.

"Roar and Sprite, tonight, we celebrate how the paths of two lonely people crossed when you met, and now you will be joined forever as you continue your journey side by side. It is this locking together of once-separate hearts, minds, bodies, and souls that brings phenomenal strength to each of you and binds you to one destiny that defies time, space, and death."

Gunnar addressed him first. "Roar, do you give your collar to your submissive, fully understanding the scope of the responsibility you are undertaking to her?"

"I do."

He then turned toward Pamela. "Sprite, do you accept Roar's collar of your own free will, fully understanding the commitment and promises you are about to enter into?"

"I do," she replied, her voice and commitment never wavering.

"Roar and Sprite, before me and these witnesses, do you both swear that the commitment you are about to enter into is absolute and will last for the rest of your lives and beyond?"

Simultaneously, they answered, "We do."

"Roar informed me earlier that the two of you have prepared individual vows to exchange at this time," Gunnar said. He nodded toward Grant who brought a pillow around and placed it between the two of them.

Kristoffer cleared his throat and recited the words he'd practiced on the drive out here until they were imprinted on his brain.

"Sprite, tonight I come to you as I am—the Dominant who has chosen you above all women to wear my collar and accept my pledge of loyalty, faithfulness, and trust. My promise is to protect and cherish you as I nurture and guide you, share all that I am and have, and bind myself to you for the rest of our lives and, indeed, into eternity."

Sprite handed the rose to Grant and knelt before Roar, looking up at him in love and trust. Her tremulous smile nearly made him tear up again.

"Master Roar, I kneel before you of my own free will, with clarity of mind, heart, and conscience. I surrender my life to you, submitting to your will in all things we have agreed will be under your authority," she said with a grin.

Forever the brat—and soon to be *his* brat forever.

Pamela's emotions almost overpowered her as the moment he would place his collar around her neck drew closer.

But she hadn't finished with her vows yet. "I vow to honor you with my every thought, word, and action. To stay with you, support you, and fulfill your needs and desires as you so allow. Sir, I gladly accept your guidance and love and, to my utmost ability, will devote myself to making you pleased with me in every way." Her voice cracked, but when he reached out to cup her cheek in reassurance, she grew stronger. She leaned into his hand, feeling cherished as his thumb brushed her cheekbone.

"I am yours, Master Roar."

Patrick presented to Roar a box that bore the now-familiar insignia of the jeweler in Big Sur. The region would always hold a special place in her heart, because it was where they had first admitted they were falling in love with each other. He opened the lid to reveal a choker lying on white satin. The round, pea-sized Big Sur jade beads had a stunning teardrop-shaped pendant in the front.

He lifted the choker out and held it in front of her. "By accepting my collar, which is to be worn every day as long as you live, know that I, as your Dominant, vow to do everything within my power to remain worthy of both you and your submission. I promise to respect and be sensitive to your needs and desires, to work with you to keep our relationship strong and vibrant, and to love, hold, honor, and support you. I will acknowledge my responsibility for the safekeeping of the profound trust you have placed in me with your surrender."

He drew a shaky breath. Seeing how nervous he was, she smiled at him. "Sprite, I accept the deeper responsibility that comes with the placing of this collar around your neck. I vow to never violate, or even *threaten* to violate, the trust you have granted me. I acknowledge and accept with all my heart the gift of your submission and surrender to me."

He lifted the collar to his lips and placed a kiss on the pendant and another on the barrel-shaped clasp. She was grateful he hadn't chosen one with a padlock. No one at the hospital would suspect this was anything other than a special necklace.

"Sprite, are you ready to accept this collar in the spirit in which it is offered?"

"Most definitely, Master Roar."

As he walked around behind her, her body began to shake with profound emotion. She blinked back tears. "As long as I remain true to you and my vows, this collar is never to be removed without my permission. Hold your head high as you accept my collar, Sprite," he commanded. She stretched to her full height as the cold beads were laid on her collarbone.

"My beloved Sprite, this collar—and any collar I choose to place around your neck from this day forward—will forever be a symbol to the two of us, those present here tonight, our BDSM community at large, as well as the universe, that you have agreed to be mine. But by wearing this collar, I expect you to continue to be the authentic person you are and to continue to grow into the person you wish to become. I will move heaven and earth to deepen your roots, honor your boundaries, stretch your limits, and give you wings to take flight—each at the appropriate time."

As he closed the clasp, sealing her to him forever, Roar's fingers brushed the back of her neck causing goose bumps to break out on her arms. He ran his warm hand over the back of her collar before squeezing her shoulder reassuringly. A sense of belonging came over her.

"Sir, I accept your collar as the outward and visible sign of your love and protection for me."

He returned to stand before her. "Look at me, Sprite." Tears streamed down her face as she met his gaze once more, but she smiled as he wiped them away. "We remain equals in a sense. I can't do this without you; you can't do this without me. Our separate halves are now one, dovetailing like the yin and the yang."

She felt whole, yet unique in her own identity, like the ancient Chinese symbol he referred to. Interconnected to give each other what they needed, but formed in such a way that the two must become one to be complete.

Roar took her hands and helped her to her feet. "We have both consented to this exchange of power and have agreed to follow the vows we spoke earlier, but unless we communicate to one another what we want and need, we won't be able to succeed. Before we move on, is there anything else you want to express at this time?"

Empowered to share, she searched for the words she wanted to speak. After a moment, she began, "Sir, it is my deepest joy to become yours in such a beautiful way, an honor I will never take for granted. Yes, I have given you authority over me and trust you to guide me on the path that is right for the two of us as we continue this journey together. Master Roar, know that you are the center of my universe, the light of my life, and the love of my heart. I place my entire being—body, mind, and spirit—into your care now and forever."

Roar seemed nonplussed by her declaration a moment before he smiled and bent to kiss her lips.

"Ahem." Gunnar smiled. "Not so fast. There's more." He resumed his officiant mantle. "The two of you have been joined for the sole purpose of loving, caring and supporting each other in the fullness of time. To symbolically show you are willing to shed blood for each other, Roar has asked me to conclude this evening with the White Rose Ceremony."

Gunnar nodded to Patrick, who lifted the cloth-covered tray revealing a full-blown, long-stemmed red rose along with two lancets. She smiled, remembering their discussion about the risk of fungal infections if they'd used the thorns of the roses. As always, he bowed to her authority in her area of expertise. She hoped he'd scrubbed his hands as thoroughly as she'd instructed him to.

Focus!

Patrick handed the red rose to Gunnar at the same time that Grant presented him with the white one Pamela had carried down the aisle.

Gunnar held up Sprite's rose first. "This white rose represents the purity of your gift of submission as well as the unity of your coming together. The petals remain slightly closed, Sprite, to show that your submission has not yet come to full bloom. In fact, it never will. Submission is ever deepening and ever growing. Therefore, you will never reach a place where you cannot open a bit more for your Dominant, Roar."

She found comfort in knowing she wasn't expected to know everything or to be perfect in her submission. As long as her heart remained pure and on track—she could improve with each passing day.

Next, Gunnar lifted the other rose. "The red rose signifies Roar's Dominance, his passion, and his desire to cherish and protect his collared submissive at all costs. The red rose is almost in full bloom to symbolize Roar's readiness to accept the responsibilities required of him."

With a twinkle in his eye toward her, Gunnar continued. "While traditionally, we might now have used the thorns of roses to shed blood, Sprite pointed out the inherent health dangers," he winked at her, and Roar smiled remembering her tirade. His alpha submissive wouldn't blindly follow and he'd better be willing to admit when he was wrong and cut his losses. "Therefore, we'll only point out the significance of the thorns."

Growing serious again, he said, "These thorns symbolize that the journey you have chosen in a lifestyle not accepted by many will not be an easy one. But there is never an easy path in this life. There will be slings and arrows you will have to fight off—but you will be able to defend against them side by side because of the commitment you have made to one another tonight."

When instructed by Gunnar, Roar picked up one of the lancets from the tray and asked for her left hand. The nondominant one, she thought, as she prepared for the finger stick. It was so much easier being on the other side of the lancet or needle.

"Look at me, Sprite."

She did so and a sense of peace came over her as she smiled at him with confidence.

I trust you, Master Roar.

"Deep breath," he commanded. As she inhaled, she felt a sting to her middle finger, but his firm hold on her kept her from jerking away. Gunnar held the red rose in front of her, and Roar guided her hand to hover above it as he squeezed two drops of blood onto the petals of the red rose.

Gunnar explained, "Sprite has shed two drops of her blood on Roar's rose to signify the giving of herself completely to him—body and soul."

Picking up the remaining lancet with her right hand, she then held her left one out between them, going a little off script but moved to do so both out of necessity to keep his hand still and a deep need to send him an important message from her heart.

"Sir, please rest your dominant hand palm up on the back of your submissive's hand." He quirked a brow, but placed his warm, tanned hand against the back of her pale one. "Remember always, Master Roar, that I am here to walk beside you and provide support to you for the rest of our journey here on this earth, and again when we are reunited in the afterlife."

His smile melted her heart.

As quickly as he had done, she lanced him, returned the lancet to the tray, and took his bloodied finger to guide it over the top of the white rose Gunnar held out to them. She squeezed two drops of blood onto the petals of the bud.

Gunnar said, "In having his own blood fall onto Sprite's rose, Dominant Roar shows his willingness to accept injury and even death in order to protect and defend Sprite. His second drop seals their unity."

Grant extended a thin red ribbon to Gunnar, who addressed submissive and Dominant. "Press your middle fingers together." The instant they touched, a jolt of pure energy washed through her.

Gunnar tied their fingers together before Sprite pressed her entire palm and other fingers against Roar's. "By pressing your wounds together, you allow separate blood to mix as one, binding you as strongly as your own family bloodlines. Sprite and Dominant Roar, you are now and forevermore the same flesh and blood."

When she saw a tear trickle down Roar's cheek, she lost control of her own, but didn't care. She could be weak as well as strong with him and still be loved.

"Continue facing one another," Gunnar began, "and repeat the following vows in one voice."

They spoke their closing vows one line at a time:

I will cherish your love today, tomorrow, and forever.
I will trust you, honor you, care for you, and protect you.
I will always be open and honest with you
and eternally grateful for your unconditional, accepting love.
I will laugh with you and cry with you.
I will love you and only you, faithfully.
Through the best and the worst,

the difficult and the easy,
whatever may come, I will always be beside you.
As I have given you my hand to hold,
I give you my life to keep.

Gunnar beamed as he announced, "Sprite—or Doctor Pamela Jeffrey, as you are known outside these walls—I am pleased to announce you are now and forevermore the collared submissive to Dominant Kristoffer Roar Larson."

As he untied their fingers, Gunnar said, "Roar, Sprite awaits you to seal this union in one more symbolic way. No, wait! That comes later." He grinned. "First, seal it with a kiss."

As if needing no more encouragement, Roar closed the gap and pulled her into his arms. His hand automatically went to her hair and pulled her head back, thrilling her. She didn't worry about what would happen with her updo. It would be coming down tonight anyway.

He ground his lips against hers in a show of dominance she melted into. Holding onto his shoulder blades as he deepened the kiss, she opened her mouth to welcome him.

The pop of a cork made her jump, and the kiss ended as Patrick poured champagne from a magnum of vintage Dom Perignon rosé. He handed each of them a flute before passing one to the others present.

Still in officiating mode, Gunnar proposed the first toast. "I'm a firm believer that we make our own destiny and that happily ever after takes work. You two worked hard to find a unique way to unite despite hardships. Kris, you above all know that life is fleeting. Pamela, your compassion has led you to seeing the horrors and suffering around us, too." She wasn't sure where this was going, but hoped he'd reach the blissful part soon. "My hope for you both is that you will seek out joy-filled moments every chance you get."

They smiled that he'd managed to end on a high note and clinked glasses. Roar raised his flute next, first addressing those in the room. "Thank you all for helping make this evening one to be remembered by us for the rest of our lives. Thank you for your support, Gunnar, through the dark times. Thank you, Grant and Patrick, for your trustworthiness and willingness to stand up with us tonight."

When he turned his attention to her, Pamela's heart nearly burst with love. "Sprite, when I placed that collar around your neck, you became the first and foremost person in my life. Yes, I'll continue to be her guardian and husband until her body leaves this world, but Tori is receiving excellent care and no longer needs me the way you do."

He took a breath. "From this moment forward, my home, my heart, my life are centered around the two of us. I'll do everything in my power to see that not a day, not a minute even, goes by that you aren't aware of my love and protection."

They intertwined their arms before drinking from their flutes, gazes locked along with hearts. "I love you, Master Roar."

"I love you, too, Sprite."

CHAPTER TWENTY-FIVE

Pamela broke down the last of the boxes she'd unpacked and surveyed the kitchen of her dreams—stainless appliances, granite countertops, and a drop-dead gorgeous view of the Red Rocks Park over the double sink.

Their wine rack was filled with what remained of the bottles they'd shipped home from their Sonoma trip this past summer. They wouldn't be taking many trips like that for the next few decades while paying off this place, but she didn't care. They'd splurge on one big trip a year and be content to spend the rest of their time here.

Hard to believe that a month ago she'd been collared, and here they were setting up their home. Their offer had been accepted two days after they'd submitted it. Preparations for the collaring ceremony had kept her so busy, she hadn't even worried.

The house had modern touches and rustic charm, suiting both their tastes. They'd been taking evening walks in the neighborhood this week after she returned from work. She was happy the bulk of unpacking for the living areas was almost finished. They still needed to shop for furniture in the spare bedrooms.

She hoped to entice her mom back to Colorado for a visit sometime, although she was a little worried that all Mom talked about anymore was Heidi's school. Pamela hoped she wouldn't do anything rash like sign on to teach there.

Tori's parents would need a room, too, when they came for visits. She'd enjoyed their enthusiasm for life when she'd met them briefly. How heartbreaking the loss of their daughter must have been, but clearly, they loved Kristoffer and wanted him to move on. She'd been welcomed by them into the family.

Pamela had recently learned the hard way how important it was not to leave anything unsaid or broken. A little more than a week ago, while watching the news, she'd found out the trauma center she'd worked at in Kunduz had been bombed—barely a month after she'd left. She'd lost two close colleagues and dozens of others. When Kristoffer had heard her scream, he came running from his office at the condo to see what had happened. So senseless, but the incident brought home the fact that no one was safe in a volatile place like that. So many humanitarian aid workers and their patients at the trauma center wouldn't be returning to their families.

Don't think about that, or you'll start crying again.

That weekend, they'd held each other even closer. He'd pointed out how it easily could have been her in the bombing if her assignment had been postponed one more month.

If she hadn't already sworn off future trips with the medical and humanitarian group, this would have made her do so.

Fortunately, they'd begun moving in right after the incident. That activity and her busy work schedule had helped keep her mind off the tragedy except for times like this when it crept back in.

This house and land had already become their oasis from the world. They were content to stay home except when one or both had to go to work. Kristoffer hadn't been called to Breckenridge all week and had done the bulk of the moving and unpacking, but he'd left the kitchen to her this weekend.

Outside, he'd set up a bench near the trickling waterfall. As soon as she came home and changed into more comfortable clothes, her assignment was to sit there and journal for half an hour. She was to write down anything she was still worried about that might encroach on their time together and then let those things go until the next day. The exercises provided her with a great deal of solace.

By then, she and Kristoffer were anxious to explore other means of stress relief. She smiled as her pulse quickened merely thinking about them. She had the feeling he was scouting every inch of their six secluded acres, as well as every corner of the house. Kristoffer had pointed out a tree this morning on their walk that was hidden away and butted up against the privacy fence where he wanted to tie her up and have his way with her. Her body tingled with excitement.

Plenty of room to raise a family, too, if they were lucky enough to have children. They'd been blessed with so much already and shouldn't be greedy, but having his baby would be the ultimate gift. As they'd agreed to attempt a natural pregnancy for a year, at least they'd agreed adoption was a viable option as well. Perhaps an orphaned child from Afghanistan or that region. A back-up plan took some of the pressure and anxiety off her shoulders.

No matter whether she birthed naturally or they adopted, the important thing was that their children would have doting parents and an extended family on both sides that loved them. They would carry the Larson name, like Pamela would as soon as the court approved her recent petition for a legal name change. She smiled remembering when she'd announced her decision to Kristoffer over dinner. There weren't many things that could leave him speechless, but that had.

Oddly enough, even without any baby Larsons, they already had a cradle. When Kristoffer had cleaned out his storage unit, the only piece of furniture he'd brought into their home was a cradle he'd inherited from FarFar. For now, it was tucked in a closet in a spare bedroom. She didn't want to see the empty cradle again unless they knew they would be able to fill it.

Noma rubbed against her leg, and she bent down to lift the fat cat into her arms and rub under her jaw where she liked being petted. They had their spoiled furbaby. When the tabby meowed, she realized this wasn't a call for affection but food, and placed a handful of the special dry cat food that the vet insisted on. She first sniffed the food cautiously and then the air with great disdain.

"Sorry, Noma, but until you lose some of that excess padding, that's all you get to eat. Doctor's orders."

As happened at least a dozen times a day still, her fingers sought out her collar, which rested warm around her neck and left her with the now-familiar sense of belonging, trust, and love. Kristoffer had made her his in the most important way that mattered.

"Where do you want this?" Kristoffer, who had been in charge of unpacking the remaining boxes in the living room, carried in her mom's housewarming gift that had been special delivered yesterday.

The fluid jade carving depicted a tall man staring lovingly into the eyes of a much shorter woman, his hands framing her face in an oh-so-dominant pose. Water lapped at their lower bodies—although Kristoffer first interpreted them as flames. When she mentioned it reminded her of a water sprite in the arms of her Viking lover, he conceded the point.

Either way, the piece was gorgeous, sensual, and hit much closer to home than her mother might have intended.

"Just set it there for now." She pointed to the kitchen counter. "I need to give a little more thought to where it fits best." The coffee table in the great room would give it more exposure to guests, but she leaned toward keeping it all to themselves in their master bedroom.

While he poured a glass of ice water, she crossed the room to wash her hands, first removing the ring she now wore on her left ring finger. Their first night here, he'd surprised her with the platinum band to wear that had been inscribed on the inside with "Roar" spelled in Norwegian runic lettering. She had only been able to decipher the two r's at either end of the word until he enlightened her.

When he'd placed it on her finger, he said it was yet another token of his love—but also a signal to any non-lifestyle men who didn't get the message to steer clear from her collar.

His.

She smiled as she dried her hands.

"What's so funny?" Kristoffer came across the room and wrapped her in his arms, cocooning her.

"Not funny, really. I was simply remembering why you gave me a ring in addition to my collar and bracelet."

He shrugged. "Call me a Viking. I lay claim to what's mine."

"If I'm not mistaken, your ancestors were renowned for laying claim to what was everyone else's, too."

He gave his Viking battle cry as he tilted her off balance and devoured her neck. Kissing her there never failed to make her wet. Then he whispered in her ear, "My sprite, rest assured my plundering and pillaging days are over. I've won the most valuable treasure of all."

She pivoted around to face him as his lips lowered to hers, barely brushing them at first before doing a fair job of plundering her mouth with his tongue. She opened her mouth to allow him to further claim her. One hand held the back of her head firmly to keep her in place, while the other glided up the inside of her thigh-length T-shirt to cup her breast. Her bra left her body the minute she returned home from work, per his instructions, although that had always been the first thing to go when she'd lived alone, too. Only now, she had instructions to go without panties around the house, too, as long as no one else but Kristoffer was there.

When he pinched and twisted her nipple, she gasped, breathing his essence into her soul. His hand lowered from her head to cup her butt and pull her against his erection, signaling to her they were finished unpacking this Sunday afternoon.

He broke away, took her hand, and tugged her toward the open-concept living room. "Let's go outside."

She was disappointed that they weren't going to play after he'd touched her so, but they still had plenty of time before she was due at the hospital in the morning.

✧   ✧   ✧

Kristoffer had been planning this scene for days, but they'd had so much work to do before Pamela started the workweek again. With four or five hours of daylight remaining, the time was now.

"Close your eyes and wait here in position three." He walked to the foyer coat closet to retrieve what he'd stowed there earlier. With a sleep mask in one hand and toy bag in the other, he returned to find her stance perfect.

Coming up behind her, he slipped the sleep mask over her eyes.

"Can you see anything?"

"Not a thing, Sir."

"Release your hands from the box hold and hold them over your head." After she had followed his instructions, he tugged her T-shirt over her head and used it to tie her hands together in front of her with a secure knot. Seeing her standing completely naked, bound, and blindfolded made him so hard he was tempted to take her upstairs to their bed and scrap the whole scene.

But he had better self-control than that.

"I'm going to take your arm and lead you. Take small steps. I'll catch you if you stumble."

He'd walked the path to the bristlecone pine tree several times to clear away any debris or obstacles. Her arm tensed when she realized he was opening the door.

"Trust me." The privacy fence would shield her nakedness from anyone outside and the nearest neighbor's house was on the opposite side of their acreage. Not that she seemed all that concerned about being naked outside.

God of Thunder, I love this woman!

He bent to whisper in her ear. "So that we don't have the neighborhood watch folks filing reports or complaints, I'm placing you in voice—and noise—restriction."

She nodded that she'd heard and understood.

"You have your safeword if you need it." But he intended to torture her senses in a pleasant way today. If she did become a little loud, they might find out they had some kinky neighbors—or would learn which close-minded ones to steer clear of. What they chose to do in the privacy of their own property was no one else's business.

When they reached the tree he'd prepared for her Friday, he stopped and took her bound hands to lift them over her head. Just a little short, so he'd have to retrieve some rope from his bag. First, he used his hands to stroke her beautiful body. Her nipples remained aroused, probably from the illicitness of the scene.

Rope in hand, he positioned her facing the tree and slung the rope over a branch stub. The other day, he'd checked the tree for any loose splinters or areas that might abrade. While gentle friction with the tree trunk would be a turn-on for them both, his goal wasn't to wear away her skin enough to cause bleeding.

With Pamela's back bared before him, he placed a kiss on the Roar tattoo. They'd gone to the tattoo artist again three weeks ago to have his Sprite tattoo added to the same spot on his body. Yet another bonding experience for the two of them.

Taking the flogger in his hand, he stroked her skin from shoulders to calves, slowly, sensuously. Gooseflesh rose on her arms as he paid them some attention, too. In no hurry, he let the kangaroo hide become a part of her. She'd told him this was her favorite. He wasn't sure if it was the way it felt or that Gunnar had left it for them on the bed the evening of her collaring.

Focus.

Her spicy scent rose from her skin. He stepped away and lightly swished the flogger tails against the skin of her shoulders, flicking her tresses. He loved her hair loose, even when it would have been sexier to see her skin pinken.

But there was plenty of exposed skin still. He let the tails slap against her ass briefly. Her hands clenched, and he heard her sharp intake of breath. So responsive. Did the tree bark bite against her breasts as she jerked and fought her restraints? Or did that only heighten her senses?

The falls now thudded against the curve above her rounded ass and on the tat. The dimples on either side of her hips mesmerized him as he increased the rhythm of his strokes. Her pale skin reddened quickly. His stiff cock throbbed.

He directed the flogger to her calves, then thighs. When he slapped her ass again, her soft panting matched the rhythm of the impacts. He worked the flogger into a frenzy against her skin. She tried to pull away from the tree, but the hand and arm restraints made it impossible.

Was the tree bark rubbing her skin? He'd check soon, but for now didn't let up. He'd like to see if he could get her into subspace. Judging by her body language and the hitches in her breath, Pamela was in the throes of passion, not pain.

If he didn't get her to subspace, he'd at least make her come.

Exploring limits with her had already given him new insights, some contradicting what he thought he knew about each of them. For instance, he'd never identified himself as being a sadist, but had gone further than ever imagined with her without either of them ending the scene. And, while not a masochist, she'd definitely enjoyed pain for pain's sake on more than one occasion. It was up to him to determine where each of their limits lay on that spectrum—both in giving and receiving. He grinned at the prospect stretching out before him for many years to come.

When her head lolled backward and her clenched hands loosened, he thought perhaps he'd succeeded in the former, helping her to reach that state of euphoria coveted by submissives, but when he slapped her ass once more with the flogger, she lifted her head and clenched her fists.

Man, he didn't want this scene with his sweet sprite to ever end.

Wanting to awaken her senses before taking her deeper, he returned the flogger to his toy bag. He reached deep inside and removed the perfect toy to bring out more gooseflesh on her tender backside.

He smiled. He couldn't wait for her response.

On fire! Her shoulders, thighs, and butt burned, but she wanted more. When he stopped, she fought back a groan and took a deep breath, instead. Her mind floated back to the scene. There had been a moment when she thought she'd reach subspace, but not yet. She'd get there one of these days because each scene they did, she came closer. Her willingness to stay in the moment and not overthink things— thanks to Master Roar's training—had made a huge difference.

She wouldn't get there if she kept dwelling on *wanting* to get there.

Master Roar took her hair and draped it over her left shoulder, baring her back. The stroke of something soft tracing a meandering path from her neck down her spine to her lower back awakened her skin even further. It tickled. A feather? Furry paddle?

As it drifted in a sashaying motion over her back, goose bumps rose on her butt cheeks in anticipation. Already so sensitive from the flogger, her skin further awakened to his touch.

She felt more alive than ever before. An outdoor scene was so elemental. In the beginning, she'd heard the sounds of the neighborhood—children playing, dogs barking, cars driving by. But her total awareness was now on the tip of an extremely soft feather. Ostrich, most likely.

Her mind remained firmly in this moment with Master Roar.

The feathery object trailed down the back of her right thigh, and she parted her legs as much as she could, but a swat to her backside with his hand told her she hadn't been given permission to change her position. She moved her feet back to where she thought they'd been before.

Disappointed that the bundle of nerves between her legs would be harder to reach from where he stood, she couldn't help but imagine the feather, or whatever was tickling her, would bring on an explosive orgasm.

Unfortunately, perhaps because she hadn't been obedient, he started back up, teasing a spot on the upper part of her ass. Her tattoo? When he changed direction again to move lower, she once again held her breath. Closer.

Yes. Keep going. So close!

However, instead of touching her between her legs, the feather flitted over her butt crack and coursed up her back yet again. When it stroked the side of her breast, her nipples hardened, sensitive from being rubbed against the bark during the flogging.

But the feathery touches wiped away the pain. The flesh rose on the side of first one breast and then the other as he meandered an erratic path over her body. She fought to stand still, but couldn't help sometimes squirming as she tried not to scream. What a rude awakening for the neighbors to find out the neighborhood had gone to pot— or kink, as the case may be.

When Master Roar traced a path inside her armpit and up the underside of her arm, she started to jerk away from the ticklish sensation but remembered her training and clenched her hands while breathing slowly, instead. There weren't many places she was ticklish, but of course, he'd found one.

When the feather stopped moving against her skin, she waited. All too soon, he began untying the rope and lifting her hands off the branch above her. Her arms protested being lowered, but he massaged her shoulders to take away some of the discomfort.

Was the scene over? He turned her around and pressed her backside against the tree. She smiled. The trunk now scraped the burning skin of her butt cheeks. Her bound hands were lifted above her head once more, and ropes secured her to about the same spot, but this time she was raised on tiptoes.

He adjusted the rope. "Feet flat on the ground. I don't want you getting a cramp."

He also placed a belt around her waist, securing her to the tree another way. Her nipples swelled as the cool breeze kissed them. So sensitive.

When she heard the tinkling of a familiar chain, she knew he'd brought out the nipple clamps. Her hands clenched in anticipation.

"Prepare for the bite of the clovers, Sprite."

Damn!

Those were well-known as the most vicious of all nipple clamps. He'd never used them on her before, but had been consistently ramping up their play in that area, one of his favorites.

She clutched her hands together and steeled herself as he pinched and twisted her nipple.

"Deep breath."

Here it comes! She inhaled too quickly, and the clamp pinched her sensitive peak on the exhalation. The initial pain made it hard to tell which type of clamp he'd used, but she hoped he wouldn't tug on the chain and tighten the clovers.

Be strong for him.

As he told her time and again, his pleasure was found in having a well-behaved, satisfied submissive.

"Breathe again. Slowly, this time."

With the second clamp on, she waited. The pain dissipated quickly. When he tugged on the chain, making her nipples dance, she braced herself for the pain to worsen.

But the pain only stimulated her. Were they actually clover clamps? Had she become accustomed to high levels of pain? Or was this just another mindfuck?

Her focus returned to the sinfully delicious things the amazing Master Roar was doing to her body in *this* moment.

The next sensation she felt was slightly prickly with a strong scent of pine. Landscapers had planted bristlecone, mugo, and pinyon pines in the yard. The needles brushed softly against her right breast. Would they prickle if he reversed direction? So far, the strokes were soft, making her almost certain it was the bristlecone. The needles caressed the curve of her breasts and then underneath. Her nipples bunched, and she let out a moan of ecstasy.

"Quiet, or suffer the consequences. You've been doing well up to now."

Without warning, what must be a second branch bit into the side of her other breast hard enough to make her hold extremely still.

She heard a swishing noise, and he began using the two branches in a flogging motion on her nipples, sometimes gently and others times harder with the occasional pinprick sensation. Her head grew light as she surrendered to the feelings. Her head lolled back against the tree trunk.

She wanted so badly to express how much she enjoyed this exquisite scene, but remained in voice restriction. The needle flogging ended abruptly, and she waited in frustration until, once more, the sides of the soft needles poked at her breasts.

An epiphany hit her. Master Roar was an expert at reading her body—the bunching of her nipples, clenching of her hands, and her incredibly relaxed posture told him all he needed to know without making any noise at all.

The soft, yet prickly, needles of the branches trailed down her sides from her breasts to her waist to her hips. Then lower still. At her thighs, she felt the sharp needles against her skin.

Touch me there!

But he stopped. She nibbled on her lip. Was he a mind reader, too? Okay, she'd quit asking for what she wanted, even in her thoughts.

He only deprived her of sensation a moment before sliding the needles up her sides, completely ignoring her mound and clit, and continuing up the undersides of her arms to her hands before starting back down. He circled her breasts once before tormenting her nipples with a light thrashing from the bristly points. The flogging lasted longer this time. Sweat broke out on her forehead as she strained to maintain control and focus on the rhythmic slapping of the needles against her swollen peaks mashed inside the clamps.

Her clit throbbed in response, begging for his attention, but she drew her focus back to the area he played with, knowing that's where he wanted it to be. The bombardment continued, and the lightheadedness encroached again.

Her mind screamed when a slight tugging at her clamps suddenly released them. The burning sensation washed through her entire body, sending her mind into a euphoric state where nothing else mattered but experiencing this glorious flogging.

"Breathe, Sprite," he whispered, his mouth now close to her ear. Pamela took a much-needed deep breath before exhaling slowly, but reveled in the primal experience. "Float back to me when you're ready."

Some corner of her mind registered his soothing voice encouraging her to soar earlier and now calling her back to him. His fingers touched her nipples as the numbness dissipated, and his mouth then ministered to the mangled peaks. He'd used almost no skin-to-skin contact with her during the scene so far, so she welcomed his touch to her breasts and nipples, however briefly it lasted.

A pungent odor assailed her nostrils. Menthol? Eucalyptus? Not something she could identify right away. His finger applied the cool, wet balm to her nipples, and the breeze kissed the areolas as well, leaving them chilled enough to cause the sensitive tips to swell even more.

Suddenly, whatever he'd applied to her skin turned fiery hot. Tiger Balm? Or arthritis medicine perhaps? Her peaks went from icy cold to burning hot in seconds. She longed for him to rub her nipples once again to disperse the heat, but instead, he began flicking the tails of a stingy pine-needle flogger against her mound, igniting a deeper fire throughout her body.

Slap, slap, slap.

"Spread your legs for me, Sprite."

She did so, feeling the pull of the rope on her arms, but only wanting to give him access to the cleft between her legs. She sucked air into her lungs as the makeshift flogger slapped against her mound and labia, sending pings to her clit that only made her want him inside her more than ever. She clenched her fingers into fists and panted as he drew her to the edge of total abandon.

So close. Almost there!

And then he stopped again.

No! Not now!

A groan of frustration nearly escaped before she controlled herself. He had to know she was beyond thinking rationally at the moment.

Sadistic, sensual tease.

She had the presence of mind to fight back her plea for release. Part of the game of sensation play was to bring her to the height of pleasure over and over before permitting her to come. But, Christ, she hoped there would be an orgasm for her at some point tonight. For him, as well. She wanted so badly to please this man who had done nothing but bring her pleasure—well, and a heavy dose of frustration. If only he would drive himself inside her and break this god-awful tension.

An itching on the side of her right breast distracted her, but she didn't think Master Roar had caused it. The more she tried to ignore it, the more it became the center of her attention. She couldn't scratch it with her hands restrained, and it wasn't in a spot where she could use the tree trunk to relieve the annoying itching.

But her focus was shot.

"Cocoa Beach, Sir."

She instantly regretted having to use her slow-down safeword and wondered what he would do.

"What's wrong, Sprite?" His husky voice sent a tingle down her body.

"I have an itch, Sir."

"Where?" He sounded like he was grinning now.

Well, to be honest, between my legs.

But she'd trust he'd take care of that less pressing one later. "On the outer side of my right breast. It doesn't hurt, but the inability to scratch it is driving me crazy. I'm afraid my focus is gone."

He surprised her by rubbing the very exact place where she itched. "There?"

"Yes!" The relief bordered on orgasmic. She nearly came undone as he continued scratching it vigorously. Best sensation ever. However, the more he scratched, the more she wanted. When he placed a kiss on the tender spot, she moaned. The kiss hadn't been sexual at all. Merely comforting.

But in her heightened state of arousal, everything was sexual!

Master Roar untied her, removed the T-shirt binding her hands, and lifted her into his arms. He carried her a ways when she heard a truck motor.

"Bloody hell. Who makes deliveries on a Sunday way up here?"

She started to giggle then sobered. What if it was someone from the hospital? She was still blindfolded with a very red, very bare butt.

"Sprite, I'm going to set you down on your feet behind this tree. Stand perfectly still. Do not take one step. Let me get rid of whoever it is."

She almost lost it again with her laughter, but managed to nod. "I'll be waiting, Sir."

He left her for less than five minutes, but she was never so relieved as when she heard the crunching of wood mulch telling her someone approached. "Now, where were we?" Hearing Master Roar's voice, her body relaxed. She hadn't realized how vulnerable she'd feel out here alone like this, even if for only a few minutes.

He lifted her into his arms again and carried her. She was curious about who had been at the door, but didn't ask. He'd tell her if and when she needed to know. When he put her down on her feet and removed her blindfold, she found them in the bedroom.

Yes!

He began stripping, never taking his eyes off her. Watching the light dance in his eyes only made her hotter.

"Remove your sneakers and socks."

Forgetting she still wore them, she sat on the edge of the bed to take off her walking shoes and socks.

He removed his boxers to reveal a cock ready for her. But after he'd removed his own shoes and socks, instead of throwing her on the bed to take her, he took her hand and pulled her to her bare feet again.

"Come with me. How's the bite?"

"What bite?"

He chuckled. "The insect bite. I'll take care of that later unless the itching gets too bad."

She'd completely forgotten about it. He led her into the master bathroom, reached inside the granite walk-in shower big enough for six, and turned on the steam feature before squirting eucalyptus oil into the slot. They'd barely begun to explore the possibilities in this wet oasis, but already had found strategically positioned jetted faucets, a foot massager, handheld shower hoses with all levels of water pressure, and numerous shower heads with varying water pressures from rain to massager. Their predecessors were serious about their shower time.

This delightful feature might have been one of the primary selling points on the house for her. They'd embarrassed their real-estate agent immensely, sending her fleeing to the patio, when Kristoffer pressed Pamela inside the shower and pinned her against the far wall with her arms over her head during their walk-through.

Before the poor woman could escape, he had said in his turned on, husky voice, staring intently at Pamela, "Yeah, this will do nicely."

She'd become wet at the promise in his voice then, but not nearly as wet as she was now.

Standing naked before him, she waited. Without a word, he pierced her with his intense blue eyes and took her hand to accompany her inside. His predatory stare made her insides melt as her nipples pebbled. The warm steam billowed around them after he closed the glass doors, making visibility nil.

"Close your eyes. Simply feel and let me take care of you."

His pampering of her, body and soul, never ceased. Lowering her eyelids, she felt him take her by the shoulders and turn her around before pressing her back against the still cold wall. She gasped, the extreme difference in temperatures between the steam and the granite shocking her system.

He lifted her left hand up to where she knew he'd installed a hook, one of the first Dom improvements he'd made on the place. Quickly trapping her wrist in a cuff, he soon did the same with the other. She hadn't seen him bring cuffs in here, but he must have stashed them earlier. She hoped they were waterproof. Leather might shrink and cut off her circulation.

He'd never taken her in here before, and she wondered if their extreme height difference would make having sex in this position difficult. She fought back a laugh as she reined in her mind.

"I'm not sure what you find amusing, my helpless sprite, but I have you where I want you now and intend to have my way with you." The sexy threat in his voice, coupled with his roaming hands touching her with more force than he'd used outside, made her body quake with tightly leashed passion.

He stepped away, and she fought to control her excitement with her slow, steady breathing. Not as easy as it sounded, but she wanted this moment to last forever—then again, she wanted to come. Now!

He teased her with a handheld hose that wetted her skin with warm spray. He squirted something on her torso. "Ack! That's cold!" The scent of her Sensual Amber shower gel permeated her senses.

"Allow me to warm you up." His lecherous tone made her stomach flip-flop even before his powerful hands zeroed in on her breasts, kneading and pinching as he spread the soap over them. She moaned.

Was she still in voice restriction? He hadn't said anything about her outburst a moment ago, but she'd try to restrain herself, just in case.

His magical hands massaged away every possible tension except the one she most wanted relieved. Over her abdomen, making her clench in anticipation of his going lower, he slickened her skin with the soapy liquid. To her chagrin, he stopped short of her mound.

Throbbing for his touch there, she managed not to groan at being deprived of her orgasm still.

"Spread your legs."

Yes!

She planted her feet as wide apart as she could, despite the strain on her arms. A staccato sound of water hitting the wall with great force told her Kristoffer must have changed the setting to massaging. Her clit throbbed in anticipation.

The hard, pulsating stream of water flicked against her nipples first, as if he were paddling her breasts. Finally, he directed the water lower to her hips, and then to her thighs, still missing the area between her legs she most wanted him to touch.

"Grrr!" she groaned.

"Did you say something, Sprite?"

"No, Sir. Only clearing my throat."

He chuckled, but instead of depriving her any longer, the pulsating jets pounded the top of her mound, the apex of her thighs, and briefly battered the area under which her clit lay hidden and waiting. Her body thrummed in anticipation.

Again, he directed the spray there from above. She didn't think she'd want to have a spray that hard going inside her vagina, but if he continued to focus on her clit, she'd come.

But he hadn't given her permission to come yet.

He brought her closer, but she fought letting her body find release. Shaking, gritting her teeth, she tried to ignore the building pressure.

And then the water stopped. Her hypersensitive body was on the verge of exploding when his fingers delved between the cleft and slipped inside her. Just as suddenly, his fingers were gone.

Not again! Don't leave me like this!

Kristoffer lifted her by the waist and lowered her onto his cock with one swift motion, filling her completely. He used the wall to keep her steady as he pounded into her, each thrust creating friction with her swollen clit. She wasn't sure how long she'd be able to hold out, but apparently, he'd reached a fever pitch, too.

"Come with me, Sprite. Let me hear you scream."

He pulled her lower body away from the wall and pummeled her, hitting her G-spot repeatedly. "Oh, Sir! Yes!" As his movements increased, she screamed and the world exploded around her.

Immediately after, Kristoffer grunted his own orgasm and spilled his semen deep inside her.

When she was coherent again, he dried them both off and carried her to their bed. She stroked his hair as he lay with his head on her chest.

"I'm not sure I'll be able to walk for a week, Sir. How am I going to do rounds or stand for hours in surgery tomorrow?"

"Don't overdo it." His thumb brushed over her navel with light strokes, threatening to ignite a fire down below again, although she was more than sated—for tonight, at least. Lying in the arms of the man she loved, ensconced in the house where they would create many more memories in the years to come, she was living a fairy-tale life she'd only dreamed of since her teen years.

Could she ever ask for more?

"Do you think the delivery person saw anything?" She'd been waiting for him to say what had been delivered, but they hadn't stopped for a minute since then.

"No. But we may have to invest in a lockable gate if we plan on playing outside much. I'd have thought a Sunday would be safe."

Clearly, she was going to have to be blunt. "What was so urgent to be delivered on a Sunday afternoon?"

"Something from Gunnar. I'll look at it tomorrow."

"When's the last time Gunnar had something delivered on a Sunday? Don't you think you should at least open it?"

"But I'd have to leave you to go get it."

"Kristoffer, if you don't, I will. I'm dying of curiosity." Intuition told her they needed to at least open it.

He sighed and walked down to wherever he'd left it, coming back into the bedroom carrying an overnight envelope. Oh, well. Probably just business. He pulled out a sheaf of legal-looking documents, and she was sure of it.

"What the—" He shuffled through several pieces of paper.

She sat up in the bed. "What's wrong?"

A slow grin spread over his face, and he met her gaze. "Gunnar's given us a collaring and housewarming gift all rolled into one."

"What kind of gift?"

Kristoffer held out the papers and across the space, she made out the letterhead of their bank. "He's paid off our mortgage. The house is ours."

How did someone pay off such an expensive house just like that? Gunnar continued to amaze her both in his wealth and his generosity.

"So we're not house poor anymore?"

"That monthly payment will free up a lot of money for us to travel or do whatever we want and still manage to save a good portion."

"How will we ever repay such generosity?"

"You don't. We're family. But I know just the place to take him for a steak dinner to celebrate."

He set the papers down and rejoined her in the bed. A strain she hadn't been aware of had been lifted. They wouldn't have to worry about scrimping to afford the house they hoped to one day fill with lots of little Larsons.

EPILOGUE

The strains of Miles Davis's "Blue in Green" played, one of Tori's favorites, moving through him as he watched the video of Tori's life pass by on the large-screen TV. Kristoffer had provided Grant with a list of the music he wanted played at the memorial service, and she'd taken care of everything beautifully.

Tori's mom had given him some baby and childhood photos to add to the slideshow for a more complete life story, but while the photos conjured up memories for him, they weren't the essence of Tori any more than the mindless shell that had lain in a bed for four years had been. Still, he was thankful he'd worked years ago on the section of images depicting his and Tori's time together. There had been so many arrangements to take care of this past week, and so many family members and friends coming to the house, that he wouldn't have had time to do it right.

The day had come to say goodbye to Tori one last time.

Until now, he hadn't looked at the photos since he'd scanned them and put the photo albums away. Last night, gathered at the house with everyone, he'd given Liz and Ron the actual albums. He held the memories in his heart and this slide show if he needed to reminisce on anniversaries. Her parents weren't high-tech at all. He didn't know why he hadn't thought to share the images with them before.

Seeing Tori's life played out before him again reminded him of all the good times they'd had together. Commencement at Penn, wedding, honeymoon to Sonoma, and so many anniversary trips back there. Photos of her at some of her Denver charity events here, hanging out with Gunnar in Breck, and enjoying wine and dinner with friends.

Vibrant, beautiful, and alive. He'd dwelled too much in the last four and a half years on her current state and had forgotten how she'd lived life to the fullest until the instant she'd been taken away from him in the wreck.

"How are you doing, Kristoffer?" Pamela walked up behind him and reached for his hand, squeezing it reassuringly.

He smiled down at her. She'd been his rock since Tori's passing. "Better, thanks to you." He kissed her cheek. "I wouldn't have gotten through this week without everything you'd done."

Pamela smiled back. "That's what we do when a loved one is hurting."

A strand of hair had slipped out of the simple bun she'd placed it in this morning. Little wonder, given the way she'd been running around all day. After feeding breakfast to the family staying at their house, she'd barely had time to dress. But, as always, she was stunning in the modest, plum-colored dress. He'd asked her not to wear black. Today was a day to celebrate Tori's transition. There'd been enough darkness in recent years.

His collar around her slim neck had been raved at by both her mother and his own, but none had been the wiser. She'd just told them it was a special gift from Kristoffer.

Thankfully, he hadn't been alone when the facility staff called a week ago. While he'd known the day would arrive eventually, hearing she'd passed peacefully in her sleep, rather than having to suffer through another bout of pneumonia, gave him some comfort. Pamela had canceled her appointments that day and stayed home with him.

Tori had finally severed the strings to the broken body that had held her earthbound all these years.

Eva Cassidy's poignant rendition of "Autumn Leaves" began playing, the last of the prelude music.

"Anytime you're ready to start, I think everyone we're expecting is here," Pamela said.

He nodded. "Let me check with Liz and Ron first."

Tori had been cremated two days ago, and her ashes sat in an urn on the table in the front of the chairs assembled for the few dozen guests. Having no church affiliation, they'd chosen to have the ceremony in the chapel at the facility so that some of the staff who had cared for her body here over the past two and a half years could attend. Rick had also come, perhaps to make sure he was holding up okay. Kristoffer hadn't visited the therapist since July, but was forever in his debt for getting him to let go of the past and stop wishing for a future that could never be. There was still a lot he had to live for, if he stayed in the present.

Pamela's calm, supportive presence had been there to help him more than anything or anyone else could. Life marched on—and sometimes it even danced along.

In the back, he found Liz standing near the table where she'd set up some of the mementos she'd kept from among Tori's personal things. "Liz, Ron, if you're ready, we can begin anytime."

Liz dabbed a tear from her eye, but her smile hadn't wavered since she'd arrived at the airport. She'd called this a bittersweet day, which summed it up well.

Unable to help himself, he hugged the woman who had been like a mother to him, too. As he embraced her, he whispered, "She passed peacefully. It's surreal how quickly she crossed over in the end after such a long ordeal, but she's free now. That's all any of us ever wanted."

"You've been a devoted husband, Kristoffer," Liz said, pulling away and reaching for Ron's hand. "You made Victoria happier than she'd ever been."

"It wasn't hard to make her happy. She had a joy for life until the end."

Ron cleared his throat. "Let's do this." He'd only seen the man cry once, when they'd arrived at the hospital the day after the accident. But Kristoffer saw tears welling up in his eyes now as he prepared to say a final goodbye to his little girl.

Kristoffer took Pamela's hand again, and they followed Tori's parents to the front row to take their seats as Sting's "Fields of Gold" played. It was the song he and Tori had danced to on their first date at a club in Philly and remained her favorite the rest of her life. Although, now the lyrics held new meaning.

He'd only added the song at the last minute after having a vivid dream in the wee hours this morning. In it, he and Tori walked beside each other in a field of barley, much like the song described. But there were differences, too. She held the strings of a huge bouquet of pink balloons filled with helium. Pink had always been her favorite color.

He thought the point of the dream was to let him know that she had been sending him signs that she'd passed on. He'd seen stray pink balloons any number of times—during her last hospitalization, on the beach walk, and finally, the night he asked Pamela to wear his collar. All had been pivotal moments for him, and if he'd been more aware, he'd have been comforted to know she was with him.

But the dream didn't end there. The golden sunlight bathed the two of them in warmth until Tori broke free, dancing toward the setting sun, laughing with glee, and flinging her arms up while still holding tight to the strings. He tried to follow, but his feet were leaden as if buried in cement, although when he looked down, he saw green grass alongside the grain field.

The next thing he knew, Pamela had joined him, wrapping her arm around his waist and squeezing him in support as they both watched Tori dance with great abandon and joy. Suddenly, she stopped, turned around, blew him a kiss, and released the balloons to the heavens. They floated higher and higher, just as they had on those other times he'd seen them, until they were out of sight. When he looked back at where Tori had stood, she'd disappeared as if enveloped by the brilliant rays. She'd been able to break free the bounds of earth.

He'd awakened abruptly enough to disturb Pamela's sleep. As he told her about the visitation dream—and he had no doubt it had been a visit from Tori—Pamela hugged and comforted him. He'd cried for the first time all week—not out of sadness, but at the beauty and peace of it. His sprite had cried, too.

Tori had found a way to break through even his logical mind and convey a message she'd tried to get across to him for a long time. He'd suspected Tori might be behind the balloons when that third one flitted by their window at the restaurant. There'd been no other explanation for one to be there at that moment. But he hadn't mentioned it to Pamela at the time. That night had been about them moving forward.

Tori had given him fourteen wonderful years. He'd never forget her or their time together, but she'd made it clear by the dream and other signs she'd sent that his place was now beside Pamela. Tori had also found a way to say goodbye to him that would make the memorial service less painful. The peace that descended on him in that moment left him able to completely say farewell to Tori and fully embrace his new life with Pamela.

Unable to fall asleep again, he and Pamela had decided to rise early and start preparing breakfast. Their house of love was filled to the brim with every guest bedroom and sofa bed occupied—Tori's parents, Maribeth, Kristoffer's mother, and Tori's college roommate all had their own room in the enormous house. Bryce and Monica, as well as Gunnar, had chosen to drive up for the day rather than stay overnight, or they'd have had to resort to air mattresses.

Mother flying out to Denver weeks before the ski season started had surprised him more than anything, but he welcomed the chance to introduce her to Pamela. As far as he could tell, they hit it off. Mother rarely dispensed compliments, but when Pamela mentioned they were invited to Connecticut for Christmas next month, he knew that was as close as he would get to an "I like your Pamela, Kristoffer."

Pamela seemed eager to go, if she wasn't on call. He'd told her they didn't have to go exactly on Christmas. Any two or three days between the holidays would be fine.

His meandering thoughts were pulled back as the facility's chaplain read from scripture, but Kristoffer had difficulty concentrating. His gaze drifted to the urn holding the cremated remains of his wife. Should he keep them in there, or should he scatter them? Somehow, after she'd been trapped in the broken vessel that had been her earthbound body for so long, he knew instinctively he needed to free her from the urn.

He'd ask Liz and Ron if they wanted to keep any of the ashes with them and then make plans to take the remainder to Sonoma—Tori's happy place. Maribeth was going to need to head back in a couple of days. He'd talk to Gunnar and Patrick, who had been thoughtful enough to attend the service today, to see if one of them might fly the three of them out there, drop off Maribeth near Carmel, and then head up to Sonoma to spread Tori's ashes.

Grace, Tori's college roommate, made her way to the lectern next. She'd flown in from New York City late last night and had to return tonight, but wanted to be here to say goodbye to her friend. According to the program, she'd chosen to read the anonymously written poem, *Miss Me, But Let Me Go.*

> *When I come to the end of the road*
> *and the sun has set for me,*
> *I want no rites in a gloom filled room.*
> *Why cry for a soul set free?*
>
> *Miss me a little, but not for long,*
> *and not with your head bowed low.*
> *Remember the love that once we shared.*
> *Miss me, but let me go.*

Not knowing the author's name made the words more poignant, as though Tori herself was speaking them. Grace continued to read, but he lost his ability to concentrate again as Tori's smiling face from the dream last night flashed before his eyes.

'Miss me, but let me go.'

Done, sweetheart. Be free.

Gunnar walked up front next. He'd asked a couple of years ago if he could say a few words, not long after Kristoffer had told him he'd been working on the ceremony. Of course, he'd said *yes.*

He wore a dark gray suit, white shirt, and a black necktie with rows of gold stripes. Upon closer inspection earlier today, Kristoffer had seen that the stripes spelled out the words United States Army over and over. He was proud to have served his country in that way and in others.

When Gunnar first tried to speak, he had to clear his throat, which made Kristoffer lose it. Gunnar never cried or showed serious emotion. Pamela squeezed his hand, and he held onto hers more tightly.

"Tori was like a little sister to me. My first one." He exchanged a grin with Pamela who smiled back. "I can't tell how much I appreciated Tori for coming along and whipping my wild, younger cousin into shape after he'd made some bad choices." Gunnar winked at someone on the other side of the room, and Kristoffer leaned forward to see Mother grinning.

Everyone laughed, including Kristoffer, who shook his head just the same. He exchanged a smile with the man who had been more like a brother to him.

Gunnar sobered. "She was taken from us too soon. Kris, I know you've stopped playing the *coulda, woulda, shoulda* game. Life doesn't always go as planned. I've lost a lot of people close to me over the years, most of them far too young, just like Tori. But in forty-eight years, I've come to understand some things I'd like to share."

He delivered the rest of his talk looking directly at Kristoffer and Pamela.

"We all have different journeys to take in this life, and none of us knows when our journey will come to an end. We can't stay here forever, so it's a given we'll all reach a point where the road ends. Sometimes, when we're really lucky, our paths converge for a time with someone who makes living worthwhile.

"We enjoy sharing the journey with them for however long we have and learn what we can, until the day our paths veer away from each other. It happens to us all. None of us has a "get out of death" card we can play. Some separations are nobody's fault. Just a part of life."

He paused, as if waiting for those words to sink in, and Kristoffer winked at him with a smile. He'd figured it out. Finally.

"But just because they're gone from our lives doesn't mean *our* journey has come to an end. The hardest steps we'll ever take are those first ones when we start down a new path alone. But, Kris, man, I'm so proud of you for opening yourself up, being vulnerable, and finding love again. It's what Tori would have wanted. And what her parents and I have been urging you to do for a long time. I'm just glad you pulled your…" He paused, almost repeating one of his favorite military expressions that Kristoffer had heard more than a few times over the years. Kristoffer shook his head and smiled. "I'm glad you got your head on straight so you could see the path in front of you leading to Pamela."

Me, too, Cuz.

Gunnar then turned his attention to the others in the room. "I'll leave you with a bit of a poem I think says better what I'm trying to convey." Kristoffer thought he was doing just fine, but Gunnar read:

"We all have different journeys,
different paths along the way.
We all were meant to learn some things,
but never meant to stay."

Gunnar returned to his seat behind Kristoffer and squeezed him on the shoulder. Surrounded by family who loved him, including the rock-solid woman seated beside him, Kristoffer marveled at his blessings.

Tori's parents and Kristoffer had chosen not to speak. They'd said all they needed to say to one another and to Tori already. The chaplain returned, everyone stood and said a prayer, and it was over.

After receiving well-wishes from the staff and conveying his utmost thanks to them, Kristoffer walked up front and picked up the urn bearing Tori's remains. As they made their way down the aisle, Pamela whispered, "We have a surprise on the lawn. Some of the more able-bodied patients got together and wanted to do a tribute to Tori."

Curious, Kristoffer nodded and, still holding Tori's urn, he, Pamela, and the other guests made their way out a side door. The patio was filled with pink helium balloons.

"Oh, Kristoffer! She's sending you a sign." Pamela rubbed his back. "Remember the one we saw together in the restaurant the night you asked me to wear your collar? I think that was from her, too."

"There actually have been others, I was just not connecting them to Tori until that one you just mentioned. They always seemed to come at turning points where I had a choice to embrace life again or bury myself in the past."

The activities director captured their attention as she explained that some of the patients wanted Tori's loved ones to join them in releasing the biodegradable balloons, each of which carried an inspiring message with Tori's name on it. The woman showed him a few of the quotes, some familiar and some new. "Each has a different saying," she explained, "and I'll provide you with the list of quotes later."

He was blown away at how thoughtful the staff and Tori's fellow patients had been—people who could never have really known her. He thanked everyone and set the urn on a nearby table when handed a pair of scissors to launch the first one. He paused first to look at the saying:

He read from the card, "This one reads: 'The wound is the place where the light enters you,' by the Middle Eastern poet Rumi."

He looked at Pamela, whose tears conveyed that she probably interpreted the message as he did. His wound had been directly to the heart—when Tori had been yanked from his life. But through that gaping wound, a beam of light—Sprite—had entered. Because he'd made a conscious decision to choose light and life over darkness and the death from his wound, she'd healed him.

When he could see beyond the moisture welling in his eyes, he felt for the place where the ribbon was tied to the balloon and cut as close as he could. As it floated away on the breeze, Iz's ukulele-accompanied rendition of "Somewhere Over the Rainbow" began to play. The uplifting music continued as others read their quote and released their balloon. The sounds of laughter and childlike joy surrounding them were yet more signs from Tori that she'd moved on.

He hoped that the balloons landed in the paths of those needing their words of hope and encouragement when at last they settled back onto the earth.

✧   ✧   ✧

Pamela and her stepmother carried another tray of finger foods out to the buffet table they'd set up in the great room. "Monica, you've been such a help to me today. I've always enjoyed our times in the kitchen."

"No thanks needed. I'm happy to help in this way."

Gunnar had offered to arrange for caterers to prepare and serve the refreshments, but her stepmother had generously offered to stay behind at the house while everyone else attended the memorial service. Monica definitely shared a service orientation with Pamela, whose mother did as well. Perhaps both women had helped influence her in her choice to give back.

The voices and laughter in the room from reminiscing about Kristoffer's and Tori's life were a welcome transition following the bittersweet service this morning. She glanced over at him as he talked with his mother. He turned to her and smiled. Butterflies unleashed in her belly at how connected they'd become.

She returned to the kitchen for another bottle of cranberry ginger ale for the punch bowl. As she neared where her parents chatted amicably together, she couldn't help but overhear Mom telling her dad about her plans to join Heidi at the Afghan school to work with the girls. She'd blown Pamela away with the announcement at dinner last night. Pamela wasn't at all happy about it after the attack on the Kunduz trauma center, but Mom wouldn't listen to her concerns any more than Pamela had listened to her dad's warnings when she'd signed on to go to dangerous places like Chad and Afghanistan over the past few years. At least Gunnar looked out for Heidi and those at the school and would help keep Pamela updated.

When she returned to the family-filled room, she saw that Kristoffer was talking with Patrick. She filled the punch bowl and turned to find Kristoffer's mother standing there. "Can I pour you a glass of punch, Mrs. Larson?"

"No, thank you, dear." Her accent sounded more British than Kristoffer's Connecticut-bordered-on-Rhode Island. Pamela had been surprised to learn the woman actually had been born in England.

Perhaps it explained her seeming to be so reserved, which he sometimes interpreted as being cold.

"Is there something else I can get you?" Pamela asked.

"I wondered if I might steal you away a moment to talk." She was dressed impeccably, right down to her pearls and shoe clips. The silver-haired matron had an aristocratic air about her, somewhat haughty, but that might be a defense mechanism. Kristoffer had doubts about how his mother felt about him, but based it primarily on his teenage years. Perhaps the two needed to come together as adults and let the past go there, as well.

"Why don't we go out on the deck? It's surprisingly warm for this time of year." Pamela took her by the elbow and guided her out through the kitchen door.

"Would you prefer to sit, dear?" Mrs. Larson asked. "Being on your feet so much today must be tiring."

Pamela thought at first she was encouraging her to sit because… No, of course not. She reassured her, "Oh, I'm used to standing long hours in my profession. But how about you?"

"No, I'm fine." She looked out over the view a moment and avoided Pamela's gaze. "I want to thank you for bringing Kris back to life. Seeing him lost and hurting was more than I could bear."

"I love him more than anything in this world. Anything I can do to bring joy back to him, I will."

The older woman turned toward her. "It takes a special woman to love a man with so many obstacles. I'm not sure we in the older generations would have been courageous enough to disregard social mores and do what makes us happy." Pamela wasn't sure if that was a backhanded compliment, but then Mrs. Larson smiled. "My son has a wild streak in him. Rebellious at times."

Pamela had only begun to see some of that in Kristoffer, but from stories Gunnar told her, he had been rambunctious at the very least.

His mother continued. "But he's as loyal as they come. He never abandons those he loves, even when he's angry with them, as he was with me after the break-up of my marriage to his father."

"I know he loves you. I had a lot of resentment toward my mother about my parents' break-up, too, but as I've matured and learned some of what happened, it's lessened. Have you ever explained to him what led to it?"

Mrs. Larson shook her head. "It didn't seem appropriate for him to know at the time, but his bloody father had a roaming eye." Pamela knew there was nothing to smile about, but now she knew where Kristoffer had picked up the British curse "bloody." "It became too much for me after a while. But Kris was just a boy. He simply idolized his father. I didn't want to come between them, although I didn't expect his father to move away and start a new family, abandoning our son. I don't see how his knowing now would even matter."

Pamela got the impression the woman rarely shared her deepest emotions with anyone, so opening up like this must have been difficult. She seemed the type to close off and compartmentalize the pain and keep a stiff upper lip, much like Kristoffer did after losing Tori.

"Mrs. Larson, he is grown up now, and I think he'd be able to handle and understand that information better." If nothing else, Pamela would like to see him grow closer to his mother. She truly must love him to have flown more than halfway across the country to be here with him this week. "Perhaps after things quiet down tonight and before you fly home tomorrow, you could take some time to share with him what you told me."

"We'll see." A noncommittal response for sure, but who could tell? "I should let you return to your guests, but I hope you and Kris will come to Connecticut for the holidays. I'd like to get to know you better and hear more about the many adventures Kris was telling me about."

Pamela smiled, surprised she'd been the topic of conversation. "I'd like that, Mrs. Larson. *Christmas in Connecticut* is one of my favorite holiday movies, too."

Mrs. Larson smiled. "I'm afraid it doesn't look quite like that these days, but it did in my youth out in the countryside."

"As soon as I have my December schedule, I'll let you know, but surely we can get away for at least a few days between Christmas and

New Year's."

✧   ✧   ✧

Overwhelmed by the day all of a sudden and running on very little sleep and copious amounts of black coffee, Kristoffer stepped outside the front door and walked to the side of the house for a few moments of solitude by the waterfall. There were no more words to speak to Tori.

He stood listening to the water and the chirping of the birds for an unknown time before deciding to go back inside and seek out Pamela's arms. He turned just as she walked up and slipped her arms around his waist.

"It's been a long week, hasn't it? Can I get you anything, Sir?"

He held onto her tightly. "Just having you beside me is all I need." They clung to each other, listening to the tinkling water tumbling over the rocks, which never failed to bring them both peace.

"Pamela, I've been blessed to be loved by two of the most amazing women in the world. I'm surrounded by family and friends who love me. My life is right where it's supposed to be. I don't know how long before the next big change, but whatever it is, I'm ready to face it head-on with you by my side."

She remained quiet so long that he became worried and pulled away. Tear tracks stained her face, but she was smiling.

Pamela cleared her throat. "I was going to wait until after everyone left, but I want you to know that sometimes change isn't bad."

What now? He really was hoping for smooth sailing for a little while.

"Sir, we're expecting a baby."

He searched her eyes, thinking perhaps he was hearing things. "For real?"

How profound, man. She just told you you're about to become a dad for the first time.

He had a million questions. "When did you find out?"

"I took a home pregnancy test the day before yesterday, but wanted to confirm it, so I had the lab at the hospital run it, too. It's definitely for real, although I'm still pinching myself that it happened so fast given our ages and—"

He bent down for a kiss, happy to hear the news, but also to keep her from reminding him any further that he'd just turned forty-two a couple weeks ago. Hell, he'd practically be drawing Social Security by the time his son or daughter graduated from college. But the elation he felt right now made him feel like twenty-something again. This child would keep him young.

Not only had life given *him* a second chance, but it had given him and Pamela a chance at bringing a new life into the world.

He broke away, concerned suddenly. "Should you be resting? God of Thunder, you've been working your ass off the past few days—even more than usual. If I'd kno—"

It was her turn to cut him off when she placed her hand over his mouth. "I'm fine! It's good for the baby if I remain active, so I'll continue to work as long as my OB agrees it's safe for us both. Based on my cycles, I should be due sometime in mid to late July, and I intend to take maternity leave at least through October."

They'd need someone to help with the baby after she returned to work. With his at-home job, they could probably arrange to have someone in-house only part-time during his crucial work times, and then he could work at night after Pamela came home. He wanted to be a hands-on dad.

Dad.

He hadn't gotten his hopes up that they'd be successful, especially not after only two months trying. But holy shit! They'd done it.

Lifting her up, he spun her around before realizing that might not be good for the baby. As he set her down, the sounds of the water trickling in their yard gave him another thought. He released her and looked down at the waterfall.

"We may need to put a fence around this to keep the baby out."

Pamela chuckled. "I think we're good for a few years before we'll let him or her run around out here unsupervised."

Their oasis suddenly seemed fraught with dangers. Surviving fatherhood might be one of the toughest things he'd ever done.

Pamela, who'd had more time to get used to the idea, continued to lay out the plan. "And if we take our trip to Norway in September, I should be able to travel by then."

He grinned, thinking she'd picked up where he'd left off in trying to plan every aspect of life. It would seem that having a baby wasn't going to slow Pamela down or make her change her routine. Kristoffer would be more cautious and see how they adjusted before making plans for an international trip like that. September wasn't the best time to be traipsing around Norway anyway.

But that she was already thinking about establishing strong roots for their baby in the place where half of Kristoffer's ancestors had called home sounded so right to him.

"We can dip baby Larson into the fjords of the motherland while there."

"Do you have any idea how cold the fjords are that time of year?"

She laughed. "Okay, maybe just the toes—enough for the baby to let out his or her first roar, just like his daddy's."

About the Author

Kallypso Masters is a full-time author and three-time *USA Today* Bestselling Author of the Rescue Me Saga (with more than one million copies in paperbacks and e-books). "My dad served in the Navy (World War II) and the Army's Signal Corps (Korea). His PTSD from the latter affected the rest of his life." As a result, Kally chose to write about members of a military "family" helping each other heal and cope after combat and life's intrusions. She also writes about the fallout from devastating traumas suffered by other characters in her ongoing saga. She knows that Happily Ever After takes maintenance, so her couples don't solve all their problems and disappear at "the end" of "their" novel, but will continue to work on real problems in their relationships in later books in the Saga. Therefore, the books in the Rescue Me Saga should be read in order because characters recur and continue their journeys throughout the series. However, there will be spinoff books and series in the future that will be written so that they can be read without reading the Rescue Me Saga first. This includes *Roar*.

Kally's emotional, realistic Romance novels emphasize ways of healing using unconventional methods. Her alpha males are dominant and attracted to strong women who can bring them to their knees. Kally has brought many readers to their knees, as well—having them experience the stories right alongside her characters. Readers often tell her they're on their third, sixth, or even twelfth read of the series because the layers are so deep that new information is revealed with each re-read.

Kally has been writing full-time since May 2011. She lives in rural Kentucky and has been married almost 33 years to the man who provided her own Happily Ever After. They have two adult children, one adorable grandson, and a rescued dog and cat.

Kally enjoys meeting readers. Check out the Appearances page on her web site to see if she'll be near you!

For more timely updates and a chance to win great prizes, get sneak peeks at unedited excerpts, and more, sign up for her newsletter (sent out via e-mail) (kallypsomasters.com/newsletter) and/or for text alerts (used ONLY for new releases of e-books or print books) at her Web site (KallypsoMasters.com).

To contact or interact with Kally,
go to Facebook (where almost all posts are public),
her Facebook Author page,
or Twitter (@kallypsomasters),
or her Web site (KallypsoMasters.com).

To join the secret Facebook group Rescue Me Saga Discussion Group, please send a friend request to Karla Paxton and she will open the door for you. (Please allow her a few days! She's a busy woman these days!) Must be 18 to join.

And feel free to e-mail Kally at kallypsomasters@gmail.com, or write to her at

Kallypso Masters
PO Box 1183
Richmond, KY 40476-1183

Get your Kally Swag!

Want to own merchandise from the Rescue Me Saga, including these Ka-thunk!® T-shirts (inspired by Adam and Karla) and the new Princess Slut® T-shirts (inspired by a scene in *Nobody's Perfect*—along with beaded evil sticks from the same book). With each order, you also will receive a bag filled with available swag items including ink pens, bookmarks (paper and magnetic), plastic hand fans, lens/cleaning cloths with the *ROAR* cover on them, vintage-cover trading cards, and more swag coming all the time! You can even order personally sign copies of her paperbacks to be sent directly to you. Kally ships internationally wherever these books and items are legal! To shop, go to kallypsomasters.com/kally_swag.

The *Rescue Me Saga*

Masters at Arms & Nobody's Angel (Combined Volume)
(First in the *Rescue Me Saga*)

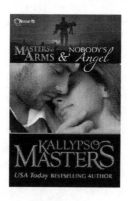

Masters at Arms is an introduction to the *Rescue Me Saga*, which needs to be read first. The book begins the journey of three men, each on a quest for honor, acceptance, and to ease his unspoken pain. Their paths cross at one of the darkest points in their lives. As they try to come to terms with the aftermath of Iraq—forging an unbreakable bond—they band together to start their own BDSM club. But will they ever truly become masters of their own fates? Or would fate become master of them?

Nobody's Angel: Marc D'Alessio might own a BDSM club with his fellow military veterans, Adam and Damián, but he keeps all women at a distance. However, when Marc rescues beautiful Angelina Giardano from a disastrous first BDSM experience at the club, an uncharacteristic attraction leaves him torn between his safe, but lonely world, and a possible future with his angel.

Angelina leaves BDSM behind, only to have her dreams plagued by the Italian angel who rescued her at the club. When she meets Marc at a bar in her hometown, she can't shake the feeling she knows him—but has no idea why he reminds her of her angel.

Nobody's Hero

(Second in the *Rescue Me Saga*)

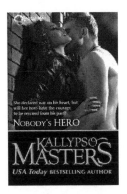

Retired Marine Master Sergeant Adam Montague has battled through four combat zones, but now finds himself retreating from Karla Paxton, who has declared war on his heart. With a significant age difference, he feels he should be her guardian and protector, not her lover. But Karla's knack for turning up in his bed at inopportune times is killing his resolve to do the right thing. Karla isn't the young girl he rescued nine years earlier—something his body reminds him of every chance it gets.

Their age difference is only part of the problem. Fifty-year-old Adam has been a collector of lost and vulnerable souls most of his life, but a secret he has run from for more than three decades has kept him emotionally unable to admit love for anyone. Will Karla be able to break through the defenses around his heart and help him put the ghosts from his past to rest? In her all-out war to get Adam to surrender his heart, will the strong-willed Goth singer offer herself as his submissive and, if so, at what cost to herself?

Nobody's Perfect

(Third in the *Rescue Me Saga*)

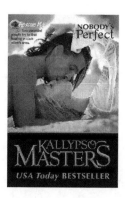

Savannah/Savi escaped eleven years of abuse at the hands of her father and finally made a safe life for herself and her daughter. But when her father once again threatens her peace of mind—and her daughter's safety—Savi runs to Damian Orlando for protection. Eight years earlier as Savannah, she shared one perfect day with Damian that changed both their young lives and resulted in a secret she no longer can hide. But being with Damian reawakens repressed memories and feelings she wants to keep buried. After witnessing a scene with Damian on Savi's first night at his private club, however, she begins to wonder if he could help her regain control of her life and reclaim her sexuality and identity.

Damian, a wounded warrior, has had his own dragons to fight in life, but has never forgotten Savannah. He will lay down his life to protect her and her daughter, but doesn't believe he can offer more than that. She deserves a whole man, something he can never be after a firefight in Iraq. Damian has turned to SM to regain control of his life and emotions and fulfills the role of Service Top to "bottoms" at the club. However, he could never deliver those services to Savi, who needs someone gentle and loving, not the man he has become.

Will two wounded survivors find love and healing in each other's arms?

Somebody's Angel

(Fourth in the *Rescue Me Saga*)

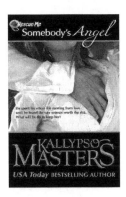

When Marc D'Alessio first rescued the curvaceous and spirited Italian Angelina Giardano at the Masters at Arms Club, he never expected her to turn his safe, controlled life upside down and pull at his long-broken heartstrings. Months later, the intense fire of their attraction still rages, but something holds him back from committing to her completely. Worse, secrets and memories from his past join forces to further complicate his relationships with family, friends, and his beautiful angel.

Angelina cannot give all of herself to someone who hides himself from her. She loves Marc, the BDSM world he brought her into, and the way their bodies respond to one another, but she needs more. Though she destroyed the wolf mask he once wore, only he can remove the mask he dons daily to hide his emotions. In a desperate attempt to break through his defenses and reclaim her connection to the man she loves, she attempts a full frontal assault that sends him into a fast retreat, leaving her nobody's angel once again.

Marc finds that running to the mountains no longer gives him solace but instead leaves him empty and alone. Angelina is the one woman worth the risk of opening his heart. Will he risk everything to become the man she deserves and the man he wants to be?

Nobody's Lost

(Fifth in the *Rescue Me Saga*)

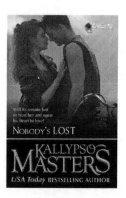

Ryder Wilson returned from serving multiple deployments, but can't leave the hell of combat behind him. Frustrated and ashamed of his inability to function in the world, unlike the veterans he had served with, Ryder retreated. When sent on a mission to protect the sister of retired Master Sergeant Adam Montague, Ryder's days of hiding out may be over. Can he fulfill his mission without failing again?

Megan Gallagher has two big-brother Marines bent on protecting her from the evils of the world, but she's tougher than they think. When her older brother sends Ryder, one of his recon Marines, to her doorstep in the wee hours one night following a break-in, she realizes he needs rescuing more than she does. A friendship forms quickly, but unexpected passions run hot and complicate her resolve never to have a romantic relationship, much less marriage. So why are her body and her heart betraying her every time he comes near?

Can these two wounded people lower their defenses long enough to allow love to grow?

Nobody's Dream

(Sixth in the *Rescue Me Saga*)

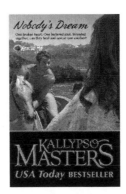

One broken heart.

One battered soul.

No one said life would be fair or easy. Quiet, Peruvian-born artist Cassie López learned this the hard way. Betrayed by the man she planned to marry, she shut herself off as far away from all but her closest friend from college...

Until the night Luke Denton came crashing into her Colorado mountain sanctuary with a vengeance. Confused by her heart's response to this kind and gentle man, Cassie pushes herself to help the cowboy recover quickly so she can send him on his way. But Luke's patience and understanding threaten to break down the very defenses she needs to survive in this world after he's gone.

Search-and-Rescue worker Luke, who lost his wife and unborn child in a tragic accident, also knows firsthand of the unfairness of life. He keeps his own nightmares at bay by focusing on his rescue activities, most recently adopting and working with abused and neglected horses.

Can two wounded people find trust and love together? Do nightmares end where dreams come true?

Made in the USA
San Bernardino, CA
08 October 2016